FYODOR M. DOSTOEVSKY

THE BROTHERS
KARAMAZOV

II

*Translated from the Russian
by Constance Garnett*

Original Illustrations by Pietro Sarto

Distributed by
HERON BOOKS

*Published by arrangement with
William Heinemann Ltd.*

13 005 10 R3

THE
GREATEST MASTERPIECES
OF
RUSSIAN LITERATURE

CONTENTS

PART III

PART IV

PART III

BOOK VII: ALYOSHA

CHAPTER I

THE BREATH OF CORRUPTION

THE body of Father Zossima was prepared for burial according to the established ritual. As is well known, the bodies of dead monks and hermits are not washed. In the words of the Church Ritual: "If any one of the monks depart in the Lord, the monk designated" (that is, whose office it is) "shall wipe the body with warm water, making first the sign of the Cross with a sponge on the forehead of the deceased, on the breast, on the hands and feet and on the knees, and that is enough." All this was done by Father Païssy, who then clothed the deceased in his monastic garb and wrapped him in his cloak, which was, according to custom, somewhat slit to allow of its being folded about him in the form of a cross. On his head he put a hood with an eight-cornered cross. The hood was left open and the dead man's face was covered with black gauze. In his hands was put an ikon of the Saviour. Towards morning he was put in the coffin which had been made ready long before. It was decided to leave the coffin all day in the cell, in the larger room in which the elder used to receive his visitors and fellow monks. As the deceased was a priest and monk of the strictest rule, the Gospel, not the Psalter, had to be read over his body by monks in holy orders. The reading was begun by Father Iosif immediately after the requiem service. Father Païssy desired later on to read the Gospel all day and night over his dead friend, but for the present he, as well as the Father Superintendent of the Hermitage, was very busy and occupied, for something extraordinary, an unheard-of, even "unseemly" excitement and impatient expectation began to be apparent in the monks, and the visitors from the monastery hostels, and the crowds of people flocking from the town. And as time went on, this grew more and more marked.

1

Both the Superintendent and Father Païssy did their utmost to calm the general bustle and agitation.

When it was fully daylight, some people began bringing their sick, in most cases children, with them from the town— as though they had been waiting expressly for this moment to do so, evidently persuaded that the dead elder's remains had a power of healing, which would be immediately made mani- fest in accordance with their faith. It was only then apparent how unquestionably everyone in our town had accepted Father Zossima during his lifetime as a great saint. And those who came were far from being all of the humbler classes.

This intense expectation on the part of believers, displayed with such haste, such openness, even with impatience and almost insistence, impressed Father Païssy as unseemly. Though he had long foreseen something of the sort, the actual manifestation of the feeling was beyond anything he had looked for. When he came across any of the monks who displayed this excitement, Father Païssy began to reprove them. ''Such immediate expectation of something extraordinary,'' he said, ''shows a levity possible to worldly people but unseemly in us.''

But little attention was paid him and Father Païssy noticed it uneasily. Yet he himself (if the whole truth must be told), secretly at the bottom of his heart, cherished almost the same hopes and could not but be aware of it, though he was indignant at the too impatient expectation around him, and saw in it light-mindedness and vanity. Nevertheless, it was particularly unpleasant to him to meet certain persons whose presence aroused in him great misgivings. In the crowd in the dead man's cell he noticed with inward aversion (for which he im- mediately reproached himself) the presence of Rakitin and of the monk from Obdorsk, who was still staying in the monastery. Of both of them Father Païssy felt for some reason suddenly suspicious—though, indeed, he might well have felt the same about others.

The monk from Obdorsk was conspicuous as the most fussy in the excited crowd. He was to be seen everywhere; every- where he was asking questions, everywhere he was listening, on all sides he was whispering with a peculiar, mysterious air. His expression showed the greatest impatience and even a sort of irritation.

As for Rakitin, he, as appeared later, had come so early to the hermitage at the special request of Madame Hohlakov.

As soon as that good-hearted but weak-minded woman, who could not herself have been admitted to the hermitage, waked and heard of the death of Father Zossima, she was overtaken with such intense curiosity that she promptly despatched Rakitin to the hermitage, to keep a careful look-out and report to her by letter every half-hour or so *"everything that takes place"*. She regarded Rakitin as a most religious and devout young man. He was particularly clever in getting round people and assuming whatever part he thought most to their taste, if he detected the slightest advantage to himself from doing so.

It was a bright, clear day and many of the visitors were thronging about the tombs, which were particularly numerous round the church and scattered here and there about the hermitage. As he walked round the hermitage, Father Païssy remembered Alyosha and that he had not seen him for some time, not since the night. And he had no sooner thought of him than he at once noticed him in the furthest corner of the hermitage garden, sitting on the tombstone of a monk who had been famous long ago for his saintliness. He sat with his back to the hermitage and his face to the wall, and seemed to be hiding behind the tombstone. Going up to him, Father Païssy saw that he was weeping quietly but bitterly, with his face hidden in his hands and that his whole frame was shaking with sobs. Father Païssy stood over him for a little.

"Enough, dear son, enough, dear," he pronounced with feeling at last. "Why do you weep? Rejoice and weep not. Don't you know that this is the greatest of his days? Think only where he is now, at this moment!"

Alyosha glanced at him, uncovering his face, which was swollen with crying like a child's, but turned away at once without uttering a word and hid his face in his hands again.

"Maybe it is well," said Father Païssy thoughtfully; "weep if you must, Christ has sent you those tears."

"Your touching tears are but a relief to your spirit and will serve to gladden your dear heart," he added to himself, walking away from Alyosha and thinking lovingly of him. He moved away quickly, however, for he felt that he too might weep looking at him.

Meanwhile the time was passing; the monastery services and the requiems for the dead followed in their due course. Father Païssy again took Father Iosif's place by the coffin and began reading the Gospel. But before three o'clock in the afternoon that something took place to which I alluded at the end of the last book, something so unexpected by all of us and so contrary to the general hope that, I repeat, this trivial incident has been minutely remembered to this day in our town and all the surrounding neighbourhood. I may add here, for myself personally, that I feel it is almost repulsive to recall that event which caused such frivolous agitation and was such a stumbling-block to many, though in reality it was the most natural and trivial matter. I should, of course, have omitted all mention of it in my story if it had not exerted a very strong influence on the heart and soul of the chief, *though future*, hero of my story, Alyosha, forming a crisis and turning-point in his spiritual development, giving a shock to his intellect, which finally strengthened it for the rest of his life and gave it a definite aim.

And so, to return to our story. When before dawn they laid Father Zossima's body in the coffin and brought it into the front room, the question of opening the windows was raised among those who were around the coffin. But this suggestion, made casually by someone, was unanswered and almost unnoticed. Some of those present may perhaps have inwardly noticed it, only to reflect that the anticipation of decay and corruption from the body of such a saint was an actual absurdity, calling for compassion (if not a smile) for the lack of faith and the frivolity it implied. For they expected something quite different.

And, behold, soon after midday there were signs of something, at first only observed in silence by those who came in and out and were evidently each afraid to communicate the thought in his mind. But by three o'clock those signs had become so clear and unmistakable that the news swiftly reached all the monks and visitors in the hermitage, promptly penetrated to the monastery, throwing all the monks into amazement, and finally, in the shortest possible time, spread to the town, exciting everyone in it, believers and unbelievers alike. The unbelievers rejoiced, and, as for the believers, some of them rejoiced even more than the unbelievers, for "men love the downfall and disgrace of the righteous", as the deceased elder had said in one of his exhortations.

The fact is that a smell of decomposition began to come from the coffin, growing gradually more marked, and by three o'clock it was quite unmistakable. In all the past history of our monastery no such scandal could be recalled, and in no other circumstances could such a scandal have been possible, as showed itself in unseemly disorder immediately after this

4

discovery among the very monks themselves. Afterwards, even many years afterwards, some sensible monks were amazed and horrified, when they recalled that day, that the scandal could have reached such proportions. For in the past, monks of very holy life had died, God-fearing old men, whose saintliness was acknowledged by all, yet from their humble coffins, too, the breath of corruption had come, naturally, as from all dead bodies, but that had caused no scandal nor even the slightest excitement. Of course there had been, in former times, saints in the monastery whose memory was carefully preserved and whose relics, according to tradition, showed no signs of corruption. This fact was regarded by the monks as touching and mysterious, and the tradition of it was cherished as something blessed and miraculous, and as a promise, by God's grace, of still greater glory from their tombs in the future.

One such, whose memory was particularly cherished, was an old monk, Job, who had died seventy years before at the age of a hundred and five. He had been a celebrated ascetic, rigid in fasting and silence, and his tomb was pointed out to all visitors on their arrival with peculiar respect and mysterious hints of great hopes connected with it. (That was the very tomb on which Father Païssy had found Alyosha sitting in the morning.) Another memory cherished in the monastery was that of the famous Father Varsonofy, who was only recently dead and had preceded Father Zossima in the eldership. He was reverenced during his lifetime as a crazy saint by all the pilgrims to the monastery. There was a tradition that both of these had laid in their coffins as though alive, that they had shown no signs of decomposition when they were buried and that there had been a holy light in their faces. And some people even insisted that a sweet fragrance came from their bodies.

Yet, in spite of these edifying memories, it would be difficult to explain the frivolity, absurdity and malice that were manifested beside the coffin of Father Zossima. It is my private opinion that several different causes were simultaneously at work, one of which was the deeply rooted hostility to the institution of elders as a pernicious innovation, an antipathy hidden deep in the hearts of many of the monks. Even more powerful was jealousy of the dead man's saintliness, so firmly established during his lifetime that it was almost a forbidden thing to question it. For though the late elder had won over many hearts, more by love than by miracles, and had gathered round him a mass of loving adherents, none the less, in fact, rather the more on that account he had awakened jealousy and so had come to have bitter enemies, secret and open, not only in the monastery but in the world outside it. He did no one any harm, but: "Why do they think him so saintly?" And that question alone, gradually repeated, gave rise at last to an intense, insatiable hatred of him. That, I believe, was why many people were extremely delighted at the smell of decomposition which came so quickly, for not a day had passed since his death. At the same time there were some among those who had been hitherto reverently devoted to the elder who were almost mortified and personally affronted by this incident. This was how the thing happened.

As soon as signs of decomposition had begun to appear, the whole aspect of the monks betrayed their secret motives in entering the cell. They went in, stayed a little while and hastened out to confirm the news to the crowd of other monks waiting outside. Some of the latter shook their heads mournfully, but others did not even care to conceal the delight which gleamed unmistakably in their malignant eyes. And now no one reproached them for it, no one raised his voice in protest, which was strange, for the majority of the monks had been devoted to the dead elder. But it seemed as though God had in this case let the majority get the upper hand for a time.

Visitors from outside, particularly of the educated class, soon went into the cell, too, with the same spying intent. Of the peasantry few went into the cell, though there were crowds of them at the gates of the hermitage. After three o'clock the rush of worldly visitors was greatly increased and this was no doubt owing to the shocking news. People were attracted who would not otherwise have come on that day and had not intended to come, and among them were some personages of high standing. But external decorum was still preserved and Father Païssy, with a stern face, continued firmly and distinctly reading aloud the Gospel, apparently not noticing what was taking place around him, though he had, in fact, observed something unusual long before. But at last the murmurs, first subdued but gradually louder and more confident, reached even him. "It shows God's judgment is not as man's," Father Païssy heard suddenly. The first to give utterance to this sentiment was a layman, an elderly official from the town, known to be a man of great piety. But he only repeated aloud what the monks had long been whispering. They had long before formulated this damning conclusion, and the worst of it was that a sort of triumphant satisfaction at that conclusion became more and more apparent every moment. Soon they began to lay aside even external decorum and almost seemed to feel they had a sort of right to discard it.

"And for what reason can *this* have happened?" some of the monks said, at first with a show of regret; "he had a small frame and his flesh was dried up on his bones, what was there to decay?"

"It must be a sign from heaven," others hastened to add, and their opinion was adopted at once without protest. For it was pointed out, too, that if the decomposition had been natural, as in the case of every dead sinner, it would have been apparent later, after a lapse of at least twenty-four hours, but this premature corruption "was in excess of nature", and so the finger of God was evident. It was meant for a sign. This conclusion seemed irresistible.

Gentle Father Iosif, the librarian, a great favourite of the dead man's, tried to reply to some of the evil speakers that "this is not held everywhere alike", and that the incorruptibility of the bodies of the just was not a dogma of the Orthodox Church but only an opinion, and that even in the most Orthodox regions, at Athos, for instance, they were not greatly confounded by the smell of corruption, and there the chief sign of the glorification of the saved was not bodily incorruptibility but the colour of the bones when the bodies have lain many years in the earth and have decayed in it. "And if the bones are yellow as wax, that is the great sign that the Lord has glorified the dead saint; if they are not yellow but black, it shows that God has not deemed him worthy of such glory—that is the belief in Athos, a great place, where the Orthodox doctrine has been preserved from of old, unbroken and in its greatest purity," said Father Iosif in conclusion.

But the meek Father's words had little effect and even provoked a mocking retort. "That's all pedantry and innovation, no use listening to it," the monks decided. "We stick to the old doctrine, there are all sorts of innovations nowadays, are we to follow them all?" added others.

"We have had as many holy fathers as they had. There they are among the Turks, they have forgotten everything. Their doctrine has long been impure and they have no bells even," the most sneering added.

Father Iosif walked away, grieving the more since he had put forward his own opinion with little confidence as though scarcely believing in it himself. He foresaw with distress that something very unseemly was beginning and that there were positive signs of disobedience. Little by little, all the sensible monks were reduced to silence like Father Iosif. And so it came to pass that all who loved the elder and had accepted with devout obedience the institution of the eldership were all at once terribly cast down and glanced timidly in one another's faces, when they met. Those who were hostile to the institution of elders, as a novelty, held up their heads proudly. "There was no smell of corruption from the late elder Varsonofy, but a sweet fragrance," they recalled malignantly. "But he gained that glory not because he was an elder but because he was a holy man."

And this was followed by a shower of criticism and even blame of Father Zossima. "His teaching was false; he taught that life is a great joy and not a vale of tears," said some of the more unreasonable. "He followed the fashionable belief, he did not recognise material fire in hell," others, still more unreasonable, added. "He was not strict in fasting, allowed himself sweet things, ate cherry jam with his tea, ladies used to send it to him. Is it for a monk of strict rule to drink tea?" could be heard among some of the envious. "He sat in pride," the most malignant declared vindictively; "he considered himself a saint and he took it as his due when people knelt before him." "He abused the sacrament of confession," the fiercest opponents of the institution of elders added in a malicious whisper. And among these were some of the oldest monks, strictest in their devotion, genuine ascetics, who had kept silent during the life of the deceased elder, but now suddenly unsealed their lips. And this was terrible, for their words had great influence on young monks who were not yet firm in their convictions. The monk from Obdorsk heard all this attentively, heaving deep sighs and nodding his head. "Yes, clearly Father Ferapont was right in his judgment yesterday," and at that moment Father Ferapont himself made his appearance, as though on purpose to increase the confusion.

I have mentioned already that he rarely left his wooden cell by the apiary. He was seldom even seen at church and they overlooked this neglect on the ground of his craziness, and did not keep him to the rules binding on all the rest. But if the whole truth is to be told, they hardly had a choice about it. For it would have been discreditable to insist on burdening with the common regulations so great an ascetic, who prayed day

8

and night (he even dropped asleep on his knees). If they had insisted, the monks would have said: "He is holier than all of us and he follows a rule harder than ours. And if he does not go to church, it's because he knows when he ought to; he has his own rule." It was to avoid the chance of these sinful murmurs Father Ferapont was left in peace,

As everyone was aware, Father Ferapont particularly disliked Father Zossima. And now the news had reached him in his hut that "God's judgment is not the same as man's", and that something had happened which was "in excess of nature". It may well be supposed that among the first to run to him with the news was the monk from Obdorsk, who had visited him the evening before and left his cell terror-stricken.

I have mentioned above that though Father Païssy, standing firm and immovable reading the Gospel over the coffin, could not hear or see what was passing outside the cell, he gauged most of it correctly in his heart, for he knew the men surrounding him well. He was not shaken by it, but awaited what would come next without fear, watching with penetration and insight for the outcome of the general excitement.

Suddenly an extraordinary uproar in the passage, in open defiance of decorum, burst on his ears. The door was flung open and Father Ferapont appeared in the doorway. Behind him there could be seen accompanying him a crowd of monks, together with many people from the town. They did not, however, enter the cell, but stood at the bottom of the steps, waiting to see what Father Ferapont would say or do. For they felt with a certain awe, in spite of their audacity, that he had not come for nothing. Standing in the doorway, Father Ferapont raised his arms, and under his right arm the keen inquisitive little eyes of the monk from Obdorsk peeped in. He alone, in his intense curiosity, could not resist running up the steps after Father Ferapont. The others, on the contrary, pressed further back in sudden alarm when the door was noisily flung open. Holding his hands aloft, Father Ferapont suddenly roared:

"Casting out I cast out!" and, turning in all directions, he began at once making the sign of the Cross at each of the four walls and four corners of the cell in succession. All who accompanied Father Ferapont immediately understood his action. For they knew he always did this wherever he went, and that he would not sit down or say a word till he had driven out the evil spirits.

"Satan, go hence! Satan, go hence!" he repeated at each

9

sign of the Cross. "Casting out I cast out!" he roared again.

He was wearing his coarse gown girt with a rope. His bare chest, covered with grey hair, could be seen under his hempen shirt. His feet were bare. As soon as he began waving his arms, the cruel irons he wore under his gown could be heard clanking.

Father Païssy paused in his reading, stepped forward and stood before him waiting.

"What have you come for, worthy Father? Why do you offend against good order? Why do you disturb the peace of the flock?" he said at last, looking sternly at him.

"What have I come for? You ask why? What is your faith?" shouted Father Ferapont crazily. "I've come here to drive out your visitors, the unclean devils. I've come to see how many have gathered here while I have been away. I want to sweep them out with a birch broom."

"You cast out the evil spirit, but perhaps you are serving him yourself," Father Païssy went on fearlessly. "And who can say of himself, 'I am holy'. Can you, Father?"

"I am unclean, not holy. I would not sit in an arm-chair and would not have them bow down to me as an idol," thundered Father Ferapont. "Nowadays folk destroy the truth faith. The dead man, your saint," he turned to the crowd, pointing with his finger to the coffin, "did not believe in devils. He gave medicine to keep off the devils. And so they have become as common as spiders in the corners. And now he has begun to stink himself. In that we see a great sign from God."

The incident he referred to was this: One of the monks was haunted in his dreams and, later on, in waking moments, by visions of evil spirits. When in the utmost terror he confided this to Father Zossima, the elder had advised continual prayer and rigid fasting. But when that was of no use, he advised him, while persisting in prayer and fasting, to take a special medicine. Many persons were shocked at the time and wagged their heads as they talked over it—and most of all Father Ferapont, to whom some of the censorious had hastened to report this "extraordinary" counsel on the part of the elder.

"Go away, Father!" said Father Païssy, in a commanding voice, "it's not for man to judge but for God. Perhaps we see here a 'sign' which neither you, nor I, nor any one of us is able to comprehend. Go, Father, and do not trouble the flock!" he repeated impressively.

"He did not keep the fasts according to the rule and there-

10

fore the sign has come. That is clear and it's a sin to hide it."
The fanatic, carried away by a zeal that outstripped his reason,
would not be quieted. "He was seduced by sweetmeats, ladies
brought them to him in their pockets, he sipped tea, he
worshipped his belly, filling it with sweet things and his
mind with haughty thoughts. . . . And for this he is put to
shame. . . ."

"You speak lightly, Father." Father Païssy too raised his
voice. "I admire your fasting and severities, but you speak
lightly like some frivolous youth, fickle and childish. Go
away, Father, I command you!" Father Païssy thundered in
conclusion.

"I will go," said Ferapont, seeming somewhat taken aback,
but still as bitter. "You learned men! You are so clever you
look down upon my humbleness. I came hither with little
learning and here I have forgotten what I did know. God Himself has preserved me in my weakness from your subtlety."

Father Païssy stood over him, waiting resolutely. Father
Ferapont paused and, suddenly leaning his cheek on his hand
despondently, pronounced in a sing-song voice, looking at the
coffin of the dead elder:

"To-morrow they will sing over him 'Our Helper and Defender'—a splendid anthem—and over me when I die all they'll
sing will be 'What earthly joy'—a little canticle," * he added
with tearful regret. "You are proud and puffed up, this is a
vain place!" he shouted suddenly like a madman, and with a
wave of his hand he turned quickly and quickly descended the
steps. The crowd awaiting him below wavered; some followed
him at once and some lingered, for the cell was still open, and
Father Païssy, following Father Ferapont on to the steps, stood
watching him. But the excited old fanatic was not completely
silenced. Walking twenty steps away, he suddenly turned towards the setting sun, raised both his arms and, as though someone had cut him down, fell to the ground with a loud scream.

"My God has conquered! Christ has conquered the setting
sun!" he shouted frantically, stretching up his hands to the
sun, and falling face downwards on the ground, he sobbed like
a little child, shaken by his tears and spreading out his arms on
the ground. Then all rushed up to him; there were exclamations

* When a monk's body is carried out from the cell to the church and
from the church to the graveyard, the canticle "What earthly joy" . . .
is sung. If the deceased was a priest as well as a monk the canticle
"Our Helper and Defender" is sung instead.

and sympathetic sobs . . . a kind of frenzy seemed to take possession of them all.

"This is the one who is a saint! This is the one who is a holy man!" some cried aloud, losing their fear. "This is he who should be an elder," others added malignantly.

"He wouldn't be an elder . . . he would refuse . . . he wouldn't serve a cursed innovation . . . he wouldn't imitate their foolery," other voices chimed in at once. And it is hard to say how far they might have gone, but at that moment the bell rang summoning them to service. All began crossing themselves at once. Father Ferapont, too, got up and crossing himself went back to his cell without looking round, still uttering exclamations which were utterly incoherent. A few followed him, but the greater number dispersed, hastening to service. Father Païssy let Father Iosif read in his place and went down. The frantic outcries of bigots could not shake him, but his heart was suddenly filled with melancholy for some special reason and he felt that. He stood still and suddenly wondered, "Why am I sad even to dejection?" and immediately grasped with surprise that his sudden sadness was due to a very small and special cause. In the crowd thronging at the entrance to the cell he had noticed Alyosha and he remembered that he had felt at once a pang at heart on seeing him. "Can that boy mean so much to my heart now?" he asked himself, wondering.

At that moment Alyosha passed him, hurrying away, but not in the direction of the church. Their eyes met. Alyosha quickly turned away his eyes and dropped them to the ground, and from the boy's look alone, Father Païssy guessed what a great change was taking place in him at that moment.

"Have you, too, fallen into temptation?" cried Father Païssy. "Can you be with those of little faith?" he added mournfully.

Alyosha stood still and gazed vaguely at Father Païssy, but quickly turned his eyes away again and again looked on the ground. He stood sideways and did not turn his face to Father Païssy, who watched him attentively.

"Where are you hastening? The bell calls to service," he asked again, but again Alyosha gave no answer.

"Are you leaving the hermitage? What! without asking leave, without asking a blessing?"

Alyosha suddenly gave a wry smile, cast a strange, very strange, look at the Father to whom his former guide, the former sovereign of his heart and mind, his beloved elder, had

12

confided him as he lay dying. And suddenly, still without speaking, waved his hand, as though not caring even to be respectful, and with rapid steps walked towards the gates away from the hermitage.

"You will come back again!" murmured Father Païssy, looking after him with sorrowful surprise.

CHAPTER II

A CRITICAL MOMENT

FATHER PAÏSSY, of course, was not wrong when he decided that his "dear boy" would come back again. Perhaps indeed, to some extent, he penetrated with insight into the true meaning of Alyosha's spiritual condition. Yet I must frankly own that it would be very difficult for me to give a clear account of that strange, vague moment in the life of the young hero I love so much. To Father Païssy's sorrowful question, "Are you too with those of little faith?" I could of course confidently answer for Alyosha, No, he is not with those of little faith. Quite the contrary. Indeed, all his trouble came from the fact that he was of great faith. But still the trouble was there and was so agonising that even long afterwards Alyosha thought of that sorrowful day as one of the bitterest and most fatal days of his life. If the question is asked: "Could all his grief and disturbance have been due only to the fact that his elder's body had shown signs of premature decomposition instead of at once performing miracles?" I must answer without beating about the bush, "Yes, it certainly was". I would only beg the reader not to be in too great a hurry to laugh at my young hero's pure heart. I am far from intending to apologise for him or to justify his innocent faith on the ground of his youth, or the little progress he had made in his studies, or any such reason. I must declare, on the contrary, that I have genuine respect for the qualities of his heart. No doubt a youth who received impressions cautiously, whose love was lukewarm, and whose mind was too prudent for his age and so of little value, such a young man might, I admit, have avoided what happened to my hero. But in some cases it is really more creditable to be carried away by an emotion, however unreasonable, which springs from a great love, than to be unmoved. And this is even truer in youth, for a young man who is always sensible

13

is to be suspected and is of little worth—that's my opinion!

"But," reasonable people will exclaim perhaps, "every young man cannot believe in such a superstition and your hero is no model for others."

To this I reply again, Yes! my hero had faith, a faith holy and steadfast, but still I am not going to apologise for him.

Though I declared above, and perhaps too hastily, that I should not explain or justify my hero, I see that some explanation is necessary for the understanding of the rest of my story. Let me say, then, it was not a question of miracles. There was no frivolous and impatient expectation of miracles in his mind. And Alyosha needed no miracles at the time, for the triumph of some preconceived idea—oh no, not at all—what he saw before all was one figure—the figure of his beloved elder, the figure of that holy man whom he revered with such adoration. The fact is that all the love that lay concealed in his pure young heart for everyone and everything had, for the past year, been concentrated—and perhaps wrongly so—on one being, his beloved elder. It is true that being had for so long been accepted by him as his ideal, that all his young strength and energy could not but turn towards that ideal, even to the forgetting at the moment "of everyone and everything". He remembered afterwards how, on that terrible day, he had entirely forgotten his brother Dmitri, about whom he had been so anxious and troubled the day before; he had forgotten, too, to take the two hundred roubles to Ilusha's father, though he had so warmly intended to do so the preceding evening. But again it was not miracles he needed but only "the higher justice" which had been in his belief outraged by the blow that had so suddenly and cruelly wounded his heart. And what does it signify that this "justice" looked for by Alyosha inevitably took the shape of miracles to be wrought immediately by the ashes of his adored teacher? Why, everyone in the monastery cherished the same thought and the same hope, even those whose intellects Alyosha revered, Father Païssy himself, for instance. And so Alyosha, untroubled by doubts, clothed his dreams too in the same form as all the rest. And a whole year of life in the monastery had formed the habit of this expectation in his heart. But it was justice, justice, he thirsted for, not simply miracles.

And now the man who should, he believed, have been exalted above everyone in the whole world, that man, instead of receiving the glory that was his due, was suddenly degraded and dishonoured! What for? Who had judged him? Who could have decreed this? Those were the questions that wrung his in-experienced and virginal heart. He could not endure without mortification, without resentment even, that the holiest of holy men should have been exposed to the jeering and spiteful mockery of the frivolous crowd so inferior to him. Even had there been no miracles, had there been nothing marvellous to justify his hopes, why this indignity, why this humiliation, why this premature decay, "in excess of nature", as the spiteful monks said. Why this "sign from heaven", which they so triumphantly acclaimed in company with Father Ferapont, and why did they believe they had gained the right to acclaim it? Where is the finger of Providence? Why did Providence hide its face "at the most critical moment" (so Alyosha thought it), as though voluntarily submitting to the blind, dumb, pitiless laws of nature?

That was why Alyosha's heart was bleeding, and, of course, as I have said already, the sting of it all was that the man he loved above everything on earth should be put to shame and humiliated! This murmuring may have been shallow and un-reasonable in my hero, but I repeat again for the third time—and am prepared to admit that it might be difficult to defend my feeling—I am glad that my hero showed himself not too reasonable at that moment, for any man of sense will always come back to reason in time, but if love does not gain the upper hand in a boy's heart at such an exceptional moment, when will it? I will not, however, omit to mention something strange, which came for a time to the surface of Alyosha's mind at this fatal and obscure moment. This new something was the harassing impression left by the conversation with Ivan, which now persistently haunted Alyosha's mind. At this moment it haunted him. Oh, it was not that something of the fundamental, elemental, so to speak, faith of his soul had been shaken. He loved his God and believed in Him steadfastly, though he was suddenly murmuring against Him. Yet a vague but tormenting and evil impression left by his conversation with Ivan the day before, suddenly revived again now in his soul and seemed forcing its way to the surface of his consciousness.

It had begun to get dusk when Rakitin, crossing the pine copse from the hermitage to the monastery, suddenly noticed Alyosha, lying face downwards on the ground under a tree, not moving and apparently asleep. He went up and called him by his name.

"You here, Alexey? Can you have . . ." he began wonder-

ing but broke off. He had meant to say: "Can you have come
to this?"

Alyosha did not look at him, but from a slight movement
Rakitin at once saw that he heard and understood him.

"What's the matter?" he went on; but the surprise in his
face gradually passed into a smile that became more and more
ironical.

"I say, I've been looking for you for the last two hours. You
suddenly disappeared. What are you about? What foolery is
this? You might just look at me . . ."

Alyosha raised his head, sat up and leaned his back against
the tree. He was not crying, but there was a look of suffering
and irritability in his face. He did not look at Rakitin, however, but looked away to one side of him.

"Do you know your face is quite changed? There's none of
your famous mildness to be seen in it. Are you angry with someone? Have they been ill-treating you?"

"Let me alone," said Alyosha suddenly, with a weary
gesture of his hand, still looking away from him.

"Oho! So that's how we are feeling! So you can shout at
people like other mortals. That is a come-down from the angels.
I say, Alyosha, you have surprised me, do you hear? I mean
it. It's long since I've been surprised at anything here. I
always took you for an educated man . . ."

Alyosha at last looked at him, but vaguely, as though scarcely
understanding what he said.

"Can you really be so upset simply because your old man
has begun to stink? You don't mean to say you seriously
believed that he was going to work miracles?" exclaimed
Rakitin, genuinely surprised again.

"I believed, I believe, I want to believe, and I will believe,
what more do you want?" cried Alyosha irritably.

"Nothing at all, my boy. Damn it all, why no schoolboy of
thirteen believes in that now. But there . . . So now you are
'n a temper with your God, you are rebelling against Him; He
hasn't given promotion, He hasn't bestowed the order of merit!
Eh, you are a set!"

Alyosha gazed a long while with his eyes half closed at
Rakitin, and there was a sudden gleam in his eyes . , but
not of anger with Rakitin.

"I am not rebelling against my God; I simply 'don't accept
His world'." Alyosha suddenly smiled a forced smile.

"How do you mean, you don't accept the world?" Rakitin

16

thought a moment over his answer. "What idiocy is this?"

Alyosha did not answer.

"Come, enough nonsense, now to business. Have you had anything to eat to-day?"

"I don't remember . . . I think I have."

"You need keeping up, to judge by your face. It makes one sorry to look at you. You didn't sleep all night either, I hear, you had a meeting in there. And then all this bobbery afterwards. Most likely you've had nothing to eat but a mouthful of holy bread. I've got some sausage in my pocket; I've brought it from the town in case of need, only you won't eat sausage. . . ."

"Give me some."

"I say! You are going it! Why, it's a regular mutiny, with barricades! Well, my boy, we must make the most of it. Come to my place . . . I shouldn't mind a drop of vodka myself, I am tired to death. Vodka is going too far for you, I suppose . . . or would you like some?"

"Give me some vodka too."

"Hullo! You surprise me, brother!" Rakitin looked at him in amazement. "Well, one way or another, vodka or sausage, this is a jolly fine chance and mustn't be missed. Come along."

Alyosha got up in silence and followed Rakitin.

"If your little brother Ivan could see this—wouldn't he be surprised! By the way, your brother Ivan set off to Moscow this morning, did you know?"

"Yes," answered Alyosha listlessly, and suddenly the image of his brother Dmitri rose before his mind. But only for a minute, and though it reminded him of something that must not be put off for a moment, some duty, some terrible obligation, even that reminder made no impression on him, did not reach his heart and instantly faded out of his mind and was forgotten. But, a long while afterwards, Alyosha remembered this.

"Your brother Ivan declared once that I was a 'liberal booby with no talents whatever'. Once you, too, could not resist letting me know I was 'dishonourable'. Well! I should like to see what your talents and sense of honour will do for you now." This phrase Rakitin finished to himself in a whisper.

"Listen!" he said aloud, "let's go by the path beyond the monastery straight to the town. H'm! I ought to go to Madame Hohlakov's, by the way. Only fancy, I've written to tell her everything that happened, and would you believe it, she

17

answered me instantly in pencil (the lady has a passion for writing notes) that 'she would never have expected *such conduct* from a man of such a reverend character as Father Zossima'. That was her very word: 'conduct'. She is angry too. Eh, you are a set! Stay!" he cried suddenly again. He suddenly stopped and taking Alyosha by the shoulder made him stop too.

"Do you know, Alyosha," he peeped inquisitively into his eyes, absorbed in a sudden new thought which had dawned on him, and though he was laughing outwardly he was evidently afraid to utter that new idea aloud, so difficult he still found it to believe in the strange and unexpected mood in which he now saw Alyosha. "Alyosha, do you know where we had better go?" he brought out at last timidly, and insinuatingly.

"I don't care . . . where you like."

"Let's go to Grushenka, eh? Will you come?" pronounced Rakitin at last, trembling with timid suspense.

"Let's go to Grushenka," Alyosha answered calmly, at once, and this prompt and calm agreement was such a surprise to Rakitin that he almost started back.

"Well! I say!" he cried in amazement, but seizing Alyosha firmly by the arm he led him along the path, still dreading that he would change his mind.

They walked along in silence, Rakitin was positively afraid to talk.

"And how glad she will be, how delighted," he muttered, but lapsed into silence again. And indeed it was not to please Grushenka he was taking Alyosha to her. He was a practical person and never undertook anything without a prospect of gain for himself. His object in this case was twofold, first a revengeful desire to see "the downfall of the righteous", and Alyosha's fall "from the saints to the sinners", over which he was already gloating in his imagination, and in the second place he had in view a certain material gain for himself, of which more will be said later.

"So the critical moment has come," he thought to himself with spiteful glee, "and we shall catch it on the hop, for it's just what we want."

CHAPTER III

GRUSHENKA lived in the busiest part of the town, near the cathedral square, in a small wooden lodge in the court-yard belonging to the house of the widow Morozov. The house was a large stone building of two storeys, old and very ugly. The widow led a secluded life with her two unmarried nieces, who were also elderly women. She had no need to let her lodge, but everyone knew that she had taken in Grushenka as a lodger, four years before, solely to please her kinsman, the merchant Samsonov, who was known to be the girl's protector. It was said that the jealous old man's object in placing his "favourite" with the widow Morozov was that the old woman should keep a sharp eye on her new lodger's conduct. But this sharp eye soon proved to be unnecessary, and in the end the widow Morozov seldom met Grushenka and did not worry her by looking after her in any way. It is true that four years had passed since the old man had brought the slim, delicate, shy, timid, dreamy, and sad girl of eighteen from the chief town of the province, and much had happened since then. Little was known of the girl's history in the town and that little was vague. Nothing more had been learnt during the last four years, even after many persons had become interested in the beautiful young woman into whom Agrafena Alexandrovna had meanwhile developed. There were rumours that she had been, at seventeen, betrayed by someone, some sort of officer, and immediately afterwards abandoned by him. The officer had gone away and afterwards married, while Grushenka had been left in poverty and disgrace. It was said, however, that though Grushenka had been raised from destitution by the old man Samsonov, she came of a respectable family belonging to the clerical class, that she was the daughter of a deacon or something of the sort.

And now after four years the sensitive, injured and pathetic little orphan had become a plump, rosy beauty of the Russian type, a woman of bold and determined character, proud and insolent. She had a good head for business, was acquisitive, saving and careful, and by fair means or foul had succeeded, it was said, in amassing a little fortune. There was only one point on which all were agreed. Grushenka was not easily to be approached, and except her aged protector there had not been one man who could boast of her favours during those four years. It was a positive fact, for there had been a good many, especially during the last two years, who had attempted to obtain those favours. But all their efforts had been in vain and some of these suitors had been forced to beat an undignified and even comic retreat, owing to the firm and ironical resistance they met from the strong-willed young person. It was known too that the young person had, especially of late, been given to what is called "speculation", and that she had shown marked abilities in that direction, so that many people began to say that she was no better than a Jew. It was not that she lent money on interest, but it was known, for instance, that she had for some time past, in partnership with old Karamazov, actually invested in the purchase of bad debts for a trifle, a tenth of their nominal value, and afterwards had made out of them ten times their value.

The old widower Samsonov, a man of large fortune, was stingy and merciless. He tyrannised over his grown-up sons, but for the last year, during which he had been ill and lost the use of his swollen legs, he had fallen greatly under the influence of his protégée, whom he had at first kept strictly and in humble surroundings "on Lenten fare", as the wits said at the time. But Grushenka had succeeded in emancipating herself, while she established in him a boundless belief in her fidelity. The old man, now long since dead, had had a large business in his day and was also a noteworthy character, miserly and hard as flint. Though Grushenka's hold upon him was so strong that he could not live without her (it had been so especially for the last two years), he did not settle any considerable fortune on her and would not have been moved to do so if she had threatened to leave him. But he had presented her with a small sum, and even that was a surprise to everyone when it became known.

"You are a wench with brains," he said to her, when he gave her eight thousand roubles, "and you must look after yourself, but let me tell you that except your yearly allowance as before, you'll get nothing more from me to the day of my death, and I'll leave you nothing in my will either."

And he kept his word; he died and left everything to his sons, whom, with their wives and children, he had treated all his life as servants. Grushenka was not even mentioned in his will. All this became known afterwards. He helped Grushenka with his advice to increase her capital and put business in her way.

20

When Fyodor Pavlovitch, who first came into contact with Grushenka over a piece of speculation, ended, to his own surprise, by falling madly in love with her, old Samsonov, gravely ill as he was, was immensely amused. It is remarkable that throughout their whole acquaintance Grushenka was absolutely and spontaneously open with the old man, and he seems to have been the only person in the world with whom she was so. Of late, when Dmitri too had come on the scene with his love, the old man left off laughing. On the contrary, he once gave Grushenka a stern and earnest piece of advice.

"If you have to choose between the two, father or son, you'd better choose the old man, if only you make sure the old scoundrel will marry you and settle some fortune on you before-hand. But don't keep on with the captain, you'll get no good out of that."

These were the very words of the old profligate, who felt already that his death was not far off and who actually died five months later.

I will note, too, in passing, that although many in our town knew of the grotesque and monstrous rivalry of the Karamazovs, father and son, the object of which was Grushenka, scarcely anyone understood what really underlay her attitude to both of them. Even Grushenka's two servants (after the catastrophe of which we will speak later) testified in court that she received Dmitri Fyodorovitch simply from fear because "he threatened to murder her". These servants were an old cook, invalidish and almost deaf, who came from Grushenka's old home, and her granddaughter, a smart young girl of twenty, who performed the duties of a maid. Grushenka lived very economically and her surroundings were anything but luxurious. Her lodge consisted of three rooms furnished with mahogany furniture in the fashion of 1820, belonging to her landlady.

It was quite dark when Rakitin and Alyosha entered her rooms, yet they were not lighted up. Grushenka was lying down in her drawing-room on the big, hard, clumsy sofa with a mahogany back. The sofa was covered with shabby and ragged leather. Under her head she had two white down pillows taken from her bed. She was lying stretched out motionless on her back with her hands behind her head. She was dressed as though expecting someone, in a black silk dress, with a dainty lace fichu on her head, which was very becoming. Over her shoulders was thrown a lace shawl pinned with a massive gold

21

brooch. She certainly was expecting someone. She lay as though impatient and weary, her face rather pale and her lips and eyes hot, restlessly tapping the arm of the sofa with the tip of her right foot. The appearance of Rakitin and Alyosha caused a slight excitement. From the hall they could hear Grushenka leap up from the sofa and cry out in a frightened voice: "Who's there?" But the maid met the visitors and at once called back to her mistress:

"It's not he, it's nothing, only other visitors."

"What can be the matter?" muttered Rakitin, leading Alyosha into the drawing-room.

Grushenka was standing by the sofa as though still alarmed. A thick coil of her dark brown hair escaped from its lace covering and fell on her right shoulder, but she did not notice it and did not put it back till she had gazed at her visitors and recognised them.

"Ah, it's you, Rakitin? You quite frightened me. Whom have you brought? Who is this with you? Good heavens, you have brought him!" she exclaimed, recognising Alyosha.

"Do send for candles!" said Rakitin, with the free-and-easy air of a most intimate friend, who is privileged to give orders in the house.

"Candles . . . of course, candles. . . . Fenya, fetch him a candle. . . . Well, you have chosen a moment to bring him!" she exclaimed again, nodding towards Alyosha and turning to the looking-glass she began quickly fastening up her hair with both hands. She seemed displeased.

"Haven't I managed to please you?" asked Rakitin, instantly almost offended.

"You frightened me, Rakitin, that's what it is." Grushenka turned with a smile to Alyosha. "Don't be afraid of me, my dear Alyosha, you can't think how glad I am to see you, my unexpected visitor. But you frightened me, Rakitin, I thought it was Mitya breaking in. You see, I deceived him just now, I made him promise to believe me and I told him a lie. I told him that I was going to spend the evening with my old man, Kuzma Kuzmitch, and should be there till late counting up his money. I always spend one whole evening a week with him making up his accounts. We lock ourselves in and he counts on the reckoning beads while I sit and put things down in the book. I am the only person he trusts. Mitya believes that I am there, but I came back and have been sitting locked in here, expecting some news. How was it Fenya let you in? Fenya, Fenya, run out to the gate, open it and look about whether the captain is to be seen! Perhaps he is hiding and spying, I am dreadfully frightened."

"There's no one there, Agrafena Alexandrovna, I've just looked out, I keep running to peep through the crack, I am in fear and trembling myself."

"Are the shutters fastened, Fenya? And we must draw the curtains—that's better!" She drew the heavy curtains herself. "He'd rush in at once if he saw a light. I am afraid of your brother Mitya to-day, Alyosha."

Grushenka spoke aloud, and though she was alarmed, she seemed very happy about something.

"Why are you so afraid of Mitya to-day?" inquired Rakitin. "I should have thought you were not timid with him, you'd twist him round your little finger."

"I tell you, I am expecting news, priceless news, so I don't want Mitya at all. And he didn't believe, I feel he didn't, that I should stay at Kuzma Kuzmitch's. He must be in his ambush now, behind Fyodor Pavlovitch's, in the garden, watching for me. And if he's there, he won't come here, so much the better! But I really have been to Kuzma Kuzmitch's. Mitya escorted me there. I told him I should stay there till midnight, and I asked him to be sure to come at midnight to fetch me home. He went away and I sat ten minutes with Kuzma Kuzmitch and came back here again. Ugh! I was afraid, I ran for fear of meeting him."

"And why are you so dressed up? What a curious cap you've got on!"

"How curious you are yourself, Rakitin! I tell you, I am expecting a message. If the message comes, I shall fly, I shall gallop away and you will see no more of me. That's why I am dressed up, so as to be ready."

"And where are you flying to?"

"If you know too much, you'll get old too soon."

"Upon my word! You are highly delighted . . . I've never seen you like this before. You are dressed up as if you were going to a ball." Rakitin looked her up and down.

"Much you know about balls."

"And do you know much about them?"

"I have seen a ball. The year before last, Kuzma Kuzmitch's son was married and I looked on from the gallery. Do you suppose I want to be talking to you, Rakitin, while a prince like this is standing here? Such a visitor! Alyosha, my dear boy, I gaze at you and can't believe my eyes. Good heavens, can you have come here to see me! To tell you the truth I never had a thought of seeing you and I didn't think that you would ever come and see me. Though this is not the moment now, I am awfully glad to see you. Sit down on the sofa, here, that's right, my bright young moon. I really can't take it in even now . . . Eh, Rakitin, if only you had brought him yesterday or the day before! But I am glad as it is! Perhaps it's better he has come now, at such a moment, and not the day before yesterday."

She gaily sat down beside Alyosha on the sofa, looking at him with positive delight. And she really was glad, she was not lying when she said so. Her eyes glowed, her lips laughed, but it was a good-natured merry laugh. Alyosha had not expected to see such a kind expression in her face. . . . He had hardly met her till the day before, he had formed an alarming idea of her, and had been horribly distressed the day before by the spiteful and treacherous trick she had played on Katerina Ivanovna. He was greatly surprised to find her now altogether different from what he had expected. And, crushed as he was by his own sorrow, his eyes involuntarily rested on her with attention. Her whole manner seemed changed for the better since yesterday, there was scarcely any trace of that mawkish sweetness in her speech, of that voluptuous softness in her movements. Everything was simple and good-natured, her gestures were rapid, direct, confiding, but she was greatly excited.

"Dear me, how everything comes together to-day!" she chattered on again. "And why I am so glad to see you, Alyosha, I couldn't say myself! If you ask me, I couldn't tell you."

"Come, don't you know why you're glad?" said Rakitin, grinning. "You used to be always pestering me to bring him, you'd some object, I suppose."

"I had a different object once, but now that's over, this is not the moment. I say, I want you to have something nice. I am so good-natured now. You sit down, too, Rakitin, why are you standing? You've sat down already? There's no fear of Rakitin's forgetting to look after himself. Look, Alyosha, he's sitting there opposite us, so offended that I didn't ask him to sit down before you. Ugh, Rakitin is such a one to take offence!" laughed Grushenka. "Don't be angry, Rakitin, I'm kind to-day. Why are you so depressed, Alyosha, are you afraid of me?'' she peeped into his eyes with merry mockery.

"He's sad. The promotion has not been given," boomed Rakitin.

"What promotion?''

"His elder stinks.''

"What? You are talking some nonsense, you want to say something nasty. Be quiet, you stupid! Let me sit on your knee, Alyosha, like this." She suddenly skipped forward and jumped, laughing, on his knee, like a nestling kitten, with her right arm about his neck. "I'll cheer you up, my pious boy. Yes, really, will you let me sit on your knee, you won't be angry? If you tell me, I'll get off?''

Alyosha did not speak. He sat afraid to move, he heard her words, "If you tell me, I'll get off", but he did not answer. But there was nothing in his heart such as Rakitin, for instance, watching him malignantly from his corner, might have expected or fancied. The great grief in his heart swallowed up every sensation that might have been aroused, and if only he could have thought clearly at that moment he would have realised that he had now the strongest armour to protect him from every lust and temptation. Yet in spite of the vague irresponsiveness of his spiritual condition and the sorrow that overwhelmed him, he could not help wondering at a new and strange sensation in his heart. This woman, this "dreadful" woman, had no terror for him now, none of that terror that had stirred in his soul at any passing thought of woman. On the contrary, this woman, dreaded above all women, sitting now on his knee, holding him in her arms, aroused in him now a quite different, unexpected, peculiar feeling, a feeling of the intensest and purest interest without a trace of fear, of his former terror. That was what instinctively surprised him.

"You've talked nonsense enough," cried Rakitin, "you'd much better give us some champagne. You owe it me, you know you do!''

"Yes, I really do. Do you know, Alyosha, I promised him champagne on the top of everything, if he'd bring you? I'll have some too! Fenya, Fenya, bring us the bottle Mitya left! Look sharp! Though I am so stingy, I'll stand a bottle, not for you, Rakitin, you're a toadstool, but he is a falcon! And though my heart is full of something very different, so be it, I'll drink with you. I long for some dissipation."

"But what is the matter with you? And what is this message, may I ask, or is it a secret?'' Rakitin put in inquisitively, doing

25

his best to pretend not to notice the snubs that were being continually aimed at him.

"Ech, it's not a secret, and you know it, too," Grushenka said, in a voice suddenly anxious, turning her head towards Rakitin, and drawing a little away from Alyosha, though she still sat on his knee with her arm round his neck. "My officer is coming, Rakitin, my officer is coming."

"I heard he was coming, but is he so near?"

"He is at Mokroe now, he'll send a messenger from there, so he wrote, I got a letter from him to-day. I am expecting the messenger every minute."

"You don't say so! Why at Mokroe?"

"That's a long story, I've told you enough."

"Mitya'll be up to something now—I say! Does he know or doesn't he?"

" 'He know!' Of course he doesn't. If he knew there would be murder. But I am not afraid of that now, I am not afraid of his knife. Be quiet, Rakitin, don't remind me of Dmitri Fyodorovitch, he has bruised my heart. And I don't want to think of that at this moment. I can think of Alyosha here, I can look at Alyosha . . . Smile at me, dear, cheer up, smile at my foolishness, at my pleasure. . . . Ah, he's smiling, he's smiling! How kindly he looks at me! And you know, Alyosha, I've been thinking all this time you were angry with me, because of the day before yesterday, because of that young lady. I was a cur, that's the truth. . . . But it's a good thing it happened so. It was a horrid thing, but a good thing too." Grushenka smiled dreamily and a little cruel line showed in her smile. "Mitya told me that she screamed out that I 'ought to be flogged'. I did insult her dreadfully. She sent for me, she wanted to make a conquest of me, to win me over with her chocolate. . . . No, it's a good thing it did end like that." She smiled again. "But I am still afraid of your being angry."

"Yes, that's really true," Rakitin put in suddenly, with genuine surprise. "Alyosha, she is really afraid of a chicken like you."

"He is a chicken to you, Rakitin . . . because you've no conscience, that's what it is! You see, I love him with all my soul, that's how it is! Alyosha, do you believe I love you with all my soul?"

"Ah, you shameless woman! She is making you a declaration, Alexey!"

"Well, what of it? I love him!"

26

"And what about your officer? And the priceless message from Mokroe?"

"That is quite different."

"That's a woman's way of looking at it!"

"Don't you make me angry, Rakitin." Grushenka caught him up hotly. "This is quite different. I love Alyosha in a different way. It's true, Alyosha, I had sly designs on you before. For I am a horrid, violent creature. But at other times I've looked upon you, Alyosha, as my conscience. I've kept thinking 'how anyone like that must despise a nasty thing like me'. I thought that the day before yesterday, as I ran home from the young lady's. I have thought of you a long time in that way, Alyosha, and Mitya knows. I've talked to him about it. Mitya understands. Would you believe it, I sometimes look at you and feel ashamed, utterly ashamed of myself. . . . And how, and since when, I began to think about you like that I can't say, I don't remember . . ."

Fenya came in and put a tray with an uncorked bottle and three glasses of champagne on the table.

"Here's the champagne!" cried Rakitin. "You're excited, Agrafena Alexandrovna, and not yourself. When you've had a glass of champagne, you'll be ready to dance. Eh, they can't even do that properly," he added, looking at the bottle. "The old woman's poured it out in the kitchen and the bottle's been brought in warm and without a cork. Well, let me have some, anyway."

He went up to the table, took a glass, emptied it at one gulp and poured himself out another.

"One doesn't often stumble upon champagne," he said, licking his lips. "Now, Alyosha, take a glass, show what you can do! What shall we drink to? The gates of paradise? Take a glass, Grushenka, you drink to the gates of paradise, too."

"What gates of paradise?"

She took a glass, Alyosha took his, tasted it and put it back.

"No, I'd better not," he smiled gently.

"And you bragged!" cried Rakitin.

"Well, if so, I won't either," chimed in Grushenka, "I really don't want any. You can drink the whole bottle alone, Rakitin. If Alyosha has some, I will."

"What touching sentimentality!" said Rakitin tauntingly, "and she's sitting on his knee, too! He's got something to grieve over, but what's the matter with you? He is rebelling against his God and ready to eat sausage . . ."

THE BROTHERS KARAMAZOV

"How so?"

"His elder died to-day—Father Zossima, the saint."

"So Father Zossima is dead," cried Grushenka. "Good God, I did not know!" She crossed herself devoutly. "Goodness, what have I been doing, sitting on his knee like this at such a moment!" She started up as though in dismay, instantly slipped off his knee and sat down on the sofa.

Alyosha bent a long wondering look upon her and a light seemed to dawn in his face.

"Rakitin," he said suddenly, in a firm and loud voice, "don't taunt me with having rebelled against God. I don't want to feel angry with you, so you must be kinder, too. I've lost a treasure such as you have never had, and you cannot judge me now. You had much better look at her—do you see how she has pity on me? I came here to find a wicked soul— I felt drawn to evil because I was base and evil myself, and I've found a true sister, I have found a treasure—a loving heart. She had pity on me just now. . . . Agrafena Alexandrovna, I am speaking of you. You've raised my soul from the depths."

Alyosha's lips were quivering and he caught his breath.

"She has saved you, it seems," laughed Rakitin spitefully. "And she meant to get you in her clutches, do you realise that?"

"Stay, Rakitin." Grushenka jumped up. "Hush, both of you. Now I'll tell you all about it. Hush, Alyosha, your words make me ashamed, for I am bad and not good—that's what I am. And you hush, Rakitin, because you are telling lies. I had the low idea of trying to get him in my clutches, but now you are lying, now it's all different. And don't let me hear anything more from you, Rakitin."

All this Grushenka said with extreme emotion.

"They are both crazy," said Rakitin, looking at them with amazement. "I feel as though I were in a madhouse. They're both getting so feeble they'll begin crying in a minute."

"I shall begin to cry, I shall," repeated Grushenka. "He called me his sister and I shall never forget that. Only let me tell you, Rakitin, though I am bad, I did give away an onion."

"An onion? Hang it all, you really are crazy."

Rakitin wondered at their enthusiasm. He was aggrieved and annoyed, though he might have reflected that each of them was just passing through a spiritual crisis such as does not come often in a lifetime. But though Rakitin was very sensitive about

28

everything that concerned himself, he was very obtuse as regards the feelings and sensations of others—partly from his youth and inexperience, partly from his intense egoism.

"You see, Alyosha," Grushenka turned to him with a nervous laugh. "I was boasting when I told Rakitin I had given away an onion, but it's not to boast I tell you about it. It's only a story, but it's a nice story. I used to hear it when I was a child from Matryona, my cook, who is still with me. It's like this: Once upon a time there was a peasant woman, and a very wicked woman she was. And she died and did not leave a single good deed behind. The devils caught her and plunged her into the lake of fire. So her guardian angel stood and wondered what good deed of hers he could remember to tell to God; 'she once pulled up an onion in her garden,' said he, 'and gave it to a beggar woman'. And God answered: 'You take that onion then, hold it out to her in the lake, and let her take hold and be pulled out. And if you can pull her out of the lake, let her come to Paradise, but if the onion breaks, then the woman must stay where she is.' The angel ran to the woman and held out the onion to her. 'Come,' said he, 'catch hold and I'll pull you out.' And he began cautiously pulling her out. He had just pulled her right out when the other sinners in the lake, seeing how she was being drawn out, began catching hold of her so as to be pulled out with her. But she was a very wicked woman and she began kicking them. 'I'm to be pulled out, not you. It's my onion, not yours.' As soon as she said that, the onion broke. And the woman fell into the lake and she is burning there to this day. So the angel wept and went away. So that's the story, Alyosha; I know it by heart, for I am that wicked woman myself. I boasted to Rakitin that I had given away an onion, but to you I'll say: 'I've done nothing but give away one onion all my life, that's the only good deed I've done.' So don't praise me, Alyosha, don't think me good, I am bad, I am a wicked woman and you make me ashamed if you praise me. Eh, I must confess everything. Listen, Alyosha. I was so anxious to get hold of you that I promised Rakitin twenty-five roubles if he would bring you to me. Stay, Rakitin, wait!"

She went with rapid steps to the table, opened a drawer. pulled out a purse and took from it a twenty-five-rouble note.

"What nonsense! What nonsense!" cried Rakitin, disconcerted.

"Take it, Rakitin, I owe it you, there's no fear of your

refusing it, you asked for it yourself." And she threw the note to him.

"Likely I should refuse it!" boomed Rakitin, obviously abashed, but carrying off his confusion with a swagger. "That will come in very handy; fools are made for wise men's profit."

"And now hold your tongue, Rakitin, what I am going to say now is not for your ears. Sit down in that corner and keep quiet. You don't like us, so hold your tongue."

"What should I like you for?" Rakitin snarled, not concealing his ill-humour. He put the twenty-five-rouble note in his pocket and he felt ashamed at Alyosha's seeing it. He had reckoned on receiving his payment later, without Alyosha's knowing of it, and now, feeling ashamed, he lost his temper. Till that moment he had thought it discreet not to contradict Grushenka too flatly in spite of her snubbing, since he had something to get out of her. But now he, too, was angry:

"One loves people for some reason, but what have either of you done for me?"

"You should love people without a reason, as Alyosha does."

"How dare he love you? How has he shown it, that you make such a fuss about it?"

Grushenka was standing in the middle of the room; she spoke with heat and there were hysterical notes in her voice.

"Hush, Rakitin, you know nothing about us! And don't dare to speak to me like that again. How dare you be so familiar! Sit in that corner and be quiet, as though you were my footman! And now, Alyosha, I'll tell you the whole truth, that you may see what a wretch I am! I am not talking to Rakitin, but to you. I wanted to ruin you, Alyosha, that's the holy truth; I quite meant to. I wanted to so much, that I bribed Rakitin to bring you. And why did I want to do such a thing? You know nothing about it, Alyosha, you turned away from me, if you passed me, you dropped your eyes. And I've looked at you a hundred times before to-day, I began asking everyone about you. Your face haunted my heart. 'He despises me,' I thought, 'he won't even look at me.' And I felt it so much at last that I wondered at myself for being so frightened of a boy. I'll get him in my clutches and laugh at him. I was full of spite and anger. Would you believe it, nobody here dares talk or think of coming to Agrafena Alexandrovna with any evil purpose. Old Kuzma is the only man I have anything to do with here, I was bound and sold to him, Satan brought us together, but there has been no one else. But looking at you, I thought I'll get him in my clutches and laugh at him. You see what a spiteful cur I am, and you called me your sister! And now that man who wronged me has come; I sit here waiting for a message from him. And do you know what that man has been to me? Five years ago, when Kuzma brought me here, I used to shut myself up, that no one might have sight or sound of me. I was a silly slip of a girl; I used to sit here sobbing, I used to lie awake all night, thinking: 'Where is he now, the man who wronged me? He is laughing at me with another woman, most likely. If only I could see him, if I could meet him again, I'd pay him out, I'd pay him out!' At night I used to lie sobbing into my pillow in the dark, and I used to brood over it, I used to tear my heart on purpose and gloat over my anger. 'I'll pay him out, I'll pay him out!' That's what I used to cry out in the dark. And when I suddenly thought that I should really do nothing to him, and that he was laughing at me then, or perhaps had utterly forgotten me, I would fling myself on the floor, melt into helpless tears, and lie there shaking till dawn. In the morning I would get up more spiteful than a dog, ready to tear the whole world to pieces. And then what do you think? I began saving money, I became hardhearted, grew stout—grew wiser, would you say? No, no one in the whole world sees it, no one knows it, but when night comes on, I sometimes lie as I did five years ago, when I was a silly girl, clenching my teeth and crying all night, thinking: 'I'll pay him out, I'll pay him out!' Do you hear? Well then, now you understand me. A month ago a letter came to me—he was coming, he was a widower, he wanted to see me. It took my breath away, then I suddenly thought: 'If he comes and whistles to call me, I shall creep back to him like a beaten dog.' I couldn't believe myself. Am I so abject? Shall I run to him or not? And I've been in such a rage with myself all this month that I am worse than I was five years ago. Do you see now, Alyosha, what a violent, vindictive creature I am? I have shown you the whole truth! I played with Mitya to keep me from running to that other. Hush, Rakitin, it's not for you to judge me, I am not speaking to you. Before you came in I was lying here waiting, brooding, deciding my whole future life and you can never know what was in my heart. Yes, Alyosha, tell your young lady not to be angry with me for what happened the day before yesterday. . . . Nobody in the whole world knows what I am going through now, and no one ever can

know. . . . For perhaps I shall take a knife with me to-day,
I can't make up my mind . . ."

And at this "tragic" phrase Grushenka broke down, hid her
face in her hands, flung herself on the sofa pillows, and sobbed
like a little child.

Alyosha got up and went to Rakitin.

"Misha," he said, "don't be angry. She wounded you, but
don't be angry. You heard what she said just now? You
mustn't ask too much of human endurance, one must be merciful."

Alyosha said this at the instinctive prompting of his heart.
He felt obliged to speak and he turned to Rakitin. If Rakitin
had not been there he would have spoken to the air. But
Rakitin looked at him ironically and Alyosha stopped short.

"You were so primed up with your elder's teaching last night
that now you have to let it off on me, Alexey, man of God!"
said Rakitin, with a smile of hatred.

"Don't laugh, Rakitin, don't smile, don't talk of the dead—
he was better than anyone in the world!" cried Alyosha, with
tears in his voice. "I didn't speak to you as a judge but as
the lowest of the judged. What am I beside her? I came here
seeking my ruin, and said to myself, 'What does it matter?'
in my cowardliness, but she, after five years in torment, as soon
as anyone says a word from the heart to her—it makes her
forget everything, forgive everything, in her tears! The man
who has wronged her has come back, he sends for her and she
forgives him everything, and hastens joyfully to meet him and
she won't take a knife with her. She won't! No, I am not like
that. I don't know whether you are, Misha, but I am not like
that. It's a lesson to me . . . She is more loving than we. . . .
Have you heard her speak of what she has just told us? No,
you haven't; if you had, you'd have understood her long ago
. . . and the person insulted the day before yesterday must
forgive her, too! She will, when she knows . . . and she shall
know . . . This soul is not yet at peace with itself, one must
be tender with it . . . there may be a treasure in that soul . . ."

Alyosha stopped, because he caught his breath. In spite of
his ill-humour Rakitin looked at him with astonishment. He
had never expected such a tirade from the gentle Alyosha.

"She's found someone to plead her cause! Why, are you
in love with her? Agrafena Alexandrovna, our monk's really
in love with you, you've made a conquest!" he cried, with a
coarse laugh.

Grushenka lifted her head from the pillow and looked at Alyosha with a tender smile shining on her tear-stained face.

"Let him alone, Alyosha, my cherub, you see what he is, he is not a person for you to speak to. Mihail Osipovitch," she turned to Rakitin, "I meant to beg your pardon for being rude to you, but now I don't want to. Alyosha, come to me, sit down here." She beckoned to him with a happy smile. "That's right, sit here. Tell me," she took him by the hand and peeped into his face, smiling, "tell me, do I love that man or not? the man who wronged me, do I love him or not? Before you came, I lay here in the dark, asking my heart whether I loved him. Decide for me, Alyosha, the time has come, it shall be as you say. Am I to forgive him or not?"

"But you have forgiven him already," said Alyosha, smiling.

"Yes, I really have forgiven him," Grushenka murmured thoughtfully. "What an abject heart! To my abject heart!" She snatched up a glass from the table, emptied it at a gulp, lifted it in the air and flung it on the floor. The glass broke with a crash. A little cruel line came into her smile.

"Perhaps I haven't forgiven him, though," she said, with a sort of menace in her voice, and she dropped her eyes to the ground as though she were talking to herself. "Perhaps my heart is only getting ready to forgive. I shall struggle with my heart. You see, Alyosha, I've grown to love my tears in these five years. . . . Perhaps I only love my resentment, not him . . ."

"Well, I shouldn't care to be in his shoes," hissed Rakitin.

"Well, you won't be, Rakitin, you'll never be in his shoes. You shall black my shoes, Rakitin, that's the place you are fit for. You'll never get a woman like me . . . and he won't either, perhaps" . . .

"Won't he? Then why are you dressed up like that?" said Rakitin, with a venomous sneer.

"Don't taunt me with dressing up, Rakitin, you don't know all that is in my heart! If I choose to tear off my finery, I'll tear it off at once, this minute," she cried in a resonant voice. "You don't know what that finery is for, Rakitin! Perhaps I shall see him and say: 'Have you ever seen me look like this before?' He left me a thin, consumptive cry-baby of seventeen. I'll sit by him, fascinate him and work him up. 'Do you see what I am like now?' I'll say to him. 'Well, and that's enough for you, my dear sir, there's many a slip twixt the cup and the lip!' That may be what the finery is for, Rakitin." Grushenka finished with a malicious laugh. "I'm violent and resentful, Alyosha, I'll tear off my finery, I'll destroy my beauty, I'll scorch my face, slash it with a knife, and turn beggar. If I choose, I won't go anywhere now to see anyone. If I choose, I'll send Kuzma back all he has ever given me, to-morrow, and all his money and I'll go out charing for the rest of my life. You think I wouldn't do it, Rakitin, that I would not dare to do it? I would, I would, I could do it directly, only don't exasperate me . . . and I'll send him about his business, I'll snap my fingers in his face, he shall never see me again!"

She uttered the last words in an hysterical scream, but broke down again, hid her face in her hands, buried it in the pillow and shook with sobs.

Rakitin got up.

"It's time we were off," he said, "it's late, we shall be shut out of the monastery."

Grushenka leapt up from her place.

"Surely you don't want to go, Alyosha!" she cried, in mournful surprise. "What are you doing to me? You stirred up my feeling, tortured me, and now you'll leave me to face this night alone!"

"He can hardly spend the night with you! Though if he wants to, let him! I'll go alone," Rakitin scoffed jeeringly.

"Hush, evil tongue!" Grushenka cried angrily at him; "you never said such words to me as he has come to say."

"What has he said to you so special?" asked Rakitin irritably.

"I can't say, I don't know. I don't know what he said to me, it went straight to my heart; he has wrung my heart. . . . He is the first one, the only one, who has pitied me, that's what it is. Why did you not come before, my angel?" She fell on her knees before him as though in a sudden frenzy. "I've been waiting all my life for someone like you, I knew that someone like you would come and forgive me. I believed that, nasty as I am, someone would really love me, not only with a shameful love!"

"What have I done to you?" answered Alyosha, bending over her with a tender smile, and gently taking her by the hands; "I only gave you an onion, nothing but a tiny little onion, that was all!"

He was moved to tears himself as he said it. At that moment there was a sudden noise in the passage, someone came into

the hall. Grushenka jumped up seeming greatly alarmed. Fenya ran noisily into the room, crying out:

"Mistress, mistress darling, a messenger has galloped up," she cried, breathless and joyful. "A carriage from Mokroe for you, Timofey the driver, with three horses, they are just putting in fresh horses. . . . A letter, here's the letter, mistress."

A letter was in her hand and she waved it in the air all the while she talked. Grushenka snatched the letter from her and carried it to the candle. It was only a note, a few lines. She read it in one instant.

"He has sent for me," she cried, her face white and distorted, with a wan smile; "he whistles! Crawl back, little dog!"

But only for one instant she stood as though hesitating; suddenly the blood rushed to her head and sent a glow to her cheeks.

"I will go," she cried; "five years of my life! Good-bye! Good-bye, Alyosha, my fate is sealed. Go, go, leave me, all of you, don't let me see you again! Grushenka is flying to a new life . . . Don't you remember evil against me either, Rakitin. I may be going to my death! Ugh! I feel as though I were drunk!"

She suddenly left them and ran into her bedroom.

"Well, she has no thoughts for us now!" grumbled Rakitin. "Let's go, or we may hear that feminine shriek again. I am sick of all these tears and cries."

Alyosha mechanically let himself be led out. In the yard stood a covered cart. Horses were being taken out of the shafts, men were running to and fro with a lantern. Three fresh horses were being led in at the open gate. But when Alyosha and Rakitin reached the bottom of the steps, Grushenka's bedroom window was suddenly opened and she called in a ringing voice after Alyosha:

"Alyosha, give my greetings to your brother Mitya and tell him not to remember evil against be, though I have brought him misery. And tell him too in my words: 'Grushenka has fallen to a scoundrel, and not to you, noble heart.' And add, too, that Grushenka loved him only one hour, only one short hour she loved him—so let him remember that hour all his life—say, 'Grushenka tells you to!' "

She ended in a voice full of sobs. The window was shut with a slam.

"Hm, hm!" growled Rakitin, laughing, "she murders your

brother Mitya and then tells him to remember it all his life!
What ferocity!"

Alyosha made no reply, he seemed not to have heard. He
walked fast beside Rakitin as though in a terrible hurry. He
was lost in thought and moved mechanically. Rakitin felt a
sudden twinge as though he had been touched on an open
wound. He had expected something quite different by bringing Grushenka and Alyosha together. Something very different
from what he had hoped for had happened.

"He is a Pole, that officer of hers," he began again, restrain-
ing himself; "and indeed he is not an officer at all now. He
served in the Customs in Siberia, somewhere on the Chinese
frontier, some puny little beggar of a Pole, I expect. Lost his
job, they say. He's heard now that Grushenka's saved a little
money, so he's turned up again—that's the explanation of the
mystery."

Again Alyosha seemed not to hear. Rakitin could not control
himself.

"Well, so you've saved the sinner?" he laughed spitefully.
"Have you turned the Magdalene into the true path? Driven
out the seven devils, eh? So you see the miracles you were
looking out for just now have come to pass!"

"Hush, Rakitin," Alyosha answered with an aching heart.

"So you despise me now for those twenty-five roubles? I've
sold my friend, you think? But you are not Christ, you know,
and I am not Judas."

"Oh, Rakitin, I assure you I'd forgotten about it," cried
Alyosha, "you remind me of it yourself . . ."

But this was the last straw for Rakitin.

"Damnation take you all and each of you!" he cried suddenly. "Why the devil did I take you up? I don't want to know
you from this time forward. Go alone, there's your road!"

And he turned abruptly into another street, leaving Alyosha
alone in the dark. Alyosha came out of the town and walked
across the fields to the monastery.

CHAPTER IV

CANA OF GALILEE

IT was very late, according to the monastery ideas, when
Alyosha returned to the hermitage; the door-keeper let him in
by a special entrance. It had struck nine o'clock—the hour of

rest and repose after a day of such agitation for all. Alyosha timidly opened the door and went into the elder's cell where his coffin was now standing. There was no one in the cell but Father Païssy, reading the Gospel in solitude over the coffin, and the young novice Porfiry, who, exhausted by the previous night's conversation and the disturbing incidents of the day, was sleeping the deep sound sleep of youth on the floor of the other room. Though Father Païssy heard Alyosha come in, he did not even look in his direction. Alyosha turned to the right from the door to the corner, fell on his knees and began to pray.

His soul was overflowing but with mingled feelings; no single sensation stood out distinctly; on the contrary, one drove out another in a slow, continual rotation. But there was a sweetness in his heart and, strange to say, Alyosha was not surprised at it. Again he saw that coffin before him, the hidden dead figure so precious to him, but the weeping and poignant grief of the morning was no longer aching in his soul. As soon as he came in, he fell down before the coffin as before a holy shrine, but joy, joy was glowing in his mind and in his heart. The one window of the cell was open, the air was fresh and cool. "So the smell must have become stronger, if they opened the window," thought Alyosha. But even this thought of the smell of corruption, which had seemed to him so awful and humiliating a few hours before, no longer made him feel miserable or indignant. He began quietly praying, but he soon felt that he was praying almost mechanically. Fragments of thought floated through his soul, flashed like stars and went out again at once, to be succeeded by others. But yet there was reigning in his soul a sense of the wholeness of things—something steadfast and comforting—and he was aware of it himself. Sometimes he began praying ardently, he longed to pour out his thankfulness and love. . . .

But when he had begun to pray, he passed suddenly to something else, and sank into thought, forgetting both the prayer and what had interrupted it. He began listening to what Father Païssy was reading, but worn out with exhaustion he gradually began to doze.

"*And the third day there was a marriage in Cana of Galilee,*" read Father Païssy. "*And the mother of Jesus was there: And both Jesus was called, and his disciples, to the marriage.*"

"Marriage? What's that; . . . A marriage!" floated whirling through Alyosha's mind. "There is happiness for her, too . . . She has gone to the feast. . . . No, she has not taken the

37

knife. . . . That was only a tragic phrase. . . . Well . . . tragic phrases should be forgiven, they must be. Tragic phrases comfort the heart . . . Without them, sorrow would be too heavy for men to bear. Rakitin has gone off to the back alley. As long as Rakitin broods over his wrongs, he will always go off to the back alley. . . . But the high road. . . . The road is wide and straight and bright as crystal, and the sun is at the end of it. . . . Ah! . . . What's being read?" . . .

"And when they wanted wine, the mother of Jesus saith unto him: 'They have no wine' " . . . Alyosha heard.

"Ah, yes, I was missing that, and I don't want to miss it, I love that passage: it's Cana of Galilee, the first miracle. . . . Ah, that miracle! Ah, that sweet miracle! It was not men's grief but their joy Christ visited, He worked His first miracle to help men's gladness. . . . 'He who loves men loves their gladness, too' . . . *He* was always repeating that, it was one of his leading ideas. . . . 'There's no living without joy,' Mitya says. . . . Yes, Mitya. . . . 'Everything that is true and good is always full of forgiveness,' he used to say that, too" . . .

"Jesus saith unto her, Woman, what has it to do with thee or me? Mine hour is not yet come."

"His mother saith unto the servants: Whatsoever he saith unto you, do it" . . .

"Do it. . . . Gladness, the gladness of some poor, very poor, people. . . . Of course they were poor, since they hadn't wine enough even at a wedding. . . . The historians write that, in those days, the people living about the Lake of Gennesareth were the poorest that can possibly be imagined . . . and another great heart, that other great being, His Mother, knew that He had come not only to make His great terrible sacrifice. She knew that His heart was open even to the simple, artless merry-making of some obscure and unlearned people, who had warmly bidden Him to their poor wedding. 'Mine hour is not yet come,' He said, with a soft smile (He must have smiled gently to her). And indeed was it to make wine abundant at poor weddings He had come down to earth? And yet He went and did as she asked him. . . . Ah, he is reading again" . . .

"Jesus saith unto them, Fill the waterpots with water. And they filled them up to the brim.

And he saith unto them, Draw out now and bear unto the Governor of the feast. And they bare it.

When the ruler of the feast had tasted the water that was made wine, and knew not whence it was; [but the servants which drew the water knew] the governor of the feast called the bridegroom,

And saith unto him: Every man at the beginning doth set forth good wine; and when men have well drunk, that which is worse; but thou hast kept the good wine until now."

"But what's this, what's this? Why is the room growing wider? . . . Ah, yes . . . It's the marriage, the wedding . . . yes, of course. Here are the guests, here are the young couple sitting, and the merry crowd and . . . Where is the wise governor of the feast? But who is this? Who? Again the walls are receding. . . . Who is getting up there from the great table? What! . . . He here, too? But he's in the coffin . . . but he's here too. He has stood up, he sees me, he is coming here. . . . God!" . . .

Yes, he came up to him, to him, he, the little, thin old man, with tiny wrinkles on his face, joyful and laughing softly. There was no coffin now, and he was in the same dress as he had worn yesterday sitting with them, when the visitors had gathered about him. His face was uncovered, his eyes were shining. How was this then, he, too, had been called to the feast. He too, at the marriage of Cana in Galilee. . . .

"Yes, my dear, I am called, too, called and bidden," he heard a soft voice saying over him. "Why have you hidden yourself here, out of sight? You come and join us too."

It was his voice, the voice of Father Zossima. And it must be he, since he called him!

The elder raised Alyosha by the hand and he rose from his knees.

"We are rejoicing," the little, thin old man went on. "We are drinking the new wine, the wine of new, great gladness; do you see how many guests? Here are the bride and bridegroom, here is the wise governor of the feast, he is tasting the new wine. Why do you wonder at me? I gave an onion to a beggar, so I, too, am here. And many here have given only an onion each—only one little onion. . . . What are all our deeds? And you, my gentle one, you, my kind boy, you too have known how to give a famished woman an onion to-day. Begin your work, dear one, begin it, gentle one! . . . Do you see our Sun, do you see Him?"

"I am afraid . . . I dare not look," whispered Alyosha.

"Do not fear Him. He is terrible in His greatness, awful

in His sublimity, but infinitely merciful. He has made Himself like unto us from love and rejoices with us. He is changing the water into wine that the gladness of the guests may not be cut short. He is expecting new guests, He is calling new ones unceasingly for ever and ever. . . . There they are bringing new wine. Do you see they are bringing the vessels? . . ."

Something glowed in Alyosha's heart, something filled it till it ached, tears of rapture rose from his soul. . . . He stretched out his hands, uttered a cry and waked up.

Again the coffin, the open window, and the soft, solemn, distinct reading of the Gospel. But Alyosha did not listen to the reading. It was strange, he had fallen asleep on his knees, but now he was on his feet, and suddenly, as though thrown forward, with three rapid steps he went right up to the coffin. His shoulder brushed against Father Païssy without his noticing it. Father Païssy raised his eyes for an instant from his book, but looked away again at once, seeing that something strange was happening to the boy. Alyosha gazed for half a minute at the coffin, at the covered, motionless dead man that lay in the coffin, with the ikon on his breast and the peaked cap with the octangular cross on his head. He had only just been hearing his voice, and that voice was still ringing in his ears. He was listening, still expecting other words, but suddenly he turned sharply and went out of the cell.

He did not stop on the steps either, but went quickly down; his soul, overflowing with rapture, yearned for freedom, space, openness. The vault of heaven, full of soft, shining stars, stretched vast and fathomless above him. The Milky Way ran in two pale streams from the zenith to the horizon. The fresh, motionless, still night enfolded the earth. The white towers and golden domes of the cathedral gleamed out against the sapphire sky. The gorgeous autumn flowers, in the beds round the house, were slumbering till morning. The silence of earth seemed to melt into the silence of the heavens. The mystery of earth was one with the mystery of the stars. . . .

Alyosha stood, gazed, and suddenly threw himself down on the earth. He did not know why he embraced it. He could not have told why he longed so irresistibly to kiss it, to kiss it all. But he kissed it weeping, sobbing and watering it with his tears, and vowed passionately to love it, to love it for ever and ever. "Water the earth with the tears of your joy and love those tears," echoed in his soul.

What was he weeping over?

40

Oh! In his rapture he was weeping even over those stars, which were shining to him from the abyss of space, and "he was not ashamed of that ecstasy". There seemed to be threads from all those innumerable worlds of God, linking his soul to them, and it was trembling all over "in contact with other worlds". He longed to forgive everyone and for everything, and to beg forgiveness. Oh, not for himself but for all men, for all and for everything. "And others are praying for me too," echoed again in his soul. But with every instant he felt clearly and, as it were, tangibly that something firm and unshakable as that vault of heaven had entered into his soul. It was as though some idea had seized the sovereignty of his mind—and it was for all his life and for ever and ever. He had fallen on the earth a weak boy, but he rose up a resolute champion, and he knew and felt it suddenly at the very moment of his ecstasy. And never, never, all his life long, could Alyosha forget that minute.

"Someone visited my soul in that hour," he used to say afterwards, with implicit faith in his words.

Within three days he left the monastery in accordance with the words of his elder, who had bidden him "sojourn in the world".

BOOK VIII: MITYA

CHAPTER I

KUZMA SAMSONOV

BUT Dmitri, to whom Grushenka, flying away to a new life, had left her last greeting, bidding him remember the hour of her love for ever, knew nothing of what had happened to her, and was at that moment in a condition of feverish agitation and activity. For the last two days he had been in such an inconceivable state of mind that he might easily have fallen ill with brain fever, as he said himself afterwards. Alyosha had not been able to find him the morning before, and Ivan had not succeeded in meeting him at the tavern on the same day. The people at his lodgings, by his orders, concealed his movements.

He had spent those two days literally rushing in all directions, "struggling with his destiny and trying to save himself", as he expressed it himself afterwards, and for some hours he even made a dash out of the town on urgent business, terrible as it was to him to lose sight of Grushenka for a moment. All this was explained afterwards in detail, and confirmed by documentary evidence; but for the present we will only note the most essential incidents of those two terrible days immediately preceding the awful catastrophe that broke so suddenly upon him.

Though Grushenka had, it is true, loved him for an hour, genuinely and sincerely, yet she tortured him sometimes cruelly and mercilessly. The worst of it was that he could never tell what she meant to do. To prevail upon her by force or kindness was also impossible: she would yield to nothing. She would only have become angry and turned away from him altogether, he knew that well already. He suspected, quite correctly, that she, too, was passing through an inward struggle, and was in a state of extraordinary indecision, that she was making up her mind to something, and unable to determine upon it. And so, not without good reason, he divined, with a sinking heart, that at moments she must simply hate him and his passion. And so, perhaps, it was, but what was distressing Grushenka he did not understand. For him the whole tormenting question lay between him and Fyodor Pavlovitch.

Here, we must note, by the way, one certain fact: he was firmly persuaded that Fyodor Pavlovitch would offer, or perhaps had offered Grushenka lawful wedlock, and did not for a moment believe that the old voluptuary hoped to gain his object for three thousand roubles. Mitya had reached this conclusion from his knowledge of Grushenka and her character. That was how it was that he could believe at times that all Grushenka's uneasiness rose from not knowing which of them to choose, which was most to her advantage.

Strange to say, during those days it never occurred to him to think of the approaching return of the "officer", that is, of the man who had been such a fatal influence in Grushenka's life, and whose arrival she was expecting with such emotion and dread. It is true that of late Grushenka had been very silent about it. Yet he was perfectly aware of a letter she had received a month ago from her seducer, and had heard of it from her own lips. He partly knew, too, what the letter contained. In a moment of spite Grushenka had shown him that letter, but to her astonishment he attached hardly any consequence to it. It would be hard to say why this was. Perhaps, weighed down by all the hideous horror of his struggle with his own father for this woman, he was incapable of imagining any danger more terrible, at any rate for the time. He simply did not believe in a suitor who suddenly turned up again after five years' disappearance, still less in his speedy arrival. Moreover, in the "officer's" first letter which had been shown to Mitya, the possibility of his new rival's visit was very vaguely suggested. The letter was very indefinite, high-flown, and full of sentimentality. It must be noted that Grushenka had concealed from him the last lines of the letter, in which his return was alluded to more definitely. He had, besides, noticed at that moment, he remembered afterwards, a certain involuntary proud contempt for this missive from Siberia on Grushenka's face. Grushenka told him nothing of what had passed later between her and this rival; so that by degrees he had completely forgotten the officer's existence.

He felt that, whatever might come later, whatever turn things might take, his final conflict with Fyodor Pavlovitch was close upon him, and must be decided before anything else. With a sinking heart he was expecting every moment Grushenka's decision, always believing that it would come suddenly, on the impulse of the moment. All of a sudden she would say to him : "Take me, I'm yours for ever," and it would be all over. He would seize her and bear her away at once to the ends of the earth. Oh, then he would bear her away at once, as far, far away as possible; to the furthest end of Russia, if not of the earth, then he would marry her, and settle down with her incognito, so that no one would know anything about them, there, here, or anywhere, Then, oh then, a new life would begin at once!

Of this different, reformed and "virtuous" life ("it must, it must be virtuous") he dreamed feverishly at every moment. He thirsted for that reformation and renewal. The filthy morass in which he had sunk of his own free will was too revolting to him, and, like very many men in such cases, he put faith above all in change of place. If only it were not for these circumstances, if only he could fly away from this accursed place—he would be altogether regenerated, would enter on a new path. That was what he believed in, and for what he was yearning.

But all this could only be on condition of the first, the *happy* solution of the question. There was another possibility, a different and awful ending. Suddenly she might say to him : "Go away! I have just come to terms with Fyodor Pavlovitch.

I am going to marry him and don't want you"—and then . . .
but then. . . . But Mitya did not know what would happen
then. Up to the last hour he didn't know. That must be said
to his credit. He had no definite intentions, had planned no
crime. He was simply watching and spying in agony, while
he prepared himself for the first, happy solution of his destiny.
He drove away any other idea, in fact. But for that ending
a quite different anxiety arose, a new, incidental, but yet fatal
and insoluble difficulty presented itself.

If she were to say to him: "I'm yours; take me away,"
how could he take her away? Where had he the means, the
money to do it? It was just at this time that all sources of
revenue from Fyodor Pavlovitch, doles which had gone on
without interruption for so many years, ceased. Grushenka
had money, of course, but with regard to this Mitya suddenly
evinced extraordinary pride; he wanted to carry her away and
begin the new life with her himself, at his own expense, not at
hers. He could not conceive of taking her money, and the very
idea caused him a pang of intense repulsion. I won't enlarge
on this fact or analyse it here, but confine myself to remarking
that this was his attitude at the moment. All this may have
arisen indirectly and unconsciously from the secret stings of his
conscience for the money of Katerina Ivanovna that he had
dishonestly appropriated. "I've been a scoundrel to one of
them, and I shall be a scoundrel again to the other directly,"
was his feeling then, as he explained after: "and when Grushenka knows, she won't care for such a scoundrel."

Where then was he to get the means, where was he to get the
fateful money? Without it, all would be lost and nothing could
be done, "and only because I hadn't the money. Oh, the
shame of it!"

To anticipate things: he did, perhaps, know where to get the
money, knew, perhaps, where it lay at that moment. I will say
no more of this here, as it will all be clear later. But his chief
trouble, I must explain however obscurely, lay in the fact that
to have that sum he knew of, to *have the right* to take it, he
must first restore Katerina Ivanovna's three thousand—if not,
"I'm a common pickpocket, I'm a scoundrel", Mitya decided.
And so he made up his mind to move heaven and earth to
return Katerina Ivanovna that three thousand, and that *first of
all*. The final stage of this decision, so to say, had been reached
only during the last hours, that is, after his last interview with
Alyosha, two days before, on the high-road, on the evening

when Grushenka had insulted Katerina Ivanovna, and Mitya, after hearing Alyosha's account of it, had admitted that he was a scoundrel, and told him to tell Katerina Ivanovna so, if it could be any comfort to her. After parting from his brother on that night, he had felt in his frenzy that it would be better "to murder and rob someone than fail to pay my debt to Katya. I'd rather everyone thought me a robber and a murderer, I'd rather go to Siberia than that Katya should have the right to say that I deceived her and stole her money, and used her money to run away with Grushenka and begin a new life! That I can't do!" So Mitya decided, grinding his teeth, and he might well fancy at times that his brain would give way. But meanwhile he went on struggling. . . .

Strange to say, though one would have supposed there was nothing left for him but despair—for what chance had he, with nothing in the world, to raise such a sum?—yet to the very end he persisted in hoping that he would get that three thousand, that the money would somehow come to him, of itself, as though it might drop from heaven. That is just how it is with people who, like Dmitri, have never had anything to do with money, except to squander what has come to them by inheritance without any effort of their own, and have no notion how money is obtained. A whirl of the most fastastic notions took possession of his brain immediately after he had parted from Alyosha two days before, and threw his thoughts into a tangle of confusion. This is how it was he pitched first on a perfectly wild enterprise. And perhaps to men of that kind in such circumstances the most impossible, fantastic schemes occur first, and seem most practical.

He suddenly determined to go to Samsonov, the merchant who was Grushenka's protector, and to propose a "scheme" to him, and by means of it to obtain from him at once the whole of the sum required. Of the commercial value of his scheme he had no doubt, not the slightest, and was only uncertain how Samsonov would look upon his freak, supposing he were to consider it from any but the commercial point of view. Though Mitya knew the merchant by sight, he was not acquainted with him and had never spoken a word to him. But for some unknown reason he had long entertained the conviction that the old reprobate, who was lying at death's door, would perhaps not at all object now to Grushenka's securing a respectable position and marrying a man "to be depended upon". And he believed not only that he would not object but that this was what he desired, and, if opportunity arose, that he would be ready to help. From some rumour, or perhaps from some stray word of Grushenka's, he had gathered further that the old man would perhaps prefer him to Fyodor Pavlovitch for Grushenka.

Possibly many of the readers of my novel will feel that in reckoning on such assistance, and being ready to take his bride, so to speak, from the hands of her protector, Dmitri showed great coarseness and want of delicacy. I will only observe that Mitya looked upon Grushenka's past as something completely over. He looked on that past with infinite pity and resolved with all the fervour of his passion that when once Grushenka told him she loved him and would marry him, it would mean the beginning of a new Grushenka and a new Dmitri, free from every vice. They would forgive one another and would begin their lives afresh. As for Kuzma Samsonov, Dmitri looked upon him as a man who had exercised a fateful influence in that remote past of Grushenka's, though she had never loved him, and who was now himself a thing of the past, completely done with and, so to say, non-existent. Besides, Mitya hardly looked upon him as a man at all, for it was known to everyone in the town that he was only a shattered wreck, whose relations with Grushenka had changed their character and were now simply paternal, and that this had been so for a long time.

In any case there was much simplicity on Mitya's part in all this, for, in spite of all his vices, he was a very simple-hearted man. It was an instance of this simplicity that Mitya was seriously persuaded that, being on the eve of his departure for the next world, old Kuzma must sincerely repent of his past relations with Grushenka, and that she had no more devoted friend and protector in the world than this, now harmless, old man.

After his conversation with Alyosha, at the cross-roads, he hardly slept all night, and, at ten o'clock next morning, he was at the house of Samsonov and telling the servant to announce him. It was a very large and gloomy old house, of two storeys, with a lodge and out-houses. In the lower storey lived Samsonov's two married sons with their families, his old sister, and his unmarried daughter. In the lodge lived two of his clerks, one of whom also had a large family. Both the lodge and the lower storey were overcrowded, but the old man kept the upper floor to himself, and would not even let the daughter live there with him, though she waited upon him, and in spite of her asthma was obliged at certain fixed hours, and at any time he might call her, to run upstairs to him from below.

This upper floor contained a number of large rooms kept purely for show, furnished in the old-fashioned merchant style, with long, monotonous rows of clumsy mahogany chairs along the walls, with glass chandeliers under shades, and gloomy mirrors on the walls. All these rooms were entirely empty and unused, for the old man kept to one room, a small, remote bedroom, where he was waited upon by an old servant with a kerchief on her head, and by a lad, who used to sit on the locker in the passage. Owing to his swollen legs, the old man could hardly walk at all, and was only rarely lifted from his leather arm-chair, when the old woman supporting him led him up and down the room once or twice. He was morose and taciturn even with this old woman.

When he was informed of the arrival of the "captain", he at once refused to see him. But Mitya persisted and sent his name up again. Samsonov questioned the lad minutely: What he looked like? Whether he was drunk? Was he going to make a row? The answer he received was: that he was sober, but wouldn't go away. The old man again refused to see him. Then Mitya, who had foreseen this, and purposely brought pencil and paper with him, wrote clearly on the piece of paper the words: "On most important business concerning Agrafena Alexandrovna," and sent it up to the old man.

After thinking a little Samsonov told the lad to take the visitor to the drawing-room, and sent the old woman downstairs with a summons to his younger son to come upstairs to him at once. This younger son, a man over six foot and of exceptional physical strength, who was closely shaven and dressed in the European style, though his father still wore a kaftan and a beard, came at once without a comment. All the family trembled before the father. The old man had sent for this giant, not because he was afraid of the "captain" (he was by no means of a timorous temper) but in order to have a witness in case of any emergency. Supported by his son and the servant-lad, he waddled at last into the drawing-room. It may be assumed that he felt considerable curiosity. The drawing-room in which Mitya was awaiting him was a vast, dreary room that laid a weight of depression on the heart. It had a double row of windows, a gallery, marbled walls, and three immense chandeliers covered with shades.

Mitya was sitting on a little chair at the entrance, awaiting his fate with nervous impatience. When the old man appeared at the opposite door, seventy feet away, Mitya jumped up at once, and with his long, military stride walked to meet him. Mitya was well dressed, in a frock-coat, buttoned up, with a round hat and black gloves in his hands, just as he had been three days before at the elder's, at the family meeting with his father and brothers. The old man waited for him, standing dignified and unbending, and Mitya felt at once that he had looked him through and through as he advanced. Mitya was greatly impressed, too, with Samsonov's immensely swollen face. His lower lip, which had always been thick, hung down now, looking like a bun. He bowed to his guest in dignified silence, motioned him to a low chair by the sofa, and, leaning on his son's arm, he began lowering himself on to the sofa opposite, groaning painfully, so that Mitya, seeing his painful exertions, immediately felt remorseful and sensitively conscious of his insignificance in the presence of the dignified person he had ventured to disturb.

"What is it you want of me, sir?" said the old man, deliberately, distinctly, severely, but courteously, when he was at last seated.

Mitya started, leapt up, but sat down again. Then he began at once speaking with loud, nervous haste, gesticulating, and in a positive frenzy. He was unmistakably a man driven into a corner, on the brink of ruin, catching at the last straw, ready to sink if he failed. Old Samsonov probably grasped all this in an instant, though his face remained cold and immovable as a statue's.

"Most honoured sir, Kuzma Kuzmitch, you have no doubt heard, more than once, of my disputes with my father, Fyodor Pavlovitch Karamazov, who robbed me of my inheritance from my mother . . . seeing the whole town is gossiping about it . . . for here everyone's gossiping of what they shouldn't . . . and besides, it might have reached you through Grushenka . . . I beg your pardon, through Agrafena Alexandrovna . . . Agrafena Alexandrovna, the lady for whom I have the highest respect and esteem . . ."

So Mitya began, and broke down at the first sentence. We will not reproduce his speech word for word, but will only summarise the gist of it. Three months ago, he said, he had of express intention (Mitya purposely used these words instead of "intentionally") consulted a lawyer in the chief town of the province, "a distinguished lawyer, Kuzma Kuzmitch, Pavel Pavlovitch

Korneplodov. You have perhaps heard of him? A man of vast intellect, the mind of a statesman . . . he knows you, too . . . spoke of you in the highest terms . . ." Mitya broke down again. But these breaks did not deter him. He leapt instantly over the gaps, and struggled on and on.

This Korneplodov, after questioning him minutely and inspecting the documents he was able to bring him (Mitya alluded somewhat vaguely to these documents, and slurred over the subject with special haste), reported that they certainly might take proceedings concerning the village of Tchermashnya, which ought, he said, to have come to him, Mitya, from his mother, and so checkmate the old villain, his father . . . "because every door was not closed and justice might still find a loop-hole". In fact, he might reckon on an additional sum of six or even seven thousand roubles from Fyodor Pavlovitch, as Tchermashnya was worth, at least, twenty-five thousand, he might say twenty-eight thousand; in fact, "thirty, thirty, Kuzma Kuzmitch, and, would you believe it? I didn't get seventeen from that heartless man!" So he, Mitya, had thrown the business up, for the time, knowing nothing about the law, but on coming here was struck dumb by a cross-claim made upon him (here Mitya went adrift again, and again took a flying leap forward). "So will not you, excellent and honoured Kuzma Kuzmitch, be willing to take up all my claims against that unnatural monster, and pay me a sum down of only three thousand? . . . You see, you cannot, in any case, lose over it. On my honour, my honour, I swear that. Quite the contrary, you may make six or seven thousand instead of three" . . . Above all, he wanted this concluded that very day.

"I'll do the business with you at a notary's, or whatever it is . . . in fact, I'm ready to do anything. . . . I'll hand over all the deeds . . . whatever you want, sign anything . . . and we could draw up the agreement at once . . . and if it were possible, if it were only possible, that very morning. . . . You could pay me that three thousand, for there isn't a capitalist in this town to compare with you, and so would save me from . . . would save me, in fact . . . for a good, I might say an honourable, action. . . . For I cherish the most honourable feelings for a certain person, whom you know well, and care for as a father. I would not have come, indeed, if it had not been as a father. And, indeed, it's a struggle of three in this business, for it's fate—that's a fearful thing, Kuzma Kuzmitch! A tragedy, Kuzma Kuzmitch, a tragedy! And as you've dropped out long ago, it's a tug-of-war between two. I'm expressing it awkwardly, perhaps, but I'm not a literary man. You see, I'm on the one side, and that monster on the other. So you must choose. It's either I or the monster. It all lies in your hands— the fate of three lives, and the happiness of two. . . . Excuse me, I'm making a mess of it, but you understand . . . I see from your venerable eyes that you understand . . . and if you don't understand, I'm done for . . . so you see!"

Mitya broke off his clumsy speech with that "so you see!" and jumping up from his seat, awaited the answer to his foolish proposal. At the last phrase he had suddenly become hopelessly aware that it had all fallen flat; above all, that he had been talking utter nonsense.

"How strange it is! On the way here it seemed all right, and now it's nothing but nonsense." The idea suddenly dawned on his despairing mind. All the while he had been talking, the old man sat motionless, watching him with an icy expression in his eyes. After keeping him for a moment in suspense, Kuzma Kuzmitch pronounced at last, in the most positive and chilling tone:

"Excuse me, we don't undertake such business."

Mitya suddenly felt his legs growing weak under him.

"What am I to do now, Kuzma Kuzmitch?" he muttered, with a pale smile. "I suppose it's all up with me—what do you think?"

"Excuse me . . ."

Mitya remained standing, staring motionless. He suddenly noticed a movement in the old man's face. He started.

"You see, sir, business of that sort's not in our line," said the old man slowly. "There's the court, and the lawyers—it's a perfect misery. But if you like, there is a man here you might apply to."

"Good heavens! Who is it? You're my salvation, Kuzma Kuzmitch," faltered Mitya.

"He doesn't live here, and he's not here just now. He is a peasant, he does business in timber. His name is Lyagavy. He's been haggling with Fyodor Pavlovitch for the last year over your copse at Tchermashnya. They can't agree on the price, maybe you've heard? Now he's come back again and is staying with the priest at Ilyinskoe, about twelve versts from the Volovya station. He wrote to me, too, about the business of the copse asking my advice. Fyodor Pavlovitch means to go and see him, himself. So if you were to be beforehand with

Fyodor Pavlovitch and to make Lyagavy the offer you've made me, he might possibly . . ."

"A brilliant idea!" Mitya interrupted ecstatically. "He's the very man, it would just suit him. He's haggling with him for it, being asked too much, and here he would have all the documents entitling him to the property itself. Ha-ha-ha!"

And Mitya suddenly went off into his short, wooden laugh, startling Samsonov.

"How can I thank you, Kuzma Kuzmitch?" cried Mitya effusively.

"Don't mention it," said Samsonov, inclining his head.

"But you don't know, you've saved me. Oh, it was a true presentiment brought me to you. . . . So now to this priest!"

"No need of thanks."

"I'll make haste and fly there. I'm afraid I've overtaxed your strength. I shall never forget it. It's a Russian says that, Kuzma Kuzmitch, a R-r-russian!"

"To be sure!"

Mitya seized his hand to press it, but there was a malignant gleam in the old man's eye. Mitya drew back his hand, but at once blamed himself for his mistrustfulness.

"It's because he's tired," he thought.

"For her sake! For her sake, Kuzma Kuzmitch! You understand that it's for her," he cried, his voice ringing through the room. He bowed, turned sharply round, and with the same long stride walked to the door without looking back. He was trembling with delight.

"Everything was on the verge of ruin and my guardian angel saved me," was the thought in his mind. And if such a business man as Samsonov (a most worthy old man, and what dignity!) had suggested this course, then . . . then success was assured. He would fly off immediately. "I will be back before night, I shall be back at night and the thing is done. Could the old man have been laughing at me?" exclaimed Mitya, as he strode towards his lodging. He could, of course, imagine nothing but that the advice was practical "from such a business man" with an understanding of the business, with an understanding of this Lyagavy (curious surname!). Or—the old man was laughing at him.

Alas! the second alternative was the correct one. Long afterwards, when the catastrophe had happened, old Samsonov himself confessed, laughing, that he had made a fool of the "captain". He was a cold, spiteful and sarcastic man, liable to violent antipathies. Whether it was the "captain's" excited face, or the foolish conviction of the "rake and spendthrift", that he, Samsonov, could be taken in by such a cock-and-bull story as his scheme, or jealousy over Grushenka, in whose name this "scapegrace" had rushed in on him with such a tale to get money—which worked on the old man I can't tell. But at the instant when Mitya stood before him, feeling his legs grow weak under him, and frantically exclaiming that he was ruined, at that moment the old man looked at him with intense spite, and resolved to make a laughing-stock of him. When Mitya had gone, Kuzma Kuzmitch, white with rage, turned to his son and bade him see to it that that beggar be never seen again, and never admitted even into the yard, or else he'd . . .

He did not utter his threat. But even his son, who often saw him enraged, trembled with fear. For a whole hour afterwards the old man was shaking with anger, and by evening he was worse, and sent for the doctor.

CHAPTER II

LYAGAVY

SO he must drive at full speed, and he had not the money for horses. He had forty kopecks, and that was all, all that was left after so many years of prosperity! But he had at home an old silver watch which had long ceased to go. He snatched it up and carried it to a Jewish watchmaker who had a shop in the market-place. The Jew gave him six roubles for it.

"And I didn't expect that," cried Mitya, ecstatically. (He was still in a state of ecstasy.) He seized his six roubles and ran home. At home he borrowed three roubles from the people of the house, who loved him so much that they were pleased to give it him, though it was all they had. Mitya in his excitement told them on the spot that his fate would be decided that day, and he described, in desperate haste, the whole scheme he had put before Samsonov, the latter's decision, his own hopes for the future, and so on. These people had been told many of their lodger's secrets before, and so looked upon him as a gentleman who was not at all proud, and almost one of themselves. Having thus collected nine roubles Mitya sent for posting-horses to take him to the Volovya station. This was how the fact came to be remembered and established that "at midday, on the day before the event, Mitya had not a farthing, and that he had sold his watch to get money and had borrowed three roubles from his landlord, all in the presence of witnesses.''

I note this fact; later on it will be apparent why I do so.

Though he was radiant with the joyful anticipation that he would at last solve all his difficulties, yet, as he drew near Volovya station, he trembled at the thought of what Grushenka might be doing in his absence. What if she made up her mind to-day to go to Fyodor Pavlovitch? This was why he had gone off without telling her and why he left orders with his landlady not to let out where he had gone, if anyone came to inquire for him.

"I must, I must get back to-night," he repeated, as he was jolted along in the cart, "and I dare say I shall have to bring this Lyagavy back here . . . to draw up the deed." So mused Mitya, with a throbbing heart, but alas! his dreams were not fated to be carried out.

To begin with, he was late, taking a short cut from Volovya station which turned out to be eighteen versts instead of twelve. Secondly, he did not find the priest at home at Ilyinskoe; he had gone off to a neighbouring village. While Mitya, setting off there with the same exhausted horses, was looking for him, it was almost dark.

The priest, a shy and amiable-looking little man, informed him at once that, though Lyagavy had been staying with him at first, he was now at Suhoy Possyolok, that he was staying the night in the forester's cottage, as he was buying timber there too. At Mitya's urgent request that he would take him to Lyagavy at once, and by so doing "save him, so to speak", the priest agreed, after some demur, to conduct him to Suhoy Possyolok; his curiosity was obviously aroused. But, unluckily, he advised their going on foot, as it would not be "much over" a verst. Mitya, of course, agreed, and marched off with his yard-long strides, so that the poor priest almost ran after him. He was a very cautious man, though not old.

Mitya at once began talking to him, too, of his plans, nervously and excitedly asking advice in regard to Lyagavy, and talking all the way. The priest listened attentively, but gave little advice. He turned off Mitya's questions with: "I don't know. Ah, I can't say. How can I tell?" and so on. When Mitya began to speak of his quarrel with his father over his inheritance, the priest was positively alarmed, as he was in some way dependent on Fyodor Pavlovitch. He inquired, however, with surprise, why he called the peasant-trader Gorstkin, Lyagavy, and obligingly explained to Mitya that, though the man's name really was Lyagavy, he was never called so, as he would be grievously offended at the name, and that he must be sure to call him Gorstkin, "or you'll do nothing with him; he won't even listen to you", said the priest in conclusion.

Mitya was somewhat surprised for a moment, and explained that that was what Samsonov had called him. On hearing this fact, the priest dropped the subject, though he would have done well to put into words his doubt whether, if Samsonov had sent him to that peasant, calling him Lyagavy, there was not something wrong about it, and he was turning him into ridicule. But Mitya had no time to pause over such trifles. He hurried, striding along, and only when he reached Suhoy Possyolok he realised that they had come not one verst, nor one and a half, but at least three. This annoyed him, but he controlled himself.

They went into the hut. The forester lived in one half of the hut, and Gorstkin was lodging in the other, the better room the other side of the passage. They went into that room and lighted a tallow candle. The hut was extremely overheated. On the table there was a samovar that had gone out, a tray with cups, an empty rum-bottle, a bottle of vodka partly full, and some half-eaten crusts of wheaten bread. The visitor himself lay stretched at full length on the bench, with his coat crushed up under his head for a pillow, snoring heavily. Mitya stood in perplexity.

"Of course I must wake him. My business is too important. I've come in such haste. I'm in a hurry to get back to-day," he said in great agitation. But the priest and the forester stood in silence, not giving their opinion. Mitya went up and began trying to wake him himself, he tried vigorously, but the sleeper did not wake.

"He's drunk," Mitya decided. "Good Lord! What am I to do? What am I to do?" And, terribly impatient, he began pulling him by the arms, by the legs, shaking his head, lifting him up and making him sit on the bench. Yet, after prolonged exertions, he could only succeed in getting the drunken man to utter absurd grunts, and violent but inarticulate oaths.

"No, you'd better wait a little," the priest pronounced at last, "for he's obviously not in a fit state."

"He's been drinking the whole day," the forester chimed in.

"Good heavens!" cried Mitya. "If only you knew how important it is to me and how desperate I am!"

"No, you'd better wait till morning," the priest repeated.

"Till morning? Mercy! that's impossible!"

And in his despair he was on the point of attacking the sleeping man again, but stopped short at once, realising the uselessness of his efforts. The priest said nothing, the sleepy forester looked gloomy.

"What terrible tragedies real life contrives for poeple," said Mitya, in complete despair. The perspiration was streaming down his face. The priest seized the moment to put before him, very reasonably, that, even if he succeeded in wakening the man, he would still be drunk and incapable of conversation. "And your business is important," he said, "so you'd certainly better put it off till morning." With a gesture of despair Mitya agreed.

"Father, I will stay here with a light, and seize the favourable moment. As soon as he wakes I'll begin. I'll pay you for the light," he said to the forester, "for the night's lodging, too; you'll remember Dmitri Karamazov. Only, Father, I don't know what we're to do with you. Where will you sleep?"

"No, I'm going home. I'll take his horse and get home," he said, indicating the forester. "And now I'll say good-bye. I wish you all success.'

So it was settled. The priest rode off on the forester's horse, delighted to escape, though he shook his head uneasily, wondering whether he ought not next day to inform his benefactor Fyodor Pavlovitch of this curious incident, "or he may in an unlucky hour hear of it, be angry, and withdraw his favour".

The forester, scratching himself, went back to his room without a word, and Mitya sat on the bench to "catch the favourable moment", as he expressed it. Profound dejection clung about his soul like a heavy mist. A profound, intense dejection! He sat thinking, but could reach no conclusion. The candle burnt dimly, a cricket chirped; it became insufferably close in the overheated room. He suddenly pictured the garden, the path behind the garden, the door of his father's house mysteriously opening and Grushenka running in. He leapt up from the bench.

"It's a tragedy!" he said, grinding his teeth. Mechanically he went up to the sleeping man and looked in his face. He was a lean, middle-aged peasant, with a very long face, flaxen curls, and a long, thin, reddish beard, wearing a blue cotton shirt and a black waistcoat, from the pocket of which peeped the chain of a silver watch. Mitya looked at his face with intense hatred, and for some unknown reason his curly hair particularly irritated him.

What was insufferably humiliating was that, after leaving things of such importance and making such sacrifices, he, Mitya, utterly worn out, should with business of such urgency be standing over this dolt on whom his whole fate depended, while he snored as though there were nothing the matter, as though he'd dropped from another planet.

"Oh, the irony of fate!" cried Mitya, and, quite losing his head, he fell again to rousing the tipsy peasant. He roused him with a sort of ferocity, pulled at him, pushed him, even beat him; but after five minutes of vain exertions, he returned to his bench in helpless despair, and sat down.

"Stupid! Stupid!" cried Mitya. "And how dishonourable it all is!" something made him add. His head began to ache horribly. "Should he fling it up and go away altogether?" he wondered. "No, wait till to-morrow now. I'll stay on purpose. What else did I come for? Besides, I've no means of going. How am I to get away from here now? Oh, the idiocy of it!"

But his head ached more and more. He sat without moving, and unconsciously dozed off and fell asleep as he sat. He seemed to have slept for two hours or more. He was waked up by his head aching so unbearably that he could have screamed. There was a hammering in his temples, and the top of his head ached. It was a long time before he could wake up fully and understand what had happened to him.

At last he realised that the room was full of charcoal fumes from the stove, and that he might die of suffocation. And the drunken peasant still lay snoring. The candle guttered and was about to go out. Mitya cried out, and ran staggering across the passage into the forester's room. The forester waked up at once, but hearing that the other room was full of fumes, to Mitya's surprise and annoyance accepted the fact with strange unconcern, though he did go to see to it.

"But he's dead, he's dead! and . . . what am I to do then?" cried Mitya frantically.

They threw open the doors, opened a window and the chimney. Mitya brought a pail of water from the passage. First he wetted his own head, then, finding a rag of some sort, dipped it into the water, and put it on Lyagavy's head. The forester still treated the matter contemptuously, and when he opened the window said grumpily:

"It'll be all right now."

He went back to sleep, leaving Mitya a lighted lantern. Mitya fussed about the drunken peasant for half an hour, wetting his head, and gravely resolved not to sleep all night. But he was so worn out that when he sat down for a moment to take breath, he closed his eyes, unconsciously stretched himself full length on the bench and slept like the dead.

It was dreadfully late when he waked. It was somewhere about nine o'clock. The sun was shining brightly in the two little windows of the hut. The curly-headed peasant was sitting on the bench and had his coat on. He had another samovar and another bottle in front of him. Yesterday's bottle had already been finished, and the new one was more than half empty. Mitya jumped up and saw at once that the cursed peasant was drunk again, hopelessly and incurably. He stared at him for a moment with wide-opened eyes. The peasant was silently and slyly watching him, with insulting composure, and even a sort of contemptuous condescension, so Mitya fancied. He rushed up to him.

"Excuse me, you see. . . . I . . . you've most likely heard from the forester here in the hut. I'm Lieutenant Dmitri Karamazov, the son of the old Karamazov whose copse you are buying."

"That's a lie!" said the peasant, calmly and confidently.

"A lie? You know Fyodor Pavlovitch?"

"I don't know any of your Fyodor Pavlovitches," said the peasant, speaking thickly.

"You're bargaining with him for the copse, for the copse. Do wake up, and collect yourself. Father Pavel of Ilyinskoe brought me here. You wrote to Samsonov, and he has sent me to you," Mitya gasped breathlessly.

"You're l—lying!" Lyagavy blurted out again. Mitya's legs went cold.

"For mercy's sake! It isn't a joke! You're drunk, perhaps. Yet you can speak and understand . . . or else . . . I understand nothing!"

"You're a painter!"

"For mercy's sake! I'm Karamazov, Dmitri Karamazov. I have an offer to make you, an advantageous offer . . . very advantageous offer, concerning the copse!"

The peasant stroked his beard importantly.

"No, you've contracted for the job and turned out a scamp. You're a scoundrel!"

"I assure you you're mistaken," cried Mitya, wringing his

hands in despair. The peasant still stroked his beard, and suddenly screwed up his eyes cunningly.

"No, you show me this: you tell me the law that allows roguery. D'you hear? You're a scoundrel! Do you understand that?"

Mitya stepped back gloomily, and suddenly "something seemed to hit him on the head", as he said afterwards. In an instant a light seemed to dawn in his mind, "a light was kindled and I grasped it all". He stood, stupefied, wondering how he, after all a man of intelligence, could have yielded to such folly, have been led into such an adventure, and have kept it up for almost twenty-four hours, fussing round this Lyagavy, wetting his head.

"Why, the man's drunk, dead drunk, and he'll go on drinking now for a week; what's the use of waiting here? And what if Samsonov sent me here on purpose? What if she? . . . Oh, God, what have I done?"

The peasant sat watching him and grinning. Another time Mitya might have killed the fool in a fury, but now he felt as weak as a child. He went quietly to the bench, took up his overcoat, put it on without a word, and went out of the hut. He did not find the forester in the next room; there was no one there. He took fifty kopecks in small change out of his pocket and put them on the table for his night's lodging, the candle, and the trouble he had given. Coming out of the hut he saw nothing but forest all round. He walked at hazard, not knowing which way to turn out of the hut, to the right or to the left. Hurrying there the evening before with the priest, he had not noticed the road. He had no revengeful feeling for anybody, even for Samsonov, in his heart. He strode along a narrow forest path, aimless, dazed, without heeding where he was going. A child could have knocked him down, so weak was he in body and soul. He got out of the forest somehow, however, and a vista of fields, bare after the harvest, stretched as far as the eye could see.

"What despair! What death all round!" he repeated, striding on and on.

He was saved by meeting an old merchant who was being driven across country in a hired trap. When he overtook him, Mitya asked the way, and it turned out that the old merchant, too, was going to Volovya. After some discussion Mitya got into the trap. Three hours later they arrived. At Volovya, Mitya at once ordered posting-horses to drive to the town, and suddenly realised that he was appallingly hungry. While the horses were being harnessed, an omelette was prepared for him. He ate it all in an instant, ate a huge hunk of bread, ate a sausage, and swallowed three glasses of vodka. After eating, his spirits and his heart grew lighter. He flew towards the town, urged on the driver, and suddenly made a new and "unalterable" plan to procure that "accursed money" before evening. "And to think, only to think that a man's life should be ruined for the sake of that paltry three thousand!" he cried, contemptuously. "I'll settle it to-day." And if it had not been for the thought of Grushenka and of what might have happened to her, which never left him, he would perhaps have become quite cheerful again. . . . But the thought of her was stabbing him to the heart every moment, like a sharp knife.

At last they arrived, and Mitya at once ran to Grushenka.

CHAPTER III

GOLD-MINES

THIS was the visit of Mitya of which Grushenka had spoken to Rakitin with such horror. She was just then expecting the "message", and was much relieved that Mitya had not been to see her that day or the day before. She hoped that "please God he won't come till I'm gone away", and he suddenly burst in on her. The rest we know already. To get him off her hands she suggested at once that he should walk with her to Samsonov's, where she said she absolutely must go "to settle his accounts", and when Mitya accompanied her at once, she said good-bye to him at the gate, making him promise to come at twelve o'clock to take her home again. Mitya, too, was delighted at this arrangement. If she were sitting at Samsonov's she could not be going to Fyodor Pavlovitch's, "if only she's not lying", he added at once. But he thought she was not lying from what he saw.

He was that sort of jealous man who, in the absence of the beloved woman, at once invents all sorts of awful fancies of what may be happening to her, and how she may be betraying him, but, when shaken, heart-broken, convinced of her faithlessness, he runs back to her; at the first glance at her face, her gay, laughing, affectionate face, he revives at once, lays aside all suspicion and with joyful shame abuses himself for his jealousy.

After leaving Grushenka at the gate he rushed home. Oh, he had so much still to do that day! But a load had been lifted from his heart, anyway.

"Now I must only make haste and find out from Smerdyakov whether anything happened there last night; whether, by any chance, she went to Fyodor Pavlovitch; ough!" floated through his mind.

Before he had time to reach his lodging, jealousy had surged up again in his restless heart.

Jealousy! "Othello was not jealous, he was trustful," observed Pushkin. And that remark alone is enough to show the deep insight of our great poet. Othello's soul was shattered and his whole outlook clouded simply because *his ideal was destroyed*. But Othello did not begin hiding, spying, peeping! He was trustful. On the contrary, he had to be led up, pushed on, excited with great difficulty before he could entertain the idea of deceit. The truly jealous man is not like that. It is impossible to picture to oneself the shame and moral degradation to which the jealous man can descend without a qualm of conscience. And yet it's not as though the jealous were all vulgar and base souls. On the contrary, a man of lofty feelings, whose love is pure and full of self-sacrifice, may yet hide under tables, bribe the vilest people, and be familiar with the lowest ignominy of spying and eavesdropping.

Othello was incapable of making up his mind to faithlessness —not incapable of forgiving it, but of making up his mind to it— though his soul was as innocent and free from malice as a babe's. It is not so with the really jealous man. It is hard to imagine what some jealous men can make up their mind to and overlook, and what they can forgive! The jealous are the readiest of all to forgive, and all women know it. The jealous man can forgive extraordinarily quickly (though, of course, after a violent scene), and he is able to forgive infidelity almost conclusively proved, the very kisses and embraces he has seen, if only he can somehow be convinced that it has all been "for the last time", and that his rival will vanish from that day forward, will depart to the ends of the earth, or that he himself will carry her away somewhere, where that dreaded rival will not get near her. Of course the reconciliation is only for an hour. For, even if the rival did disappear next day, he would invent another one and would be jealous of him. And one might wonder what there was in a love that had to be so watched over, what a love could be worth that needed such strenuous guard-

60

ing. But that the jealous will never understand. And yet among them are men of noble hearts. It is remarkable, too, that those very men of noble hearts, standing hidden in some cupboard, listening and spying, never feel the stings of conscience at that moment, anyway, though they understand clearly enough with their "noble hearts" the shameful depths to which they have voluntarily sunk.

At the sight of Grushenka, Mitya's jealousy vanished and for an instant he became trustful and generous, and positively despised himself for his evil feelings. But that only proved that, in his love for that woman, there was an element of something far higher than he himself imagined, that it was not only a sensual passion, not only the "curve of her body", of which he had talked to Alyosha. But as soon as Grushenka had gone Mitya began to suspect her of all the low cunning of faithlessness, and he felt no sting of conscience at it.

And so jealousy surged up in him again. He had, in any case, to make haste. The first thing to be done was to get hold of at least a small, temporary loan of money. The nine roubles had almost all gone on his expedition. And, as we all know, one can't take a step without money. But he had thought over in the cart where he could get a loan. He had a brace of fine duelling pistols in a case, which he had not pawned till then because he prized them above all his possessions.

In the "Metropolis" tavern he had some time since made acquaintance with a young official and had learnt that this very opulent bachelor was passionately fond of weapons. He used to buy pistols, revolvers, daggers, hang them on his wall and show them to acquaintances. He prided himself on them, and was quite a specialist on the mechanism of the revolver. Mitya, without stopping to think, went straight to him, and offered to pawn his pistols to him for ten roubles. The official, delighted, began trying to persuade him to sell them outright. But Mitya would not consent, so the young man gave him ten roubles, protesting that nothing would induce him to take interest. They parted friends.

Mitya was in haste; he rushed towards Fyodor Pavlovitch's by the back way, to his arbour, to get hold of Smerdyakov as soon as possible. In this way the fact was established that three or four hours before a certain event, of which I shall speak later on, Mitya had not a farthing, and pawned for ten roubles a possession he valued, though, three hours later, he was in possession of thousands. . . . But I am anticipating. From

Marya Kondratyevna (the woman living near Fyodor Pavlovitch's) he learned the very disturbing fact of Smerdyakov's illness. He heard the story of his fall in the cellar, his fit, the doctor's visit, Fyodor Pavlovitch's anxiety; he heard with interest, too, that his brother Ivan had set off that morning for Moscow.

"Then he must have driven through Volovya before me," thought Dmitri, but he was terribly distressed about Smerdyakov. "What will happen now? Who'll keep watch for me? Who'll bring me word?" he thought. He began greedily questioning the women whether they had seen anything the evening before. They quite understood what he was trying to find out, and completely reassured him. No one had been there. Ivan Fyodorovitch had been there the night; everything had been perfectly as usual. Mitya grew thoughtful. He would certainly have to keep watch to-day, but where? Here or at Samsonov's gate? He decided that he must be on the look-out both here and there, and meanwhile . . . meanwhile . . . The difficulty was that he had to carry out the new plan that he had made on the journey back. He was sure of its success, but he must not delay acting upon it. Mitya resolved to sacrifice an hour to it: "in an hour I shall know everything, I shall settle everything, and then, then, first of all to Samsonov's. I'll inquire whether Grushenka's there and instantly be back here again, stay till eleven, and then to Samsonov's again to bring her home." This was what he decided.

He flew home, washed, combed his hair, brushed his clothes, dressed, and went to Madame Hohlakov's. Alas! he had built his hopes on her. He had resolved to borrow three thousand from that lady. And what was more, he felt suddenly convinced that she would not refuse to lend it to him. It may be wondered why, if he felt so certain, he had not gone to her at first, one of his own sort, so to speak, instead of to Samsonov, a man he did not know, who was not of his own class, and to whom he hardly knew how to speak.

But the fact was that he had never known Madame Hohlakov well, and had seen nothing of her for the last month, and that he knew she could not endure him. She had detested him from the first because he was engaged to Katerina Ivanovna, while she had, for some reason, suddenly conceived the desire that Katerina Ivanovna should throw him over, and marry the "charming, chivalrously refined Ivan, who had such excellent manners". Mitya's manners she detested. Mitya positively laughed at her, and had once said about her that she was just as lively and at her ease as she was uncultivated. But that morning in the cart a brilliant idea had struck him: "If she is so anxious I should not marry Katerina Ivanovna (and he knew she was positively hysterical upon the subject) why should she refuse me now that three thousand, just to enable me to leave Katya and get away from her for ever? These spoilt fine ladies, if they set their hearts on anything, will spare no expense to satisfy their caprice. Besides, she's so rich," Mitya argued.

As for his "plan" it was just the same as before; it consisted of the offer of his rights to Tchermashnya—but not with a commercial object, as it had been with Samsonov, not trying to allure the lady with the possibility of making a profit of six or seven thousand—but simply as a security for the debt. As he worked out this new idea, Mitya was enchanted with it, but so it always was with him in all his undertakings, in all his sudden decisions. He gave himself up to every new idea with passionate enthusiasm. Yet, when he mounted the steps of Madame Hohlakov's house he felt a shiver of fear run down his spine. At that moment he saw fully, as a mathematical certainty, that this was his last hope, that if this broke down, nothing else was left him in the world but to "rob and murder someone for the three thousand". It was half-past seven when he rang at the bell.

At first fortune seemed to smile upon him. As soon as he was announced he was received with extraordinary rapidity. "As though she were waiting for me," thought Mitya, and as soon as he had been led to the drawing-room, the lady of the house herself ran in, and declared at once that she was expecting him.

"I was expecting you! I was expecting you! Though I'd no reason to suppose you would come to see me, as you will admit yourself. Yet, I did expect you. You may marvel at my instinct, Dmitri Fyodorovitch, but I was convinced all the morning that you would come."

"That is certainly wonderful, Madam," observed Mitya, sitting down limply, "but I have come to you on a matter of great importance. . . . On a matter of supreme importance for me, that is, Madam . . . for me alone . . . and I hasten . . ."

"I know you've come on most important business, Dmitri Fyodorovitch; it's not a case of presentiment, no reactionary harking back to the miraculous (have you heard about Father Zossima?). This is a case of mathematics: you couldn't help coming, after all that has passed with Katerina Ivanovna; you couldn't, you couldn't, that's a mathematical certainty.'

"The realism of actual life, Madam, that's what it is. But allow me to explain . . ."

"Realism indeed, Dmitri Fyodorovitch. I'm all for realism now. I've seen too much of miracles. You've heard that Father Zossima is dead?"

"No, Madam, it's the first time I've heard of it." Mitya was a little surprised. The image of Alyosha rose to his mind.

"Last night, and only imagine . . ."

"Madam," said Mitya, "I can imagine nothing except that I'm in a desperate position, and that if you don't help me, everything will come to grief, and I first of all. Excuse me for the triviality of the expression, but I'm in a fever . . ."

"I know, I know that you're in a fever. You could hardly fail to be, and whatever you may say to me, I know beforehand. I have long been thinking over your destiny, Dmitri Fyodorovitch, I am watching over it and studying it. . . . Oh, believe me, I'm an experienced doctor of the soul, Dmitri Fyodorovitch."

"Madam, if you are an experienced doctor, I'm certainly an experienced patient," said Mitya, with an effort to be polite, "and I feel that if you are watching over my destiny in this way, you will come to my help in my ruin, and so allow me at least to explain to you the plan with which I have ventured to come to you . . . and what I am hoping of you. . . . I have come, Madam . . ."

"Don't explain it. It's of secondary importance. But as for help, you're not the first I have helped, Dmitri Fyodorovitch. You have most likely heard of my cousin, Madame Belmesov. Her husband was ruined, 'had come to grief', as you characteristically express it, Dmitri Fyodorovitch. I recommended him to take to horse-breeding, and now he's doing well. Have you any idea of horse-breeding, Dmitri Fyodorovitch?"

"Not the faintest, Madam; ah, Madam, not the faintest!" cried Mitya, in nervous impatience, positively starting from his seat. "I simply implore you, Madam, to listen to me. Only give me two minutes of free speech that I may just explain to you everything, the whole plan with which I have come. Besides I am short of time. I'm in a fearful hurry," Mitya cried hysterically, feeling that she was just going to begin talking again, and hoping to cut her short. "I have come in despair . . . in the last gasp of despair, to beg you to lend me the sum of three thousand, a loan, but on safe, most safe security, Madam, with the most trustworthy guarantees! Only let me explain . . ."

"You must tell me all that afterwards, afterwards!" Madame Hohlakov with a gesture demanded silence in her turn, "and whatever you may tell me, I know it all beforehand; I've told you so already. You ask for a certain sum, for three thousand, but I can give you more, immeasurably more, I will save you, Dmitri Fyodorovitch, but you must listen to me."

Mitya started from his seat again.

"Madam, will you really be so good?" he cried, with strong feeling. "Good God, you've saved me! You have saved a man from a violent death, from a bullet. . . . My eternal gratitude . . ."

"I will give you more, infinitely more than three thousand!" cried Madame Hohlakov, looking with a radiant smile at Mitya's ecstasy.

"Infinitely? But I don't need so much. I only need that fatal three thousand, and on my part I can give security for that sum with infinite gratitude, and I propose a plan which . . ."

"Enough, Dmitri Fyodorovitch, it's said and done." Madame Hohlakov cut him short, with the modest triumph of beneficence: "I have promised to save you, and I will save you. I will save you as I did Belmesov. What do you think of the gold-mines, Dmitri Fyodorovitch?"

"Of the gold-mines, Madam? I have never thought anything about them."

"But I have thought of them for you. Thought of them over and over again. I have been watching you for the last month. I've watched you a hundred times as you've walked past, saying to myself: that's a man of energy who ought to be at the gold-mines. I've studied your gait and come to the conclusion: that's a man who would find gold."

"From my gait, Madam?" said Mitya, smiling.

"Yes, from your gait. You surely don't deny that character can be told from the gait, Dmitri Fyodorovitch? Science supports the idea. I'm all for science and realism now. After all this business with Father Zossima, which has so upset me, from this very day I'm a realist and I want to devote myself to practical usefulness. I'm cured. 'Enough!' as Turgenev says."

"But, Madam, the three thousand you so generously promised to lend me . . ."

"It is yours, Dmitri Fyodorovitch," Madame Hohlakov cut

in at once. "The money is as good as in your pocket, not three thousand but three million, Dmitri Fyodorovitch, in less than no time. I'll make you a present of the idea: you shall find gold-mines, make millions, return and become a leading man, and wake us up and lead us to better things. Are we to leave it all to the Jews? You will found institutions and enterprises of all sorts. You will help the poor, and they will bless you. This is the age of railways, Dmitri Fyodorovitch. You'll become famous and indispensable to the Department of Finance, which is so badly off at present. The depreciation of the rouble keeps me awake at night, Dmitri Fyodorovitch; people don't know that side of me . . ."

"Madam, Madam!" Dmitri interrupted, with an uneasy presentiment. "I shall indeed, perhaps, follow your advice, your wise advice, Madam. . . . I shall perhaps set off . . . to the gold-mines. . . . I'll come and see you again about it . . . many times, indeed . . . but now, that three thousand you so generously . . . oh, that would set me free, and if you could to-day . . . you see, I haven't a minute, a minute to lose to-day . . ."

"Enough, Dmitri Fyodorovitch, enough!" Madame Hohlakov interrupted emphatically. "The question is, will you go to the gold-mines or not; have you quite made up your mind? Answer yes or no."

"I will go, Madam, afterwards. . . . I'll go where you like . . . but now . . ."

"Wait!" cried Madam Hohlakov. And jumping up and running to a handsome bureau with numerous drawers, she began pulling out one drawer after another, looking for something with desperate haste.

"The three thousand," thought Mitya, his heart almost stopping, "and at the instant . . . without any papers or formalities . . . that's doing things in gentlemanly style! She's a splendid woman, if only she didn't talk so much!"

"Here!" cried Madame Hohlakov, running back joyfully to Mitya, "here is what I was looking for!"

It was a tiny silver ikon on a cord, such as is sometimes worn next the skin with a cross.

"This is from Kiev, Dmitri Fyodorovitch," she went on reverently, "from the relics of the Holy Martyr, Varvara. Let me put it on your neck myself, and with it dedicate you to a new life, to a new career."

And she actually put the cord round his neck, and began arranging it. In extreme embarrassment, Mitya bent down

and helped her, and at last he got it under his neck-tie and collar through his shirt to his chest.

"Now you can set off," Madame Hohlakov pronounced, sitting down triumphantly in her place again.

"Madam, I am so touched. I don't know how to thank you, indeed . . . for such kindness, but . . . If only you knew how precious time is to me. . . . That sum of money, for which I shall be indebted to your generosity. . . . Oh, Madam, since you are so kind, so touchingly generous to me" (Mitya exclaimed impulsively), "then let me reveal to you . . . though, of course, you've known it a long time . . . that I love somebody here. . . . I have been false to Katya . . . Katerina Ivanovna, I should say. . . . Oh, I've behaved inhumanly, dishonourably to her, but I fell in love here with another woman . . . a woman whom you, Madam, perhaps despise, for you know everything already, but whom I cannot leave on any account, and therefore that three thousand now . . ."

"Leave everything, Dmitri Fyodorovitch," Madame Hohlakov interrupted in the most decisive tone. "Leave everything, especially women. Gold-mines are your goal, and there's no place for women there. Afterwards, when you come back rich and famous, you will find the girl of your heart in the highest society. That will be a modern girl, a girl of education and advanced ideas. By that time the dawning woman question will have gained ground, and the new woman will have appeared."

"Madam, that's not the point, not at all. . . ." Mitya clasped his hands in entreaty.

"Yes it is, Dmitri Fyodorovitch, just what you need; the very thing you're yearning for, though you don't realise it yourself. I am not at all opposed to the present woman movement, Dmitri Fyodorovitch. The development of woman, and even the political emancipation of woman in the near future—that's my ideal. I've a daughter myself, Dmitri Fyodorovitch, people don't know that side of me. I wrote a letter to the author, Shtchedrin, on that subject. He has taught me so much, so much about the vocation of women. So last year I sent him an anonymous letter of two lines: 'I kiss and embrace you, my teacher, for the modern woman. Persevere.' And I signed myself, 'a Mother'. I thought of signing myself 'a contemporary mother', and hesitated, but I stuck to the simple 'Mother'; there's more moral beauty in that, Dmitri Fyodorovitch. And the word 'contemporary' might have reminded him of '*The*

THE BROTHERS KARAMAZOV

Contemporary'—a painful recollection owing to the censorship. . . . Good heavens, what is the matter?"

"Madam!" cried Mitya, jumping up at last, clasping his hands before her in hopeless entreaty. "You will make me weep if you delay what you have so generously . . ."

"Oh, do weep, Dmitri Fyodorovitch, do weep! That's a noble feeling . . . such a path lies open before you! Tears will ease your heart, and later on you will return rejoicing. You will hasten to me from Siberia on purpose to share your joy with me . . ."

"But allow me, too!" Mitya cried suddenly. "For the last time I entreat you, tell me, can I have the sum you promised me to-day? if not, when may I come for it?"

"What sum, Dmitri Fyodorovitch?"

"The three thousand you promised me . . . that you so generously . . ."

"Three thousand? Roubles? Oh, no, I haven't got three thousand," Madame Hohlakov announced with serene amazement. Mitya was stupefied.

"Why, you said just now . . . you said . . . you said it was as good as it my hands . . ."

"Oh, no, you misunderstood me, Dmitri Fyodorovitch. In that case you misunderstood me. I was talking of the gold-mines. It's true I promised you more, infinitely more than three thousand, I remember it all now, but I was referring to the gold-mines."

"But the money? The three thousand?" Mitya exclaimed, awkwardly.

"Oh, if you meant money, I haven't any. I haven't a penny, Dmitri Fyodorovitch. I'm quarrelling with my steward about it, and I've just borrowed five hundred roubles from Miüsov, myself. No, no, I've no money. And, do you know, Dmitri Fyodorovitch, if I had I wouldn't lend it to you. In the first place I never lend money. Lending money means losing friends. And I wouldn't give it to you particularly. I wouldn't give it you, because I like you and want to save you, for all you need is the gold-mines, the gold-mines, the gold-mines!"

"Oh, the devil!" roared Mitya, and with all his might brought his fist down on the table.

"Aie! Aie!" cried Madame Hohlakov, alarmed, and she flew to the other end of the drawing-room.

Mitya spat on the ground, and strode rapidly out of the room, out of the house, into the street, into the darkness! He walked

68

like one possessed, and beating himself on the breast, on the spot where he had struck himself two days previously, before Alyosha, the last time he saw him in the dark, on the road. What those blows upon his breast signified, *on that spot*, and what he meant by it—that was, for the time, a secret which was known to no one in the world, and had not been told even to Alyosha. But that secret meant for him more than disgrace; it meant ruin, suicide. So he had determined, if he did not get hold of the three thousand that would pay his debt to Katerina Ivanovna, and so remove from his breast, from *that spot on his breast*, the shame he carried upon it, that weighed on his conscience. All this will be fully explained to the reader later on, but now that his last hope had vanished, this man, so strong in appearance, burst out crying like a little child a few steps from the Hohlakovs' house. He walked on, and not knowing what he was doing, wiped away his tears with his fist. In this way he reached the square, and suddenly became aware that he had stumbled against something. He heard a piercing wail from an old woman whom he had almost knocked down.

"Good Lord, you've nearly killed me! Why don't you look where you're going, scapegrace?"

"Why, it's you!" cried Mitya, recognising the old woman in the dark. It was the old servant who waited on Samsonov, whom Mitya had particularly noticed the day before.

"And who are you, my good sir?" said the old woman in quite a different voice. "I don't know you in the dark."

"You live at Kuzma Kuzmitch's. You're the servant there?"

"Just so, sir, I was only running out to Prohoritch's . . . But I don't know you now."

"Tell me, my good woman, is Agrafena Alexandrovna there now?" said Mitya, beside himself with suspense. "I saw her to the house some time ago."

"She has been there, sir. She stayed a little while, and went off again."

"What? Went away?" cried Mitya. "When did she go?"

"Why, as soon as she came. She only stayed a minute. She only told Kuzma Kuzmitch a tale that made him laugh, and then she ran away."

"You're lying, damn you!" roared Mitya.

"Aie! Aie!" shrieked the old woman, but Mitya had vanished.

He ran with all his might to the house where Grushenka lived.

At the moment he reached it Grushenka was on her way to Mokroe. It was not more than a quarter of an hour after her departure.

Fenya was sitting with her grandmother, the old cook, Matryona, in the kitchen when "the captain" ran in. Fenya uttered a piercing shriek on seeing him.

"You scream?" roared Mitya. "Where is she?"

But without giving the terror-stricken Fenya time to utter a word, he fell all of a heap at her feet.

"Fenya, for Christ's sake, tell me, where is she?"

"I don't know. Dmitri Fyodorovitch, my dear, I don't know. You may kill me, but I can't tell you." Fenya swore and protested. "You went out with her yourself not long ago . . ."

"She came back!"

"Indeed she didn't. By God I swear she didn't come back."

"You're lying!" shouted Mitya. "From your terror I know where she is."

He rushed away. Fenya in her fright was glad she had got off so easily. But she knew very well that it was only that he was in such haste, or she might not have fared so well. But as he ran, he surprised both Fenya and old Matryona by an unexpected action. On the table stood a brass mortar, with a pestle in it, a small brass pestle, not much more than six inches long. Mitya already had opened the door with one hand when, with the other, he snatched up the pestle and thrust it in his side pocket.

"Oh Lord! He's going to murder someone!" cried Fenya, flinging up her hands.

CHAPTER IV

IN THE DARK

WHERE was he running? "Where could she be except at Fyodor Pavlovitch's? She must have run straight to him from Samsonov's, that was clear now. The whole intrigue, the whole deceit was evident." . . . It all rushed whirling through his mind. He did not run to Marya Kondratyevna's . "There was no need to go there . . . not the slightest need . . . he must raise no alarm . . . they would run and tell directly.

. . . Marya Kondratyevna was clearly in the plot, Smerdyakov too, he too, all had been bought over!''

He formed another plan of action: he ran a long way round Fyodor Pavlovitch's house, crossing the lane, running down Dmitrovsky Street, then over the little bridge, and so came straight to the deserted alley at the back, which was empty and uninhabited, with, on one side, the hurdle fence of a neighbour's kitchen-garden, on the other, the strong high fence that ran all round Fyodor Pavlovitch's garden. Here he chose a spot, apparently the very place, where, according to the tradition, he knew Lizaveta had once climbed over it: ''If she could climb over it,'' the thought, God knows why, occurred to him, ''surely I can.'' He did in fact jump up, and instantly contrived to catch hold of the top of the fence. Then he vigorously pulled himself up and sat astride of it. Close by, in the garden, stood the bath-house, but from the fence he could see the lighted windows of the house too.

''Yes, the old man's bedroom is lighted up. She's there!'' and he leapt from the fence into the garden. Though he knew Grigory was ill and very likely Smerdyakov, too, and that there was no one to hear him, he instinctively hid himself, stood still and began to listen. But there was dead silence on all sides and, as though of design, complete stillness, not the slightest breath of wind.

''And naught but the whispering silence,'' the line for some reason rose to his mind. ''If only no one heard me jump over the fence! I think not.'' Standing still for a minute, he walked softly over the grass in the garden, avoiding the trees and shrubs. He walked slowly, creeping stealthily at every step, listening to his own footsteps. It took him five minutes to reach the lighted window. He remembered that just under the window there were several thick and high bushes of elder and white beam. The door from the house into the garden, on the left-hand side, was shut; he had carefully looked purposely to see, in passing. At last he reached the bushes and hid behind them. He held his breath. ''I must wait now,'' he thought, ''to reassure them, in case they heard my footsteps and are listening . . . if only I don't cough or sneeze.''

He waited two minutes. His heart was beating violently, and, at moments, he could scarcely breathe. ''No, this throbbing at my heart won't stop,'' he thought. ''I can't wait any longer.'' He was standing behind a bush in the shadow. The light of the window fell on the front part of the bush.

"How red the white-beam berries are!" he murmured, not knowing why. Softly and noiselessly, step by step, he approached the window, and raised himself on tiptoe. All Fyodor Pavlovitch's bedroom lay open before him. It was not a large room, and was divided in two parts by a red screen, "Chinese", as Fyodor Pavlovitch used to call it. The word "Chinese" flashed into Mitya's mind, "and behind the screen is Grushenka", thought Mitya. He began watching Fyodor Pavlovitch, who was wearing his new striped-silk dressing-gown, which Mitya had never seen, and a silk cord with tassels round the waist. A clean, dandified shirt of fine linen with gold studs peeped out under the collar of the dressing-gown. On his head Fyodor Pavlovitch had the same red bandage which Alyosha had seen.

"He has got himself up," thought Mitya.

His father was standing near the window, apparently lost in thought. Suddenly he jerked up his head, listened a moment, and, hearing nothing, went up to the table, poured out half a glass of brandy from a decanter, and drank it off. Then he uttered a deep sigh, again stood still a moment, walked carelessly up to the looking-glass on the wall, with his right hand raised the red bandage on his forehead a little, and began examining his bruises and scars, which had not yet disappeared.

"He's alone," thought Mitya, "in all probability he's alone."

Fyodor Pavlovitch moved away from the looking-glass, turned suddenly to the window and looked out. Mitya instantly slipped away into the shadow.

"She may be there behind the screen. Perhaps she's asleep by now," he thought, with a pang at his heart. Fyodor Pavlovitch moved away from the window. "He's looking for her out of the window, so she's not there. Why should he stare out into the dark? He's wild with impatience" . . . Mitya slipped back at once, and fell to gazing in at the window again. The old man was sitting down at the table, apparently disappointed. At last he put his elbow on the table, and laid his right cheek against his hand. Mitya watched him eagerly.

"He's alone, he's alone!" he repeated again. "If she were here, his face would be different."

Strange to say, a queer, irrational vexation rose up in his heart that she was not here. "It's not that she's not here," he explained to himself, immediately, "but that I can't tell for certain whether she is or not." Mitya remembered afterwards that his mind was, at that moment, exceptionally clear, that he took in everything to the slightest detail, and missed no point. But a feeling of misery, the misery of uncertainty and indecision, was growing in his heart with every instant. "Is she here or not?" The angry doubt filled his heart, and suddenly, making up his mind, he put out his hand and softly knocked on the window frame. He knocked the signal the old man had agreed upon with Smerdyakov, twice slowly and then three times more quickly, the signal that meant "Grushenka is here!"

The old man started, jerked up his head, and, jumping up quickly, ran to the window. Mitya slipped away into the shadow. Fyodor Pavlovitch opened the window and thrust his whole head out.

"Grushenka, is it you? Is it you?" he said, in a sort of trembling half-whisper. "Where are you, my angel, where are you?" He was fearfully agitated and breathless.

"He's alone," Mitya decided.

"Where are you?" cried the old man again; and he thrust his head out further, thrust it out to the shoulders, gazing in all directions, right and left. "Come here, I've a little present for you. Come, I'll show you . . ."

"He means the three thousand," thought Mitya.

"But where are you? Are you at the door? I'll open it directly."

And the old man almost climbed out of the window, peering out to the right, where there was a door into the garden, trying to see into the darkness. In another second he would certainly have run out to open the door without waiting for Grushenka's answer.

Mitya looked at him from the side without stirring. The old man's profile that he loathed so, his pendent Adam's apple, his hooked nose, his lips that smiled in greedy expectation, were all brightly lighted up by the slanting lamplight falling on the left from the room. A horrible fury of hatred suddenly surged up in Mitya's heart: "There he was, his rival, the man who had tormented him, had ruined his life!" It was a rush of that sudden, furious, revengeful anger of which he had spoken, as though foreseeing it, to Alyosha four days ago in the arbour, when, in answer to Alyosha's question: "How can you say you'll kill our father?" "I don't know, I don't know," he had said then. "Perhaps I shall not kill him, perhaps I shall. I'm afraid he'll suddenly be so loathsome to me at that moment.

I hate his double chin, his nose, his eyes, his shameless grin. I feel a personal repulsion. That's what I'm afraid of, that's what may be too much for me" . . . This personal repulsion was growing unendurable. Mitya was beside himself, he suddenly pulled the brass pestle out of his pocket.

"God was watching over me then," Mitya himself said afterwards. At that very moment Grigory waked up on his bed of sickness. Earlier in the evening he had undergone the treatment which Smerdyakov had described to Ivan. He had rubbed himself all over with vodka mixed with a secret very strong decoction, had drunk what was left of the mixture while his wife repeated a "certain prayer" over him, after which he had gone to bed. Marfa Ignatyevna had tasted the stuff, too, and, being unused to strong drink, slept like the dead beside her husband.

But Grigory waked up in the night, quite suddenly, and, after a moment's reflection, though he immediately felt a sharp pain in his back, he sat up in bed. Then he deliberated again, got up and dressed hurriedly. Perhaps his conscience was uneasy at the thought of sleeping while the house was unguarded "in such perilous times". Smerdyakov, exhausted by his fit, lay motionless in the next room. Marfa Ignatyevna did not stir. "The stuff's been too much for the old woman," Grigory thought, glancing at her, and groaning, he went out on the steps. No doubt he only intended to look out from the steps, for he was hardly able to walk, the pain in his back and his right leg was intolerable. But he suddenly remembered that he had not locked the little gate into the garden that evening. He was the most punctual and precise of men, a man who adhered to an unchangeable routine, and habits that lasted for years. Limping and writhing with pain he went down the steps and towards the garden. Yes, the gate stood wide open. Mechanically he stepped into the garden. Perhaps he fancied something, perhaps caught some sound, and, glancing to the left, he saw his master's window open. No one was looking out of it then.

"What's it open for? It's not summer now," thought Grigory, and suddenly, at that very instant, he caught a glimpse of something extraordinary before him in the garden. Forty paces in front of him a man seemed to be running in the dark, a sort of shadow was moving very fast.

"Good Lord!" cried Grigory, beside himself, and forgetting

THE BROTHERS KARAMAZOV

the pain in his back, he hurried to intercept the running figure. He took a short cut, evidently he knew the garden better; the flying figure went towards the bath-house, ran behind it and rushed to the garden fence. Grigory followed, not losing sight of him, and ran, forgetting everything. He reached the fence at the very moment the man was climbing it. Grigory cried out, beside himself, pounced on him, and clutched his leg in his two hands.

Yes, his foreboding had not deceived him. He recognised him, it was he, the "monster", the "parricide".

"Parricide!" the old man shouted so that the whole neighbourhood could hear, but he had not time to shout more, he fell at once, as though struck by lightning.

Mitya jumped back into the garden and bent over the fallen man. In Mitya's hands was a brass pestle, and he flung it mechanically in the grass. The pestle fell two paces from Grigory, not in the grass but on the path, in a most conspicuous place. For some seconds he examined the prostrate figure before him. The old man's head was covered with blood. Mitya put out his hand and began feeling it. He remembered afterwards clearly that he had been awfully anxious to make sure whether he had broken the old man's skull or simply stunned him with the pestle. But the blood was flowing horribly; and in a moment Mitya's fingers were drenched with the hot stream. He remembered taking out of his pocket the clean white handkerchief with which he had provided himself for his visit to Madame Hohlakov, and putting it to the old man's head, senselessly trying to wipe the blood from his face and temples. But the handkerchief was instantly soaked with blood.

"Good heavens! what am I doing it for?" thought Mitya, suddenly pulling himself together. "If I have broken his skull, how can I find out now? And what difference does it make now?" he added, hopelessly. "If I've killed him, I've killed him . . . you've come to grief, old man, so there you must lie!" he said aloud. And suddenly, turning to the fence, he vaulted over it into the lane and fell to running—the handkerchief soaked with blood he held, crushed up, in his right fist, and, as he ran, he thrust it into the back pocket of his coat. He ran headlong, and the few passers-by who met him in the dark, in the streets, remembered afterwards that they had met a man running that night. He flew back again to the widow Morozov's house.

Immediately after he had left it, that evening, Fenya had rushed to the chief porter, Nazar Ivanovitch, and besought him, for Christ's sake, "not to let the captain in again to-day or to-morrow". Nazar Ivanovitch promised, but went upstairs to his mistress who had suddenly sent for him, and meeting his nephew, a boy of twenty, who had recently come from the country, on the way up told him to take his place, but forgot to mention "the captain". Mitya, running up to the gate, knocked. The lad instantly recognised him, for Mitya had more than once tipped him. Opening the gate at once, he let him in, and hastened to inform him with a good-humoured smile that "Agrafena Alexandrovna is not at home now, you know."

"Where is she then, Prohor?" asked Mitya, stopping short.

"She set off this evening, some two hours ago, with Timofey, to Mokroe."

"What for?" cried Mitya.

"That I can't say. To see some officer. Someone invited her and horses were sent to fetch her."

Mitya left him, and ran like a madman to Fenya.

CHAPTER V

A SUDDEN RESOLUTION

SHE was sitting in the kitchen with her grandmother; they were both just going to bed. Relying on Nazar Ivanovitch, they had not locked themselves in. Mitya ran in, pounced on Fenya and seized her by the throat.

"Speak at once! Where is she? With whom is she now, at Mokroe?" he roared furiously.

Both the women squealed.

"Aie! I'll tell you. Aie, Dmitri Fyodorovitch, darling. I'll tell you everything directly, I won't hide anything," gabbled Fenya, frightened to death; "she's gone to Mokroe, to her officer."

"What officer?" roared Mitya.

"To her officer, the same one she used to know, the one who threw her over five years ago," cackled Fenya, as fast as she could speak.

Mitya withdrew the hands with which he was squeezing her throat. He stood facing her, pale as death, unable to utter a word, but his eyes showed that he realised it all, all, from the first word, and guessed the whole position. Poor Fenya was not in a condition at that moment to observe whether he understood or not. She remained sitting on the trunk as she had been when he ran into the room, trembling all over, holding her hands out before her as though trying to defend herself. She seemed to have grown rigid in that position. Her wide-opened, scared eyes were fixed immovably upon him. And to make matters worse, both his hands were smeared with blood. On the way, as he ran, he must have touched his forehead with them, wiping off the perspiration, so that on his forehead and his right cheek were blood-stained patches. Fenya was on the verge of hysterics. The old cook had jumped up and was staring at him like a mad woman, almost unconscious with terror.

Mitya stood for a moment, then mechanically sank on to a chair next to Fenya. He sat, not reflecting but, as it were, terror-stricken, benumbed. Yet everything was clear as day: that officer, he knew about him, he knew everything perfectly, he had known it from Grushenka herself, had known that a letter had come from him a month before. So that for a month, for a whole month, this had been going on in secret from him, till the very arrival of this new man, and he had never thought of him! But how could he, how could he not have thought of him? Why was it he had forgotten this officer, like that, forgotten him as soon as he heard of him? That was the question that faced him like some monstrous thing. And he looked at this monstrous thing with horror, growing cold with horror.

But suddenly, as gently and mildly as a gentle and affectionate child, he began speaking to Fenya as though he had utterly forgotten how he had scared and hurt her just now. He fell to questioning Fenya with an extreme preciseness, astonishing in his position, and though the girl looked wildly at his blood-stained hands, she, too, with wonderful readiness and rapidity, answered every question as though eager to put the whole truth and nothing but the truth before him. Little by little, even with a sort of enjoyment, she began explaining every detail, not wanting to torment him, but, as it were, eager to be of the utmost service to him. She described the whole of that day in great detail: the visit of Rakitin and Alyosha, how she, Fenya, had stood on the watch, how the mistress had set off, and how she had called out of the window to Alyosha to give him, Mitya, her greetings, and to tell him "to remember for ever how she had loved him for an hour'.

Hearing of the message, Mitya suddenly smiled, and there was a flush of colour on his pale cheeks. At the same moment Fenya said to him, not a bit afraid now to be inquisitive:

"Look at your hands, Dmitri Fyodorovitch. They're all over blood!"

"Yes," answered Mitya mechanically. He looked carelessly at his hands and at once forgot them and Fenya's question.

He sank into silence again. Twenty minutes had passed since he had run in. His first horror was over, but evidently some new fixed determination had taken possession of him. He suddenly stood up, smiling dreamily.

"What has happened to you, sir?" said Fenya, pointing to his hands again. She spoke compassionately, as though she felt very near to him now in his grief. Mitya looked at his hands again.

"That's blood, Fenya," he said, looking at her with a strange expression. "That's human blood, and, my God! why was it shed? But. . . . Fenya . . . there's a fence here" (he looked at her as though setting her a riddle), "a high fence, and terrible to look at. But, at dawn to-morrow, when the sun rises, Mitya will leap over that fence. . . . You don't understand what fence, Fenya, and, never mind. . . . You'll hear to-morrow and understand . . . and now, good-bye. I won't stand in her way. I'll step aside, I know how to step aside. Live, my joy. . . . You loved me for an hour, remember Mityenka Karamazov so for ever. . . . She always used to call me Mityenka, do you remember?"

And with those words he went suddenly out of the kitchen. Fenya was almost more frightened at this sudden departure than she had been when he ran in and attacked her.

Just ten minutes later Dmitri went into Pyotr Ilyitch Perhotin, the young official with whom he had pawned his pistols. It was by now half-past eight, and Pyotr Ilyitch had finished his evening tea and had just put his coat on again to go to the "Metropolis" to play billiards. Mitya caught him coming out.

Seeing him with his face all smeared with blood, the young man uttered a cry of surprise.

"Good heavens! What is the matter?"

"I've come for my pistols," said Mitya, "and brought you

the money. And thanks very much. I'm in a hurry, Pyotr Ilyitch, please make haste."

Pyotr Ilyitch grew more and more surprised; he suddenly caught sight of a bundle of bank-notes in Mitya's hand, and, what was more, he had walked in holding the notes as no one walks in and no one carries money: he had them in his right hand, and held them outstretched as if to show them. Perhotin's servant-boy, who met Mitya in the passage, said afterwards that he walked into the passage in the same way, with the money outstretched in his hand, so he must have been carrying them like that even in the street. They were all rainbow-coloured hundred-rouble notes, and the fingers holding them were covered with blood.

When Pyotr Ilyitch was questioned later on as to the sum of money, he said that it was difficult to judge at a glance, but that it might have been two thousand, or perhaps three, but it was a big, "fat" bundle. "Dmitri Fyodorovitch," so he testified afterwards, "seemed unlike himself, too; not drunk, but, as it were, exalted, lost to everything, but at the same time, as it were, absorbed, as though pondering and searching for something and unable to come to a decision. He was in great haste, answered abruptly and very strangely, and at moments seemed not at all dejected but quite cheerful."

"But what *is* the matter with you? What's wrong?" cried Pyotr Ilyitch, looking wildly at his guest. "How is it that you're all covered with blood? Have you had a fall? Look at yourself!"

He took him by the elbow and led him to the glass.

Seeing his blood-stained face, Mitya started and scowled wrathfully.

"Damnation! That's the last straw," he muttered angrily, hurriedly changing the notes from his right hand to the left, and impulsively jerked the handkerchief out of his pocket. But the handkerchief turned out to be soaked with blood, too (it was the handkerchief he had used to wipe Grigory's face). There was scarcely a white spot on it, and it had not merely begun to dry but had stiffened into a crumpled ball and could not be pulled part. Mitya threw it angrily on the floor.

"Oh, damn it!" he said. "Haven't you a rag of some sort . . . to wipe my face?"

"So you're only stained, not wounded? You'd better wash," said Pyotr Ilyitch. "Here's a wash-stand. I'll pour you out some water."

"A wash-stand? That's all right . . . but where am I to put this?"

With the strangest perplexity he indicated his bundle of hundred-rouble notes, looking inquiringly at Pyotr Ilyitch as though it were for him to decide what he, Mitya, was to do with his own money.

"In your pocket, or on the table here. They won't be lost."

"In my pocket? Yes, in my pocket. All right. . . . But, I say, that's all nonsense," he cried, as though suddenly coming out of his absorption. "Look here, let's first settle that business of the pistols. Give them back to me. Here's your money . . . because I am in great need of them . . . and I haven't a minute, a minute, to spare."

And taking the topmost note from the bundle he held it out to Ptoyr Ilyitch.

"But I shan't have change enough. Haven't you less?"

"No," said Mitya, looking again at the bundle, and as though not trusting his own words he turned over two or three of the topmost ones.

"No, they're all alike," he added, and again he looked inquiringly at Pyotr Ilyitch.

"How have you grown so rich?" the latter asked. "Wait, I'll send my boy to Plotnikov's—they close late—to see if they will change it. Here, Misha!" he called into the passage.

"To Plotnikov's shop—first-rate!" cried Mitya, as though struck by an idea. "Misha," he turned to the boy as he came in, "look here, run to Plotnikov's and tell them that Dmitri Fyodorovitch sends his greetings, and will be there directly. . . . But listen, listen, tell them to have champagne, three dozen bottles, ready before I come, and packed as it was to take to Mokroe. I took four dozen with me then," he added (suddenly addressing Pyotr Ilyitch); "they know all about it, don't you trouble, Misha," he turned again to the boy. "Stay, listen; tell them to put in cheese, Strasbourg pies, smoked fish, ham, caviare, and everything, everything they've got, up to a hundred roubles, or a hundred and twenty as before. . . . But wait: don't let them forget dessert—sweets, pears, water-melons, two or three or four—no, one melon's enough, and chocolate, candy, toffee, fondants; in fact, everything I took to Mokroe before, three hundred roubles' worth with the champagne . . . let it be just the same again. And remember, Misha, if you are called Misha. . . . His name is Misha, isn't it?" He turned to Pyotr Ilyitch again.

"Wait a minute," Pyotr Ilyitch intervened, listening and watching him uneasily, "you'd better go yourself and tell them. He'll muddle it."

"He will, I see he will! Eh, Misha! Why, I was going to kiss you for the commission. . . . If you don't make a mistake, there's ten roubles for you, run along, make haste. . . . Champagne's the chief thing, let them bring up champagne. And brandy, too, and red and white wine, and all I had then. . . . They know what I had then."

"But listen!" Pyotr Ilyitch interrupted with some impatience. "I say, let him simply run and change the money and tell them not to close, and you go and tell them. . . . Give him your note. Be off, Misha! Put your best leg forward!"

Pyotr Ilyitch seemed to hurry Misha off on purpose, because the boy remained standing with his mouth and eyes wide open, apparently understanding little of Mitya's orders, gazing up with amazement and terror at his blood-stained face and the trembling blood-stained fingers that held the notes.

"Well, now come and wash," said Pyotr Ilyitch, sternly. "Put the money on the table or else in your pocket. . . . That's right, come along. But take off your coat."

And beginning to help him off with his coat, he cried out again:

"Look, your coat's covered with blood, too!"

"That . . . it's not the coat. It's only a little here on the sleeve. . . . And that's only here where the handkerchief lay. It must have soaked through. I must have sat on the handkerchief at Fenya's, and the blood's come through," Mitya explained at once with a childlike unconsciousness that was astounding. Pyotr Ilyitch listened, frowning.

"Well, you must have been up to something; you must have been fighting with someone," he muttered.

They began to wash. Pyotr Ilyitch held the jug and poured out the water. Mitya, in desperate haste, scarcely soaped his hands (they were trembling, and Pyotr Ilyitch remembered it afterwards). But the young official insisted on his soaping them thoroughly and rubbing them more. He seemed to exercise more and more sway over Mitya, as time went on. It may be noted in passing that he was a young man of sturdy character.

"Look, you haven't got your nails clean. Now rub your face; here, on your temples, by your ear. . . . Will you go in that shirt? Where are you going? Look, all the cuff of your right sleeve is covered with blood."

"Yes, it's all bloody," observed Mitya, looking at the cuff of his shirt.

"Then change your shirt."

"I haven't time. You see I'll . . ." Mitya went on with the same confiding ingenuousness, drying his face and hands on the towel, and putting on his coat. "I'll turn it up at the wrist. It won't be seen under the coat. . . . You see!"

"Tell me now, what game have you been up to? Have you been fighting with someone? In the tavern again, as before? Have you been beating that captain again?" Pyotr Ilyitch asked him reproachfully. "Whom have you been beating now . . . or killing, perhaps?"

"Nonsense!" said Mitya.

"Why 'nonsense'?"

"Don't worry," said Mitya, and he suddenly laughed. "I smashed an old woman in the market-place just now."

"Smashed? An old woman?"

"An old man!" cried Mitya, looking Pyotr Ilyitch straight in the face, laughing, and shouting at him as though he were deaf.

"Confound it! An old woman, an old man. . . . Have you killed someone?"

"We made it up. We had a row—and made it up. In a place I know of. We parted friends. A fool. . . . He's forgiven me. . . . He's sure to have forgiven me by now . . . if he had got up, he wouldn't have forgiven me"—Mitya suddenly winked—"only, damn him, you know, I say, Pyotr Ilyitch, damn him! Don't you worry about him! I don't want to just now!" Mitya snapped out, resolutely.

"Whatever do you want to go picking quarrels with everyone for? . . . Just as you did with that captain over some nonsense. . . . You've been fighting and now you're rushing off on the spree—that's you all over! Three dozen champagne —what do you want all that for?"

"Bravo! Now give me the pistols. Upon my honour I've no time now. I should like to have a chat with you, my dear boy, but I haven't the time. And there's no need, it's too late for talking. Where's my money? Where have I put it?" he cried, thrusting his hands into his pockets.

"You put it on the table . . . yourself. . . . Here it is. Had you forgotten? Money's like dirt or water to you, it seems. Here are your pistols. It's an odd thing, at six o'clock you pledged them for ten roubles, and now you've got thousands. Two or three, I should say."

"Three, you bet," laughed Mitya, stuffing the notes into the side pocket of his trousers.

"You'll lose it like that. Have you found a gold-mine?"

"The mines? The gold-mines?" Mitya shouted at the top of his voice and went off in a roar of laughter. "Would you like to go to the mines, Perhotin? There's a lady here who'll stump up three thousand for you if only you'll go. She did it for me, she's so awfully fond of gold-mines. Do you know Madame Hohlakov?"

"I don't know her, but I've heard of her and seen her. Did she really give you three thousand? Did she really?" said Pyotr Ilyitch, eyeing him dubiously.

"As soon as the sun rises to-morrow, as soon as Phœbus, ever young, flies upwards, praising and glorifying God, you go to her, this Madame Hohlakov, and ask her whether she did stump up that three thousand or not. Try and find out."

"I don't know on what terms you are . . . since you say it so positively, I suppose she did give it to you. You've got the money in your hand, but instead of going to Siberia you're spending it all. . . . Where are you really off to now, eh?"

"To Mokroe."

"To Mokroe? But it's night!"

"Once the lad had all, now the lad has naught," cried Mitya suddenly.

"How 'naught'? You say that with all those thousands!"

"I'm not talking about thousands. Damn thousands! I'm taking of the female character.

> 'Fickle is the heart of woman
> Treacherous and full of vices;'

I agree with Ulysses. That's what he says."

"I don't understand you!"

"Am I drunk?"

"Not drunk, but worse."

"I'm drunk in spirit, Pyotr Ilyitch, drunk in spirit! But that's enough!"

"What are you doing, loading the pistol?"

"I'm loading the pistol."

Unfastening the pistol-case, Mitya actually opened the powder horn, and carefully sprinkled and rammed in the charge. Then he took the bullet and before inserting it, held it in two fingers in front of the candle.

"Why are you looking at the bullet?" asked Pyotr Ilyitch, watching him with uneasy curiosity.

"Oh, a fancy. Why, if you meant to put that bullet in your brain, would you look at it or not?"

"Why look at it?"

"It's going into my brain, so it's interesting to look and see what it's like. But that's foolishness, a moment's foolishness. Now that's done," he added, putting in the bullet and driving it home with the ramrod. "Pyotr Ilyitch, my dear fellow, that's nonsense, all nonsense, and if only you knew what nonsense! Give me a little piece of paper now."

"Here's some paper."

"No, a clean new piece, writing paper. That's right."

And taking a pen from the table, Mitya rapidly wrote two lines, folded the paper in four, and thrust it in his waistcoat pocket. He put the pistols in the case, locked it up, and kept it in his hand. Then he looked at Pyotr Ilyitch with a slow, thoughtful smile.

"Now let's go," he said.

"Where are we going? No, wait a minute. . . . Are you thinking of putting that bullet in your brain, perhaps?" Pyotr Ilyitch asked uneasily.

"I was fooling about the bullet! I want to live. I love life! You may be sure of that. I love golden-haired Phœbus and his warm light. . . . Dear Pyotr Ilyitch, do you know how to step aside?"

"What do you mean by 'stepping aside'?"

"Making way. Making way for a dear creature, and for one I hate. And to let the one I hate become dear—that's what 'making way' means! And to say to them: God bless you, go your way, pass on, while I . . ."

"While you?"

"That's enough, let's go."

"Upon my word. I'll tell someone to prevent your going there," said Pyotr Ilyitch, looking at him. "What are you going to Mokroe for, now?"

"There's a woman there, a woman. That's enough for you. You shut up."

"Listen, though you're such a savage I've always liked you. . . . I feel anxious."

"Thanks, old fellow. I'm a savage, you say. Savages,

84

savages! That's what I am always saying. Savages! Why, here's Misha! I was forgetting him."

Misha ran in, post-haste, with a handful of notes in change, and reported that everyone was in a bustle at the Plotnikovs': "They're carrying down the bottles, and the fish, and the tea; it will all be ready directly." Mitya seized ten roubles and handed it to Pyotr Ilyitch, then tossed another ten-rouble note to Misha.

"Don't dare to do such a thing!" cried Pyotr Ilyitch. "I won't have it in my house, it's a bad, demoralising habit. Put your money away. Here, put it here, why waste it? It would come in handy to-morrow, and I dare say you'll be coming to me to borrow ten roubles again. Why do you keep putting the notes in your side pocket? Ah, you'll lose them!"

"I say, my dear fellow, let's go to Mokroe together."

"What should I go for?"

"I say, let's open a bottle at once, and drink to life! I want to drink, and especially to drink with you. I've never drunk with you, have I?"

"Very well, we can go to the 'Metropolis'. I was just going there."

"I haven't time for that. Let's drink at the Plotnikovs', in the back room. Shall I ask you a riddle?"

"Ask away."

Mitya took the piece of paper out of his waistcoat pocket, unfolded it and showed it. In a large, distinct hand was written:

"I punish myself for my whole life, my whole life I punish!"

"I certainly will speak to someone. I'll go at once," said Pyotr Ilyitch, after reading the paper.

"You won't have time, my dear boy, come and have a drink. March!"

Plotnikovs' shop was at the corner of the street, next door but one to Pyotr Ilyitch's. It was the largest grocery shop in our town, and by no means a bad one, belonging to some rich merchants. They kept everything that could be got in a Petersburg shop—grocery of all sorts, wines "bottled by the brothers Eliseyev", fruits, cigars, tea, coffee, sugar, and so on. There were three shop-assistants and two errand boys always employed. Though our part of the country had grown poorer, the landowners had gone away, and trade had got worse, yet the grocery stores flourished as before, every year with increasing prosperity; there were plenty of purchasers for their goods.

They were awaiting Mitya with impatience in the shop. They had vivid recollections of how he had bought, three or four weeks ago, wine and goods of all sorts to the value of several hundred roubles paid for in cash (they would never have let him have anything on credit, of course). They remembered that then, as now, he had had a bundle of hundred-rouble notes in his hand, and had scattered them at random, without bargaining, without reflecting, or caring to reflect what use so much wine and provisions would be to him. The story was told all over the town that, driving off then with Grushenka to Mokroe, he had "spent three thousand in one night and the following day, and had come back from the spree without a penny". He had picked up a whole troop of gipsies (encamped in our neighbourhood at the time), who for two days got money without stint out of him while he was drunk, and drank expensive wine without stint. People used to tell, laughing at Mitya, how he had given champagne to grimy-handed peasants, and feasted the village women and girls on sweets and Strasbourg pies. Though to laugh at Mitya to his face was rather a risky proceeding, there was much laughter behind his back, especially in the tavern, at his own ingenuous public avowal that all he had got out of Grushenka by this "escapade" was "permission to kiss her foot, and that was the utmost she had allowed him".

By the time Mitya and Pyotr Ilyitch reached the shop, they found a cart with three horses harnessed abreast with bells, and with Andrey, the driver, ready waiting for Mitya at the entrance. In the shop they had almost entirely finished packing one box of provisions, and were only waiting for Mitya's arrival to nail it down and put it in the cart. Pyotr Ilyitch was astounded.

"Where did this cart come from in such a hurry?" he asked Mitya.

"I met Andrey as I ran to you, and told him to drive straight here to the shop. There's no time to lose. Last time I drove with Timofey, but Timofey now has gone on before me with the witch. Shall we be very late, Andrey?"

"They'll only get there an hour at most before us, not even that maybe. I got Timofey ready to start. I know how he'll go. Their pace won't be ours, Dmitri Fyodorovitch. How could it be? They won't get there an hour earlier!" Andrey, a lanky, red-haired, middle-aged driver, wearing a full-skirted coat, and with a kaftan on his arm, replied warmly:

"Fifty roubles for vodka if we're only an hour behind them."

"I warrant the time, Dmitri Fyodorovitch. Ech, they won't be half an hour before us, let alone an hour."

Though Mitya bustled about seeing after things, he gave his orders strangely, as it were disconnectedly, and inconsecutively. He began a sentence and forgot the end of it. Pyotr Ilyitch found himself obliged to come to the rescue.

"Four hundred roubles' worth, not less than four hundred roubles' worth, just as it was then," commanded Mitya. "Four dozen champagne, not a bottle less."

"What do you want with so much? What's it for? Stay!" cried Pyotr Ilyitch. "What's this box. What's in it? Surely there isn't four hundred roubles' worth here?"

The officious shopmen began explaining with oily politeness that the first box contained only half a dozen bottles of champagne, and only "the most indispensable articles" such as savouries, sweets, toffee, &c. But the main part of the goods ordered would be packed and sent off, as on the previous occasion, in a special cart, also with three horses, travelling at full speed, so that it would arrive not more than an hour later than Dmitri Fyodorovitch himself.

"Not more than an hour! Not more than an hour! And put in more toffee and fondants. The girls there are so fond of it," Mitya insisted hotly.

"The fondants are all right. But what do you want with four dozen of champagne? One would be enough," said Pyotr Ilyitch, almost angry. He began bargaining, asking for a bill of the goods, and refused to be satisfied. But he only succeeded in saving a hundred roubles. In the end it was agreed that only three hundred roubles' worth should be sent.

"Well, you may go to the devil!" cried Pyotr Ilyitch, on second thoughts. "What's it to do with me? Throw away your money, since it's cost you nothing."

"This way, my economist, this way, don't be angry." Mitya drew him into a room at the back of the shop. "They'll give us a bottle here directly. We'll taste it. Ech, Pyotr Ilyitch, come along with me, for you're a nice fellow, the sort I like."

Mitya sat down on a wicker chair, before a little table, covered with a dirty dinner napkin. Pyotr Ilyitch sat down opposite, and the champagne soon appeared, and oysters were suggested to the gentlemen. "First-class oysters, the last lot in."

"Hang the oysters. I don't eat them. And we don't need anything," cried Pyotr Ilyitch, almost angrily.

"There's no time for oysters," said Mitya. "And I'm not hungry. Do you know, friend," he said suddenly, with feeling, "I never have liked all this disorder."

"Who does like it? Three dozen champagne for peasants, upon my word, that's enough to make anyone angry!"

"That's not what I mean. I'm talking of a higher order. There's no order in me, no higher order. But . . . that's all over. There's no need to grieve about it. It's too late, damn it! My whole life has been disorder, and one must set it in order. Is that a pun, eh?"

"You're raving, not making puns!"

> " 'Glory be to God in Heaven,
>   Glory be to God in me' . . .

"That verse came from my heart once, it's not a verse but a tear. . . . I made it myself . . . not while I was pulling the captain's beard, though" . . . .

"Why do you bring him in all of a sudden?"

"Why do I bring him in? Foolery! All things come to an end; all things are made equal. That's the long and short of it."

"You know, I keep thinking of your pistols."

"That's all foolery, too! Drink, and don't be fanciful. I love life. I've loved life too much, shamefully much. Enough! Let's drink to life, dear boy, I propose the toast. Why am I pleased with myself? I'm a scoundrel, but I'm satisfied with myself. And yet I'm tortured by the thought that I'm a scoundrel, but satisfied with myself. I bless the creation. I'm ready to bless God and His creation directly, but . . . I must kill one noxious insect for fear it should crawl and spoil life for others. . . . Let us drink to life, dear brother. What can be more precious than life? Nothing! To life, and to one queen of queens!"

"Let's drink to life and to your queen, too, if you like."

They drank a glass each. Although Mitya was excited and expansive, yet he was melancholy, too. It was as though some heavy, overwhelming anxiety were weighing upon him.

"Misha . . . here's your Misha come! Misha, come here, my boy, drink this glass to Phœbus, the golden-haired, of to-morrow morn . . ."

"What are you giving it him for?" cried Pyotr Ilyitch, irritably.

"Yes, yes, yes, let me! I want to!"

"E—ech!"

Misha emptied the glass, bowed, and ran out.

"He'll remember it afterwards," Mitya remarked. "Woman, I love woman! What is woman? The queen of creation! My heart is sad, my heart is sad, Pyotr Ilyitch. Do you remember Hamlet? 'I am very sorry, good Horatio! Alas, poor Yorick!' Perhaps that's me, Yorick? Yes, I'm Yorick now, and a skull afterwards."

Pyotr Ilyitch listened in silence. Mitya, too, was silent for a while.

"What dog's that you've got here?" he asked the shopman, casually, noticing a pretty little lap-dog with dark eyes, sitting in the corner.

"It belongs to Varvara Alexyevna, the mistress," answered the clerk. "She brought it and forgot it here. It must be taken back to her."

"I saw one like it . . . in the regiment . . ." murmured Mitya dreamily, "only that one had its hind leg broken. . . . By the way, Pyotr Ilyitch, I wanted to ask you: have you ever stolen anything in your life?"

"What a question!"

"Oh, I didn't mean anything. From somebody's pocket, you know. I don't mean government money, everyone steals that, and no doubt you do, too" . . .

"You go to the devil."

"I'm talking of other peoples' money. Stealing straight out of a pocket. Out of a purse, eh?"

"I stole twenty kopecks from my mother when I was nine years old. I took it off the table on the sly, and held it tight in my hand."

"Well, and what happened?"

"Oh, nothing. I kept it three days, then I felt ashamed, confessed, and gave it back."

"And what then?"

"Naturally I was whipped. But why do you ask? Have you stolen something?"

"I have," said Mitya, winking slyly.

"What have you stolen?" inquired Pyotr Ilyitch curiously.

"I stole twenty kopecks from my mother when I was nine years old, and gave it back three days after."

As he said this, Mitya suddenly got up.

"Dmitri Fyodorovitch, won't you come now?" called Andrey from the door of the shop.

"Are you ready? We'll come!" Mitya started. "A few more last words and . . . Andrey, a glass of vodka at starting. Give him some brandy as well! That box" (the one with the pistols) "put under my seat. Good-bye, Pyotr Ilyitch, don't remember evil against me."

"But you're coming back to-morrow?"

"Of course."

"Will you settle the little bill now?" cried the clerk, springing forward.

"Oh yes, the bill. Of course."

He pulled the bundle of notes out of his pocket again, picked out three hundred roubles, threw them on the counter, and ran hurriedly out of the shop. Everyone followed him out, bowing and wishing him good luck. Andrey, coughing from the brandy he had just swallowed, jumped up on the box. But Mitya was only just taking his seat when suddenly, to his surprise, he saw Fenya before him. She ran up panting, clasped her hands before him with a cry, and plumped down at his feet.

"Dmitri Fyodorovitch, dear good Dmitri Fyodorovitch, don't harm my mistress. And it was I told you all about it. . . . And don't murder him, he came first, he's hers! He'll marry Agrafena Alexandrovna now. That's why he's come back from Siberia. Dmitri Fyodorovitch, dear, don't take a fellow creature's life!"

"Tut—tut—tut! That's it, is it? So you're off there to make trouble!" muttered Pyotr Ilyitch. "Now it's all clear, as clear as daylight. Dmitri Fyodorovitch, give me your pistols at once if you mean to behave like a man," he shouted aloud to Mitya. "Do you hear, Dmitri?"

"The pistols? Wait a bit, brother, I'll throw them into the pool on the road," answered Mitya. "Fenya, get up, don't kneel to me. Mitya won't hurt anyone, the silly fool won't hurt anyone again. But I say, Fenya," he shouted, after having taken his seat, "I hurt you just now, so forgive me and have pity on me, forgive a scoundrel. . . . But it doesn't matter if you don't. It's all the same now. Now then, Andrey, look alive, fly along full speed!"

Andrey whipped up the horses, and the bells began ringing.

"Good-bye, Pyotr Ilyitch! My last tear is for you! . . ."

"He's not drunk, but he keeps babbling like a lunatic,"

Pyotr Ilyitch thought as he watched him go. He had half a mind to stay and see the cart packed with the remaining wines and provisions, knowing that they would deceive and defraud Mitya. But, suddenly feeling vexed with himself, he turned away with a curse and went to the tavern to play billiards.

"He's a fool, though he's a good fellow," he muttered as he went. "I've heard of that officer, Grushenka's former flame. Well, if he has turned up. . . . Ech, those pistols! Damn it all! I'm not his nurse! Let them do what they like! Besides, it'll all come to nothing. They're a set of brawlers, that's all. They'll drink and fight, fight and make friends again. They are not men who do anything real. What does he mean by 'I'm stepping aside, I'm punishing myself'? It'll come to nothing! He's shouted such phrases a thousand times, drunk, in the taverns. But now he's not drunk. 'Drunk in spirit'— they're fond of fine phrases, the villains. Am I his nurse? He must have been fighting, his face was all over blood. With whom? I shall find out at the 'Metropolis'. And his handkerchief was soaked in blood. . . . It's still lying on my floor. . . . Hang it!"

He reached the tavern in a bad humour and at once made up a game. The game cheered him. He played a second game, and suddenly began telling one of his partners that Dmitri Karamazov had come in for some cash again—something like three thousand roubles, and had gone to Mokroe again to spend it with Grushenka. . . . This news roused singular interest in his listeners. They all spoke of it, not laughing but with a strange gravity. They left off playing.

"Three thousand? But where can he have got three thousand?"

Questions were asked. The story of Madame Hohlakov's present was received with scepticism.

"Hasn't he robbed his old father, that's the question?"

"Three thousand! There's something odd about it."

"He boasted aloud that he would kill his father; we all heard him, here. And it was three thousand he talked about . . ."

Pyotr Ilyitch listened. All at once he became short and dry in his answers. He said not a word about the blood on Mitya's face and hands, though he had meant to speak of it at first.

They began a third game, and by degrees the talk about Mitya died away. But by the end of the third game Pyotr Ilyitch felt no more desire for billiards; he laid down the cue, and without having supper as he had intended, he walked out of the tavern. When he reached the market-place he stood still in perplexity, wondering at himself. He realised that what he wanted was to go to Fyodor Pavlovitch's and find out if anything had happened there. "On account of some stupid nonsense—as it's sure to turn out—am I going to wake up the household and make a scandal? Fooh! damn it, is it my business to look after them?"

In a very bad humour he went straight home, and suddenly remembered Fenya. "Damn it all! I ought to have questioned her just now," he thought, with vexation, "I should have heard everything." And the desire to speak to her, and so find out, became so pressing and importunate that when he was half-way home he turned abruptly and went towards the house where Grushenka lodged. Going up to the gate he knocked. The sound of the knock in the silence of the night sobered him and made him feel annoyed. And no one answered him; everyone in the house was asleep.

"And I shall be making a fuss!" he thought, with a feeling of positive discomfort. But instead of going away altogether, ne fell to knocking again with all his might, filling the street with clamour.

"Not coming? Well, I will knock them up, I will!" he muttered at each knock, fuming at himself, but at the same time he redoubled his knocks on the gate.

CHAPTER VI

"I AM COMING, TOO!"

BUT Dmitri Fyodorovitch was speeding along the road. It was a little more than twenty versts to Mokroe, but Andrey's three horses galloped at such a pace that the distance might be covered in an hour and a quarter. The swift motion revived Mitya. The air was fresh and cool, there were big stars shining in the sky. It was the very night, and perhaps the very hour, in which Alyosha fell on the earth, and rapturously swore to love it for ever and ever.

All was confusion, confusion, in Mitya's soul, but although many things were goading his heart, at that moment his whole being was yearning for her, his queen, to whom he was flying to look on her for the last time. One thing I can say for certain; his heart did not waver for one instant. I shall perhaps not be

believed when I say that this jealous lover felt not the slightest jealousy of this new rival, who seemed to have sprung out of the earth. If any other had appeared on the scene, he would have been jealous at once, and would perhaps have stained his fierce hands with blood again. But as he flew through the night, he felt no envy, no hostility even, for the man who had been her first lover. . . . It is true he had not yet seen him.

"Here there was no room for dispute: it was her right and his; this was her first love which, after five years, she had not forgotten; so she had loved him only for those five years, and I, how do I come in? What right have I? Step aside, Mitya, and make way! What am I now? Now everything is over apart from the officer—even if he had not appeared, everything would be over . . ."

These words would roughly have expressed his feelings, if he had been capable of reasoning. But he could not reason at that moment. His present plan of action had arisen without reasoning. At Fenya's first words, it had sprung from feeling, and been adopted in a flash, with all its consequences. And yet, in spite of his resolution, there was confusion in his soul, an agonising confusion: his resolution did not give him peace. There was so much behind that tortured him. And it seemed strange to him, at moments, to think that he had written his own sentence of death with pen and paper: "I punish myself," and the paper was lying there in his pocket, ready; the pistol was loaded; he had already resolved how, next morning, he would meet the first warm ray of "golden-haired Phœbus".

And yet he could not be quit of the past, of all that he had left behind and that tortured him. He felt that miserably, and the thought of it sank into his heart with despair. There was one moment when he felt an impulse to stop Andrey, to jump out of the cart, to pull out his loaded pistol, and to make an end of everything without waiting for the dawn. But that moment flew by like a spark. The horses galloped on, "devouring space", and as he drew near his goal, again the thought of her, of her alone, took more and more complete possession of his soul, chasing away the fearful images that had been haunting it. Oh, how he longed to look upon her, if only for a moment, if only from a distance!

"She's now with *him*," he thought, "now I shall see what she looks like with him, her first love, and that's all I want." Never had this woman, who was such a fateful influence in his life, aroused such love in his breast, such new and unknown feeling, surprising even to himself, a feeling tender to devout-ness, to self-effacement before her! "I will efface myself!" he said, in a rush of almost hysterical ecstasy.

They had been galloping nearly an hour. Mitya was silent, and though Andrey was, as a rule, a talkative peasant, he did not utter a word, either. He seemed afraid to talk, he only whipped up smartly his three lean, but mettlesome, bay horses. Suddenly Mitya cried out in horrible anxiety:

"Andrey! What if they're asleep?"

This thought fell upon him like a blow. It had not occurred to him before.

"It may well be that they're gone to bed, by now, Dmitri Fyodorovitch."

Mitya frowned as though in pain. Yes, indeed . . . he was rushing there . . . with such feelings . . . while they were asleep . . . she was asleep, perhaps, there too. . . . An angry feeling surged up in his heart.

"Drive on, Andrey! Whip them up! Look alive!" he cried, beside himself.

"But maybe they're not in bed!" Andrey went on after a pause. "Timofey said there were a lot of them there . . "

"At the station?"

"Not at the posting-station, but at Plastunov's, at the inn, where they let out horses, too."

"I know. So you say there are a lot of them? How's that? Who are they?" cried Mitya, greatly dismayed at this unex-pected news.

"Well, Timofey was saying they're all gentlefolk. Two from our town—who they are I can't say—and there are two others, strangers, maybe more besides. I didn't ask particularly. They've set to playing cards, so Timofey said."

"Cards?"

"So, maybe they're not in bed if they're at cards. It's most likely not more than eleven."

"Quicker, Andrey! Quicker!" Mitya cried again, nervously.

"May I ask something, sir?" said Andrey, after a pause. "Only I'm afraid of angering you, sir."

"What is it?"

"Why, Fenya threw herself at your feet just now, and begged you not to harm her mistress, and someone else, too . . . so you see, sir . . . It's I am taking you there . . . forgive me, sir, it's my conscience . . . maybe it's stupid of me to speak of it . . ."

94

Mitya suddenly seized him by the shoulders from behind.
"Are you a driver?" he asked frantically.
"Yes, sir . . ."
"Then you know that one has to make way. What would
you say to a driver who wouldn't make way for anyone but
would just drive on and crush people? No, a driver mustn't
run over people. One can't run over a man. One can't spoil
people's lives. And if you have spoilt a life—punish yourself.
. . . If only you've spoilt, if only you've ruined anyone's
life—punish yourself and go away."
These phrases burst from Mitya almost hysterically. Though
Andrey was surprised at him, he kept up the conversation.
"That's right, Dmitri Fyodorovitch, you're quite right, one
mustn't crush or torment a man, or any kind of creature, for
every creature is created by God. Take a horse, for instance,
for some folks, even among us drivers, drive anyhow. Nothing
will restrain them, they just force it along."
"To hell?" Mitya interrupted, and went off into his abrupt,
short laugh. "Andrey, simple soul," he seized him by the
shoulders again, "tell me, will Dmitri Fyodorovitch Karamazov
go to hell, or not, what do you think?"
"I don't know, darling, it depends on you, for you are . . .
you see, sir, when the Son of God was nailed on the Cross and
died, He went straight down to hell from the Cross, and set
free all sinners that were in agony. And the devil groaned, because he thought that he would get no more sinners in hell.
And God said to him, then, 'Don't groan, for you shall have all
the mighty of the earth, the rulers, the chief judges, and the
rich men, and shall be filled up as you have been in all the ages
till I come again.' Those were His very words . . ."
"A peasant legend! Capital! Whip up the left, Andrey!"
"So you see, sir, who it is hell's for," said Andrey, whipping
up the left horse, "but you're like a little child . . . that's how
we look on you . . . and though you're hasty-tempered, sir,
yet God will forgive you for your kind heart."
"And you, do you forgive me, Andrey?"
"What should I forgive you for, sir? You've never done me
any harm."
"No, for everyone, for everyone, you here alone, on the
road, will you forgive me for everyone? Speak, simple peasant
heart!"
"Oh, sir! I feel afraid of driving you, your talk is so
strange."

But Mitya did not hear. He was frantically praying and muttering to himself.

"Lord, receive me, with all my lawlessness, and do not condemn me. Let me pass by Thy judgment . . . do not condemn me, for I have condemned myself, do not condemn me, for I love Thee, O Lord. I am a wretch, but I love Thee. If Thou sendest me to hell, I shall love Thee there, and from there I shall cry out that I love Thee for ever and ever. . . . But let me love to the end. . . . Here and now for just five hours . . . till the first light of Thy day . . . for I love the queen of my soul . . . I love her and I cannot help loving her. Thou seest my whole heart. . . . I shall gallop up, I shall fall before her and say, 'You are right to pass on and leave me. Farewell and forget your victim . . . never fret yourself about me!'."

"Mokroe!" cried Andrey, pointing ahead with his whip.

Through the pale darkness of the night loomed a solid black mass of buildings, flung down, as it were, in the vast plain. The village of Mokroe numbered two thousand inhabitants, but at that hour all were asleep, and only here and there a few lights still twinkled.

"Drive on, Andrey, I come!" Mitya exclaimed, feverishly.

"They're not asleep," said Andrey again, pointing with his whip to the Plastunovs' inn, which was at the entrance to the village. The six windows, looking on the street, were all brightly lighted up.

"They're not asleep," Mitya repeated joyously. "Quicker, Andrey! Gallop! Drive up with a dash! Set the bells ringing! Let all know that I have come. I'm coming! I'm coming, too!"

Andrey lashed his exhausted team into a gallop, drove with a dash and pulled up his steaming, panting horses at the high flight of steps.

Mitya jumped out of the cart just as the inn-keeper, on his way to bed, peeped out from the steps, curious to see who had arrived.

"Trifon Borissovitch, is that you?"

The inn-keeper bent down, looked intently, ran down the steps, and rushed up to the guest with obsequious delight.

"Dmitri Fyodorovitch, your honour! Do I see you again?"

Trifon Borissovitch was a thick-set, healthy peasant, of middle height, with a rather fat face. His expression was severe and uncompromising, especially with the peasants of Mokroe, but he had the power of assuming the most obsequious

countenance, when he had an inkling that it was to his interest.
He dressed in Russian style, with a shirt buttoning down on one
side, and a full-skirted coat. He had saved a good sum of
money, but was for ever dreaming of improving his position.
More than half the peasants were in his clutches, everyone in
the neighbourhood was in debt to him. From the neighbouring
landowners he bought and rented lands which were worked by
the peasants, in payment of debts which they could never shake
off. He was a widower, with four grown-up daughters. One of
them was already a widow and lived in the inn with her two
children, his grandchildren, and worked for him like a char-
woman. Another of his daughters was married to a petty official
and in one of the rooms of the inn, on the wall, could be seen,
among the family photographs, a miniature photograph of this
official in uniform and official epaulettes. The two younger
daughters used to wear fashionable blue or green dresses, fitting
tightly at the back, and with trains a yard long, on Church holidays or when they went to pay visits. But next morning they
would get up at dawn, as usual, sweep out the room with a
birch broom, empty the slops, and clean up after lodgers.

In spite of the thousands of roubles he had saved, Trifon
Borissovitch was very fond of emptying the pockets of a
drunken guest, and, remembering that not a month ago he had,
in twenty-four hours, made two if not three hundred roubles out
of Dmitri, when he had come on his escapade with Grushenka,
he met him now with eager welcome, scenting his prey the
moment Mitya drove up to the steps.

"Dmitri Fyodorovitch, dear sir, we see you once more!"

"Stay, Trifon Borissovitch," began Mitya, "first and fore-
most, where is she?"

"Agrafena Alexandrovna?" The inn-keeper understood at
once, looking sharply into Mitya's face. "She's here, too . . ."

"With whom? With whom?"

"Some strangers. One is an official gentleman, a Pole, to
judge from his speech. He sent the horses for her from here;
and there's another with him, a friend of his, or a fellow
traveller, there's no telling. They're dressed like civilians."

"Well, are they feasting? Have they money?"

"Poor sort of a feast! Nothing to boast of, Dmitri Fyodorovitch."

"Nothing to boast of? And who are the others?"

"They're two gentlemen from the town. . . . They've come
back from Tcherny, and are putting up here. One's quite a

97

young gentleman, a relative of Mr. Miüsov, he must be, but I've forgotten his name . . . and I expect you know the other, too, a gentleman called Maximov. He's been on a pilgrimage, so he says, to the monastery in the town. He's travelling with this young relation of Mr. Miüsov."

"Is that all?"

"Yes."

"Stay, listen, Trifon Borissovitch. Tell me the chief thing: What of her? How is she?"

"Oh, she's only just come. She's sitting with them."

"Is she cheerful? Is she laughing?"

"No, I think she's not laughing much. She's sitting quite dull. She's combing the young gentleman's hair."

"The Pole—the officer?"

"He's not young, and he's not an officer, either. Not him, sir. It's the young gentleman that's M. Miüsov's relation . . . I've forgotten his name."

"Kalganov?"

"That's it, Kalganov!"

"All right. I'll see for myself. Are they playing cards?"

"They have been playing, but they've left off. They've been drinking tea, the official gentleman asked for liqueurs."

"Stay, Trifon Borissovitch, stay, my good soul. I'll see for myself. Now answer one more question: are the gypsies here?"

"You can't have the gypsies now, Dmitri Fyodorovitch. The authorities have sent them away. But we've Jews that play the cymbals and the fiddle in the village, so one might send for them. They'd come."

"Send for them. Certainly send for them!" cried Mitya. "And you can get the girls together as you did then, Marya especially, Stepanida, too, and Arina. Two hundred roubles for a chorus!"

"Oh, for a sum like that I can get all the village together, though by now they're asleep. Are the peasants here worth such kindness, Dmitri Fyodorovitch, or the girls either? To spend a sum like that on such coarseness and rudeness! What's the good of giving a peasant a cigar to smoke, the stinking ruffian! And the girls are all lousy. Besides, I'll get my daughters up for nothing, let alone a sum like that. They've only just gone to bed, I'll give them a kick and set them singing for you. You gave the peasants champagne to drink the other day, e-ech!"

For all his pretended compassion for Mitya, Trifon Borissovitch had hidden half a dozen bottles of champagne on the last occasion, and had picked up a hundred-rouble note under the table, and it had remained in his clutches.

"Trifon Borissovitch, I sent more than one thousand flying last time I was here. Do you remember?"

"You did send it flying. I may well remember. You must have left three thousand behind you."

"Well, I've come to do the same again, do you see?"

And he pulled out his roll of notes, and held them up before the inn-keeper's nose.

"Now, listen and remember. In an hour's time the wine will arrive, savouries, pies, and sweets—bring them all up at once. That box Andrey has got is to be brought up at once, too. Open it, and hand champagne immediately. And the girls, we must have the girls, Marya especially."

He turned to the cart and pulled out the box of pistols.

"Here, Andrey, let's settle. Here's fifteen roubles for the drive, and fifty for vodka . . . for your readiness, for your love. . . . Remember Karamazov!"

"I'm afraid, sir," faltered Andrey. "Give me five roubles extra, but more I won't take. Trifon Borissovitch, bear witness. Forgive my foolish words . . ."

"What are you afraid of?" asked Mitya, scanning him. "Well, go to the devil, if that's it!" he cried, flinging him five roubles. "Now, Trifon Borissovitch, take me up quietly and let me first get a look at them, so that they don't see me. Where are they? In the blue room?"

Trifon Borissovitch looked apprehensively at Mitya, but at once obediently did his bidding. Leading him into the pasage, he went himself into the first large room, adjoining that in which the visitors were sitting, and took the light away. Then he stealthily led Mitya in, and put him in a corner in the dark, whence he could freely watch the company without being seen. But Mitya did not look long, and, indeed, he could not see them. He saw her, his heart throbbed violently, and all was dark before his eyes.

She was sitting sideways to the table in a low chair, and beside her, on the sofa, was the pretty youth, Kalganov. She was holding his hand and seemed to be laughing, while he, seeming vexed and not looking at her, was saying something in a loud voice to Maximov, who sat the other side of the table, facing Grushenka. Maximov was laughing violently at something. On the sofa sat *he*, and on a chair by the sofa there was another stranger. The one on the sofa was lolling backwards, smoking a pipe, and Mitya had an impression of a stoutish, broad-faced, short little man, who was apparently angry about something. His friend, the other stranger, struck Mitya as extraordinarily tall, but he could make out nothing more. He caught his breath. He could not bear it for a minute, he put the pistol-case on a chest, and with a throbbing heart he walked, feeling cold all over, straight into the blue room to face the company.

"Aie!" shrieked Grushenka, the first to notice him.

CHAPTER VII

THE FIRST AND RIGHTFUL LOVER

WITH his long, rapid strides, Mitya walked straight up to the table.

"Gentlemen," he said in a loud voice, almost shouting, yet stammering at every word, "I . . . I'm all right! Don't be afraid!" he exclaimed, "I—there's nothing the matter," he turned suddenly to Grushenka, who had shrunk back in her chair towards Kalganov, and clasped his hand tightly. "I . . . I'm coming, too. I'm here till morning. Gentlemen, may I stay with you till morning? Only till morning, for the last time, in this same room?"

So he finished, turning to the fat little man, with the pipe, sitting on the sofa. The latter removed his pipe from his lips with dignity and observed severely:

"*Panie*, we're here in private. There are other rooms."

"Why, it's you, Dmitri Fyodorovitch! What do you mean?" answered Kalganov suddenly. "Sit down with us. How are you?"

"Delighted to see you, dear . . . and precious fellow, I always thought a lot of you," Mitya responded, joyfully and eagerly, at once holding out his hand across the table.

"Aie! How tight you squeeze! You've quite broken my fingers," laughed Kalganov.

"He always squeezes like that, always," Grushenka put in gaily, with a timid smile, seeming suddenly convinced from Mitya's face that he was not going to make a scene. She was watching him with intense curiosity and still some uneasiness. She was impressed by something about him, and indeed the last thing she expected of him was that he would come in and speak like this at such a moment.

"Good evening," Maximov ventured blandly, on the left. Mitya rushed up to him, too.

"Good evening. You're here, too! How glad I am to find you here, too! Gentlemen, gentlemen, I . . ." (He addressed the Polish gentleman with the pipe again, evidently taking him for the most important person present.) "I flew here. . . . I wanted to spend my last day, my last hour in this room, in this very room . . . where I, too, adored . . . my queen. . . . Forgive me, *panie*," he cried wildly, "I flew here and vowed. . . . Oh, don't be afraid, it's my last night! Let's drink to our good understanding. They'll bring the wine at once. . . . I brought this with me." (Something made him pull out his bundle of notes.) "Allow me, *panie*. I want to have music, singing, a revel, as we had before. But the worm, the unnecessary worm, will crawl away, and there'll be no more of him. I will commemorate my day of joy on my last night."

He was almost choking. There was so much, so much he wanted to say, but strange exclamations were all that came from his lips. The Pole gazed fixedly at him, at the bundle of notes in his hand; looked at Grushenka, and was in evident perplexity.

"If my suverin lady is permitting . . ." he was beginning,

"What does 'suverin' mean? 'Sovereign,' I suppose?" interrupted Grushenka. "I can't help laughing at you, the way you talk. Sit down, Mitya, what are you talking about? Don't frighten us, please. You won't frighten us, will you? If you won't, I am glad to see you . . ."

"Me, me frighten you?" cried Mitya, flinging up his hands. "Oh, pass me by, go your way, I won't hinder you!" . . .

And suddenly he surprised them all, and no doubt himself as well, by flinging himself on a chair, and bursting into tears, turning his head away to the opposite wall, while his arms clasped the back of the chair tightly, as though embracing it.

"Come, come, what a fellow you are!" cried Grushenka reproachfully. "That's just how he comes to see me—he begins talking, and I can't make out what he means. He cried like that once before, and now he's crying again! It's shameful! Why are you crying? *As though you had anything to cry for!*" she added enigmatically, emphasising each word with some irritability.

"I . . . I'm not crying. . . . Well, good evening!" He

instantly turned round in his chair, and suddenly laughed, not his abrupt, wooden laugh, but a long, quivering, inaudible nervous laugh.

"Well, there you are again. . . . Come, cheer up, cheer up!" Grushenka said to him persuasively. "I'm very glad you've come, very glad, Mitya, do you hear, I'm very glad? I want him to stay here with us," she said peremptorily, addressing the whole company, though her words were obviously meant for the man sitting on the sofa. "I wish it, I wish it! And if he goes away I shall go, too!" she added, with flashing eyes.

"What my queen commands is law!" pronounced the Pole, gallantly kissing Grushenka's hand. "I beg you, *panie,* to join our company," he added politely, addressing Mitya.

Mitya was jumping up with the obvious intention of delivering another tirade, but the words did not come.

"Let's drink, *panie,*" he blurted out instead of making a speech. Everyone laughed.

"Good heavens! I thought he was going to begin again!" Grushenka exclaimed nervously. "Do you hear, Mitya?" she went on insistently, "don't prance about, but it's nice you've brought the champagne. I want some myself, and I can't bear liqueurs. And best of all, you've come yourself. We were fearfully dull here. . . . You've come for a spree again, I suppose? But put your money in your pocket. Where did you get such a lot?"

Mitya had been, all this time, holding in his hand the crumpled bundle of notes on which the eyes of all, especially of the Poles, were fixed. In confusion he thrust them hurriedly into his pocket. He flushed. At that moment the inn-keeper brought in an uncorked bottle of champagne, and glasses on a tray. Mitya snatched up the bottle, but he was so bewildered that he did not know what to do with it. Kalganov took it from him and poured out the champagne.

"Another! Another bottle!" Mitya cried to the inn-keeper, and, forgetting to clink glasses with the Pole whom he had so solemnly invited to drink to their good understanding, he drank off his glass without waiting for anyone else. His whole countenance suddenly changed. The solemn and tragic expression with which he had entered vanished completely, and a look of something childlike came into his face. He seemed to have become suddenly gentle and subdued. He looked shyly and happily at everyone, with a continual nervous little laugh, and the blissful expression of a dog who has done wrong, been punished, and forgiven. He seemed to have forgotten everything, and was looking round at everyone with a childlike smile of delight. He looked at Grushenka, laughing continually, and bringing his chair close up to her. By degrees he had gained some idea of the two Poles, though he had formed no definite conception of them yet.

The Pole on the sofa struck him by his dignified demeanour and his Polish accent; and, above all, by his pipe. "Well, what of it? It's a good thing he's smoking a pipe," he reflected. The Pole's puffy, middle-aged face, with its tiny nose and two very thin, pointed, dyed and impudent-looking moustaches, had not so far roused the faintest doubts in Mitya. He was not even particularly struck by the Pole's absurd wig made in Siberia, with love-locks foolishly combed forward over the temples. "I suppose it's all right, since he wears a wig," he went on, musing blissfully. The other, younger Pole, who was staring insolently and defiantly at the company and listening to the conversation with silent contempt, still only impressed Mitya by his great height, which was in striking contrast to the Pole on the sofa. "If he stood up he'd be six foot three." The thought flitted through Mitya's mind. It occurred to him, too, that this Pole must be the friend of the other, as it were, a "bodyguard", and no doubt the big Pole was at the disposal of the little Pole with the pipe. But this all seemed to Mitya perfectly right and not to be questioned. In his mood of doglike submissiveness all feeling of rivalry had died away.

Grushenka's mood and the enigmatic tone of some of her words he completely failed to grasp. All he understood, with thrilling heart, was that she was kind to him, that she had forgiven him, and made him sit by her. He was beside himself with delight, watching her sip her glass of champagne. The silence of the company seemed somehow to strike him, however, and he looked round at everyone with expectant eyes.

"Why are we sitting here though, gentlemen? Why don't you begin doing something?" his smiling eyes seemed to ask.

"He keeps talking nonsense, and we were all laughing," Kalganov began suddenly, as though divining his thought, and pointing to Maximov.

Mitya immediately stared at Kalganov and then at Maximov.

"He's talking nonsense!" he laughed his short, wooden laugh, seeming suddenly delighted at something—"ha, ha!"

"Yes. Would you believe it, he will have it that all our cavalry officers in the 'twenties married Polish women. That's awful rot, isn't it?"

"Polish women?" repeated Mitya, perfectly ecstatic.

Kalganov was well aware of Mitya's attitude to Grushenka, and he guessed about the Pole, too, but that did not so much interest him, perhaps did not interest him at all; what he was interested in was Maximov. He had come here with Maximov by chance, and he met the Poles here at the inn for the first time in his life. Grushenka he knew before, and had once been with someone to see her; but she had not taken to him. But here she looked at him very affectionately: before Mitya's arrival she had been making much of him, but he seemed somehow to be unmoved by it. He was a boy, not over twenty, dressed like a dandy, with a very charming fair-skinned face, and splendid thick, fair hair. From his fair face looked out beautiful pale blue eyes, with an intelligent and sometimes even deep expression, beyond his age indeed, although the young man sometimes looked and talked quite like a child, and was not at all ashamed of it, even when he was aware of it himself. As a rule he was very wilful, even capricious, though always friendly. Sometimes there was something fixed and obstinate in his expression. He would look at you and listen, seeming all the while to be persistently dreaming over something else. Often he was listless and lazy, at other times he would grow excited, sometimes, apparently, over the most trivial matters.

"Only imagine, I've been taking him about with me for the last four days," he went on, indolently drawling his words, quite naturally though, without the slightest affectation. "Ever since your brother, do you remember? shoved him off the carriage and sent him flying. That made me take an interest in him at the time, and I took him into the country, but he keeps talking such rot I'm ashamed to be with him. I'm taking him back."

"The gentleman has not seen Polish ladies, and says what is impossible," the Pole with the pipe observed to Maximov.

He spoke Russian fairly well, much better, anyway, than he pretended. If he used Russian words, he always distorted them into a Polish form.

"But I was married to a Polish lady myself," tittered Maximov.

"But did you serve in the cavalry? You were talking about

104

the cavalry. Were you a cavalry officer?" put in Kalganov at once.

"Was he a cavalry officer indeed? Ha, ha!" cried Mitya, listening eagerly, and turning his inquiring eyes to each as he spoke, as though there were no knowing what he might hear from each.

"No, you see," Maximov turned to him. "What I mean is that those pretty Polish ladies . . . when they danced the mazurka with our Uhlans . . . when one of them dances a mazurka with a Uhlan she jumps on his knee like a kitten . . . a little white one . . . and the pan-father and pan-mother look on and allow it. . . . They allow it . . . and next day the Uhlan comes and offers her his hand. . . . That's how it is . . . offer her his hand, he—he!" Maximov ended, tittering.

"The *pan* is a *lajdak!*" The tall Pole on the chair growled suddenly and crossed one leg over the other. Mitya's eye was caught by his huge greased boot, with its thick, dirty sole. The dress of both the Poles looked rather greasy.

"Well, now it's *lajdak!* What's he scolding about?" said Grushenka, suddenly vexed.

"*Pani* Agrippina, what the gentleman saw in Poland were servant girls, and not ladies of good birth," the Pole with the pipe observed to Grushenka.

"You can reckon on that," the tall Pole snapped contemptuously.

"What next! Let him talk! People talk, why hinder them? It makes it cheerful," Grushenka said crossly.

"I'm not hindering them, *pani*," said the Pole in the wig, with a long look at Grushenka, and relapsing into dignified silence he sucked his pipe again.

"No, no. The Polish gentleman spoke the truth." Kalganov got excited again, as though it were a question of vast import. "He's never been in Poland, so how can he talk about it? I suppose you weren't married in Poland, were you?"

"No, in the Province of Smolensk. Only, a Uhlan had brought her to Russia before that, my future wife, with her mamma and her aunt, and another female relation with a grown-up son. He brought her straight from Poland and gave her up to me. He was a lieutenant in our regiment, a very nice young man. At first he meant to marry her himself. But he didn't marry her, because she turned out to be lame."

"So you married a lame woman?" cried Kalganov.

"Yes. They both deceived me a little bit at the time, and

concealed it. I thought she was hopping; she kept hopping . . .
I thought it was for fun."

"So pleased she was going to marry you!" yelled Kalganov,
in a ringing, childish voice.

"Yes, so pleased. But it turned out to be quite a different
cause. Afterwards, when we were married, after the wedding,
that very evening, she confessed, and very touchingly asked
forgiveness. 'I once jumped over a puddle when I was a child,'
she said, 'and injured my leg.' He—he!"

Kalganov went off into the most childish laughter, almost
falling on the sofa. Grushenka, too, laughed. Mitya was at
the pinnacle of happiness.

"Do you know, that's the truth, he's not lying now," exclaimed Kalganov, turning to Mitya; "and do you know,
he's been married twice; it's his first wife he's talking about.
But his second wife, do you know, ran away, and is alive
now."

"Is it possible?" said Mitya, turning quickly to Maximov,
with an expression of the utmost astonishment.

"Yes. She did run away. I've had that unpleasant experience," Maximov modestly assented, "with a *monsieur*. And
what was worse, she'd had all my little property transferred to
her beforehand. 'You're an educated man,' she said to me.
'You can always get your living.' She settled my business with
that. A venerable bishop once said to me: 'One of your wives
was lame, but the other was too light-footed.' He-he!"

"Listen, listen!" cried Kalganov, bubbling over, "if he's
telling lies—and he often is—he's only doing it to amuse us all.
There's no harm in that, is there? You know, I sometimes like
him. He's awfully low, but it's natural to him, eh? Don't you
think so? Some people are low from self-interest, but he's
simply so, from nature. Only fancy, he claims (he was arguing about it all the way yesterday) that Gogol wrote *'Dead
Souls'* about him. Do you remember, there's a landowner
called Maximov in it, whom Nozdryov thrashed. He was
charged, do you remember, 'for inflicting bodily injury with
rods on the landowner Maximov in a drunken condition'.
Would you believe it, he claims that he was that Maximov and
that he was beaten! Now can it be so? Tchitchikov made his
journey, at the very latest, at the beginning of the 'twenties, so
that the dates don't fit. He couldn't have been thrashed then,
he couldn't, could he?"

It was difficult to imagine what Kalganov was excited about, but his excitement was genuine. Mitya followed his lead without protest.

"Well, but if they did thrash him!" he cried, laughing.

"It's not that they thrashed me exactly, but what I mean is . . ." put in Maximov.

"What do you mean? Either they thrashed you or they didn't."

"What o'clock is it, *panie?*" the Pole with the pipe asked his tall friend, with a bored expression. The other shrugged his shoulders in reply. Neither of them had a watch.

"Why not talk? Let other people talk. Mustn't other people talk because you're bored?" Grushenka flew at him with evident intention of finding fault. Something seemed for the first time to flash upon Mitya's mind. This time the Pole answered with unmistakable irritability.

"*Pani*, I didn't oppose it. I didn't say anything."

"All right then. Come, tell us your story," Grushenka cried to Maximov. "Why are you all silent?"

"There's nothing to tell, it's all so foolish," answered Maximov at once, with evident satisfaction, mincing a little. "Besides, all that's by way of allegory in Gogol, for he's made all the names have a meaning. Nozdryov was really called Nosov, and Kuvshinikov had quite a different name, he was called Shkvornev. Fenardi really was called Fenardi, only he wasn't an Italian but a Russian, and Mamsel Fernadi was a pretty girl with her pretty little legs in tights, and she had a little short skirt with spangles, and she kept turning round and round, only not for four hours but for four minutes only, and she bewitched everyone . . ."

"But what were you beaten for?" cried Kalganov.

"For Piron!" answered Maximov.

"What Piron?" cried Mitya.

"The famous French writer, Piron. We were all drinking then, a big party of us, in a tavern, at that very fair. They'd invited me, and first of all I began quoting epigrams. 'Is that you, Boileau? What a funny get-up!' and Boileau answers that he's going to a masquerade, that is to the baths, he-he! And they took it to themselves, so I made haste to repeat another, very sarcastic, well known to all educated people:

> '*Yes, Sappho and Phaon are we!*
> *But one grief is weighing on me.*
> *You don't know your way to the sea!*'

"They were still more offended and began abusing me in the most unseemly way for it. And as ill-luck would have it, to set things right I began telling a very cultivated anecdote about Piron, how he was not accepted into the French Academy, and to avenge himself wrote his own epitaph:

'Ci-gît Piron qui ne fut rien
Pas même académicien.'

They seized me and thrashed me."

"But what for? What for?"

"For my education. People can thrash a man for anything," Maximov concluded, briefly and sententiously.

"Eh, that's enough! That's all stupid, I don't want to listen. I thought it would be amusing," Grushenka cut them short, suddenly.

Mitya started, and at once left off laughing. The tall Pole rose upon his feet, and with the haughty air of a man bored and out of his element, began pacing from corner to corner of the room, his hands behind his back.

"Ah, he can't sit still," said Grushenka, looking at him contemptuously. Mitya began to feel anxious. He noticed, besides, that the Pole on the sofa was looking at him with an irritable expression.

"*Panie!*" cried Mitya, "let's drink! and the other *pan,* too! Let us drink."

In a flash he had pulled three glasses towards him, and filled them with champagne.

"To Poland, *panovie,* I drink to your Poland!" cried Mitya.

"I shall be delighted, *panie,*" said the Pole on the sofa, with dignity and affable condescension, and he took his glass.

"And the other *pan,* what's his name? Drink, most illustrious, take your glass!" Mitya urged.

"Pan Vrublevsky," put in the Pole on the sofa.

Pan Vrublevsky came up to the table, swaying as he walked.

"To Poland, *panovie!*" cried Mitya, raising his glass. "Hurrah!"

All three drank. Mitya seized the bottle and again poured out three glasses.

"Now to Russia, *panovie,* and let us be brothers!"

"Pour out some for us," said Grushenka; "I'll drink to Russia, too!"

"So will I," said Kalganov.

"And I would, too . . . to Russia, the old grandmother!" tittered Maximov.

"All! All!" cried Mitya. "Trifon Borissovitch, some more bottles!"

The other three bottles Mitya had brought with him were put on the table. Mitya filled the glasses.

"To Russia! Hurrah!" he shouted again. All drank the toast except the Poles, and Grushenka tossed off her whole glass at once. The Poles did not touch theirs,

"How's this, *panovie?*" cried Mitya, "won't you drink it?"

Pan Vrublevsky took the glass, raised it, and said with a resonant voice:

"To Russia as she was before 1772."

"Come, that's better!" cried the other Pole, and they both emptied their glasses at once.

"You're fools, you *panovie,*" broke suddenly from Mitya.

"*Panie!*" shouted both the Poles, menacingly, setting on Mitya like a couple of cocks. Pan Vrublevsky was specially furious.

"Can one help loving one's own country?" he shouted,

"Be silent! Don't quarrel! I won't have any quarrelling!" cried Grushenka imperiously, and she stamped her foot on the floor. Her face glowed, her eyes were shining. The effects of the glass she had just drunk were apparent. Mitya was terribly alarmed.

"*Panovie,* forgive me! It was my fault, I'm sorry. Vrublevsky, *panie* Vrublevsky, I'm sorry."

"Hold your tongue, you, anyway! Sit down, you stupid!" Grushenka scolded with angry annoyance.

Everyone sat down, all were silent, looking at one another.

"Gentlemen, I was the cause of it all," Mitya began again, unable to make anything of Grushenka's words. "Come, why are we sitting here? What shall we do . . , to amuse ourselves again?"

"Ach, it's certainly anything but amusing!" Kalganov mumbled lazily.

"Let's play faro again, as we did just now," Maximov tittered suddenly.

"Faro? Splendid!" cried Mitya. "If only the *panovie* . . ."

"It's lite, *panovie,*" the Pole on the sofa responded, as it were unwillingly.

"That's true," assented Pan Vrublevsky.

"Lite? What do you mean by 'lite'?" asked Grushenka.

"Late, *pani!* 'a late hour' I mean," the Pole on the sofa explained.

"It's always late with them. They can never do anything!" Grushenka almost shrieked in her anger. "They're dull themselves, so they want others to be dull. Before you came, Mitya, they were just as silent and kept turning up their noses at me."

"My goddess!" cried the Pole on the sofa, "I see you're not well-disposed to me, that's why I'm gloomy. I'm ready, *panie,*" added he, addressing Mitya,

"Begin, *panie,*" Mitya assented, pulling his notes out of his pocket, and laying two hundred-rouble notes on the table. "I want to lose a lot to you. Take your cards. Make the bank."

"We'll have cards from the landlord, *panie,*" said the little Pole, gravely and emphatically.

"That's much the best way," chimed in Pan Vrublevsky.

"From the landlord? Very good, I understand, let's get them from him. Cards!" Mitya shouted to the landlord.

The landlord brought in a new, unopened pack, and informed Mitya that the girls were getting ready, and that the Jews with the cymbals would most likely be here soon; but the cart with the provisions had not yet arrived. Mitya jumped up from the table and ran into the next room to give orders, but only three girls had arrived, and Marya was not there yet. And he did not know himself what orders to give and why he had run out. He only told them to take out of the box the presents for the girls, the sweets, the toffee and the fondants. "And vodka for Andrey, vodka for Andrey!" he cried in haste. "I was rude to Andrey!"

Suddenly Maximov, who had followed him out, touched him on the shoulder.

"Give me five roubles," he whispered to Mitya. "I'll stake something at faro, too, he-he!"

"Capital! Splendid! Take ten, here!"

Again he took all the notes out of his pocket and picked out one for ten roubles. "And if you lose that, come again, come again."

"Very good," Maximov whispered joyfully, and he ran back again, Mitya too, returned, apologising for having kept them waiting. The Poles had already sat down, and opened the pack. They looked much more amiable, almost cordial. The Pole on the sofa had lighted another pipe and was preparing to throw. He wore an air of solemnity.

"To your places, gentlemen," cried Pan Vrublevsky.

"No, I'm not going to play any more," observed Kalganov, "I've lost fifty roubles to them just now,"

"The *pan* had no luck, perhaps he'll be lucky this time," the Pole on the sofa observed in his direction.

"How much in the bank? To correspond?" asked Mitya.

"That's according, *panie,* maybe a hundred, maybe two hundred, as much as you will stake."

"A million!" laughed Mitya.

"The Pan Captain has heard of Pan Podvysotsky, perhaps?"

"What Podvysotsky?"

"In Warsaw there was a bank and anyone comes and stakes against it. Podvysotsky comes, sees a thousand gold pieces, stakes against the bank. The banker says, '*Panie* Podvysotsky, are you laying down the gold, or must we trust to your honour?' 'To my honour, *panie,*' says Podvysotsky. 'So much the better.' The banker throws the dice. Podvysotsky wins. 'Take it, *panie,*' says the banker, and pulling out the drawer he gives him a million. 'Take it, *panie,* this is your gain.' There was a million in the bank. 'I didn't know that,' says Podvysotsky. '*Panie* Podvysotsky,' said the banker, 'you pledged your honour and we pledged ours.' Podvysotsky took the million."

"That's not true," said Kalganov.

"*Panie* Kalganov, in gentlemanly society one doesn't say such things."

"As if a Polish gambler would give away a million!" cried Mitya, but checked himself at once, "Forgive me, *panie,* it's my fault again, he would, he would give away a million, for honour, for Polish honour. You see how I talk Polish, ha-ha! Here, I stake ten roubles, the knave leads."

"And I put a rouble on the queen, the queen of hearts, the pretty little *panienotchka,* he-he!" laughed Maximov, pulling out his queen, and, as though trying to conceal it from everyone, he moved right up and crossed himself hurriedly under the table. Mitya won. The rouble won, too.

"A corner!" cried Mitya.

"I'll bet another rouble, a 'single' stake," Maximov muttered gleefully, hugely delighted at having won a rouble.

"Lost!" shouted Mitya. "A 'double' on the seven!"

The seven too was trumped.

"Stop!" cried Kalganov suddenly.

"Double! Double!" Mitya doubled his stakes, and each time he doubled the stake the card he doubled was trumped by the Poles. The rouble stakes kept winning.

"On the double!" shouted Mitya furiously.

"You've lost two hundred, *panie*. Will you stake another hundred?" the Pole on the sofa inquired.

"What? Lost two hundred already? Then another two hundred! All doubles!"

And pulling his money out of his pocket, Mitya was about to fling two hundred roubles on the queen, but Kalganov covered it with his hand.

"That's enough!" he shouted in his ringing voice.

"What's the matter?" Mitya stared at him.

"That's enough! I don't want you to play any more. Don't!"

"Why?"

"Because I don't. Hang it, come away. That's why. I won't let you go on playing."

Mitya gazed at him in astonishment.

"Give it up, Mitya. He may be right. You've lost a lot as it is," said Grushenka, with a curious note in her voice. Both the Poles rose from their seats with a deeply offended air.

"Are you joking, *panie?*" said the short man, looking severely at Kalganov.,

"How dare you!" Pan Vrublevsky, too, growled at Kalganov.

"Don't dare to shout like that," cried Grushenka. "Ah, you turkey-cocks!"

Mitya looked at each of them in turn. But something in Grushenka's face suddenly struck him, and at the same instant something new flashed into his mind—a strange new thought!

"*Pani* Agrippina," the little Pole was beginning, crimson with anger, when Mitya suddenly went up to him and slapped him on the shoulder.

"Most illustrious, two words with you."

"What do you want?"

"In the next room, I've two words to say to you, something pleasant, very pleasant. You'll be glad to hear it."

The little *pan* was taken aback and looked apprehensively at Mitya. He agreed at once, however, on condition that Pan Vrublevsky went with them.

"The body-guard? Let him come, and I want him, too. I must have him!" cried Mitya. "March, *panovie!*"

"Where are you going?" asked Grushenka anxiously.

"We'll be back in one moment," answered Mitya.

There was a sort of boldness, a sudden confidence shining in his eyes. His face had looked very different when he entered the room an hour before.

He led the Poles, not into the large room where the chorus of girls was assembling and the table was being laid, but into the bedroom on the right, where the trunks and packages were kept, and there were two large beds, with pyramids of cotton pillows on each. There was a lighted candle on a small deal table in the corner. The small man and Mitya sat down to this table, facing each other, while the huge Vrublevsky stood beside them, his hands behind his back. The Poles looked severe but were evidently inquisitive.

"What can I do for you, *panie?*" lisped the little Pole.

"Well, look here, *panie,* I won't keep you long. There's money for you," he pulled out his notes. "Would you like three thousand? Take it and go your way."

The Pole gazed open-eyed at Mitya, with a searching look.

"Three thousand, *panie?*" He exchanged glances with Vrublevsky.

"Three, *panovie,* three! Listen, *panie,* I see you're a sensible man. Take three thousand and go to the devil, and Vrublevsky with you—d'you hear? But, at once, this very minute, and for ever. You understand that, *panie,* for ever. Here's the door, you go out of it. What have you got there, a greatcoat, a fur coat? I'll bring it out to you. They'll get the horses out directly, and then—good-bye, *panie!*"

Mitya awaited an answer with assurance. He had no doubts. An expression of extraordinary resolution passed over the Pole's face.

"And the money, *panie?*"

"The money, *panie?* Five hundred roubles I'll give you this moment for the journey, and as a first instalment, and two thousand five hundred to-morrow, in the town—I swear on my honour, I'll get it, I'll get it at any cost!" cried Mitya.

The Poles exchanged glances again. The short man's face looked more forbidding.

"Seven hundred, seven hundred, not five hundred, at once, this minute, cash down!" Mitya added, feeling something wrong. "What's the matter, *panie?* Don't you trust me? I can't give you the whole three thousand straight off. If I give it, you may come back to her to-morrow. . . . Besides, I haven't the three thousand with me. I've got it at home in the town," faltered Mitya, his spirit sinking at every word he uttered. "Upon my word, the money's there, hidden."

113

In an instant an extraordinary sense of personal dignity showed itself in the little man's face.

"What next?" he asked ironically. "For shame!" and he spat on the floor. Pan Vrublevsky spat too.

"You do that, *panie*," said Mitya, recognising with despair that all was over, "because you hope to make more out of Grushenka? You're a couple of capons, that's what you are!"

"This is a mortal insult!" The little Pole turned as red as a crab, and he went out of the room, briskly, as though unwilling to hear another word. Vrublevsky swung out after him, and Mitya followed, confused and crestfallen. He was afraid of Grushenka, afraid that the *pan* would at once raise an outcry. And so indeed he did. The Pole walked into the room and threw himself in a theatrical attitude before Grushenka.

"*Pani* Agrippina, I have received a mortal insult!" he exclaimed. But Grushenka suddenly lost all patience, as though they had wounded her in the tenderest spot.

"Speak Russian! Speak Russian!" she cried, "not another word of Polish! You used to talk Russian. You can't have forgotten it in five years."

She was red with passion.

"*Pani* Agrippina . . ."

"My name's Agrafena, Grushenka, speak Russian or I won't listen!"

The Pole gasped with offended dignity, and quickly and pompously delivered himself in broken Russian:

"*Pani* Agrafena, I came here to forget the past and forgive it, to forget all that has happened till to-day . . ."

"Forgive? Came here to forgive me?" Grushenka cut him short, jumping up from her seat.

"Just so, *pani*, I'm not pusillanimous, I'm magnanimous. But I was astounded when I saw your lovers. Pan Mitya offered me three thousand, in the other room, to depart. I spat in the *pan's* face."

"What? He offered you money for me?" cried Grushenka, hysterically. "Is it true, Mitya? How dare you? Am I for sale?"

"*Panie, panie!*" yelled Mitya, "she's pure and shining, and I have never been her lover! That's a lie . . ."

"How dare you defend me to him?" shrieked Grushenka. "It wasn't virtue kept me pure, and it wasn't that I was afraid of Kuzma, but that I might hold up my head when I met him,

114

and tell him he's a scoundrel. And did he actually refuse the money?"

"He took it! He took it!" cried Mitya; "only he wanted to get the whole three thousand at once, and I could only give him seven hundred straight off."

"I see: he heard I had money, and came here to marry me!"

"*Pani* Agrippina!" cried the little Pole. "I'm—a knight, I'm—a nobleman, and not a *lajdak*. I came here to make you my wife and I find you a different woman, perverse and shameless."

"Oh, go back where you came from! I'll tell them to turn you out and you'll be turned out," cried Grushenka, furious. "I've been a fool, a fool, to have been miserable these five years! And it wasn't for his sake, it was my anger made me miserable. And this isn't he at all! Was he like this? It might be his father! Where did you get your wig from? He was a falcon, but this is a gander. He used to laugh and sing to me. . . . And I've been crying for five years, damned fool, abject, shameless I was!"

She sank back in her low chair and hid her face in her hands. At that instant the chorus of Mokroe girls began singing in the room on the left—a rollicking dance song.

"A regular Sodom!" Vrublevsky roared suddenly. "Landlord, send the shameless hussies away!"

The landlord, who had been for some time past inquisitively peeping in at the door, hearing shouts and guessing that his guests were quarrelling, at once entered the room.

"What are you shouting for? D'you want to split your throat?" he said, addressing Vrublevsky, with surprising rudeness.

"Animal!' bellowed Pan Vrublevsky.

"Animal! And what sort of cards were you playing with just now? I gave you a pack and you hid it. You played with marked cards! I could send you to Siberia for playing with false cards, d'you know that, for it's just the same as false banknotes . . ."

And going up to the sofa he thrust his fingers between the sofa-back and the cushion, and pulled out an unopened pack of cards.

"Here's my pack unopened!"

He held it up and showed it to all in the room. "From where I stood I saw him slip my pack away, and put his in place of it —you're a cheat and not a gentleman!"

"And I twice saw the *pan* change a card!" cried Kalganov.

"How shameful! How shameful!" exclaimed Grushenka, clasping her hands, and blushing for genuine shame. "Good Lord, he's come to that!"

"I thought so, too!" said Mitya. But before he had uttered the words, Vrublevsky, with a confused and infuriated face, shook his fist at Grushenka, shouting:

"You low harlot!"

Mitya flew at him at once, clutched him in both hands, lifted him in the air, and in one instant had carried him into the room on the right, from which they had just come.

"I've laid him on the floor, there," he announced, returning at once, gasping with excitement. "He's struggling, the scoundrel! But he won't come back, no fear of that!" . . .

He closed one half of the folding doors, and holding the other ajar called out to the little Pole:

"Most illustrious, will you be pleased to retire as well?"

"My dear Dmitri Fyodorovitch," said Trifon Borissovitch, "make them give you back your money you lost. It's as good as stolen from you."

"I don't want my fifty roubles back," Kalganov declared suddenly.

"I don't want my two hundred, either," cried Mitya, "I wouldn't take it for anything! Let him keep it as a consolation."

"Bravo, Mitya! You're a trump, Mitya!" cried Grushenka, and there was a note of fierce anger in the exclamation.

The little *pan*, crimson with fury, but still mindful of his dignity, was making for the door, but he stopped short and said suddenly, addressing Grushenka:

"*Pani*, if you want to come with me, come. If not, good-bye."

And swelling with indignation and importance he went to the door. This was a man of character: he had so good an opinion of himself that, after all that had passed, he still expected that she would marry him. Mitya slammed the door after him.

"Lock it," said Kalganov. But the key clicked on the other side, they had locked it from within.

"That's capital!" exclaimed Grushenka relentlessly. "Serve them right!"

CHAPTER VIII

DELIRIUM

WHAT followed was almost an orgy, a feast to which all were welcome. Grushenka was the first to call for wine.

"I want to drink. I want to be quite drunk, as we were before. Do you remember, Mitya, do you remember how we made friends here last time?"

Mitya himself was almost delirious, feeling that his happiness was at hand. But Grushenka was continually sending him away from her:

"Go and enjoy yourself. Tell them to dance, to make merry, let the stove and cottage dance'; as we had it last time," she kept exclaiming. She was tremendously excited. And Mitya hastened to obey her. The chorus were in the next room. The room in which they had been sitting till that moment was too small, and was divided in two by cotton curtains, behind which was a huge bed with a puffy feather mattress and a pyramid of cotton pillows. In the four rooms for visitors there were beds. Grushenka settled herself just at the door. Mitya set an easy chair for her. She had sat in the same place to watch the dancing and singing "the time before", when they had made merry there. All the girls who had come had been there then; the Jewish band with fiddles and zithers had come, too, and at last the long-expected cart had arrived with the wines and provisions.

Mitya bustled about. All sorts of people began coming into the room to look on, peasants and their women, who had been roused from sleep and attracted by the hopes of another marvellous entertainment such as they had enjoyed a month before. Mitya remembered their faces, greeting and embracing everyone he knew. He uncorked bottles and poured out wine for everyone who presented himself. Only the girls were very eager for the champagne. The men preferred rum, brandy, and, above all, hot punch. Mitya had chocolate made for all the girls, and ordered that three samovars should be kept boiling all night to provide tea and punch for everyone to help himself.

An absurd chaotic confusion followed, but Mitya was in his natural element, and the more foolish it became the more his spirits rose. If the peasants had asked him for money at that moment he would have pulled out his notes and given them away right and left. This was probably why the landlord, Trifon Borissovitch, kept hovering about Mitya to protect him. He seemed to have given up all idea of going to bed that night, though he drank little, only one glass of punch, and kept a sharp look-out on Mitya's interests after his own fashion. He intervened in the nick of time, civilly and obsequiously persuading Mitya not to give away "cigars and Rhine wine", and, above all, money to the peasants as he had done before. He was very indignant, too, at the peasant girls drinking liqueur, and eating sweets.

"They're a lousy lot, Dmitri Fyodorovitch," he said. "I'd give them a kick, every one of them, and they'd take it as an honour—that's all they're worth!"

Mitya remembered Andrey again, and ordered punch to be sent out to him. "I was rude to him just now," he repeated with a sinking, softened voice. Kalganov did not want to drink, and at first did not care for the girls singing; but after he had drunk a couple of glasses of champagne he became extraordinarily lively, strolling about the room, laughing and praising the music and the songs, admiring everyone and everything. Maximov, blissfully drunk, never left his side. Grushenka, too, was beginning to get drunk. Pointing to Kalganov, she said to Mitya:

"What a dear, charming boy he is!"

And Mitya, delighted, ran to kiss Kalganov and Maximov. Oh, great were his hopes! She had said nothing yet, and seemed, indeed, purposely to refrain from speaking. But she looked at him from time to time with caressing and passionate eyes. At last she suddenly gripped his hand and drew him vigorously to her. She was sitting at the moment in the low chair by the door.

"How was it you came just now, eh? How you walked in! . . . I *was* frightened. So you wanted to give me up to him, did you? Did you really want to?"

"I didn't want to spoil your happiness!" Mitya faltered blissfully. But she did not need his answer.

"Well, go and enjoy yourself . . ." she sent him away once more. "Don't cry, I'll call you back again."

He would run away, and she listened to the singing and looked at the dancing, though her eyes followed him wherever he went. But in another quarter of an hour she would call him once more and again he would run back to her.

"Come, sit beside me, tell me, how did you hear about me, and my coming here yesterday? From whom did you first hear it?"

And Mitya began telling her about it, disconnectedly, incoherently, feverishly. He spoke strangely, often frowning, and stopping abruptly.

"What are you frowning at?" she asked.

"Nothing. . . . I left a man ill there. I'd give ten years of my life for him to get well, to know he was all right!"

"Well, never mind him, if he's ill. So you meant to shoot yourself to-morrow! What a silly boy! What for? I like such reckless fellows as you," she lisped, with a rather halting tongue. "So you would go any length for me, eh? Did you really mean to shoot yourself to-morrow, you stupid? No, wait a little. To-morrow I may have something to say to you. . . . I won't say it to-day, but to-morrow. You'd like it to be to-day? No, I don't want to to-day. Come, go along now, go and amuse yourself."

Once, however, she called him, as it were, puzzled and uneasy.

"Why are you sad? I see you're sad. . . . Yes, I see it," she added, looking intently into his eyes. "Though you keep kissing the peasants and shouting, I see something. No, be merry. I'm merry; you be merry, too. . . . I love somebody here. Guess who it is. Ah, look, my boy has fallen asleep, poor dear, he's drunk."

She meant Kalganov. He was, in fact, drunk, and had dropped asleep for a moment, sitting on the sofa. But he was not merely drowsy from drink; he felt suddenly dejected, or, as he said, "bored". He was intensely depressed by the girls' songs, which, as the drinking went on, gradually became coarse and more reckless. And the dances were as bad. Two girls dressed up as bears, and a lively girl called Stepanida, with a stick in her hand, acted the part of keeper, and began to "show them".

"Look alive, Marya, or you'll get the stick!"

The bears rolled on the ground at last in the most unseemly fashion, amid roars of laughter from the closely packed crowd of men and women.

"Well, let them! Let them!" said Grushenka sententiously, with an ecstatic expression on her face. "When they do get a day to enjoy themselves, why shouldn't folks be happy?"

Kalganov looked as though he had been besmirched with dirt.

"It's swinish, all this peasant foolery," he murmured, moving away; "it's the games they play when it's light all night in summer."

He particularly disliked one "new" song to a jaunty dance-tune. It described how a gentleman came and tried his luck with the girls, to see whether they would love him:

> *"The master came to try the girls:*
> *Would they love him, would they not?"*

But the girls could not love the master.

> *"He would beat me cruelly*
> *And such love won't do for me."*

Then a gipsy comes along and he, too, tries:

> *"The gipsy came to try the girls:*
> *Would they love him, would they not?"*

But they couldn't love the gipsy either:

> *"He would be a thief, I fear,*
> *And would cause me many a tear."*

And many more men come to try their luck, among them a soldier:

> *"The soldier came to try the girls:*
> *Would they love him, would they not?"*

But the soldier is rejected with contempt, in two indecent lines, sung with absolute frankness and producing a furore in the audience. The song ends with a merchant:

> *"The merchant came to try the girls:*
> *Would they love him, would they not?"*

And it appears that he wins their love because:

> *"The merchant will make gold for me*
> *And his queen I'll gladly be."*

Kalganov was positively indignant.

"That's just a song of yesterday," he said aloud. "Who writes such things for them? They might just as well have had a railwayman or a Jew come to try his luck with the girls; they'd have carried all before them."

And, almost as though it were a personal affront, he declared, on the spot, that he was bored, sat down on the sofa and immediately fell asleep. His pretty little face looked rather pale, as it fell back on the sofa cushion.

"Look how pretty he is," said Grushenka, taking Mitya up to him. "I was combing his hair just now; his hair's like flax, and so thick . . ."

And, bending over him tenderly, she kissed his forehead. Kalganov instantly opened his eyes, looked at her, stood up, and with the most anxious air inquired where was Maximov?

"So that's who it is you want." Grushenka laughed. "Stay with me a minute. Mitya, run and find his Maximov."

Maximov, it appeared, could not tear himself away from the girls, only running away from time to time to pour himself out a glass of liqueur. He had drunk two cups of chocolate. His face was red, and his nose was crimson; his eyes were moist, and mawkishly sweet. He ran up and announced that he was going to dance the "sabotière".

"They taught me all those well-bred, aristocratic dances when I was little . . ."

"Go, go with him, Mitya, and I'll watch from here how he dances," said Grushenka.

"No, no, I'm coming to look on, too," exclaimed Kalganov, brushing aside in the most naïve way Grushenka's offer to sit with him. They all went to look on. Maximov danced his dance. But it roused no great admiration in anyone but Mitya. It consisted of nothing but skipping and hopping, kicking up the feet, and at every skip Maximov slapped the upturned sole of his foot. Kalganov did not like it at all, but Mitya kissed the dancer.

"Thanks. You're tired perhaps! What are you looking for here? Would you like some sweets? A cigar, perhaps?"

"A cigarette."

"Don't you want a drink?"

"I'll just have a liqueur. . . . Have you any chocolates?"

"Yes, there's a heap of them on the table there. Choose one, my dear soul!"

"I like one with vanilla . . . for old people. He-he!"

121

"No, brother, we've none of that special sort."

"I say," the old man bent down to whisper in Mitya's ear. "That girl there, little Marya, he-he! How would it be if you were to help me make friends with her?"

"So that's what you're after! No, brother, that won't do!"

"I'd do no harm to anyone," Maximov muttered disconsolately.

"Oh, all right, all right. They only come here to dance and sing, you know, brother. But damn it all, wait a bit! . . . Eat and drink and be merry, meanwhile. Don't you want money?"

"Later on perhaps," smiled Maximov.

"All right, all right . . ."

Mitya's head was burning. He went outside to the wooden balcony which ran round the whole building on the inner side, overlooking the court-yard. The fresh air revived him. He stood alone in a dark corner, and suddenly clutched his head in both hands. His scattered thoughts came together; his sensations blended into a whole and threw a sudden light into his mind. A fearful and terrible light! "If I'm to shoot myself, why not now?" passed through his mind. "Why not go for the pistols, bring them here, and here, in this dark, dirty corner, make an end?" Almost a minute he stood, undecided. A few hours earlier, when he had been dashing here, he was pursued by disgrace, by the theft he had committed, and that blood, that blood! . . . But yet it was easier for him then. Then everything was over: he had lost her, given her up. She was gone for him—oh, then his death sentence had been easier for him; at least it had seemed necessary, inevitable. For what had he to stay on earth for?

But now? Was it the same as then? Now one phantom, one terror at least was at an end: that first, rightful lover, that fateful figure had vanished, leaving no trace. The terrible phantom had turned into something so small, so comic; it had been carried into the bedroom and locked in. It would never return. She was ashamed, and from her eyes he could see now whom she loved. Now he had everything to make life happy . . . but he could not go on living, he could not; oh, damnation! "Oh, God! restore to life the man I knocked down at the fence! Let this fearful cup pass from me! Lord, Thou hast wrought miracles for such sinners as me! But what, what if the old man's alive? Oh, then the shame of the other disgrace I would wipe away. I would restore the stolen money. I'd give it back; I'd get it somehow. . . . No trace of that shame will remain except in my heart for ever! But no, no; oh, impossible cowardly dreams! Oh, damnation!"

Yet there was a ray of light and hope in his darkness. He jumped up and ran back to the room—to her, to her, his queen for ever! Was not one moment of her love worth all the rest of life, even in the agonies of disgrace? This wild question clutched at his heart. "To her, to her alone, to see her, to hear her, to think of nothing, to forget everything, if only for that night, for an hour, for a moment!" Just as he turned from the balcony into the passage, he came upon the landlord, Trifon Borissovitch. He thought he looked gloomy and worried, and fancied he had come to find him.

"What is it, Trifon Borissovitch? Are you looking for me?"

"No, sir." The landlord seemed disconcerted. "Why should I be looking for you? Where have you been?"

"Why do you look so glum? You're not angry, are you? Wait a bit, you shall soon get to bed. . . . What's the time?"

"It'll be three o'clock. Past three, it must be."

"We'll leave off soon. We'll leave off."

"Don't mention it; it doesn't matter. Keep it up as long as you like . . ."

"What's the matter with him?" Mitya wondered for an instant, and he ran back to the room where the girls were dancing. But she was not there. She was not in the blue room either; there was no one but Kalganov asleep on the sofa. Mitya peeped behind the curtain—she was there. She was sitting in the corner, on a trunk. Bent forward, with her head and arms on the bed close by, she was crying bitterly, doing her utmost to stifle her sobs that she might not be heard. Seeing Mitya, she beckoned him to her, and when he ran to her she grasped his hand tightly.

"Mitya, Mitya, I loved him, you know. How I have loved him these five years, all that time! Did I love him or only my own anger? No, him, him! It's a lie that it was my anger I loved and not him. Mitya, I was only seventeen then; he was so kind to me, so merry; he used to sing to me. . . . Or so it seemed to a silly girl like me. . . . And now, O Lord, it's not the same man. Even his face is not the same; he's different altogether. I shouldn't have known him. I drove here with Timofey, and all the way I was thinking how I should meet him, what I should say to him, how we should look at one another. My soul was faint, and all of a sudden it was just as though he had emptied a pail of dirty water over me. He talked to me like a schoolmaster, all so grave and learned; he met me so solemnly that I was struck dumb. I couldn't get a word in. At first I thought he was ashamed to talk before his great big Pole. I sat staring at him and wondering why I couldn't say a word to him now. It must have been his wife that ruined him; you know, he threw me up to get married. She must have changed him like that. Mitya, how shameful it is! Oh, Mitya I'm ashamed, I'm ashamed for all my life. Curse it, curse it, curse those five years!"

And again she burst into tears, but clung tightly to Mitya's hand and did not let it go.

"Mitya darling, stay, don't go away. I want to say one word to you," she whispered, and suddenly raised her face to him. "Listen, tell me whom it is I love? I love one man here. Who is that man? That's what you must tell me."

A smile lighted up her face that was swollen with weeping, and her eyes shone in the half-darkness.

"A falcon flew in, and my heart sank. 'Fool! that's the man you love!' That was what my heart whispered to me at once. You came in and all grew bright. What's he afraid of? I wondered. For you were frightened; you couldn't speak. It's not them he's afraid of—could you be frightened of anyone? It's me he's afraid of, I thought, only me. So Fenya told you, you little stupid, how I called to Alyosha out of the window that I'd loved Mityenka for one hour, and that I was going now to love . . another. Mitya, Mitya, how could I be such a fool as to think I could love anyone after you? Do you forgive me, Mitya? Do you forgive me or not? Do you love me? Do you love me?" She jumped up and held him with both hands on his shoulders. Mitya, dumb with rapture, gazed into her eyes, at her face, at her smile, and suddenly clasped her tightly in his arms and kissed her passionately.

"You will forgive me for having tormented you? It was through spite I tormented you all. It was for spite I drove the old man out of his mind. . . . Do you remember how you drank at my house one day and broke the wineglass? I remembered that and I broke a glass to-day and drank 'to my vile heart'. Mitya, my falcon, why don't you kiss me? He kissed me once, and now he draws back and looks and listens. Why listen to me? Kiss me, kiss me hard, that's right. If you love, well then love! I'll be your slave now, your slave for the rest of my life. It's sweet to be a slave. Kiss me! Beat me, ill-treat me, do what you will with me. . . . And I do deserve to suffer. Stay, wait, afterwards, I won't have that . . ." she suddenly thrust him away. "Go along, Mitya, I'll come and have some wine, I want to be drunk, I'm going to get drunk and dance; I must, I must!" She tore herself away from him and disappeared behind the curtain. Mitya followed like a drunken man.

"Yes, come what may—whatever may happen now, for one minute, I'd give the whole world," he thought. Grushenka did, in fact, toss off a whole glass of champagne at one gulp, and became at once very tipsy. She sat down in the same chair as before, with a blissful smile on her face. Her cheeks were glowing, her lips were burning, her flashing eyes were moist; there was passionate appeal in her eyes. Even Kalganov felt a stir at the heart and went up to her.

"Did you feel how I kissed you when you were asleep just now?" she said thickly. "I'm drunk now, that's what it is. . . . And aren't you drunk? And why isn't Mitya drinking? Why don't you drink, Mitya? I'm drunk, and you don't drink . . ."

"I am drunk! I'm drunk as it is . . . drunk with you . . . and now I'll be drunk with wine, too."

He drank off another glass, and—he thought it strange himself—that glass made him completely drunk. He was suddenly drunk, although till that moment he had been quite sober, he remembered that. From that moment everything whirled about him as though he were delirious. He walked, laughed, talked to everybody, without knowing what he was doing. Only one persistent burning sensation made itself felt continually, "like a red-hot coal in his heart," he said afterwards. He went up to her, sat beside her, gazed at her, listened to her. . . . She became very talkative, kept calling everyone to her, and beckoned to different girls out of the chorus. When the girl came up, she either kissed her or made the sign of the Cross over her. In another minute she might have cried. She was greatly amused by the "little old man", as she called Maximov. He ran up every minute to kiss her hands, "each little finger", and finally he danced another dance to an old song, which he sang himself. He danced with special vigour to the refrain:

> "*The little pig says—umph! umph! umph!*
> *The little calf says—moo, moo, moo,*
> *The little duck says—quack, quack, quack,*

The little goose says—ga, ga, ga.
The hen goes strutting through the porch
Troo-roo-roo-roo-roo, she'll say,
Troo-roo-roo-roo-roo, she'll say!

"Give him something, Mitya," said Grushenka. "Give him a present, he's poor, you know. Ah, the poor, the insulted. . . . Do you know, Mitya, I shall go into a nunnery. No, I really shall one day. Alyosha said something to me to-day that I shall remember all my life. . . . Yes. . . . But to-day let us dance. To-morrow to the nunnery, but to-day we'll dance. I want to play to-day, good people, and what of it? God will forgive us. If I were God I'd forgive everyone: 'My dear sinners, from this day forth I forgive you.' I'm going to beg forgiveness: 'Forgive me, good people, a silly wench.' I'm a beast, that's what I am. But I want to pray. I gave a little onion. Wicked as I've been, I want to pray. Mitya, let them dance, don't stop them. Everyone in the world is good. Everyone—even the worst of them. The world's a nice place. Though we're bad the world's all right. We're good and bad, good and bad. . . . Come tell me, I've something to ask you; come here everyone, and I'll ask you: Why am I so good? You know I am good. I'm very good. . . . Come, why am I so good?"

So Grushenka babbled on, getting more and more drunk. At last she announced that she was going to dance too. She got up from her chair, staggering. "Mitya, don't give me any more wine—if I ask you, don't give it to me. Wine doesn't give peace. Everything's going round, the stove, and everything. I want to dance. Let everyone see how I dance . . . let them see how beautifully I dance . . ."

She really meant it. She pulled a white cambric handkerchief out of her pocket, and took it by one corner in her right hand, to wave it in the dance. Mitya ran to and fro, the girls were quiet, and got ready to break into a dancing song at the first signal. Maximov, hearing that Grushenka wanted to dance, squealed with delight, and ran skipping about in front of her, humming:

> *"With legs so slim and sides so trim*
> *And its little tail curled tight."*

But Grushenka waved her handkerchief at him and drove him away.

"Sh-h! Mitya, why don't they come? Let everyone come . . . to look on. Call them in, too, that were locked in. . . . Why did you lock them in? Tell them I'm going to dance. Let them look on, too . . ."

Mitya walked with a drunken swagger to the locked door, and began knocking to the Poles with his fist.

"Hi, you . . . Podvysotskys! Come, she's going to dance. She calls you."

"*Lajdak!*" one of the Poles shouted in reply.

"You're a *lajdak* yourself! You're a little scoundrel, that's what you are."

"Leave off laughing at Poland," said Kalganov sententiously. He too was drunk.

"Be quiet, boy! If I call him a scoundrel, it doesn't mean that I called all Poland so. One *lajdak* doesn't make a Poland. Be quiet, my pretty boy, eat a sweetmeat."

"Ach, what fellows! As though they were not men. Why won't they make friends?" said Grushenka, and went forward to dance. The chorus broke into "Ah, my porch, my new porch!" Grushenka flung back her head, half opened her lips, smiled, waved her handkerchief, and suddenly, with a violent lurch, stood still in the middle of the room, looking bewildered.

"I'm weak . . ." she said in an exhausted voice. "Forgive me. . . . I'm weak, I can't. . . . I'm sorry."

She bowed to the chorus, and then began bowing in all directions.

"I'm sorry. . . . Forgive me . . ."

"The lady's been drinking. The pretty lady has been drinking," voices were heard saying.

"The lady's drunk too much," Maximov explained to the girls, giggling.

"Mitya, lead me away . . . take me," said Grushenka helplessly. Mitya pounced on her, snatching her up in his arms, and carried the precious burden through the curtains.

"Well, now I'll go," thought Kalganov, and walking out of the blue room, he closed the two halves of the door after him. But the orgy in the larger room went on and grew louder and louder. Mitya laid Grushenka on the bed and kissed her on the lips.

"Don't touch me . . ." she faltered, in an imploring voice. "Don't touch me, till I'm yours. . . . I've told you I'm yours, but don't touch me . . . spare me. . . . With them here, with them close, you mustn't. He's here. It's nasty here . . ."

"I'll obey you! I won't think of it . . . I worship you!" muttered Mitya. "Yes, it's nasty here, it's abominable."

And still holding her in his arms, he sank on his knees by the bedside.

"I know, though you're a brute, you're generous," Grushenka articulated with difficulty. "It must be honourable . . . it shall be honourable for the future . . . and let us be honest, let us be good, not brutes, but good . . . take me away, take me far away, do you hear? I don't want it to be here, but far, far away . . ."

"Oh, yes, yes, it must be!" said Mitya, pressing her in his arms. "I'll take you and we'll fly away. . . . Oh, I'd give my whole life for one year only to know about that blood!"

"What blood?" asked Grushenka, bewildered.

"Nothing," muttered Mitya, through his teeth. "Grusha, you wanted to be honest, but I'm a thief. But I've stolen money from Katya. . . . Disgrace, a disgrace!"

"From Katya, from that young lady? No, you didn't steal it. Give it her back, take it from me. . . . Why make a fuss? Now everything of mine is yours. What does money matter? We shall waste it, anyway. . . . Folks like us are bound to waste money. But we'd better go and work the land. I want to dig the earth with my own hands. We must work, do you hear? Alyosha said so. I won't be your mistress, I'll be faithful to you, I'll be your slave, I'll work for you. We'll go to the young lady and bow down to her together, so that she may forgive us, and then we'll go away. And if she won't forgive us, we'll go, anyway. Take her money and love me. . . . Don't love her. . . . Don't love her any more. If you love her, I shall strangle her. . . . I'll put out both her eyes with a needle . . ."

"I love you. I love only you. I'll love you in Siberia . . ."

"Why Siberia? Never mind, Siberia if you like. I don't care . . . we'll work . . . there's snow in Siberia. . . . I love driving in the snow . . . and must have bells. . . . Do you hear, there's a bell ringing? Where is that bell ringing? There are people coming. . . . Now it's stopped."

She closed her eyes, exhausted, and suddenly fell asleep for an instant. There had certainly been the sound of a bell in the distance, but the ringing had ceased. Mitya let his head sink on her breast. He did not notice that the bell had ceased ringing, nor did he notice that the songs had ceased, and that in-

stead of singing and drunken clamour there was absolute stillness in the house. Grushenka opened her eyes.

"What's the matter? Was I asleep? Yes . . . a bell . . . I've been asleep and dreamt I was driving over the snow with bells, and I dozed. I was with someone I loved, with you. And far, far away. I was holding you and kissing you, nestling close to you. I was cold, and the snow glistened. . . . You know how the snow glistens at night when the moon shines. It was as though I was not on earth. I woke up, and my dear one is close to me. How sweet that is . . ."

"Close to you," murmured Mitya, kissing her dress, her bosom, her hands. And suddenly he had a strange fancy: it seemed to him that she was looking straight before her, not at him, not into his face, but over his head, with an intent, almost uncanny fixity. An expression of wonder, almost of alarm, came suddenly into her face.

"Mitya, who is that looking at us?" she whispered.

Mitya turned, and saw that someone had, in fact, parted the curtains and seemed to be watching them. And not one person alone, it seemed.

He jumped up and walked quickly to the intruder.

"Here, come to us, come here," said a voice, speaking not loudly but firmly and peremptorily.

Mitya passed to the other side of the curtain and stood stockstill. The room was filled with people, but not those who had been there before. An instantaneous shiver ran down his back, and he shuddered. He recognised all those people instantly. That tall, stout old man in the overcoat and forage cap with a cockade—was the police captain, Mihail Makarovitch. And that "consumptive-looking" trim dandy, "who always has such polished boots"—that was the deputy prosecutor. "He has a chronometer worth four hundred roubles; he showed it to me." And that small young man in spectacles. . . . Mitya forgot his surname, though he knew him, had seen him: he was the "investigating lawyer", from the "school of jurisprudence", who had only lately come to the town. And this man—the inspector of police, Mavriky Mavrikyevitch, a man he knew well. And those fellows with the brass plates on, why are they here? And those other two . . . peasants. . . . And there at the door Kalganov with Trifon Borissovitch. . . .

"Gentlemen! What's this for, gentlemen?" began Mitya, but suddenly, as though beside himself, not knowing what he was doing, he cried aloud, at the top of his voice:

"I un—der—stand!"

The young man in spectacles moved forward suddenly, and stepping up to Mitya, began with dignity, though hurriedly:

"We have to make . . . in brief, I beg you to come this way, this way to the sofa. . . . It is absolutely imperative that you should give an explanation."

"The old man!" cried Mitya frantically. "The old man and his blood! . . . I understand."

And he sank, almost fell, on a chair close by, as though he had been mown down by a scythe.

"You understand? He understands it! Monster and parricide! Your father's blood cries out against you!" the old captain of police roared suddenly, stepping up to Mitya.

He was beside himself, crimson in the face and quivering all over.

"This is impossible!" cried the small young man. "Mihail Makarovitch, Mihail Makarovitch, this won't do! . . . I beg you'll allow me to speak. I should never have expected such behaviour from you . . ."

"This is delirium, gentlemen, raving delirium," cried the captain of police; "look at him: drunk, at this time of night, in the company of a disreputable woman, with the blood of his father on his hands. . . . It's delirium! . . ."

"I beg you most earnestly, dear Mihail Makarovitch, to restrain your feelings," the prosecutor said in a rapid whisper to the old police captain, "or I shall be forced to resort to . . . ."

But the little lawyer did not allow him to finish. He turned to Mitya, and delivered himself in a loud, firm, dignified voice:

"Ex-Lieutenant Karamazov, it is my duty to inform you that you are charged with the murder of your father, Fyodor Pavlovitch Karamazov, perpetrated this night . . ."

He said something more, and the prosecutor, too, put in something, but though Mitya heard them he did not understand them. He stared at them all with wild eyes.

BOOK IX: THE PRELIMINARY INVESTIGATION

CHAPTER I

THE BEGINNING OF PERHOTIN'S OFFICIAL CAREER

PYOTR ILYITCH PERHOTIN, whom we left knocking at the strong locked gates of the widow Morozov's house, ended, of course, by making himself heard. Fenya, who was still excited by the fright she had had two hours before, and too much "upset" to go to bed, was almost frightened into hysterics on hearing the furious knocking at the gate. Though she had herself seen him drive away, she fancied that it must be Dmitri Fyodorovitch knocking again, no one else could knock so savagely. She ran to the house-porter, who had already waked up and gone out to the gate, and began imploring him not to open it. But having questioned Pyotr Ilyitch, and learned that he wanted to see Fenya on very "important business", the man made up his mind at last to open. Pyotr Ilyitch was admitted into Fenya's kitchen, but the girl begged him to allow the house-porter to be present, "because of her misgivings". He began questioning her and at once learnt the most vital fact, that is, that when Dmitri Fyodorovitch had run out to look for Grushenka, he had snatched up a pestle from the mortar, and that when he returned the pestle was not with him and his hands were smeared with blood.

"And the blood was simply flowing, dripping from him, dripping!" Fenya kept exclaiming. This horrible detail was simply the product of her disordered imagination. But although not "dripping", Pyotr Ilyitch had himself seen those hands stained with blood, and had helped to wash them. Moreover, the question he had to decide was not how soon the blood had dried but where Dmitri Fyodorovitch had run with the pestle, or rather, whether it really was to Fyodor Pavlovitch's, and how he could satisfactorily ascertain. Pyotr Ilyitch persisted in returning to this point, and though he found out nothing conclusive, yet he carried away a conviction that Dmitri Fyodorovitch could have gone nowhere but to his father's house, and that therefore something must have happened there.

"And when he came back," Fenya added with excitement, "I told him the whole story, and then I began asking him:

131

'Why have you got blood on your hands, Dmitri Fyodorovitch?' and he answered that that was human blood, and that he had just killed someone. He confessed it all to me, and suddenly ran off like a madman. I sat down and began thinking, where's he run off to now like a madman? He'll go to Mokroe, I thought, and kill my mistress there. I ran out to beg him not to kill her. I was running to his lodgings, but I looked at Plotinkov's shop, and saw him just setting off, and there was no blood on his hands then." (Fenya had noticed this and remembered it.) Fenya's old grandmother confirmed her evidence as far as she was capable. After asking some further questions, Pyotr Ilyitch left the house, even more upset and uneasy than he had been when he entered it.

The most direct and the easiest thing for him to do would have been to go straight to Fyodor Pavlovitch's, to find out whether anything had happened there, and if so, what; and only to go to the police captain, as Pyotr Ilyitch firmly intended doing, when he had satisfied himself of the fact. But the night was dark, Fyodor Pavlovitch's gates were strong, and he would have to knock again. His acquaintance with Fyodor Pavlovitch was of the slightest, and what if, after he had been knocking, they opened to him, and nothing had happened, and Fyodor Pavlovitch in his jeering way would go telling the story all over the town, how a stranger, called Perhotin, had broken in upon him at midnight to ask if anyone had killed him. It would make a scandal. And scandal was what Pyotr Ilyitch dreaded more than anything in the world.

Yet the feeling that possessed him was so strong that though he stamped his foot angrily and swore at himself, he set off again, not to Fyodor Pavlovitch's but to Madame Hohlakov's. He decided that if she denied having just given Dmitri Fyodorovitch three thousand roubles, he would go straight to the police captain, but if she admitted having given him the money, he would go home and let the matter rest till next morning.

It is, of course, perfectly evident that there was even more likelihood of causing scandal by going at eleven o'clock at night to a fashionable lady, a complete stranger, and perhaps rousing her from her bed to ask her an amazing question, than by going to Fyodor Pavlovitch. But that is just how it is, sometimes, especially in cases like the present one, with the decisions of the most precise and phlegmatic people. Pyotr Ilyitch was by no means phlegmatic at that moment. He remembered all his life how a haunting uneasiness gradually gained possession of him, growing more and more painful and driving him on, against his will. Yet he kept cursing himself, of course, all the way for going to this lady, but "I will get to the bottom of it, I will!" he repeated for the tenth time, grinding his teeth, and he carried out his intention.

It was exactly eleven o'clock when he entered Madame Hohlakov's house. He was admitted into the yard pretty quickly, but, in response to his inquiry whether the lady was still up, the porter could give no answer, except that she was usually in bed by that time.

"Ask at the top of the stairs. If the lady wants to receive you, she'll receive you. If she won't, she won't."

Pyotr Ilyitch went up, but did not find things so easy here. The footman was unwilling to take in his name, but finally called a maid. Pyotr Ilyitch politely but insistently begged her to inform her lady that an official, living in the town, called Perhotin, had called on particular business, and that, if it were not of the greatest importance, he would not have ventured to come. "Tell her in those words, in those words exactly," he asked the girl.

She went away. He remained waiting in the entry. Madame Hohlakov herself was already in her bedroom, though not yet asleep. She had felt upset ever since Mitya's visit, and had a presentiment that she would not get through the night without the sick headache which always, with her, followed such excitement. She was surprised on hearing the announcement from the maid. She irritably declined to see him, however, though the unexpected visit at such an hour, of an "official living in the town", who was a total stranger, roused her feminine curiosity intensely. But this time Pyotr Ilyitch was as obstinate as a mule. He begged the maid most earnestly to take another message in these very words:

"That he had come on business of the greatest importance, and that Madame Hohlakov might have cause to regret it later if she refused to see him now."

"I plunged headlong," he described it afterwards.

The maid, gazing at him in amazement, went to take his message again. Madame Hohlakov was impressed. She thought a little, asked what he looked like, and learned that he was "very well dressed, young and so polite". We may note, parenthetically, that Pyotr Ilyitch was a rather good-looking young man, and well aware of the fact. Madame Hohlakov made up her mind to see him. She was in her dressing-gown

133

and slippers, but she flung a black shawl over her shoulders. "The official" was asked to walk into the drawing-room, the very room in which Mitya had been received shortly before. The lady came to meet her visitor, with a sternly inquiring countenance, and, without asking him to sit down, began at once with the question:

"What do you want?"

"I have ventured to disturb you, madam, on a matter concerning our common acquaintance, Dmitri Fyodorovitch Karamazov," Perhotin began.

But he had hardly uttered the name when the lady's face showed signs of acute irritation. She almost shrieked, and interrupted him in a fury:

"How much longer am I to be worried by that awful man?" she cried hysterically. "How dare you, sir, how could you venture to disturb a lady who is a stranger to you, in her own house at such an hour! . . . And to force yourself upon her to talk of a man who came here, to this very drawing-room, only three hours ago, to murder me, and went stamping out of the room, as no one would go out of a decent house. Let me tell you, sir, that I shall lodge a complaint against you, that I will not let it pass. Kindly leave me at once . . . I am a mother. . . . I . . . I . . ."

"Murder! then he tried to murder you, too?"

"Why, has he killed somebody else?" Madame Hohlakov asked impulsively.

"If you would kindly listen, madam, for half a moment, I'll explain it all in a couple of words," answered Perhotin firmly. "At five o'clock this afternoon Dmitri Fyodorovitch borrowed ten roubles from me, and I know for a fact he had no money. Yet at nine o'clock he came to see me with a bundle of hundred-rouble notes in his hand, about two or three thousand roubles. His hands and face were all covered with blood, and he looked like a madman. When I asked him where he had got so much money, he answered that he had just received it from you, that you had given him a sum of three thousand to go to the gold-mines . . ."

Madame Hohlakov's face assumed an expression of intense and painful excitement.

"Good God! He must have killed his old father!" she cried, clasping her hands. "I have never given him money, never! Oh, run, run! . . . Don't say another word! Save the old man . . . run to his father . . . run!"

"Excuse me, madam, then you did not give him money? You remember for a fact that you did not give him any money?"

"No, I didn't, I didn't! I refused to give it him, for he could not appreciate it. He ran out in a fury, stamping. He rushed at me, but I slipped away . . . And let me tell you, as I wish to hide nothing from you now, that he positively spat at me. Can you fancy that! But why are we standing? Ah, sit down. . . . Excuse me, I . . . or better run, run, you must run and save the poor old man from an awful death!"

"But if he has killed him already?"

"Ah, good heavens, yes! Then what are we to do now? What do you think we must do now?"

Meantime she had made Pyotr Ilyitch sit down and sat down herself, facing him. Briefly, but fairly clearly, Pyotr Ilyitch told her the history of the affair, that part of it at least which he had himself witnessed. He described, too, his visit to Fenya, and told her about the pestle. All these details produced an overwhelming effect on the distracted lady, who kept uttering shrieks and covering her face with her hands. . . .

"Would you believe it, I foresaw all this! I have that special faculty, whatever I imagine comes to pass. And how often I've looked at that awful man and always thought, that man will end by murdering me. And now it's happened . . . that is, if he hasn't murdered me, but only his own father, it's only because the finger of God preserved me, and what's more, he was ashamed to murder me because, on this very place, I put the holy ikon from the relics of the holy martyr, Saint Varvara, on his neck. . . . And to think how near I was to death at that minute, I went close up to him and he stretched out his neck to me! . . . Do you know, Pyotr Ilyitch (I think you said your name was Pyotr Ilyitch), I don't believe in miracles, but that ikon and this unmistakable miracle with me now—that shakes me, and I'm ready to believe in anything you like. Have you heard about Father Zossima? . . . But I don't know what I'm saying . . . and only fancy, with the ikon on his neck he spat at me. . . . He only spat, it's true, he didn't murder me and . . . he dashed away! But what shall we do, what must we do now? What do you think?"

Pyotr Ilyitch got up, and announced that he was going straight to the police captain, to tell him all about it, and leave him to do what he thought fit.

"Oh, he's an excellent man, excellent! Mihail Makarovitch, I know him. Of course, he's the person to go to. How practical you are, Pyotr Ilyitch! How well you've thought of everything! I should never have thought of it in your place!"

"Especially as I know the police captain very well, too," observed Pyotr Ilyitch, who still continued to stand, and was obviously anxious to escape as quickly as possible from the impulsive lady, who would not let him say good-bye and go away.

"And be sure, be sure," she prattled on, "to come back and tell me what you see there, and what you find out . . . what comes to light . . . how they'll try him . . . and what he's condemned to . . . Tell me, we have no capital punishment, have we? But be sure to come, even if it's at three o'clock at night, at four, at half-past four. . . . Tell them to wake me, to wake me, to shake me if I don't get up . . . But, good heavens, I shan't sleep! But wait, hadn't I better come with you?"

"N—no. But if you would write three lines with your own hand, stating that you did not give Dmitri Fyodorovitch money, it might, perhaps, be of use . . . in case it's needed . . ."

"To be sure!" Madame Hohlakov skipped, delighted, to her bureau. "And you know I'm simply struck, amazed at your resourcefulness, your good sense in such affairs. Are you in the service here? I'm delighted to think that you're in the service here!"

And still speaking, she scribbled on half a sheet of notepaper the following lines:

"I've never in my life lent to that unhappy man, Dmitri Fyodorovitch Karamazov (for, in spite of all, he is unhappy) three thousand roubles to-day. I've never given him money, never! That I swear by all that's holy!

"K. HOHLAKOV."

"Here's the note!" she turned quickly to Pyotr Ilyitch. "Go, save him. It's a noble deed on your part!"

And she made the sign of the Cross three times over him. She ran out to accompany him to the passage.

"How grateful I am to you! You can't think how grateful I am to you for having come to me, first. How is it I haven't met you before? I shall feel flattered at seeing you at my house in the future. How delightful it is that you are living here! . . . Such precision! Such practical ability! . . . They must appreciate you, they must understand you. If there's anything I can do, believe me . . . oh, I love young people! I'm

136

in love with young people! The younger generation are the
one prop of our suffering country. Her one hope. . . . Oh, go,
go!" . . .

But Pyotr Ilyitch had already run away or she would not
have let him go so soon. Yet Madame Hohlakov had made a
rather agreeable impression on him, which had somewhat
softened his anxiety at being drawn into such an unpleasant
affair. Tastes differ, as we all know. "She's by no means so
elderly," he thought, feeling pleased; "on the contrary, I should
have taken her for her daughter."

As for Madame Hohlakov she was simply enchanted by the
young man. "Such sense! such exactness! in so young a man!
in our day! and all that with such manners and appearance!
People say the young people of to-day are no good for anything,
but here's an example!" etc. etc. So she simply forgot this
"dreadful affair", and it was only as she was getting into bed
that, suddenly recalling "how near death she had been", she
exclaimed: "Ah, it is awful, awful!"

But she fell at once into a sound, sweet sleep.

I would not, however, have dwelt on such trivial and
irrelevant details if this eccentric meeting of the young official
with the by no means elderly widow had not subsequently
turned out to be the foundation of the whole career of that
practical and precise young man. His story is remembered to
this day with amazement in our town, and I shall perhaps have
something to say about it when I have finished my long history
of the Brothers Karamazov.

CHAPTER II

THE ALARM

OUR police captain, Mihail Makarovitch Makarov, a retired
lieutenant-colonel, was a widower and an excellent man.
He had only come to us three years previously, but had won
general esteem, chiefly because he "knew how to keep society
together". He was never without visitors, and could not have
got on without them. Someone or other was always dining
with him; he never sat down to table without guests. He gave
regular dinners, too, on all sorts of occasions, sometimes most
surprising ones. Though the fare was not *recherché*, it was

abundant. The fish pies were excellent, and the wine made up in quantity for what it lacked in quality.

The first room his guests entered was a well-fitted billiard-room, with pictures of English racehorses, in black frames on the walls, an essential decoration, as we all know, for a bachelor's billiard-room. There was card-playing every evening at his house, if only at one table. But at frequent intervals, all the society of our town, with the mammas and young ladies, assembled at his house to dance. Though Mihail Makarovitch was a widower, he did not live alone. His widowed daughter lived with him, with her two unmarried daughters, grown-up girls, who had finished their education. They were of agreeable appearance and lively character, and though everyone knew they would have no dowry, they attracted all the young men of fashion to their grandfather's house.

Mihail Makarovitch was by no means very efficient in his work, though he performed his duties no worse than many others. To speak plainly, he was a man of rather narrow education. His understanding of the limits of his administrative power could not always be relied upon. It was not so much that he failed to grasp certain reforms enacted during the present reign, as that he made conspicuous blunders in his interpretation of them. This was not from any special lack of intelligence but from carelessness, for he was always in too great a hurry to go into the subject.

"I have the heart of a soldier rather than of a civilian," he used to say of himself. He had not even formed a definite idea of the fundamental principles of the reforms connected with the emancipation of the serfs, and only picked it up, so to speak, from year to year, involuntarily increasing his knowledge by practice. And yet he was himself a landowner. Pyotr Ilyitch knew for certain that he would meet some of Mihail Makarovitch's visitors there that evening, but he didn't know which. As it happened, at that moment the prosecutor, and Varvinsky, our district doctor, a young man who had only just come to us from Petersburg after taking a brilliant degree at the Academy of Medicine, were playing whist at the police captain's. Ippolit Kirillovitch, the prosecutor (he was really the deputy prosecutor, but we always called him the prosecutor), was rather a peculiar man, of about five-and-thirty, inclined to be consumptive, and married to a fat and childless woman. He was vain and irritable, though he had a good intellect, and even a kind heart. It seemed that all that was wrong with him was that he had a better opinion of himself than his ability warranted. And that made him seem constantly uneasy. He had, moreover, certain higher, even artistic, leanings towards psychology: for instance, a special study of the human heart, a special knowledge of the criminal and his crime. He cherished a grievance on this ground, considering that he had been passed over in the service, and being firmly persuaded that in higher spheres he had not been properly appreciated, and had enemies. In gloomy moments he even threatened to give up his post and practise as a barrister in criminal cases. The unexpected Karamazov case agitated him profoundly: "It was a case that might well be talked about all over Russia." But I am anticipating.

Nikolay Parfenovitch Nelyudov, the young investigating lawyer who had only come from Petersburg two months before, was sitting in the next room with the young ladies. People talked about it afterwards and wondered that all the gentlemen should, as though intentionally, on the evening of "the crime" have been gathered together at the house of the executive authority. Yet it was perfectly simple and happened quite naturally.

Ippolit Kirillovitch's wife had had toothache for the last two days, and he was obliged to go out to escape from her groans. The doctor, from the very nature of his being, could not spend an evening except at cards. Nikolay Parfenovitch Nelyudov had been intending for three days past to drop in that evening at Mihail Makarovitch's, so to speak casually, so as slyly to startle the eldest granddaughter, Olga Mihailovna, by showing that he knew her secret, that he knew it was her birthday, and that she was trying to conceal it on purpose, so as not to be obliged to give a dance. He anticipated a great deal of merriment, many playful jests about her age, and her being afraid to reveal it, about his knowing her secret and telling everybody, and so on. The charming young man was a great adept at such teasing; the ladies had christened him "the naughty man", and he seemed to be delighted at the name. He was extremely well bred, however, of good family, education and feelings, and, though leading a life of pleasure, his sallies were always innocent and in good taste. He was short and delicate-looking. On his white, slender, little fingers he always wore a number of big, glittering rings. When he was engaged in his official duties he always became extraordinarily grave, as though realising his position and the sanctity of the obligations laid upon him. He had a special gift for mystifying murderers and other criminals

139

of the peasant class during interrogation, and if he did not win their respect, he certainly succeeded in arousing their wonder.

Pyotr Ilyitch was simply dumbfounded when he went into the police captain's. He saw instantly that everyone knew. They had positively thrown down their cards, all were standing up and talking. Even Nikolay Parfenovitch had left the young ladies and ran in, looking strenuous and ready for action. Pyotr Ilyitch was met with the astounding news that old Fyodor Pavlovitch really had been murdered that evening in his own house, murdered and robbed. The news had only just reached them in the following manner.

Marfa Ignatyevna, the wife of old Grigory, who had been knocked senseless near the fence, was sleeping soundly in her bed and might well have slept till morning after the draught she had taken. But all of a sudden she waked up, no doubt roused by a fearful epileptic scream from Smerdyakov, who was lying in the next room unconscious. That scream always preceded his fits, and always terrified and upset Marfa Ignatyevna. She could never get accustomed to it. She jumped up and ran half-awake to Smerdyakov's room. But it was dark there, and she could only hear the invalid beginning to gasp and struggle. Then Marfa Ignatyevna herself screamed out and was going to call her husband, but suddenly realised that when she had got up he was not beside her in bed. She ran back to the bedstead and began groping with her hands, but the bed was really empty. Then he must have gone out—where? She ran to the steps and timidly called him. She got no answer, of course, but she caught the sound of groans far away in the garden in the darkness. She listened. The groans were repeated, and it was evident they came from the garden.

"Good Lord! Just as it was with Lizaveta Smerdyashtchaya!" she thought distractedly. She went timidly down the steps and saw that the gate into the garden was open.

"He must be out there, poor dear," she thought. She went up to the gate and all at once she distinctly heard Grigory calling her by name, "Marfa! Marfa!" in a weak, moaning, dreadful voice.

"Lord, preserve us from harm!" Marfa Ignatyevna murmured, and ran towards the voice, and that was how she found Grigory. But she found him not by the fence where he had been knocked down but about twenty paces off. It appeared later that he had crawled away on coming to himself, and probably had been a long time getting so far, losing consciousness several times. She noticed at once that he was covered with blood, and screamed at the top of her voice. Grigory was muttering incoherently:

"He has murdered . . . his father murdered. . . . Why scream, silly . . . run . . . fetch someone . . ."

But Marfa continued screaming, and seeing that her master's window was open and that there was a candle alight in the window, she ran there and began calling Fyodor Pavlovitch. But peeping in at the window, she saw a fearful sight. Her master was lying on his back, motionless, on the floor. His light-coloured dressing-gown and white shirt were soaked with blood. The candle on the table brightly lighted up the blood and the motionless dead face of Fyodor Pavlovitch. Terror-stricken, Marfa rushed away from the window, ran out of the garden, drew the bolt of the big gate, and ran headlong by the back way to the neighbour, Marya Kondratyevna. Both mother and daughter were asleep, but they waked up at Marfa's desperate and persistent screaming and knocking at the shutter. Marfa, shrieking and screaming incoherently, managed to tell them the main fact, and to beg for assistance. It happened that Foma had come back from his wanderings and was staying the night with them. They got him up immediately and all three ran to the scene of the crime. On the way, Marya Kondratyevna remembered that at about eight o'clock she heard a dreadful scream from their garden, and this was no doubt Grigory's scream, "Parricide!" uttered when he caught hold of Mitya's leg.

"Some one person screamed out and then was silent," Marya Kondratyevna explained as she ran. Running to the place where Grigory lay, the two women with the help of Foma carried him to the lodge. They lighted a candle and saw that Smerdyakov was no better, that he was writhing in convulsions, his eyes fixed in a squint, and that foam was flowing from his lips. They moistened Grigory's forehead with water mixed with vinegar, and the water revived him at once. He asked immediately:

"Is the master murdered?"

Then Foma and both the women ran to the house and saw this time that not only the window but also the door into the garden was wide open, though Fyodor Pavlovitch had for the last week locked himself in every night and did not allow even Grigory to come in on any pretext. Seeing that door open, they were afraid to go in to Fyodor Pavlovitch "for fear anything should happen afterwards". And when they returned to Grigory, the old man told them to go straight to the police captain. Marya Kondratyevna ran there and gave the alarm to the whole party at the police captain's. She arrived only five minutes before Pyotr Ilyitch, so that his story came, not as his own surmise and theory but as the direct confirmation, by a witness, of the theory held by all, as to the identity of the criminal (a theory he had in the bottom of his heart refused to believe till that moment).

It was resolved to act with energy. The deputy police inspector of the town was commissioned to take four witnesses, to enter Fyodor Pavlovitch's house and there to open an inquiry on the spot, according to the regular forms, which I will not go into here. The district doctor, a zealous man, new to his work, almost insisted on accompanying the police captain, the prosecutor, and the investigating lawyer.

I will note briefly that Fyodor Pavlovitch was found to be quite dead, with his skull battered in. But with what? Most likely with the same weapon with which Grigory had been attacked later. And immediately that weapon was found, Grigory, to whom all possible medical assistance was at once given, described in a weak and breaking voice how he had been knocked down. They began looking with a lantern by the fence and found the brass pestle dropped in a most conspicuous place on the garden path. There were no signs of disturbance in the room where Fyodor Pavlovitch was lying. But by the bed, behind the screen, they picked up from the floor a big and thick envelope with the inscription: "A present of three thousand roubles for my angel Grushenka, if she is willing to come." And below had been added by Fyodor Pavlovitch: "For my little chicken." There were three seals of red sealing-wax on the envelope, but it had been torn open and was empty: the money had been removed. They found also on the floor a piece of narrow pink ribbon with which the envelope had been tied up.

One piece of Pyotr Ilyitch's evidence made a great impression on the prosecutor and the investigating magistrate, namely, his idea that Dmitri Fyodorovitch would shoot himself before daybreak, that he had resolved to do so, had spoken of it to Pyotr Ilyitch, had taken the pistols, loaded them before him, written a letter, put it in his pocket, etc. When Pyotr Ilyitch, though still unwilling to believe in it, threatened to tell someone so as to prevent the suicide, Mitya had answered grinning: "You'll be too late." So they must make haste to Mokroe to find the criminal, before he really did shoot himself.

"That's clear, that's clear!" repeated the prosecutor in great excitement. "That's just the way with mad fellows like that: 'I shall kill myself to-morrow, so I'll make merry till I die!' "

The story of how he had bought the wine and provisions excited the prosecutor more than ever.

"Do you remember the fellow that murdered a merchant called Olsufyev, gentlemen? He stole fifteen hundred, went at once to have his hair curled, and then, without even hiding the money, carrying it almost in his hand in the same way, he went off to the girls."

All were delayed, however, by the inquiry, the search, and the formalities, etc., in the house of Fyodor Pavlovitch. It all took time and so, two hours before starting, they sent on ahead to Mokroe the officer of the rural police, Mavriky Mavrikyevitch Schmertsov, who had arrived in the town the morning before to get his pay. He was instructed to avoid raising the alarm when he reached Mokroe, but to keep constant watch over the "criminal" till the arrival of the proper authorities, to procure also witnesses for the arrest, police constables, and so on. Mavriky Mavrikyevitch did as he was told, preserving his incognito, and giving no one but his old acquaintance, Trifon Borissovitch, the slightest hint of his secret business. He had spoken to him just before Mitya met the landlord in the balcony, looking for him in the dark, and noticed at once a change in Trifon Borissovitch's face and voice. So neither Mitya nor any one else knew that he was being watched. The box with the pistols had been carried off by Trifon Borissovitch and put in a suitable place. Only after four o'clock, almost at sunrise, all the officials, the police captain, the prosecutor, the investigating lawyer, drove up in two carriages, each drawn by three horses. The doctor remained at Fyodor Pavlovitch's to make a post-mortem next day on the body. But he was particularly interested in the condition of the servant, Smerdyakov.

"Such violent and protracted epileptic fits, recurring continually for twenty-four hours, are rarely to be met with, and are of interest to science," he declared enthusiastically to his companions, and, as they left, they laughingly congratulated him on his find. The prosecutor and the investigating lawyer distinctly remembered the doctor's saying that Smerdyakov could not outlive the night.

After these long but, I think, necessary explanations, we will return to that moment of our tale at which we broke off.

CHAPTER III

THE SUFFERINGS OF A SOUL. THE FIRST ORDEAL

A ND so Mitya sat looking wildly at the people round him, not understanding what was said to him. Suddenly he got up, flung up his hands and shouted aloud:

"I'm not guilty! I'm not guilty of that blood! I'm not guilty of my father's blood. . . . I meant to kill him. But I'm not guilty. Not I."

But he had hardly said this before Grushenka rushed from behind the curtain and flung herself at the police captain's feet.

"It was my fault! Mine! My wickedness!" she cried, in a heart-rending voice, bathed in tears, stretching out her clasped hands towards them. "He did it through me. I tortured him and drove him to it. I tortured that poor old man that's dead, too, in my wickedness, and brought him to this! It's my fault, mine first, mine most, my fault!"

"Yes, it's your fault! You're the chief criminal! You fury! You harlot! You're the most to blame!" shouted the police captain, threatening her with his hand. But he was quickly and resolutely suppressed. The prosecutor positively seized hold of him.

"This is absolutely irregular, Mihail Makarovitch!" he cried. "You are positively hindering the inquiry. . . . You're ruining the case . . ." he almost gasped.

"Follow the regular course! Follow the regular course!" cried Nikolay Parfenovitch, fearfully excited too, "otherwise it's absolutely impossible! . . ."

"Judge us together!" Grushenka cried frantically, still kneeling. "Punish us together. I will go with him now, if it's to death!"

"Grusha, my life, my blood, my holy one!" Mitya fell on his knees beside her and held her tight in his arms. "Don't believe her," he cried, "she's not guilty of anything, of any blood, of anything!"

He remembered afterwards that he was forcibly dragged away from her by several men, and that she was led out, and that when he recovered himself he was sitting at the table.

Beside him and behind him stood the men with metal plates. Facing him on the other side of the table sat Nikolay Parfenovitch, the investigating lawyer. He kept persuading him to drink a little water out of a glass that stood on the table.

"That will refresh you, that will calm you. Be calm, don't be frightened," he added, extremely politely. Mitya (he remembered it afterwards) became suddenly intensely interested in his big rings, one with an amethyst and another with a transparent bright yellow stone, of great brilliance. And long afterwards he remembered with wonder how those rings had riveted his attention through all those terrible hours of interrogation, so that he was utterly unable to tear himself away from them and dismiss them, as things that had nothing to do with his position. On Mitya's left side, in the place where Maximov had been sitting at the beginning of the evening, the prosecutor was now seated, and on Mitya's right hand, where Grushenka had been, was a rosy-cheeked young man in a sort of shabby hunting-jacket, with ink and paper before him. This was the secretary of the investigating lawyer, who had brought him with him. The police captain was now standing by the window at the other end of the room, beside Kalganov, who was sitting there.

"Drink some water," said the investigating lawyer softly, for the tenth time.

"I have drunk it, gentlemen, I have . . . but . . . come, gentlemen, crush me, punish me, decide my fate!" cried Mitya, staring with terribly fixed wide-open eyes at the investigating lawyer.

"So you positively declare that you are not guilty of the death of your father, Fyodor Pavlovitch?" asked the investigating lawyer, softly but insistently.

"I am not guilty. I am guilty of the blood of another old man, but not of my father's. And I weep for it! I killed, I killed the old man and knocked him down. . . . But it's hard to have to answer for that murder with another, a terrible murder of which I am not guilty. . . . It's a terrible accusation, gentlemen, a knockdown blow. But who has killed my father, who has killed him? Who can have killed him if I didn't? It's marvellous, extraordinary, impossible."

"Yes, who can have killed him?" the investigating lawyer was beginning, but Ippolit Kirillovitch, the prosecutor, glancing at him, addressed Mitya.

"You need not worry yourself about the old servant, Grigory Vassilyevitch. He is alive, he has recovered, and in spite of the terrible blows inflicted, according to his own and your evidence, by you, there seems no doubt that he will live, so the doctor says, at least."

"Alive? He's alive?" cried Mitya, flinging up his hands. His face beamed. "Lord, I thank Thee for the miracle Thou hast wrought for me, a sinner and evil-doer. That's an answer to my prayer. I've been praying all night." And he crossed himself three times. He was almost breathless.

"So from this Grigory we have received such important evidence concerning you that . . ." the prosecutor would have continued, but Mitya suddenly jumped up from his chair.

"One minute, gentlemen, for God's sake, one minute; I will run to her——"

"Excuse me, at this moment it's quite impossible," Nikolay Parfenovitch almost shrieked. He, too, leapt to his feet. Mitya was seized by the men with the metal plates, but he sat down of his own accord. . . .

"Gentlemen, what a pity! I wanted to see her for one minute only; I wanted to tell her that it has been washed away, it has gone, that blood that was weighing on my heart all night, and that I am not a murderer now! Gentlemen, she is my betrothed!" he said ecstatically and reverently, looking round at them all. "Oh, thank you, gentlemen! Oh, in one minute you have given me new life, new heart! . . . That old man used to carry me in his arms, gentlemen. He used to wash me in the tub when I was a baby three years old, abandoned by everyone, he was like a father to me! . . ."

"And so you . . ." the investigating lawyer began.

"Allow me, gentlemen, allow me one minute more," interposed Mitya, putting his elbows on the table and covering his face with his hands. "Let me have a moment to think, let me breathe, gentlemen. All this is horribly upsetting, horribly. A man is not a drum, gentlemen!"

"Drink a little more water," murmured Nikolay Parfenovitch.

Mitya took his hands from his face and laughed. His eyes were confident. He seemed completely transformed in a moment. His whole bearing was changed; he was once more the equal of these men, with all of whom he was acquainted, as though they had all met the day before, when nothing had happened, at some social gathering. We may note in passing that, on his first arrival, Mitya had been made very welcome at the police captain's, but later, during the last month especially,

Mitya had hardly called at all, and when the police captain met him, in the street, for instance, Mitya noticed that he frowned and only bowed out of politeness. His acquaintance with the prosecutor was less intimate, though he sometimes paid his wife, a nervous and fanciful lady, visits of politeness, without quite knowing why, and she always received him graciously and had, for some reason, taken an interest in him up to the last. He had not had time to get to know the investigating lawyer, though he had met him and talked to him twice, each time about the fair sex.

"You're a most skilful lawyer, I see, Nikolay Parfenovitch," cried Mitya, laughing gaily, "but I can help you now. Oh, gentlemen, I feel like a new man, and don't be offended at my addressing you so simply and directly. I'm rather drunk, too, I'll tell you that frankly. I believe I've had the honour and pleasure of meeting you, Nikolay Parfenovitch, at my kinsman Miüsov's. Gentlemen, gentlemen, I don't pretend to be on equal terms with you. I understand, of course, in what character I am sitting before you. Oh, of course, there's a horrible suspicion . . . hanging over me . . . if Grigory has given evidence. . . . A horrible suspicion! It's awful, awful, I understand that! But to business, gentlemen, I am ready, and we will make an end of it in one moment; for, listen, listen, gentlemen! Since I know I'm innocent, we can put an end to it in a minute. Can't we? Can't we?"

Mitya spoke much and quickly, nervously and effusively, as though he positively took his listeners to be his best friends.

"So, for the present, we will write that you absolutely deny the charge brought against you," said Nikolay Parfenovitch, impressively, and bending down to the secretary he dictated to him in an undertone what to write.

"Write it down? You want to write that down? Well, write it; I consent, I give my full consent, gentlemen, only . . . do you see. . . . Stay, stay, write this. Of disorderly conduct I am guilty, of violence on a poor old man I am guilty. And there is something else at the bottom of my heart, of which I am guilty, too—but that you need not write down" (he turned suddenly to the secretary); "that's my personal life, gentlemen, that doesn't concern you, the bottom of my heart, that's to say. . . . But of the murder of my old father I'm not guilty. That's a wild idea. It's quite a wild idea! . . . I will prove you that and you'll be convinced directly. . . . You will laugh, gentlemen. You'll laugh yourself at your suspicion! . . ."

147

"Be calm, Dmitri Fyodorovitch," said the investigating lawyer, evidently trying to allay Mitya's excitement by his own composure. "Before we go on with our inquiry, I should like, if you will consent to answer, to hear you confirm the statement that you disliked your father, Fyodor Pavlovitch, that you were involved in continual disputes with him. Here at least, a quarter of an hour ago, you exclaimed that you wanted to kill him: 'I didn't kill him,' you said, 'but I wanted to kill him'!"

"Did I exclaim that? Ach, that may be so, gentlemen! Yes, unhappily, I did want to kill him . . . many times I wanted to . . . unhappily, unhappily!"

"You wanted to. Would you consent to explain what motives precisely led you to such a sentiment of hatred for your parent?"

"What is there to explain, gentlemen?" Mitya shrugged his shoulders sullenly, looking down. "I have never concealed my feelings. All the town knows about it—everyone knows in the tavern. Only lately I declared them in Father Zossima's cell. . . . And the very same day, in the evening I beat my father. I nearly killed him, and I swore I'd come again and kill him, before witnesses. . . . Oh, a thousand witnesses! I've been shouting it aloud for the last month, anyone can tell you that! . . . The fact stares you in the face, it speaks for itself, it cries aloud, but feelings, gentlemen, feelings are another matter. You see, gentlemen" (Mitya frowned), "it seems to me that about feelings you've no right to question me. I know that you are bound by your office, I quite understand that, but that's my affair, my private, intimate affair, yet . . . since I haven't concealed my feelings in the past . . . in the tavern, for instance, I've talked to everyone, so . . . so I won't make a secret of it now. You see, I understand, gentlemen, that there are terrible facts against me in this business. I told everyone that I'd kill him, and now, all of a sudden, he's been killed. So it must have been me! Ha, ha! I can make allowances for you, gentlemen, I can quite make allowances. I'm struck all of a heap myself, for who can have murdered him if not I? That's what it comes to, isn't it? If not I, who can it be, who? Gentlemen, I want to know, I insist on knowing!" he exclaimed suddenly. "Where was he murdered? How was he murdered? How, and with what? Tell me," he asked quickly, looking at the two lawyers.

"We found him in his study, lying on his back on the floor, with his head battered in," said the prosecutor.

148

"That's horrible!" Mitya shuddered and, putting his elbows on the table, hid his face in his right hand.

"We will continue," interposed Nikolay Parfenovitch. "So what was it that impelled you to this sentiment of hatred? You have asserted in public, I believe, that it was based upon jealousy?"

"Well, yes, jealousy. And not only jealousy."

"Disputes about money?"

"Yes, about money, too."

"There was a dispute about three thousand roubles, I think, which you claimed as part of your inheritance?"

"Three thousand! More, more," cried Mitya hotly; "more than six thousand, more than ten, perhaps. I told everyone so, shouted it at them. But I made up my mind to let it go at three thousand. I was desperately in need of that three thousand . . . so the bundle of notes for three thousand that I knew he kept under his pillow, ready for Grushenka, I considered as simply stolen from me. Yes, gentlemen, I looked upon it as mine, as my own property . . ."

The prosecutor looked significantly at the investigating lawyer, and had time to wink at him on the sly.

"We will return to that subject later," said the lawyer promptly. "You will allow us to note that point and write it down; that you looked upon that money as your own property?"

"Write it down, by all means. I know that's another fact that tells against me, but I'm not afraid of facts and I tell them against myself. Do you hear? Do you know, gentlemen, you take me for a different sort of man from what I am," he added, suddenly, gloomy and dejected. "You have to deal with a man of honour, a man of the highest honour; above all—don't lose sight of it—a man who's done a lot of nasty things but has always been, and still is, honourable at bottom, in his inner being. I don't know how to express it. That's just what's made me wretched all my life, that I yearned to be honourable, that I was, so to say, a martyr to a sense of honour, seeking for it with a lantern, with the lantern of Diogenes and yet, all my life I've been doing filthy things like all of us, gentlemen . . . that is like me alone. That was a mistake, like me alone, me alone! . . . Gentlemen, my head aches . . ." His brows contracted with pain. "You see, gentlemen, I couldn't bear the look of him, there was something in him ignoble, impudent, trampling on everything sacred, something sneering and irreverent, loathsome, loathsome. But now that he's dead, I feel differently."

"How do you mean?"

"I don't feel differently, but I wish I hadn't hated him so."

"You feel penitent?"

"No, not penitent, don't write that. I'm not much good myself, I'm not very beautiful, so I had no right to consider him repulsive. That's what I mean. Write that down, if you like."

Saying this Mitya became very mournful. He had grown more and more gloomy as the inquiry continued.

At that moment another unexpected scene followed. Though Grushenka had been removed, she had not been taken far away, only into the room next but one from the blue room, in which the examination was proceeding. It was a little room with one window, next beyond the large room in which they had danced and feasted so lavishly. She was sitting there with no one by her but Maximov, who was terribly depressed, terribly scared, and clung to her side, as though for security. At their door stood one of the peasants with a metal plate on his breast. Grushenka was crying, and suddenly her grief was too much for her, she jumped up, flung up her arms, and with a loud wail of sorrow rushed out of the room to him, to her Mitya, and so unexpectedly that they had not time to stop her. Mitya, hearing her cry, trembled, jumped up, and with a yell rushed impetuously to meet her, not knowing what he was doing. But they were not allowed to come together, though they saw one another. He was seized by the arms. He struggled, and tried to tear himself away. It took three or four men to hold him. She was seized too, and he saw her stretching out her arms to him, crying aloud as they carried her away. When the scene was over he came to himself again, sitting in the same place as before, opposite the investigating lawyer, and crying out to them:

"What do you want with her? Why do you torment her? She's done nothing, nothing! . . ."

The lawyers tried to soothe him. About ten minutes passed like this. At last Mihail Makarovitch, who had been absent, came hurriedly into the room, and said in a loud and excited voice to the prosecutor:

"She's been removed, she's downstairs. Will you allow me to say one word to this unhappy man, gentlemen? In your presence, gentlemen, in your presence."

"By all means, Mihail Makarovitch," answered the investigating lawyer. "In the present case we have nothing against it."

"Listen, Dmitri Fyodorovitch, my dear fellow," began the police captain, and there was a look of warm, almost fatherly, feeling for the luckless prisoner on his excited face. "I took your Agrafena Alexandrovna downstairs myself, and confided her to the care of the landlord's daughters, and that old fellow Maximov is with her all the time. And I soothed her, do you hear? I soothed and calmed her. I impressed on her that you have to clear yourself, so she mustn't hinder you, must not depress you, or you may lose your head and say the wrong thing in your evidence. In fact, I talked to her and she understood. She's a sensible girl, my boy, a good-hearted girl, she would have kissed my old hands, begging help for you. She sent me herself, to tell you not to worry about her. And I must go, my dear fellow, I must go and tell her that you are calm and comforted about her. And so you must be calm, do you understand? I was unfair to her; she is a Christian soul, gentlemen, yes, I tell you, she's a gentle soul, and not to blame for anything. So what am I to tell her, Dmitri Fyodorovitch, will you sit quiet or not?"

The good-natured police captain said a great deal that was irregular, but Grushenka's suffering, a fellow creature's suffering, touched his good-natured heart, and tears stood in his eyes. Mitya jumped up and rushed towards him.

"Forgive me, gentlemen, oh, allow me, allow me!" he cried. "You've the heart of an angel, an angel, Mihail Makarovitch, I thank you for her. I will, I will be calm, cheerful, in fact. Tell her, in the kindness of your heart, that I am cheerful, quite cheerful, that I shall be laughing in a minute, knowing that she has a guardian angel like you. I shall have done with all this directly, and as soon as I'm free, I'll be with her, she'll see, let her wait. Gentlemen," he said, turning to the two lawyers, "now I'll open my whole soul to you; I'll pour out everything. We'll finish this off directly, finish it off gaily. We shall laugh at it in the end, shan't we? But, gentlemen, that woman is the queen of my heart. Oh, let me tell you that. That one thing I'll tell you now. . . . I see I'm with honourable men. She is my light, she is my holy one, and if only you knew! Did you hear her cry: 'I'll go to death with you'? And what have I, a penniless beggar, done for her? Why such love for me? How can a clumsy, ugly brute like me, with my ugly face,

151

deserve such love, that she is ready to go to exile with me? And how she fell down at your feet for my sake, just now! . . . and yet she's proud and has done nothing! How can I help adoring her, how can I help crying out and rushing to her as I did just now? Gentlemen, forgive me! But now, now I am comforted."

And he sank back in his chair and covered his face with his hands, burst into tears. But they were happy tears. He recovered himself instantly. The old police captain seemed much pleased, and the lawyers also. They felt that the examination was passing into a new phase. When the police captain went out, Mitya was positively gay.

"Now, gentlemen, I am at your disposal, entirely at your disposal. And if it were not for all these trivial details, we should understand one another in a minute. I'm at those details again. I'm at your disposal, gentlemen, but I declare that we must have mutual confidence, you in me and I in you, or there'll be no end to it. I speak in your interests. To business, gentlemen, to business, and don't rummage in my soul; don't tease me with trifles, but only ask me about facts and what matters, and I will satisfy you at once. And damn the details!"

So spoke Mitya. The interrogation began again.

CHAPTER IV

THE SECOND ORDEAL

"YOU don't know how you encourage us, Dmitri Fyodorovitch, by your readiness to answer," said Nikolay Parfenovitch, with an animated air, and obvious satisfaction beaming in his very prominent, short-sighted, light grey eyes, from which he had removed his spectacles a moment before. "And you have made a very just remark about the mutual confidence, without which it is sometimes positively impossible to get on in cases of such importance, if the suspected party really hopes and desires to defend himself and is in a position to do so. We, on our side, will do everything in our power, and you can see for yourself how we are conducting the case. You approve, Ippolit Kirillovitch?" He turned to the prosecutor.

"Oh, undoubtedly," replied the prosecutor. His tone was somewhat cold, compared with Nikolay Parfenovitch's impulsiveness.

I will note once for all that Nikolay Parfenovitch, who had but lately arrived among us, had from the first felt marked respect for Ippolit Kirillovitch, our prosecutor, and had become almost his bosom friend. He was almost the only person who put implicit faith in Ippolit Kirillovitch's extraordinary talents as a psychologist and orator and in the justice of his grievance. He had heard of him in Petersburg. On the other hand, young Nikolay Parfenovitch was the only person in the whole world whom our "unappreciated" prosecutor genuinely liked. On their way to Mokroe they had time to come to an understanding about the present case. And now as they sat at the table, the sharp-witted junior caught and interpreted every indication on his senior colleague's face, at half a word, at a glance, or at a wink.

"Gentlemen, only let me tell my own story and don't interrupt me with trivial questions and I'll tell you everything in a moment," said Mitya excitedly.

"Excellent! Thank you. But before we proceed to listen to your communication, will you allow me to inquire as to another little fact of great interest to us? I mean the ten roubles you borrowed yesterday at about five o'clock on the security of your pistols, from your friend, Pyotr Ilyitch Perhotin."

"I pledged them, gentlemen. I pledged them for ten roubles. What more? That's all about it. As soon as I got back to town I pledged them."

"You got back to town? Then had you been out of town?"

"Yes, I went a journey of forty versts into the country. Didn't you know?"

The prosecutor and Nikolay Parfenovitch exchanged glances.

"Well, how would it be if you began your story with a systematic description of all you did yesterday, from the morning onwards? Allow us, for instance, to inquire why you were absent from the town, and just when you left and when you came back—all those facts."

"You should have asked me like that from the beginning," cried Mitya, laughing aloud, "and, if you like, we won't begin from yesterday but from the morning of the day before; then you'll understand how, why, and where I went. I went the day before yesterday, gentlemen, to a merchant of the town, called Samsonov, to borrow three thousand roubles from him on safe security. It was a pressing matter, gentlemen, it was a sudden necessity."

"Allow me to interrupt you," the prosecutor put in politely.

"Why were you in such pressing need for just that sum, three thousand?"

"Oh, gentlemen, you needn't go into details, how, when and why, and why just so much money, and not so much, and all that rigmarole. Why, it'll run to three volumes and then you'll want an epilogue!"

Mitya said all this with the good-natured but impatient familiarity of a man who is anxious to tell the whole truth and is full of the best intentions.

"Gentlemen!"—he corrected himself hurriedly—"don't be vexed with me for my restiveness, I beg you again. Believe me once more, I feel the greatest respect for you and understand the true position of affairs. Don't think I'm drunk. I'm quite sober now. And, besides, being drunk would be no hindrance. It's with me, you know, like the saying: 'When he is sober, he is a fool; when he is drunk, he is a wise man.' Ha, ha! But I see, gentlemen, it's not the proper thing to make jokes to you, till we've had our explanation, I mean. And I've my own dignity to keep up, too. I quite understand the difference for the moment. I am, after all, in the position of a criminal, and so, far from being on equal terms with you. And it's your business to watch me. I can't expect you to pat me on the head for what I did to Grigory, for one can't break old men's heads with impunity. I suppose you'll put me away for him for six months, or a year perhaps, in a house of correction. I don't know what the punishment is—but it will be without loss of the rights of my rank, without loss of my rank, won't it? So you see, gentlemen, I understand the distinction between us. . . . But you must see that you could puzzle God Himself with such questions. 'How did you step? Where did you step? When did you step? And on what did you step?' I shall get mixed up if you go on like this, and you will put it all down against me. And what will that lead to? To nothing! And even if it's nonsense I'm talking now, let me finish, and you, gentlemen, being men of honour and refinement, will forgive me! I'll finish by asking you, gentlemen, to drop that conventional method of questioning. I mean, beginning from some miserable trifle, how I got up, what I had for breakfast, how I spat, and where I spat, and so distracting the attention of the criminal, suddenly stun him with an overwhelming question: 'Whom did you murder? Whom did you rob?' Ha, ha! That's your regulation method, that's where all your cunning comes in. You can put peasants off their guard like that, but not me.

I know the tricks. I've been in the service, too. Ha, ha, ha! You're not angry, gentlemen? You forgive my impertinence?" he cried, looking at them with a good-nature that was almost surprising. "It's only Mitya Karamazov, you know, so you can overlook it. It would be inexcusable in a sensible man; but you can forgive it in Mitya. Ha, ha!"

Nikolay Parfenovitch listened, and laughed too. Though the prosecutor did not laugh, he kept his eyes fixed keenly on Mitya, as though anxious not to miss the least syllable, the slightest movement, the smallest twitch of any feature of his face.

"That's how we have treated you from the beginning," said Nikolay Parfenovitch, still laughing. "We haven't tried to put you out by asking how you got up in the morning and what you had for breakfast. We began, indeed, with questions of the greatest importance."

"I understand. I saw it and appreciated it, and I appreciate still more your present kindness to me, an unprecedented kindness, worthy of your noble hearts. We three here are gentlemen, and let everything be on the footing of mutual confidence between educated, well-bred people, who have the common bond of noble birth and honour. In any case, allow me to look upon you as my best friends at this moment of my life, at this moment when my honour is assailed. That's no offence to you, gentlemen, is it?"

"On the contrary. You've expressed all that so well, Dmitri Fyodorovitch," Nikolay Parfenovitch answered with dignified approbation.

"And enough of those trivial questions, gentlemen, all those tricky questions!" cried Mitya enthusiastically. "Or there's simply no knowing where we shall get to! Is there?"

"I will follow your sensible advice entirely," the prosecutor interposed, addressing Mitya. "But I don't withdraw my question, however. It is now vitally important for us to know exactly why you needed that sum, I mean precisely three thousand."

"Why I needed it? . . . Oh, for one thing and another. . . . Well, it was to pay a debt."

"A debt to whom?"

"That I absolutely refuse to answer, gentlemen. Not because I couldn't, or because I shouldn't dare, or because it would be damaging, for it's all a paltry matter and absolutely trifling, but—I won't, because it's a matter of principle: that's my private life, and I won't allow any intrusion into my private life. That's my principle. Your question has no bearing on the case, and whatever has nothing to do with the case is my private affair. I wanted to pay a debt. I wanted to pay a debt of honour, but to whom I won't say."

"Allow me to make a note of that," said the prosecutor.

"By all means. Write down that I won't say, that I won't. Write that I should think is dishonourable to say. Ech! you can write it: you've nothing else to do with your time."

"Allow me to caution you, sir, and to remind you once more, if you are unaware of it," the prosecutor began, with a peculiar and stern impressiveness, "that you have a perfect right not to answer the questions put to you now, and we, on our side, have no right to extort an answer from you if you decline to give it for one reason or another. That is entirely a matter for your personal decision. But it is our duty, on the other hand, in such cases as the present, to explain and set before you the degree of injury you will be doing yourself by refusing to give this or that piece of evidence. After which I will beg you to continue."

"Gentlemen, I'm not angry . . . I . . ." Mitya muttered in a rather disconcerted tone. "Well, gentlemen, you see, that Samsonov to whom I went then . . ."

We will, of course, not reproduce his account of what is known to the reader already. Mitya was impatiently anxious not to omit the slightest detail. At the same time he was in a hurry to get it over. But as he gave his evidence it was written down, and therefore they had continually to pull him up. Mitya disliked this, but submitted; got angry, though still good-humouredly. He did, it is true, exclaim, from time to time: "Gentlemen, that's enough to make an angel out of patience!" Or: "Gentlemen, it's no good your irritating me."

But even though he exclaimed he still preserved for a time his genially expansive mood. So he told them how Samsonov had made a fool of him two days before. (He had completely realised by now that he had been fooled.) The sale of his watch for six roubles to obtain money for the journey was something new to the lawyers. They were at once greatly interested, and even, to Mitya's intense indignation, thought it necessary to write the fact down as a secondary confirmation of the circumstance that he had hardly a farthing in his pocket at the time. Little by little Mitya began to grow surly. Then, after describing his journey to see Lyagavy, the night spent in the stifling hut, and so on, he came to his return to the town. Here he began, without being particularly urged, to give a minute account of the agonies of jealousy he endured on Grushenka's account.

He was heard with silent attention. They inquired particularly into the circumstance of his having a place of ambush in Marya Kondratyevna's house at the back of Fyodor Pavlovitch's garden to keep watch on Grushenka, and of Smerdyakov's bringing him information. They laid particular stress on this, and noted it down. Of his jealousy he spoke warmly and at length, and though inwardly ashamed at exposing his most intimate feelings, so to speak, to "public ignominy", he evidently overcame his shame in order to tell the truth. The frigid severity, with which the investigating lawyer, and still more the prosecutor, stared intently at him as he told his story, disconcerted him at last considerably.

"That boy, Nikolay Parfenovitch, to whom I was talking nonsense about women only a few days ago, and that sickly prosecutor are not worth my telling this to," he reflected mournfully. "It's ignominious. 'Be patient, humble, hold thy peace.'" He wound up his reflections with that line. But he pulled himself together to go on again. When he came to telling of his visit to Madame Hoklakov, he regained his spirits and even wished to tell a little anecdote of that lady which had nothing to do with the case. But the investigating lawyer stopped him, and civilly suggested that he should pass on to "more essential matters". At last, when he described his despair and told them how, when he left Madame Hohlakov's, he thought that he'd "get three thousand if he had to murder someone to do it", they stopped him again and noted down that he had "meant to murder someone". Mitya let them write it without protest. At last he reached the point in his story when he learned that Grushenka had deceived him and had returned from Samsonov's as soon as he left her there, though she had said that she would stay there till midnight.

"If I didn't kill Fenya then, gentlemen, it was only because I hadn't time," broke from him suddenly at that point in his story. That, too, was carefully written down. Mitya waited gloomily, and was beginning to tell how he ran into his father's garden when the investigating lawyer suddenly stopped him, and opening the big portfolio that lay on the sofa beside him he brought out the brass pestle.

"Do you recognise this object?" he asked, showing it to Mitya.

"Oh, yes," he laughed gloomily. "Of course I recognise it. Let me have a look at it. . . . Damn it, never mind!"

"You have forgotten to mention it," observed the investigating lawyer.

"Hang it all, I shouldn't have concealed it from you. Do you suppose I could have managed without it? It simply escaped my memory."

"Be so good as to tell us precisely how you came to arm yourself with it."

"Certainly I will be so good, gentlemen."

And Mitya described how he took the pestle and ran.

"But what object had you in view in arming yourself with such a weapon?"

"What object? No object. I just picked it up and ran off."

"What for, if you had no object?"

Mitya's wrath flared up. He looked intently at "the boy" and smiled gloomily and malignantly. He was feeling more and more ashamed at having told "such people" the story of his jealousy so sincerely and spontaneously.

"Bother the pestle!" broke from him suddenly.

"But still . . ."

"Oh, to keep off dogs. . . . Oh, because it was dark. . . . In case anything turned up."

"But have you ever on previous occasions taken a weapon with you when you went out, since you're afraid of the dark?"

"Ugh! damn it all, gentlemen! There's positively no talking to you!" cried Mitya, exasperated beyond endurance, and turning to the secretary, crimson with anger, he said quickly, with a note of fury in his voice:

"Write down at once . . . at once . . . 'that I snatched up the pestle to go and kill my father . . . Fyodor Pavlovitch . . . by hitting him on the head with it!' Well, now are you satisfied, gentlemen? Are your minds relieved?" he said, glaring defiantly at the lawyers.

"We quite understand that you made that statement just now through exasperation with us and the questions we put to you, which you consider trivial, though they are, in fact, essential," the prosecutor remarked drily in reply.

"Well, upon my word, gentlemen! Yes, I took the pestle. . . . What does one pick things up for at such moments? I don't know what for. I snatched it up and ran—that's all. For to me, gentlemen, *passons*, or I declare I won't tell you any more."

158

He sat with his elbows on the table and his head in his hand. He sat sideways to them and gazed at the wall, struggling against a feeling of nausea. He had, in fact, an awful inclination to get up and declare that he wouldn't say another word, "not if you hang me for it".

"You see, gentlemen," he said at last, with difficulty controlling himself, "you see. I listen to you and am haunted by a dream. . . . It's a dream I have sometimes, you know. . . . I often dream it—it's always the same . . . that someone is hunting me, someone I'm awfully afraid of . . . that he's hunting me in the dark, in the night . . . tracking me, and I hide somewhere from him, behind a door or cupboard, hide in a degrading way, and the worst of it is, he always knows where I am, but he pretends not to know where I am on purpose, to prolong my agony, to enjoy my terror. . . . That's just what you're doing now. It's just like that!"

"Is that the sort of thing you dream about?" inquired the prosecutor.

"Yes, it is. Don't you want to write it down?" said Mitya, with a distorted smile.

"No; no need to write it down. But still you do have curious dreams."

"It's not a question of dreams now, gentlemen—this is realism, this is real life! I'm a wolf and you're the hunters. Well, hunt him down!"

"You are wrong to make such comparisons . . ." began Nikolay Parfenovitch, with extraordinary softness.

"No, I'm not wrong, not at all!" Mitya flared up again, though his outburst of wrath had obviously relieved his heart. He grew more good-humoured at every word. "You may not trust a criminal or a man on trial tortured by your questions, but an honourable man, the honourable impulses of the heart (I say that boldly!)—no! That you must believe; you have no right indeed . . . but—

> 'Be silent, heart,
> Be patient, humble, hold thy peace.'

Well, shall I go on?" he broke off gloomily.

"If you'll be so kind," answered Nikolay Parfenovitch.

CHAPTER V

THE THIRD ORDEAL

THOUGH Mítya spoke sullenly, it was evident that he was trying more than ever not to forget or miss a single detail of his story. He told them how he had leapt over the fence into his father's garden; how he had gone up to the window; told them all that had passed under the window. Clearly, precisely, distinctly, he described the feelings that troubled him during those moments in the garden when he longed so terribly to know whether Grushenka was with his father or not. But, strange to say, both the lawyers listened now with a sort of awful reserve, looked coldly at him, asked few questions. Mítya could gather nothing from their faces.

"They're angry and offended," he thought. "Well, bother them!"

When he described how he made up his mind at last to make the "signal" to his father that Grushenka had come, so that he should open the window, the lawyers paid no attention to the word "signal", as though they entirely failed to grasp the meaning of the word in this connection: so much so, that Mítya noticed it. Coming at last to the moment when, seeing his father peering out of the window, his hatred flared up and he pulled the pestle out of his pocket, he suddenly, as though of design, stopped short. He sat gazing at the wall and was aware that their eyes were fixed upon him.

"Well?" said the investigating lawyer. "You pulled out the weapon and . . . and what happened then?"

"Then? Why, then I murdered him . . . hit him on the head and cracked his skull. . . . I suppose that's your story. That's it!"

His eyes suddenly flashed. All his smothered wrath suddenly flamed up with extraordinary violence in his soul.

"Our story?" repeated Nikolay Parfenovitch. "Well—and yours?"

Mítya dropped his eyes and was a long time silent.

"My story, gentlemen? Well, it was like this," he began softly. "Whether it was someone's tears, or my mother prayed to God, or a good angel kissed me at that instant, I don't know. But the devil was conquered. I rushed from the window and ran to the fence. My father was alarmed and, for the first time, he saw me then, cried out, and sprang back from the

160

window. I remember that very well. I ran across the garden to the fence . . . and there Grigory caught me, when I was sitting on the fence."

At that point he raised his eyes at last and looked at his listeners. They seemed to be staring at him with perfectly unruffled attention. A sort of paroxysm of indignation seized on Mitya's soul.

"Why, you're laughing at me at this moment, gentlemen!" he broke off suddenly.

"What makes you think that?" observed Nikolay Parfenovitch.

"You don't believe one word—that's why! I understand, of course, that I have come to the vital point. The old man's lying there now with his skull broken, while I—after dramatically describing how I wanted to kill him, and how I snatched up the pestle—I suddenly run away from the window. A romance! Poetry! As though one could believe a fellow on his word. Ha, ha! You are scoffers, gentlemen!"

And he swung round on his chair so that it creaked.

"And did you notice," asked the prosecutor suddenly, as though not observing Mitya's excitement, "did you notice, when you ran away from the window, whether the door into the garden was open?"

"No, it was not open."

"It was not?"

"It was shut. And who could open it? Bah! the door. Wait a bit!" He seemed suddenly to bethink himself, and almost with a start:

"Why, did you find the door open?"

"Yes, it was open."

"Why, who could have opened it if you did not open it yourselves?" cried Mitya, greatly astonished.

"The door stood open, and your father's murderer undoubtedly went in at that door, and, having committed the crime, went out again by the same door," the prosecutor pronounced deliberately, as though chiselling out each word separately. "That is perfectly clear. The murder was committed in the room and *not through the window;* that is absolutely certain from the examination that has been made, from the position of the body, and everything. There can be no doubt of that circumstance."

Mitya was absolutely dumbfounded.

"But that's utterly impossible!" he cried, completely at a

loss. "I . . . I didn't go in. . . . I tell you positively, definitely, the door was shut the whole time I was in the garden, and when I ran out of the garden. I only stood at the window and saw him through the window. That's all, that's all. . . . I remember to the last minute. And if I didn't remember, it would be just the same. I know it, for no one knew the signals except Smerdyakov, and me, and the dead man. And he wouldn't have opened the door to anyone in the world without the signals."

"Signals? What signals?" asked the prosecutor, with greedy, almost hysterical curiosity. He instantly lost all trace of his reserve and dignity. He asked the question with a sort of cringing timidity. He scented an important fact of which he had known nothing, and was already filled with dread that Mitya might be unwilling to disclose it.

"So you didn't know!" Mitya winked at him with a malicious and mocking smile. "What if I won't tell you? From whom could you find out? No one knew about the signals except my father, Smerdyakov, and me: that was all. Heaven knew, too, but it won't tell you. But it's an interesting fact. There's no knowing what you might build on it. Ha, ha! Take comfort, gentlemen. I'll reveal it. You've some foolish idea in your hearts. You don't know the man you have to deal with! You have to do with a prisoner who gives evidence against himself, to his own damage! Yes, for I'm a man of honour and you—are not."

The prosecutor swallowed this without a murmur. He was trembling with impatience to hear the new fact. Minutely and diffusely Mitya told them everything about the signals invented by Fyodor Pavlovitch for Smerdyakov. He told them exactly what every tap on the window meant, tapped the signals on the table, and when Nikolay Parfenovitch said that he supposed he, Mitya, had tapped the signal "Grushenka has come", when he tapped to his father, he answered precisely that he had tapped that signal, that "Grushenka had come".

"So now you can build up your tower," Mitya broke off, and again turned away from them contemptuously.

"So no one knew of the signals but your dead father, you, and the valet Smerdyakov? And no one else?" Nikolay Parfenovitch inquired once more.

"Yes. The valet Smerdyakov, and heaven. Write down about heaven. That may be of use. Besides, you will need God yourselves."

162

And they had already, of course, begun writing it down. But while they wrote, the prosecutor said suddenly, as though pitching on a new idea:

"But if Smerdyakov also knew of these signals and you absolutely deny all responsibility for the death of your father, was it not he, perhaps, who knocked the signal agreed upon, induced your father to open to him, and then . . . . committed the crime?"

Mitya turned upon him a look of profound irony and intense hatred. His silent stare lasted so long that it made the prosecutor blink.

"You've caught the fox again," commented Mitya at last; you've got the beast by the tail. Ha, ha! I see through you, Mr. Prosecutor. You thought, of course, that I should jump at that, catch at your prompting, and shout with all my might. 'Aie, it's Smerdyakov; he's the murderer'. Confess that's what you thought. Confess, and I'll go on."

But the prosecutor did not confess. He held his tongue and waited.

"You're mistaken. I'm not going to shout 'It's Smerdyakov'," said Mitya.

"And you don't even suspect him?"

"Why, do you suspect him?"

"He is suspected, too."

Mitya fixed his eyes on the floor.

"Joking apart," he brought out gloomily. "Listen. From the very beginning, almost from the moment when I ran out to you from behind the curtain, I've had the thought of Smerdyakov in my mind. I've been sitting here, shouting that I'm innocent and thinking all the time 'Smerdyakov!' I can't get Smerdyakov out of my head. In fact, I, too, thought of Smerdyakov just now; but only for a second. Almost at once I thought: 'No, it's not Smerdyakov.' It's not his doing, gentlemen."

"In that case is there anybody else you suspect?" Nikolay Parfenovitch inquired cautiously.

"I don't know anyone it could be, whether it's the hand of Heaven or of Satan, but . . . not Smerdyakov," Mitya jerked out with decision.

"But what makes you affirm so confidently and emphatically that it's not he?"

"From my conviction—my impression. Because Smerdyakov is a man of the most abject character and a coward. He's not a coward, he's the epitome of all the cowardice in the world

163

walking on two legs. He has the heart of a chicken. When he talked to me, he was always trembling with fear I should kill him, though I never raised my hand against him. He fell at my feet and blubbered; he has kissed these very boots, literally, beseeching me 'not to frighten him'. Do you hear? 'Not to frighten him.' What a thing to say! Why, I offered him money. He's a puling chicken—sickly, epileptic, weak-minded —a child of eight could thrash him. He has no character worth talking about. It's not Smerdyakov, gentlemen. He doesn't care for money; he wouldn't take my presents. Besides, what motive had he for murdering the old man? Why, he's very likely his son, you know—his natural son. Do you know that?''

"We have heard that legend. But you are your father's son, too, you know; yet you yourself told everyone you meant to murder him.''

"That's a thrust! And a nasty, mean one, too! I'm not afraid! Oh, gentlemen, isn't it too base of you to say that to my face? It's base, because I told you that myself. I not only wanted to murder him, but I might have done it. And, what's more, I went out of my way to tell you of my own accord that I nearly murdered him. But, you see, I didn't murder him; you see, my guardian angel saved me—that's what you've not taken into account. And that's why it's so base of you. For I didn't kill him, I didn't kill him! Do you hear, I did not kill him.''

He was almost choking. He had not been so moved before during the whole interrogation.

"And what has he told you, gentlemen—Smerdyakov, I mean?'' he added suddenly, after a pause. "May I ask that question?''

"You may ask any question,'' the prosecutor replied with frigid severity, "any question relating to the facts of the case, and we are, I repeat, bound to answer every inquiry you make. We found the servant Smerdyakov, concerning whom you inquire, lying unconscious in his bed, in an epileptic fit of extreme severity, that has recurred, possibly, ten times. The doctor who was with us told us, after seeing him, that he may possibly not outlive the night.''

"Well, if that's so, the devil must have killed him,'' broke suddenly from Mitya, as though until that moment he had been asking himself: "Was it Smerdyakov or not?''

"We will come back to this later,'' Nikolay Parfenovitch

decided. "Now, wouldn't you like to continue your statement?"

Mitya asked for a rest. His request was courteously granted. After resting, he went on with his story. But he was evidently depressed. He was exhausted, mortified and morally shaken. To make matters worse the prosecutor exasperated him, as though intentionally, by vexatious interruptions about "trifling points". Scarcely had Mitya described how, sitting on the wall, he had struck Grigory on the head with the pestle, while the old man had hold of his left leg, and how he had then jumped down to look at him, when the prosecutor stopped him to ask him to describe exactly how he was sitting on the wall. Mitya was surprised.

"Oh, I was sitting like this, astride, one leg on one side of the wall and one on the other."

"And the pestle?"

"The pestle was in my hand."

"Not in your pocket? Do you remember that precisely? Was it a violent blow you gave him?"

"It must have been a violent one. But why do you ask?"

"Would you mind sitting on the chair just as you sat on the wall then and showing us just how you moved your arm, and in what direction?"

"You're making fun of me, aren't you?" asked Mitya, looking haughtily at the speaker; but the latter did not flinch.

Mitya turned abruptly, sat astride on his chair, and swung his arm.

"This was how I struck him! That's how I knocked him down! What more do you want?"

"Thank you. May I trouble you now to explain why you jumped down, with what object, and what you had in view?"

"Oh, hang it! . . . I jumped down to look at the man I'd hurt . . . I don't know what for!"

"Thought you were so excited and were running away?"

"Yes, though I was excited and running away."

"You wanted to help him?"

"Help! . . . Yes, perhaps I did want to help him. . . . I don't remember."

"You don't remember? Then you didn't quite know what you were doing?"

"Not at all. I remember everything—every detail. I jumped down to look at him, and wiped his face with my handkerchief."

"We have seen your handkerchief. Did you hope to restore him to consciousness?"

"I don't know whether I hoped it. I simply wanted to make sure whether he was alive or not."

"Ah! You wanted to be sure? Well, what then?"

"I'm not a doctor. I couldn't decide. I ran away thinking I'd killed him. And now he's recovered."

"Excellent," commented the prosecutor. "Thank you. That's all I wanted. Kindly proceed."

Alas! it never entered Mitya's head to tell them, though he remembered it, that he had jumped back from pity, and standing over the prostrate figure had even uttered some words of regret: "You've came to grief, old man—there's no help for it. Well, there you must lie."

The prosecutor could only draw one conclusion: that the man had jumped back "at such a moment and in such excitement simply with the object of ascertaining whether the *only* witness of his crime were dead; that he must therefore have been a man of great strength, coolness, decision and foresight even at such a moment," . . . and so on. The prosecutor was satisfied: "I've provoked the nervous fellow by 'trifles' and he has said more than he meant to."

With painful effort Mitya went on. But this time he was pulled up immediately by Nikolay Parfenovitch.

"How came you to run to the servant, Fedosya Markovna, with your hands so covered with blood, and, as it appears, your face too?"

"Why, I didn't notice the blood at all at the time," answered Mitya.

"That's quite likely. It does happen sometimes." The prosecutor exchanged glances with Nikolay Parfenovitch.

"I simply didn't notice. You're quite right there, prosecutor," Mitya assented suddenly.

Next came the account of Mitya's sudden determination to "step aside" and make way for their happiness. But he could not make up his mind to open his heart to them as before, and tell them about "the queen of his soul". He disliked speaking of her before these chilly persons "who were fastening on him like bugs". And so in response to their reiterated questions he answered briefly and abruptly:

"Well, I made up my mind to kill myself. What had I left to live for? That question stared me in the face. Her first rightful lover had come back, the man who wronged her but

166

who'd hurried back to offer his love, after five years and atone for the wrong with marriage. . . . So I knew it was all over for me. . . . And behind me disgrace, and that blood— Grigory's. . . . What had I to live for? So I went to redeem the pistols I had pledged, to load them and put a bullet in my brain to-morrow."

"And a grand feast the night before?"

"Yes, a grand feast the night before. Damn it all, gentlemen! Do make haste and finish it. I meant to shoot myself not far from here, beyond the village, and I'd planned to do it at five o'clock in the morning. And I had a note in my pocket already. I wrote it at Perhotin's when I loaded my pistols. Here's the letter. Read it! It's not for you I tell it," he added contemptuously. He took it from his waistcoat pocket and flung it on the table. The lawyers read it with curiosity, and, as is usual, added it to the papers connected with the case.

"And you didn't even think of washing your hands at Perhotin's? You were not afraid then of arousing suspicion?"

"What suspicion? Suspicion or not, I should have galloped here just the same and shot myself at five o'clock, and you wouldn't have been in time to do anything. If it hadn't been for what's happened to my father, you would have known nothing about it, and wouldn't have come here. Oh, it's the devil's doing. It was the devil murdered father, it was through the devil that you found it out so soon. How did you manage to get here so quickly? It's marvellous, a dream!"

"Mr. Perhotin informed us that when you came to him, you held in your hands . . . your blood-stained hands . . . your money . . . a lot of money . . . . a bundle of hundred-rouble notes, and that his servant boy saw it too."

"That's true, gentlemen. I remember it was so."

"Now, there's one little point presents itself. Can you inform us," Nikolay Parfenovitch began, with extreme gentleness, "where did you get so much money all of a sudden, when it appears from the facts, from the reckoning of time, that you had not been home?"

The prosecutor's brows contracted at the question being asked so plainly, but he did not interrupt Nikolay Parfenovitch.

"No, I didn't go home," answered Mitya, apparently perfectly composed, but looking at the floor.

"Allow me then to repeat my question," Nikolay Parfenovitch went on as though creeping up to the subject. "Where were you able to procure such a sum all at once, when, by your own confession, at five o'clock the same day you . . ."

"I was in want of ten roubles and pledged my pistols with Perhotin, and then went to Madame Hohlakov to borrow three thousand which she wouldn't give me, and so on, and all the rest of it," Mitya interrupted sharply. "Yes, gentlemen, I was in want of it, and suddenly thousands turned up, eh? Do you know, gentlemen, you're both afraid now, 'What if he won't tell us where he got it?' That's just how it is. I'm not going to tell you, gentlemen. You've guessed right. You'll never know," said Mitya, chipping out each word with extraordinary determination. The lawyers were silent for a moment.

"You must understand, Mr. Karamazov, that it is of vital importance for us to know," said Nikolay Parfenovitch, softly and suavely.

"I understand; but still I won't tell you."

The prosecutor, too, intervened, and again reminded him that the prisoner was at liberty to refuse to answer questions if he thought it to his interest, and so on. But in view of the damage he might do himself by his silence, especially in a case of such importance as . . .

"And so on, gentlemen, and so on. Enough! I've heard that rigmarole before," Mitya interrupted again. "I can see for myself how important it is, and that this is the vital point, and still I won't say."

"What is it to us? It's not our business, but yours. You are doing yourself harm," observed Nikolay Parfenovitch nervously.

"You see, gentlemen, joking apart"—Mitya lifted his eyes and looked firmly at them both—"I had an inkling from the first that we should come to loggerheads at this point. But at first, when I began to give my evidence, it was all still far away and misty; it was all floating, and I was so simple that I began with the supposition of mutual confidence existing between us. Now I can see for myself that such confidence is out of the question, for in any case we were bound to come to this cursed stumbling-block. And now we've come to it! It's impossible and there's an end of it! But I don't blame you. You can't believe it all simply on my word. I understand that, of course."

He relapsed into gloomy silence.

"Couldn't you, without abandoning your resolution to be silent about the chief point, could you not, at the same time, give us some slight hint as to the nature of the motives which are strong enough to induce you to refuse to answer, at a crisis so full of danger to you?"

Mitya smiled mournfuly, almost dreamily.

"I'm much more good-natured than you think, gentlemen. I'll tell you the reason why and give you that hint, though you don't deserve it. I won't speak of that, gentlemen, because it would be a stain on my honour. The answer to the question where I got the money would expose me to far greater disgrace than the murder and robbing of my father, if I had murdered and robbed him. That's why I can't tell you. I can't, for fear of disgrace. What, gentlemen, are you going to write that down?"

"Yes, we'll write it down," lisped Nikolay Parfenovitch.

"You ought not to write that down about 'disgrace'. I only told you that in the goodness of my heart. I needn't have told you. I made you a present of it, so to speak, and you pounce upon it at once. Oh well, write—write what you like," he concluded, with scornful disgust. "I'm not afraid of you and I can still hold up my head before you."

"And can't you tell us the nature of that disgrace?" Nikolay Parfenovitch hazarded.

The prosecutor frowned darkly.

"No, no, *c'est fini,* don't trouble yourselves. It's not worth while soiling one's hands. I have soiled myself enough through you as it is. You're not worth it—no one is . . . Enough, gentlemen. I'm not going on."

This was said too peremptorily. Nikolay Parfenovitch did not insist further, but from Ippolit Kirillovitch's eyes he saw that he had not given up hope.

"Can you not, at least, tell us what sum you had in your hands when you went into Mr. Perhotin's—how many roubles exactly?"

"I can't tell you that."

"You spoke to Mr. Perhotin, I believe, of having received three thousand from Madame Hohlakov."

"Perhaps I did. Enough, gentlemen. I won't say how much I had."

"Will you be so good then as to tell us how you came here and what you have done since you arrived?"

"Oh! you might ask the people here·about that. But I'll tell you if you like."

He proceeded to do so, but we won't repeat his story. He told it drily and curtly. Of the raptures of his love he said nothing, but told them that he abandoned his determination to shoot himself, owing to "new factors in the case". He told the story without going into motives or details. And this time the lawyers did not worry him much. It was obvious that there was no essential point of interest to them here.

"We shall verify all that. We will come back to it during the examination of the witnesses, which will, of course, take place in your presence," said Nikolay Parfenovitch in conclusion. "And now allow me to request you to lay on the table everything in your possession, especialy all the money you still have about you."

"My money, gentlemen? Certainly. I understand that that is necessary. I'm surprised, indeed, that you haven't inquired about it before. It's true I couldn't get away anywhere. I'm sitting here where I can be seen. But here's my money—count it—take it. That's all, I think."

He turned it all out of his pocket; even the small change—two pieces of twenty copecks—he pulled out of his waistcoat pocket. They counted the money, which amounted to eight hundred and thirty-six roubles and forty copecks.

"And is that all?" asked the investigating lawyer.

"Yes."

"You stated just now in your evidence that you spent three hundred roubles at Plotnikovs'. You gave Perhotin ten, your driver twenty, here you lost two hundred, then . . ."

Nikolay Parfenovitch reckoned it all up. Mitya helped him readily. They recollected every farthing and included it in the reckoning. Nikolay Parfenovitch hurriedly added up the total.

"With this eight hundred you must have had about fifteen hundred at first?"

"I suppose so," snapped Mitya.

"How is it they all assert there was much more?"

"Let them assert it."

"But you asserted it yourself."

"Yes, I did, too."

"We will compare all this with the evidence of other persons not yet examined. Don't be anxious about your money. It will be properly taken care of and be at your disposal at the conclusion of . . . what is beginning . . . if it appears, or, so to speak, is proved that you have undisputed right to it. Well, and now . . ."

Nikolay Parfenovitch suddenly got up, and informed Mitya

firmly that it was his duty and obligation to conduct a minute and thorough search "of your clothes and everything else . . ."

"By all means, gentlemen. I'll turn out all my pockets, if you like."

And he did, in fact, begin turning out his pockets.

"It will be necessary to take off your clothes, too."

"What! Undress? Ugh! Damn it! Won't you search me as I am? Can't you?"

"It's utterly impossible, Dmitri Fyodorovitch. You must take off your clothes."

"As you like," Mitya submitted gloomily; "only, please, not here, but behind the curtains. Who will search them?"

"Behind the curtains, of course."

Nikolay Parfenovitch bent his head in assent. His small face wore an expression of peculiar solemnity.

CHAPTER VI

THE PROSECUTOR CATCHES MITYA

SOMETHING utterly unexpected and amazing to Mitya followed. He could never, even a minute before, have conceived that anyone could behave like that to him, Mitya Karamazov. What was worst of all, there was something humiliating in it, and on their side something "supercilious and scornful". It was nothing to take off his coat, but he was asked to undress further, or rather not asked but "commanded", he quite understood that. From pride and contempt he submitted without a word. Several peasants accompanied the lawyers and remained on the same side of the curtain. "To be ready if force is required," thought Mitya, "and perhaps for some other reason, too."

"Well, must I take off my shirt, too?" he asked sharply, but Nikolay Parfenovitch did not answer. He was busily engaged with the prosecutor in examining the coat, the trousers, the waistcoat and the cap; and it was evident that they were both much interested in the scrutiny. "They make no bones about it," thought Mitya, "they don't keep up the most elementary politeness."

"I ask you for the second time—need I take off my shirt or not?" he said, still more sharply and irritably.

"Don't trouble yourself. We will tell you what to do,"

Nikolay Parfenovitch said, and his voice was positively peremptory, or so it seemed to Mitya.

Meantime a consultation was going on in undertones between the lawyers. There turned out to be on the coat, especially on the left side at the back, a huge patch of blood, dry, and still stiff. There were bloodstains on the trousers, too. Nikolay Parfenovitch, moreover, in the presence of the peasant witnesses, passed his fingers along the collar, the cuffs, and all the seams of the coat and trousers, obviously looking for something—money, of course. He didn't even hide from Mitya his suspicion that he was capable of sewing money up in his clothes.

"He treats me not as an officer but as a thief," Mitya muttered to himself. They communicated their ideas to one another with amazing frankness. The secretary, for instance, who was also behind the curtain, fussing about and listening, called Nikolay Parfenovitch's attention to the cap, which they were also fingering.

"You remember Gridyenko, the copying-clerk," observed the secretary. "Last summer he received the wages of the whole office, and pretended to have lost the money when he was drunk. And where was it found? Why, in just such pipings in his cap. The hundred-rouble notes were screwed up in little rolls and sewed in the piping."

Both the lawyers remembered Gridyenko's case perfectly, and so laid aside Mitya's cap, and decided that all his clothes must be more thoroughly examined later.

"Excuse me," cried Nikolay Parfenovitch, suddenly, noticing that the right cuff of Mitya's shirt was turned in, and covered with blood, "excuse me, what's that, blood?"

"Yes," Mitya jerked out.

"That is, what blood . . . and why is the cuff turned in?"

Mitya told him how he had got the sleeve stained with blood looking after Grigory, and had turned it inside when he was washing his hands at Perhotin's.

"You must take off your shirt, too. That's very important as material evidence."

Mitya flushed red and flew into a rage.

"What! am I to stay naked?" he shouted.

"Don't disturb yourself. We will arrange something. And meanwhile take off your socks."

"You're not joking? Is that really necessary?" Mitya's eyes flashed.

172

"We are in no mood for joking," answered Nikolay Parfeno-vitch sternly.

"Well, if I must . . ." muttered Mitya, and sitting down on the bed, he took off his socks. He felt unbearably awkward. All were clothed, while he was naked, and strange to say, when he was undressed he felt somehow guilty in their presence, and was almost ready to believe himself that he was inferior to them, and that now they had a perfect right to despise him.

"When all are undressed, one is somehow not ashamed, but when one's the only one undressed and everybody is looking, it's degrading," he kept repeating to himself, again and again. "It's like a dream, I've sometimes dreamed of being in such degrading positions." It was a misery to him to take off his socks. They were very dirty, and so were his underclothes, and now everyone could see it. And what was worse, he disliked his feet. All his life he had thought both his big toes hideous. He particularly loathed the coarse, flat, crooked nail on the right one, and now they would all see it. Feeling intolerably ashamed made him, at once and intentionally, rougher. He pulled off his shirt, himself.

"Would you like to look anywhere else if you're not ashamed to?"

"No, there's no need to, at present."

"Well, am I to stay naked like this?" he added savagely.

"Yes, that can't be helped for the time . . . Kindly sit down here for a while. You can wrap yourself in a quilt from the bed, and I . . . I'll see to all this."

All the things were shown to the witnesses. The report of the search was drawn up, and at last Nikolay Parfenovitch went out, and the clothes were carried out after him. Ippolit Kirillovitch went out, too. Mitya was left alone with the peasants, who stood in silence, never taking their eyes off him. Mitya wrapped himself up in the quilt. He felt cold. His bare feet stuck out, and he couldn't pull the quilt over so as to cover them. Nikolay Parfenovitch seemed to be gone a long time, "an insufferable time". "He thinks of me as a puppy," thought Mitya, gnash-ing his teeth. "That rotten prosecutor has gone, too, con-temptuous no doubt, it disgusts him to see me naked!"

Mitya imagined, however, that his clothes would be examined and returned to him. But what was his indignation when Nikolay Parfenovitch came back with quite different clothes, brought in behind him by a peasant.

"Here are clothes for you," he observed airily, seeming well

satisfied with the success of his mission. "Mr. Kalganov has
kindly provided these for this unusual emergency, as well as
a clean shirt. Luckily he had them all in his trunk. You can
keep your own socks and underclothes."

Mitya flew into a passion.

"I won't have other people's clothes!" he shouted menacingly, "give me my own!"

"It's impossible!"

"Give me my own. Damn Kalganov and his clothes, too!"

It was a long time before they could persuade him. But they
succeeded somehow in quieting him down. They impressed
upon him that, his clothes being stained with blood, must be
"included with the other material evidence", and that they
"had not even the right to let him have them now . . . taking
into consideration the possible outcome of the case". Mitya
at last understood this. He subsided into gloomy silence and
hurriedly dressed himself. He merely observed, as he put them
on, that the clothes were much better than his old ones, and
that he disliked "gaining by the change". It was, besides,
"ridiculously narrow. Am I to be dressed up like a fool . . .
for your amusement?"

They urged upon him again that he was exaggerating, that
Kalganov was only a little taller, so that only the trousers might
be a little too long. But the coat turned out to be really tight
in the shoulders.

"Damn it all! I can hardly button it," Mitya grumbled.
"Be so good as to tell Mr. Kalganov from me that I didn't ask
for his clothes, and it's not my doing that they've dressed me
up like a clown."

"He quite understands that, and is sorry . . . I mean, not
sorry to lend you his clothes, but sorry about all this business,"
mumbled Nikolay Parfenovitch.

"Confound his sorrow! Well, where now, or am I to go on
sitting here?"

He was asked to go back to the "other room". Mitya went
in, scowling with anger, and trying to avoid looking at anyone.
Dressed in another man's clothes he felt himself disgraced, even
in the eyes of the peasants, and of Trifon Borissovitch, whose
face appeared, for some reason, in the doorway, and vanished
immediately. "He's come to look at me dressed up," thought
Mitya. He sat down on the same chair as before. He had
an absurd nightmarish feeling, as though he were out of his
mind.

"Well, what now? Are you going to flog me? That's all that's left for you," he said, clenching his teeth and addressing the prosecutor. He would not turn to Nikolay Parfenovitch, as though he disdained to speak to him.

"He looked too closely at my socks, and turned them inside out on purpose to show everyone how dirty they were—the scoundrel!"

"Well, now we must proceed to the examination of witnesses," observed Nikolay Parfenovitch, as though in reply to Mitya's question.

"Yes," said the prosecutor thoughtfully, as though reflecting on something.

"We've done what we could in your interest, Dmitri Fyodorovitch," Nikolay Parfenovitch went on, "but having received from you such an uncompromising refusal to explain to us the source from which you obtained the money found upon you, we are, at the present moment . . ."

"What is the stone in your ring?" Mitya interrupted suddenly, as though awakening from a reverie. He pointed to one of the three large rings adorning Nikolay Parfenovitch's right hand.

"Ring?" repeated Nikolay Parfenovitch, with surprise.

"Yes, that one . . . on your middle finger, with the little veins in it, what stone is that?" Mitya persisted, like a peevish child.

"That's a smoky topaz," said Nikolay Parfenovitch, smiling. "Would you like to look at it? I'll take it off . . ."

"No, don't take it off," cried Mitya furiously, suddenly waking up, and angry with himself. "Don't take it off . . . there's no need. . . . Damn it. . . . Gentlemen, you've sullied my heart! Can you suppose that I would conceal it from you, if I really had killed my father, that I would shuffle, lie, and hide myself? No, that's not like Dmitri Karamazov, that he couldn't do, and if I were guilty, I swear I shouldn't have waited for your coming, or for the sunrise as I meant at first, but should have killed myself before this, without waiting for the dawn! I know that about myself now. I couldn't have learnt so much in twenty years as I've found out in this accursed night! . . . And should I have been like this on this night, and at this moment, sitting with you, could I have talked like this, could I have moved like this, could I have looked at you and at the world like this, if I had really been the murderer of my father, when the very thought of having accidentally killed

175

Grigory gave me no peace all night—not from fear—oh, not simply from fear of your punishment? The disgrace of it! And you expect me to be open with such scoffers as you, who see nothing and believe in nothing, blind moles and scoffers, and to tell you another nasty thing I've done, another disgrace, even if that would save me from your accusation! No, better Siberia! The man who opened the door to my father and went in at that door, he killed him, he robbed him. Who was he?—I'm racking my brains and can't think who. But I can tell you it was not Dmitri Karamazov, and that's all I can tell you, and that's enough, enough, leave me alone. . . . Exile me, punish me, but don't bother me any more. I'll say no more. Call your witnesses!"

Mitya uttered his sudden monologue as though he were determined to be absolutely silent for the future. The prosecutor watched him the whole time and only when he had ceased speaking, observed, as though it were the most ordinary thing, with the most frigid and composed air:

"Oh, about the open door of which you spoke just now, we may as well inform you, by the way, now, of a very interesting piece of evidence of the greatest importance both to you and to us, that has been given us by Grigory, the old man you wounded. On his recovery, he clearly and emphatically stated, in reply to our questions, that when, on coming out to the steps, and hearing a noise in the garden, he made up his mind to go into it through the little gate which stood open, before he noticed you running, as you have told us already, in the dark from the open window where you saw your father, he, Grigory, glanced to the left, and, while noticing the open window, observed at the same time, much nearer to him, the door, standing wide open—that door which you have stated to have been shut the whole time you were in the garden. I will not conceal from you that Grigory himself confidently affirms and bears witness that you must have run from that door, though, of course, he did not see you do so with his own eyes, since he only noticed you first some distance away in the garden, running towards the fence."

Mitya had leapt up from his chair half-way through this speech.

"Nonsense!" he yelled, in a sudden frenzy, "it's a bare-faced lie. He couldn't have seen the door open because it was shut. He's lying!"

"I consider it my duty to repeat that he is firm in his statement. He does not waver. He adheres to it. We've cross-examined him several times."

"Precisely. I have cross-examined him several times," Nikolay Parfenovitch confirmed warmly.

"It's false, false! It's either an attempt to slander me, or the hallucination of a madman," Mitya still shouted. "He's simply raving, from loss of blood, from the wound. He must have fancied it when he came to. . . . He's raving."

"Yes, but he noticed the open door, not when he came to after his injuries but before that, as soon as he went into the garden from the lodge."

"But it's false, it's false! It can't be so! He's slandering me from spite. . . . He couldn't have seen it . . . I didn't come from the door," gasped Mitya.

The prosecutor turned to Nikolay Parfenovitch and said to him impressively:

"Confront him with it."

"Do you recognise this object?"

Nikolay Parfenovitch laid upon the table a large and thick official envelope, on which three seals still remained intact. The envelope was empty, and slit open at one end. Mitya stared at it with open eyes.

"It . . . it must be that envelope of my father's, the envelope that contained the three thousand roubles . . . and if there's inscribed on it, allow me, 'For my little chicken' . . . yes—three thousand!" he shouted, "do you see, three thousand, do you see?"

"Of course, we see. But we didn't find the money in it. It was empty, and lying on the floor by the bed, behind the screen."

For some seconds Mitya stood as though thunderstruck.

"Gentlemen, it's Smerdyakov!" he shouted suddenly, at the top of his voice. "It's he who's murdered him! He's robbed him! No one else knew where the old man hid the envelope. It's Smerdyakov, that's clear, now!"

"But you, too, knew of the envelope and that it was under the pillow."

"I never knew it. I've never seen it. This is the first time I've looked at it. I'd only heard of it from Smerdyakov. . . . He was the only one who knew where the old man kept it hidden, I didn't know . . ." Mitya was completely breathless.

"But you told us yourself that the envelope was under your

177

deceased father's pillow. You especially stated that it was under the pillow, so you must have known it."

"We've got it written down," confirmed Nikolay Parfenovitch.

"Nonsense! It's absurd! I'd no idea it was under the pillow. And perhaps it wasn't under the pillow at all. . . . It was just a chance guess that it was under the pillow. What does Smerdyakov say? Have you asked him where it was? What does Smerdyakov say? that's the chief point. . . . And I went out of my way to tell lies against myself. . . . I told you without thinking that it was under the pillow, and now you . . . Oh, you know how one says the wrong thing, without meaning it. No one knew but Smerdyakov, only Smerdyakov, and no one else. . . . He didn't even tell me where it was! But it's his doing, his doing; there's no doubt about it, he murdered him, that's as clear as daylight now," Mitya exclaimed more and more frantically, repeating himself incoherently, and growing more and more exasperated and excited. "You must understand that, and arrest him at once. . . . He must have killed him while I was running away and while Grigory was unconscious, that's clear now. . . . He gave the signal and father opened to him . . . for no one but he knew the signal, and without the signal father would never have opened the door. . . ."

"But you're again forgetting the circumstance," the prosecutor observed, still speaking with the same restraint, though with a note of triumph, "that there was no need to give the signal if the door already stood open when you were there, while you were in the garden . . ."

"The door, the door!" muttered Mitya, and he stared speechless at the prosecutor. He sank back helpless in his chair. All were silent.

"Yes, the door! . . . It's a nightmare! God is against me!" he exclaimed, staring before him in complete stupefaction.

"Come, you see," the prosecutor went on, with dignity, "and you can judge for yourself, Dmitri Fyodorovitch. On the one hand we have the evidence of the open door from which you ran out, a fact which overwhelms you and us. On the other side your incomprehensible, persistent, and, so to speak, obdurate silence with regard to the source from which you obtained the money which was so suddenly seen in your hands, when only three hours earlier, on your own showing, you pledged your pistols for the sake of ten roubles! In view of all these facts.

judge for yourself. What are we to believe, and what can we depend upon? And don't accuse us of being 'frigid, cynical, scoffing people', who are incapable of believing in the generous impulses of your heart. . . . Try to enter into our position . . ."

Mitya was indescribably agitated. He turned pale.

"Very well!" he exclaimed suddenly, "I will tell you my secret. I'll tell you where I got the money! . . . I'll reveal my shame, that I may not have to blame myself or you hereafter."

"And believe me, Dmitri Fyodorovitch," put in Nikolay Parfenovitch, in a voice of almost pathetic delight, "that every sincere and complete confession on your part at this moment may, later on, have an immense influence in your favour, and may, indeed, moreover . . ."

But the prosecutor gave him a slight shove under the table, and he checked himself in time. Mitya, it is true, had not heard him.

CHAPTER VII

MITYA'S GREAT SECRET. RECEIVED WITH HISSES

"GENTLEMEN," he began, still in the same agitation, "I want to make a full confession: that money was *my own*."

The lawyers' faces lengthened. That was not at all what they expected.

"How do you mean?" faltered Nikolay Parfenovitch, "when at five o'clock on the same day, from your own confession . . ."

"Damn five o'clock on the same day and my own confession. That's nothing to do with it now! That money was my own, my own, that is, stolen by me . . . not mine, I mean, but stolen by me, and it was fifteen hundred roubles, and I had it on me all the time, all the time . . ."

"But where did you get it?"

"I took it off my neck, gentlemen, off this very neck . . . it was here, round my neck, sewn up in a rag, and I'd had it round my neck a long time, it's a month since I put it round my neck . . . to my shame and disgrace!"

"And from whom did you . . . appropriate it?"

"You mean, 'steal it'? Speak out plainly now. Yes, I consider that I practically stole it, but, if you prefer, I 'appropriated it'. I consider I stole it. And last night I stole it finally."

"Last night? But you said that it's a month since you . . . obtained it? . . ."

179

"Yes. But not from my father. Not from my father, don't be uneasy. I didn't steal it from my father, but from her. Let me tell you without interrupting. It's hard to do, you know. You see, a month ago, I was sent for by Katerina Ivanovna, formerly my betrothed. Do you know her?"

"Yes, of course."

"I know you know her. She's a noble creature, noblest of the noble. But she has hated me ever so long, oh, ever so long . . . and hated me with good reason, good reason!"

"Katerina Ivanovna!" Nikolay Parfenovitch exclaimed, with wonder. The prosecutor, too, stared.

"Oh, don't take her name in vain! I'm a scoundrel to bring her into it. Yes, I've seen that she hated me . . . a long while. . . . From the very first, even that evening at my lodging . . . but enough, enough. You're unworthy even to know of that. No need of that at all. . . . I need only tell you that she sent for me a month ago, gave me three thousand roubles to send off to her sister and another relation in Moscow (as though she couldn't have sent it off herself!), and I . . . it was just at that fatal moment in my life when I . . . Well, in fact, when I'd just come to love another, *her*, she's sitting down below now, Grushenka. I carried her off here to Mokroe then, and wasted here in two days half that damned three thousand, but the other half I kept on me. Well, I've kept that other half, that fifteen hundred like a locket round my neck, but yesterday I undid it, and spent it. What's left of it, eight hundred roubles, is in your hands now, Nikolay Parfenovitch. That's the change out of the fifteen hundred I had yesterday."

"Excuse me. How's that? Why, when you were here a month ago you spent three thousand, not fifteen hundred, everybody knows that."

"Who knows it? Who counted the money? Did I let any-one count it?"

"Why, you told everyone yourself that you'd spent exactly three thousand."

"It's true, I did. I told the whole town so, and the whole town said so. And here, at Mokroe, too, everyone reckoned it was three thousand. Yet I didn't spend three thousand but fifteen hundred. And the other fifteen hundred I sewed into a little bag. That's how it was, gentlemen. That's where I got that money yesterday . . ."

"This is almost miraculous," murmured Nikolay Parfeno-vitch.

"Allow me to inquire," observed the prosecutor at last, "have you informed anyone whatever of this circumstance before, I mean that you had fifteen hundred left about you a month ago?"

"I told no one."

"That's strange. Do you mean absolutely no one?"

"Absolutely no one. No one and nobody."

"What was your reason for this reticence? What was your motive for making such a secret of it? To be more precise: You have told us at last your secret, in your words, so 'disgraceful', though in reality—that is, of course, comparatively speaking—this action, that is, the appropriation of three thousand roubles belonging to someone else, and, of course, only for a time is, in my view at least, only an act of the greatest recklessness and not so disgraceful, when one takes into consideration your character. . . . Even admitting that it was an action in the highest degree discreditable, still, 'discreditable' is not 'disgraceful' . . . Many people have already guessed, during this last month, about the three thousand of Katerina Ivanovna's that you have spent, and I had heard the legend myself, apart from your confession. . . . Mihail Makarovitch, for instance, had heard it, too, so that, indeed, it was scarcely a legend but the gossip of the whole town. There are indications too, if I am not mistaken, that you confessed this yourself to someone, I mean that the money was Katerina Ivanovna's, and so it's extremely surprising to me that hitherto, that is, up to the present moment, you have made such an extraordinary secret of the fifteen hundred you say you put by, apparently connecting a feeling of positive horror with that secret. . . . It's not easy to believe that it could cost you such distress to confess such a secret. . . . You cried out, just now, that Siberia would be better than confessing it . . ."

The prosecutor ceased speaking. He was provoked. He did not conceal his vexation, which was almost anger, and gave vent to all his accumulated spleen, without choosing words, disconnectedly and incoherently.

"It's not the fifteen hundred that's the disgrace, but that I put it apart from the rest of the three thousand," said Mitya firmly.

"Why," smiled the prosecutor irritably. "What is there disgraceful, to your thinking, in your having set aside half of the three thousand you had discreditably, if you prefer, 'disgracefully', appropriated? Your taking the three thousand is more important than what you did with it. And by the way, why did you do that—why did you set apart that half, for what purpose, for what object did you do it? Can you explain that to us?"

"Oh, gentlemen, the purpose is the whole point!" cried Mitya. "I put it aside because I was vile, that is, because I was calculating, and to be calculating in such a case is vile . . . and that vileness has been going on a whole month."

"It's incomprehensible."

"I wonder at you. But I'll make it clearer. Perhaps it really is incomprehensible. You see, attend to what I say. I appropriate three thousand entrusted to my honour, I spend it on a spree, say I spend it all, and next morning I go to her and say, 'Katya, I've done wrong, I've squandered your three thousand'. Well, is that right? No, it's not right—it's dishonest and cowardly, I'm a beast, with no more self-control than a beast, that's so, isn't it? But still I'm not a thief! Not a downright thief, you'll admit! I squandered it, but I didn't steal it. Now a second, rather more favourable alternative: follow me carefully, or I may get confused again—my head's going round— and so, for the second alternative: I spend here only fifteen hundred out of the three thousand, that is, only half. Next day I go and take that half to her: 'Katya, take this fifteen hundred from me, I'm a low beast, and an untrustworthy scoundrel, for I've wasted half the money, and I shall waste this, too, so keep me from temptation!' Well, what of that alternative? I should be a beast and a scoundrel, and whatever you like; but not a thief, not altogether a thief, or I should not have brought back what was left but have kept that, too. She would see at once that since I brought back half, I should pay back what I'd spent, that I should never give up trying to, that I should work to get it and pay it back. So in that case I should be a scoundrel, but not a thief, you may say what you like, not a thief!"

"I admit that there is a certain distinction," said the prosecutor, with a cold smile. "But it's strange that you see such a vital difference."

"Yes, I see a vital difference! Every man may be a scoundrel, and perhaps every man is a scoundrel, but not everyone can be a thief, it takes an arch-scoundrel to be that. Oh, of course, I don't know how to make these fine distinctions . . . but a thief is lower than a scoundrel, that's my conviction. Listen, I carry the money about me a whole month, I may make up my mind to give it back to-morrow, and I'm a scoundrel no longer, but I cannot make up my mind, you see, though I'm making up my mind every day, and every day spurring myself on to do it, and yet for a whole month I can't bring myself to it, you see. Is that right to your thinking, is that right?''

"Certainly, that's not right, that I can quite understand, and that I don't dispute,'' answered the prosecutor, with reserve. "And let us give up all discussions of these subtleties and distinctions, and, if you will be so kind, get back to the point. And the point is, that you have still not told us, although we've asked you, why, in the first place, you halved the money, squandering one half and hiding the other? For what purpose exactly did you hide it, what did you mean to do with that fifteen hundred? I insist upon that question, Dmitri Fyodorovitch.''

"Yes, of course!'' cried Mitya, striking himself on the forehead; "forgive me, I'm worrying you, and am not explaining the chief point, or you'd understand in a minute, for it's just the motive of it that's the disgrace! You see, it was all to do with the old man, my dead father. He was always pestering Agrafena Alexandrovna, and I was jealous; I thought then that she was hesitating between me and him. So I kept thinking every day, suppose she were to make up her mind all of a sudden, suppose she were to leave off tormenting me, and were suddenly to say to me, 'I love you, not him; take me to the other end of the world'. And I'd only forty kopecks; how could I take her away, what could I do? Why, I'd be lost. You see, I didn't know her then, I didn't understand her, I thought she wanted money, and that she wouldn't forgive my poverty. And so I fiendishly counted out the half of that three thousand, sewed it up, calculating on it, sewed it up before I was drunk, and after I had sewn it up I went off to get drunk on the rest. Yes, that was base. Do you understand now?''

Both the lawyers laughed aloud.

"I should have called it sensible and moral on your part not to have squandered it all,'' chuckled Nikolay Parfenovitch, "for after all what does it amount to?''

"Why, that I stole it, that's what it amounts to! Oh, God, you horrify me by not understanding! Every day that I had that fifteen hundred sewn up round my neck, every day and every hour I said to myself, 'You're a thief! you're a thief!' Yes, that's why I've been so savage all this month, that's why I fought in the tavern, that's why I attacked my father, it was because I felt I was a thief. I couldn't make up my mind, I didn't dare even to tell Alyosha, my brother, about that fifteen hundred: I felt I was such a scoundrel and such a pickpocket. But, do you know, while I carried it I said to myself at the same time every hour: 'No, Dmitri Fyodorovitch, you may yet not be a thief.' Why? Because I might go next day and pay back that fifteen hundred to Katya. And only yesterday I made up my mind to tear my amulet off my neck, on my way from Fenya's to Perhotin. I hadn't been able till that moment to bring myself to it. And it was only when I tore it off that I became a downright thief, a thief and a dishonest man for the rest of my life. Why? Because, with that I destroyed, too, my dream of going to Katya and saying, 'I'm a scoundrel, but not a thief!' Do you understand now? Do you understand?''

"What was it made you decide to do it yesterday?" Nikolay Parfenovitch interrupted.

"Why? It's absurd to ask. Because I had condemned myself to die at five o'clock this morning, here, at dawn. I thought it made no difference whether I died a thief or a man of honour. But I see it's not so, it turns out that it does make a difference. Believe me, gentlemen, what has tortured me most during this night has not been the thought that I'd killed the old servant, and that I was in danger of Siberia just when my love was being rewarded, and Heaven was open to me again. Oh, that did torture me, but not in the same way; not so much as the damned consciousness that I had torn that damned money off my breast at last and spent it, and had become a downright thief! Oh, gentlemen, I tell you again, with a bleeding heart, I have learnt a great deal this night. I have learnt that it's not only impossible to live a scoundrel but impossible to die a scoundrel. . . . No, gentlemen, one must die honest . . .''

Mitya was pale. His face had a haggard and exhausted look, in spite of his being intensely excited.

"I am beginning to understand you, Dmitri Fyodorovitch,'' the prosecutor said slowly, in a soft and almost compassionate tone. "But all this, if you'll excuse my saying so, is a matter of nerves, in my opinion . . . your overwrought nerves, that's what it is. And why, for instance, should you not have saved yourself such misery for almost a month, by going and returning that fifteen hundred to the lady who had entrusted it to you? And why could you not have explained things to her, and in view of your position, which you describe as being so awful, why could you not have had recourse to the plan which would so naturally have occurred to one's mind, that is, after honourably confessing your errors to her, why could you not have asked her to lend you the sum needed for your expenses, which, with her generous heart, she would certainly not have refused you in your distress, especially if it had been with some guarantee, or even on the security you offered to the merchant Samsonov, and to Madame Hohlakov. I suppose you still regard that security as of value?"

Mitya suddenly crimsoned.

"Surely you don't think me such an out-and-out scoundrel as that? You can't be speaking in earnest?" he said, with indignation, looking the prosecutor straight in the face, and seeming unable to believe his ears.

"I assure you I'm in earnest. . . . Why do you imagine I'm not serious?" It was the prosecutor's turn to be surprised.

"Oh, how base that would have been! Gentlemen, do you know, you are torturing me! Let me tell you everything, so be it. I'll confess all my infernal wickedness, but to put you to shame, and you'll be surprised yourself at the depths of ignominy to which a medley of human passions can sink. You must know that I already had that plan myself, that plan you spoke of, just now, prosecutor! Yes, gentlemen, I, too, have had that thought in my mind all this current month, so that I was on the point of deciding to go to Katya—I was mean enough for that. But to go to her, to tell her of my treachery, and for that very treachery, to carry it out, for the expenses of that treachery, to beg for money from her, Katya (to beg, do you hear? to beg), and to go straight from her to run away with the other, the rival, who hated and insulted her—to think of it! You must be mad, prosecutor!"

"Mad I am not, but I did speak in haste, without thinking . . . of that feminine jealousy . . . if there could be jealousy in this case, as you assert . . . yes, perhaps there is something of the kind," said the prosecutor, smiling.

"But that would have been so infamous!" Mitya brought his fist down on the table fiercely. "That would have been filthy beyond everything! Yes, do you know that she might have given me that money, yes, and she would have given it, too; she'd have been certain to give it, to be avenged on me; she'd have given it to satisfy her vengeance, to show her contempt for me, for hers is an infernal nature, too, and she's a woman of great wrath. I'd have taken the money, too, oh, I should have taken it; I should have taken it, and then, for the rest of my life . . . oh, God! Forgive me, gentlemen, I'm making such an outcry because I've had that thought in my mind so lately, only the day before yesterday, that night when I was having all that bother with Lyagavy, and afterwards yesterday, all day yesterday, I remember, till that happened . . ."

"Till what happened?" put in Nikolay Parfenovitch inquisitively, but Mitya did not hear it.

"I have made you an awful confession," Mitya said gloomily in conclusion. "You must appreciate it, and what's more, you must respect it, for if not, if that leaves your souls untouched, then you've simply no respect for me, gentlemen, I tell you that, and I shall die of shame at having confessed it to men like you! Oh, I shall shoot myself! Yes, I see, I see already that you don't believe me. What! you want to write that down, too?" he cried in dismay.

"Yes, what you said just now," said Nikolay Parfenovitch, looking at him in surprise, "that is, that up to the last hour you were still contemplating going to Katerina Ivanovna to beg that sum from her. . . . I assure you, that's a very important piece of evidence for us, Dmitri Fyodorovitch, I mean for the whole case . . . and particularly for you, particularly important for you."

"Have mercy, gentlemen!" Mitya flung up his hands. 'Don't write that, anyway; have some shame. Here I've torn my heart asunder before you, and you seize the opportunity and are fingering the wounds in both halves. . . . Oh, my God!"

In despair he hid his face in his hands.

"Don't worry yourself so, Dmitri Fyodorovitch," observed the prosecutor, "everything that is written down will be read over to you afterwards, and what you don't agree to we'll alter as you like. But now I'll ask you one little question for the second time. Has no one, absolutely no one, heard from you of that money you sewed up? That, I must tell you, is almost impossible to believe."

"No one, no one, I told you so before, or you've not understood anything! Let me alone!"

"Very well, this matter is bound to be explained, and there's plenty of time for it, but meantime, consider; we have perhaps a dozen witnesses that you yourself spread it abroad, and even shouted almost everywhere about the three thousand you'd spent here; three thousand, not fifteen hundred. And now, too, when you got hold of the money you had yesterday, you gave many people to understand that you had brought three thousand with you."

"You've got not dozens but hundreds of witnesses, two hundred witnesses, two hundred have heard it, thousands have heard it!" cried Mitya.

"Well, you see, all bear witness to it. And the word *all* means something."

"It means nothing. I talked rot, and everyone began repeating it."

"But what need had you to 'talk rot', as you call it?"

"The devil knows. From bravado perhaps . . . at having wasted so much money. . . . To try and forget that money I had sewn up, perhaps . . . yes, that was why . . . damn it . . . how often will you ask me that question? Well, I told a fib, and that was the end of it, once I'd said it, I didn't care to correct it. What does a man tell lies for sometimes?"

"That's very difficult to decide, Dmitri Fyodorovitch, what makes a man tell lies," observed the prosecutor impressively. "Tell me, though, was that 'amulet', as you call it, on your neck a big thing?"

"No, not big."

"How big, for instance?"

"If you fold a hundred-rouble note in half, that would be the size."

"You'd better show us the remains of it. You must have them somewhere."

"Damnation, what nonsense! I don't know where they are."

"But excuse me: where and when did you take it off your neck? According to your own evidence you didn't go home."

"When I was going from Fenya's to Perhotin's on the way I tore it off my neck and took out the money."

"In the dark?"

"What should I want a light for? I did it with my fingers in one minute."

"Without scissors, in the street?"

"In the market-place, I think it was. Why scissors? It was an old rag. It was torn in a minute."

"Where did you put it afterwards?"

"I dropped it there."

"Where was it, exactly?"

"In the market-place, in the market-place! The devil knows whereabouts. What do you want to know for?"

"That's extremely important, Dmitri Fyodorovitch. It

187

would be material evidence in your favour. How it is you don't understand that? Who helped you to sew it up a month ago?"

"No one helped me. I did it myself."

"Can you sew?"

"A soldier has to know how to sew. No knowledge was needed to do that."

"Where did you get the material, that is, the rag in which you sewed the money?"

"Are you laughing at me?"

"Not at all. And we are in no mood for laughing, Dmitri Fyodorovitch."

"I don't know where I got the rag from—somewhere, I suppose."

"I should have thought you couldn't have forgotten it?"

"Upon my word, I don't remember. I might have torn a bit off my linen."

"That's very interesting. We might find in your lodgings to-morrow the shirt or whatever it is from which you tore the rag. What sort of rag was it, cloth or linen?"

"Goodness only knows what it was. Wait a bit. . . . I believe I didn't tear it off anything. It was a bit of calico. . . . I believe I sewed it up in a cap of my landlady's."

"In your landlady's cap?"

"Yes, I took it from her."

"How did you get it?"

"You see, I remember once taking a cap for a rag, perhaps to wipe my pen on. I took it without asking, because it was a worthless rag. I tore it up, and I took the notes and sewed them up in it. I believe it was in that very rag I sewed it. An old piece of calico, washed a thousand times."

"And you remember that for certain now?"

"I don't know whether for certain. I think it was in the cap. But hang it, what does it matter?"

"In that case your landlady will remember that the thing was lost?"

"No, she won't, she didn't miss it. It was an old rag, I tell you, an old rag not worth a farthing."

"And where did you get the needle and thread?"

"I'll stop now. I won't say any more. Enough of it!" said Mitya, losing his temper at last.

"It's strange that you should have so completely forgotten where you threw the pieces in the market-place."

"Give orders for the market-place to be swept to-morrow,

and perhaps you'll find it," said Mitya sneering. "Enough, gentlemen, enough!" he decided, in an exhausted voice. "I see you don't believe me! Not for a moment! It's my fault, not yours. I ought not to have been so ready. Why, why did I degrade myself by confessing my secret to you? It's a joke to you. I see that from your eyes. You led me on to it, prosecutor! Sing a hymn of triumph if you can. . . . Damn you, you torturers!"

He bent his head, and hid his face in his hands. The lawyers were silent. A minute later he raised his head and looked at them almost vacantly. His face expressed now complete, hopeless despair, and he sat mute and passive as though hardly conscious of what was happening. In the meantime they had to finish what they were about. They had immediately to begin examining the witnesses. It was by now eight o'clock in the morning. The lights had been extinguished long ago. Mihail Makarovitch and Kalganov, who had been continually in and out of the room all the while the interrogation had been going on, had now both gone out again. The lawyers, too, looked very tired. It was a wretched morning, the whole sky was overcast, and the rain streamed down in bucketfuls. Mitya gazed blankly out of the window.

"May I look out of window?" he asked Nikolay Parfenovitch, suddenly.

"Oh, as much as you like," the latter replied.

Mitya got up and went to the window. The rain lashed against the little greenish panes of the window. He could see the muddy road just below the window, and further away, in the rainy mist, a row of poor, black, dismal huts, looking even blacker and poorer in the rain. Mitya thought of "Phœbus the golden-haired", and how he had meant to shoot himself at his first ray. "Perhaps it would be even better on a morning like this," he thought with a smile, and suddenly, flinging his hand downwards, he turned to his "torturers".

"Gentlemen," he cried, "I see that I am lost! But she? Tell me about her, I beseech you. Surely she need not be ruined with me? She's innocent, you know, she was out of her mind when she cried last night, 'It's all my fault!' She's done nothing nothing! I've been grieving over her all night as I sat with you. . . . Can't you, won't you tell me what you are going to do with her now?"

"You can set your mind quite at rest on that score, Dmitri Fyodorovitch," the prosecutor answered at once, with evident alacrity. "We have, so far, no grounds for interfering with the lady in whom you are so interested. I trust that it may be the same in the later development of the case. . . . On the contrary, we'll do everything that lies in our power in that matter. Set your mind completely at rest."

"Gentlemen, I thank you. I knew that you were honest, straightforward people in spite of everything. You've taken a load off my heart. . . . Well, what are we to do now? I'm ready."

"Well, we ought to make haste. We must pass to examining the witnesses without delay. That must be done in your presence and therefore . . ."

"Shouldn't we have some tea first?" interposed Nikolay Parfenovitch, "I think we've deserved it!"

They decided that if tea were ready downstairs (Mihail Makarovitch had, no doubt, gone down to get some) they would have a glass and then "go on and on", putting off their proper breakfast until a more favourable opportunity. Tea really was ready below, and was soon brought up. Mitya at first refused the glass that Nikolay Parfenovitch politely offered him, but afterwards he asked for it himself and drank it greedily. He looked surprisingly exhausted. It might have been supposed from his herculean strength that one night of carousing, even accompanied by the most violent emotions, could have had little effect on him. But he felt that he could hardly hold his head up, and from time to time all the objects about him seemed heaving and dancing before his eyes. "A little more and I shall begin raving," he said to himself.

CHAPTER VIII

THE EVIDENCE OF THE WITNESSES. THE BABE

THE examination of the witnesses began. But we will not continue our story in such detail as before. And so we will not dwell on how Nikolay Parfenovitch impressed on every witness called that he must give his evidence in accordance with truth and conscience, and that he would afterwards have to repeat his evidence on oath, how every witness was called upon to sign the protocol of his evidence, and so on. We will only note that the point principally insisted upon in the examination was the question of the three thousand roubles, that is, was the sum spent here, at Mokroe, by Mitya on the first occasion, a month before, three thousand or fifteen hundred? And again had he spent three thousand or fifteen hundred yesterday? Alas, all the evidence given by everyone turned out to be against Mitya. There was not one in his favour, and some witnesses introduced new, almost crushing facts, in contradiction of his, Mitya's story.

The first witness examined was Trifon Borissovitch. He was not in the least abashed as he stood before the lawyers. He had, on the contrary, an air of stern and severe indignation with the accused, which gave him an appearance of truthfulness and personal dignity. He spoke little, and with reserve, waited to be questioned, answered precisely and deliberately. Firmly and unhesitatingly he bore witness that the sum spent a month before could not have been less than three thousand, that all the peasants about here would testify that they had heard the sum of three thousand mentioned by Dmitri Fyodorovitch himself. "What a lot of money he flung away on the gipsy girls alone. He wasted a thousand, I dare say, on them alone."

"I don't believe I gave them five hundred," was Mitya's gloomy comment on this. "It's a pity I didn't count the money at the time, but I was drunk . . ."

Mitya was sitting sideways with his back to the curtains. He listened gloomily, with a melancholy and exhausted air, as though he would say:

"Oh, say what you like. It makes no difference now."

"More than a thousand went on them, Dmitri Fyodorovitch," retorted Trifon Borissovitch firmly. "You flung it about at random and they picked it up. They were a rascally, thievish lot, horse-stealers, they've been driven away from here, or maybe they'd bear witness themselves how much they got from you. I saw the sum in your hands, myself—count it I didn't, you didn't let me, that's true enough—but by the look of it I should say it was far more than fifteen hundred . . . fifteen hundred indeed! We've seen money too. We can judge of amounts . . ."

As for the sum spent yesterday he asserted that Dmitri Fyodorovitch had told him, as soon as he arrived, that he had brought three thousand with him.

"Come now, is that so, Trifon Borissovitch?" replied Mitya. "Surely I didn't declare so positively that I'd brought three thousand?"

"You did say so, Dmitri Fyodorovitch. You said it before Andrey. Andrey himself is still here. Send for him. And in the hall, when you were treating the chorus, you shouted straight out that you would leave your sixth thousand here— that is, with what you spent before, we must understand. Stepan and Semyon heard it, and Pyotr Fomitch Kalganov, too, was standing beside you at the time. Maybe he'd remember it . . ."

The evidence as to the "sixth" thousand made an extraordinary impression on the two lawyers. They were delighted with this new method of reckoning, three and three made six, three thousand then and three now made six, that was clear.

They questioned all the peasants suggested by Trifon Borissovitch, Stepan and Semyon, the driver Andrey, and Kalganov. The peasants and the driver unhesitatingly confirmed Trifon Borissovitch's evidence. They noted down, with particular care, Andrey's account of the conversation he had had with Mitya on the road: " 'Where,' says he, 'am I, Dmitri Fyodorovitch, going, to Heaven or to Hell, and shall I be forgiven in the next world or not?' "

The psychological Ippolit Kirillovitch heard this with a subtle smile, and ended by recommending that these remarks as to where Dmitri Fyodorovitch would go should be "included in the case".

Kalganov, when called, came in reluctantly, frowning and ill-humoured, and he spoke to the lawyers as though he had never met them before in his life, though they were acquaintances whom he had been meeting every day for a long time past. He began by saying that "he knew nothing about it and didn't want to". But it appeared that he had heard of the "sixth" thousand, and he admitted that he had been standing close by at the moment. As far as he could see he "didn't know" how much money Mitya had in his hands. He affirmed that the Poles had cheated at cards. In reply to reiterated questions he stated that after the Poles had been turned out, Mitya's position with Agrafena Alexandrovna had certainly improved, and that she had said that she loved him. He spoke of Agrafena Alexandrovna with reserve and respect, as though she had been a lady of the best society, and did not once allow himself to call her Grushenka. In spite of the young man's obvious repugnance at giving evidence, Ippolit Kirillovitch examined him at great length, and only from him learnt all the details of what made up Mitya's "romance", so to say, on that night.

192

Mitya did not once pull Kalganov up. At last they let the young man go, and he left the room with unconcealed indignation.

The Poles, too, were examined. Though they had gone to bed in their room, they had not slept all night, and on the arrival of the police officers they hastily dressed and got ready, realising that they would certainly be sent for. They gave their evidence with dignity, though not without some uneasiness. The little Pole turned out to be a retired official of the twelfth class, who had served in Siberia as a veterinary surgeon. His name was Mussyalovitch. Pan Vrublevsky turned out to be an un-certificated dentist. Although Nikolay Parfenovitch asked them questions on entering the room they both addressed their answers to Mihail Makarovitch, who was standing on one side, taking him in their ignorance for the most important person and in command, and addressed him at every word as "Pan Colonel". Only after several reproofs from Mihail Makarovitch himself, they grasped that they had to address their answers only to Nikolay Parfenovitch. It turned out that they could speak Russian quite correctly except for their accent in some words. Of his relations with Grushenka, past and present, Pan Mussyalovitch spoke proudly and warmly, so that Mitya was roused at once and declared that he would not allow the "scoundrel" to speak like that in his presence! Pan Mussyalovitch at once called attention to the word "scoundrel", and begged that it should be put down in the protocol. Mitya fumed with rage.

"He's a scoundrel! A scoundrel! You can put that down. And put down, too, that, in spite of the protocol, I still declare that he's a scoundrel!" he cried.

Though Nikolay Parfenovitch did insert this in the protocol, he showed the most praiseworthy tact and management. After sternly reprimanding Mitya, he cut short all further inquiry into the romantic aspect of the case, and hastened to pass to what was essential. One piece of evidence given by the Poles roused special interest in the lawyers: that was how, in that very room, Mitya had tried to buy off Pan Mussyalovitch, and had offered him three thousand roubles to resign his claims, seven hundred roubles down and the remaining two thousand three hundred "to be paid next day in the town". He had sworn at the time that he had not the whole sum with him at Mokroe, but that his money was in the town. Mitya observed hotly that he had not said that he would be sure to pay him the remainder next day in the town. But Pan Vrublevsky confirmed the statement, and Mitya, after thinking for a moment, admitted, frowning, that it must have been as the Poles stated, that he had been excited at the time, and might indeed have said so.

The prosecutor positively pounced on this piece of evidence. It seemed to establish for the prosecution (and they did, in fact, base this deduction on it) that half, or a part of the three thousand that had come into Mitya's hands might really have been left somewhere hidden in the town, or even, perhaps, somewhere here, in Mokroe. This would explain the circumstance, so baffling for the prosecution, that only eight hundred roubles were to be found in Mitya's hands. This circumstance had been the one piece of evidence which, insignificant as it was, had hitherto told, to some extent, in Mitya's favour. Now this one piece of evidence in his favour had broken down. In answer to the prosecutor's inquiry, where he would have got the remaining two thousand three hundred roubles, since he himself had denied having more than fifteen hundred, Mitya confidently replied that he had meant to offer the "little chap" not money but a formal deed of conveyance of his rights to the village of Tchermashnya, those rights which he had already offered to Samsonov and Madame Hohlakov. The prosecutor positively smiled at the "innocence of this subterfuge".

"And you imagine he would have accepted such a deed as a substitute for two thousand three hundred roubles in cash?"

"He certainly would have accepted it," Mitya declared warmly. "Why, look here, he might have grabbed not two thousand but four or six for it. He would have put his lawyers, Poles and Jews, on to the job, and might have got, not three thousand but the whole property out of the old man."

The evidence of Pan Mussyalovitch was, of course, entered into the protocol in the fullest detail. Then they let the Poles go. The incident of the cheating at cards was hardly touched upon. Nikolay Parfenovitch was too well pleased with them, as it was, and did not want to worry them with trifles, moreover, it was nothing but a foolish, drunken quarrel over cards. There had been drinking and disorder enough, that night. . . . So the two hundred roubles remained in the pockets of the Poles.

Then old Maximov was summoned. He came in timidly, approached with little steps, looking very dishevelled and depressed. He had, all this time, taken refuge below with Grushenka, sitting dumbly beside her, and "now and then he'd begin blubbering over her and wiping his eyes with a

blue check handkerchief", as Mihail Makarovitch described
afterwards. So that she, herself, began trying to pacify and
comfort him. The old man at once confessed that he had done
wrong, that he had borrowed "ten roubles in my poverty",
from Dmitri Fyodorovitch's and that he was ready to pay it back.
To Nikolay Parfenovitch's direct question, had he noticed how
much money Dmitri Fyodorovitch held in his hand, as he must
have been able to see the sum better than anyone when he
took the note from him, Maximov, in the most positive manner,
declared that there was twenty thousand.

"Have you seen ever as much as twenty thousand before,
then?" inquired Nikolay Parfenovitch, with a smile.

"To be sure I have, not twenty, but seven, when my wife
mortgaged my little property. She'd only let me look at it from
a distance, boasting of it to me. It was a very thick bundle,
all rainbow-coloured notes. And Dmitri Fyodorovitch's were all
rainbow-coloured . . ."

He was not kept long. At last it was Grushenka's turn.
Nikolay Parfenovitch was obviously apprehensive of the effect
her appearance might have on Mitya, and he muttered a few
words of admonition to him, but Mitya bowed his head in
silence, giving him to understand "that he would not make a
scene". Mihail Makarovitch, himself, led Grushenka in. She
entered with a stern and gloomy face, that looked almost composed, and sat down quietly on the chair offered her by
Nikolay Parfenovitch. She was very pale, she seemed to be
cold, and wrapped herself closely in her magnificent black
shawl. She was suffering from a slight feverish chill—the first
symptom of the long illness which followed that night. Her
grave air, her direct earnest look and quiet manner made a very
favourable impression on everyone. Nikolay Parfenovitch was
even a little bit "fascinated". He admitted himself, when talking about it afterwards, that only then had he seen "how handsome the woman was", for, though he had seen her several
times before, he had always looked upon her as something of a
"provincial hetaira". "She has the manners of the best
society," he said enthusiastically, gossiping about her in a circle
of ladies. But this was received with positive indignation by
the ladies, who immediately called him a "naughty man", to
his great satisfaction.

As she entered the room, Grushenka only glanced for an
instant at Mitya, who looked at her uneasily. But her face
reassured him at once. After the first inevitable inquiries and

warnings, Nikolay Parfenovitch asked her, hesi ng a little, but preserving the most courteous manner, cn what terms she was with the retired lieutenant, Dmitri Fyodorovitch Karamazov. To this Grushenka firmly and quietly replied:

"He was an acquaintance. He came to see me as an acquaintance during the last month." To further inquisitive questions she answered plainly and with complete frankness that, though "at times' she had thought him attractive, she had not loved him, but had won his heart as well as his old father's "in my nasty spite", that she had seen that Mitya was very jealous of Fyodor Pavlovitch and everyone else; but that had only amused her. She had never meant to go to Fyodor Pavlovitch, she had simply been laughing at him. "I had no thoughts for either of them all this last month. I was expecting another man who had wronged me. But I think," she said in conclusion, "that there's no need for you to inquire about that, nor for me to answer you, for that's my own affair."

Nikolay Parfenovitch immediately acted upon this hint. He again dismissed the "romantic" aspect of the case and passed to the serious one, that is, to the question of most importance, concerning the three thousand roubles. Grushenka confirmed the statement that three thousand roubles had certainly been spent on the first carousal at Mokroe, and though she had not counted the money herself, she had heard that it was three thousand from Dmitri Fyodorovitch's own lips.

"Did he tell you that alone, or before someone else, or did you only hear him speak of it to others in your presence?" the prosecutor inquired immediately.

To which Grushenka replied that she had heard him say so before other people, and had heard him say so when they were alone.

"Did he say it to you alone once or several times?" inquired the prosecutor, and learned that he had told Grushenka so several times.

Ippolit Kirillovitch was very well satisfied with this piece of evidence. Further examination elicited that Grushenka knew, too, where that money had come from, and that Dmitri Fyodorovitch had got it from Katerina Ivanovna.

"And did you never, once, hear that the money spent a month ago was not three thousand, but less, and that Dmitri Fyodorovitch had saved half that sum for his own use?"

"No, I never heard that," answered Grushenka.

It was explained further that Mitya had, on the contrary, often told her that he hadn't a farthing.

"He was always expecting to get some from his father," said Grushenka in conclusion.

"Did he never say before you . . . casually, or in a moment of irritation," Nikolay Parfenovitch put in suddenly, "that he intended to make an attempt on his father's life?"

"Ach, he did say so," sighed Grushenka.

"Once or several times?"

"He mentioned it several times, always in anger."

"And did you believe he would do it?"

"No, I never believed it," she answered firmly. "I had faith in his noble heart."

"Gentlemen, allow me," cried Mitya suddenly, "allow me to say one word to Agrafena Alexandrovna, in your presence."

"You can speak," Nikolay Parfenovitch assented.

"Agrafena Alexandrovna!" Mitya got up from his chair, "have faith in God and in me. I am not guilty of my father's murder!"

Having uttered these words Mitya sat down again on his chair. Grushenka stood up and crossed herself devoutly before the ikon.

"Thanks be to Thee, O Lord," she said, in a voice thrilled with emotion, and still standing, she turned to Nikolay Parfenovitch and added:

"As he has spoken now, believe it! I know him. He'll say anything as a joke or from obstinacy, but he'll never deceive you against his conscience. He's telling the whole truth, you may believe it."

"Thanks, Agrafena Alexandrovna, you've given me fresh courage," Mitya responded in a quivering voice.

As to the money spent the previous day, she declared that she did not know what sum it was, but had heard him tell several people that he had three thousand with him. And to the question where he got the money she said that he had told her that he had "stolen" it from Katerina Ivanovna, and that she had replied to that that he hadn't stolen it, and that he must pay the money back the next day. On the prosecutor's asking her emphatically whether the money he said he had stolen from Katerina Ivanovna was what he had spent yesterday, or what he had squandered here a month ago, she declared that he meant the money spent a month ago, and that that was how she understood him.

Grushenka was at last released, and Nikolay Parfenovitch informed her impulsively that she might at once return to the town and that if he could be of any assistance to her, with horses, for example, or if she would care for an escort he . . . would be . . .

"I thank you sincerely," said Grushenka, bowing to him, "I'm going with this old gentleman, I am driving him back to town with me, and meanwhile, if you'll allow me, I'll wait below to hear what you decide about Dmitri Fyodorovitch."

She went out. Mitya was calm, and even looked more cheerful, but only for a moment. He felt more and more oppressed by a strange physical weakness. His eyes were closing with fatigue. The examination of the witnesses was, at last, over. They proceeded to a final revision of the protocol. Mitya got up, moved from his chair to the corner by the curtain, lay down on a large chest covered with a rug, and instantly fell asleep.

He had a strange dream, utterly out of keeping with the place and the time.

He was driving somewhere in the steppes, where he had been stationed long ago, and a peasant was driving him in a cart with a pair of horses, through snow and sleet. He was cold, it was early in November, and the snow was falling in big wet flakes, melting as soon as it touched the earth. And the peasant drove him smartly, he had a fair, long beard. He was not an old man, somewhere about fifty, and he had on a grey peasant's smock. Not far off was a village, he could see the black huts, and half the huts were burnt down, there were only the charred beams sticking up. And as they drove in, there were peasant women drawn up along the road, a lot of women, a whole row, all thin and wan, with their faces a sort of brownish colour, especially one at the edge, a tall, bony woman, who looked forty but might have been only twenty, with a long thin face. And in her arms was a little baby crying. And her breasts seemed so dried up that there was not a drop of milk in them. And the child cried and cried, and held out its little bare arms, with its little fists blue from cold.

"Why are they crying? Why are they crying?" Mitya asked, as they dashed gaily by.

"It's the babe," answered the driver, "the babe's weeping."

And Mitya was struck by his saying, in his peasant way, "the babe", and he liked the peasant's calling it a "babe". There seemed more pity in it.

"But why is it weeping?" Mitya persisted stupidly, "why are its little arms bare? Why don't they wrap it up?"

"The babe's cold, its little clothes are frozen and don't warm it."

"But why is it? Why?" foolish Mitya still persisted.

"Why, they're poor people, burnt out. They've no bread. They're begging because they've been burnt out."

"No, no," Mitya, as it were, still did not understand. "Tell me why it is those poor mothers stand there. Why are people poor? Why is the babe poor? Why is the steppe barren? Why don't they hug each other and kiss? Why don't they sing songs of joy? Why are they so dark from black misery? Why don't they feed the babe?"

And he felt that, though his questions were unreasonable and senseless, yet he wanted to ask just that, and he had to ask it just in that way. And he felt that a passion of pity, such as he had never known before, was rising in his heart, that he wanted to cry, that he wanted to do something for them all, so that the babe should weep no more, so that the dark-faced, dried-up mother should not weep, that no one should shed tears again from that moment, and he wanted to do it at once, at once, regardless of all obstacles, with all the recklessness of the Karamazovs.

"And I'm coming with you. I won't leave you now for the rest of my life, I'm coming with you," he heard close beside him Grushenka's tender voice, thrilling with emotion. And his heart glowed, and he struggled forward towards the light, and he longed to live, to live, to go on and on, towards the new, beckoning light, and to hasten, hasten, now, at once!

"What! Where?" he exclaimed opening his eyes, and sitting up on the chest, as though he had revived from a swoon, smiling brightly. Nikolay Parfenovitch was standing over him, suggesting that he should hear the protocol read aloud and sign it. Mitya guessed that he had been asleep an hour or more, but he did not hear Nikolay Parfenovitch. He was suddenly struck by the fact that there was a pillow under his head, which hadn't been there when he had leant back, exhausted, on the chest.

"Who put that pillow under my head? Who was so kind?" he cried, with a sort of ecstatic gratitude, and tears in his voice, as though some great kindness had been shown him.

He never found out who this kind man was, perhaps one of the peasant witnesses, or Nikolay Parfenovitch's little secretary had compassionately thought to put a pillow under his head, but his whole soul was quivering with tears. He went to the table and said that he would sign whatever they liked.

"I've had a good dream, gentlemen," he said in a strange voice, with a new light, as of joy, in his face.

CHAPTER IX

THEY CARRY MITYA AWAY

WHEN the protocol had been signed, Nikolay Parfenovitch turned solemnly to the prisoner and read him the "Committal", setting forth that in such a year, on such a day, in such a place, the investigating lawyer of such-and-such a district court, having examined so-and-so (to wit, Mitya) accused of this and of that (all charges were carefully written out) and having considered that the accused, not pleading guilty to the charge made against him had brought forward nothing in his defence, while the witnesses, so-and-so, and so-and-so, and the circumstances such-and-such testify against him, acting in accordance with such-and-such articles of the Statute Book, and so on, has ruled, that, in order to preclude such-and-such (Mitya) from all means of evading pursuit and judgment he be detained in such-and-such a prison, where he hereby notifies to the accused and communicates a copy of this same "Committal" to the deputy prosecutor, and so on, and so on.

In brief, Mitya was informed that he was, from that moment, a prisoner, and that he would be driven at once to the town, and there shut up in a very unpleasant place. Mitya listened attentively, and only shrugged his shoulders.

"Well, gentlemen, I don't blame you. I'm ready. . . . I understand that there's nothing else for you to do."

Nikolay Parfenovitch informed him gently that he would be escorted at once by the rural police officer, Mavriky Mavrikyevitch, who happened to be on the spot. . . .

"Stay," Mitya interrupted, suddenly, and impelled by uncontrollable feeling he pronounced, addressing all in the room.

"Gentlemen, we're all cruel, we're all monsters, we all make men weep, and mothers, and babes at the breast, but of all, let it be settled here, now, of all I am the lowest reptile! I've sworn to amend, and every day I've done the same filthy things. I understand now that such men as I need a blow, a blow of destiny to catch them as with a noose, and bind them by a force from without. Never, never should I have risen of myself! But the thunderbolt has fallen. I accept the torture of accusation, and my public shame, I want to suffer and by suffering I shall be purified. Perhaps I shall be purified, gentlemen? But listen, for the last time, I am not guilty of my father's blood. I accept my punishment, not because I killed him but because I meant to kill him, and perhaps I really might have killed him. Still, I mean to fight it out with you, I warn you of that. I'll fight it out with you to the end, and then God will decide. Good-bye, gentlemen, don't be vexed with me for having shouted at you during the examination. Oh, I was still such a fool then. . . . In another minute I shall be a prisoner, but now, for the last time, as a free man, Dmitri Karamazov offers you his hand. Saying good-bye to you, I say it to all men."

His voice quivered and he streched out his hand, but Nikolay Parfenovitch, who happened to stand nearest to him, with a sudden, almost nervous movement, hid his hands behind his back. Mitya instantly noticed this, and started. He let his outstretched hand fall at once.

"The preliminary inquiry is not yet over," Nikolay Parfenovitch faltered, somewhat embarrassed. "We will continue it in the town, and I, for my part, of course, am ready to wish you all success . . . in your defence. . . . As a matter of fact, Dmitri Fyodorovitch, I've always been disposed to regard you as, so to speak, more unfortunate than guilty. All of us here, if I may make bold to speak for all, we are all ready to recognise that you are, at bottom, a young man of honour, but, alas, one who has been carried away by certain passions to a somewhat excessive degree . . ."

Nikolay Parfenovitch's little figure was positively majestic by the time he had finished speaking. It struck Mitya that in another minute this "boy" would take his arm, lead him to another corner, and renew their conversation about "girls". But many quite irrelevant and inappropriate thoughts sometimes occur even to a prisoner when he is being led out to execution.

"Gentlemen, you are good, you are humane, may I see *her* to say 'good-bye' for the last time?" asked Mitya.

"Certainly, but considering . . . in fact, now it's impossible except in the presence of . . ."

"Oh well, if it must be so, it must!"

201

Grushenka was brought in, but the farewell was brief and of few words and did not at all satisfy Nikolay Parfenovitch. Grushenka made a deep bow to Mitya.

"I have told you I am yours, and I will be yours. I will follow you for ever, wherever they may send you. Farewell; you are guiltless, though you've been your own undoing."

Her lips quivered, tears flowed from her eyes.

"Forgive me, Grusha, for my love, for ruining you, too, with my love."

Mitya would have said something more, but he broke off and went out. He was at once surrounded by men who kept a constant watch on him. At the bottom of the steps to which he had driven up with such a dash the day before with Andrey's three horses, two carts stood in readiness. Mavriky Mavrikyevitch, a sturdy, thick-set man with a wrinkled face, was annoyed about something, some sudden irregularity. He was shouting angrily. He asked Mitya to get into the cart with somewhat excessive surliness.

"When I stood him drinks in the tavern, the man had quite a different face," thought Mitya, as he got in. At the gates there was a crowd of people, peasants, women and drivers. Trifon Borissovitch came down the steps too. All stared at Mitya.

"Forgive me at parting, good people!" Mitya shouted suddenly from the cart.

"Forgive us too!" he heard two or three voices.

"Good-bye to you, too, Trifon Borissovitch!"

But Trifon Borissovitch did not even turn round. He was, perhaps, too busy. He, too, was shouting and fussing about something. It appeared that everything was not yet ready in the second cart, in which two constables were to accompany Mavriky Mavrikyevitch. The peasant who had been ordered to drive the second cart was pulling on his smock, stoutly maintaining that it was not his turn to go, but Akim's. But Akim was not to be seen. They ran to look for him. The peasant persisted and besought them to wait.

"You see what our peasants are, Mavriky Mavrikyevitch. They've no shame!" exclaimed Trifon Borissovitch. "Akim gave you twenty-five kopecks the day before yesterday. You've drunk it all and now you cry out. I'm simply surprised at your good-nature with our low peasants, Mavriky Mavrikyevitch, that's all I can say."

"But what do we want a second cart for?" Mitya put in.

"Let's start with the one, Mavriky Mavrikyevitch. I won't be unruly, I won't run away from you, old fellow. What do we want an escort for?"

"I'll trouble you, sir, to learn how to speak to me if you've never been taught. I'm not 'old fellow' to you, and you can keep your advice for another time!" Mavriky Mavrikyevitch snapped out savagely, as though glad to vent his wrath.

Mitya was reduced to silence. He flushed all over. A moment later he felt suddenly very cold. The rain had ceased, but the dull sky was still overcast with clouds, and a keen wind was blowing straight in his face.

"I've taken a chill," thought Mitya, twitching his shoulders.

At last Mavriky Mavrikyevitch, too, got into the cart, sat down heavily, and, as though without noticing it, squeezed Mitya into the corner. It is true that he was out of humour and greatly disliked the task that had been laid upon him.

"Good-bye, Trifon Borissovitch!" Mitya shouted again, and felt himself that he had not called out this time from good-nature but involuntarily, from resentment.

But Trifon Borissovitch stood proudly, with both hands behind his back, and staring straight at Mitya with a stern and angry face, he made no reply.

"Good-bye, Dmitri Fyodorovitch, good-bye!" he heard all at once the voice of Kalganov, who had suddenly darted out. Running up to the cart he held out his hand to Mitya. He had no cap on.

Mitya had time to seize and press his hand.

"Good-bye, dear fellow! I shan't forget your generosity," he cried warmly.

But the cart moved and their hands parted. The bell began ringing and Mitya was driven off.

Kalganov ran back, sat down in a corner, bent his head, hid his face in his hands, and burst out crying. For a long while he sat like that, crying as though he were a little boy instead of a young man of twenty. Oh, he believed almost without doubt in Mitya's guilt.

"What are these people? What can men be after this?" he exclaimed incoherently, in bitter despondency, almost despair. At that moment he had no desire to live.

"Is it worth it? Is it worth it?" exclaimed the boy in his grief.

PART IV

BOOK X: THE BOYS

CHAPTER I

KOLYA KRASSOTKIN

IT was the beginning of November. There had been a hard frost, eleven degrees Réaumur, without snow, but a little dry snow had fallen on the frozen ground during the night, and a keen dry wind was lifting and blowing it along the dreary streets of our town, especially about the market-place. It was a dull morning, but the snow had ceased.

Not far from the market-place, close to Plotnikov's shop, there stood a small house, very clean both without and within. It belonged to Madame Krassotkin, the widow of a former provincial secretary, who had been dead for fourteen years. His widow, still a nice-looking woman of thirty-two, was living in her neat little house on her private means. She lived in respectable seclusion; she was of a soft but fairly cheerful disposition. She was about eighteen at the time of her husband's death; she had been married only a year and had just borne him a son. From the day of his death she had devoted herself heart and soul to the bringing up of her precious treasure, her boy Kolya. Though she had loved him passionately those fourteen years, he had caused her far more suffering than happiness. She had been trembling and fainting with terror almost every day, afraid he would fall ill, would catch cold, do something naughty, climb on a chair and fall off it, and so on and so on. When Kolya began going to school, the mother devoted herself to studying all the sciences with him so as to help him, and go through his lessons with him. She hastened to make the acquaintance of the teachers and their wives, even made up to Kolya's schoolfellows, and fawned upon them in the hope of thus saving Kolya from being teased, laughed at, or beaten by them. She went so far that the boys actually began to mock at him on her account, and taunt him with being a "mother's darling".

But the boy could take his own part. He was a resolute

boy, "tremendously strong", as was rumoured in his class, and soon proved to be the fact; he was agile, strong-willed, and of an audacious and enterprising temper. He was good at lessons, and there was a rumour in the school that he could beat the teacher, Dardanelov, at arithmetic and universal history. Though he looked down upon everyone, he was a good comrade and not supercilious. He accepted his schoolfellows' respect as his due, but was friendly with them. Above all, he knew where to draw the line. He could restrain himself on occasion, and in his relations with the teachers he never overstepped that last mystic limit beyond which a prank becomes an unpardonable breach of discipline. But he was as fond of mischief on every possible occasion as the smallest boy in the school, and not so much for the sake of mischief as for creating a sensation, inventing something, doing something effective and conspicuous. He was extremely vain. He knew how to make even his mother give way to him; he was almost despotic in his control of her. She gave way to him, oh, she had given way to him for years. The one thought unendurable to her was that her boy had no great love for her. She was always fancying that Kolya was "unfeeling" to her, and at times, dissolving into hysterical tears, she used to reproach him with his coldness. The boy disliked this, and the more demonstrations of feeling were demanded of him the more he seemed intentionally to avoid them. Yet it was not intentional on his part but instinctive—it was his character. His mother was mistaken; he was very fond of her. He only disliked "sheepish sentimentality", as he expressed it in his schoolboy language.

There was a book-case in the house containing a few books that had been his father's. Kolya was fond of reading, and had read several of them by himself. His mother did not mind that and only wondered sometimes at seeing the boy stand for hours by the book-case poring over a book instead of going to play. And in that way Kolya read some things unsuitable for his age.

Though the boy, as a rule, knew where to draw the line in his mischief, he had of late begun to play pranks that caused his mother serious alarm. It is true there was nothing vicious in what he did, but a wild mad recklessness.

It happened that July, during the summer holidays, that the mother and son went to another district, forty-five miles away, to spend a week with a distant relation, whose husband was an official at the railway station (the very station, the nearest

one to our town, from which a month later Ivan Fyodorovitch
Karamazov set off for Moscow). There Kolya began by carefully
investigating every detail connected with the railway, knowing
that he could impress his schoolfellows when he got home with
his newly acquired knowledge. But there happened to be some
other boys in the place with whom he soon made friends. Some
of them were living at the station, others in the neighbourhood;
there were six or seven of them, all between twelve and fifteen,
and two of them came from our town. The boys played together,
and on the fourth or fifth day of Kolya's stay at the station, a
mad bet was made by the foolish boys. Kolya, who was almost
the youngest of the party and rather looked down upon by the
others in consequence, was moved by vanity or by reckless
bravado to bet them two roubles that he would lie down between
the rails at night when the eleven o'clock train was due, and
would lie there without moving while the train rolled over him
at full speed. It is true they made a preliminary investigation,
from which it appeared that it was possible to lie so flat between
the rails that the train could pass over without touching, but
to lie there was no joke! Kolya maintained stoutly that he
would. At first they laughed at him, called him a little liar, a
braggart, but that only egged him on. What piqued him most
was that these boys of fifteen turned up their noses at him too
superciliously, and were at first disposed to treat him as "a
small boy", not fit to associate with them, and that was an
unendurable insult.

And so it was resolved to go in the evening, half a mile from
the station, so that the train might have time to get up full speed
after leaving the station. The boys assembled. It was a pitch-
dark night without a moon. At the time fixed, Kolya lay down
between the rails. The five others who had taken the bet waited
among the bushes below the embankment, their hearts beating
with suspense, which was followed by alarm and remorse. At
last they heard in the distance the rumble of the train leaving
the station. Two red lights gleamed out of the darkness; the
monster roared as it approached.

"Run, run away from the rails," the boys cried to Kolya
from the bushes, breathless with terror. But it was too late: the
train darted up and flew past. The boys rushed to Kolya. He
lay without moving. They began pulling at him, lifting him up.
He suddenly got up and walked away without a word. Then he
explained that he had lain there as though he were insensible to
frighten them, but the fact was that he really had lost conscious-

206

ness, as he confessed long after to his mother. In this way his reputation as "a desperate character" was established for ever. He returned home to the station as white as a sheet. Next day he had a slight attack of nervous fever, but he was in high spirits and well pleased with himself. The incident did not become known at once, but when they came back to the town it penetrated to the school and even reached the ears of the masters. But then Kolya's mother hastened to entreat the masters on her boy's behalf, and in the end Dardanelov, a respected and influential teacher, exerted himself in his favour, and the affair was ignored.

Dardanelov was a middle-aged bachelor, who had been passionately in love with Madame Krassotkin for many years past, and had once already, about a year previously, ventured, trembling with fear and the delicacy of his sentiments, to offer her most respectfully his hand in marriage. But she refused him resolutely, feeling that to accept him would be an act of treachery to her son, though Dardanelov had, to judge from certain mysterious symptoms, reason for believing that he was not an object of aversion to the charming but too chaste and tender-hearted widow. Kolya's mad prank seemed to have broken the ice, and Dardanelov was rewarded for his inter-cession by a suggestion of hope. The suggestion, it is true, was a faint one, but then Dardanelov was such a paragon of purity and delicacy that it was enough for the time being to make him perfectly happy. He was fond of the boy, though he would have felt it beneath him to try to win him over, and was severe and strict with him in class. Kolya, too, kept him at a respectful distance. He learned his lessons perfectly; he was second in his class, was reserved with Dardanelov, and the whole class firmly believed that Kolya was so good at universal history that he could "beat" even Dardanelov. Kolya did in-deed ask him the question, "Who founded Troy?" to which Dardanelov had made a very vague reply, referring to the move-ments and migrations of races, to the remoteness of the period, to the mythical legends. But the question, "Who had founded Troy?" that is, what individuals, he could not answer, and even for some reason regarded the question as idle and frivolous. But the boys remained convinced that Dardanelov did not know who founded Troy. Kolya had read of the founders of Troy in Smaragdov, whose history was among the books in his father's book-case. In the end all the boys became interested in the question, who it was that had founded Troy, but Krassotkin would not tell his secret, and his reputation for knowledge remained unshaken.

After the incident on the railway a certain change came over Kolya's attitude to his mother. When Anna Fyodorovna (Madame Krassotkin) heard of her son's exploit, she almost went out of her mind with horror. She had such terrible attacks of hysterics, lasting with intervals for several days that Kolya, seriously alarmed at last, promised on his honour that such pranks should never be repeated. He swore on his knees before the holy image, and swore by the memory of his father, at Madame Krassotkin's instance, and the "manly" Kolya burst into tears like a boy of six. And all that day the mother and son were constantly rushing into each other's arms sobbing. Next day Kolya woke up as "unfeeling" as before, but he had become more silent, more modest, sterner, and more thoughtful.

Six weeks later, it is true, he got into another scrape, which even brought his name to the ears of our Justice of the Peace, but it was a scrape of quite another kind, amusing, foolish, and he did not, as it turned out, take the leading part in it but was only implicated in it. But of this later. His mother still fretted and trembled, but the more uneasy she became, the greater were the hopes of Dardanelov. It must be noted that Kolya understood and divined what was in Dardanelov's heart and, of course, despised him profoundly for his "feelings"; he had in the past been so tactless as to show this contempt before his mother, hinting vaguely that he knew what Dardanelov was after. But from the time of the railway incident his behaviour in this respect also was changed; he did not allow himself the remotest allusion to the subject and began to speak more respectfully of Dardanelov before his mother, which the sensitive woman at once appreciated with boundless gratitude. But at the slightest mention of Dardanelov by a visitor in Kolya's presence, she would flush as pink as a rose. At such moments Kolya would either stare out of the window scowling, or would investigate the state of his boots, or would shout angrily for "Perezvon", the big, shaggy, mangy dog which he had picked up a month before, brought home, and kept for some reason secretly indoors, not showing him to any of his schoolfellows. He bullied him frightfully, teaching him all sorts of tricks, so that the poor dog howled for him whenever he was absent at school, and when he came in, whined with delight, rushed about as if he were crazy, begged, lay down on the ground pretending to be dead, and so on; in fact, showed all the tricks he had taught him, not at the word of command but simply from the zeal of his excited and grateful heart.

I have forgotten, by the way, to mention that Kolya Krassotkin was the boy stabbed with a penknife by the boy already known to the reader as the son of Captain Snegiryov. Ilusha had been defending his father when the schoolboys jeered at him, shouting the nickname "wisp of tow".

CHAPTER II

CHILDREN

AND so on that frosty, snowy, and windy day in November, Kolya Krassotkin was sitting at home. It was Sunday and there was no school. It had just struck eleven, and he particularly wanted to go out "on very urgent business", but he was left alone in charge of the house, for it so happened that all its elder inmates were absent owing to a sudden and singular event. Madame Krassotkin had let two little rooms, separated from the rest of the house by a passage, to a doctor's wife with her two small children. This lady was the same age as Anna Fyodorovna, and a great friend of hers. Her husband, the doctor, had taken his departure twelve months before, going first to Orenburg and then to Tashkend, and for the last six months she had not heard a word from him. Had it not been for her friendship with Madame Krassotkin, which was some consolation to the forsaken lady, she would certainly have completely dissolved away in tears. And now, to add to her misfortunes, Katerina, her only servant, was suddenly moved the evening before to announce, to her mistress's amazement, that she proposed to bring a child into the world before morning. It seemed almost miraculous to everyone that no one had noticed the probability of it before. The astounded doctor's wife decided to move Katerina while there was still time to an establishment in the town kept by a midwife for such emergencies. As she set great store by her servant, she promptly carried out this plan and remained there looking after her. By the morning all Madame Krassotkin's friendly sympathy and energy were called upon to render assistance and appeal to someone for help in the case.

So both the ladies were absent from home, the Krassotkins' servant, Agafya, had gone out to the market, and Kolya was thus left for a time to protect and look after "the kids", that is, the son and daughter of the doctor's wife, who were left alone. Kolya was not afraid of taking care of the house; besides, he had Perezvon, who had been told to lie flat, without moving, under the bench in the hall. Every time Kolya, walking to and fro through the rooms, came into the hall, the dog shook his head and gave two loud and insinuating taps on the floor with his tail, but alas! the whistle did not sound to release him. Kolya looked sternly at the luckless dog, who relapsed again into obedient rigidity. The one thing that troubled Kolya was "the kids". He looked, of course, with the utmost scorn on Katerina's unexpected adventure, but he was very fond of the bereaved "kiddies", and had already taken them a picture-book. Nastya, the elder, a girl of eight, could read, and Kostya, the boy, aged seven, was very fond of being read to by her. Krassotkin could, of course, have provided more diverting entertainment for them. He could have made them stand side by side and played soldiers with them, or send them hiding all over the house. He had done so more than once before and was not above doing it, so much so that a report once spread at school that Krassotkin played horses with the little lodgers at home, prancing with his head on one side like a trace-horse. But Krassotkin haughtily parried this thrust, pointing out that to play horses with boys of one's own age, boys of thirteen, would certainly be disgraceful "at this date", but that he did it for the sake of "the kids" because he liked them, and no one had a right to call him to account for his feelings. The two "kids" adored him.

But on this occasion he was in no mood for games. He had very important business of his own before him, something almost mysterious. Meanwhile time was passing and Agafya, with whom he could have left the children, would not come back from market. He had several times already crossed the passage, opened the door of the lodgers' room and looked anxiously at the kids who were sitting over the book, as he had bidden them. Every time he opened the door they grinned at him, hoping he would come in and would do something delightful and amusing. But Kolya was bothered and did not go in.

At last it struck eleven and he made up his mind, once for all, that if that "damned" Agafya did not come back within ten minutes he should go out without waiting for her, making the kids "promise", of course, to be brave when he was away, not to be naughty, not to cry from fright. With this idea he put on

210

his wadded winter overcoat with its catskin fur collar, slung his satchel round his shoulder, and, regardless of his mother's constantly reiterated entreaties that he should always put on galoshes in such cold weather, he looked at them contemptuously as he crossed the hall and went out with only his boots on. Perezvon, seeing him in his outdoor clothes, began tapping vigorously on the floor with his tail, nervously. Twitching all over, he even uttered a plaintive whine. But Kolya, seeing his dog's passionate excitement, decided that it was a breach of discipline, kept him for another minute under the bench, and only when he had opened the door into the passage he whistled for him. The dog leapt up like a mad creature and rushed bounding before him rapturously.

Kolya opened the door to peep at the kids. They were both sitting as before at the table, not reading but warmly disputing about something. The children often argued together about various exciting problems of life, and Nastya, being the elder, always got the best of it. If Kostya did not agree with her, he almost always appealed to Kolya Krassotkin, and his verdict was regarded as infallible by both of them. This time the kids' discussion rather interested Krassotkin, and he stood still in the passage to listen. The children saw he was listening and that made them dispute with even greater energy.

"I shall never, never believe," Nastya prattled, "that the old women find babies among the cabbages in the kitchen garden. It's winter now and there are no cabbages, and so the old woman couldn't have taken Katerina a daughter."

Kolya whistled to himself.

"Or perhaps they do bring babies from somewhere, but only to those who are married."

Kostya stared at Nastya and listened, pondering profoundly.

"Nastya, how silly you are," he said at last, firmly and calmly. "How can Katerina have a baby when she isn't married?"

Nastya was exasperated.

"You know nothing about it," she snapped irritably. "Perhaps she has a husband, only he is in prison, so now she's got a baby."

"But is her husband in prison?" the matter-of-fact Kostya inquired gravely.

"Or, I tell you what," Nastya interrupted impulsively, completely rejecting and forgetting her first hypothesis. "She hasn't a husband, you are right there, but she wants to be married,

211

and so she's been thinking of getting married, and thinking and thinking of it till now she's got it, that is, not a husband but a baby."

"Well, perhaps so," Kostya agreed, entirely vanquished. "But you didn't say so before. So how could I tell?"

"Come, kiddies," said Kolya, stepping into the room. "You're terrible people, I see."

"And Perezvon with you!" grinned Kostya, and began snapping his fingers and calling Perezvon.

"I am in a difficulty, kids," Krassotkin began solemnly, "and you must help me. Agafya must have broken her leg, since she has not turned up till now, that's certain. I must go out. Will you let me go?"

The children looked anxiously at one another. Their smiling faces showed signs of uneasiness, but they did not yet fully grasp what was expected of them.

"You won't be naughty while I am gone? You won't climb on the cupboard and break your legs? You won't be frightened alone and cry?"

A look of profound despondency came into the children's faces.

"And I could show you something as a reward, a little copper cannon which can be fired with real gunpowder."

The children's faces instantly brightened. "Show us the cannon," said Kostya, beaming all over.

Krassotkin put his hand in his satchel, and pulling out a little bronze cannon stood it on the table.

"Ah, you are bound to ask that! Look, it's on wheels." He rolled the toy along on the table. "And it can be fired off, too. It can be loaded with shot and fired off."

"And it could kill anyone?"

"It can kill anyone; you've only got to aim at anybody," and Krassotkin explained where the powder had to be put, where the shot should be rolled in, showed a tiny hole like a touch-hole, and told them that it kicked when it was fired.

The children listened with intense interest. What particularly struck their imagination was that the cannon kicked.

"And have you got any powder?" Nastya inquired.

"Yes."

"Show us the powder, too," she drawled, with a smile of entreaty.

Krassotkin dived again into his satchel and pulled out a small flask containing a little real gunpowder. He had some shot, too,

212

in a screw of paper. He even uncorked the flask and shook a little powder into the palm of his hand.

"One has to be careful there's no fire about, or it would blow up and kill us all," Krassotkin warned them sensationally.

The children gazed at the powder with an awe-stricken alarm that only intensified their enjoyment. But Kostya liked the shot better.

"And does the shot burn?" he inquired.

"No, it doesn't."

"Give me a little shot," he asked in an imploring voice.

"I'll give you a little shot; here, take it, but don't show it to your mother till I come back, or she'll be sure to think it's gunpowder, and will die of fright and give you a thrashing."

"Mother never does whip us," Nastya observed at once.

"I know, I only said it to finish the sentence. And don't you ever deceive your mother except just this once, until I come back. And so, kiddies, can I go out? You won't be frightened and cry when I'm gone?"

"We sha—all cry," drawled Kostya, on the verge of tears already.

"We shall cry, we shall be sure to cry," Nastya chimed in, with timid haste.

"Oh, children, children, how fraught with peril are your years! There's no help for it, chickens, I shall have to stay with you I don't know how long. And time is passing, time is passing, oogh!"

"Tell Perezvon to pretend to be dead!" Kostya begged.

"There's no help for it, we must have recourse to Perezvon. *Ici*, Perezvon." And Kolya began giving orders to the dog, who performed all his tricks.

He was a rough-haired dog, of medium size, with a coat of a sort of lilac-grey colour. He was blind in his right eye, and his left ear was torn. He whined and jumped, stood and walked on his hind legs, lay on his back with his paws in the air, rigid as though he were dead. While this last performance was going on, the door was opened and Agafya, Madame Krassotkin's servant, a stout woman of forty, marked with small-pox, appeared in the doorway. She had come back from market and had a bag full of provisions in her hand. Holding up the bag of provisions in her left hand she stood still to watch the dog. Though Kolya had been so anxious for her return, he did not cut short the performance, and after keeping Perezvon dead for the usual time, at last he whistled to him. The dog jumped up and began bounding about in his joy at having done his duty.

"Only think, a dog!" Agafya observed sententiously.

"Why are you late, female?" asked Krassotkin sternly.

"Female, indeed! Go on with you, you brat."

"Brat?"

"Yes, a brat. What is it to you if I'm late; if I'm late, you may be sure I have good reason," muttered Agafya, busying herself about the stove, without a trace of anger or displeasure in her voice. She seemed quite pleased in fact, to enjoy a skirmish with her merry young master.

"Listen, you frivolous old woman," Krassotkin began, getting up from the sofa, "can you swear by all you hold sacred in the world and something else besides, that you will watch vigilantly over the kids in my absence? I am going out."

"And what am I going to swear for?" laughed Agafya. "I shall look after them without that."

"No, you must swear on your eternal salvation. Else I shan't go."

"Well, don't, then. What does it matter to me? It's cold out; stay at home."

"Kids," Kolya turned to the children, "this woman will stay with you till I come back or till your mother comes, for she ought to have been back long ago. She will give you some lunch, too. You'll give them something, Agafya, won't you?"

"That I can do."

"Good-bye, chickens, I go with my heart at rest. And you, granny," he added gravely, in an undertone, as he passed Agafya, "I hope you'll spare their tender years and not tell them any of your old woman's nonsense about Katerina. *Ici,* Perezvon!"

"Get along with you!" retorted Agafya, really angry this time. "Ridiculous boy! You want a whipping for saying such things, that's what you want!"

CHAPTER III

THE SCHOOLBOY

BUT Kolya did not hear her. At last he could go out. As he went out at the gate he looked round him, shrugged up his shoulders, and saying "It is freezing", went straight along the street and turned off to the right towards the market-place. When he reached the last house but one before the market-place he stopped at the gate, pulled a whistle out of his pocket, and whistled with all his might as though giving a signal. He had not to wait more than a minute before a rosy-cheeked boy of about eleven, wearing a warm, neat, and even stylish coat, darted out to meet him. This was Smurov, a boy in the preparatory class (two classes below Kolya Krassotkin's), son of a well-to-do official. Apparently he was forbidden by his parents to associate with Krassotkin, who was well known to be a desperately naughty boy, so Smurov was obviously slipping out on the sly. He was—if the reader has not forgotten—one of the group of boys who two months before had thrown stones at Ilusha. He was the one who told Alyosha Karamazov about Ilusha.

"I've been waiting for you for the last hour, Krassotkin," said Smurov stolidly, and the boys strode towards the market-place.

"I am late," answered Krassotkin. "I was detained by circumstances. You won't be thrashed for coming with me?"

"Come, I say, I'm never thrashed! And you've got Perezvon with you?"

"Yes."

"You're taking him, too?"

"Yes."

"Ah! if it were only Zhutchka!"

"That's impossible. Zhutchka's non-existent. Zhutchka is lost in the mists of obscurity."

"Ah! couldn't we do this?" Smurov suddenly stood still. "You see, Ilusha says that Zhutchka was a shaggy, greyish, smoky-looking dog like Perezvon. Couldn't you tell him this is Zhutchka, and he might believe you?"

"Boy, shun a lie, that's one thing; even with a good object—that's another. Above all, I hope you've not told them anything about my coming."

"Heaven forbid! I know what I am about. But you won't comfort him with Perezvon," said Smurov, with a sigh. "You know his father, the captain, 'the wisp of tow', told us that he was going to bring him a real mastiff pup, with a black nose, to-day. He thinks that would comfort Ilusha; but I doubt it."

"And how is Ilusha?"

"Ah, he is bad, very bad! I believe he's in consumption: he

is quite conscious, but his breathing! His breathing's gone wrong. The other day he asked to have his boots on to be led round the room. He tried to walk, but he couldn't stand. 'Ah, I told you before, father,' he said, 'that those boots were no good. I could never walk properly in them.' He fancied it was his boots that made him stagger, but it was simply weakness, really. He won't live another week. Herzenstube is looking after him. Now they are rich again—they've got heaps of money."

"They are rogues."

"Who are rogues?"

"Doctors and the whole crew of quacks collectively, and also, of course, individually. I don't believe in medicine. It's a useless institution. I mean to go into all that. But what's that sentimentality you've got up there? The whole class seems to be there every day?"

"Not the whole class: it's only ten of our fellows who go to see him every day. There's nothing in that."

"What I don't understand in all this is the part that Alexey Karamazov is taking in it. His brother's going to be tried to-morrow or next day for such a crime, and yet he has so much time to spend on sentimentality with boys."

"There's no sentimentality about it. You are going yourself now to make it up with Ilusha."

"Make it up with him? What an absurd expression! But I allow no one to analyse my actions."

"And how pleased Ilusha will be to see you! He has no idea that you are coming. Why was it, why was it you wouldn't come all this time?" Smurov cried, with sudden warmth.

"My dear boy, that's my business, not yours. I am going of myself because I choose to, but you've all been hauled there by Alexey Karamazov—there's a difference, you know. And how do you know? I may not be going to make it up at all. It's a stupid expression."

"It's not Karamazov at all; it's not his doing. Our fellows began going there of themselves. Of course, they went with Karamazov at first. And there's been nothing of that sort—no silliness. First one went, and then another. His father was awfully pleased to see us. You know, he will simply go out of his mind if Ilusha dies. He sees that Ilusha's dying. And he seems so glad we've made it up with Ilusha. Ilusha asked after you, that was all. He just asks and says no more. His father will go out of his mind or hang himself. He behaved like a mad-man before. You know he is a very decent man. We made a mistake then. It's all the fault of that murderer who beat him then."

"Karamazov's a riddle to me all the same. I might have made his acquaintance long ago, but I like to have a proper pride in some cases. Besides, I have a theory about him which I must work out and verify."

Kolya subsided into dignified silence. Smurov, too, was silent. Smurov, of course, worshipped Krassotkin and never dreamed of putting himself on a level with him. Now he was tremendously interested at Kolya's saying that he was "going of himself" to see Ilusha. He felt that there must be some mystery in Kolya's suddenly taking it into his head to go to him that day. They crossed the market-place, in which at that hour were many loaded waggons from the country and a great number of live fowls. The market women were selling rolls, cottons and threads, etc., in their booths. These Sunday markets were naïvely called "fairs" in the town, and there were many such fairs in the year.

Perezvon ran about in the wildest spirits, sniffing about first one side, then the other. When he met other dogs they zealously smelt each other over according to the rules of canine etiquette.

"I like to watch such realistic scenes, Smurov," said Kolya suddenly. "Have you noticed how dogs sniff at one another when they meet? It seems to be a law of their nature."

"Yes; it's a funny habit."

"No, it's not funny; you are wrong there. There's nothing funny in nature, however funny it may seem to man with his prejudices. If dogs could reason and criticise us they'd be sure to find just as much that would be funny to them, if not far more, in the social relations of men, their masters—far more, indeed. I repeat that because I am convinced that there is far more foolishness among us. That's Rakitin's idea—a remarkable idea. I am a Socialist, Smurov."

"And what is a Socialist?" asked Smurov.

"That's when all are equal and all have property in common, there are no marriages, and everyone has any religion and laws he likes best, and all the rest of it. You are not old enough to understand that yet. It's cold, though."

"Yes, twelve degrees of frost. Father looked at the thermometer just now."

"Have you noticed, Smurov, that in the middle of winter we don't feel so cold even when there are fifteen or eighteen degrees of frost as we do now, in the beginning of winter, when there is a sudden frost of twelve degrees, especially when there is not much snow. It's because people are not used to it. Everything is habit with men, everything even in their social and political relations. Habit is the great motive-power. What a funny-looking peasant!"

Kolya pointed to a tall peasant, with a good-natured countenance, in a long sheepskin coat, who was standing by his waggon, clapping together his hands, in their shapeless leather gloves, to warm them. His long fair beard was all white with frost.

"That peasant's beard's frozen," Kolya cried in a loud provocative voice as he passed him.

"Lots of people's beards are frozen," the peasant replied, calmly and sententiously.

"Don't provoke him," observed Smurov.

"It's all right; he won't be cross; he's a nice fellow. Good-bye, Matvey."

"Good-bye."

"Is your name Matvey?"

"Yes. Didn't you know?"

"No, I didn't. It was a guess."

"You don't say so! You are a schoolboy, I suppose?"

"Yes."

"You get whipped, I expect?"

"Nothing to speak of—sometimes."

"Does it hurt?"

"Well, yes, it does."

"Ech, what a life!" The peasant heaved a sigh from the bottom of his heart.

"Good-bye, Matvey."

"Good-bye. You are a nice chap, that you are."

The boys went on.

"That was a nice peasant," Kolya observed to Smurov. "I like talking to the peasants, and am always glad to do them justice."

"Why did you tell a lie, pretending we are thrashed?" asked Smurov.

"I had to say that to please him."

"How do you mean?"

"You know, Smurov, I don't like being asked the same thing twice. I like people to understand at the first word. Some things can't be explained. According to a peasant's notions, schoolboys are whipped, and must be whipped. What would a

218

schoolboy be if he were not whipped? And if I were to tell him we are not, he'd be disappointed. But you don't understand that. One has to know how to talk to the peasants."

"Only don't tease them, please, or you'll get into another scrape as you did about that goose."

"So you're afraid?"

"Don't laugh, Kolya. Of course I'm afraid. My father would be awfully cross. I am entirely forbidden to go out with you."

"Don't be uneasy, nothing will happen this time. Hullo, Natasha!" he shouted to a market woman in one of the booths.

"Call me Natasha! What next? My name is Marya," the middle-aged market woman shouted at him.

"I am so glad it's Marya. Good-bye!"

"Ah, you young rascal! A brat like you to carry on so!"

"I'm in a hurry. I can't stay now. You shall tell me next Sunday." Kolya waved his hand at her, as though she had attacked him and not he her.

"I've nothing to tell you next Sunday. You set upon me, you impudent young monkey. I didn't say anything," bawled Marya. "You want a whipping, that's what you want, you saucy jackanapes!"

There was a roar of laughter among the other market women round her. Suddenly a man in a violent rage darted out from the arcade of shops close by. He was a young man, not a native of the town, with dark, curly hair and a long, pale face, marked with smallpox. He wore a long blue coat and a peaked cap, and looked like a merchant's clerk. He was in a state of stupid excitement and brandished his fist at Kolya.

"I know you!" he cried angrily, "I know you!"

Kolya stared at him. He could not recall when he could have had a row with the man. But he had been in so many rows in the street that he could hardly remember them all.

"Do you?" he asked sarcastically.

"I know you! I know you!" the man repeated idiotically.

"So much the better for you. Well, it's time I was going. Good-bye."

"You are at your saucy pranks again?" cried the man. "You are at your saucy pranks again? I know, you are at it again!"

"It's not your business, brother, if I am at my saucy pranks again," said Kolya, standing still and scanning him.

"Not my business?"

"No; it's not your business."

"Whose then? Whose then? Whose then?"

"It's Trifon Nikititch's business, not yours."

"What Trifon Nikititch?" asked the youth, staring with loutish amazement at Kolya, but still as angry as ever.

Kolya scanned him gravely.

"Have you been to the Church of the Ascension?" he suddenly asked him, with stern emphasis.

"What Church of Ascension? What for? No, I haven't," said the young man, somewhat taken aback.

"Do you know Sabaneyev?" Kolya went on even more emphatically and even more severely.

"What Sabaneyev? No, I don't know him."

"Well then, you can go to the devil," said Kolya, cutting short the conversation, and turning sharply to the right he strode quickly on his way as though he disdained further conversation with a dolt who did not even know Sabaneyev.

"Stop, heigh! What Sabaneyev?" The young man recovered from his momentary stupefaction and was as excited as before. "What did he say?" He turned to the market women with a silly stare.

The women laughed.

"You can never tell what he's after," said one of them.

"What Sabaneyev is it he's talking about?" the young man repeated, still furious and brandishing his right arm.

"It must be a Sabaneyev who worked for the Kuzmitchovs, that's who it must be," one of the women suggested.

The young man stared at her wildly.

"For the Kuzmitchovs?" repeated another woman. "But his name wasn't Trifon. His name's Kuzma, not Trifon; but the boy said Trifon Nikititch, so it can't be the same."

"His name is not Trifon and not Sabaneyev, it's Tchizhov," put in suddenly a third woman, who had hitherto been silent, listening gravely. "Alexey Ivanitch is his name. Tchizhov, Alexey Ivanitch."

"Not a doubt about it, it's Tchizhov," a fourth woman emphatically confirmed the statement.

The bewildered youth gazed from one to another.

"But what did he ask for, what did he ask for, good people?" he cried almost in desperation. " 'Do you know Sabaneyev?' says he. And who the devil's to know who is Sabaneyev?"

"You're a senseless fellow. I tell you it's not Sabaneyev but Tchizhov, Alexey Ivanitch Tchizhov, that's who it is!" one of the women shouted at him impressively.

"What Tchizhov? Who is he? Tell me, if you know."

"That tall, snivelling fellow who used to sit in the market in the summer."

"And what's your Tchizhov to do with me, good people, eh?"

"How can I tell what he's to do with you?" put in another. "You ought to know yourself what you want with him, if you make such a clamour about him. He spoke to you, he did not speak to us, you stupid. Don't you really know him?"

"Know whom?"

"Tchizhov."

"The devil take Tchizhov and you with him. I'll give him a hiding, that I will. He was laughing at me!"

"Will give Tchizhov a hiding! More likely he will give you one. You are a fool, that's what you are!"

"Not Tchizhov, not Tchizhov, you spiteful, mischievous woman. I'll give the boy a hiding. Catch him, catch him, he was laughing at me!"

The women guffawed. But Kolya was by now a long way off, marching along with a triumphant air. Smurov walked beside him, looking round at the shouting group far behind. He, too, was in high spirits, though he was still afraid of getting into some scrape in Kolya's company.

"What Sabaneyev did you mean?" he asked Kolya, foreseeing what his answer would be.

"How do I know? Now there'll be a hubbub among them all day. I like to stir up fools in every class of society. There's another blockhead, that peasant there. You know, they say 'there's no one stupider than a stupid Frenchman', but a stupid Russian shows it in his face just as much. Can't you see it all over his face that he is a fool, that peasant, eh?"

"Let him alone, Kolya. Let's go on."

"Nothing could stop me, now I am once off. Hey, good morning, peasant!"

A sturdy-looking peasant, with a round, simple face and grizzled beard, who was walking by, raised his head and looked at the boy. He seemed not quite sober.

"Good morning, if you are not laughing at me," he said deliberately in reply.

"And if I am?" laughed Kolya.

"Well, a joke's a joke. Laugh away. I don't mind. There's no harm in a joke."

"I beg your pardon, brother, it was a joke."

221

"Well, God forgive you!"

"Do you forgive me, too?"

"I quite forgive you. Go along."

"I say, you seem a clever peasant."

"Cleverer than you," the peasant answered unexpectedly, with the same gravity.

"I doubt it," said Kolya, somewhat taken aback.

"It's true though."

"Perhaps it is."

"It is, brother."

"Good-bye, peasant!"

"Good-bye!"

"There are all sorts of peasants," Kolya observed to Smurov, after a brief silence. "How could I tell I had hit on a clever one? I am always ready to recognise intelligence in the peasantry."

In the distance the cathedral clock struck half-past eleven. The boys made haste and they walked as far as Captain Snegiryov's lodging, a considerable distance, quickly and almost in silence. Twenty paces from the house Kolya stopped and told Smurov to go on ahead and ask Karamazov to come out to him.

"One must sniff round a bit first," he observed to Smurov.

"Why ask him to come out?" Smurov protested. "You go in; they will be awfully glad to see you. What's the sense of making friends in the frost out here?"

"I know why I want to see him out here in the frost," Kolya cut him short in the despotic tone he was fond of adopting with "small boys", and Smurov ran to do his bidding.

CHAPTER IV

THE LOST DOG

KOLYA leaned against the fence with an air of dignity, waiting for Alyosha to appear. Yes, he had long wanted to meet him. He had heard a great deal about him from the boys, but hitherto he had always maintained an appearance of disdainful indifference when he was mentioned, and he had even "criticised" what he heard about Alyosha. But secretly he had a great longing to make his acquaintance; there was something sympathetic and attractive in all he was told about Alyosha. So the present moment was important: to begin with, he had to show himself at his best, to show his independence. "Or he'll think of me as thirteen and take me for a boy, like the rest of them. And what are these boys to him? I shall ask him when I get to know him. It's a pity I am so short, though. Tuzikov is younger than I am, yet he is half a head taller. But I have a clever face. I am not good-looking. I know I'm hideous, but I've a clever face. I mustn't talk too freely; if I fall into his arms all at once, he may think . . . Tfoo! how horrible if he should think . . . !"

Such were the thoughts that excited Kolya while he was doing his utmost to assume the most independent air. What distressed him most was his being so short; he did not mind so much his "hideous" face as being so short. On the wall in a corner at home he had the year before made a pencil mark to show his height, and every two months since, he anxiously measured himself against it to see how much he had gained. But, alas! he grew very slowly, and this sometimes reduced him almost to despair. His face was in reality by no means "hideous"; on the contrary, it was rather attractive, with a fair, pale skin, freckled. His small, lively grey eyes had a fearless look, and often glowed with feeling. He had rather high cheek-bones; small, very red, but not very thick lips; his nose was small and unmistakably turned up. "I've a regular pug-nose, a regular pug-nose," Kolya used to mutter to himself when he looked in the looking-glass, and he always left it with indignation. "But perhaps I haven't got a clever face?" he sometimes thought, doubtful even of that. But it must not be supposed that his mind was preoccupied with his face and his height. On the contrary, however bitter the moments before the looking-glass were to him, he quickly forgot them, and forgot them for a long time, "abandoning himself entirely to ideas and to real life", as he formulated it to himself.

Alyosha came out quickly and hastened up to Kolya. Before he reached him, Kolya could see that he looked delighted. "Can he be so glad to see me?" Kolya wondered, feeling pleased. We may note here, in passing, that Alyosha's appearance had undergone a complete change since we saw him last. He had abandoned his cassock and was wearing now a well-cut coat, a soft, round hat, and his hair had been cropped short. All this was very becoming to him, and he looked quite handsome. His charming face always had a good-humoured expression; but there was a gentleness and serenity in his good humour. To Kolya's surprise, Alyosha came out to him just as he was, without an overcoat. He had evidently come in haste. He held out his hand to Kolya at once.

"Here you are at last! How anxious we've been to see you!"

"There were reasons which you shall know directly. Anyway, I am glad to make your acquaintance. I've long been hoping for an opportunity, and have heard a great deal about you," Kolya muttered, a little breathless.

"We should have met, anyway. I've heard a great deal about you, too; but you've been a long time coming here."

"Tell me, how are things going?"

"Ilusha is very ill. He is certainly dying."

"How awful! You must admit that medicine is a fraud, Karamazov," cried Kolya warmly.

"Ilusha has mentioned you often, very often, even in his sleep, in delirium, you know. One can see that you used to be very, very dear to him . . . before the incident . . . with the knife . . . Then there's another reason. . . . Tell me, is that your dog?"

"Yes, Perezvon."

"Not Zhutchka?" Alyosha looked at Kolya with eyes full of pity. "Is she lost for ever?"

"I know you would all like it to be Zhutchka. I've heard all about it." Kolya smiled mysteriously. "Listen, Karamazov, I'll tell you all about it. That's what I came for; that's what I asked you to come out here for, to explain the whole episode to you before we go in," he began, with animation. "You see, Karamazov, Ilusha came into the preparatory class last spring. Well, you know what our preparatory class is—a lot of small boys. They began teasing Ilusha at once. I am two classes higher up, and, of course, I only look on at them from a distance. I saw the boy was weak and small, but he wouldn't give in to them; he fought with them. I saw he was proud, and his eyes were full of fire. I like children like that. And they teased him all the more. The worst of it was he was horribly dressed at the time, his breeches were too small for him; and there were holes in his boots. They worried him about it; they jeered at him. That I can't stand. I stood up for him at once, and gave it to them hot. I beat them, but they adore me, do you know, Karamazov?" Kolya boasted impulsively; "but I am always fond of children. I've two chickens on my hands at home now —that's what detained me to-day. So they left off beating Ilusha and I took him under my protection. I saw the boy was proud. I tell you that, the boy was proud; but in the end he became slavishly devoted to me: he did my slightest bidding, obeyed me as though I were God, tried to copy me In the intervals between the classes he used to run to me at once, and I'd go about with him. On Sundays, too. They always laugh when an older boy makes friends with a younger one like that; but that's a prejudice. If it's my fancy, that's enough. I am teaching him, developing him. Why shouldn't I develop him if I like him? Here you, Karamazov, have taken up with all these nestlings. I see you want to influence the younger generation— to develop them, to be of use to them, and I assure you this trait in your character, which I knew by hearsay, attracted me more than anything. Let us get to the point, though. I noticed that there was a sort of softness and sentimentality coming over the boy, and you know I have a positive hatred of this sheepish sentimentality, and I have had it from a baby. There were contradictions in him, too: he was proud, but he was slavishly devoted to me, and yet all at once his eyes would flash and he'd refuse to agree with me; he'd argue, fly into a rage. I used sometimes to propound certain ideas; I could see that it was not so much that he disagreed with the ideas but that he was simply rebelling against me, because I was cool in responding to his endearments. And so, in order to train him properly, the tenderer he was, the colder I became. I did it on purpose: that was my idea. My object was to form his character, to lick him into shape, to make a man of him . . . and besides . . . no doubt, you understand me at a word. Suddenly I noticed for three days in succession he was downcast and dejected, not because of my coldness but for something else, something more important. I wondered what the tragedy was. I have pumped him and found out that he had somehow got to know Smerdyakov, who was footman to your late father—it was before his death, of course—and he taught the little fool a silly trick—that is, a brutal, nasty trick. He told him to take a piece of bread, to stick a pin in it, and throw it to one of those hungry dogs who snap up anything without biting it, and then to watch and see what would happen. So they prepared a piece of bread like that and threw it to Zhutchka, that shaggy dog there's been such a fuss about. The people of the house it belonged to never fed it at all, though it barked all day. (Do you like that stupid barking, Karamazov? I can't stand it.) So it rushed at the bread, swallowed it, and began to squeal; it turned round and round and ran away, squealing as it ran out of sight. That was Ilusha's own account of it. He confessed it to me, and cried bitterly. He hugged me, shaking all over. He kept on repeating, 'He ran away squealing': the sight of that haunted him. He was tormented by remorse, I could see that. I took it seriously. I determined to give him a lesson for other things as well. So I must confess I wasn't quite straightforward, and pretended to be more indignant perhaps than I was. 'You've done a nasty thing,' I said, 'you are a scoundrel. I won't tell of it, of course, but I shall have nothing more to do with you for a time. I'll think it over and let you know through Smurov (that's the boy who's just come with me; he's always ready to do anything for me) whether I will have anything to do with you in the future or whether I give you up for good as a scoundrel.' He was tremendously upset. I must own I felt I'd gone too far as I spoke, but there was no help for it. I did what I thought best at the time. A day or two after, I sent Smurov to tell him that I would not speak to him again. That's what we call it when two schoolfellows refuse to have anything more to do with one another. Secretly I only meant to send him to Coventry for a few days and then, if I saw signs of repentance, to hold out my hand to him again. That was my intention. But what do you think happened? He heard Smurov's message, his eyes flashed. 'Tell Krassotkin from me,' he cried, 'that I will throw bread with pins to all the dogs—all—all of them!' 'So he's going in for a little temper. We must smoke it out of him.' And I began to treat him with contempt: whenever I met him I turned away or smiled sarcastically. And just then that affair with his father happened. You remember? You must realise that he was fearfully worked up by what had happened already. The boys, seeing I'd given him up, set on him and taunted him, shouting: 'Wisp of tow, wisp of tow!' And he had soon regular skirmishes with them, which I am very sorry for. They seem to have given him one very bad beating. One day he flew at them all as they were coming out of school. I stood a few yards off, looking on. And, I swear, I don't remember that I laughed; it was quite the other way, I felt awfully sorry for him, in another minute I would have run up to take his part. But he suddenly met my eyes. I don't know what he fancied; but he pulled out a pen-knife, rushed at me, and struck at my thigh, here in my right leg. I didn't move. I don't mind owning I am plucky some-times, Karamazov. I simply looked at him contemptuously, as though to say, 'This is how you repay all my kindness! Do it again, if you like, I'm at your service.' But he didn't stab me

226

again; he broke down, he was frightened at what he had done, he threw away the knife, burst out crying, and ran away. I did not sneak on him, of course, and I made them all keep quiet, so it shouldn't come to the ears of the masters. I didn't even tell my mother till it had healed up. And the wound was a mere scratch. And then I heard that the same day he'd been throwing stones and had bitten your finger—but you understand now what a state he was in! Well, it can't be helped: it was stupid of me not to come and forgive him—that is, to make it up with him—when he was taken ill. I am sorry for it now. But I had a special reason. So now I've told you all about it . . . but I'm afraid it was stupid of me."

"Oh, what a pity," exclaimed Alyosha, with feeling, "that I didn't know before what terms you were on with him, or I'd have come to you long ago to beg you to go to him with me. Would you believe it, when he was feverish he talked about you in delirium. I didn't know how much you were to him! And you've really not succeeded in finding that dog? His father and the boys have been hunting all over the town for it. Would you believe it, since he's been ill, I've three times heard him repeat with tears, 'It's because I killed Zhutchka, father, that I am ill now. God is punishing me for it.' He can't get that idea out of his head. And if the dog were found and proved to be alive, one might almost fancy the joy would cure him. We have all rested our hopes on you."

"Tell me, what made you hope that I should be the one to find him?" Kolya asked, with great curiosity. "Why did you reckon on me rather than anyone else?"

"There was a report that you were looking for the dog, and that you would bring it when you'd found it. Smurov said something of the sort. We've all been trying to persuade Ilusha that the dog is alive, that it's been seen. The boys brought him a live hare: he just looked at it, with a faint smile, and asked them to set it free in the fields. And so we did. His father has just this moment come back, bringing him a mastiff pup, hoping to comfort him with that; but I think it only makes it worse."

"Tell me, Karamazov, what sort of man is the father? I know him, but what do you make of him—a mountebank, a buffoon?"

"Oh, no; there are people of deep feeling who have been somehow crushed. Buffoonery in them is a form of resentful irony against those to whom they daren't speak the truth, from having been for years humiliated and intimidated by them. Believe me, Krassotkin, that sort of buffoonery is sometimes tragic in the extreme. His whole life now is centred in Ilusha, and if Ilusha dies, he will either go mad with grief or kill himself. I feel almost certain of that when I look at him now."

"I understand you, Karamazov. I see you understand human nature," Kolya added, with feeling.

"And as soon as I saw you with a dog, I thought it was Zhutchka you were bringing."

"Wait a bit, Karamazov, perhaps we shall find it yet; but this is Perezvon. I'll let him go in now and perhaps it will amuse Ilusha more than the mastiff pup. Wait a bit, Karamazov, you will know something in a minute. But, I say, I am keeping you here!" Kolya cried suddenly. "You've no overcoat on in this bitter cold. You see what an egoist I am. Oh, we are all egoists, Karamazov!"

"Don't trouble; it is cold, but I don't often catch cold. Let us go in though, and, by the way, what is your name? I know you are called Kolya, but what else?"

"Nikolay—Nikolay Ivanovitch Krassotkin, or, as they say in official documents, 'Krassotkin son'." Kolya laughed for some reason, but added suddenly: "Of course I hate my name Nikolay."

"Why so?"

"It's so trivial, so ordinary."

"You are thirteen?" asked Alyosha.

"No, fourteen—that is, I shall be fourteen very soon, in a fortnight. I'll confess one weakness of mine, Karamazov, just to you, since it's our first meeting, so that you may understand my character at once. I hate being asked my age, more than that . . . and in fact . . . there's a libellous story going about me, that last week I played robbers with the preparatory boys. It's a fact that I did play with them, but it's a perfect libel to say I did it for my own amusement. I have reasons for believing that you've heard the story; but I wasn't playing for my own amusement, it was for the sake of the children, because they couldn't think of anything to do by themselves. But they've always got some silly tale. This is an awful town for gossip, I can tell you."

"But what if you had been playing for your own amusement, what's the harm?"

"Come, I say, for my own amusement! You don't play horses, do you?"

"But you must look at it like this," said Alyosha, smiling. "Grown-up people go to the theatre and there the adventures of all sorts of heroes are represented—sometimes there are robbers and battles, too—and isn't that just the same thing, in a different form, of course? And young people's games of soldiers or robbers in their play-time are also art in its first stage. You know, they spring from the growing artistic instincts of the young. And sometimes these games are much better than performances in the theatre, the only difference is that people go there to look at actors, while in these games the young people are the actors themselves. But that's only natural."

"You think so? Is that your idea?" Kolya looked at him intently. "Oh, you know, that's rather an interesting view. When I go home, I'll think it over. I'll admit I thought I might learn something from you. I've come to learn of you, Karamazov," Kolya concluded, in a voice full of spontaneous feeling.

"And I of you," said Alyosha, smiling and pressing his hand.

Kolya was much pleased with Alyosha. What struck him most was that he treated him exactly like an equal and that he talked to him just as if he were "quite grown up".

"I'll show you something directly, Karamazov; it's a theatrical performance, too," he said, laughing nervously. "That's why I've come."

"Let us go first to the people of the house, on the left. All the boys leave their coats in there, because the room is small and hot."

"Oh, I'm only coming in for a minute. I'll keep on my overcoat. Perezvon will stay here in the passage and be dead. *Ici*, Perezvon, lie down and be dead! You see how he's dead. I'll go in first and explore, then I'll whistle to him when I think fit, and you'll see he'll dash in like mad. Only Smurov must not forget to open the door at the moment. I'll arrange it all and you'll see something."

CHAPTER V

BY ILUSHA'S BEDSIDE

THE room inhabited by the family of the retired captain Snegiryov is already familiar to the reader. It was close and crowded at that moment with a number of visitors. Several boys were sitting with Ilusha, and though all of them like Smurov were prepared to deny that it was Alyosha who had brought them and reconciled them with Ilusha, it was really the fact. All the art he had used had been to take them, one by one, to Ilusha, without "sheepish sentimentality", appearing to do so casually and without design. It was a great consolation to Ilusha in his suffering. He was greatly touched by seeing the almost tender affection and sympathy shown him by these boys, who had been his enemies. Krassotkin was the only one missing and his absence was a heavy load on Ilusha's heart. Perhaps the bitterest of all his bitter memories was his stabbing Krassotkin, who had been his one friend and protector. Clever little Smurov, who was the first to make it up with Ilusha, thought it was so. But when Smurov hinted to Krassotkin that Alyosha wanted to come and see him about something, the latter cut him short, bidding Smurov tell "Karamazov" at once that he knew best what to do, that he wanted no one's advice, and that if he went to see Ilusha he would choose his own time for he had "his own reasons".

That was a fortnight before this Sunday. That was why Alyosha had not been to see him, as he had meant to. But though he waited, he sent Smurov to him twice again. Both times Krassotkin met him with a curt, impatient refusal, sending Alyosha a message not to bother him any more, that if he came himself, he, Krassotkin, would not go to Ilusha at all. Up to the very last day, Smurov did not know that Kolya meant to go to Ilusha that morning, and only the evening before, as he parted from Smurov, Kolya abruptly told him to wait at home for him next morning, for he would go with him to the Snegiryovs, but warned him on no account to say he was coming, as he wanted to drop in casually. Smurov obeyed. Smurov's fancy that Kolya would bring back the lost dog was based on the words Kolya had dropped that "they must be asses not to find the dog, if it were alive". When Smurov, waiting for an opportunity, timidly hinted at his guess about the dog, Krassotkin flew into a violent rage. "I'm not such an ass as to go hunting about the town for other people's dogs when I've got a dog of my own! And how can you imagine a dog could be alive after swallowing a pin? Sheepish sentimentality, that's what it is!"

For the last fortnight Ilusha had not left his little bed under the ikons in the corner. He had not been to school since the day he met Alyosha and bit his finger. He was taken ill the same day, though for a month afterwards he was sometimes able to get up and walk about the room and passage. But latterly he had become so weak that he could not move without help from his father. His father was terribly concerned about him. He even gave up drinking and was almost crazy with terror that his boy would die. And often, especially after leading him round the room on his arm and putting him back to bed, he would run to a dark corner in the passage and, leaning his head against the wall, he would break into paroxysms of violent weeping, stifling his sobs that they might not be heard by Ilusha.

Returning to the room, he would usually begin doing something to amuse and comfort his precious boy, he would tell him stories, funny anecdotes, or would mimic comic people he had happened to meet, even imitate the howls and cries of animals. But Ilusha could not bear to see his father fooling and playing the buffoon. Though the boy tried not to show how he disliked it, he saw with an aching heart that his father was an object of contempt, and he was continually haunted by the memory of the "wisp of tow" and that "terrible day".

Nina, Ilusha's gentle, crippled sister, did not like her father's buffoonery either (Varvara had been gone for some time past to Petersburg to study at the University). But the half imbecile mother was greatly diverted and laughed heartily when her husband began capering about or performing something. It was the only way she could be amused, all the rest of the time she was grumbling and complaining that now everyone had forgotten her, that no one treated her with respect, that she was slighted and so on. But during the last few days she had completely changed. She began looking constantly at Ilusha's bed in the corner and seemed lost in thought. She was more silent, quieter, and, if she cried, she cried quietly so as not to be heard. The captain noticed the change in her with mournful perplexity. The boys' visits at first only angered her, but later on their merry shouts and stories began to divert her, and at last she liked them so much that, if the boys had given up coming, she would have felt dreary without them. When the children told some story or played a game, she laughed and clapped her hands. She called some of them to her and kissed them. She was particularly fond of Smurov.

As for the captain, the presence in his room of the children, who came to cheer up Ilusha, filled his heart from the first with ecstatic joy. He even hoped that Ilusha would now get over his depression, and that that would hasten his recovery. In spite of his alarm about Ilusha, he had not, till lately, felt one minute's doubt of his boy's ultimate recovery.

He met his little visitors with homage, waited upon them hand and foot, he was ready to be their horse and even began letting them ride on his back, but Ilusha did not like the game and it was given up. He began buying little things for them, gingerbread and nuts, gave them tea and cut them sandwiches. It must be noted that all this time he had plenty of money. He had taken the two hundred roubles from Katerina Ivanovna just as Alyosha had predicted he would. And afterwards Katerina Ivanovna, learning more about their circumstances and Ilusha's illness, visited them herself, made the acquaintance of the family and succeeded in fascinating the half imbecile mother. Since then she had been lavish in helping them, and the captain, terror-stricken at the thought that his boy might be dying, forgot his pride and humbly accepted her assistance.

All this time Doctor Henzenstube, who was called in by Katerina Ivanovna, came punctually every other day, but little was gained by his visits and he dosed the invalid mercilessly. But on that Sunday morning a new doctor was expected, who had come from Moscow, where he had a great reputation. Katerina Ivanovna had sent for him from Moscow at great expense, not expressly for Ilusha but for another object of which more will be said in its place hereafter. But, as he had come, she had asked him to see Ilusha as well, and the captain had been told to expect him. He hadn't the slightest idea that Kolya Krassotkin was coming, though he had long wished for a visit from the boy for whom Ilusha was fretting.

At the moment when Krassotkin opened the door and came into the room, the captain and all the boys were round Ilusha's bed, looking at a tiny mastiff pup, which had only been born the day before, though the captain had bespoken it a week ago to comfort and amuse Ilusha, who was still fretting over the lost and probably dead Zhutchka. Ilusha, who had heard three days before that he was to be presented with a puppy, not an ordinary puppy but a pedigree mastiff (a very important point, of course), tried from delicacy of feeling to pretend that he was pleased. But his father and the boys could not help seeing that the puppy only served to recall to his little heart the thought of the unhappy dog he had killed. The puppy lay beside him feebly moving and he, smiling sadly, stroked it with his thin, pale, wasted hand. Clearly he liked the puppy, but . . . it wasn't Zhutchka; if he could have had Zhutchka and the puppy, too, then he would have been completely happy.

"Krassotkin!" cried one of the boys suddenly. He was the first to see him come in.

Krassotkin's entrance made a general sensation, the boys moved away and stood on each side of the bed, so that he could get a full view of Ilusha. The captain ran eagerly to meet Kolya.

"Please come in . . . you are welcome!" he said hurriedly. "Ilusha, Mr. Krassotkin has come to see you!"

But Krassotkin, shaking hands with him hurriedly, instantly showed his complete knowledge of the manners of good society. He turned first to the captain's wife sitting in her armchair, who was very ill-humoured at the moment and was grumbling that the boys stood between her and Ilusha's bed and did not let her see the new puppy. With the greatest courtesy he made her a bow, scraping his foot and then, turning to Nina, he made her, as the only other lady present, a similar bow. This polite behaviour made an extremely favourable impression on the deranged lady.

"There, you can see at once he is a young man that has been well brought up," she commented aloud, throwing up her hands; "but as for our other visitors, they come in one on the top of another."

"How do you mean, mamma, 'one on top of another', how is that?" muttered the captain affectionately, though a little anxious on her account.

"That's how they ride in. They get on each other's shoulders in the passage and prance in like that on a respectable family. Strange sort of visitors!"

"But who's come in like that, mamma?"

"Why, that boy came in riding on that one's back and this one on that one's."

Kolya was already by Ilusha's bedside. The sick boy turned visibly paler. He raised himself in the bed and looked intently at Kolya. Kolya had not seen his little friend for two months, and he was rather overwhelmed at the sight of him. He had never imagined that he would see such a wasted, yellow face, such enormous, feverishly glowing eyes and such thin little hands. He saw, with grieved surprise, Ilusha's rapid, hard breathing and dry lips. He stepped close to him, held out his hand and, almost overwhelmed, he said:

"Well, old man . . . how are you?" But his voice failed

233

him, he couldn't achieve an appearance of ease; his face suddenly twitched and the corners of his mouth quivered. Ilusha smiled a pitiful little smile, still unable to utter a word. Something moved Kolya to raise his hand and pass it over Ilusha's hair.

"Never mind!" he murmured softly to him to cheer him up, or perhaps not knowing why he said it. For a minute they were silent again.

"Hullo, so you've got a new puppy?" Kolya said suddenly, in a most callous voice.

"Ye-es," answered Ilusha in a long whisper, gasping for breath.

"A black nose, that means he'll be fierce, a good house-dog," Kolya observed gravely and stolidly, as if the only thing he cared about was the puppy and its black nose. But in reality he still had to do his utmost to control his feelings not to burst out crying like a child, and do what he would he could not control it. "When it grows up, you'll have to keep it on the chain, I'm sure."

"He'll be a huge dog!" cried out of the boys.

"Of course he will," "a mastiff," "large," "like this," "as big as a calf," shouted several voices.

"As big as a calf, as a real calf," chimed in the captain. "I got one like that on purpose, one of the fiercest breeds, and his parents are huge and very fierce, they stand as high as this from the floor. . . . Sit down here, on Ilusha's bed, or here on the bench. You are welcome, we've been hoping to see you a long time . . . You were so kind as to come with Alexey Fyodorovitch?"

Krassotkin sat on the edge of the bed, at Ilusha's feet. Though he had perhaps prepared a free-and-easy opening for the conversation on his way, now he completely lost the thread of it.

"No . . . I came with Perezvon. I've got a dog now, called Perezvon. A Slavonic name. He's out there . . . if I whistle, he'll run in. I've brought a dog too," he said, addressing Ilusha all at once . "Do you remember Zhutchka, old man?" he suddenly fired the question at him.

Ilusha's little face quivered. He looked with an agonised expression at Kolya. Alyosha, standing at the door, frowned and signed to Kolya not to speak of Zhutchka, but he did not or would not notice.

"Where . . . is Zhutchka?" Ilusha asked in a broken voice.

"Oh well, my boy, your Zhutchka's lost and done for!"

Ilusha did not speak, but he fixed an intent gaze once more on Kolya. Alyosha, catching Kolya's eye, signed to him vigorously again, but he turned away his eyes, pretending not to have noticed.

"It must have run away and died somewhere. It must have died after a meal like that," Kolya pronounced pitilessly, though he seemed a little breathless. "But I've got a dog, Perezvon . . . A Slavonic name. . . . I've brought him to show you."

"I don't want him!" said Ilusha suddenly.

"No, no, you really must see him. . . it will amuse you. I brought him on purpose. . . . He's the same sort of shaggy dog. . . . You allow me to call in my dog, madam?" He suddenly addressed Madame Snegiryov, with inexplicable excitement in his manner.

"I don't want him, I don't want him!" cried Ilusha, with a mournful break in his voice. There was a reproachful light in his eyes.

"You'd better," the captain started up from the chest by the wall on which he had just sat down, "you'd better . . . another time," he muttered, but Kolya could not be restrained. He hurriedly shouted to Smurov: "Open the door," and as soon as it was open, he blew his whistle. Perezvon dashed headlong into the room.

"Jump, Perezvon, beg! Beg!" shouted Kolya, jumping up, and the dog stood erect on its hind legs by Ilusha's bedside. What followed was a surprise to everyone: Ilusha started, lurched violently forward, bent over Perezvon and gazed at him, faint with suspense.

"It's . . . Zhutchka!" he cried suddenly, in a voice breaking with joy and suffering.

"And who did you think it was?" Krassotkin shouted with all his might, in a ringing, happy voice, and bending down he seized the dog and lifted him up to Ilusha.

"Look, old man, you see, blind of one eye and the left ear is torn, just the marks you described to me. It was by that I found him. I found him directly. He did not belong to anyone!" he explained, turning quickly to the captain, to his wife, to Alyosha and then again to Ilusha. "He used to live in the Fedotovs' backyard. Though he made his home there, they did not feed him. He was a stray dog that had run away from the village . . . I found him. . . . You see, old man, he couldn't have swallowed what you gave him. If he had, he must have died, he must have! So he must have spat it out, since he is alive. You did not see him do it. But the pin pricked his tongue, that is why he squealed. He ran away squealing and you thought he'd swallowed it. He might well squeal, because the skin of dogs' mouths is so tender . . . tenderer than in men, much tenderer!" Kolya cried impetuously, his face glowing and radiant with delight. Ilusha could not speak. White as a sheet, he gazed open-mouthed at Kolya, with his great eyes almost starting out of his head. And if Krassotkin, who had no suspicion of it, had known what a disastrous and fatal effect such a moment might have on the sick child's health, nothing would have induced him to play such a trick on him. But Alyosha was perhaps the only person in the room who realised it. As for the captain he behaved like a small child.

"Zhutchka! It's Zhutchka!" he cried in a blissful voice, "Ilusha, this is Zhutchka, your Zhutchka! Mamma, this is Zhutchka!" He was almost weeping.

"And I never guessed!" cried Smurov regretfully. "Bravo, Krassotkin, I said he'd find the dog and here he's found him."

"Here he's found him!" another boy repeated gleefully.

"Krassotkin's a brick!" cried a third voice.

"He's a brick, he's a brick!" cried the other boys, and they began clapping.

"Wait, wait," Krassotkin did his utmost to shout above them all. "I'll tell you how it happened, that's the whole point. I found him, I took him home and hid him at once. I kept him locked up at home and did not show him to anyone till to-day. Only Smurov has known for the last fortnight, but I assured him this dog was called Perezvon and he did not guess. And meanwhile I taught the dog all sorts of tricks. You should only see all the things he can do! I trained him so as to bring you a well-trained dog, in good condition, old man, so as to be able to say to you: 'See, old man, what a fine dog your Zhutchka is now!' Haven't you a bit of meat, he'll show you a trick that will make you die with laughing. A piece of meat, haven't you got any?"

The captain ran across the passage to the landlady, where the cooking was done. Not to lose precious time, Kolya, in desperate haste, shouted to Perezvon, "Dead"! And the dog immediately turned round and lay on his back with his four paws in the air. The boys laughed, Ilusha looked on with the same

suffering smile, but the person most delighted with the dog's performance was "mamma". She laughed at the dog and began snapping her fingers and calling it: "Perezvon, Perezvon!"

"Nothing will make him get up, nothing!" Kolya cried triumphantly, proud of his success. "He won't move for all the shouting in the world, but if I call to him he'll jump up in a minute. *Ici*, Perezvon!" The dog leapt up and bounded about, whining with delight. The captain ran back with a piece of cooked beef.

"Is it hot?" Kolya inquired hurriedly, with a businesslike air, taking the meat. "Dogs don't like hot things. No, it's all right. Look, everybody, look, Ilusha, look, old man; why aren't you looking? He does not look at him now I've brought him."

The new trick consisted in making the dog stand motionless with his nose out and putting a tempting morsel of meat just on his nose. The luckless dog had to stand without moving, with the meat on his nose, as long as his master chose to keep him, without a movement, perhaps for half an hour. But he kept Perezvon only for a brief moment.

"Paid for!" cried Kolya, and the meat passed in a flash from the dog's nose to his mouth. The audience, of course, expressed enthusiasm and surprise.

"Can you really have put off coming all this time simply to train the dog?" exclaimed Alyosha, with an involuntary note of reproach in his voice.

"Simply for that!" answered Kolya, with perfect simplicity. "I wanted to show him in all his glory."

"Perezvon! Perezvon!" called Ilusha suddenly, snapping his thin fingers and beckoning to the dog.

"What is it? Let him jump up on the bed! *Ici*, Perezvon!" Kolya slapped the bed and Perezvon darted up by Ilusha. The boy threw both arms round his head and Perezvon instantly licked his cheek. Ilusha crept close to him, stretched himself out in bed and hid his face in the dog's shaggy coat.

"Dear, dear!" kept exclaiming the captain. Kolya sat down again on the edge of the bed.

"Ilusha, I can show you another trick. I've brought you a little cannon. You remember, I told you about it before and you said how much you'd like to see it. Well, here, I've brought it to you."

And Kolya hurriedly pulled out of his satchel the little bronze cannon. He hurried, because he was happy himself. Another time he would have waited till the sensation made by Perezvon had passed off, now he hurried on regardless of all consideration. "You are all happy now," he felt, "so here's something to make you happier!" He was perfectly enchanted himself.

"I've been coveting this thing for a long while; it's for you, old man, it's for you. It belonged to Morozov, it was of no use to him, he had it from his brother. I swopped a book from father's book-case for it, "A Kinsman of Mahomet, or Salutary Folly', a scandalous book published in Moscow a hundred years ago, before they had any censorship. And Morozov has a taste for such things. He was grateful to me, too . . ."

Kolya held the cannon in his hand so that all could see and admire it. Ilusha raised himself, and, with his right arm still round the dog, he gazed enchanted at the toy. The sensation was even greater when Kolya announced that he had gunpowder, too, and that it could be fired off at once "if it won't alarm the ladies". "Mamma" immediately asked to look at the toy closer and her request was granted. She was much pleased with the little bronze cannon on wheels and began rolling it to and fro on her lap. She readily gave permission for the cannon to be fired, without any idea of what she had been asked. Kolya showed the powder and the shot. The captain, as a military man, undertook to load it, putting in a minute quantity of powder. He asked that the shot might be put off till another time. The cannon was put on the floor, aiming towards an empty part of the room, three grains of powder were thrust into the touch-hole and a match was put to it. A magnificent explosion followed. Mamma was startled, but at once laughed with delight. The boys gazed in speechless triumph. But the captain, looking at Ilusha, was more enchanted than any of them. Kolya picked up the cannon and immediately presented it to Ilusha, together with the powder and the shot.

"I got it for you, for you! I've been keeping it for you a long time," he repeated once more in his delight.

"Oh, give it to me! No, give me the cannon!" Mamma began begging like a little child. Her face showed a piteous fear that she would not get it. Kolya was disconcerted. The captain fidgeted uneasily.

"Mamma, mamma," he ran to her, "the cannon's yours, of course, but let Ilusha have it, because it's a present to him, but it's just as good as yours. Ilusha will always let you play with it, it shall belong to both of you, both of you."

"No, I don't want it to belong to both of us, I want it to be mine altogether, not Ilusha's," persisted mamma, on the point of tears.

"Take it, mother, here, keep it!" Ilusha cried. "Krassotkin, may I give it to my mother?" he turned to Krassotkin with an imploring face, as though he were afraid he might be offended at his giving his present to someone else.

"Of course you may," Krassotkin assented heartily, and, taking the cannon from Ilusha, he handed it himself to mamma with a polite bow. She was so touched that she cried.

"Ilusha darling, he's the one who loves his mamma!" she said tenderly, and at once began wheeling the cannon to and fro on her lap again.

"Mamma, let me kiss your hand." The captain darted up to her at once and did so.

"And I never saw such a charming fellow as this nice boy," said the grateful lady, pointing to Krassotkin.

"And I'll bring you as much powder as you like, Ilusha. We make the powder ourselves now. Borovikov found out how it's made—twenty-four parts of saltpetre, ten of sulphur and six of birchwood charcoal. It's all pounded together, mixed into a paste with water and rubbed through a tammy sieve—that's how it's done."

"Smurov told me about your powder, only father says it's not real gunpowder," responded Ilusha.

"Not real?" Kolya flushed. "It burns. I don't know, of course."

"No, I didn't mean that," put in the captain with a guilty face. "I only said that real powder is not made like that, but that's nothing, it can be made so."

"I don't know, you know best. We lighted some in a pomatum pot, it burned splendidly, it all burnt away leaving only a tiny ash. But that was only the paste, and if you rub it through . . . . but of course you know best, I don't know. . . . And Bulkin's father thrashed him on account of our powder, did you hear?" he turned to Ilusha.

"Yes," answered Ilusha. He listened to Kolya with immense interest and enjoyment.

"We had prepared a whole bottle of it and he used to keep it under his bed. His father saw it. He said it might explode, and thrashed him on the spot. He was going to make a complaint against me to the masters. He is not allowed to go about with me now, no one is allowed to go about with me now. Smurov is not allowed to either, I've got a bad name with everyone. They say I'm a 'desperate character'," Kolya smiled scornfully. "It all began from what happened on the railway."

"Ah, we've heard of that exploit of yours, too," cried the captain. "How could you lie still on the line? Is it possible you weren't the least afraid, lying there under the train? Weren't you frightened?"

The captain was abject in his flattery of Kolya.

"N-not particularly," answered Kolya carelessly. "What's blasted my reputation more than anything here was that cursed goose," he said, turning again to Ilusha. But though he assumed an unconcerned air as he talked, he still could not control himself and was continually missing the note he tried to keep up.

"Ah! I heard about the goose!" Ilusha laughed, beaming all over. "They told me, but I don't understand. Did they really take you to the court?"

"The most stupid, trivial affair, they made a mountain of a mole-hill as they always do," Kolya began carelessly. "I was walking through the market-place here one day, just when they'd driven in the geese. I stopped and looked at them. All at once a fellow, who is an errand boy at Plotnikov's now, looked at me and said: 'What are you looking at the geese for?' I looked at him, he was a stupid, moon-faced fellow of twenty. I am always on the side of the peasantry, you know. I like talking to the peasants. . . . We've dropped behind the peasants—that's an axiom. I believe you are laughing, Karamazov?"

"No, heaven forbid, I am listening," said Alyosha with a most good-natured air, and the sensitive Kolya was immediately reassured.

"My theory, Karamazov, is clear and simple," he hurried on again, looking pleased. "I believe in the people and am always glad to give them their due, but I am not for spoiling them, that is a *sine qua non* . . . But I was telling you about the goose. So I turned to the fool and answered: 'I am wondering what the goose thinks about.' He looked at me quite stupidly: 'And what does the goose think about?' he asked. 'Do you see that cartful of oats?' I said. 'The oats are dropping out of the sack, and the goose has put its neck right under the wheel to gobble them up—do you see?' 'I see that quite well,' he said. 'Well,' said I, 'if that cart were to move on a little, would it break the goose's neck or not? 'It'd be sure to break it,' and he grinned all over his face, highly delighted. 'Come on then,' said I, 'let's try.' 'Let's,' he said. And it did not take us long to arrange: he stood at the bridle without being noticed, and I stood on one side to direct the goose. And the owner wasn't looking, he was talking to someone, so I had nothing to do, the goose thrust its head in after the oats of itself, under the cart, just under the wheel. I winked at the lad, he tugged at the bridle, and crack! The goose's neck was broken in half. And, as luck would have it, all the peasants saw us at that moment and they kicked up a shindy at once. 'You did that on purpose!' 'No, not on purpose.' 'Yes, you did, on purpose!' Well, they shouted, 'Take him to the justice of the peace!' They took me, too. 'You were there, too,' they said, 'you helped, you're known all over the market!' And, for some reason, I really am known all over the market,'' Kolya added conceitedly. ''Wo all went off to the justice's, they brought the goose, too. The fellow was crying in a great funk, simply blubbering like a woman. And the farmer kept shouting that you could kill any number of geese like that. Well, of course, there were witnesses. The justice of the peace settled it in a minute: that the farmer was to be paid a rouble for the goose, and the fellow to have the goose. And he was warned not to play such pranks again. And the fellow kept blubbering like a woman. 'It wasn't me,' he said, 'it was he egged me on,' and he pointed to me. I answered with the utmost composure that I hadn't egged him on, that I simply stated the general proposition, had spoken hypothetically. The justice of the peace smiled and was vexed with himself at once for having smiled. 'I'll complain to your masters of you, so that for the future you mayn't waste your time on such general propositions, instead of sitting at your books and learning your lessons.' He didn't complain to the masters, that was a joke, but the matter was noised abroad and came to the ears of the masters. Their ears are long, you know! The classical master, Kolbasnikov, was particularly shocked about it, but Dardanelov got me off again. But Kolbasnikov is savage with everyone now like a green ass. Did you know, Ilusha, he is just married, got a dowry of a thousand roubles, and his bride's a regular fright of the first rank and the last degree. The third-class fellows wrote an epigram on it.

> 'Astounding news has reached the class
> Kolbasnikov has been an ass.'

And so on, awfully funny, I'll bring it to you later on. I say nothing against Dardanelov, he is a learned man, there's no doubt about it. I respect men like that and it's not because he stood up for me.''

"But you took him down about the founders of Troy!" Smurov put in suddenly, unmistakably proud of Krassotkin at such a moment. He was particularly pleased with the story of the goose.

"Did you really take him down?" the captain inquired, in a flattering way. "On the question who founded Troy? We heard of it, Ilusha told me about it at the time.''

"He knows everything, father, he knows more than any of us!" put in Ilusha; "he only pretends to be like that, but really he is top in every subject . . .''

Ilusha looked at Kolya with infinite happiness.

"Oh, that's all nonsense about Troy, a trivial matter. I consider this an unimportant question,'' said Kolya with haughty humility. He had by now completely recovered his dignity, though he was still a little uneasy. He felt that he was greatly excited and that he had talked about the goose, for instance, with too little reserve, while Alyosha had looked serious and had not said a word all the time. And the vain boy began by degrees to have a rankling fear that Alyosha was silent because he despised him, and thought he was showing off before him. If he dared to think anything like that Kolya would . . .

"I regard the question as quite a trivial one," he rapped out again, proudly.

"And I know who founded Troy," a boy, who had not spoken before, said suddenly, to the surprise of everyone. He was silent and seemed to be shy. He was a pretty boy of about eleven, called Kartashov. He was sitting near the door. Kolya looked at him with dignified amazement.

The fact was that the identity of the founders of Troy had become a secret for the whole school, a secret which could only be discovered by reading Smaragdov, and no one had Smaragdov but Kolya. One day when Kolya's back was turned Kartashov hastily opened Smaragdov, which lay among Kolya's books, and immediately lighted on the passage relating to the foundation of Troy. This was a good time ago, but he felt uneasy and could not bring himself to announce publicly that he, too, knew who had founded Troy, afraid of what might happen and of Krassotkin's somehow putting him to shame over it. But now he couldn't resist saying it. For weeks he had been longing to.

"Well, who did found it?" asked Kolya, turning to him with

haughty superciliousness. He saw from his face that he really did know and at once made up his mind how to take it. There was, so to speak, a discordant note in the general harmony.

"Troy was founded by Teucer, Dardanus, Ilius and Tros," the boy rapped out at once, and in the same instant he blushed, blushed so, that it was painful to look at him. But the boys stared at him, stared at him for a whole minute, and then all the staring eyes turned at once and were fastened upon Kolya, who was still scanning the audacious boy with disdainful composure.

"In what sense did they found it?" he deigned to comment at last. "And what is meant by founding a city or a state? What did they do?—did they go and each lay a brick, do you suppose?"

There was laughter. The offending boy turned from pink to crimson. He was silent and on the point of tears. Kolya held him so for a minute.

"Before you talk of a historical event like the foundation of a nationality, you must first understand what you mean by it," he admonished him in stern incisive tones. "But I attach no consequence to these old wives' tales and I don't think much of universal history in general," he added carelessly, addressing the company generally.

"Universal history?" the captain inquired, looking almost scared.

"Yes, universal history! It's the study of the successive follies of mankind and nothing more. The only subjects I respect are mathematics and natural science," said Kolya. He was showing off and he stole a glance at Alyosha, his was the only opinion he was afraid of there. But Alyosha was still silent and still serious as before. If Alyosha had said a word it would have stopped him, but Alyosha was silent and "it might be the silence of contempt" and that finally irritated Kolya.

"The classical languages, too . . . they are simply madness, nothing more. You seem to disagree with me again, Karamazov?"

"I don't agree," said Alyosha, with a faint smile.

"The study of the classics, if you ask my opinion, is simply a police measure, that's simply why it has been introduced into our schools." By degrees Kolya began to get breathless again. "Latin and Greek were introduced because they are a bore and because they stupefy the intellect. It was dull before, so what could they do to make things duller? It was senseless enough

243

before, so what could they do to make it more senseless? So they thought of Greek and Latin. That's my opinion, I hope I shall never change it," Kolya finished abruptly. His cheeks were flushed.

"That's true," assented Smurov suddenly, in a ringing tone of conviction. He had listened attentively.

"And yet he is first in Latin himself," cried one of the group of boys suddenly.

"Yes, father, he says that and yet he is first in Latin," echoed Ilusha.

"What of it?" Kolya thought fit to defend himself, though the praise was very sweet to him. "I am fagging away at Latin because I have to, because I promised my mother to pass my examination, and I think that whatever you do, it's worth doing it well. But in my soul I have a profound contempt for the classics and all that fraud. . . . You don't agree, Karamazov?"

"Why 'fraud'?" Alyosha smiled again.

"Well, all the classical authors have been translated into all languages, so it was not for the sake of studying the classics they introduced Latin, but solely as a police measure, to stupefy the intelligence. So what can one call it but a fraud?"

"Why, who taught you all this?" cried Alyosha, surprised at last.

"In the first place I am capable of thinking for myself without being taught. Besides, what I said just now about the classics being translated our teacher Kolbasnikov has said to the whole of the third class."

"The doctor has come!" cried Nina, who had been silent till then.

A carriage belonging to Madame Hohlakov drove up to the gate. The captain, who had been expecting the doctor all the morning, rushed headlong out to meet him. "Mamma" pulled herself together and assumed a dignified air. Alyosha went up to Ilusha and began setting his pillows straight. Nina, from her invalid chair, anxiously watched him putting the bed tidy. The boys hurriedly took leave. Some of them promised to come again in the evening. Kolya called Perezvon and the dog jumped off the bed.

"I won't go away, I won't go away," Kolya said hastily to Ilusha. "I'll wait in the passage and come back when the doctor's gone, I'll come back with Perezvon."

But by now the doctor had entered, an important-looking person with long, dark whiskers and a shiny, shaven chin, wearing a bearskin coat. As he crossed the threshold he stopped, taken aback; he probably fancied he had come to the wrong place. "How is this? Where am I?" he muttered, not removing his coat nor his peaked sealskin cap. The crowd, the poverty of the room, the washing hanging on a line in the corner, puzzled him. The captain, bent double, was bowing low before him.

"It's here, sir, here, sir," he muttered cringingly; "it's here, you've come right, you were coming to us . . ."

"Sne-gi-ryov?" the doctor said loudly and pompously. "Mr. Snegiryov—is that you?"

"That's me, sir!"

"Ah!"

The doctor looked round the room with a squeamish air once more and threw off his coat, displaying to all eyes the grand decoration at his neck. The captain caught the fur coat in the air, and the doctor took off his cap.

"Where is the patient?" he asked emphatically.

CHAPTER VI

PRECOCITY

"WHAT do you think the doctor will say to him?" Kolya asked quickly. "What a repulsive mug though, hasn't he? I can't endure medicine!"

"Ilusha is dying. I think that's certain," answered Alyosha mournfully.

"They are rogues! Medicine's a fraud! I am glad to have made your acquaintance though, Karamazov. I wanted to know you for a long time. I am only sorry we meet in such sad circumstances."

Kolya had a great inclination to say something even warmer and more demonstrative, but he felt ill at ease. Alyosha noticed this, smiled, and pressed his hand.

"I've long learned to respect you as a rare person," Kolya muttered again, faltering and uncertain. "I have heard you are a mystic and have been in the monastery. I know you are a mystic, but . . . that hasn't put me off. Contact with real life will cure you. . . . It's always so with characters like yours."

'What do you mean by mystic? Cure me of what?" Alyosha was rather astonished.

"Oh, God and all the rest of it."

"What, don't you believe in God?"

"Oh, I've nothing against God. Of course, God is only a hypothesis, but . . . I admit that He is needed . . . for the order of the universe and all that . . . and that if there were no God He would have to be invented," added Kolya, beginning to blush. He suddenly fancied that Alyosha might think he was trying to show off his knowledge and to prove that he was "grown up". "I haven't the slightest desire to show off my knowledge to him," Kolya thought indignantly. And all of a sudden he felt horribly annoyed.

"I must confess I can't endure entering on such discussions," he said, with a final air. "It's possible for one who doesn't believe in God to love mankind, don't you think so? Voltaire didn't believe in God and loved mankind." ("I am at it again," he thought to himself.)

"Voltaire believed in God, though not very much, I think, and I don't think he loved mankind very much either," said Alyosha quietly, gently, and quite naturally, as though he were talking to someone of his own age, or even older. Kolya was particularly struck by Alyosha's apparent diffidence about his opinion of Voltaire. He seemed to be leaving the question for him, little Kolya, to settle.

"Have you read Voltaire?" Alyosha finished.

"No, not to say 'read'. . . . But I've read *Candide* in the Russian translation . . . in an absurd, grotesque, old translation". . . . ("At it again! again!")

"And did you understand it?"

"Oh, yes, everything. . . . That is . . . Why do you suppose I shouldn't understand it? There's a lot of nastiness in it, of course. . . . Of course I can understand that it's a philosophical novel and written to advocate an idea. . . ." Kolya was getting mixed by now. "I am a Socialist, Karamazov, I am an incurable Socialist," he announced suddenly, apropos of nothing.

"A Socialist?" laughed Alyosha. "But when have you had time to become one? Why, I thought you are only thirteen?"

Kolya winced.

"In the first place I am not thirteen, but fourteen, fourteen in a fortnight," he flushed angrily, "and in the second place I am at a complete loss to understand what my age has to do with it. The question is, what are my convictions, not what is my age, isn't it?"

"When you are older, you'll understand for yourself the influence of age on convictions. I fancied, too, that you were not expressing your own ideas," Alyosha anwered serenely and modestly, but Kolya interrupted him hotly:

"Come, you want obedience and mysticism. You must admit that the Christian religion, for instance, has only been of use to the rich and the powerful to keep the lower classes in slavery, that's so, isn't it?"

"Ah, I know where you read that, and I am sure someone told you so!" cried Alyosha.

"I say, what makes you think I read it? And certainly no one told me so. I can think for myself. . . . I am not opposed to Christ, if you like. He was a most humane person, and if He were alive to-day, He would be found in the ranks of the revolutionists, and would perhaps play a conspicuous part. . . . There's no doubt about that."

"Oh, where, where did you get that from? What fool have you made friends with?" exclaimed Alyosha.

"Come, the truth will out! It has so chanced that I have often talked to Mr. Rakitin, of course, but . . . old Byelinsky said that, too, so they say."

"Byelinsky? I don't remember. He hasn't written that anywhere."

"If he didn't write it, they say he said it. I heard that from a . . . but never mind."

"And have you read Byelinsky?"

"Well, no . . . I haven't read all of him, but . . . I read the passage about Tatyana, why she didn't go off with Onyegin."

"Didn't go off with Onyegin? Surely you don't . . . understand that already?"

"Why, you seem to take me for little Smurov," said Kolya, with a grin of irritation. "But please don't suppose I am such a revolutionist. I often disagree with Mr. Rakitin. Though I mention Tatyana, I am not at all for the emancipation of women. I acknowledge that women are a subject race and must obey. *Les femmes tricottent*, as Napoleon said." Kolya, for some reason, smiled. "And on that question at least I am quite of one mind with that pseudo-great man. I think, too, that to leave one's own country and fly to America is mean, worse than mean—silly. Why go to America when one may be of great service to humanity here? Now especially. There's

247

a perfect mass of fruitful activity open to us. That's what I answered."

"What do you mean? Answered whom? Has someone suggested your going to America already?"

"I must own, they've been at me to go, but I declined. That's between ourselves, of course, Karamazov; do you hear, not a word to anyone. I say this only to you. I am not at all anxious to fall into the clutches of the secret police and take lessons at the Chain bridge:

> *'Long will you remember*
> *The house at the Chain bridge.'*

Do you remember? It's splendid. Why are you laughing? You don't suppose I am fibbing, do you?" ("What if he should find out that I've only that one number of *The Bell* in father's bookcase, and haven't read any more of it?" Kolya thought, with a shudder.)

"Oh no, I am not laughing and don't suppose for a moment that you are lying. No, indeed, I can't suppose so, for all this, alas! is perfectly true. But tell me, have you read Pushkin, Onyegin, for instance? . . . You spoke just now of Tatyana."

"No, I haven't read it yet, but I want to read it. I have no prejudices, Karamazov; I want to hear both sides. What makes you ask?"

"Oh, nothing."

"Tell me, Karamazov, have you an awful contempt for me?" Kolya rapped out suddenly and drew himself up before Alyosha, as though he were on drill. "Be so kind as to tell me, without beating about the bush."

"I have a contempt for you?" Alyosha looked at him wondering. "What for? I am only sad that a charming nature such as yours should be perverted by all this crude nonsense before you have begun life."

"Don't be anxious about my nature," Kolya interrupted, not without complacency. "But it's true that I am stupidly sensitive, crudely sensitive. You smiled just now, and I fancied you seemed to . . ."

"Oh, my smile meant something quite different. I'll tell you why I smiled. Not long ago I read the criticism made by a German who had lived in Russia on our students and schoolboys of to-day. 'Show a Russian schoolboy,' he writes, 'a map of the stars, which he knows nothing about, and he will give you back the map next day with corrections on it.' No knowledge and unbounded conceit—that's what the German meant to say about the Russian schoolboy."

"Yes, that's perfectly right," Kolya laughed suddenly, "exactly so! Bravo the German. But he did not see the good side, what do you think? Conceit, maybe, that comes from youth, that will be corrected if need be, but, on the other hand, there is an independent spirit almost from childhood, boldness of thought and conviction, and not the spirit of these sausage-makers, grovelling before authority. . . . But the German was right all the same. Bravo the German! But Germans want strangling all the same. Though they are so good at science and learning they must be strangled."

"Strangled, what for?" smiled Alyosha.

"Well, perhaps I am talking nonsense, I agree. I am awfully childish sometimes, and when I am pleased about anything I can't restrain myself and am ready to talk any stuff. But, I say, we are chattering away here about nothing, and that doctor has been a long time in there. But perhaps he's examining the mamma and that poor crippled Nina. I liked that Nina, you know. She whispered to me suddenly as I was coming away: 'Why didn't you come before?' And in such a voice, so reproachfully! I think she is awfully nice and pathetic."

"Yes, yes! Well, you'll be coming often, you will see what she is like. It would do you a great deal of good to know people like that, to learn to value a great deal which you will find out from knowing these people," Alyosha observed warmly. "That would have more effect on you than anything."

"Oh, how I regret and blame myself for not having come sooner!" Kolya exclaimed, with bitter feeling.

"Yes, it's a great pity. You saw for yourself how delighted the poor child was to see you. And how he fretted for you to come!"

"Don't tell me! You make it worse! But it serves me right. What kept me from coming was my conceit, my egoistic vanity, and the beastly wilfulness, which I never can get rid of, though I've been struggling with it all my life. I see that now. I am a beast in lots of ways, Karamazov!"

"No, you have a charming nature, though it's been distorted, and I quite understand why you have had such an influence on this generous, morbidly sensitive boy," Alyosha answered warmly.

"And you say that to me!" cried Kolya; "and would you

believe it, I thought—I've thought several times since I've been here—that you despised me! If only you knew how I prize your opinion!"

"But are you really so sensitive? At your age! Would you believe it, just now, when you were telling your story, I thought, as I watched you, that you must be very sensitive!"

"You thought so? What an eye you've got, I say! I bet that was when I was talking about the goose. That was just when I was fancying you had a great contempt for me for being in such a hurry to show off, and for a moment I quite hated you for it, and began talking like a fool. Then I fancied—just now, here—when I said that if there were no God He would have to be invented, that I was in too great a hurry to display my knowledge, especially as I got that phrase out of a book. But I swear I wasn't showing off out of vanity, though I really don't know why, because I was so pleased, yes, I believe it was because I was so pleased . . . though it's perfectly disgraceful for anyone to be gushing directly they are pleased, I know that. But I am convinced now that you don't despise me; it was all my imagination. Oh, Karamazov, I am profoundly unhappy. I sometimes fancy all sorts of things, that everyone is laughing at me, the whole world, and then I feel ready to overturn the whole order of things."

"And you worry everyone about you," smiled Alyosha.

"Yes, I worry everyone about me, especially my mother. Karamazov, tell me, am I very ridiculous now?"

"Don't think about that, don't think of it at all!" cried Alyosha. "And what does 'ridiculous' mean? Isn't everyone constantly being or seeming ridiculous? Besides, nearly all clever people now are fearfully afraid of being ridiculous, and that makes them unhappy. All I am surprised at is that you should be feeling that so early, though I've observed it for some time past, and not only in you. Nowadays the very children have begun to suffer from it. It's almost a sort of insanity. The devil has taken the form of that vanity and entered into the whole generation; it's simply the devil," added Alyosha, without a trace of the smile that Kolya, staring at him, expected to see. "You are like everyone else," said Alyosha, in conclusion, "that is, like very many others. Only you must not be like everybody else, that's all."

"Even if everyone is like that?"

"Yes, even if everyone is like that. You be the only one not like it. You really are not like everyone else, here you are not ashamed to confess to something bad and even ridiculous. And who will admit so much in these days? No one. And people have even ceased to feel the impulse to self-criticism. Don't be like everyone else, even if you were the only one."

"Splendid! I was not mistaken in you. You know how to console one. Oh, how I have longed to know you, Karamazov. I've long been eager for this meeting. Can you really have thought about me, too? You said just now that you thought of me, too."

"Yes, I'd heard of you and had thought of you, too . . . and if it's partly vanity that makes you ask, it doesn't matter."

"Do you know, Karamazov, our talk has been like a declaration of love," said Kolya, in a bashful and melting voice. "That's not ridiculous, is it?"

"Not at all ridiculous, and if it were, it wouldn't matter, because it's been a good thing." Alyosha smiled brightly.

"But do you know, Karamazov, you must admit that you are a little ashamed yourself, now. . . . I see it by your eyes." Kolya smiled with a sort of sly happiness.

"Why ashamed?"

"Well, why are you blushing?"

"It was you made me blush," laughed Alyosha, and he really did blush. "Oh well, I am a little, goodness knows why. I don't know . . ." he muttered almost embarrassed.

"Oh, how I love you and admire you at this moment just because you are rather ashamed! Because you are just like me," cried Kolya, in positive ecstasy. His cheeks glowed, his eyes beamed.

"You know, Kolya, you will be very unhappy in your life," something made Alyosha say suddenly.

"I know, I know. How you know it all beforehand!" Kolya agreed at once.

"But you will bless life on the whole, all the same."

"Just so, hurrah! You are a prophet. Oh, we shall get on together, Karamazov! Do you know, what delights me most is that you treat me quite like an equal. But we are not equals, no, we are not, you are better! But we shall get on. Do you know, all this last month I've been saying to myself, 'Either we shall be friends at once, for ever, or we shall part enemies to the grave!'"

"And saying that, of course, you loved me," Alyosha laughed gaily.

"I did. I loved you awfully. I've been loving and dreaming of you. And how do you know it all beforehand? Ah, here's the doctor. Goodness! What will he tell us? Look at his face!"

CHAPTER VII

ILUSHA

THE doctor came out of the room again, muffled in his fur coat and with his cap on his head. His face looked almost angry and disgusted, as though he were afraid of getting dirty. He cast a cursory glance round the passage, looking sternly at Alyosha and Kolya as he did so. Alyosha waved from the door to the coachman, and the carriage that had brought the doctor drove up. The captain darted out after the doctor, and, bowing apologetically, stopped him to get the last word. The poor fellow looked utterly crushed; there was a scared look in his eyes.

"Your Excellency, your Excellency . . . is it possible?" he began, but could not go on and clasped his hands in despair. Yet he still gazed imploringly at the doctor, as though a word from him might still change the poor boy's fate.

"I can't help it, I am not God!" the doctor answered off-hand, though with the customary impressiveness.

"Doctor . . . your Excellency . . . and will it be soon, soon?"

"You must be prepared for anything," said the doctor in emphatic and incisive tones, and dropping his eyes, he was about to step out to the coach.

"Your Excellency, for Christ's sake," the terror-stricken captain stopped him again. "Your Excellency! but can nothing, absolutely nothing save him now?"

"It's not in my hands now," said the doctor impatiently, "but, h'm . . ." he stopped suddenly. "If you could, for instance . . . send . . . your patient . . . at once, without delay" (the words "at once, without delay", the doctor uttered with an almost wrathful sternness that made the captain start), "to Syracuse, the change to the new be-ne-ficial climatic conditions might possibly affect . . ."

"To Syracuse!" cried the captain, unable to grasp what was said.

"Syracuse is in Sicily," Kolya jerked out suddenly in explanation. The doctor looked at him.

"Sicily! your Excellency," faltered the captain, "but you've seen"—he spread out his hands, indicating his surroundings— "mamma and my family?"

"N-no, Sicily is not the place for the family, the family should go to the Caucasus in the early spring . . . your daughter must go to the Caucasus, and your wife . . . after a course of the waters in the Caucasus for her rheumatism . . . must be sent straight to Paris to the mental specialist Lepelletier; I could give you a note to him, and then . . . there might be a change . . ."

"Doctor, doctor! But you see!" The captain flung wide his hands again despairingly, indicating the bare wooden walls of the passage.

"Well, that's not my business," grinned the doctor. "I have only told you the answer of medical science to your question as to possible treatment. As for the rest, to my regret. . . ."

"Don't be afraid, apothecary, my dog won't bite you," Kolya rapped out loudly, noticing the doctor's rather uneasy glance at Perezvon, who was standing in the doorway. There was a wrathful note in Kolya's voice. He used the word apothecary instead of doctor on purpose, and, as he explained afterwards, "I used it to insult him".

"What's that?" The doctor flung up his head, staring with surprise at Kolya. "Who's this?" he addressed Alyosha, as though asking him to explain.

"It's Perezvon's master, don't worry about me," Kolya said incisively again.

"Perezvon?"* repeated the doctor, perplexed.

"He hears the bell, but where it is he cannot tell. Good-bye, we shall meet in Syracuse."

"Who's this? Who's this?" The doctor flew into a terrible rage.

"He is a schoolboy, doctor, he is a mischievous boy; take no notice of him," said Alyosha, frowning and speaking quickly. "Kolya, hold your tongue!" he cried to Krassotkin. "Take no notice of him, doctor," he repeated, rather impatiently.

"He wants a thrashing, a good thrashing!" The doctor stamped in a perfect fury.

"And you know, apothecary, my Perezvon might bite!" said Kolya, turning pale, with quivering voice and flashing eyes. "*Ici*, Perezvon!"

* *I.e.* a chime of bells.

"Kolya, if you say another word I'll have nothing more to do with you," Alyosha cried peremptorily.

"There is only one man in the world who can command Nikolay Krassotkin—this is the man." (Kolya pointed to Alyosha.) "I obey him, good-bye!"

He stepped forward, opened the door, and quickly went into the inner room. Perezvon flew after him. The doctor stood still for five seconds in amazement, looking at Alyosha; then, with a curse, he went out quickly to the carriage, repeating aloud: "This is . . . this is . . . I don't know what it is!" The captain darted forward to help him into the carriage. Alyosha followed Kolya into the room. He was already by Ilusha's bed-side. The sick boy was holding his hand and calling for his father. A minute later the captain, too, came back.

"Father, father, come . . . we . . ." Ilusha faltered in violent excitement, but apparently unable to go on, he flung his wasted arms round his father and Kolya, uniting them in one embrace, and hugging them as tightly as he could. The captain suddenly began to shake with dumb sobs, and Kolya's lips and chin twitched.

"Father, father! How sorry I am for you!" Ilusha moaned bitterly.

"Ilusha . . . darling . . . the doctor said . . . you would be all right . . . we shall be happy . . . the doctor . . ." the captain began.

"Ah, father! I know what the new doctor said to you about me. . . . I saw!" cried Ilusha, and again he hugged them both with all his strength, hiding his face on his father's shoulder.

"Father, don't cry, and when I die get a good boy, another one . . . choose one of them all, a good one, call him Ilusha and love him instead of me . . ."

"Hush, old man, you'll get well," Krassotkin cried suddenly, in a voice that sounded angry.

"But don't ever forget me, father," Ilusha went on, "come to my grave . . . and, father, bury me by our big stone, where we used to go for our walk, and come to me there with Krassotkin in the evening . . . and Perezvon . . . I shall expect you. . . . Father, father!"

His voice broke. They were all three silent, still embracing. Nina was crying, quietly in her chair, and at last, seeing them all crying, "mamma", too, burst into tears.

"Ilusha! Ilusha!" she exclaimed.

Krassotkin suddenly released himself from Ilusha's embrace.

"Good-bye, old man, mother expects me back to dinner," he said quickly. "What a pity I did not tell her! She will be dreadfully anxious. . . . But after dinner I'll come back to you for the whole day, for the whole evening, and I'll tell you all sorts of things, all sorts of things. And I'll bring Perezvon, but now I will take him with me, because he will begin to howl when I am away and bother you. Good-bye!"

And he ran out into the passage. He didn't want to cry, but in the passage he burst into tears. Alyosha found him crying.

"Kolya, you must be sure to keep your word and come, or he will be terribly disappointed," Alyosha said emphatically.

"I will! Oh, how I curse myself for not having come before," muttered Kolya, crying, and no longer ashamed of it.

At that moment the captain flew out of the room, and at once locked the door behind him. His face looked frenzied, his lips were trembling. He stood before the two lads and flung up his arms.

"I don't want a good boy! I don't want another boy!" he muttered in a wild whisper, clenching his teeth. "If I forget thee, Jerusalem, may my tongue . . ." he broke off with a sob and sank on his knees before the wooden bench. Pressing his fists against his head, he began sobbing with absurd whimpering cries, doing his utmost that his cries should not be heard in the room.

Kolya ran out into the street.

"Good-bye, Karamazov! Will you come yourself?" he cried sharply and angrily to Alyosha.

"I will certainly come in the evening."

"What was that he said about Jerusalem? . . . What did he mean by that?"

"It's from the Bible. 'If I forget thee, Jerusalem,' that is, if I forget all that is most precious to me, if I let anything take its place, then may . . ."

"I understand, that's enough! Mind you come! *Ici,* Perezvon!" he cried, with positive ferocity to the dog, and with rapid strides he went home.

BOOK XI: IVAN

CHAPTER I

AT GRUSHENKA'S

ALYOSHA went towards the cathedral square to the widow Morozov's house to see Grushenka, who had sent Fenya to him early in the morning with an urgent message begging him to come. Questioning Fenya, Alyosha learned that her mistress had been particularly distressed since the previous day. During the two months that had passed since Mitya's arrest, Alyosha had called frequently at the widow Morozov's house, both from his own inclination and to take messages for Mitya. Three days after Mitya's arrest, Grushenka was taken very ill and was ill for nearly five weeks. For one whole week she was unconscious. She was very much changed—thinner and a little sallow, though she had for the past fortnight been well enough to go out. But to Alyosha her face was even more attractive than before, and he liked to meet her eyes when he went in to her. A look of firmness and intelligent purpose had developed in her face. There were signs of a spiritual transformation in her, and a steadfast, fine and humble determination that nothing could shake could be discerned in her. There was a small vertical line between her brows which gave her charming face a look of concentrated thought, almost austere at the first glance. There was scarcely a trace of her former frivolity.

It seemed strange to Alyosha, too, that in spite of the calamity that had overtaken the poor girl, betrothed to a man who had been arrested for a terrible crime, almost at the instant of their betrothal, in spite of her illness and the almost inevitable sentence hanging over Mitya, Grushenka had yet not lost her youthful cheerfulness. There was a soft light in the once proud eyes, though at times they gleamed with the old vindictive fire when she was visited by one disturbing thought stronger than ever in her heart. The object of that uneasiness was the same as ever—Katerina Ivanovna, of whom Grushenka had even raved when she lay in delirium.. Alyosha knew that she was fearfully jealous of her. Yet Katerina Ivanovna had not once visited Mitya in his prison, though she might have done it whenever she liked. All this made a difficult problem for Alyosha, for he was the only person to whom Grushenka opened her heart and from whom she was continually asking advice. Sometimes he was unable to say anything.

Full of anxiety he entered her lodging. She was at home. She had returned from seeing Mitya half an hour before, and from the rapid movement with which she leapt up from her chair to meet him he saw that she had been expecting him with great impatience. A pack of cards dealt for a game of "fools" lay on the table. A bed had been made up on the leather sofa on the other side and Maximov lay, half-reclining, on it. He wore a dressing-gown and a cotton nightcap, and was evidently ill and weak, though he was smiling blissfully. When the home-less old man returned with Grushenka from Mokroe two months before, he had simply stayed on and was still staying with her. He arrived with her in rain and sleet, sat down on the sofa, drenched and scared, and gazed mutely at her with a timid, appealing smile. Grushenka, who was in terrible grief and in the first stage of fever, almost forgot his existence in all she had to do the first half-hour after her arrival. Suddenly she chanced to look at him intently: he laughed a pitiful, helpless little laugh. She called Fenya and told her to give him something to eat. All that day he sat in the same place, almost without stirring. When it got dark and the shutters were closed, Fenya asked her mistress:

"Is the gentleman going to stay the night, mistress?"

"Yes; make him a bed on the sofa," answered Grushenka.

Questioning him more in detail, Grushenka learned from him that he had literally nowhere to go, and that "Mr. Kalganov, my benefactor, told me straight that he wouldn't receive me again and gave me five roubles."

"Well, God bless you, you'd better stay then," Grushenka decided in her grief, smiling compassionately at him. Her smile wrung the old man's heart and his lips twitched with grateful tears. And so the destitute wanderer had stayed with her ever since. He did not leave the house even when she was ill. Fenya and her grandmother, the cook, did not turn him out, but went on serving him meals and making up his bed on the sofa. Grushenka had grown used to him, and coming back from see-ing Mitya (whom she had begun to visit in prison before she was really well) she would sit down and begin talking to "Maxi-mushka" about trifling matters, to keep her from thinking of her sorrow. The old man turned out to be a good story-teller on occasions, so that at last he became necessary to her. Grushenka saw scarcely anyone else beside Alyosha, who did not come every day and never stayed long. Her old merchant lay seriously ill at this time, "at his last gasp", as they said in the town, and he did, in fact, die a week after Mitya's trial. Three weeks before his death, feeling the end approaching, he made his sons, their wives and children, come upstairs to him at last and bade them not leave him again. From that moment he gave strict orders to his servants not to admit Grushenka and to tell her if she came, "The master wishes you long life and happiness and tells you to forget him". But Grushenka sent almost every day to inquire after him.

"You've come at last!" she cried, flinging down the cards and joyfully greeting Alyosha, "and Maximushka's been scaring me that perhaps you wouldn't come. Ah, how I need you! Sit down at the table. What will you have—coffee?"

"Yes, please," said Alyosha, sitting down at the table. "I am very hungry."

"That's right. Fenya, Fenya, coffee," cried Grushenka. "It's been made a long time ready for you. And bring some little pies, and mind they are hot. Do you know, we've had a storm over those pies to-day. I took them to the prison for him, and would you believe it, he threw them back to me: he would not eat them. He flung one of them on the floor and stamped on it. So I said to him: 'I shall leave them with the warder; if you don't eat them before evening, it will be that your venomous spite is enough for you!' With that I went away. We quarrelled again, would you believe it? Whenever I go we quarrel."

Grushenka said all this in one breath in her agitation. Maximov, feeling nervous, at once smiled and looked on the floor.

"What did you quarrel about this time?" asked Alyosha.

"I didn't expect it in the least. Only fancy, he is jealous of the Pole. 'Why are you keeping him?' he said. 'So you've begun keeping him.' He is jealous, jealous of me all the time, jealous eating and sleeping! He even took it into his head to be jealous of Kuzma last week."

"But he knew about the Pole before?"

"Yes, but there it is. He has known about him from the very beginning, but to-day he suddenly got up and began scolding about him. I am ashamed to repeat what he said. Silly fellow! Rakitin went in as I came out. Perhaps Rakitin is egging him on. What do you think?" she added carelessly.

258

"He loves you, that's what it is; he loves you so much. And now he is particularly worried."

"I should think he might be, with the trial to-morrow. And I went to him to say something about to-morrow, for I dread to think what's going to happen then. You say that he is worried, but how worried I am! And he talks about the Pole! He's too silly! Hs is not jealous of Maximushka yet, any-way."

"My wife was dreadfully jealous over me, too," Maximov put in his word.

"Jealous of you?" Grushenka laughed in spite of herself. "Of whom could she have been jealous?"

"Of the servant girls."

"Hold your tongue, Maximushka, I am in no laughing mood now, I feel angry. Don't ogle the pies. I shan't give you any; they are not good for you, and I won't give you any vodka either. I have to look after him, too, just as though I kept an almshouse," she laughed.

"I don't deserve your kindness. I am a worthless creature," said Maximov, with tears in his voice. "You would do better to spend your kindness on people of more use than me."

"Ech, everyone is of use, Maximushka, and how can we tell who's of most use? If only that Pole didn't exist, Alyosha. He's taken it into his head to fall ill, too, to-day. I've been to see him also. And I shall send him some pies, too, on purpose. I hadn't sent him any, but Mitya accused me of it, so now I shall send some! Ah, here's Fenya with a letter! Yes, it's from the Poles—begging again!"

Pan Mussyalovitch had indeed sent an extremely long and characteristically eloquent letter in which he begged her to lend him three roubles. In the letter was enclosed a receipt for the sum, with a promise to repay it within three months, signed by Pan Vrublevsky as well. Grushenka had received many such letters, accompanied by such receipts, from her former lover during the fortnight of her convalescence. But she knew that the two Poles had been to ask after her health during her ill-ness. The first letter Grushenka got from them was a long one, written on large note-paper and with a big family crest on the seal. It was so obscure and rhetorical that Grushenka put it down before she had read half, unable to make head or tail of it. She could not attend to letters then. The first letter was followed next day by another in which Pan Mussyalovitch begged her for a loan of two thousand roubles for a very short

THE BROTHERS KARAMAZOV

period. Grushenka left that letter, too, unanswered. A whole
series of letters had followed—one every day—all as pompous
and rhetorical, but the loan asked for, gradually diminishing,
dropped to a hundred roubles, then to twenty-five, to ten, and
finally Grushenka received a letter in which both the Poles
begged her for only one rouble and included a receipt signed
by both.

Then Grushenka suddenly felt sorry for them, and at dusk
she went round herself to their lodging. She found the two
Poles in great poverty, almost destitution, without food or fuel,
without cigarettes, in debt to their landlady. The two hundred
roubles they had carried off from Mitya at Mokroe had soon
disappeared. But Grushenka was surprised at their meeting
her with arrogant dignity and self-assertion, with the greatest
punctilio and pompous speeches. Grushenka simply laughed,
and gave her former admirer ten roubles. Then, laughing, she
told Mitya of it and he was not in the least jealous. But ever
since, the Poles had attached themselves to Grushenka and
bombarded her daily with requests for money and she had
always sent them small sums. And now that day Mitya had
taken it into his head to be fearfully jealous.

"Like a fool, I went round to him just for a minute, on the
way to see Mitya, for he is ill, too, my Pole," Grushenka began
again, with nervous haste. "I was laughing, telling Mitya
about it. 'Fancy,' I said, 'my Pole had the happy thought to
sing his old songs to me to the guitar. He thought I would be
touched and marry him!' Mitya leapt up swearing. . . . So
there, I'll send them the pies! Fenya, is it that little girl they've
sent? Here, give her three roubles and pack a dozen pies up in
a paper and tell her to take them. And you, Alyosha, be sure
to tell Mitya that I did send them the pies."

"I wouldn't tell him for anything," said Alyosha, smiling.

"Ech! You think he is unhappy about it. Why, he's jealous
on purpose. He doesn't care," said Grushenka bitterly.

"On purpose?" queried Alyosha.

"I tell you you are silly, Alyosha. You know nothing about
it, with all your cleverness. I am not offended that he is jealous
of a girl like me. I would be offended if he were not jealous. I
am like that. I am not offended at jealousy. I have a fierce
heart, too. I can be jealous myself. Only what offends me
is that he doesn't love me at all. I tell you he is jealous now
on purpose. Am I blind? Don't I see? He began talking to me
just now of that woman, of Katerina, saying she was this and

that, how she had ordered a doctor from Moscow for him, to try to save him; how she had ordered the best counsel, the most learned one, too. So he loves her, if he'll praise her to my face, more shame to him! He's treated me badly himself, so he attacked me, to make out I am in fault first and to throw it all on me. 'You were with your Pole before me, so I can't be blamed for Katerina,' that's what it amounts to. He wants to throw the whole blame on me. He attacked me on purpose, on purpose, I tell you, but I'll . . ."

Grushenka could not finish saying what she would do. She hid her eyes in her handkerchief and sobbed violently.

"He doesn't love Katerina Ivanovna," said Alyosha firmly.

"Well, whether he loves her or not, I'll soon find out for myself," said Grushenka, with a menacing note in her voice, taking the handkerchief from her eyes. Her face was distorted. Alyosha saw sorrowfully that from being mild and serene it had become sullen and spiteful.

"Enough of this foolishness," she said suddenly; "it's not for that I sent for you. Alyosha darling, to-morrow—what will happen to-morrow? That's what worries me! And it's only me it worries! I look at everyone and no one is thinking of it. No one cares about it. Are you thinking about it even? To-morrow he'll be tried, you know. Tell me, how will he be tried? You know it's the valet, the valet killed him! Good heavens! Can they condemn him in place of the valet and will no one stand up for him? They haven't troubled the valet at all, have they?"

"He's been severely cross-examined," observed Alyosha thoughtfully; "but everyone came to the conclusion it was not he. Now he is lying very ill. He has been ill ever since that attack. Really ill," added Alyosha.

"Oh dear! couldn't you go to that counsel yourself and tell him the whole thing by yourself? He's been brought from Petersburg for three thousand roubles, they say."

"We gave these three thousand together—Ivan, Katerina Ivanovna and I—but she paid two thousand for the doctor from Moscow herself. The counsel Fetyukovitch would have charged more, but the case has become known all over Russia; it's talked of in all the papers and journals. Fetyukovitch agreed to come more for the glory of the thing, because the case has become so notorious. I saw him yesterday."

"Well? Did you talk to him?" Grushenka put in eagerly.

"He listened and said nothing. He told me that he had

261

already formed his opinion. But he promised to give my words consideration."

"Consideration! Ah, they are swindlers! They'll ruin him. And why did she send for the doctor?"

"As an expert. They want to prove that Mitya's mad and committed the murder when he didn't know what he was doing"; Alyosha smiled gently; "but Mitya won't agree to that."

"Yes; but that would be the truth if he had killed him!" cried Grushenka. "He was mad then, perfectly mad, and that was my fault, wretch that I am! But, of course, he didn't do it, he didn't do it! And they are all against him, the whole town. Even Fenya's evidence went to prove he had done it. And the people at the shop, and that official, and at the tavern, too, before, people had heard him say so! They are all, all against him, all crying out against him."

"Yes, there's a fearful accumulation of evidence," Alyosha observed grimly.

"And Grigory—Grigory Vassilyevitch—sticks to his story that the door was open, persists that he saw it—there's no shaking him. I went and talked to him myself. He's rude about it, too."

"Yes, that's perhaps the strongest evidence against him," said Alyosha.

"And as for Mitya's being mad, he certainly seems like it now," Grushenka began, with a peculiarly anxious and mysterious air. "Do you know, Alyosha, I've been wanting to talk to you about it for a long time. I go to him every day and simply wonder at him. Tell me, now, what do you suppose he's always talking about? He talks and talks and I can make nothing of it. I fancied he was talking of something intellectual that I couldn't understand in my foolishness. Only he suddenly began talking to me about a babe—that is, about some child. 'Why is the babe poor?' he said. 'It's for that babe I am going to Siberia now. I am not a murderer, but I must go to Siberia!' What that meant, what babe, I couldn't tell for the life of me. Only I cried when he said it, because he said it so nicely. He cried himself, and I cried, too. He suddenly kissed me and made the sign of the Cross over me. What did it mean, Alyosha? Tell me. What is this babe?"

"It must be Rakitin, who's been going to see him lately," smiled Alyosha, "though . . . that's not Rakitin's doing. I didn't see Mitya yesterday. I'll see him to-day."

THE BROTHERS KARAMAZOV

"No, it's not Rakitin; it's his brother Ivan Fyodorovitch
upsetting him. It's his going to see him, that's what it is,"
Grushenka began, and suddenly broke off. Alyosha gazed at
her in amazement.

"Ivan's going? Has he been to see him? Mitya told me
himself that Ivan hasn't been once."

"There . . . there! What a girl I am! Blurting things out!"
exclaimed Grushenka, confused and suddenly blushing. "Stay,
Alyosha, hush! Since I've said so much I'll tell the whole
truth—he's been to see him twice, the first time directly he
arrived. He galloped here from Moscow at once, of course
before I was taken ill; and the second time was a week ago.
He told Mitya not to tell you about it, under any circumstances;
and not to tell anyone, in fact. He came secretly."

Alyosha sat plunged in thought, considering something. The
news evidently impressed him.

"Ivan doesn't talk to me of Mitya's case," he said slowly.
"He's said very little to me these last two months. And whenever I go to see him, he seems vexed at my coming, so I've not
been to him for the last three weeks. Hm! . . . if he were there
a week ago . . . there certainly has been a change in Mitya
this week."

"There has been a change," Grushenka assented quickly.
"They have a secret, they have a secret! Mitya told me himself there was a secret, and such a secret that Mitya can't rest.
Before then, he was cheerful—and, indeed, he is cheerful now—
but when he shakes his head like that, you know, and strides
about the room and keeps pulling at the hair on his right temple
with his right hand, I know there is something on his mind
worrying him. . . . I know! He was cheerful before, though,
indeed, he is cheerful to-day."

"But you said he was worried."

"Yes, he is worried and yet cheerful. He keeps on being
irritable for a minute and then cheerful and then irritable again.
And you know, Alyosha, I am constantly wondering at him—
with this awful thing hanging over him, he sometimes laughs
at such trifles as though he were a baby himself."

"And did he really tell you not to tell me about Ivan? Did
he say, 'Don't tell him'?"

"Yes, he told me, 'Don't tell him'. It's you that Mitya's
most afraid of. Because it's a secret: he said himself it was a
secret. Alyosha darling, go to him and find out what their
secret is and come and tell me," Grushenka besought him, with

263

sudden eagerness. "Set my mind at rest that I may know the worst that's in store for me. That's why I sent for you."

"You think it's something to do with you? If it were, he wouldn't have told you there was a secret."

"I don't know. Perhaps he wants to tell me but doesn't dare to. He warns me. There is a secret, he tells me, but he won't tell me what it is."

"What do you think yourself?"

"What do I think? It's the end for me, that's what I think. They all three have been plotting my end, for Katerina's in it. It's all Katerina, it all comes from her. 'She is this and that' means that I am not. He tells me that beforehand—warns me. He is planning to throw me over, that's the whole secret. They've planned it together, the three of them — Mitya, Katerina, and Ivan Fyodorovitch. Alyosha, I've been wanting to ask you a long time. A week ago he suddenly told me that Ivan was in love with Katerina, because he often goes to see her. Did he tell me the truth or not? Tell me, on your conscience, tell me the worst."

"I won't tell you a lie. Ivan is not in love with Katerina Ivanovna, I think."

"Oh, that's what I thought! He is lying to me, shameless deceiver, that's what he is! And he was jealous of me just now, so as to put the blame on me afterwards. He is stupid, he can't disguise what he is doing; he is so open, you know. . . . But I'll give it to him, I'll give it to him! 'You believe I did it,' he said. He said that to me, to me. He reproached me with that! God forgive him! You wait, I'll make it hot for Katerina at the trial! I'll just say a word then . . . I'll tell everything then!"

And again she cried bitterly.

"This I can tell you for certain, Grushenka," Alyosha said, getting up. "First, that he loves you, loves you more than anyone in the world, and you only, believe me. I know. I do know. The second thing is that I don't want to worm his secret out of him, but if he'll tell me of himself to-day, I shall tell him straight out that I have promised to tell you. Then I'll come to you to-day and tell you. Only . . . I fancy . . . Katerina Ivanovna has nothing to do with it, and that the secret is about something else. That's certain. It isn't likely it's about Katerina Ivanovna, it seems to me. Good-bye for now."

Alyosha shook hands with her. Grushenka was still crying. He saw that she put little faith in his consolation, but she was

better for having had her sorrow out, for having spoken of it.
He was sorry to leave her in such a state of mind, but he was in
haste. He had a great many things to do still.

CHAPTER II

THE INJURED FOOT

THE first of these things was at the house of Madame
Hohlakov, and he hurried there to get it over as quickly
as possible and not be too late for Mitya. Madame Hohlakov
had been slightly ailing for the last three weeks: her foot had
for some reason swollen up, and though she was not in bed,
she lay all day half reclining on the couch in her boudoir, in a
fascinating but decorous *déshabillé*. Alyosha had once noted
with innocent amusement that, in spite of her illness, Madame
Hohlakov had begun to be rather dressy—top-knots, ribbons,
loose wrappers, had made their appearance, and he had an
inkling of the reason, though he dismissed such ideas from his
mind as frivolous. During the last two months the young
official, Perhotin, had become a regular visitor at the house.

Alyosha had not called for four days and he was in haste to
go straight to Lise, as it was with her he had to speak, for Lise
had sent a maid to him the previous day, specially asking him
to come to her "about something very important", a request
which, for certain reasons, had interest for Alyosha. But while
the maid went to take his name in to Lise, Madame Hohlakov
heard of his arrival from someone, and immediately sent to
beg him to come to her "just for one minute". Alyosha reflected that it was better to accede to the mamma's request, or
else she would be sending down to Lise's room every minute
that he was there. Madame Hohlakov was lying on a couch.
She was particularly smartly dressed and was evidently in a
state of extreme nervous excitement. She greeted Alyosha with
cries of rapture.

"It's ages, ages, perfect ages since I've seen you! It's a
whole week—only think of it! Ah, but you were here only
four days ago, on Wednesday. You have come to see Lise.
I'm sure you meant to slip into her room on tiptoe, without
my hearing you. My dear, dear Alexey Fyodorovitch, if you
only knew how worried I am about her! But of that later,
though that's the most important thing, of that later. Dear

Alexey Fyodorovitch, I trust you implicitly with my Lise. Since the death of Father Zossima—God rest his soul! (she crossed herself)—I look upon you as a monk, though you look charming in your new suit. Where did you find such a tailor in these parts? No, no, that's not the chief thing—of that later. Forgive me for sometimes calling you Alyosha; an old woman like me may take liberties," she smiled coquettishly; "but that will do later, too. The important thing is that I shouldn't forget what is important. Please remind me of it yourself. As soon as my tongue runs away with me, you just say 'the important thing?' Ach! how do I know now what is of most importance? Ever since Lise took back her promise— her childish promise, Alexey Fyodorovitch—to marry you, you've realised, of course, that it was only the playful fancy of a sick child who had been so long confined to her chair— thank God, she can walk now! . . . that new doctor Katya sent for from Moscow for your unhappy brother, who will to- morrow . . . But why speak of to-morrow? I am ready to die at the very thought of to-morrow. Ready to die of curiosity. . . . That doctor was with us yesterday and saw Lise. . . . I paid him fifty roubles for the visit. But that's not the point, that's not the point again. You see, I'm mixing everything up. I am in such a hurry. Why am I in a hurry? I don't under- stand. It's awful how I seem growing unable to understand anything. Everything seems mixed up in a sort of tangle. I am afraid you are so bored you will jump up and run away, and that will be all I shall see of you. Goodness! Why are we sitting here and no coffee? Yulia, Glafira, coffee!"

Alyosha made haste to thank her, and said that he had only just had coffee.

"Where?"

"At Agrafena Alexandrovna's."

"At . . . at that woman's? Ah, it's she has brought ruin on everyone. I know nothing about it though. They say she has become a saint, though it's rather late in the day. She had better have done it before. What use is it now? Hush, hush, Alexey Fyodorovitch, for I have so much to say to you that I am afraid I shall tell you nothing. This awful trial . . . I shall certainly go, I am making arrangements. I shall be carried there in my chair; besides, I can sit up. I shall have people with me. And, you know, I am a witness. How shall I speak, how shall I speak? I don't know what I shall say. One has to take an oath, hasn't one?"

"Yes; but I don't think you will be able to go."

"I can sit up. Ah, you put me out! Ah! this trial, this savage act, and then they are all going to Siberia, some are getting married, and all this so quickly, so quickly, everything's changing, and at last—nothing. All grow old and have death to look forward to. Well, so be it! I am weary. This Katya, *cette charmante personne*, has disappointed all my hopes. Now she is going to follow one of your brothers to Siberia, and your other brother is going to follow her, and will live in the nearest town, and they will all torment one another. It drives me out of my mind. Worst of all—the publicity. The story has been told a million times over in all the papers in Moscow and Petersburg. Ah! yes, would you believe it, there's a paragraph that I was 'a dear friend' of your brother's——, I can't repeat the horrid word. Just fancy, just fancy!"

"Impossible! Where was the paragraph? What did it say?"

"I'll show you directly. I got the paper and read it yesterday. Here, in the Petersburg paper *Gossip*. The paper began coming out this year. I am awfully fond of gossip, and I take it in, and now it pays me out—this is what gossip comes to! Here it is, here, this passage. Read it."

And she handed Alyosha a sheet of newspaper which had been under her pillow.

It was not exactly that she was upset, she seemed overwhelmed, and perhaps everything really was mixed up in a tangle in her head. The paragraph was very typical, and must have been a great shock to her, but, fortunately perhaps, she was unable to keep her mind fixed on any one subject at that moment, and so might race off in a minute to something else and quite forget the newspaper.

Alyosha was well aware that the story of the terrible case had spread all over Russia. And, good heavens! what wild rumours about his brother, about the Karamazovs, and about himself he had read in the course of those two months, among other equally credible items. One paper had even stated that he had gone into a monastery and become a monk, in horror at his brother's crime. Another contradicted this, and stated that he and his elder, Father Zossima, had broken into the monastery chest and "made tracks from the monastery". The present paragraph in the paper *Gossip* was under the heading, "The Karamazov Case at Skotoprigonyevsk". (That, alas! was the name of our little town. I had hitherto kept it concealed.) It was brief, and Madame Hohlakov was not directly mentioned in it. No names appeared, in fact. It was merely stated that the criminal, whose approaching trial was making such a sensation—retired army captain, an idle swaggerer, and reactionary bully—was continually involved in amorous intrigues, and particularly popular with certain ladies "who were pining in solitude". One such lady, a pining widow, who tried to seem young though she had a grown-up daughter, was so fascinated by him that only two hours before the crime she offered him three thousand roubles, on condition that he would elope with her to the gold-mines. But the criminal, counting on escaping punishment, had preferred to murder his father to get the three thousand rather than go off to Siberia with the middle-aged charms of his pining lady. This playful paragraph finished, of course, with an outburst of generous indignation at the wickedness of parricide and at the lately abolished institution of serfdom. Reading it with curiosity, Alyosha folded up the paper and handed it back to Madame Hohlakov.

"Well, that must be me," she hurried on again. "Of course I am meant. Scarcely more than an hour before, I suggested gold-mines to him, and here they talk of 'middle-aged charms' as though that were my motive! He writes that out of spite! God Almighty forgive him for the 'middle-aged charms', as I forgive him! You know it's . . . Do you know who it is? It's your friend Rakitin."

"Perhaps," said Alyosha, "though I've heard nothing about it."

"It's he, it's he! No 'perhaps' about it. You know I turned him out of the house. . . . You know all that story, don't you?"

"I know that you asked him not to visit you for the future, but why it was I haven't heard . . . from you, at least."

"Ah, then you've heard it from him! He abuses me, I suppose, abuses me dreadfully?"

"Yes, he does; but then he abuses everyone. But why you've given him up I haven't heard from him either. I meet him very seldom now, indeed. We are not friends."

"Well, then, I'll tell you all about it. There's no help for it, I'll confess, for there is one point in which I was perhaps to blame. Only a little, little point, so little that perhaps it doesn't count. You see, my dear boy"—Madame Hohlakov suddenly looked arch and a charming, though enigmatic, smile played about her lips—"you see, I suspect . . . You must forgive me, Alyosha. I am like a mother to you. . . . No, no; quite the contrary. I speak to you now as though you were

268

my father—'mother's' quite out of place. Well, it's as though I were confessing to Father Zossima, that's just it. I called you a monk just now. Well, that poor young man, your friend Rakitin (mercy on us! I can't be angry with him. I feel cross, but not very), that frivolous young man, would you believe it, seems to have taken it into his head to fall in love with me. I only noticed it later. At first—a month ago—he only began to come oftener to see me, almost every day; though, of course, we were acquainted before. I knew nothing about it . . . and suddenly it dawned upon me, and I began to notice things with surprise. You know, two months ago that modest, charming, excellent young man, Pyotr Ilyitch Perhotin, who's in the service here, began to be a regular visitor at the house. You met him here ever so many times yourself. And he is an excellent, earnest young man, isn't he? He comes once every three days, not every day (though I should be glad to see him every day), and always so well dressed. Altogether, I love young people, Alyosha, talented, modest, like you, and he has almost the mind of a statesman, he talks so charmingly, and I shall certainly, certainly try to get promotion for him. He is a future diplomat. On that awful day he almost saved me from death by coming in the night. And your friend Rakitin comes in such boots, and always stretches them out on the carpet. . . . He began hinting at his feelings, in fact, and one day, as he was going, he squeezed my hand terribly hard. My foot began to swell directly after he pressed my hand like that. He had met Pyotr Ilyitch here before, and would you believe it, he is always gibing at him, growling at him, for some reason. I simply looked at the way they went on together and laughed inwardly. So I was sitting here alone—no, I was laid up then. Well, I was lying here alone and suddenly Rakitin comes in, and only fancy! brought me some verses of his own composition—a short poem, on my bad foot: that is, he described my foot in a poem. Wait a minute—how did it go?

'A captivating little foot.'

It began somehow like that. I can never remember poetry. I've got it here. I'll show it to you later. But it's a charming thing—charming; and, you know, it's not only about the foot, it had a good moral, too, a charming idea, only I've forgotten it; in fact, it was just the thing for an album. So, of course, I thanked him, and he was evidently flattered. I'd hardly had

269

time to thank him when in comes Pyotr Ilyitch, and Rakitin suddenly looked as black as night. I could see that Pyotr Ilyitch was in the way, for Rakitin certainly wanted to say something after giving me the verses. I had a presentiment of it; but Pyotr Ilyitch came in. I showed Pyotr Ilyitch the verses and didn't say who was the author. But I am convinced that he guessed, though he won't own it to this day, and declares he had no idea. But he says that on purpose. Pyotr Ilyitch began to laugh at once, and fell to criticising it. 'Wretched doggerel,' he said they were, 'some divinity student must have written them,' and with such vehemence, such vehemence! Then, instead of laughing, your friend flew into a rage. 'Good gracious!' I thought, 'they'll fly at each other.' 'It was I who wrote them,' said he. 'I wrote them as a joke,' he said, 'for I think it degrading to write verses. . . . But they are good poetry. They want to put a monument to your Pushkin for writing about women's feet, while I wrote with a moral purpose, and you,' said he, 'are an advocate of serfdom. You've no humane ideas,' said he. 'You have no modern, enlightened feelings, you are uninfluenced by progress, you are a mere official,' he said, 'and you take bribes.' Then I began screaming and imploring them. And, you know, Pyotr Ilyitch is anything but a coward. He at once took up the most gentlemanly tone, looked at him sarcastically, listened, and apologised. 'I'd no idea,' said he. 'I shouldn't have said it, if I had known. I should have praised it. Poets are all so irritable,' he said. In short, he laughed at him under the cover of the most gentlemanly tone. He explained to me afterwards that it was all sarcastic. I thought he was in earnest. Only as I lay there, just as before you now, I thought, 'Would it, or would it not, be the proper thing for me to turn Rakitin out for shouting so rudely at a visitor in my house?' And, would you believe it, I lay here, shut my eyes, and wondered, would it be the proper thing or not. I kept worrying and worrying, and my heart began to beat, and I couldn't make up my mind whether to make an outcry or not. One voice seemed to be telling me, 'Speak,' and the other, 'No, don't speak'. And no sooner had the second voice said that than I cried out, and fainted. Of course, there was a fuss. I got up suddenly and said to Rakitin: 'It's painful for me to say it, but I don't wish to see you in my house again.' So I turned him out. Ah! Alexey Fyodorovitch, I know myself I did wrong. I was putting it on. I wasn't angry with him at all, really; but I suddenly fancied—that was what did it—that

270

it would be such a fine scene. . . . And yet, believe me, it was quite normal, for I really shed tears and cried for several days afterwards, and then suddenly, one afternoon, I forgot all about it. So it's a fortnight since he's been here, and I kept wondering whether he would come again. I wondered even yesterday, then suddenly last night came this *Gossip*. I read it and gasped. Who could have written it? He must have written it. He went home, sat down, wrote it on the spot, sent it, and they put it in. It was a fortnight ago, you see. But, Alyosha, it's awful how I keep talking and don't say what I want to say. Ah! the words come of themselves."

"It's very important for me to be in time to see my brother to-day," Alyosha faltered.

"To be sure, to be sure! You bring it all back to me. Listen, what is an aberration?"

"What aberration?" asked Alyosha, wondering.

"In the legal sense. An aberration in which everything is pardonable. Whatever you do you will be acquitted at once."

"What do you mean?"

"I'll tell you. This Katya . . . Ah! she is a charming, charming creature, only I never can make out whom it is she is in love with. She was with me some time ago and I couldn't get anything out of her. Especially as she won't talk to me except on the surface now. She is always talking about my health and nothing else, and she takes up such a tone with me, too. I simply said to myself: 'Well, so be it. I don't care' . . . Oh, yes. I was talking of aberration. This doctor has come. You know a doctor has come? Of course you know it—the one who discovers madmen. You wrote for him. No, it wasn't you, but Katya. It's all Katya's doing. Well, you see, a man may be sitting perfectly sane and suddenly have an aberration. He may be conscious and know what he is doing and yet be in a state of aberration. And there's no doubt that Dmitri Fyodorovitch was suffering from aberration. They found out about aberration as soon as the law courts were reformed. It's all the good effect of the reformed law courts. The doctor has been here and questioned me about that evening, about the gold mines. 'How did he seem then?' he asked me. He must have been in a state of aberration. He came in shouting: 'Money, money, three thousand! Give me three thousand!' and then went away and immediately did the murder. 'I don't want to murder him,' he said, and he suddenly went and murdered him.

271

That's why they'll acquit him, because he struggled against it and yet he murdered him."

"But he didn't murder him," Alyosha interrupted rather sharply. He felt more and more sick with anxiety and impatience.

"Yes, I know it was that old man Grigory murdered him."

"Grigory?" cried Alyosha.

"Yes, yes; it was Grigory. He lay as Dmitri Fyodorovitch struck him down, and then got up, saw the door open, went in and killed Fyodor Pavlovitch."

"But why, why?"

"Suffering from aberration. When he recovered from the blow Dmitri Fyodorovitch gave him on the head, he was suffering from aberration: he went and committed the murder. As for his saying he didn't, he very likely doesn't remember. Only, you know, it'll be better, ever so much better, if Dmitri Fyodorovitch murdered him. And that's how it must have been, though I say it was Grigory. It certainly was Dmitri Fyodorovitch, and that's better, ever so much better! Oh! not better that a son should have killed his father, I don't defend that. Children ought to honour their parents, and yet it would be better if it were he, as you'd have nothing to cry over then, for he did it when he was unconscious or rather when he was conscious, but did not know what he was doing. Let them acquit him—that's so humane, and would show what a blessing reformed law courts are. I know nothing about it, but they say they have been so a long time. And when I heard it yesterday, I was so struck by it that I wanted to send for you at once. And if he is acquitted, make him come straight from the law courts to dinner with me, and I'll have a party of friends, and we'll drink to the reformed law courts. I don't believe he'd be dangerous; besides, I'll invite a great many friends, so that he could always be led out if he did anything. And then he might be made a justice of the peace or something in another town, for those who have been in trouble themselves make the best judges. And, besides, who isn't suffering from aberration nowadays?—you, I, all of us are in a state of aberration, and there are ever so many examples of it: a man sits singing a song, suddenly something annoys him, he takes a pistol and shoots the first person he comes across, and no one blames him for it. I read that lately, and all the doctors confirm it. The doctors are always confirming; they confirm anything. Why, my Lise is in a state of aberration. She made me cry again yesterday, and the day before, too, and to-day I suddenly realised that it's all due to aberration. Oh, Lise grieves me so. I believe she's quite mad. Why did she send for you? Did she send for you or did you come of yourself?"

"Yes, she sent for me, and I am just going to her." Alyosha got up resolutely.

"Oh, my dear, dear Alexey Fyodorovitch, perhaps that's what's most important," Madame Hohlakov cried, suddenly bursting into tears. "God knows I trust Lise to you with all my heart, and it's no matter her sending for you on the sly, without telling her mother. But forgive me, I can't trust my daughter so easily to your brother Ivan Fyodorovitch, though I still consider him the most chivalrous young man. But only fancy, he's been to see Lise and I knew nothing about it!"

"How? What? When?" Alyosha was exceedingly surprised. He had not sat down again and listened standing.

"I will tell you, that's perhaps why I asked you to come, for I don't know now why I did ask you to come. Well, Ivan Fyodorovitch has been to see me twice, since he came back from Moscow. First time he came as a friend to call on me, and the second time Katya was here and he came because he heard she was here. I didn't, of course, expect him to come often, knowing what a lot he has to do as it is, *vous comprenez, cette affaire et la mort terrible de votre papa.* But I suddenly heard he'd been here again, not to see me but to see Lise. That's six days ago now. He came, stayed five minutes, and went away. And I didn't hear of it till three days afterwards, from Glafira, so it was a great shock to me. I sent for Lise directly. She laughed. 'He thought you were asleep,' she said, 'and came in to me to ask after your health.' Of course, that's how it happened. But Lise, Lise, mercy on us, how she distresses me! Would you believe it, one night, four days ago, just after you saw her last time, and had gone away, she suddenly had a fit, screaming, shrieking hysterics! Why is it I never have hysterics? Then, next day another fit and the same thing on the third, and yesterday too, and then yesterday that aberration. She suddenly screamed out: 'I hate Ivan Fyodorovitch. I insist on your never letting him come to the house again.' I was struck dumb at these amazing words, and answered: 'On what grounds could I refuse to see such an excellent young man, a young man of such learning too, and so unfortunate,' for all this business is a misfortune, isn't it? She suddenly burst out laughing at my words, and so rudely, you know. Well, I was pleased, I thought I had amused her and the fits would pass off, especially as I wanted to refuse to see Ivan Fyodorovitch, anyway, on account of his strange visits without my knowledge, and meant to ask him for an explanation. But early this morning Lise waked up and flew into a passion with Yulia and, would you believe it, slapped her in the face. That's monstrous, I am always polite to my servants. And an hour later she was hugging Yulia's feet and kissing them. She sent a message to me, that she wasn't coming to me at all, and would never come and see me again, and when I dragged myself down to her, she rushed to kiss me, crying, and as she kissed me she pushed me out of the room without saying a word, so I couldn't find out what was the matter. Now, dear Alexey Fyodorovitch, I rest all my hopes on you, and, of course, my whole life is in your hands. I simply beg you to go to Lise and find out everything from her, as you alone can, and come back and tell me—me, her mother, for you understand it will be the death of me, simply the death of me, if this goes on, or else I shall run away. I can stand no more. I have patience; but I may lose patience, and then . . . then something awful will happen. Ah, dear me! At last, Pyotr Ilyitch!'' cried Madame Hohlakov, beaming all over as she saw Perhotin enter the room. ''You are late, you are late! Well, sit down, speak, put us out of suspense. What does the counsel say? Where are you off to, Alexey Fyodorovitch?''

''To Lise.''

''Oh, yes. You won't forget, you won't forget what I asked you? It's a question of life and death!''

''Of course I won't forget, if I can . . . but I am so late,'' muttered Alyosha, beating a hasty retreat.

''No, be sure, be sure to come in; don't say 'if you can'. I shall die if you don't,'' Madame Hohlakov called after him, but Alyosha had already left the room.

CHAPTER III

A LITTLE DEMON

GOING to Lise, he found her half reclining in the invalid chair, in which she had been wheeled when she was unable to walk. She did not move to meet him, but her sharp keen eyes were simply riveted on his face. There was a feverish look in her eyes, her face was pale and yellow. Alyosha was amazed at the change that had taken place in her in three days. She was positively thinner. She did not hold out her hand to him. He touched the thin, long fingers which lay motionless on her dress, then he sat down facing her, without a word.

"I know you are in a hurry to get to the prison," Lise said curtly, "and mamma's kept you for hours, she's just been telling you about me and Yulia."

"How do you know?" asked Alyosha.

"I've been listening. Why do you stare at me? I want to listen and I do listen, there's no harm in that. I don't apologise."

"You are upset about something?"

"On the contrary, I am very happy. I've only just been reflecting for the thirtieth time what a good thing it is I refused you and shall not be your wife. You are not fit to be a husband. If I were to marry you and give you a note to take to the man I loved after you, you'd take it and be sure to give it to him and bring an answer back, too. If you were forty, you would still go on taking my love-letters for me."

She suddenly laughed.

"There is something spiteful and yet open-hearted about you," Alyosha smiled to her.

"The open-heartedness consists in my not being ashamed of myself with you. What's more, I don't want to feel ashamed with you, just with you. Alyosha, why is it I don't respect you? I am very fond of you, but I don't respect you. If I respected you, I shouldn't talk to you without shame, should I?"

"No."

"But do you believe that I am not ashamed with you?"

"No, I don't believe it."

Lise laughed nervously again; she spoke rapidly.

"I sent your brother, Dmitri Fyodorovitch, some sweets in prison. Alyosha, you know, you are quite pretty! I shall love you awfully for having so quickly allowed me not to love you."

"Why did you send for me to-day, Lise?"

"I wanted to tell you of a longing I have. I should like some-one to torture me, marry me and then torture me, deceive me and go away. I don't want to be happy."

"You are in love with disorder?"

"Yes, I want disorder. I keep wanting to set fire to the house. I keep imagining how I'll creep up and set fire to the house on the sly, it must be on the sly. They'll try to put it out, but it'll go on burning. And I shall know and say nothing. Ah, what silliness! And how bored I am!"

She waved her hand with a look of repulsion.

"It's your luxurious life," said Alyosha softly.

"Is it better, then, to be poor?"

"Yes, it is better."

"That's what your monk taught you. That's not true. Let me be rich and all the rest poor. I'll eat sweets and drink cream and not give any to anyone else. Ach, don't speak, don't say anything," she shook her hand at him, though Alyosha had not opened his mouth. "You've told me all that before, I know it all by heart. It bores me. If I am ever poor I shall murder somebody, and even if I am rich I may murder someone, perhaps—why do nothing? But do you know, I should like to reap, cut the rye? I'll marry you, and you shall become a peasant, a real peasant; we'll keep a colt, shall we? Do you know Kalganov?"

"Yes."

"He is always wandering about dreaming. He says, why live in real life? it's better to dream. One can dream the most delightful things, but real life is a bore. But he'll be married soon, for all that, he's been making love to me already. Can you spin tops?"

"Yes."

"Well, he's just like a top: he wants to be wound up and set spinning and then to be lashed, lashed, lashed with a whip. If I marry him I'll keep him spinning all his life. You are not ashamed to be with me?"

"No."

"You are awfully cross because I don't talk about holy things. I don't want to be holy. What will they do to one in the next world for the greatest sin? You must know all about that."

"God will censure you." Alyosha was watching her steadily.

"That's just what I should like. I would go up and they would censure me and I would burst out laughing in their faces. I should dreadfully like to set fire to the house, Alyosha, to our house, you still don't believe me?"

"Why? There are children of twelve years of age who have a longing to set fire to something and they do set things on fire, too. It's a sort of disease."

"That's not true, that's not true, there may be children, but that's not what I mean."

"You take evil for good; it's a passing crisis, it's the result of your illness, perhaps."

"You do despise me, though! It's simply that I don't want to do good. I want to do evil, and it has nothing to do with illness."

"Why do evil?"

"So that everything might be destroyed. Ah, how nice it would be if everything were destroyed! You know, Alyosha, I sometimes think of doing a fearful lot of harm and everything bad, and I should do it for a long while on the sly and suddenly everyone would find it out. Everyone will stand round and point their fingers at me and I would look at them all. That would be awfully nice. Why would it be so nice, Alyosha?"

"I don't know. It's a craving to destroy something good or, as you say, to set fire to something. It happens sometimes."

"I not only say it, I shall do it."

"I believe you."

"Ah, how I love you for saying you believe me. And you are not lying one little bit. But perhaps you think that I am saying all this on purpose to annoy you?"

"No, I don't think that . . . though perhaps there is a little desire to do that in it, too."

"There is a little. I never can tell lies to you," she declared, with a strange fire in her eyes.

What struck Alyosha above everything was her earnestness. There was not a trace of humour or jesting in her face now, though, in old days, fun and gaiety never deserted her even at her most "earnest" moments.

"There are moments when people love crime," said Alyosha thoughtfully.

"Yes, yes! You have uttered my thought, they love crime, everyone loves crime, they love it always, not at some 'moments'. You know, it's as though people have made an agreement to lie about it and have lied about it ever since. They all declare that they hate evil, but secretly they all love it."

"And are you still reading nasty books?"

"Yes, I am. Mamma reads them and hides them under her pillow and I steal them."

"Aren't you ashamed to destroy yourself?"

"I want to destroy myself. There's a boy here, who lay down between the railway lines when the train was passing. Lucky fellow! Listen, your brother is being tried now for murdering his father and everyone loves his having killed his father."

"Loves his having killed his father?"

"Yes, loves it, everyone loves it! Everybody says it's so awful, but secretly they simply love it. I for one love it."

"There is some truth in what you say about everyone," said Alyosha softly.

"Oh, what ideas you have!" Lise shrieked in delight. "And you a monk, too! You wouldn't believe how I respect you, Alyosha, for never telling lies. Oh, I must tell you a funny dream of mine. I sometimes dream of devils. It's night, I am in my room with a candle and suddenly there are devils all over the place, in all the corners, under the table, and they open the doors, there's a crowd of them behind the doors and they want to come and seize me. And they are just coming, just seizing me. But I suddenly cross myself and they all draw back, though they don't go away altogether, they stand at the doors and in the corners, waiting. And suddenly I have a frightful longing to revile God aloud, and so I begin, and then they come crowding back to me, delighted, and seize me again and I cross myself again and they all draw back. It's awful fun, it takes one's breath away."

"I've had the same dream, too," said Alyosha suddenly.

"Really?" cried Lise, surprised. "I say, Alyosha, don't laugh, that's awfully important. Could two different people have the same dream?"

"It seems they can."

"Alyosha, I tell you, it's awfully important," Lise went on, with really excessive amazement. "It's not the dream that's important but your having the same dream as me. You never lie to me, don't lie now: is it true? You are not laughing?"

"It's true."

Lise seemed extraordinarily impressed and for half a minute she was silent.

"Alyosha, come and see me, come and see me more often," she said suddenly in a supplicating voice.

"I'll always come to see you, all my life," answered Alyosha firmly.

"You are the only person I can talk to, you know," Lise began again. "I talk to no one but myself and you. Only you in the whole world. And to you more readily than to myself. And I am not a bit ashamed with you, not a bit. Alyosha, why am I not ashamed with you, not a bit? Alyosha, is it true that at Easter the Jews steal a child and kill it?"

"I don't know."

"There's a book here in which I read about the trial of a Jew, who took a child four years old and cut off the fingers from both hands, and then crucified him on the wall, hammered nails into him and crucified him, and afterwards, when he was tried, he said that the child died soon, within four hours. That was 'soon'! He said the child moaned, kept on moaning and he stood admiring it. That's nice!"

"Nice?"

"Nice, I sometimes imagine that it was I who crucified him. He would hang there moaning and I would sit opposite him eating pineapple compote. I am awfully fond of pineapple compote. Do you like it?"

Alyosha looked at her in silence. Her pale, sallow face was suddenly contorted, her eyes burned.

"You know, when I read about that Jew I shook with sobs all night. I kept fancying how the little thing cried and moaned (a child four years old understands, you know) and all the while the thought of pineapple compote haunted me. In the morning I wrote a letter to a certain person, begging him *particularly* to come and see me. He came and I suddenly told him all about the child and the pineapple compote. *All* about it, *all*, and said that it was nice. He laughed and said it really was nice. Then he got up and went away. He was only here five minutes. Did he despise me? Did he despise me? Tell me, tell me, Alyosha, did he despise me or not?" She sat up on the couch, with flashing eyes.

"Tell me," Alyosha asked suddenly, "did you send for that person?"

"Yes, I did."

"Did you send him a letter?"

"Yes."

"Simply to ask about that, about that child?"

"No, not about that at all. But when he came I asked him about that at once. He answered, laughed, got up and went away."

"That person behaved honourably," Alyosha murmured.

"And did he despise me? Did he laugh at me?"

"No, for perhaps he believes in the pineapple compote himself. He is very ill now, too, Lise."

"Yes, he does believe in it," said Lise, with flashing eyes.

"He doesn't despise anyone," Alyosha went on. "Only he does not believe anyone. If he doesn't believe in people, of course he does despise them."

279

"Then he despises me, me?"

"You, too."

"Good," Lise seemed to grind her teeth. "When he went out laughing I felt that it was nice to be despised. The child with fingers cut off is nice and to be despised is nice . . ." And she laughed in Alyosha's face, a feverish malicious laugh.

"Do you know, Alyosha, do you know, I should like . . . Alyosha, save me!" she suddenly jumped from the couch, rushed to him and seized him with both hands. "Save me!" she almost groaned. "Is there anyone in the world I could tell what I've told you? I've told you the truth, the truth. I shall kill myself, because I loathe everything! I don't want to live, because I loathe everything! I loathe everything, everything. Alyosha, why don't you love me in the least?" she finished in a frenzy.

"But I do love you!" answered Alyosha warmly.

"And will you weep over me, will you?"

"Yes."

"Not because I won't be your wife, but simply weep for me?"

"Yes."

"Thank you! It's only your tears I want. Everyone else may punish me and trample me underfoot, everyone, everyone, not excepting *anyone*. For I don't love anyone. Do you hear, not anyone! On the contrary, I hate him! Go, Alyosha, it's time you went to your brother," she tore herself away from him suddenly.

"How can I leave you like this?" said Alyosha, almost in alarm.

"Go to your brother, the prison will be shut, go, here's your hat. Give my love to Mitya, go! go!"

And she almost forcibly pushed Alyosha out of the door. He looked at her with pained surprise, when he was suddenly aware of a letter in his right hand, a tiny letter folded up tight and sealed. He glanced at it and instantly read the address: "To Ivan Fyodorovitch Karamazov". He looked quickly at Lise. Her face had become almost menacing.

"Give it to him, you must give it to him!" she ordered him, trembling and beside herself. "To-day, at once, or I'll poison myself! That's why I sent for you."

And she slammed the door quickly. The bolt clicked. Alyosha put the note in his pocket and went straight downstairs, without going back to Madame Hohlakov, forgetting her, in fact. As soon as Alyosha had gone, Lise unbolted the door, opened it a little, put her finger in the crack and slammed the door with all her might, pinching her finger. Ten seconds after, releasing her finger, she walked softly, slowly to her chair, sat up straight in it and looked intently at her blackened finger and at the blood that oozed from under the nail. Her lips were quivering and she kept whispering rapidly to herself:

"I am a wretch, wretch, wretch, wretch!"

CHAPTER IV

A HYMN AND A SECRET

IT was quite late (days are short in November) when Alyosha rang at the prison gate. It was beginning to get dusk. But Alyosha knew that he would be admitted without difficulty. Things were managed in our little town, as everywhere else. At first, of course, on the conclusion of the preliminary inquiry, relations and a few other persons could only obtain interviews with Mitya by going through certain inevitable formalities. But later, though the formalities were not relaxed, exceptions were made for some, at least, of Mitya's visitors. So much so, that sometimes the interviews with the prisoner in the room set aside for the purpose were practically *tête-à-tête*.

These exceptions, however, were few in number; only Grushenka, Alyosha and Rakitin were treated like this. But the captain of the police, Mihail Mihailovitch, was very favourably disposed to Grushenka. His abuse of her at Mokroe weighed on the old man's conscience, and when he learned the whole story, he completely changed his view of her. And, strange to say, though he was firmly persuaded of his guilt, yet after Mitya was once in prison, the old man came to take a more and more lenient view of him. "He was a man of good heart, perhaps," he thought, "who had come to grief from drinking and dissipation." His first horror had been succeeded by pity. As for Alyosha, the police captain was very fond of him and had known him for a long time. Rakitin, who had of late taken to coming very often to see the prisoner, was one of the most intimate acquaintances of the "police captain's young ladies", as he called them, and was always hanging about their house. He gave lessons in the house of the police superintendent, too.

who, though scrupulous in the performance of his duties, was a a kind-hearted old man. Alyosha, again, had an intimate acquaintance of long standing with the superintendent, who was fond of talking to him, generally on sacred subjects. He respected Ivan Fyodorovitch, and stood in awe of his opinion, though he was a great philosopher himself; "self-taught", of course. But Alyosha had an irresistible attraction for him. During the last year the old man had taken to studying the Apocryphal Gospels, and constantly talking over his impressions with his young friend. He used to come and see him in the monastery and discussed for hours together with him and with the monks. So even if Alyosha were late at the prison, he had only to go to the superintendent and everything was made easy. Besides, everyone in the prison, down to the humblest warder, had grown used to Alyosha. The sentry, of course, did not trouble him so long as the authorities were satisfied.

When Mitya was summoned from his cell, he always went downstairs, to the place set aside for interviews. As Alyosha entered the room he came upon Rakitin, who was just taking leave of Mitya. They were both talking loudly. Mitya was laughing heartily as he saw him out, while Rakitin seemed grumbling. Rakitin did not like meeting Alyosha, especially of late. He scarcely spoke to him, and bowed to him stiffly. Seeing Alyosha enter now, he frowned and looked away, as though he were entirely absorbed in buttoning his big, warm, fur-trimmed overcoat. Then he began looking at once for his umbrella.

"I must mind not to forget my belongings," he muttered, simply to say something.

"Mind you don't forget other people's belongings," said Mitya, as a joke, and laughed at once at his own wit. Rakitin fired up instantly.

"You'd better give that advice to your own family, who've always been a slave-driving lot, and not to Rakitin," he cried, suddenly trembling with anger.

"What's the matter? I was joking," cried Mitya. "Damn it all! They are all like that," he turned to Alyosha, nodding towards Rakitin's hurriedly retreating figure. "He was sitting here, laughing and cheerful, and all at once he boils up like that. He didn't even nod to you. Have you broken with him completely? Why are you so late? I've not been simply waiting but thirsting for you the whole morning. But never mind. We'll make up for it now."

"Why does he come here so often? Surely you are not such great friends?" asked Alyosha. He, too, nodded at the door through which Rakitin had disappeared.

"Great friends with Ratikin? No, not as much as that. Is it likely—a pig like that? He considers I am . . . a blackguard. They can't understand a joke either, that's the worst of such people. They never understand a joke, and their souls are dry, dry and flat; they remind me of prison walls when I was first brought here. But he is a clever fellow, very clever. Well, Alexey, it's all over with me now."

He sat down on the bench and made Alyosha sit down beside him.

"Yes, the trial's to-morrow. Are you so hopeless, brother?" Alyosha said, with an apprehensive feeling.

"What are you talking about?" said Mitya, looking at him rather uncertainly. "Oh, you mean the trial! Damn it all! Till now we've been talking of things that don't matter, about this trial, but I haven't said a word to you about the chief thing. Yes, the trial is to-morrow; but it wasn't the trial I meant, when I said it was all over with me. Why do you look at me so critically?"

"What do you mean, Mitya?"

"Ideas, ideas, that's all! Ethics! What is ethics?"

"Ethics?" asked Alyosha, wondering.

"Yes; is it a science?"

"Yes, there is such a science . . . but . . . I confess I can't explain to you what sort of science it is."

"Rakitin knows. Rakitin knows a lot, damn him! He's not going to be a monk. He means to go to Petersburg. There he'll go in for criticism of an elevating tendency. Who knows, he may be of use and make his own career, too. Ough! they are first-rate, these people, at making a career! Damn ethics. I am done for, Alexey, I am, you man of God! I love you more than anyone. It makes my heart yearn to look at you. Who was Karl Bernard?"

"Karl Bernard?" Alyosha was surprised again.

"No, not Karl. Stay, I made a mistake. Claude Bernard. What was he? Chemist or what?"

"He must be a savant," answered Alyosha; "but I confess I can't tell you much about him, either. I've heard of him as a savant, but what sort I don't know."

"Well, damn him, then! I don't know either," swore Mitya. "A scoundrel of some sort, most likely. They are all scoundrels.

And Rakitin will make his way. Rakitin will get on anywhere; he is another Bernard. Ugh, these Bernards! They are all over the place."

"But what is the matter?" Alyosha asked insistently.

"He wants to write an article about me, about my case, and so begin his literary career. That's what he comes for; he said so himself. He wants to prove some theory. He wants to say, 'He couldn't help murdering his father, he was corrupted by his environment', and so on. He explained it all to me. He is going to put in a tinge of Socialism, he says. But there, damn the fellow, he can put in a tinge, if he likes, I don't care. He can't bear Ivan, he hates him. He's not fond of you, either. But I can't turn him out, for he is a clever fellow. Awfully conceited though. I said to him just now: 'The Karamazovs are not blackguards but philosophers; for all true Russians are philosophers, and though you've studied, you are not a philosopher—you are a low fellow'. He laughed, so maliciously. And I said to him: *'De ideabus non est disputandum'*. Isn't that rather good? I can set up for being a classic, you see!" Mitya laughed suddenly.

"Why is it all over with you? You said so just now," Alyosha interposed.

"Why is it all over with me? Hm! . . . The fact of it is . . . if you take it as a whole, I am sorry to lose God—that's why it is."

"What do you mean by 'sorry to lose God'?"

"Imagine: inside, in the nerves, in the head—that is, these nerves are there in the brain . . . (damn them!) there are sort of little tails, the little tails of those nerves, and as soon as they begin quivering . . . that is, you see, I look at something with my eyes and then they begin quivering, those little tails . . . and when they quiver, then an image appears . . . it doesn't appear at once, but an instant, a second, passes . . . and then something like a moment appears; that is, not a moment —devil take the moment!—but an image; that is, an object, or an action, damn it! That's why I see and then think, because of those tails, not at all because I've got a soul, and that I am some sort of image and likeness. All that is nonsense! Rakitin explained it all to me yesterday, brother, and it simply bowled me over. It's magnificent, Alyosha, this science! A new man's arising—that I understand. . . . And yet I am sorry to lose God!"

"Well, that's a good thing, anyway," said Alyosha.

"That I am sorry to lose God? It's chemistry, brother, chemistry! There's no help for it, your reverence, you must make way for chemistry. And Rakitin does dislike God. Ough! doesn't he dislike Him! That's the sore point with all of them. But they conceal it. They tell lies. They pretend. 'Will you preach this in your reviews?' I asked him. 'Oh well, if I did it openly, they won't let it through,' he said. He laughed. 'But what will become of men then?' I asked him, 'without God and immortal life? All things are lawful then, they can do what they like?' 'Didn't you know?' he said laughing, 'a clever man can do what he likes,' he said. 'A clever man knows his way about, but you've put your foot in it, committing a murder, and now you are rotting in prison.' He says that to my face! A regular pig! I used to kick such people out, but now I listen to them. He talks a lot of sense, too. Writes well. He began reading me an article last week. I copied out three lines of it. Wait a minute. Here it is."

Mitya hurriedly pulled out a piece of paper from his pocket and read:

" 'In order to determine this question, it is above all essential to put one's personality in contradiction to one's reality.' Do you understand that?"

"No, I don't," said Alyosha. He looked at Mitya and listened to him with curiosity.

"I don't understand either. It's dark and obscure, but intellectual. 'Everyone writes like that now,' he says, 'it's the effect of their environment.' They are afraid of the environment. He writes poetry, too, the rascal. He's written in honour of Madame Hohlakov's foot. Ha, ha, ha!"

"I've heard about it," said Alyosha.

"Have you? And have you heard the poem?"

"No."

"I've got it. Here it is. I'll read it to you. You don't know —I haven't told you—there's quite a story about it. He's a rascal! Three weeks ago he began to tease me. 'You've got yourself into a mess, like a fool, for the sake of three thousand, but I'm going to collar a hundred and fifty thousand. I am going to marry a widow and buy a house in Petersburg.' And he told me he was courting Madame Hohlakov. She hadn't much brains in her youth, and now at forty she has lost what she had. 'But she's awfully sentimental,' he says; 'that's how I shall get hold of her. When I marry her I shall take her to Petersburg and there I shall start a newspaper.' And his mouth was simply watering, the beast, not for the widow but for the hundred and fifty thousand. And he made me believe it. He came to see me every day. 'She is coming round,' he declared. He was beaming with delight. And then, all of a sudden, he was turned out of the house. Perhotin's carrying everything before him, bravo! I could kiss the silly old noodle for turning him out of the house. And he had written this doggerel. 'It's the first time I've soiled my hands with writing poetry,' he said. 'It's to win her heart, so it's in a good cause. When I get hold of the silly woman's fortune, I can be of great social utility.' They have this social justification for every nasty thing they do! 'Anyway, it's better than your Pushkin's poetry,' he said, 'for I've managed to advocate enlightenment even in that.' I understand what he means about Pushkin, I quite see that, if he really was a man of talent and only wrote about women's feet. But wasn't Rakitin stuck up about his doggerel! The vanity of these fellows! 'On the convalescence of the swollen foot of the object of my affections'—he thought of that for a title. He's a waggish fellow.

A captivating little foot,
Though swollen and red and tender!
The doctors come and plasters put,
But still they cannot mend her.

Yet 'tis not for her foot I dread—
A theme for Pushkin's muse more fit—
It's not her foot, it is her head:
I tremble for her loss of wit!

For as her foot swells, strange to say,
Her intellect is on the wane—
Oh, for some remedy I pray
That may restore both foot and brain!

He is a pig, a regular pig, but he's very arch, the rascal! And he really has put in a progressive idea. And wasn't he angry when she kicked him out! He was gnashing his teeth!"

"He's taken his revenge already," said Alyosha. "He's written a paragraph about Madame Hohlakov."

And Alyosha told him briefly about the paragraph in *Gossip*.

"That's his doing, that's his doing!" Mitya assented, frowning. "That's him! These paragraphs . . . I know . . . the

insulting things that have been written about Grushenka, for
instance. . . . And about Katya, too. . . . Hm!"

He walked across the room with a harassed air.

"Brother, I cannot stay long," Alyosha said, after a pause.
"To-morrow will be a great and awful day for you, the judgment of God will be accomplished . . . I am amazed at you,
you walk about here, talking of I don't know what . . ."

"No, don't be amazed at me," Mitya broke in warmly. "Am
I to talk of that stinking dog? Of the murderer? We've talked
enough of him. I don't want to say more of the stinking son of
Stinking Lizaveta! God will kill him, you will see. Hush!"

He went up to Alyosha excitedly and kissed him. His eyes
glowed.

"Rakitin wouldn't understand it," he began in a sort of ex-
altation; "but you, you'll understand it all. That's why I was
thirsting for you. You see, there's so much I've been wanting to
tell you for ever so long, here, within these peeling walls, but I
haven't said a word about what matters most; the moment never
seems to have come. Now I can wait no longer. I must pour out
my heart to you. Brother, these last two months I've found in
myself a new man. A new man has risen up in me. He was hidden
in me, but would never have come to the surface if it hadn't
been for this blow from heaven. I am afraid! And what do I
care if I spend twenty years in the mines, breaking out ore with
a hammer? I am not a bit afraid of that—it's something else I
am afraid of now: that that new man may leave me. Even
there, in the mines, underground, I may find a human heart in
another convict and murderer by my side, and I may make
friends with him, for even there one may live and love and
suffer. One may thaw and revive a frozen heart in that convict,
one may wait upon him for years, and at last bring up from the
dark depths of a lofty soul a feeling, suffering creature; one
may bring forth an angel, create a hero! There are so many
of them, hundreds of them, and we are all to blame for them.
Why was it I dreamed of that 'babe' at such a moment? 'Why
is the babe so poor?' That was a sign to me at that moment.
It's for the babe I'm going. Because we are all responsible for
all. For all the 'babes', for there are big children as well as
little children. All are 'babes'. I go for all, because someone
must go for all. I didn't kill father, but I've got to go. I accept
it. It's all come to me here, here, within these peeling walls.
There are numbers of them there, hundreds of them underground, with hammers in their hands. Oh yes, we shall be in

chains and there will be no freedom, but then, in our great sorrow, we shall rise again to joy, without which man cannot live nor God exist, for God gives joy: it's His privilege—a grand one. Ah, man should be dissolved in prayer! What should I be underground there without God? Rakitin's laughing! If they drive God from the earth we shall shelter Him underground. One cannot exist in prison without God; it's even more impossible than out of prison. And then we men underground will sing from the bowels of the earth a glorious hymn to God, with Whom is joy. Hail to God and His joy! I love Him!"

Mitya was almost gasping for breath as he uttered his wild speech. He turned pale, his lips quivered, and tears rolled down his cheeks.

"Yes, life is full, there is life even underground," he began again. "You wouldn't believe, Alexey, how I want to live now, what a thirst for existence and consciousness has sprung up in me within these peeling walls. Rakitin doesn't understand that; all he cares about is building a house and letting flats. But I've been longing for you. And what is suffering? I am not afraid of it, even if it were beyond reckoning. I am not afraid of it now. I was afraid of it before. Do you know, perhaps I won't answer at the trial at all. . . . And I seem to have such strength in me now that I think I could stand anything, any suffering, only to be able to say and to repeat to myself every moment, 'I exist'. In thousands of agonies—I exist. I'm tormented on the rack—but I exist! Though I sit alone in a pillar—I exist! I see the sun, and if I don't see the sun I know it's there. And there's a whole life in that, in knowing that the sun is there. Alyosha, my angel, all these philosophies are the death of me. Damn them! Brother Ivan . . ."

"What of brother Ivan?" interrupted Alyosha, but Mitya did not hear.

"You see, I never had any of these doubts before, but it was all hidden away in me. It was perhaps just because ideas I did not understand were surging up in me, that I used to drink and fight and rage. It was to stifle them in myself, to still them, to smother them. Ivan is not Rakitin, there is an idea in him. Ivan is a sphinx and is silent; he is always silent. It's God that's worrying me. That's the only thing that's worrying me. What if He doesn't exist? What if Rakitin's right—that it's an idea made up by men? Then, if He doesn't exist, man is the chief of the earth, of the universe. Magnificent! Only how is he

going to be good without God? That's the question. I always
come back to that. For whom is man going to love then? To
whom will he be thankful? To whom will he sing the hymn?
Rakitin laughs. Rakitin says that one can love humanity without God. Well, only a snivelling idiot can maintain that. I
can't understand it. Life's easy for Rakitin. 'You'd better
think about the extension of civic rights, or even of keeping
down the price of meat. You will show your love for humanity
more simply and directly by that than by philosophy.' I
answered him, 'Well, but you, without a God, are more likely
to raise the price of meat, if it suits you, and make a rouble on
every kopeck'. He lost his temper. But after all, what is goodness? Answer me that, Alexey. Goodness is one thing with me
and another with a Chinaman, so it's a relative thing. Or isn't
it? Is it not relative? A treacherous question! You won't
laugh if I tell you it's kept me awake two nights. I only wonder
now how people can live and think nothing about it. Vanity!
Ivan has no God. He has an idea. It's beyond me. But he is
silent. I believe he is a Freemason. I asked him, but he is silent.
I wanted to drink from the springs of his soul—he was silent.
But once he did drop a word."

"What did he say?" Alyosha took it up quickly.

"I said to him: 'Then everything is lawful, if it is so?' He
frowned. 'Fyodor Pavlovitch, our papa,' he said, 'was a pig,
but his ideas were right enough.' That was what he dropped.
That was all he said. That was going one better than Rakitin."

"Yes," Alyosha assented bitterly. "When was he with you?"

"Of that later, now I must speak of something else. I have
said nothing about Ivan to you before. I put it off to the last.
When my business here is over and the verdict has been given,
then I'll tell you something. I'll tell you everything. We've
something tremendous on hand. . . . And you shall be my
judge in it. But don't begin about that now; be silent. You
talk of to-morrow, of the trial; but, would you believe it, I
know nothing about it."

"Have you talked to the counsel?"

"What's the use of the counsel? I told him all about it.
He's a soft, city-bred rogue—a Bernard! But he doesn't believe
me—not a bit of it. Only imagine, he believes I did it. I see it.
'In that case,' I asked him, 'why have you come to defend me?'
Hang them all! They've got a doctor down, too, want to prove
I'm mad. I won't have that! Katerina Ivanovna wants to do
her 'duty' to the end, whatever the strain!" Mitya smiled

bitterly. "The cat! Hard-hearted creature! She knows that I said of her at Mokroe that she was a woman of 'great wrath'. They repeated it. Yes, the facts against me have grown numerous as the sands of the sea. Grigory sticks to his point. Grigory's honest, but a fool. Many people are honest because they are fools: that's Rakitin's idea. Grigory's my enemy. And there are some people who are better as foes than friends. I mean Katerina Ivanovna. I am afraid, oh, I am afraid she will tell how she bowed to the ground after that four thousand. She'll pay it back to the last farthing. I don't want her sacrifice; they'll put me to shame at the trial. I wonder how I can stand it. Go to her, Alyosha, ask her not to speak of that in the court, can't you? But, damn it all, it doesn't matter! I shall get through somehow. I don't pity her. It's her own doing. She deserves what she gets. I shall have my own story to tell, Alexey." He smiled bitterly again. "Only . . . only Grusha, Grusha! Good Lord! Why should she have such suffering to bear?" he exclaimed suddenly, with tears. "Grusha's killing me; the thought of her's killing me, killing me. She was with me just now . . ."

"She told me she was very much grieved by you to-day."

"I know. Confound my temper! It was jealousy. I was sorry, I kissed her as she was going. I didn't ask her forgiveness."

"Why didn't you?" exclaimed Alyosha.

Suddenly Mitya laughed almost mirthfully.

"God preserve you, my dear boy, from ever asking forgiveness for a fault from a woman you love. From one you love especially, however greatly you may have been in fault. For a woman—devil only knows what to make of a woman! I know something about them, anyway. But try acknowledging you are in fault to a woman. Say, 'I am sorry, forgive me', and a shower of reproaches will follow! Nothing will make her forgive you simply and directly, she'll humble you to the dust, bring forward things that have never happened, recall everything, forget nothing, add something of her own, and only then forgive you. And even the best, the best of them do it. She'll scrape up all the scrapings and load them on your head. They are ready to flay you alive, I tell you, every one of them, all these angels without whom we cannot live! I tell you plainly and openly, dear boy, every decent man ought to be under some woman's thumb. That's my conviction—not conviction but feeling. A man ought to be magnanimous, and it's no disgrace to a man! No disgrace to a hero, not even a Cæsar! But don't ever beg her pardon all the same for anything. Remember that rule given you by your brother Mitya, who's come to ruin through women. No, I'd better make it up to Grusha somehow, without begging pardon. I worship her, Alexey, worship her. Only she doesn't see it. No, she still thinks I don't love her enough. And she tortures me, tortures me with her love. The past was nothing! In the past it was only those infernal curves of hers that tortured me, but now I've taken all her soul into my soul and through her I've become a man myself. Will they marry us? If they don't, I shall die of jealousy. I imagine something every day. . . . What did she say to you about me?"

Alyosha repeated all Grushenka had said to him that day. Mitya listened, made him repeat things, and seemed pleased.

"Then she is not angry at my being jealous?" he exclaimed. "She is a regular woman! 'I've a fierce heart myself!' Ah, I love such fierce hearts, though I can't bear anyone's being jealous of me. I can't endure it. We shall fight. But I shall love her, I shall love her infinitely. Will they marry us? Do they let convicts marry? That's the question. And without her I can't exist . . ."

Mitya walked frowning across the room. It was almost dark. He suddenly seemed terribly worried.

"So there's a secret, she says, a secret? We have got up a plot against her, and Katya is mixed up in it, she thinks. No, my good Grushenka, that's not it. You are very wide of the mark, in your foolish feminine way. Alyosha darling, well, here goes! I'll tell you our secret!"

He looked round, went close up quickly to Alyosha, who was standing before him, and whispered to him with an air of mystery, though in reality no one could hear them: the old warder was dozing in the corner, and not a word could reach the ears of the soldiers on guard.

"I will tell you all our secret," Mitya whispered hurriedly. "I meant to tell you later, for how could I decide on anything without you? You are everything to me. Though I say that Ivan is superior to us, you are my angel. It's your decision will decide it. Perhaps it's you that are superior and not Ivan. You see, it's a question of conscience, question of the higher conscience—the secret is so important that I can't settle it myself, and I've put it off till I could speak to you. But, anyway, it's too early to decide now, for we must wait for the verdict. As soon as the verdict is given, you shall decide my fate. Don't decide it now. I'll tell you now. You listen, but don't decide. Stand and keep quiet. I won't tell you everything. I'll only tell you the idea, without details, and you keep quiet. Not a question, not a movement. You agree? But, goodness, what shall I do with your eyes? I'm afraid your eyes will tell me your decision, even if you don't speak. Oo! I'm afraid! Alyosha, listen! Ivan suggests my *escaping*. I won't tell you the details: it's all been thought out: it can all be arranged. Hush, don't decide. I should go to America with Grusha. You know I can't live without Grusha! What if they won't let her follow me to Siberia? Do they let convicts get married? Ivan thinks not. And without Grusha what should I do there underground with a hammer? I should only smash my skull with the hammer! But, on the other hand, my conscience? I should have run away from suffering. A sign has come, I reject the sign. I have a way of salvation and I turn my back on it. Ivan says that in America, 'with the good-will', I can be of more use than underground. But what becomes of our hymn from underground? What's America? America is vanity again! And there's a lot of swindling in America, too, I expect. I should have run away from crucifixion! I tell you, you know, Alexey, because you are the only person who can understand this. There's no one else. It's folly, madness to others, all I've told you of the hymn. They'll say I'm out of my mind or a fool. I am not out of my mind and I am not a fool. Ivan understands about the hymn, too. He understands, only he doesn't answer—he doesn't speak. He doesn't believe in the hymn. Don't speak, don't speak. I see how you look! You have already decided. Don't decide, spare me! I can't live without Grusha. Wait till after the trial!"

Mitya ended beside himself. He held Alyosha with both hands on his shoulders, and his yearning, feverish eyes were fixed on his brother's.

"They don't let convicts marry, do they?" he repeated for the third time in a supplicating voice.

Alyosha listened with extreme surprise and was deeply moved.

"Tell me one thing," he said, "is Ivan very keen on it, and whose idea was it?"

"His, his, and he is very keen on it. He didn't come to see me at first, then he suddenly came a week ago and he began about it straight away. He is awfully keen on it. He doesn't ask me, but orders me to escape. He doesn't doubt of my obeying him, though I showed him all my heart as I have to you, and told him about the hymn, too. He told me he'd arrange it; he's found out about everything. But of that later. He's simply set on it. It's all a matter of money: he'll pay ten thousand for escape and give me twenty thousand for America. And he says we can arrange a magnificent escape for ten thousand."

"And he told you on no account to tell me?" Alyosha asked again.

"To tell no one, and especially not you; on no account to tell you. He is afraid, no doubt, that you'll stand before me as my conscience. Don't tell him I told you. Don't tell him, for anything."

"You are right," Alyosha pronounced; "it's impossible to decide anything before the trial is over. After the trial you'll decide of yourself. Then you'll find that new man in yourself and he will decide."

"A new man, or a Bernard who'll decide à la Bernard, for I believe I'm a contemptible Bernard myself," said Mitya, with a bitter grin.

"But, brother, have you no hope then of being acquitted?"

Mitya shrugged his shoulders nervously and shook his head.

"Alyosha darling, it's time you were going," he said, with a sudden haste. "There's the superintendent shouting in the yard. He'll be here directly. We are late; it's irregular. Embrace me quickly. Kiss me! Sign me with the Cross, darling, for the Cross I have to bear to-morrow."

They embraced and kissed.

"Ivan," said Mitya suddenly, "suggests my escaping; but, of course, he believes I did it."

A mournful smile came on to his lips.

"Have you asked him whether he believes it?" asked Alyosha.

"No, I haven't. I wanted to, but I couldn't. I hadn't the courage. But I saw it from his eyes. Well, good-bye!"

Once more they kissed hurriedly, and Alyosha was just going out when Mitya suddenly called him back.

"Stand facing me! That's right!" And again he seized Alyosha, putting both hands on his shoulders. His face became suddenly quite pale, so that it was dreadfully apparent, even through the gathering darkness. His lips twitched, his eyes fastened upon Alyosha.

"Alyosha, tell me the whole truth, as you would before God.

Do you believe I did it? Do you, do you in yourself, believe it? The whole truth, don't lie!" he cried desperately.

Everything seemed heaving before Alyosha, and he felt something like a stab at his heart.

"Hush! What do you mean?" he faltered helplessly.

"The whole truth, the whole, don't lie!" repeated Mitya.

"I've never for one instant believed that you were the murderer!" broke in a shaking voice from Alyosha's breast, and he raised his right hand in the air, as though calling God to witness his words.

Mitya's whole face was lighted up with bliss.

"Thank you!" he articulated slowly, as though letting a sigh escape him after fainting. "Now you have given me new life. Would you believe it, till this moment I've been afraid to ask you, you, even you. Well, go! You've given me strength for to-morrow. God bless you! Come, go along! Love Ivan!" were Mitya's last words.

Alyosha went out in tears. Such distrustfulness in Mitya, such lack of confidence even to him, to Alyosha—all this suddenly opened before Alyosha an unsuspected depth of hopeless grief and despair in the soul of his unhappy brother. Intense, infinite compassion overwhelmed him instantly. There was a poignant ache in his torn heart. "Love Ivan"—he suddenly recalled Mitya's words. And he was going to Ivan. He badly wanted to see Ivan all day. He was as much worried about Ivan as about Mitya, and more than ever now.

CHAPTER V

NOT YOU, NOT YOU!

ON the way to Ivan he had to pass the house where Katerina Ivanovna was living. There was light in the windows. He suddenly stopped and resolved to go in. He had not seen Katerina Ivanovna for more than a week. But now it struck him that Ivan might be with her, especially on the eve of the terrible day. Ringing, and mounting the staircase, which was dimly lighted by a Chinese lantern, he saw a man coming down, and as they met, he recognised him as his brother. So he was just coming from Katerina Ivanovna.

"Ah, it's only you," said Ivan dryly. "Well, good-bye! You are going to her?"

"Yes."

"I don't advise you to; she's upset and you'll upset her more."

A door was instantly flung open above, and a voice cried suddenly:

"No, no! Alexey Fyodorovitch, have you come from him?"

"Yes, I have been with him."

"Has he sent me any message? Come up, Alyosha, and you, Ivan Fyodorovitch, you must come back, you must. Do you hear?"

There was such a peremptory note in Katya's voice that Ivan, after a moment's hesitation, made up his mind to go back with Alyosha.

"She was listening," he murmured angrily to himself, but Alyosha heard it.

"Excuse my keeping my greatcoat on," said Ivan, going into the drawing-room. "I won't sit down. I won't stay more than a minute."

"Sit down, Alexey Fyodorovitch," said Katerina Ivanovna, though she remained standing. She had changed very little during this time, but there was an ominous gleam in her dark eyes. Alyosha remembered afterwards that she had struck him as particularly handsome at that moment.

"What did he ask you to tell me?"

"Only one thing," said Alyosha, looking her straight in the face, "that you would spare yourself and say nothing at the trial of what" (he was a little confused) ". . . passed between you . . . at the time of your first acquaintance . . . in that town."

"Ah! that I bowed down to the ground for that money!" She broke into a bitter laugh. "Why, is he afraid for me or for himself? He asks me to spare—whom? Him or myself? Tell me, Alexey Fyodorovitch!"

Alyosha watched her intently, trying to understand her.

"Both yourself and him," he answered softly.

"I am glad to hear it," she snapped out maliciously, and she suddenly blushed.

"You don't know me yet, Alexey Fyodorovitch," she said menacingly. "And I don't know myself yet. Perhaps you'll want to trample me under foot after my examination to-morrow."

"You will give your evidence honourably," said Alyosha; "that's all that's wanted."

"Women are often dishonourable," she snarled. "Only an

295

THE BROTHERS KARAMAZOV

hour ago I was thinking I felt afraid to touch that monster . . .
as though he were a reptile . . . but no, he is still a human
being to me! But did he do it? Is he the murderer?" she
cried, all of a sudden, hysterically, turning quickly to Ivan.
Alyosha saw at once that she had asked Ivan that question
before, perhaps only a moment before he came in, and not for
the first time but for the hundredth, and that they had ended
by quarrelling.

"I've been to see Smerdyakov. . . . It was you, you who
persuaded me that he murdered his father. It's only you I
believed!" she continued, still addressing Ivan. He gave her
a sort of strained smile. Alyosha started at her tone. He had
not suspected such familiar intimacy between them.

"Well, that's enough, anyway," Ivan cut short the conversation. "I am going. I'll come to-morrow." And turning at once,
he walked out of the room and went straight downstairs.

With an imperious gesture, Katerina Ivanovna seized Alyosha
by both hands.

"Follow him! Overtake him! Don't leave him alone for a
minute!" she said, in a hurried whisper. "He's mad! Don't
you know that he's mad? He is in a fever, nervous fever. The
doctor told me so. Go, run after him. . . ."

Alyosha jumped up and ran after Ivan, who was not fifty
paces ahead of him.

"What do you want?" He turned quickly on Alyosha, seeing
that he was running after him. "She told you to catch me up,
because I'm mad. I know it all by heart," he added irritably.

"She is mistaken, of course; but she is right that you are ill,"
said Alyosha. "I was looking at your face just now. You look
very ill, Ivan."

Ivan walked on without stopping. Alyosha followed him.

"And do you know, Alexey Fyodorovitch, how people do go
out of their mind?" Ivan asked in a voice suddenly quiet, without a trace of irritation, with a note of the simplest curiosity.

"No, I don't. I suppose there are all kinds of insanity."

"And can one observe that one's going mad oneself?"

"I imagine one can't see oneself clearly in such circumstances," Alyosha answered, with surprise.

Ivan paused for half a minute.

"If you want to talk to me, please change the subject," he
said suddenly.

"Oh, while I think of it, I have a letter for you," said
Alyosha timidly, and he took Lise's note from his pocket and

held it out to Ivan. They were just under a lamp-post. Ivan recognised the handwriting at once.

"Ah, from that little demon!" he laughed maliciously, and, without opening the envelope, he tore it into bits and threw it in the air. The bits were scattered by the wind.

"She's not sixteen yet, I believe, and already offering herself," he said contemptuously, striding along the street again.

"How do you mean, 'offering herself'?" exclaimed Alyosha.

"As wanton women offer themselves, to be sure."

"How can you, Ivan, how can you?" Alyosha cried warmly in a grieved voice. "She is a child; you are insulting a child! She is ill; she is very ill, too. She is on the verge of insanity, too, perhaps . . . I had hoped to hear something from you . . . that would save her."

"You'll hear nothing from me. If she is a child I am not her nurse. Be quiet, Alexey. Don't go on about her. I am not even thinking about it."

They were silent again for a moment.

"She will be praying all night now to the Mother of God to show her how to act to-morrow at the trial," he said sharply and angrily again.

"You . . . you mean Katerina Ivanovna?"

"Yes. Whether she's to save Mitya or ruin him. She'll pray for light from above. She can't make up her mind for herself, you see. She has not had time to decide yet. She takes me for her nurse, too. She wants me to sing lullabies to her."

"Katerina Ivanovna loves you, brother," said Alyosha sadly.

"Perhaps; but I am not very keen on her."

"She is suffering. Why do you . . . sometimes say things to her that give her hope?" Alyosha went on, with timid reproach. "I know that you've given her hope. Forgive me for speaking to you like this," he added.

"I can't behave to her as I ought—break off altogether and tell her so straight out," said Ivan irritably. "I must wait till sentence is passed on the murderer. If I break off with her now, she will avenge herself on me by ruining that scoundrel to-morrow at the trial, for she hates him and knows she hates him. It's all a lie—lie upon lie! As long as I don't break off with her, she goes on hoping, and she won't ruin that monster, knowing how I want to get him out of trouble. If only that damned verdict would come!"

The words "murderer" and "monster" echoed painfully in Alyosha's heart.

297

"But how can she ruin Mitya?" he asked, pondering on Ivan's words. "What evidence can she give that would ruin Mitya?"

"You don't know that yet. She's got a document in her hands, in Mitya's own writing, that proves conclusively that he did murder Fyodor Pavlovitch."

"That's impossible!" cried Alyosha.

"Why is it impossible? I've read it myself."

"There can't be such a document!" Alyosha repeated warmly. "There can't be, because he's not the murderer. It's not he murdered father, not he!"

Ivan suddenly stopped.

"Who is the murderer then, according to you?" he asked, with apparent coldness. There was even a supercilious note in his voice.

"You know who," Alyosha pronounced in a low, penetrating voice.

"Who? You mean the myth about that crazy idiot, the epileptic, Smerdyakov?"

Alyosha suddenly felt himself trembling all over.

"You know who," broke helplessly from him. He could scarcely breathe.

"Who? Who?" Ivan cried almost fiercely. All his restraint suddenly vanished.

"I only know one thing," Alyosha went on, still almost in a whisper, *"it wasn't you* killed father."

"Not you! What do you mean by 'not you'?" Ivan was thunderstruck.

"It was not you killed father, not you!" Alyosha repeated firmly.

The silence lasted for half a minute.

"I know I didn't. Are you raving?" said Ivan, with a pale, distorted smile. His eyes were riveted on Alyosha. They were standing again under a lamp-post.

"No, Ivan. You've told yourself several times that you are the murderer."

"When did I say so? I was in Moscow. . . . When have I said so?" Ivan faltered helplessly.

"You've said so to yourself many times, when you've been alone during these two dreadful months," Alyosha went on, softly and distinctly as before. Yet he was speaking now, as it were, not of himself, not of his own will, but obeying some irresistible command. "You have accused yourself and have confessed to yourself that you are the murderer and no one else. But you didn't do it: you are mistaken: you are not the murderer. Do you hear? It was not you! God has sent me to tell you so."

They were both silent. The silence lasted a whole long minute. They were both standing still, gazing into each other's eyes. They were both pale. Suddenly Ivan began trembling all over, and clutched Alyosha's shoulder.

"You've been in my room!" he whispered hoarsely. "You've been there at night, when he came. . . . Confess . . . have you seen him, have you seen him?"

"Whom do you mean—Mitya?" Alyosha asked, bewildered.

"Not him, damn the monster!" Ivan shouted, in a frenzy. "Do you know that he visits me? How did you find out? Speak!"

"Who is *he?* I don't know whom you are talking about," Alyosha faltered, beginning to be alarmed.

"Yes, you do know . . . or how could you . . . ? It's impossible that you don't know."

Suddenly he seemed to check himself. He stood still and seemed to reflect. A strange grin contorted his lips.

"Brother," Alyosha began again, in a shaking voice, "I have said this to you because you'll believe my word, I know that. I tell you once and for all, it's not you. You hear, once for all! God has put it into my heart to say this to you, even though it may make you hate me from this hour."

But by now Ivan had apparently regained his self-control.

"Alexey Fyodorovitch," he said, with a cold smile, "I can't endure prophets and epileptics—messengers from God especially—and you know that only too well. I break off all relations with you from this moment and probably for ever. I beg you to leave me at this turning. It's the way to your lodgings, too. You'd better be particularly careful not to come to me to-day! Do you hear?"

He turned and walked on with a firm step, not looking back.

"Brother," Alyosha called after him, "if anything happens to you to-day, turn to me before anyone!"

But Ivan made no reply. Alyosha stood under the lamp-post at the cross-roads till Ivan had vanished into the darkness. Then he turned and walked slowly homewards. Both Alyosha and Ivan were living in lodgings; neither of them was willing to live in Fyodor Pavlovitch's empty house. Alyosha had a furnished room in the house of some working people. Ivan lived some distance from him. He had taken a roomy and fairly comfortable lodge attached to a fine house that belonged to a well-to-do lady, the widow of an official. But his only attendant was a deaf and rheumatic old crone who went to bed at six o'clock every evening and got up at six in the morning. Ivan had become remarkably indifferent to his comforts of late, and very fond of being alone. He did everything for himself in the one room he lived in, and rarely entered any of the other rooms in his abode.

He reached the gate of the house and had his hand on the bell when he suddenly stopped. He felt that he was trembling all over with anger. Suddenly he let go of the bell, turned back with a curse, and walked with rapid steps in the opposite direction. He walked a mile and a half to a tiny, slanting, wooden house, almost a hut, where Marya Kondratyevna, the neighbour who used to come to Fyodor Pavlovitch's kitchen for soup and to whom Smerdyakov had once sung his songs and played on the guitar, was now lodging. She had sold their little house, and was now living here with her mother. Smerdyakov, who was ill—almost dying—had been with them ever since Fyodor Pavlovitch's death. It was to him Ivan was going now, drawn by a sudden and irresistible prompting.

CHAPTER VI

THE FIRST INTERVIEW WITH SMERDYAKOV

THIS was the third time that Ivan had been to see Smerdyakov since his return from Moscow. The first time he had seen him and talked to him was on the first day of his arrival, then he had visited him once more, a fortnight later. But his visits had ended with that second one, so that it was now over a month since he had seen him. And he had scarcely heard anything of him.

Ivan had only returned five days after his father's death, so that he was not present at the funeral, which took place the day before he came back. The cause of his delay was that Alyosha, not knowing his Moscow address, had to apply to Katerina Ivanovna to telegraph to him, and she, not knowing his address either, telegraphed to her sister and aunt, reckoning on Ivan's going to see them as soon as he arrived in Moscow. But he did not go to them till four days after his arrival. When he got the telegram he had, of course, set off post-haste to our town. The first to meet him was Alyosha, and Ivan was greatly surprised to find that, in opposition to the general opinion of the town, he refused to entertain a suspicion against Mitya, and spoke openly of Smerdyakov as the murderer. Later on, after seeing the police captain and the prosecutor, and hearing the details of the charge and the arrest, he was still more surprised at Alyosha, and ascribed his opinion only to his exaggerated brotherly feeling and sympathy with Mitya, of whom Alyosha, as Ivan knew, was very fond.

By the way, let us say a word or two of Ivan's feeling to his brother Dmitri. He positively disliked him, at most felt sometimes a compassion for him, and even that was mixed with great contempt, almost repugnance. Mitya's whole personality, even his appearance, was extremely unattractive to him. Ivan looked with indignation on Katerina Ivanovna's love for his brother. Yet he went to see Mitya on the first day of his arrival, and that interview, far from shaking Ivan's belief in his guilt, positively strengthened it. He found his brother agitated, nervously excited. Mitya had been talkative, but very absent-minded and incoherent. He used violent language, accused Smerdyakov, and was fearfully muddled. He talked principally about the three thousand roubles, which he said had been "stolen" from him by his father.

"The money was mine, it was my money," Mitya kept repeating. "Even if I had stolen it, I should have had the right."

He hardly contested the evidence against him, and if he tried to turn a fact to his advantage, it was in an absurd and incoherent way. He hardly seemed to wish to defend himself to Ivan or anyone else. Quite the contrary, he was angry and proudly scornful of the charges against him; he was continually firing up and abusing everyone. He only laughed contemptuously at Grigory's evidence about the open door, and declared that it was "the devil that opened it". But he could not bring forward any coherent explanation of the fact. He even succeeded in insulting Ivan during their first interview, telling him sharply that it was not for people who declared that "everything was lawful" to suspect and question him. Altogether he was anything but friendly with Ivan on that occasion. Immediately after that interview with Mitya, Ivan went for the first time to see Smerdyakov.

In the railway train on his way from Moscow, he kept thinking of Smerdyakov and of his last conversation with him on the

THE BROTHERS KARAMAZOV

evening before he went away. Many things seemed to him puzzling and suspicious. But when he gave his evidence to the investigating lawyer Ivan said nothing, for the time, of that conversation. He put that off till he had seen Smerdyakov, who was at that time in the hospital.

Doctor Herzenstube and Varvinsky, the doctor he met in the hospital, confidently asserted, in reply to Ivan's persistent questions, that Smerdyakov's epileptic attack was unmistakably genuine, and were surprised indeed at Ivan asking whether he might not have been shamming on the day of the catastrophe. They gave him to understand that the attack was an exceptional one, the fits persisting and recurring several times, so that the patient's life was positively in danger, and it was only now, after they had applied remedies, that they could assert with confidence that the patient would survive. "Though it might well be," added Doctor Herzenstube, "that his reason would be impaired for a considerable period, if not permanently." On Ivan's asking impatiently whether that meant that he was now mad, they told him that this was not yet the case, in the full sense of the word, but that certain abnormalities were perceptible. Ivan decided to find out for himself what those abnormalities were.

At the hospital he was at once allowed to see the patient. Smerdyakov was lying on a truckle bed in a separate ward. There was only one other bed in the room, and in it lay a tradesman of the town, swollen with dropsy, who was obviously almost dying; he could be no hindrance to their conversation. Smerdyakov grinned uncertainly on seeing Ivan, and for the first instant seemed nervous. So at least Ivan fancied. But that was only momentary. For the rest of the time he was struck, on the contrary, by Smerdyakov's composure. From the first glance Ivan had no doubt that he was very ill. He was very weak; he spoke slowly, seeming to move his tongue with difficulty; he was much thinner and sallower. Throughout the interview, which lasted twenty minutes, he kept complaining of headache and of pain in all his limbs. His thin emasculate face seemed to have become so tiny; his hair was ruffled, and his crest of curls in front stood up in a thin tuft. But in the left eye, which was screwed up and seemed to be insinuating something, Smerdyakov showed himself unchanged. "It's always worth while speaking to a clever man." Ivan was reminded of that at once. He sat down on the stool at his feet. Smerdyakov, with painful effort, shifted his position in bed, but he was not

302

the first to speak. He remained dumb, and did not even look much interested.

"Can you talk to me?" asked Ivan. "I won't tire you much."

"Certainly I can," mumbled Smerdyakov, in a faint voice. "Has your honour been back long?" he added patronisingly, as though encouraging a nervous visitor.

"I only arrived to-day. . . . To see the mess you are in here."

Smerdyakov sighed.

"Why do you sigh, you knew of it all along?" Ivan blurted out.

Smerdyakov was stolidly silent for a while.

"How could I help knowing? It was clear beforehand. But how could I tell it would turn out like that?"

"What would turn out? Don't prevaricate! You've fore-told you'd have a fit; on the way down to the cellar, you know. You mentioned the very spot."

"Have you said so at the examination yet?" Smerdyakov queried, with composure.

Ivan felt suddenly angry.

"No, I haven't yet, but I certainly shall. You must explain a great deal to me, my man, and let me tell you, I am not going to let you play with me!"

"Why should I play with you, when I put my whole trust in you, as in God Almighty?" said Smerdyakov, with the same composure, only for a moment closing his eyes.

"In the first place," began Ivan, "I know that epileptic fits can't be foretold beforehand. I've inquired, don't try to take me in. You can't foretell the day and the hour. How was it you told me the day and the hour beforehand, and about the cellar, too? How could you tell that you would fall down the cellar stairs in a fit, if you didn't sham a fit on pur-pose?"

"I had to go to the cellar, anyway, several times a day, in-deed," Smerdyakov drawled deliberately. "I fell from the garret just in the same way a year ago. It's quite true you can't foretell the day and hour of a fit beforehand, but you can always have a presentiment of it."

"But you did foretell the day and the hour!"

"In regard to my epilepsy, sir, you had much better inquire of the doctors here. You can ask them whether it was a real fit or a sham; it's no use my saying any more about it."

303

"And the cellar? How could you know beforehand of the cellar?"

"You don't seem able to get over that cellar! As I was going down to the cellar, I was in terrible dread and doubt. What frightened me most was losing you and being left without defence in all the world. So I went down into the cellar thinking, 'Here, it'll come on directly, it'll strike me down directly, shall I fall?' And it was through this fear that I suddenly felt the spasm that always comes . . . and so I went flying. All that and all my previous conversation with you at the gate the evening before, when I told you how frightened I was and spoke of the cellar, I told all that to Doctor Herzenstube and Nikolay Parfenovitch, the investigating lawyer, and it's all been written down in the protocol. And the doctor here, Mr. Varvinsky, maintained to all of them that it was just the thought of it brought it on, the apprehension that I might fall. It was just then that the fit seized me. And so they've written it down, that it's just how it must have happened, simply from my fear."

As he finished, Smerdyakov drew a deep breath, as though exhausted.

"Then you have said all that in your evidence?" said Ivan, somewhat taken aback. He had meant to frighten him with the threat of repeating their conversation, and it appeared that Smerdyakov had already reported it all himself.

"What have I to be afraid of? Let them write down the whole truth," Smerdyakov pronounced firmly.

"And have you told them every word of our conversation at the gate?"

"No, not to say every word."

"And did you tell them that you can sham fits, as you boasted then?"

"No, I didn't tell them that either."

"Tell me now, why did you send me then to Tchermashnya?"

"I was afraid you'd go away to Moscow, Tchermashnya is nearer, anyway."

"You are lying, you suggested my going away yourself; you told me to get out of the way of trouble."

"That was simply out of affection and my sincere devotion to you, foreseeing trouble in the house, to spare you. Only I wanted to spare myself even more. That's why I told you to get out of harm's way, that you might understand that there would be trouble in the house, and would remain at home to protect your father."

"You might have said it more directly, you blockhead!" Ivan suddenly fired up.

"How could I have said it more directly then? It was simply my fear that made me speak, and you might have been angry, too. I might well have been apprehensive that Dmitri Fyodorovitch would make a scene and carry away that money, for he considered it as good as his own, but who could tell that it would end in a murder like this? I thought that he would only carry off the three thousand that lay under the master's mattress in the envelope, and you see, he's murdered him. How could you guess it either, sir?"

"But if you say yourself that it couldn't be guessed, how could I have guessed and stayed at home? You contradict yourself!" said Ivan, pondering.

"You might have guessed from my sending you to Tchermashnya and not to Moscow."

"How could I guess it from that?"

Smerdyakov seemed much exhausted, and again he was silent for a minute.

"You might have guessed from the fact of my asking you not to go to Moscow, but to Tchermashnya, that I wanted to have you nearer, for Moscow's a long way off, and Dmitri Fyodorovitch, knowing you are not far off, would not be so bold. And if anything had happened, you might have come to protect me, too, for I warned you of Grigory Vassilyevitch's illness, and that I was afraid of having a fit. And when I explained those knocks to you, by means of which one could go in to the deceased, and that Dmitri Fyodorovitch knew them all through me, I thought that you would guess yourself that he would be sure to do something, and so wouldn't go to Tchermashnya even, but would stay."

"He talks very coherently," thought Ivan, "though he does mumble; what's the derangement of his faculties that Herzenstube talked of?"

"You are cunning with me, damn you," he exclaimed, getting angry.

"But I thought at the time that you quite guessed," Smerdyakov parried, with the simplest air.

"If I'd guessed, I should have stayed," cried Ivan.

"Why, I thought that it was because you guessed that you went away in such a hurry, only to get out of trouble, only to run away and save yourself in your fright."

"You think that everyone is as great a coward as yourself?"

"Forgive me, I thought you were like me."

"Of course, I ought to have guessed," Ivan said in agitation, "and I did guess there was some mischief brewing on your part . . . only you are lying, you are lying again," he cried, suddenly recollecting. "Do you remember how you went up to the carriage and said to me, 'It's always worth while speaking to a clever man'? So you were glad I went away, since you praised me?"

Smerdyakov sighed again and again. A trace of colour came into his face.

"If I was pleased," he articulated rather breathlessly, "it was simply because you agreed not to go to Moscow, but to Tchermashnya. For it was nearer, anyway. Only when I said these words to you, it was not by way of praise but of reproach. You didn't understand it."

"What reproach?"

"Why, that foreseeing such a calamity you deserted your own father, and would not protect us, for I might have been taken up any time for stealing that three thousand."

"Damn you!" Ivan swore again. "Stay, did you tell the prosecutor and the investigating lawyer about those knocks?"

"I told them everything just as it was."

Ivan wondered inwardly again.

"If I thought of anything then," he began again, "it was solely of some wickedness on your part. Dmitri might kill him, but that he would steal—I did not believe that then. . . . But I was prepared for any wickedness from you. You told me yourself you could sham a fit. What did you say that for?"

"It was just through my simplicity, and I never have shammed a fit on purpose in my life. And I only said so then to boast to you. It was just foolishness. I liked you so much then, and was open-hearted with you."

"My brother directly accuses you of the murder and theft."

"What else is left for him to do?" said Smerdyakov, with a bitter grin. "And who will believe him with all the proofs against him? Grigory Vassilyevitch saw the door open. What can he say after that? But never mind him! He is trembling to save himself."

He slowly ceased speaking, and suddenly, as though on reflection, added:

"And look here again. He wants to throw it on me and make out that it is the work of my hands—I've heard that already. But as to my being clever at shamming a fit: should I have

306

told you beforehand that I could sham one if I really had had such a design against your father? If I had been planning such a murder, could I have been such a fool as to give such evidence against myself beforehand? And to his son, too! Upon my word! Is that likely? As if that could be, such a thing has never happened. No one hears this talk of ours now, except Providence itself, and if you were to tell of it to the prosecutor and Nikolay Parfenovitch you might defend me completely by doing so, for who would be likely to be such a criminal if he is so open-hearted beforehand? Anyone can see that."

"Well," and Ivan got up to cut short the conversation, struck by Smerdyakov's last argument. "I don't suspect you at all, and I think it's absurd indeed to suspect you. On the contrary, I am grateful to you for setting my mind at rest. Now I am going, but I'll come again. Meanwhile, good-bye. Get well. Is there anything you want?"

"I am very thankful for everything. Marfa Ignatyevna does not forget me, and provides me anything I want, according to her kindness. Good people visit me every day."

"Good-bye. But I shan't say anything of your being able to sham a fit, and I don't advise you to, either," something made Ivan say suddenly.

"I quite understand. And if you don't speak of that, I shall say nothing of that conversation of ours at the gate."

Then it happened that Ivan went out, and only when he had gone a dozen steps along the corridor, he suddenly felt that there was an insulting significance in Smerdyakov's last words. He was almost on the point of turning back, but it was only a passing impulse, and muttering, "Nonsense!" he went out of the hospital.

His chief feeling was one of relief at the fact that it was not Smerdyakov, but Mitya, who had committed the murder, though he might have been expected to feel the opposite. He did not want to analyse the reason for this feeling, and even felt a positive repugnance at prying into his sensations. He felt as though he wanted to make haste to forget something. In the following days he became convinced of Mitya's guilt, as he got to know all the weight of evidence against him. There was evidence of people of no importance, Fenya and her mother, for instance, but the effect of it was almost overpowering. As to Perhotin, the people at the tavern, and at Plotnikov's shop, as well as the witnesses at Mokroe, their evidence seemed conclusive. It was the details that were so damning. The secret of

THE BROTHERS KARAMAZOV

the knocks impressed the lawyers almost as much as Grigory's evidence as to the open door. Grigory's wife, Marfa, in answer to Ivan's questions, declared that Smerdyakov had been lying all night the other side of the partition wall, "He was not three paces from our bed," and that although she was a sound sleeper she waked several times and heard him moaning, "He was moaning the whole time, moaning continually."

Talking to Herzenstube, and giving it as his opinion that Smerdyakov was not mad, but only rather weak, Ivan only evoked from the old man a subtle smile.

"Do you know how he spends his time now?" he asked, "learning lists of French words by heart. He has an exercise-book under his pillow with the French words written out in Russian letters for him by someone, he, he, he!"

Ivan ended by dismissing all doubts. He could not think of Dmitri without repulsion. Only one thing was strange, however. Alyosha persisted that Dmitri was not the murderer, and that "in all probability" Smerdyakov was. Ivan always felt that Alyosha's opinion meant a great deal to him, and so he was astonished at it now. Another thing that was strange was that Alyosha did not make any attempt to talk about Mitya with Ivan, that he never began on the subject and only answered his questions. This, too, struck Ivan particularly.

But he was very much preoccupied at that time with something quite apart from that. On his return from Moscow, he abandoned himself hopelessly to his mad and consuming passion for Katerina Ivanovna. This is not the time to begin to speak of this new passion of Ivan's, which left its mark on all the rest of his life: this would furnish the subject for another novel, which I may perhaps never write. But I cannot omit to mention here that when Ivan, on leaving Katerina Ivanovna with Alyosha, as I've related already, told him: "I am not keen on her," it was an absolute lie: he loved her madly, though at times he hated her so that he might have murdered her. Many causes helped to bring about this feeling. Shattered by what had happened with Mitya, she rushed on Ivan's return to meet him as her one salvation. She was hurt, insulted and humiliated in her feelings. And here the man had come back to her, who had loved her so ardently before (oh, she knew that very well), and whose heart and intellect she considered so superior to her own. But the sternly virtuous girl did not abandon herself altogether to the man she loved, in spite of the Karamazov violence of his passions and the great fascination he had for her.

She was continually tormented at the same time by remorse for having deserted Mitya, and in moments of discord and violent anger (and they were numerous) she told Ivan so plainly. This was what he had called to Alyosha "lies upon lies". There was, of course, much that was false in it, and that angered Ivan more than anything. . . . But of all this later.

He did, in fact, for a time almost forget Smerdyakov's existence, and yet, a fortnight after his first visit to him, he began to be haunted by the same strange thoughts as before. It's enough to say that he was continually asking himself, why was it that on that last night in Fyodor Pavlovitch's house he had crept out on to the stairs like a thief and listened to hear what his father was doing below? Why had he recalled that afterwards with repulsion; why, next morning, had he been suddenly so depressed on the journey; why, as he reached Moscow, had he said to himself "I am a scoundrel"? And now he almost fancied that these tormenting thoughts would make him even forget Katerina Ivanovna, so completely did they take possession of him again. It was just after fancying this that he met Alyosha in the street. He stopped him at once, and put a question to him:

"Do you remember when Dmitri burst in after dinner and beat father, and afterwards I told you in the yard that I reserved 'the right to desire' . . . tell me, did you think then that I desired father's death or not?"

"I did think so," answered Alyosha softly.

"It was so, too; it was not a matter of guessing. But didn't you fancy then that what I wished was just that 'one reptile should devour another'; that is, just that Dmitri should kill father, and as soon as possible . . . and that I myself was even prepared to help to bring that about?"

Alyosha turned rather pale, and looked silently into his brother's face.

"Speak!" cried Ivan. "I want above everything to know what you thought then. I want the truth, the truth!"

He drew a deep breath, looking angrily at Alyosha before his answer came.

"Forgive me, I did think that, too, at the time," whispered Alyosha, and he did not add one softening phrase.

"Thanks," snapped Ivan, and, leaving Alyosha, he went quickly on his way. From that time Alyosha noticed that Ivan began obviously to avoid him and seemed even to have taken a dislike to him, so much so that Alyosha gave up going to see him. Immediately after that meeting with him, Ivan had not gone home, but went straight to Smerdyakov again.

CHAPTER VII

THE SECOND VISIT TO SMERDYAKOV

BY that time Smerdyakov had been discharged from the hospital. Ivan knew his new lodging, the dilapidated little wooden house, divided in two by a passage on one side of which lived Marya Kondratyevna and her mother, and on the other, Smerdyakov. No one knew on what terms he lived with them, whether as a friend or as a lodger. It was supposed afterwards that he had come to stay with them as Marya Kondratyevna's betrothed, and was living there for a time without paying for board or lodging. Both mother and daughter had the greatest respect for him and looked upon him as greatly superior to themselves.

Ivan knocked, and, on the door being opened, went into the passage. By Marya Kondratyevna's directions he went straight to the better room on the left, occupied by Smerdyakov. There was a tiled stove in the room and it was extremely hot. The walls were gay with blue paper, which was a good deal used, however, and in the cracks under it cockroaches swarmed in amazing numbers, so that there was a continual rustling from them. The furniture was very scanty: two benches against each wall and two chairs by the table. The table of plain wood was covered with a cloth with pink patterns on it. There was a pot of geranium on each of the two little windows. In the corner there was a case of ikons. On the table stood a little copper samovar with many dents in it, and a tray with two cups. But Smerdyakov had finished tea and the samovar was out. He was sitting at the table on a bench. He was looking at an exercise-book and slowly writing with a pen. There was a bottle of ink by him and a flat iron candlestick, but with a composite candle. Ivan saw at once from Smerdyakov's face that he had completely recovered from his illness. His face was fresher, fuller, his hair stood up jauntily in front and was plastered down at the sides. He was sitting in a parti-coloured, wadded dressing-gown, rather dirty and frayed, however. He had spectacles on his nose, which Ivan had never seen him wearing before. This trifling circumstance suddenly redoubled

Ivan's anger: "A creature like that and wearing spectacles."

Smerdyakov slowly raised his head and looked intently at his visitor through his spectacles; then he slowly took them off and rose from the bench, but by no means respectfully, almost lazily, doing the least possible required by common civility. All this struck Ivan instantly, he took it all in and noted it at once—most of all the looks in Smerdyakov's eyes, positively malicious, churlish and haughty. "What do you want to intrude for?" it seemed to say; "we settled everything then, why have you come again?" Ivan could scarcely control himself.

"It's hot here," he said, still standing, and unbuttoned his overcoat.

"Take off your coat," Smerdyakov conceded.

Ivan took off his coat and threw it on a bench with trembling hands. He took a chair, moved it quickly to the table and sat down. Smerdyakov managed to sit down on his bench before him.

"To begin with, are we alone?" Ivan asked sternly and impulsively. "Can they overhear us in there?"

"No one can hear anything. You've seen for yourself: there's a passage."

"Listen, my good fellow, what was that you babbled, as I was leaving the hospital, that if I said nothing about your faculty of shamming fits, you wouldn't tell the investigating lawyer all our conversation at the gate? What do you mean by *all?* What could you mean by it? Were you threatening me? Have I entered into some sort of compact with you? Do you suppose I am afraid of you?"

Ivan said this in a perfect fury, giving him to understand with obvious intention that he scorned any subterfuge or indirectness and meant to show his cards. Smerdyakov's eyes gleamed resentfully, his left eye winked and he at once gave his answer, with his habitual composure and deliberation: "You want to have everything above board; very well, you shall have it," he seemed to say.

"This is what I meant then, and this is why I said that, that you, knowing beforehand of this murder of your own parent, left him to his fate, and that people mightn't after that conclude any evil about your feelings and perhaps of something else, too—that's what I promised not to tell the authorities."

Though Smerdyakov spoke without haste and obviously controlling himself, yet there was something in his voice, determined and emphatic, resentful and insolently defiant. He stared impudently at Ivan. A mist passed before Ivan's eyes for the first moment.

"How? What? Are you out of your mind?"

"I'm perfectly in possession of all my faculties."

"Do you suppose I *knew* of the murder?" Ivan cried at last, and he brought his fist violently on the table. "What do you mean by 'something else, too'? Speak, scoundrel!"

Smerdyakov was silent and still scanned Ivan with the same insolent stare.

"Speak, you stinking rogue, what is that 'something else, too'?"

"The 'something else' I meant was that you probably too were very desirous of your parent's death."

Ivan jumped up and struck him with all his might on the shoulder, so that he fell back against the wall. In an instant his face was bathed in tears. Saying, "It's a shame, sir, to strike a sick man," he dried his eyes with a very dirty blue check handkerchief and sank into quiet weeping. A minute passed.

"That's enough! Leave off," Ivan said peremptorily, sitting down again. "Don't put me out of all patience."

Smerdyakov took the rag from his eyes. Every line of his puckered face reflected the insult he had just received.

"So you thought then, you scoundrel, that together with Dmitri I meant to kill my father?"

"I didn't know what thoughts were in your mind then," said Smerdyakov resentfully; "and so I stopped you then at the gate to sound you on that very point."

"To sound what, what?"

"Why, that very circumstance, whether you wanted your father to be murdered or not?"

What infuriated Ivan more than anything was the aggressive, insolent tone to which Smerdyakov persistently adhered.

"It was you murdered him?" he cried suddenly.

Smerdyakov smiled contemptuously.

"You know of yourself, for a fact, that it wasn't I murdered him. And I should have thought that there was no need for a sensible man to speak of it again."

"But why, why had you such a suspicion about me at the time?"

"As you know already, it was simply from fear. For I was in such a position, shaking with fear, that I suspected everyone. I resolved to sound you, too, for I thought if you wanted the same as your brother, then the business was as good as settled and I should be crushed like a fly, too."

"Look here, you didn't say that a fortnight ago."

"I meant the same when I talked to you in the hospital, only I thought you'd understand without wasting words, and that being such a sensible man you wouldn't care to talk of it openly."

"What next? Come answer, answer, I insist: what was it . . . what could I have done to put such a degrading suspicion into your mean soul?"

"As for the murder, you couldn't have done that and didn't want to, but as for wanting someone else to do it, that was just what you did want."

"And how coolly, how coolly he speaks! But why should I have wanted it, what grounds had I for wanting it?"

"What grounds had you? What about the inheritance?" said Smerdyakov sarcastically, and as it were vindictively. "Why, after your parent's death there was at least forty thousand to come to each of you, and very likely more, but if Fyodor Pavlovitch got married then to that lady, Agrafena Alexandrovna, she would have had all his capital made over to her directly after the wedding, for she's plenty of sense, so that your parent would not have left you two roubles between the three of you. And were they far from a wedding, either? Not a hair's-breadth: that lady had only to lift her little finger and he would have run after her to church, with his tongue out."

Ivan restrained himself with painful effort.

"Very good," he commented at last, "you see, I haven't jumped up, I haven't knocked you down, I haven't killed you. Speak on. So, according to you, I had fixed on Dmitri to do it, I was reckoning on him?"

"How could you help reckoning on him? If he killed him, then he would lose all the rights of a nobleman, his rank and property, and would go off to exile, so his share of the inheritance would come to you and your brother Alexey Fyodorovitch, in equal parts, so you'd each have not forty but sixty thousand each. There's not a doubt you did reckon on Dmitri Fyodorovitch."

"What I put up with from you! Listen, scoundrel, if I had reckoned on anyone then, it would have been on you, not on Dmitri, and I swear I did expect some wickedness from you . . . at the time. . . . I remember my impression!"

"I thought, too, for a minute, at the time, that you were

reckoning on me as well," said Smerdyakov, with a sarcastic grin. "So that it was just by that more than anything you showed me what was in your mind. For if you had a foreboding about me and yet went away, you as good as said to me: 'You can murder my parent, I won't hinder you!'"

"You scoundrel! So that's how you understood it!"

"It was all that going to Tchermashnya. Why! You were meaning to go to Moscow and refused all your father's entreaties to go to Tchermashnya—and simply at a foolish word from me you consented at once! What reason had you to consent to Tchermashnya? Since you went to Tchermashnya with no reason, simply at my word, it shows that you must have expected something from me."

"No, I swear I didn't!" shouted Ivan, grinding his teeth.

"You didn't? Then you ought, as your father's son, to have had me taken to the lock-up and thrashed at once for my words then . . . or at least, to have given me a punch in the face on the spot, but you were not a bit angry, if you please, and at once in a friendly way acted on my foolish word and went away, which was utterly absurd, for you ought to have stayed to save your parent's life. How could I help drawing my conclusions?"

Ivan sat scowling, both his fists convulsively pressed on his knees.

"Yes, I am sorry I didn't punch you in the face," he said with a bitter smile. "I couldn't have taken you to the lock-up just then. Who would have believed me and what charge could I bring against you? But the punch in the face . . . oh, I'm sorry I didn't think of it. Though blows are forbidden, I should have pounded your ugly face to a jelly."

Smerdyakov looked at him almost with relief.

"In the ordinary occasions of life," he said in the same complacent and sententious tone in which he had taunted Grigory and argued with him about religion at Fyodor Pavlovitch's table, "in the ordinary occasions of life, blows on the face are forbidden nowadays by law and people have given them up, but in exceptional occasions of life people still fly to blows, not only among us but all over the world, be it even the fullest Republic of France, just as in the time of Adam and Eve, and they never will leave off, but you, even in an exceptional case, did not dare."

"What are you learning French words for?" Ivan nodded towards the exercise book lying on the table.

"Why shouldn't I learn them so as to improve my education,

supposing that I may myself chance to go some day to those happy parts of Europe."

"Listen, monster," Ivan's eyes flashed and he trembled all over. "I am not afraid of your accusations, you can say what you like about me, and if I don't beat you to death, it's simply because I suspect you of that crime and I'll drag you to justice. I'll unmask you."

"To my thinking, you'd better keep quiet, for what can you accuse me of, considering my absolute innocence; and who would believe you? Only if you begin, I shall tell everything, too, for I must defend myself."

"Do you think I am afraid of you now?"

"If the court doesn't believe all I've said to you just now, the public will, and you will be ashamed."

"That's as much as to say, 'It's always worth while speaking to a sensible man', eh?" snarled Ivan.

"You hit the mark, indeed. And you'd better be sensible."

Ivan got up, shaking all over with indignation, put on his coat, and without replying further to Smerdyakov, without even looking at him, walked quickly out of the cottage. The cool evening air refreshed him. There was a bright moon in the sky. A nightmare of ideas and sensations filled his soul. "Shall I go at once and give information against Smerdyakov? But what information can I give? He is not guilty, anyway. On the contrary, he'll accuse me. And in fact why did I set off for Tchermashnya then? What for? What for?" Ivan asked himself. "Yes, of course, I was expecting something and he is right . . ." And he remembered for the hundredth time how, on that last night in his father's house, he had listened on the stairs. But he remembered it now with such anguish that he stood still on the spot as though he had been stabbed. "Yes, I expected it then, that's true! I wanted the murder, I did want the murder! Did I want the murder? Did I want it? I must kill Smerdyakov! If I don't dare kill Smerdyakov now, life is not worth living!"

Ivan did not go home, but went straight to Katerina Ivanovna and alarmed her by his appearance. He was like a madman. He repeated all his conversation with Smerdyakov, every syllable of it. He couldn't be calmed, however much she tried to soothe him: he kept walking about the room, speaking strangely, disconnectedly. At last he sat down, put his elbows on the table, leaned his head on his hands and pronounced this strange sentence: "If it's not Dmitri but Smerdyakov who's the murderer, I share his guilt, for I put him up to it. Whether I did, I don't know yet. But if he is the murderer, and not Dmitri, then, of course, I am the murderer, too."

When Katerina Ivanovna heard that, she got up from her seat without a word, went to her writing-table, opened a box standing on it, took out a sheet of paper and laid it before Ivan. This was the document of which Ivan spoke to Alyosha later on as a "conclusive proof" that Dmitri had killed his father. This was the letter written by Mitya to Katerina Ivanovna when he was drunk, on the very evening he met Alyosha at the cross-roads on the way to the monastery, after the scene at Katerina Ivanovna's, when Grushenka had insulted her. Then, parting from Alyosha, Mitya had rushed to Grushenka. I don't know whether he saw her, but in the evening he was at the "Metropolis", where he got thoroughly drunk. Then he asked for pen and paper and wrote a document of weighty consequences to himself. It was a wordy, disconnected, frantic letter, a drunken letter in fact. It was like the talk of a drunken man, who, on his return home, begins with extraordinary heat telling his wife or one of his household how he has just been insulted, what a rascal had just insulted him, what a fine fellow he is on the other hand, and how he will pay that scoundrel out; and all that at great length, with great excitement and incoherence, with drunken tears and blows on the table. The letter was written on a dirty piece of ordinary paper of the cheapest kind. It had been provided by the tavern and there were figures scrawled on the back of it. There was evidently not space enough for his drunken verbosity and Mitya not only filled the margins but had written the last line right across the rest. The letter ran as follows:

"FATAL KATYA! To-morrow I will get the money and repay your three thousand and farewell, woman of great wrath, but farewell too my love! Let us make an end! To-morrow I shall try and get it from everyone, and if I can't borrow it, I give you my word of honour I shall go to my father and break his skull and take the money from under the pillow, if only Ivan has gone. If I have to go to Siberia for it, I'll give you back your three thousand. And farewell. I bow down to the ground before you, for I've been a scoundrel to you. Forgive me! No, better not forgive me, you'll be happier and so shall I! Better Siberia than your love, for I love another woman and you got to know her too well to-day, so how can you forgive? I will

316

murder the man who's robbed me! I'll leave you all and go to the East so as to see no one again. Not *her* either, for you are not my only tormentress, she is too. Farewell!"

"PS.—I write my curse, but I adore you! I hear it in my heart. One string is left, and it vibrates. Better tear my heart in two! I shall kill myself, but first of all that cur. I shall tear three thousand from him and fling it to you. Though I've been a scoundrel to you, I am not a thief! You can expect three thousand. The cur keeps it under his mattress, in pink ribbon. I am not a thief, but I'll murder my thief. Katya, don't look disdainful. Dmitri is not a thief; but a murderer! He has murdered his father and ruined himself to hold his ground, rather than endure your pride. And he doesn't love you.

"PPS.—I kiss your feet, farewell! PPPS.—Katya, pray to God that someone'll give me the money. Then I shall not be steeped in gore, and if no one does—I shall! Kill me!

"Your slave and enemy,
"D. KARAMAZOV."

When Ivan read this "document" he was convinced. So then it was his brother, not Smerdyakov. And if not Smerdyakov, then not he, Ivan. This letter at once assumed in his eyes the aspect of a logical proof. There could be no longer the slightest doubt of Mitya's guilt. The suspicion never occurred to Ivan, by the way, that Mitya might have committed the murder in conjunction with Smerdyakov, and indeed such a theory did not fit in with the facts. Ivan was completely reassured. The next morning he only thought of Smerdyakov and his gibes with contempt. A few days later he positively wondered how he could have been so horribly distressed at his suspicions. He resolved to dismiss him with contempt and forget him. So passed a month. He made no further inquiry about Smerdyakov, but twice he happened to hear that he was very ill and out of his mind.

"He'll end in madness," the young doctor, Varvinsky, observed about him and Ivan remembered this. During the last week of that month Ivan himself began to feel very ill. He went to consult the Moscow doctor who had been sent for by Katerina Ivanovna just before the trial. And just at that time his relations with Katerina Ivanovna became acutely strained. They were like two enemies in love with one another. Katerina Ivanovna's "returns" to Mitya, that is, her brief but violent revulsions of feeling in his favour, drove Ivan to perfect frenzy.

Strange to say, until that last scene described above, when Alyosha came from Mitya to Katerina Ivanovna, Ivan had never once, during that month, heard her express a doubt of Mitya's guilt, in spite of those "returns" that were so hateful to him. It is remarkable, too, that while he felt that he hated Mitya more and more every day, he realised that it was not on account of Katya's "returns" that he hated him, but just *because he was the murderer of his father*. He was conscious of this and fully recognised it to himself.

Nevertheless, he went to see Mitya ten days before the trial and proposed to him a plan of escape—a plan he had obviously thought over a long time. He was partly impelled to do this by a sore place still left in his heart from a phrase of Smerdyakov, that it was to his, Ivan's, advantage that his brother should be convicted, as that would increase his inheritance and Alyosha's from forty to sixty thousand roubles. He determined to sacrifice thirty thousand on arranging Mitya's escape. On his return from seeing him, he was very mournful and dispirited; he suddenly began to feel that he was anxious for Mitya's escape, not only to heal that sore place by sacrificing thirty thousand, but for another reason. "Is it because I am as much a murderer at heart?" he asked himself. Something very deep down seemed burning and rankling in his soul. His pride above all suffered cruelly all that month. But of that later. . . .

When, after his conversation with Alyosha, Ivan suddenly decided with his hand on the bell of his lodging to go to Smerdyakov, he obeyed a sudden and peculiar impulse of indignation. He suddenly remembered how Katerina Ivanovna had only just cried out to him in Alyosha's presence: "It was you, you, persuaded me of his [that is, Mitya's] guilt!" Ivan was thunderstruck when he recalled it. He had never once tried to persuade her that Mitya was the murderer; on the contrary, he had suspected himself, in her presence, that time when he came back from Smerdyakov. It was *she*, she, who had produced that "document" and proved his brother's guilt. And now she suddenly exclaimed: "I've been at Smerdyakov's myself!" When had she been there? Ivan had known nothing of it. So she was not at all sure of Mitya's guilt! And what could Smerdyakov have told her? What, what, had he said to her? His heart burned with violent anger. He could not understand how he could, half an hour before, have let those words pass and not have cried out at the moment. He let go of the bell and rushed off to Smerdyakov. "I shall kill him perhaps this time," he thought on the way.

CHAPTER VIII

THE THIRD AND LAST INTERVIEW WITH SMERDYAKOV

WHEN he was half-way there, the keen dry wind that had been blowing early that morning rose again, and a fine dry snow began falling thickly. It did not lie on the ground, but was whirled about by the wind, and soon there was a regular snowstorm. There were scarcely any lamp-posts in the part of the town where Smerdyakov lived. Ivan strode alone in the darkness, unconscious of the storm, instinctively picking out his way. His head ached and there was a painful throbbing in his temples. He felt that his hands were twitching convulsively. Not far from Marya Kondratyevna's cottage, Ivan suddenly came upon a solitary drunken little peasant. He was wearing a coarse and patched coat, and was walking in zigzags, grumbling and swearing to himself. Then suddenly he would begin singing in a husky drunken voice:

> *"Ach, Vanka's gone to Petersburg*
> *I won't wait till he comes back."*

But he broke off every time at the second line and began swearing again; then he would begin the same song again. Ivan felt an intense hatred for him before he had thought about him at all. Suddenly he realised his presence and felt an irresistible impulse to knock him down. At that moment they met, and the peasant with a violent lurch fell full tilt against Ivan, who pushed him back furiously. The peasant went flying backwards and fell like a log on the frozen ground. He uttered one plaintive "O-oh!" and then was silent. Ivan stepped up to him. He was lying on his back, without movement or consciousness. "He will be frozen," thought Ivan, and he went on his way to Smerdyakov's.

In the passage, Marya Kondratyevna, who ran out to open the door with a candle in her hand, whispered that Smerdyakov was very ill: "it's not that he's laid up, but he seems not himself, and he even told us to take the tea away; he wouldn't have any."

"Why, does he make a row?" asked Ivan coarsely.

"Oh dear no, quite the contrary, he's very quiet. Only

please don't talk to him too long," Marya Kondratyevna begged him. Ivan opened the door and stepped into the room.

It was overheated as before, but there were changes in the room. One of the benches at the side had been removed, and in its place had been put a large old mahogany leather sofa, on which a bed had been made up, with fairly clean white pillows. Smerdyakov was sitting on the sofa, wearing the same dressing-gown. The table had been brought out in front of the sofa, so that there was hardly room to move. On the table lay a thick book in yellow cover, but Smerdyakov was not reading it. He seemed to be sitting doing nothing. He met Ivan with a slow silent gaze, and was apparently not at all surprised at his coming. There was a great change in his face; he was much thinner and sallower. His eyes were sunken and there were blue marks under them.

"Why, you really are ill?" Ivan stopped short. "I won't keep you long, I won't even take off my coat. Where can one sit down?"

He went to the other end of the table, moved up a chair and sat down on it.

"Why do you look at me without speaking? I've only come with one question, and I swear I won't go without an answer. Has the young lady, Katerina Ivanovna, been with you?"

Smerdyakov still remained silent, looking quietly at Ivan as before. Suddenly, with a motion of his hand, he turned his face away.

"What's the matter with you?" cried Ivan.

"Nothing."

"What do you mean by 'nothing'?"

"Yes, she has. It's no matter to you. Let me alone."

"No, I won't let you alone. Tell me, when was she here?"

"Why, I'd quite forgotten about her," said Smerdyakov, with a scornful smile, and turning his face to Ivan again, he stared at him with a look of frenzied hatred, the same look that he had fixed on him at their last interview, a month before.

"You seem very ill yourself, your face is sunken; you don't look like yourself," he said to Ivan.

"Never mind my health, tell me what I ask you."

"But why are your eyes so hollow? The whites are quite yellow. Are you so worried?" He smiled contemptuously and suddenly laughed outright.

"Listen, I've told you I won't go away without an answer," Ivan cried, intensely irritated.

"Why do you keep pestering me? Why do you torment me?" said Smerdyakov, with a look of suffering.

"Damn it! I've nothing to do with you. Just answer my question and I'll go away."

"I've no answer to give you," said Smerdyakov, looking down again.

"You may be sure I'll make you answer!"

"Why are you so uneasy?" Smerdyakov stared at him, not simply with contempt, but almost with a repulsion. "Is this because the trial begins to-morrow? Nothing will happen to you, can't you believe that at last? Go home, go to bed and sleep in peace, don't be afraid of anything."

"I don't understand you. . . . What have I to be afraid of to-morrow?" Ivan articulated in astonishment, and suddenly a chill breath of fear did in fact pass over his soul. Smerdyakov measured him with his eyes.

"You don't understand?" he drawled reproachfully. "It's a strange thing a sensible man should care to play such a farce!"

Ivan looked at him speechless. The startling, incredibly supercilious tone of this man who had once been his valet was extraordinary in itself. He had not taken such a tone even at their last interview.

"I tell you, you've nothing to be afraid of. I won't say anything about you, there's no proof against you. I say, how your hands are trembling. Why are your fingers moving like that? Go home, *you* did not murder him."

Ivan started. He remembered Alyosha.

"I know it was not I," he faltered.

"Do you?" Smerdyakov caught him up again.

Ivan jumped up and seized him by the shoulder.

"Tell me everything, you viper! Tell me everything!"

Smerdyakov was not in the least scared. He only riveted his eyes on Ivan with insane hatred.

"Well, it was you who murdered him, if that's it," he whispered furiously.

Ivan sank back on his chair, as though pondering something. He laughed malignantly.

"You mean my going away? What you talked about last time?"

"You stood before me last time and understood it all, and you understand it now."

"All I understand is that you are mad."

"Aren't you tired of it? Here we are face to face; what's the use of going on keeping up a farce to each other? Are you still trying to throw it all on me, to my face? *You* murdered him; you are the real murderer, I was only your instrument, your faithful servant, and it was following your words I did it."

"*Did* it? Why, did you murder him?" Ivan turned cold.

Something seemed to give way in his brain, and he shuddered all over with a cold shiver. Then Smerdyakov himself looked at him wonderingly; probably the genuineness of Ivan's horror struck him.

"You don't mean to say you really did not know?" he faltered mistrustfully, looking with a forced smile into his eyes. Ivan still gazed at him, and seemed unable to speak.

> *Ach, Vanka's gone to Petersburg*
> *I won't wait till he comes back,*

suddenly echoed in his head.

"Do you know, I am afraid that you are a dream, a phantom sitting beside me," he muttered.

"There's no phantom here, but only us two and one other. No doubt he is here, that third, between us."

"Who is he? Who is here? What third person?" Ivan cried in alarm, looking about him, his eyes hastily searching in every corner.

"That third is God Himself, Providence. He is the third beside us now. Only don't look for him, you won't find him."

"It's a lie that you killed him!" Ivan cried madly. "You are mad, or teasing me again!"

Smerdyakov, as before, watched him curiously, with no sign of fear. He could still scarcely get over his incredulity; he still fancied that Ivan knew everything and was trying to "throw it all on him to his face."

"Wait a minute," he said at last in a weak voice, and suddenly bringing up his left leg from under the table, he began turning up his trouser leg. He was wearing long white stockings and slippers. Slowly he took off his garter and fumbled to the bottom of his stocking. Ivan gazed at him, and suddenly shuddered in a paroxysm of terror.

"He's mad!" he cried, and rapidly jumping up, he drew back, so that he knocked his back against the wall and stood up against it, stiff and straight. He looked with insane terror at Smerdyakov, who, entirely unaffected by his terror, continued fumbling in his stocking, as though he were making an effort to get hold of something with his fingers and pull it out. At last he got hold of it and began pulling it out. Ivan saw that it was a piece of paper, or perhaps a roll of papers. Smerdyakov pulled it out and laid it on the table.

"Here," he said quietly.

"What is it?" responded Ivan, trembling.

"Kindly look at it," Smerdyakov answered, still in the same low tone.

Ivan stepped up to the table, took up the roll of paper and began unfolding it, but suddenly he drew back his fingers, as though from contact with a loathsome reptile.

"Your hands keep twitching," observed Smerdyakov, and he deliberately unfolded the bundle himself. Under the wrapper were three packets of hundred-rouble notes.

"They are all here, all the three thousand roubles; you need not count them. Take them," Smerdyakov suggested to Ivan, nodding at the notes. Ivan sank back in his chair. He was as white as a handkerchief.

"You frightened me . . . with your stocking," he said, with a strange grin.

"Can you really not have known till now?" Smerdyakov asked once more.

"No, I did not know. I kept thinking of Dmitri. Brother, brother! Ach!" He suddenly clutched his head in both hands.

"Listen. Did you kill him alone? With my brother's help or without?"

"It was only with you, with your help, I killed him, and Dmitri Fyodorovitch is quite innocent."

"All right, all right. Talk about me later. Why do I keep on trembling? I can't speak properly."

"You were bold enough then. You said 'everything was lawful', and how frightened you are now," Smerdyakov muttered in surprise. "Won't you have some lemonade? I'll ask for some at once. It's very refreshing. Only I must hide this first."

And again he motioned at the notes. He was just going to get up and call at the door to Marya Kondratyevna to make some lemonade and bring it them, but, looking for something to cover up the notes that she might not see them, he first took out his handkerchief, and as it turned out to be very dirty, took up the big yellow book that Ivan had noticed at first lying on the table, and put it over the notes. The book was "The Sayings of the Holy Father Isaac the Syrian". Ivan read it mechanically.

"I won't have any lemonade," he said. "Talk of me later. Sit down and tell me how you did it. Tell me all about it."

"You'd better take off your greatcoat, or you'll be too hot."

Ivan, as though he'd only just thought of it, took off his coat, and, without getting up from his chair, threw it on the bench.

"Speak, please, speak."

He seemed calmer. He waited, feeling sure that Smerdyakov would tell him *all* about it.

"How it was done?" sighed Smerdyakov. "It was done in a most natural way, following your very words."

"Of my words later," Ivan broke in again, apparently with complete self-possession, firmly uttering his words, and not shouting as before. "Only tell me in detail how you did it. Everything, as it happened. Don't forget anything. The details, above everything, the details, I beg you."

"You'd gone away, then I fell into the cellar."

"In a fit or in a sham one?"

"A sham one, naturally. I shammed it all. I went quietly down the steps to the very bottom and lay down quietly, and as I lay down I gave a scream, and struggled, till they carried me out."

"Stay! And were you shamming all along, afterwards, and in the hospital?"

"No, not at all. Next day, in the morning, before they took me to the hospital, I had a real attack and a more violent one than I've had for years. For two days I was quite unconscious."

"All right, all right. Go on."

"They laid me on the bed. I knew I'd be the other side of the partition, for whenever I was ill Marfa Ignatyevna used to put me there, near them. She's always been very kind to me, from my birth up. At night I moaned, but quietly. I kept expecting Dmitri Fyodorovitch to come."

"Expecting him? To come to you?"

"Not to me. I expected him to come into the house, for I'd no doubt that he'd come that night, for being without me and getting no news, he'd be sure to come and climb over the fence, as he used to do, and do something."

"And if he hadn't come?"

"Then nothing would have happened. I should never have brought myself to it without him."

"All right, all right . . . speak more intelligibly, don't hurry; above all, don't leave anything out!"

"I expected him to kill Fyodor Pavlovitch. I thought that was certain, for I had prepared him for it . . . during the last few days. . . . He knew about the knocks, that was the chief thing. With his suspiciousness and the fury which had been growing in him all those days, he was bound to get into the house by means of those taps. That was inevitable, so I was expecting him."

"Stay," Ivan interrupted, "if he had killed him, he would have taken the money and carried it away; you must have considered that. What would you have got by it afterwards? I don't see."

"But he would never have found the money. That was only what I told him, that the money was under the mattress. But that wasn't true. It had been lying in a box. And afterwards I suggested to Fyodor Pavlovitch, as I was the only person he trusted, to hide the envelope with the notes in the corner behind the ikons, for no one would have guessed that place, especially if they came in a hurry. So that's where the envelope lay, in the corner behind the ikons. It would have been absurd to keep it under the mattress; the box, anyway, could be locked. But all believe it was under the mattress. A stupid thing to believe. So if Dmitri Fyodorovitch had committed the murder, finding nothing, he would either have run away in a hurry, afraid of every sound, as always happens with murderers, or he would have been arrested. So I could always have clambered up to the ikons and have taken away the money next morning or even that night, and it would have all been put down to Dmitri Fyodorovitch. I could reckon upon that."

"But what if he did not kill him, but only knocked him down?"

"If he did not kill him, of course I would not have ventured to take the money, and nothing would have happened. But I calculated that he would beat him senseless, and I should have time to take it then, and then I'd make out to Fyodor Pavlovitch that it was no one but Dmitri Fyodorovitch who had taken the money after beating him."

"Stop . . . I am getting mixed. Then it was Dmitri after all who killed him, you only took the money?"

"No, he didn't kill him. Well, I might as well have told you

325

now that he was the murderer. . . . But I don't want to lie to you now, because . . . because if you really haven't understood till now, as I see for myself, and are not pretending, so as to throw your guilt on me to my very face, you are still responsible for it all, since you knew of the murder and charged me to do it, and went away knowing all about it. And so I want to prove to your face this evening that you are the only real murderer in the whole affair, and I am not the real murderer, though I did kill him. You are the rightful murderer."

"Why, why, am I a murderer? Oh, God!" Ivan cried, unable to restrain himself at last, and forgetting that he had put off discussing himself till the end of the conversation. "You still mean that Tchermashnya? Stay, tell me, why did you want my consent, if you really took Tchermashnya for consent? How will you explain that now?"

"Assured of your consent, I should have known that you wouldn't have made an outcry over those three thousand being lost, even if I'd been suspected, instead of Dmitri Fyodorovitch, or as his accomplice; on the contrary, you would have protected me from others. . . . And when you got your inheritance you would have rewarded me when you were able, all the rest of your life. For you'd have received your inheritance through me, seeing that if he had married Agrafena Alexandrovna, you wouldn't have had a farthing."

"Ah! Then you intended to worry me all my life afterwards," snarled Ivan. "And what if I hadn't gone away then, but had informed against you?"

"What could you have informed? That I persuaded you to go to Tchermashnya? That's all nonsense. Besides, after our conversation you would either have gone away or have stayed. If you had stayed, nothing would have happened. I should have known that you didn't want it done, and should have attempted nothing. As you went away, it meant you assured me that you wouldn't dare to inform against me at the trial, and that you'd overlook my having the three thousand. And, indeed, you couldn't have prosecuted me afterwards, because then I should have told it all in the court; that is, not that I had stolen the money or killed him—I shouldn't have said that—but that you'd put me up to the theft and the murder, though I didn't consent to it. That's why I needed your consent, so that you couldn't have cornered me afterwards, for what proof could you have had? I could always have cornered you, revealing your eagerness for your father's death, and I tell you the public would all have believed it, and you would have been ashamed for the rest of your life."

"Was I so eager then, was I?" Ivan snarled again.

"To be sure you were, and by your consent you silently sanctioned my doing it." Smerdyakov looked resolutely at Ivan. He was very weak and spoke slowly and wearily, but some hidden inner force urged him on. He evidently had some design. Ivan felt that.

"Go on," he said. "Tell me what happened that night."

"What more is there to tell? I lay there and I thought I heard the master shout. And before that Grigory Vassilyevitch had suddenly got up and came out, and he suddenly gave a scream, and then all was silence and darkness. I lay there waiting, my heart beating; I couldn't bear it. I got up at last, went out. I saw the window open on the left into the garden, and I stepped to the left to listen whether he was sitting there alive, and I heard the master moving about, sighing, so I knew he was alive. Ech! I thought. I went to the window and shouted to the master: 'It's I.' And he shouted to me: 'He's been, he's been; he's run away.' He meant Dmitri Fyodorovitch had been. 'He's killed Grigory!' 'Where?' I whispered. 'There, in the corner,' he pointed. He was whispering, too. 'Wait a bit,' I said. I went to the corner of the garden to look, and there I came upon Grigory Vassilyevitch lying by the wall, covered with blood, senseless. So it's true that Dmitri Fyodorovitch has been here, was the thought that came into my head, and I determined on the spot to make an end of it, as Grigory Vassilyevitch, even if he were alive, would see nothing of it, as he lay there senseless. The only risk was that Marfa Ignatyevna might wake up. I felt that at the moment, but the longing to get it done came to me, till I could scarcely breathe. I went back to the window to the master and said: 'She's here, she's come; Agrafena Alexandrovna has come, wants to be let in.' And he started like a baby. 'Where is she?' he fairly gasped, but couldn't believe it. 'She's standing there,' said I. 'Open.' He looked out of the window at me, half believing and half distrustful, but afraid to open. 'Why, he is afraid of me now,' I thought. And it was funny. I bethought me to knock on the window frame those taps we'd agreed upon as a signal that Grushenka had come, in his presence, before his eyes. He didn't seem to believe my words, but as soon as he heard the taps, he ran at once to open the door. He opened it. I would have gone in, but he stood in the way to prevent me passing. 'Where

THE BROTHERS KARAMAZOV

is she? Where is she?' He looked at me, all of a tremble. Well,
thought I, if he's so frightened of me as all that, it's a bad
look-out! And my legs went weak with fright that he wouldn't
let me in or would call out, or Marfa Ignatyevna would run up,
or something else might happen. I don't remember now, but
I must have stood pale, facing him. I whispered to him: 'Why,
she's there, there, under the window, how is it you don't see
her?' I said. 'Bring her then, bring her.' 'She's afraid,' said
I, 'she was frightened at the noise, she's hidden in the bushes;
go and call to her yourself from the study.' He ran to the
window, put the candle in the window. 'Grushenka,' he cried,
'Grushenka, are you here?' Though he cried that, he didn't
want to lean out of the window, he didn't want to move away
from me, for he was panic-stricken; he was so frightened he
didn't dare to turn his back on me. 'Why, here she is,' said
I. I went up to the window and leaned right out of it. 'Here
she is, she's in the bush, laughing at you, don't you see her?'
He suddenly believed it; he was all of a shake—he was awfully
crazy about her—and he leaned right out of the window. I
snatched up that iron paper-weight from his table; do you
remember, weighing about three pounds? I swung it and hit
him on the top of the skull with the corner of it. He didn't
even cry out. He only sank down suddenly, and I hit him again
and a third time. And the third time I knew I'd broken his
skull. He suddenly rolled on his back, face upwards, covered
with blood. I looked round. There was no blood on me, not
a spot. I wiped the paper-weight, put it back, went up to the
ikons, took the money out of the envelope, and flung the
envelope on the floor and the pink ribbon beside it. I went out
into the garden all of a tremble, straight to the apple tree with
a hollow in it—you know that hollow? I'd marked it long before
and put a rag and a piece of paper ready in it. I wrapped all
the notes in the rag and stuffed it deep down in the hole. And
there it stayed for over a fortnight. I took it out later, when
I came out of the hospital. I went back to my bed, lay down
and thought: 'If Grigory Vassilyevitch has been killed outright,
it may be a bad job for me, but if he is not killed and recovers,
it will be first-rate, for then he'll bear witness that Dmitri
Fyodorovitch has been here, and so he must have killed him and
taken the money.' Then I began groaning with suspense and
impatience, so as to wake Marfa Ignatyevna as soon as possible. At last she got up, and she rushed to me, but when she
saw Grigory Vassilyevitch was not there, she ran out, and I

heard her scream in the garden. And that set it all going and set my mind at rest."

He stopped. Ivan had listened all the time in dead silence without stirring or taking his eyes off him. As he told his story Smerdyakov glanced at him from time to time, but for the most part his eyes averted. When he had finished he was evidently agitated and was breathing hard. The perspiration stood out on his face. But it was impossible to tell whether it was remorse he was feeling, or what.

"Stay!" cried Ivan, pondering. "What about the door? If he only opened the door to you, how could Grigory have seen it open before? For Grigory saw it before you went."

It was remarkable that Ivan spoke quite amicably, in a different tone, not angry as before, so if anyone had opened the door at that moment and peeped in at them, he would certainly have concluded that they were talking peaceably about some ordinary, though interesting, subject.

"As for that door and Grigory Vassilyevitch's having seen it open, that's only his fancy," said Smerdyakov, with a wry smile. "He is not a man, I assure you, but an obstinate mule. He didn't see it, but fancied he had seen it, and there's no shaking him. It's just our luck he took that notion into his head, for they can't fail to convict Dmitri Fyodorovitch after that."

"Listen . . ." said Ivan, beginning to seem bewildered again and making an effort to grasp something. "Listen. There are a lot of questions I want to ask you, but I forget them . . . I keep forgetting and getting mixed up. Yes. Tell me this at least, why did you open the envelope and leave it there on the floor? Why didn't you simply carry off the envelope? . . . When you were telling me, I thought you spoke about it as though it were the right thing to do . . . but why, I can't understand . . ."

"I did that for a good reason. For if a man had known all about it, as I did for instance, if he'd seen those notes before, and perhaps had put them in that envelope himself, and had seen the envelope sealed up and addressed, with his own eyes, if such a man had done the murder, what should have made him tear open the envelope afterwards, especially in such desperate haste, since he'd know for certain the notes must be in the envelope? No, if the robber had been someone like me, he'd simply have put the envelope straight in his pocket and got away with it as fast as he could. But it'd be quite different with

329

Dmitri Fyodorovitch. He only knew about the envelope by hearsay; he had never seen it, and if he'd found it, for instance, under the mattress, he'd have torn it open as quickly as possible to make sure the notes were in it. And he'd have thrown the envelope down, without having time to think that it would be evidence against him. Because he was not an habitual thief and had never directly stolen anything before, for he is a gentleman born, and if he did bring himself to steal it, it would not be regular stealing, but simply taking what was his own, for he'd told the whole town he meant to before, and had even bragged aloud before everyone that he'd go and take his property from Fyodor Pavlovitch. I didn't say that openly to the prosecutor when I was being examined, but, quite the contrary, I brought him to it by a hint, as though I didn't see it myself, and as though he'd thought of it himself and I hadn't prompted him; so that Mr. Prosecutor's mouth positively watered at my suggestion."

"But can you possibly have thought of all that on the spot?" cried Ivan, overcome with astonishment. He looked at Smerdyakov again with alarm.

"Mercy on us! Could anyone think of it all in such a desperate hurry? It was all thought out beforehand."

"Well . . . well, it was the devil helped you!" Ivan cried again. "No, you are not a fool, you are far cleverer than I thought . . ."

He got up, obviously intending to walk across the room. He was in terrible distress. But as the table blocked his way, and there was hardly room to pass between the table and the wall, he only turned round where he stood and sat down again. Perhaps the impossibility of moving irritated him, as he suddenly cried out almost as furiously as before:

"Listen, you miserable, contemptible creature! Don't you understand that if I haven't killed you, it's simply because I am keeping you to answer to-morrow at the trial. God sees," Ivan raised his hand, "perhaps I, too, was guilty; perhaps I really had a secret desire for my father's . . . death, but I swear I was not as guilty as you think, and perhaps I didn't urge you on at all. No, no, I didn't urge you on! But no matter. I will give evidence against myself to-morrow at the trial. I'm determined to! I shall tell everything, everything. But we'll make our appearance together. And whatever you may say against me at the trial, whatever evidence you give, I'll face it, I am not afraid of you. I'll confirm it all myself!

But you must confess, too! You must, you must, we'll go together. That's how it shall be!"

Ivan said this solemnly and resolutely, and from his flashing eyes alone it could be seen that it would be so.

"You are ill, I see, you are quite ill. Your eyes are yellow," Smerdyakov commented, without the least irony, with apparent sympathy in fact.

"We'll go together," Ivan repeated. "And if you won't go, no matter, I'll go alone."

Smerdyakov paused as though pondering.

"There'll be nothing of the sort, and you won't go," he concluded at last positively.

"You don't understand me," Ivan exclaimed reproachfully.

"You'll be too much ashamed, if you confess it all. And, what's more, it will be no use at all, for I shall say straight out that I never said anything of the sort to you, and that you are either ill (and it looks like it, too), or that you're so sorry for your brother that you are sacrificing yourself to save him and have invented it all against me, for you've always thought no more of me than if I'd been a fly. And who will believe you, and what single proof have you got?"

"Listen, you showed me those notes just now to convince me."

Smerdyakov lifted the book off the notes and laid it on one side.

"Take that money away with you," Smerdyakov sighed.

"Of course I shall take it. But why do you give it to me, if you committed the murder for the sake of it?" Ivan looked at him with great surprise.

"I don't want it," Smerdyakov articulated in a shaking voice, with a gesture of refusal. "I did have an idea of beginning a new life with that money in Moscow or, better still, abroad. I did dream of it, chiefly because 'all things are lawful'. That was quite right what you taught me, for you talked a lot to me about that. For if there's no everlasting God, there's no such thing as virtue, and there's no need of it. You were right there. So that's how I looked at it."

"Did you come to that of yourself?" asked Ivan, with a wry smile.

"With your guidance."

"And now, I suppose, you believe in God, since you are giving back the money?"

"No, I don't believe," whispered Smerdyakov.

"Then why are you giving it back?"

"Leave off . . . that's enough!" Smerdyakov waved his hand again. "You used to say yourself that everything was lawful, so now why are you so upset, too? You even want to go and give evidence against yourself. . . . Only there'll be nothing of the sort! You won't go to give evidence," Smerdyakov decided, with conviction.

"You'll see," said Ivan.

"It isn't possible. You are very clever. You are fond of money, I know that. You like to be respected, too, for you're very proud; you are far too fond of female charms, too, and you mind most of all about living in undisturbed comfort, without having to depend on anyone—that's what you care most about. You won't want to spoil your life for ever by taking such a disgrace on yourself. You are like Fyodor Pavlovitch, you are more like him than any of his children; you've the same soul as he had."

"You are not a fool," said Ivan, seeming struck. The blood rushed to his face. "You are serious now!" he observed, looking suddenly at Smerdyakov with a different expression.

"It was your pride made you think I was a fool. Take the money."

Ivan took the three rolls of notes and put them in his pocket without wrapping them in anything.

"I shall show them at the court to-morrow," he said.

"Nobody will believe you, as you've plenty of money of your own; you may simply have taken it out of your cash-box and brought it to the court."

Ivan rose from his seat.

"I repeat," he said, "the only reason I haven't killed you is that I need you for to-morrow, remember that, don't forget it!"

"Well, kill me. Kill me now," Smerdyakov said, all at once looking strangely at Ivan. "You won't dare do that even!" he added, with a bitter smile. "You won't dare to do anything, you, who used to be so bold!"

"Till to-morrow," cried Ivan, and moved to go out.

"Stay a moment. . . . Show me those notes again."

Ivan took out the notes and showed them to him. Smerdyakov looked at them for ten seconds.

"Well, you can go," he said, with a wave of his hand. "Ivan Fyodorovitch!" he called after him again.

"What do you want?" Ivan turned without stopping.

"Good-bye!"

"Till to-morrow!" Ivan cried again, and he walked out of the cottage.

The snowstorm was still raging. He walked the first few steps boldly, but suddenly began staggering. "It's something physical," he thought with a grin. Something like joy was springing up in his heart. He was conscious of unbounded resolution; he would make an end of the wavering that had so tortured him of late. His determination was taken, "and now it will not be changed", he thought, with relief. At that moment he stumbled against something and almost fell down. Stopping short, he made out at his feet the peasant he had knocked down, still lying senseless and motionless. The snow had almost covered his face. Ivan seized him and lifted him in his arms. Seeing a light in the little house to the right he went up, knocked at the shutters, and asked the man to whom the house belonged to help him carry the peasant to the police-station, promising him three roubles. The man got ready and came out. I won't describe in detail how Ivan succeeded in his object, bringing the peasant to the police-station and arranging for a doctor to see him at once, providing with a liberal hand for the expenses. I will only say that this business took a whole hour, but Ivan was well content with it. His mind wandered and worked incessantly.

"If I had not taken my decision so firmly for to-morrow," he reflected, with satisfaction, "I should not have stayed a whole hour to look after the peasant, but should have passed by, without caring about his being frozen. I am quite capable of watching myself, by the way," he thought at the same instant, with still greater satisfaction, "although they have decided that I am going out of my mind!"

Just as he reached his own house he stopped short, asking himself suddenly hadn't he better go at once now to the prosecutor and tell him everything. He decided the question by turning back to the house. "Everything together to-morrow!" he whispered to himself, and, strange to say, almost all his gladness and self-satisfaction passed in one instant.

As he entered his own room he felt something like a touch of ice on his heart, like a recollection or, more exactly, a reminder, of something agonising and revolting that was in that room now, at that moment, and had been there before. He sank wearily on his sofa. The old woman brought him a samovar; he made tea, but did not touch it. He sat on the sofa and felt giddy. He felt that he was ill and helpless. He was beginning to drop asleep, but got up uneasily and walked across the room to shake off his drowsiness. At moments he fancied he was delirious, but it was not illness that he thought of most. Sitting down again, he began looking round, as though searching for something. This happened several times. At last his eyes were fastened intently on one point. Ivan smiled, but an angry flush suffused his face. He sat a long time in his place, his head propped on both arms, though he looked sideways at the same point, at the sofa that stood against the opposite wall. There was evidently something, some object, that irritated him there, worried him and tormented him.

CHAPTER IX

THE DEVIL. IVAN'S NIGHTMARE

I AM not a doctor, but yet I feel that the moment has come when I must inevitably give the reader some account of the nature of Ivan's illness. Anticipating events I can say at least one thing: he was at that moment on the very eve of an attack of brain fever. Though his health had long been affected, it had offered a stubborn resistance to the fever which in the end gained complete mastery over it. Though I know nothing of medicine, I venture to hazard the suggestion that he really had perhaps, by a terrible effort of will, succeeded in delaying the attack for a time, hoping, of course, to check it completely. He knew that he was unwell, but he loathed the thought of being ill at that fatal time, at the approaching crisis in his life, when he needed to have all his wits about him, to say what he had to say boldly and resolutely and "to justify himself to himself".

He had, however, consulted the new doctor, who had been brought from Moscow by a fantastic notion of Katerina Ivanovna's to which I have referred already. After listening to him and examining him, the doctor came to the conclusion that he was actually suffering from some disorder of the brain, and was not at all surprised by an admission which Ivan had reluctantly made him. "Hallucinations are quite likely in your condition," the doctor opined, "though it would be better to verify them . . . you must take steps at once, without a moment's delay, or things will go badly with you." But Ivan did not follow this judicious advice and did not take to his bed to be nursed. "I am walking about, so I am strong enough; if

I drop, it'll be different then, anyone may nurse me who likes, he decided, dismissing the subject.

And so he was sitting almost conscious himself of his delirium and, as I have said already, looking persistently at some object on the sofa against the opposite wall. Someone appeared to be sitting there, though goodness knows how he had come in, for he had not been in the room when Ivan came into it, on his return from Smerdyakov. This was a person or, more accurately speaking, a Russian gentleman of a particular kind, no longer young, *qui faisait la cinquantaine,* as the French say, with rather long, still thick, dark hair, slightly streaked with grey and a small pointed beard. He was wearing a brownish reefer jacket, rather shabby, evidently made by a good tailor though, and of a fashion at least three years old, that had been discarded by smart and well-to-do people for the last two years. His linen and his long scarf-like neck-tie were all such as are worn by people who aim at being stylish, but on closer inspection his linen was not over-clean and his wide scarf was very threadbare. The visitor's check trousers were of excellent cut, but were too light in colour and too tight for the present fashion. His soft fluffy white hat was out of keeping with the season.

In brief there was every appearance of gentility on straitened means. It looked as though the gentleman belonged to that class of idle landowners who used to flourish in the times of serfdom. He had unmistakably been, at some time, in good and fashionable society, had once had good connections, had possibly preserved them indeed, but, after a gay youth, becoming gradually impoverished on the abolition of serfdom, he had sunk into the position of a poor relation of the best class, wandering from one good old friend to another and received by them for his companionable and accommodating disposition and as being, after all, a gentleman who could be asked to sit down with anyone, though, of course, not in a place of honour. Such gentlemen of accommodating temper and dependent position, who can tell a story, take a hand at cards, and who have a distinct aversion for any duties that may be forced upon them, are usually solitary creatures, either bachelors or widowers. Sometimes they have children, but if so, the children are always being brought up at a distance, at some aunt's, to whom these gentlemen never allude in good society, seeming ashamed of the relationship. They gradually lose sight of their children altogether, though at intervals they receive a birthday or Christmas letter from them and sometimes even answer it.

The countenance of the unexpected visitor was not so much good-natured as accommodating and ready to assume any amiable expression as occasion might arise. He had no watch, but he had a tortoise-shell lorgnette on a black ribbon. On the middle finger of his right hand was a massive gold ring with a cheap opal stone in it.

Ivan was angrily silent and would not begin the conversation. The visitor waited and sat exactly like a poor relation who had come down from his room to keep his host company at tea, and was discreetly silent, seeing that his host was frowning and pre-occupied. But he was ready for any affable conversation as soon as his host should begin it. All at once his face expressed a sudden solicitude.

"I say," he began to Ivan, "excuse me, I only mention it to remind you. You went to Smerdyakov's to find out about Katerina Ivanovna, but you came away without finding out anything about her, you probably forgot . . ."

"Ah, yes," broke from Ivan, and his face grew gloomy with uneasiness. "Yes, I'd forgotten . . . but it doesn't matter now, never mind, till to-morrow," he muttered to himself, "and you," he added, addressing his visitor, "I should have remem-bered that myself in a minute, for that was just what was tormenting me! Why do you interfere, as if I should believe that you prompted me, and that I didn't remember it of myself?"

"Don't believe it then," said the gentleman, smiling amicably, "what's the good of believing against your will? Besides, proofs are no help to believing, especially material proofs. Thomas believed, not because he saw Christ risen but because he wanted to believe, before he saw. Look at the spiritualists, for instance. . . . I am very fond of them . . . only fancy, they imagine that they are serving the cause of religion, because the devils show them their horns from the other world. That, they say, is a material proof, so to speak, of the existence of another world. The other world and material proofs, what next? And if you come to that, does proving there's a devil prove that there's a God? I want to join an idealist society. I'll lead the opposition in it, I'll say I am a realist, but not a materialist, he-he!"

"Listen," Ivan suddenly got up from the table. "I seem to be delirious . . . I am delirious, in fact, talk any nonsense you like, I don't care! You won't drive me to fury, as you did last time. But I feel somehow ashamed . . . I want to walk about the room . . . I sometimes don't see you and don't even hear your voice as I did last time, but I always guess what you are prating, for it's I, *I myself speaking, not you.* Only I don't know whether I was dreaming last time or whether I really saw you. I'll wet a towel and put it on my head and perhaps you'll vanish into air."

Ivan went into the corner, took a towel, and did as he said, and with a wet towel on his head began walking up and down the room.

"I am so glad you treat me so familiarly," the visitor began.

"Fool," laughed Ivan, "do you suppose I should stand on ceremony with you. I am in good spirits now, though I've a pain in my forehead . . . and in the top of my head . . . only please don't talk philosophy, as you did last time. If you can't take yourself off, talk of something amusing. Talk gossip, you are a poor relation, you ought to talk gossip. What a nightmare to have! But I am not afraid of you. I'll get the better of you. I won't be taken to a madhouse!"

"*C'est charmant,* poor relation. Yes, I am in my natural shape. For what am I on earth but a poor relation? By the way, I am listening to you and am rather surprised to find you are actually beginning to take me for something real, not simply your fancy, as you persisted in declaring last time . . ."

"Never for one minute have I taken you for reality," Ivan cried, with a sort of fury. "You are a lie, you are my illness, you are a phantom. It's only that I don't know how to destroy you and I see I must suffer for a time. You are my hallucination. You are the incarnation of myself, but only of one side of me . . . of my thoughts and feelings, but only the nastiest and stupidest of them. From that point of view you might be of interest to me, if only I had time to waste on you . . ."

"Excuse me, excuse me, I'll catch you. When you flew out at Alyosha under the lamp-post this evening and shouted to him, 'You learnt it from *him!* How do you know that *he* visits me?' You were thinking of me then. So for one brief moment you did believe that I really exist," the gentleman laughed blandly.

"Yes, that was a moment of weakness . . . but I couldn't believe in you. I don't know whether I was asleep or awake last time. Perhaps I was only dreaming then and didn't see you really at all . . ."

337

"And why were you so surly with Alyosha just now? He is a dear; I've treated him badly over Father Zossima."

"Don't talk of Alyosha! How dare you, you flunkey!" Ivan laughed again.

"You scold me, but you laugh—that's a good sign. But you are ever so much more polite than you were last time, and I know why: that great resolution of yours . . ."

"Don't speak of my resolution," cried Ivan savagely.

"I understand, I understand, *c'est noble, c'est charmant*, you are going to defend your brother and to sacrifice yourself . . . *C'est chevaleresque.*"

"Hold your tongue, I'll kick you!"

"I shan't be altogether sorry, for then my object will be attained. If you kick me, you must believe in my reality, for people don't kick ghosts. Joking apart, it doesn't matter to me, scold if you like, though it's better to be a trifle more polite even to me. 'Fool, flunkey!' what words!"

"Scolding you, I scold myself," Ivan laughed again, "you are myself, myself, only with a different face. You just say what I am thinking . . . and are incapable of saying anything new!"

"If I am like you in my way of thinking, it's all to my credit," the gentleman declared, with delicacy and dignity.

"You choose out only my worst thoughts, and what's more, the stupid ones. You are stupid and vulgar. You are awfully stupid. No, I can't put up with you! What am I to do, what am I to do?" Ivan said through his clenched teeth.

"My dear friend, above all things I want to behave like a gentleman and to be recognised as such," the visitor began in an access of deprecating and simple-hearted pride, typical of a poor relation. "I am poor, but . . . I won't say very honest, but . . . it's an axiom generally accepted in society that I am a fallen angël. I certainly can't conceive how I can ever have been an angel. If I ever was, it must have been so long ago that there's no harm in forgetting it. Now I only prize the reputation of being a gentlemanly person and live as I can, trying to make myself agreeable. I love men genuinely, I've been greatly calumniated! Here when I stay with you from time to. time, my life gains a kind of reality, and that's what I like most of all. You see, like you, I suffer from the fantastic and so I love the realism of earth. Here, with you, everything is circumscribed, here all is formulated and geometrical, while we have nothing but indeterminate equations! I wander about here

dreaming. I like dreaming. Besides, on earth I become superstitious. Please don't laugh, that's just what I like, to become
superstitious. I adopt all your habits here: I've grown fond of
going to the public baths, would you believe it? and I go and
steam myself with merchants and priests. What I dream of is
becoming incarnate once for all and irrevocably in the form
of some merchant's wife weighing eighteen stone, and of believing all she believes. My ideal is to go to church and offer a
candle in simple-hearted faith, upon my word it is. Then there
would be an end to my sufferings. I like being doctored too; in
the spring there was an outbreak of smallpox and I went and
was vaccinated in a foundling hospital—if only you knew how
I enjoyed myself that day. I subscribed ten roubles to the
cause of the Slavs! . . . But you are not listening. Do you
know, you are not at all well this evening? I know you went
yesterday to that doctor . . . well, what about your health?
What did the doctor say?"

"Fool!" Ivan snapped out.

"But you are clever, anyway. You are scolding again? I
didn't ask out of sympathy. You needn't answer. Now rheumatism has come in again . . ."

"Fool!" repeated Ivan.

"You keep saying the same thing; but I had such an attack
of rheumatism last year that I remember it to this day."

"The devil have rheumatism!"

"Why not, if I sometimes put on fleshly form? I put on
fleshly form and I take the consequences. Satan *sum et nihil
humanum a me alienum puto.*"

"What, what? Satan *sum et nihil humanum* . . . that's not
bad for the devil!"

"I am glad I've pleased you at last."

"But you didn't get that from me," Ivan stopped suddenly,
seeming struck. "That never entered my head, that's strange."

"*C'est du nouveau, n'est-ce pas?* This time I'll act honestly
and explain to you. Listen, in dreams and especially in night-
mares, from indigestion or anything, a man sees sometimes such
artistic visions, such complex and real actuality, such events,
even a whole world of events, woven into such a plot, with
such unexpected details from the most exalted matters to the
last button on a cuff, as I swear Leo Tolstoy has never invented.
Yet such dreams are sometimes seen, not by writers but by the
most ordinary people, officials, journalists, priests. . . . The
subject is a complete enigma. A statesman confessed to me,

indeed, that all his best ideas came to him when he was asleep. Well, that's how it is now, though I am your hallucination, yet just as in a nightmare, I say original things which had not entered your head before. So I don't repeat your ideas, yet I am only your nightmare, nothing more."

"You are lying, your aim is to convince me you exist apart and are not my nightmare, and now you are asserting you are a dream."

"My dear fellow, I've adopted a special method to-day, I'll explain it to you afterwards. Stay, where did I break off? Oh, yes! I caught cold then, only not here but yonder."

"Where is yonder? Tell me, will you be here long? Can't you go away?" Ivan exclaimed almost in despair. He ceased walking to and fro, sat down on the sofa, leaned his elbows on the table again and held his head tight in both hands. He pulled the wet towel off and flung it away in vexation. It was evidently of no use.

"Your nerves are out of order," observed the gentleman, with a carelessly easy, though perfectly polite, air. "You are angry with me even for being able to catch cold, though it happened in a most natural way. I was hurrying then to a diplomatic *soirée* at the house of a lady of high rank in Petersburg, who was aiming at influence in the Ministry. Well, an evening suit, while tie, gloves, though I was God knows where and had to fly through space to reach your earth. . . . Of course, it took only an instant, but you know a ray of light from the sun takes full eight minutes, and fancy in an evening suit and open waistcoat! Spirits don't freeze, but when one's in fleshly form, well . . . in brief, I didn't think, and set off, and you know in those ethereal spaces, in the water that is above the firmament, there's such a frost . . . at least one can't call it frost, you can fancy, 150° below zero! You know the game the village girls play—they invite the unwary to lick an axe in thirty degrees of frost, the tongue instantly freezes to it and the dupe tears the skin off, so it bleeds. But that's only in 30°, in 150° I imagine it would be enough to put your finger on the axe and it would be the end of it . . . if only there could be an axe there."

"And can there be an axe there?" Ivan interrupted, carelessly and disdainfully. He was exerting himself to the utmost not to believe in the delusion and not to sink into complete insanity.

"An axe?" the guest interrupted in surprise.

"Yes, what would become of an axe there?" Ivan cried

suddenly, with a sort of savage and insistent obstinacy.

"What would become of an axe in space? *Quelle idée!* If it were to fall to any distance, it would begin, I think, flying round the earth without knowing why, like a satellite. The astronomers would calculate the rising and the setting of the axe, *Gatzuk* would put it in his calendar, that's all."

"You are stupid, awfully stupid," said Ivan peevishly. "Fib more cleverly or I won't listen. You want to get the better of me by realism, to convince me that you exist, but I don't want to believe you exist! I won't believe it!"

"But I am not fibbing, it's all the truth; the truth is unhappily hardly ever amusing. I see you persist in expecting something big of me, and perhaps something fine. That's a great pity, for I only give what I can . . ."

"Don't talk philosophy, you ass!"

"Philosophy, indeed, when all my right side is numb and I am moaning and groaning. I've tried all the medical faculty: they can diagnose beautifully, they have the whole of your disease at their finger-tips, but they've no idea how to cure you. There was an enthusiastic little student here, 'You may die,' said he, 'but you'll know perfectly what disease you are dying of!' And then what a way they have of sending people to specialists! 'We only diagnose,' they say, 'but go to such-and-such a specialist, he'll cure you.' The old doctor who used to cure all sorts of diseases has completely disappeared, I assure you, now there are only specialists, and they all advertise in the newspapers. If anything is wrong with your nose, they send you to Paris: there, they say, is a European specialist who cures noses. If you go to Paris, he'll look at your nose; 'I can only cure your right nostril,' he'll tell you, 'for I don't cure the left nostril, that's not my speciality, but go to Vienna, there there's a specialist who will cure your left nostril.' What are you to do? I fell back on popular remedies, a German doctor advised me to rub myself with honey and salt in the bath-house. Solely to get an extra bath I went, smeared myself all over and it did me no good at all. In despair I wrote to Count Mattei in Milan. He sent me a book and some drops, bless him! and, only fancy, Hoff's malt extract cured me! I bought it by accident, drank a bottle and a half of it, and I was ready to dance, it took it away completely. I made up my mind to write to the papers to thank him, I was prompted by a feeling of gratitude, and only fancy, it led to no end of a bother: not a single paper would take my letter. 'It would be very reactionary,' they said, 'no one will believe it. *Le diable n'existe point.* You'd better remain anonymous,' they advised me. What use is a letter of thanks if it's anonymous? I laughed with the men at the newspaper office, 'it's reactionary to believe in God in our days,' I said, 'but I am the devil, so I may be believed in.' 'We quite understand that,' they said. 'Who doesn't believe in the devil? Yet it won't do, it might injure our reputation. As a joke, if you like.' But I thought as a joke it wouldn't be very witty. So it wasn't printed. And do you know, I have felt sore about it to this day. My best feelings, gratitude, for instance, are literally denied me simply from my social position."

"Philosophical reflections again?" Ivan snarled malignantly.

"God preserve me from it, but one can't help complaining sometimes. I am a slandered man. You upbraid me every moment with being stupid. One can see you are young. My dear fellow, intelligence isn't the only thing! I have naturally a kind and merry heart. 'I also write vaudevilles of all sorts.' You seem to take me for Hlestakov grown old, but my fate is a far more serious one. Before time was, by some decree which I could never make out, I was predestined 'to deny' and yet I am genuinely good-hearted and not at all inclined to negation. 'No, you must go and deny, without denial there's no criticism and what would a journal be without a column of criticism?' Without criticism it would be nothing but one 'hosannah'. But nothing but hosannah is not enough for life, the hosannah must be tried in the crucible of doubt and so on, in the same style. But I don't meddle in that, I didn't create it, I am not answerable for it. Well, they've chosen their scapegoat, they've made me write the column of criticism and so life was made possible. We understand that comedy; I, for instance, simply ask for annihilation. No, live, I am told, for there'd be nothing without you. If everything in the universe were sensible, nothing would happen. There would be no events without you, and there must be events. So against the grain I serve to produce events and do what's irrational because I am commanded to. For all their indisputable intelligence, men take this farce as something serious, and that is their tragedy. They suffer, of course . . . but then they live, they live a real life, not a fantastic one, for suffering is life. Without suffering what would be the pleasure of it? It would be transformed into an endless church service; it would be holy, but tedious. But what about me? I suffer, but still, I don't live. I am x in an indeterminate equation. I am a sort of phantom in life who has lost all beginning and end, and who has even forgotten his own name. You are laughing—no, you are not laughing, you are angry again. You are for ever angry, all you care about is intelligence, but I repeat again that I would give away all this super-stellar life, all the ranks and honours, simply to be transformed into the soul of a merchant's wife weighing eighteen stone and set candles at God's shrine."

"Then even you don't believe in God?" said Ivan, with a smile of hatred.

"What can I say—that is, if you are in earnest . . ."

"Is there a God or not?" Ivan cried, with the same savage intensity.

"Ah, then you are in earnest! My dear fellow, upon my word I don't know. There! I've said it now!"

"You don't know, but you see God? No, you are not someone apart, you are myself, you are I and nothing more! You are rubbish, you are my fancy!"

"Well, if you like, I have the same philosophy as you, that would be true. *Je pense, donc je suis*, I know that for a fact, all the rest, all these worlds, God and even Satan—all that is not proved, to my mind. Does all that exist of itself, or is it only an emanation of myself, a logical development of my ego which alone has existed for ever? But I make haste to stop, for I believe you will be jumping up to beat me directly."

"You'd better tell me some anecdote!" said Ivan miserably.

"There is an anecdote precisely on our subject, or rather a legend, not an anecdote. You reproach me with unbelief, you see, you say, yet you don't believe. But, my dear fellow, I am not the only one like that. We are all in a muddle over there now and all through your science. Once there used to be atoms, five senses, four elements, and then everything hung together somehow. There were atoms in the ancient world even, but since we've learned that you've discovered the chemical molecule and protoplasm and the devil knows what, we had to lower our crest. There's a regular muddle, and, above all, superstition, scandal; there's as much scandal among us as among you, you know; a little more in fact, and spying, indeed, for we have our secret police department where private information is received. Well, this wild legend belongs to our middle ages—not yours, but ours—and no one believes it even among us, except the old ladies of eighteen stone, not your old ladies I mean, but ours. We've everything you have, I am revealing one of our secrets out of friendship for you; though it's forbidden. This legend is about Paradise. There was, they say, here on earth a thinker and philosopher. He rejected everything, 'laws, conscience, faith', and, above all, the future life. He died; he expected to go straight to darkness and death and he found a future life before him. He was astounded and indignant. 'This is against my principles!' he said. And he was punished for that . . . that is, you must excuse me, I am just repeating what I heard myself, it's only a legend . . . he was sentenced to walk a quadrillion kilometres in the dark (we've adopted the metric system, you know) and when he has finished that quadrillion, the gates of heaven would be opened to him and he'll be forgiven . . ."

"And what tortures have you in the other world besides the quadrillion kilometres?" asked Ivan, with a strange eagerness.

"What tortures? Ah, don't ask. In old days we had all sorts, but now they have taken chiefly to moral punishments— 'the stings of conscience' and all that nonsense. We got that, too, from you, from the softening of your manners. And who's the better for it? Only those who have got no conscience, for how can they be tortured by conscience when they have none? But decent people who have conscience and a sense of honour suffer for it. Reforms, when the ground has not been prepared for them, especially if they are institutions copied from abroad, do nothing but mischief! The ancient fire was better. Well, this man, who was condemned to the quadrillion kilometres, stood still, looked round and lay down across the road. 'I won't go, I refuse on principle!' Take the soul of an enlightened Russian atheist and mix it with the soul of the prophet Jonah, who sulked for three days and nights in the belly of the whale, and you get the character of that thinker who lay across the road."

"What did he lie on there?"

"Well, I suppose there was something to lie on. You are not laughing?"

"Bravo!" cried Ivan, still with the same strange eagerness. Now he was listening with an unexpected curiosity. "Well, is he lying there now?"

"That's the point, that he isn't. He lay there almost a thousand years and then he got up and went on."

"What an ass!" cried Ivan, laughing nervously and still seeming to be pondering something intently. "Does it make any difference whether he lies there for ever or walks the quadrillion kilometres? It would take a billion years to walk it?"

"Much more than that, I haven't got a pencil and paper or I could work it out. But he got there long ago, and that's where the story begins."

"What, he got there? But how did he get the billion years to do it?"

"Why, you keep thinking of our present earth! But our present earth may have been repeated a billion times. Why, it's become extinct, been frozen; cracked, broken to bits, disintegrated into its elements, again 'the water above the firmament', then again a comet, again a sun, again from the sun it becomes earth—and the same sequence may have been repeated endlessly, and exactly the same to every detail, most unseemly and insufferably tedious . . ."

"Well, well, what happened when he arrived?"

"Why, the moment the gates of Paradise were open and he walked in, before he had been there two seconds, by his watch (though to my thinking his watch must have long dissolved into its elements on the way), he cried out that those two seconds were worth walking not a quadrillion kilometres but a quadrillion of quadrillions, raised to the quadrillionth power! In fact, he sang 'hosannah' and overdid it so, that some persons there of lofty ideas wouldn't shake hands with him at first— he'd become too rapidly reactionary, they said. The Russian temperament. I repeat, it's a legend. I give it for what it's worth. So that's the sort of ideas we have on such subjects even now."

"I've caught you!" Ivan cried, with an almost childish delight, as though he had succeeded in remembering something at last. "That anecdote about the quadrillion years I made up myself! I was seventeen then, I was at the high school. I made up that anecdote and told it to a schoolfellow called Korovkin, it was at Moscow. . . . The anecdote is so characteristic that I couldn't have taken it from anywhere. I thought I'd forgotten it . . . but I've unconsciously recalled it—I recalled it myself—it was not you telling it! Thousands of things are unconsciously remembered like that even when people are being taken to execution . . . it's come back to me in a dream. You are that dream! You are a dream, not a living creature!"

"From the vehemence with which you deny my existence," laughed the gentleman, "I am convinced that you believe in me."

"Not in the slightest! I haven't a hundredth part of a gram of faith in you!"

"But you have the thousandth of a grain. Homeopathic doses perhaps are the strongest. Confess that you have faith even to the ten-thousandth of a grain."

"Not for one minute," cried Ivan furiously. "But I should like to believe in you," he added strangely.

"Aha! There's an admission! But I am good-natured. I'll come to your assistance again. Listen, it was I caught you, not you me. I told you your anecdote you'd forgotten, on purpose, so as to destroy your faith in me completely."

"You are lying. The object of your visit is to convince me of your existence!"

"Just so. But hesitation, suspense, conflict between belief and disbelief—is sometimes such torture to a conscientious man, such as you are, that it's better to hang oneself at once. Knowing that you are inclined to believe in me, I administered some disbelief by telling you that anecdote. I lead you to belief and disbelief by turns, and I have my motive in it. It's the new method. As soon as you disbelieve in me completely, you'll begin assuring me to my face that I am not a dream but a reality. I know you. Then I shall have attained my object, which is an honourable one. I shall sow in you only a tiny grain of faith and it will grow into an oak-tree—and such an oak-tree that, sitting on it, you will long to enter the ranks of 'the hermits in the wilderness and the saintly women', for that is what you are secretly longing for. You'll dine on locusts, you'll wander into the wilderness to save your soul!"

"Then it's for the salvation of my soul you are working, is it, you scoundrel?"

"One must do a good work sometimes. How ill-humoured you are!"

"Fool! did you ever tempt those holy men who ate locusts and prayed seventeen years in the wilderness till they were overgrown with moss?"

"My dear fellow, I've done nothing else. One forgets the whole world and all the worlds, and sticks to one such saint, because he is a very precious diamond. One such soul, you know, is sometimes worth a whole constellation. We have our system of reckoning, you know. The conquest is priceless! And some of them, on my word, are not inferior to you in culture, though you won't believe it. They can contemplate such depths of belief and disbelief at the same moment that sometimes it

really seems that they are within a hair's-breadth of being
'turned upside down', as the actor Gorbunov says."

"Well, did you get your nose pulled?" *

"My dear fellow," observed the visitor sententiously, "it's
better to get off with your nose pulled than without a nose at all.
As an afflicted marquis observed not long ago (he must have
been treated by a specialist) in confession to his spiritual father
—a Jesuit. I was present, it was simply charming. 'Give me
back my nose!' he said, and he beat his breast. 'My son,' said
the priest evasively, 'all things are accomplished in accordance
with the inscrutable decrees of Providence, and what seems a
misfortune sometimes leads to extraordinary, though un-
apparent, benefits. If stern destiny has deprived you of your
nose, it's to your advantage that no one can ever pull you by
your nose. 'Holy father, that's no comfort,' cried the despairing marquis. 'I'd be delighted to have my nose pulled every
day of my life, if it were only in its proper place.' 'My son,'
sighs the priest, 'you can't expect every blessing at once. This
is murmuring against Providence, who even in this has not forgotten you, for if you repine as you repined just now, declaring
you'd be glad to have your nose pulled for the rest of your life,
your desire has already been fulfilled indirectly, for when you
lost your nose, you were led by the nose.' "

"Fool, how stupid!" cried Ivan.

"My dear friend, I only wanted to amuse you. But I swear
that's the genuine Jesuit casuistry and I swear that it all happened word for word as I've told you. It happened lately and
gave me a great deal of trouble. The unhappy young man shot
himself that very night when he got home. I was by his side
till the very last moment. Those Jesuist confessionals are really
my most delightful diversion at melancholy moments. Here's
another incident that happened only the other day. A little
blonde Norman girl of twenty—a buxom, unsophisticated beauty
that would make your mouth water—comes to an old priest.
She bends down and whispers her sin into the grating. 'Why,
my daughter, have you fallen again already?' cries the priest.
'O Sancta Maria, what do I hear! Not the same man this time,
how long is this going on? Aren't you ashamed?' *'Ah, mon
père,'* answers the sinner, with tears of penitence, *'ça lui fait
tant de plaisir, et à moi si peu de peine!'* Fancy, such an answer!
I drew back. It was the cry of nature, better than innocence

* Literally: "Did you get off with a long nose made at you?"—a
proverbial expression in Russia for failure.—TRANSLATOR.

itself, if you like. I absolved her sin on the spot and was turning to go, but I was forced to turn back. I heard the priest at the grating making an appointment with her for the evening— though he was an old man hard as flint, he fell in an instant! It was nature, the truth of nature asserted its rights! What, you are turning up your nose again? Angry again? I don't know how to please you . . . ."

"Leave me alone, you are beating on my brain like a haunting nightmare," Ivan moaned miserably, helpless before his apparition. "I am bored with you, agonisingly and insufferably. I would give anything to be able to shake you off!"

"I repeat, moderate your expectations, don't demand of me 'everything great and noble' and you'll see how well we shall get on," said the gentleman impressively. "You are really angry with me for not having appeared to you in a red glow, with thunder and lightning, with scorched wings, but have shown myself in such a modest form. You are wounded, in the first place, in your æsthetic feelings, and, secondly, in your pride. How could such a vulgar devil visit such a great man as you! Yes, there is that romantic strain in you, that was so derided by Byelinsky. I can't help it, young man, as I got ready to come to you I did think as a joke of appearing in the figure of a retired general who had served in the Caucasus, with a star of the Lion and the Sun on my coat. But I was positively afraid of doing it, for you'd have thrashed me for daring to pin the Lion and the Sun on my coat, instead of, at least, the Polar Star or the Sirius. And you keep on saying I am stupid, but, mercy on us! I make no claim to be equal to you in intelligence. Mephistopheles declared to Faust that he desired evil, but did only good. Well, he can say what he likes, it's quite the opposite with me. I am perhaps the one man in all creation who loves the truth and genuinely desires good. I was there when the Word, Who died on the Cross, rose up into Heaven bearing on His bosom the soul of the penitent thief. I heard the glad shrieks of the cherubim singing and shouting hosannah and the thunderous rapture of the seraphim which shook heaven and all creation, and I swear to you by all that's sacred, I longed to join the choir and shout hosannah with them all. The word had almost escaped me, had almost broken from my lips . . . you know how susceptible and æsthetically impressionable I am. But common sense—oh, a most unhappy trait in my character—kept me in due bounds and I let the moment pass! For what would have happened, I reflected, what would have

happened after my hosannah? Everything on earth would have been extinguished at once and no events could have occurred. And so, solely from a sense of duty and my social position, I was forced to suppress the good moment and to stick to my nasty task. Somebody takes all the credit of what's good for himself, and nothing but nastiness is left for me. But I don't envy the honour of a life of idle imposture, I am not ambitious. Why am I, of all creatures in the world, doomed to be cursed by all decent people and even to be kicked, for if I put on mortal form I am bound to take such consequences sometimes? I know, of course, there's a secret in it, but they won't tell me the secret for anything, for then perhaps, seeing the meaning of it, I might bawl hosannah, and the indispensable minus would disappear at once, and good sense would reign supreme throughout the whole world. And that, of course, would mean the end of everything, even of magazines and newspapers, for who would take them in? I know that at the end of all things 1 shall be reconciled. I, too, shall walk my quadrillion and learn the secret. But till that happens I am sulking and fulfil my destiny though it's against the grain—that is, to ruin thousands for the sake of saving one. How many souls have had to be ruined and how many honourable reputations destroyed for the sake of that one righteous man, Job, over whom they made such a fool of me in old days. Yes, till the secret is revealed, there are two sorts of truths for me—one, their truth, yonder, which I know nothing about so far and the other my own. And there's no knowing which will turn out the better. . . . Are you asleep?"

"I might well be," Ivan groaned angrily. "All my stupid ideas—outgrown, thrashed out long ago, and flung aside like a dead carcass—you present to me as something new!"

"There's no pleasing you! And I thought I should fascinate you by my literary style. That hosannah in the skies really wasn't bad, was it? And then that ironical tone à la Heine eh?"

"No, I was never such a flunkey! How then could my soul beget a flunkey like you?"

"My dear fellow, I know a most charming and attractive young Russian gentleman, a young thinker and a great lover of literature and art, the author of a promising poem entitled 'The Grand Inquisitor'. I was only thinking of him!"

"I forbid you to speak of 'The Grand Inquisitor'," cried Ivan, crimson with shame.

"And the 'Geological Cataclysm'. Do you remember? That was a poem, now!"

"Hold your tongue, or I'll kill you!"

"You'll kill me? No, excuse me, I will speak. I came to treat myself to that pleasure. Oh, I love the dreams of my ardent young friends, quivering with eagerness for life! 'There are new men,' you decided last spring, when you were meaning to come here, 'they propose to destroy everything and begin with cannibalism. Stupid fellows! they didn't ask my advice! I maintain that nothing need be destroyed, that we only need to destroy the idea of God in man, that's how we have to set to work. It's that, that we must begin with. Oh, blind race of men who have no understanding! As soon as men have all of them denied God—and I believe that period, analogous with geological periods, will come to pass—the old conception of the universe will fall of itself without cannibalism and what's more, the old morality, and everything will begin anew. Men will unite to take from life all it can give, but only for joy and happiness in the present world. Man will be lifted up with a spirit of divine Titanic pride and the man-god will appear. From hour to hour extending his conquest of nature infinitely by his will and his science, man will feel such lofty joy from hour to hour in doing it that it will make up for all his old dreams of the joys of heaven. Everyone will know that he is mortal and will accept death proudly and serenely like a god. His pride will teach him that it's useless for him to repine at life's being a moment, and he will love his brother without need of reward. Love will be sufficient only for a moment of life, but the very consciousness of its momentariness will intensify its fire, which now is dissipated in dreams of eternal love beyond the grave' . . . and so on and so on in the same style. Charming!"

Ivan sat with his eyes on the floor, and his hands pressed to his ears, but he began trembling all over. The voice continued:

"The question now is, my young thinker reflected, is it possible that such a period will ever come? If it does, everything is determined and humanity is settled for ever. But as, owing to man's inveterate stupidity, this cannot come about for at least a thousand years, everyone who recognises the truth even now may legitimately order his life as he pleases, on the new principles. In that sense, 'all things are lawful' for him. What's more, even if this period never comes to pass, since there is anyway no God and no immortality, the new man may well become the man-god, even if he is the only one in the

350

whole world, and promoted to his new position, he may light-heartedly overstep all the barriers of the old morality of the old slave-man, if necessary. There is no law for God. Where God stands, the place is holy. Where I stand will be at once the fore-most place . . . 'all things are lawful' and that's the end of it! That's all very charming; but if you want to swindle why do you want a moral sanction for doing it? But that's our modern Russian all over. He can't bring himself to swindle without a moral sanction. He is so in love with truth . . ."

The visitor talked, obviously carried away by his own eloquence, speaking louder and louder and looking ironically at his host. But he did not succeed in finishing; Ivan suddenly snatched a glass from the table and flung it at the orator.

"*Ah, mais c'est bête enfin,*" cried the latter, jumping up from the sofa and shaking the drops of tea off himself. "He remembers Luther's inkstand! He takes me for a dream and throws glasses at a dream! It's like a woman! I suspected you were only pretending to stop up your ears."

A loud, persistent knocking was suddenly heard at the window. Ivan jumped up from the sofa.

"Do you hear? You'd better open," cried the visitor; "it's your brother Alyosha with the most interesting and surprising news, I'll be bound!"

"Be silent, deceiver, I knew it was Alyosha, I felt he was coming, and of course he has not come for nothing; of course he brings 'news'," Ivan exclaimed frantically.

"Open, open to him. There's a snowstorm and he is your brother. *Monsieur sait-il le temps qu'il fait? Ce n'est pas à mettre un chien dehors.*"

The knocking continued. Ivan wanted to rush to the window, but something seemed to fetter his arms and legs. He strained every effort to break his chains, but in vain. The knocking at the window grew louder and louder. At last the chains were broken and Ivan leapt up from the sofa. He looked round him wildly. Both candles had almost burnt out, the glass he had just thrown at his visitor stood before him on the table, and there was no one on the sofa opposite. The knocking on the window-frame went on persistently, but it was by no means so loud as it had seemed in his dream; on the contrary, it was quite subdued.

"It was not a dream! No, I swear it was not a dream, it all happened just now!" cried Ivan. He rushed to the window and opened the movable pane.

"Alyosha, I told you not to come," he cried fiercely to his brother. "In two words, what do you want? In two words, do you hear?"

"An · hour ago Smerdyakov hanged himself," Alyosha answered from the yard.

"Come round to the steps, I'll open at once," said Ivan, going to open the door to Alyosha.

CHAPTER X

"IT WAS HE WHO SAID THAT"

ALYOSHA coming in told Ivan that a little over an hour ago Marya Kondratyevna had run to his rooms and informed him Smerdyakov had taken his own life. "I went in to clear away the samovar and he was hanging on a nail in the wall." On Alyosha's inquiring whether she had informed the police, she answered that she had told no one, "but I flew straight to you, I've run all the way". She seemed perfectly crazy, Alyosha reported, and was shaking like a leaf. When Alyosha ran with her to the cottage, he found Smerdyakov still hanging. On the table lay a note: "I destroy my life of my own will and desire, so as to throw no blame on anyone." Alyosha left the note on the table and went straight to the police captain and told him all about it. "And from him I've come straight to you," said Alyosha, in conclusion, looking intently into Ivan's face. He had not taken his eyes off him while he told his story, as though struck by something in his expression.

"Brother," he cried suddenly, "you must be terribly ill. You look and don't seem to understand what I tell you."

"It's a good thing you came," said Ivan, as though brooding, and not hearing Alyosha's exclamation. "I knew he had hanged himself."

"From whom?"

"I don't know. But I knew. Did I know? Yes, he told me. He told me so just now."

Ivan stood in the middle of the room, and still spoke in the same brooding tone, looking at the ground.

"Who is *he?*" asked Alyosha, involuntarily looking round.

"He's slipped away."

Ivan raised his head and smiled softly.

"He was afraid of you, of a dove like you. You are a 'pure

352

cherub'. Dmitri calls you a cherub. Cherub! . . . the thunderous rapture of the seraphim. What are seraphim? Perhaps a whole constellation. But perhaps that constellation is only a chemical molecule. There's a constellation of the Lion and the Sun. Don't you know it?"

"Brother, sit down," said Alyosha in alarm. "For goodness' sake, sit down on the sofa! You are delirious; put your head on the pillow, that's right. Would you like a wet towel on your head? Perhaps it will do you good."

"Give me the towel: it's here on the chair. I just threw it down there."

"It's not here. Don't worry yourself. I know where it is— here," said Alyosha, finding a clean towel folded up and unused, by Ivan's dressing-table in the other corner of the room. Ivan looked strangely at the towel: recollection seemed to come back to him for an instant.

"Stay"—he got up from the sofa—"an hour ago I took that new towel from there and wetted it. I wrapped it round my head and threw it down here . . . How is it it's dry? There was no other."

"You put that towel on your head?" asked Alyosha.

"Yes, and walked up and down the room an hour ago . . . Why have the candles burnt down so? What's the time?"

"Nearly twelve."

"No, no, no!" Ivan cried suddenly. "It was not a dream. He was here; he was sitting here, on that sofa. When you knocked at the window, I threw a glass at him . . . this one. Wait a minute. I was asleep last time, but this dream was not a dream. It has happened before. I have dreams now, Alyosha . . . yet they are not dreams, but reality. I walk about, talk and see . . . though I am asleep. But he was sitting here, on that sofa there. . . . He is frightfully stupid, Alyosha, frightfully stupid." Ivan laughed suddenly and began pacing about the room.

"Who is stupid? Of whom are you talking, brother?" Alyosha asked anxiously again.

"The devil! He's taken to visiting me. He's been here twice, almost three times. He taunted me with being angry at his being a simple devil and not Satan, with scorched wings, in thunder and lightning. But he is not Satan: that's a lie. He is an impostor. He is simply a devil—a paltry, trivial devil. He goes to the baths. If you undressed him, you'd be sure to find he had a tail, long and smooth like a Danish dog's, a yard long, dun colour. . . . Alyosha, you are cold. You've been in the snow. Would you like some tea? What? Is it cold? Shall I tell her to bring some? *Ce n'est pas à mettre un chien dehors . . .*"

Alyosha ran to the washing-stand, wetted the towel, persuaded Ivan to sit down again, and put the wet towel round his head. He sat down beside him.

"What were you telling me just now about Lise?" Ivan began again. (He was becoming very talkative.) "I like Lise. I said something nasty about her. It was a lie. I like her . . . I am afraid for Katya to-morrow. I am more afraid of her than of anything. On account of the future. She will cast me off to-morrow and trample me underfoot. She thinks that I am ruining Mitya from jealousy on her account! Yes, she thinks that! But it's not so. To-morrow the cross, but not the gallows. No, I shan't hang myself. Do you know, I can never commit suicide, Alyosha. Is it because I am base? I am not a coward. Is it from love of life? How did I know that Smerdyakov had hanged himself? Yes, it was *he* told me so."

"And you are quite convinced that there has been someone here?" asked Alyosha.

"Yes, on that sofa in the corner. You would have driven him away. You did drive him away: he disappeared when you arrived. I love your face, Alyosha. Did you know that I loved your face? And *he* is myself, Alyosha. All that's base in me, all that's mean and contemptible. Yes, I am a romantic. He guessed it . . . though it's a libel. He is frightfully stupid; but it's to his advantage. He has cunning, animal cunning—he knew how to infuriate me. He kept taunting me with believing in him, and that was how he made me listen to him. He fooled me like a boy. He told me a great deal that was true about myself, though. I should never have owned it to myself. Do you know, Alyosha," Ivan added in an intensely earnest and confidential tone, "I should be awfully glad to think that it was *he* and not I."

"He has worn you out," said Alyosha, looking compassionately at his brother.

"He's been teasing me. And you know he does it so cleverly, so cleverly. 'Conscience! What is conscience? I make it up for myself. Why am I tormented by it? From habit. From the universal habit of mankind for the seven thousand years. So let us give it up, and we shall be gods.' It was he said that, it was he said that!"

"And not you, not you?" Alyosha could not help crying,

looking frankly at his brother. "Never mind him, anyway; have done with him and forget him. And let him take with him all that you curse now, and never come back!"

"Yes, but he is spiteful. He laughed at me. He was impudent, Alyosha," Ivan said, with a shudder of offence. "But he was unfair to me, unfair to me about lots of things. He told lies about me to my face. 'Oh, you are going to perform an act of heroic virtue: to confess you murdered your father, that the valet murdered him at your instigation.' "

"Brother," Alyosha interposed, "restrain yourself. It was not you murdered him. It's not true!"

"That's what he says, he, and he knows it. 'You are going to perform an act of heroic virtue, and you don't believe in virtue; that's what tortures you and makes you angry, that's why you are so vindictive.' He said that to me about me and he knows what he says."

"It's you say that, not he," exclaimed Alyosha mournfully, "and you say it because you are ill and delirious, tormenting yourself."

"No, he knows what he says. 'You are going from pride,' he says. 'You'll stand up and say it was I killed him, and why do you writhe with horror? You are lying! I despise your opinion, I despise your horror!' He said that about me. 'And do you know you are longing for their praise—"he is a criminal, a murderer, but what a generous soul; he wanted to save his brother and he confessed." ' That's a lie, Alyosha!" Ivan cried suddenly, with flashing eyes. "I don't want the low rabble to praise me, I swear I don't! That's a lie! That's why I threw the glass at him and it broke against his ugly face."

"Brother, calm yourself, stop!" Alyosha entreated him.

"Yes, he knows how to torment one. He's cruel," Ivan went on, unheeding. "I had an inkling from the first what he came for. 'Granting that you go through pride, still you had a hope that Smerdyakov might be convicted and sent to Siberia, and Mitya would be acquitted, while you would only be punished with *moral* condemnation' ('Do you hear?' he laughed then)— 'and some people will praise you. But now Smerdyakov's dead, he has hanged himself, and who'll believe you alone? But yet you are going, you are going, you'll go all the same, you've decided to go. What are you going for now?' That's awful, Alyosha. I can't endure such questions. Who dare ask me such questions?"

"Brother," interposed Alyosha. His heart sank with terror,

but he still seemed to hope to bring Ivan to reason, "how could he have told you of Smerdyakov's death before I came, when no one knew of it and there was no time for anyone to know of it?"

"He told me," said Ivan firmly, refusing to admit a doubt. "It was all he did talk about, if you come to that. 'And it would be all right if you believed in virtue,' he said. 'No matter if they disbelieve you, you are going for the sake of principle. But you are a little pig like Fyodor Pavlovitch and what do you want with virtue? Why do you want to go meddling if your sacrifice is of no use to anyone? Because you don't know yourself why you go! Oh, you'd give a great deal to know yourself why you go! And can you have made up your mind? You've not made up your mind. You'll sit all night deliberating whether to go or not. But you will go; you know you'll go. You know that whichever way you decide, the decision does not depend on you. You'll go because you won't dare not to go. Why won't you dare? You must guess that for yourself. That's a riddle for you!' He got up and went away. You came and he went. He called me a coward, Alyosha! *Le mot de l'énigme* is that I am a coward. 'It is not for such eagles to soar above the earth.' It was he added that—he! And Smerdyakov said the same. He must be killed! Katya despises me. I've seen that for a month past. Even Lise will begin to despise me! 'You are going in order to be praised.' That's a brutal lie! And you despise me too, Alyosha. Now I am going to hate you again! And I hate the monster, too! I hate the monster! I don't want to save the monster. Let him rot in Siberia! He's begun singing a hymn! Oh, to-morrow I'll go, stand before them, and spit in their faces!"

He jumped up in a frenzy, flung off the towel, and fell to pacing up and down the room again. Alyosha recalled what he had just said. "I seem to be sleeping awake. . . . I walk, I speak, I see, but I am asleep." It seemed to be just like that now. Alyosha did not leave him. The thought passed through his mind to run for a doctor, but he was afraid to leave his brother alone: there was no one to whom he could leave him. By degrees Ivan lost consciousness completely at last. He still went on talking, talking incessantly, but quite incoherently, and even articulated his words with difficulty. Suddenly he staggered violently; but Alyosha was in time to support him. Ivan let him lead him to his bed. Alyosha undressed him some-how and put him to bed. He sat watching over him for another two hours. The sick man slept soundly, without stirring, breathing softly and evenly. Alyosha took a pillow and lay down on the sofa, without undressing.

As he fell asleep he prayed for Mitya and Ivan. He began to understand Ivan's illness. "The anguish of a proud determination. An earnest conscience!" God, in Whom he disbelieved, and His truth were gaining mastery over his heart, which still refused to submit. "Yes," the thought floated through Alyosha's head as it lay on the pillow, "yes, if Smerdyakov is dead, no one will believe Ivan's evidence; but he will go and give it." Alyosha smiled softly. "God will conquer!" he thought. "He will either rise up in the light of truth, or . . . he'll perish in hate, revenging on himself and on everyone his having served the cause he does not believe in," Alyosha added bitterly, and again he prayed for Ivan.

BOOK XII: A JUDICIAL ERROR

CHAPTER I

THE FATAL DAY

AT ten o'clock in the morning of the day following the events I have described, the trial of Dmitri Karamazov began in our district court.

I hasten to emphasise the fact that I am far from esteeming myself capable of reporting all that took place at the trial in full detail, or even in the actual order of events. I imagine that to mention everything with full explanation would fill a volume, even a very large one. And so I trust I may not be reproached for confining myself to what struck me. I may have selected as of most interest what was of secondary importance, and may have omitted the most prominent and essential details. But I see I shall do better not to apologise. I will do my best and the reader will see for himself that I have done all I can.

And, to begin with, before entering the court, I will mention what surprised me most on that day. Indeed, as it appeared later, everyone was surprised at it, too. We all knew that the affair had aroused great interest, that everyone was burning with impatience for the trial to begin, that it had been a subject of talk, conjecture, exclamation and surmise for the last two months in local society. Everyone knew, too, that the case had become known throughout Russia, but yet we had not imagined that it had aroused such burning, such intense interest in everyone, not only among ourselves but all over Russia. This became evident at the trial this day.

Visitors had arrived not only from the chief town of our province but from several other Russian towns, as well as from Moscow and Petersburg. Among them were lawyers, ladies, and even several distinguished personages. Every ticket of admission had been snatched up. A special place behind the table at which the three judges sat was set apart for the most distinguished and important of the men visitors; a row of arm-chairs had been placed there—something exceptional, which had never been allowed before. A large proportion—not less than half of the public—were ladies. There was such a large number of lawyers from all parts that they did not know where to seat them, for every ticket had long since been eagerly sought for and distributed. I saw at the end of the room, behind the platform, a special partition hurriedly put up, behind which all these lawyers were admitted, and they thought themselves lucky to have standing room there, for all chairs had been removed for the sake of space, and the crowd behind the partition stood throughout the case closely packed, shoulder to shoulder.

Some of the ladies, especially those who came from a distance, made their appearance in the gallery very smartly dressed, but the majority of the ladies were oblivious even of dress. Their faces betrayed hysterical, intense, almost morbid curiosity. A peculiar fact—established afterwards by many observations—was that almost all the ladies, or at least the vast majority of them, were on Mitya's side and in favour of his being acquitted. This was perhaps chiefly owing to his reputation as a conqueror of female hearts. It was known that two women rivals were to appear in the case. One of them—Katerina Ivanovna—was an object of general interest. All sorts of extraordinary tales were told about her, amazing anecdotes of her passion for Mitya, in spite of his crime. Her pride and "aristocratic connections" were particularly insisted upon (she had called upon scarcely anyone in the town). People said she intended to petition the Government for leave to accompany the criminal to Siberia and to be married to him somewhere in the mines. The appearance of Grushenka in court was awaited with no less impatience. The public was looking forward with anxious curiosity to the meeting of the two rivals—the proud aristocratic girl and "the hetaira". But Grushenka was a more familiar figure to the ladies of the district than Katerina Ivanovna. They had already seen "the woman who had ruined Fyodor Pavlovitch and his unhappy son", and all, almost without exception, wondered how father and son could be so in love with "such a very common, ordinary Russian girl, who was not even pretty".

In brief, there was a great deal of talk. I know for a fact that there were several serious family quarrels on Mitya's account in our town. Many ladies quarrelled violently with their husbands over differences of opinion about the dreadful case, and it was only natural that the husbands of these ladies, far from being favourably disposed to the prisoner, should enter the court bitterly prejudiced against him. In fact, one may say pretty certainly that the masculine, as distinguished from the feminine part of the audience were biassed against the prisoner. There were numbers of severe, frowning, even vindictive faces. Mitya, indeed, had managed to offend many people during his stay in the town. Some of the visitors were, of course, in excellent spirits and quite unconcerned as to the fate of Mitya personally. But all were interested in the trial, and the majority of the men were certainly hoping for the conviction of the criminal, except perhaps the lawyers, who were more interested in the legal than in the moral aspect of the case.

Everybody was excited at the presence of the celebrated lawyer, Fetyukovitch. His talent was well known, and this was not the first time he had defended notorious criminal cases in the provinces. And if he defended them, such cases became celebrated and long remembered all over Russia. There were stories, too, about our prosecutor and about the President of the Court. It was said that Ippolit Kirillovitch was in a tremor at meeting Fetyukovitch, and that they had been enemies from the beginning of their careers in Petersburg; that though our sensitive prosecutor, who always considered that he had been aggrieved by someone in Petersburg because his talents had not been properly appreciated, was keenly excited over the Karamazov case, and was even dreaming of rebuilding his flagging fortunes by means of it, Fetyukovitch, they said, was his one anxiety. But these rumours were not quite just. Our prosecutor was not one of those men who lose heart in face of danger. On the contrary, his self-confidence increased with the increase of danger. It must be noted that our prosecutor was in general too hasty and morbidly impressionable. He would put his whole soul into some case and work at it as though his whole fate and his whole fortune depended on its result. This was the subject of some ridicule in the legal world, for just by this characteristic our prosecutor had gained a wider notoriety than could have been expected from his modest position. People laughed particularly at his passion for psychology. In my opinion, they were wrong, and our prosecutor was, I believe, a character of greater depth than was generally supposed. But with his delicate health he had failed to make his mark at the outset of his career and had never made up for it later.

As for the President of Court, I can only say that he was a humane and cultured man, who had a practical knowledge of his work and progressive views. He was rather ambitious, but did not concern himself greatly about his future career. The great aim of his life was to be a man of advanced ideas. He was, too, a man of connections and property. He felt, as we learnt afterwards, rather strongly about the Karamazov case, but from a social, not from a personal standpoint. He was interested in it as a social phenomenon, in its classification and its character as a product of our social conditions, as typical of the national character, and so on, and so on. His attitude to the personal aspect of the case, to its tragic significance and the persons involved in it, including the prisoner, was rather indifferent and abstract, as was perhaps fitting, indeed.

The court was packed and overflowing long before the judges made their appearance. Our court is the best hall in the town —spacious, lofty, and good for sound. On the right of the judges, who were on a raised platform, a table and two rows of chairs had been put ready for the jury. On the left was the place for the prisoner and the counsel for the defence. In the middle of the court, near the judges, was a table with the "material proofs". On it lay Fyodor Pavlovitch's white silk dressing-gown, stained with blood; the fatal brass pestle with which the supposed murder had been committed; Mitya's shirt, with a blood-stained sleeve; his coat, stained with blood in patches over the pocket in which he had put his handkerchief; the handkerchief itself, stiff with blood and by now quite yellow; the pistol loaded by Mitya at Perhotin's with a view to suicide, and taken from him on the sly at Mokroe by Trifon Borissovitch; the envelope in which the three thousand roubles had been put ready for Grushenka, the narrow pink ribbon with which it had been tied, and many other articles I don't remember. In the body of the hall, at some distance, came the seats for the public. But in front of the balustrade a few chairs had been placed for witnesses who remained in the court after giving their evidence.

At ten o'clock the three judges arrived—the President, one honorary justice of the peace, and one other. The prosecutor, of course, entered immediately after. The President was a short, stout, thick-set man of fifty, with a dyspeptic complexion, dark hair turning grey and cut short, and a red ribbon, of what Order I don't remember. The prosecutor struck me and the others, too, as looking particularly pale, almost green. His face seemed to have grown suddenly thinner, perhaps in a single night, for I had seen him looking as usual only two days before. The President began with asking the court whether all the jury were present.

But I see I can't go on like this, partly because some things I did not hear, others I did not notice, and others I have forgotten, but most of all because, as I have said before, I have literally no time or space to mention everything that was said and done. I only know that neither side objected to very many of the jury-men. I remember the twelve jurymen—four were petty officials of the town, two were merchants, and six peasants and artisans of the town. I remember, long before the trial, questions were continually asked with some surprise, especially by ladies: "Can such a delicate, complex and psychological case be submitted for decision to petty officials and even peasants?" and "What can an official, still more a peasant, understand in such an affair?" All the four officials in the jury were, in fact, men of no consequence and of low rank. Except one who was rather younger, they were grey-headed men, little known in society, who had vegetated on a pitiful salary, and who probably had elderly, unpresentable wives and crowds of children, perhaps even without shoes and stockings. At most, they spent their leisure over cards and, of course, had never read a single book. The two merchants looked respectable, but were strangely silent and stolid. One of them was close-shaven, and was dressed in European style; the other had a small, grey beard, and wore a red ribbon with some sort of a medal upon it on his neck. There is no need to speak of the artisans and the peasants. The artisans of Skotoprigonyevsk are almost peasants, and even work on the land. Two of them also wore European dress, and, perhaps for that reason, were dirtier and more uninviting-looking than the others. So that one might well wonder, as I did as soon as I had looked at them, "what men like that could possibly make of such a case?" Yet their faces made a strangely imposing, almost menacing, impression; they were stern and frowning.

At last the President opened the case of the murder of Fyodor Pavlovitch Karamozov. I don't quite remember how he described him. The court usher was told to bring in the prisoner, and Mitya made his appearance. There was a hush through the court. One could have heard a fly. I don't know how it was with others, but Mitya made a most unfavourable impression on me. He looked an awful dandy in a brand-new frock-coat. I heard afterwards that he had ordered it in Moscow expressly for the occasion from his own tailor, who had his measure. He wore immaculate black kid gloves and exquisite linen. He walked in with his yard-long strides, looking stiffly straight in front of him, and sat down in his place with a most unperturbed air.

At the same moment the counsel for defence, the celebrated Fetyukovitch, entered, and a sort of subdued hum passed through the court. He was a tall, spare man, with long thin legs, with extremely long, thin, pale fingers, clean-shaven face, demurely brushed, rather short hair, and thin lips that were at times curved into something between a sneer and a smile. He looked about forty. His face would have been pleasant if it had not been for his eyes, which, in themselves small and inexpressive, were set remarkably close together, with only the thin, long nose as a dividing line between them. In fact, there was something strikingly birdlike about his face. He was in evening dress and white tie.

I remember the President's first questions to Mitya, about his name, his calling, and so on. Mitya answered sharply, and his voice was so unexpectedly loud that it made the President start and look at the prisoner with surprise. Then followed a list of persons who were to take part in the proceedings—that is, of the witnesses and experts. It was a long list. Four of the witnesses were not present—Miüsov, who had given evidence at the preliminary inquiry, but was now in Paris; Madame Hohlakov and Maximov, who were absent through illness; and Smerdyakov, through his sudden death, of which an official statement from the police was presented. The news of Smerdyakov's death produced a sudden stir and whisper in the court. Many of the audience, of course, had not heard of the sudden suicide. What struck people most was Mitya's sudden outburst.

As soon as the statement of Smerdyakov's death was made, he cried out aloud from his place:

"He was a dog and died like a dog!"

I remember how his counsel rushed to him, and how the President addressed him, threatening to take stern measures if such an irregularity were repeated. Mitya nodded and in a subdued voice repeated several times abruptly to his counsel, with no show of regret:

"I won't again, I won't. It escaped me. I won't do it again."

And, of course, this brief episode did him no good with the jury or the public. His character was displayed, and it spoke for itself. It was under the influence of this incident that the opening statement was read. It was rather short, but circumstantial. It only stated the chief reasons why he had been arrested, why he must be tried, and so on. Yet it made a great impression on me. The clerk read it loudly and distinctly. The whole tragedy was suddenly unfolded before us, concentrated, in bold relief in a fatal and pitiless light. I remember how, immediately after it had been read, the President asked Mitya in a loud impressive voice:

"Prisoner, do you plead guilty?"

Mitya suddenly rose from his seat.

"I plead guilty to drunkenness and dissipation," he exclaimed, again in a startling, almost frenzied voice, "to idleness and debauchery. I meant to become an honest man for good, just at the moment when I was struck down by fate. But I am not guilty of the death of that old man, my enemy and my father. No, no, I am not guilty of robbing him! I could not be. Dmitri Karamazov is a scoundrel, but not a thief."

He sat down again, visibly trembling all over. The President again briefly but impressively admonished him to answer only what was asked, and not to go off into irrelevant exclamations. Then he ordered the case to proceed. All the witnesses were led up to take the oath. Then I saw them all together. The brothers of the prisoner were, however, allowed to give evidence without taking the oath. After an exhortation from the priest and the President, the witnesses were led away and were made to sit as far as possible apart from one another. Then they began calling them up one by one.

CHAPTER II

DANGEROUS WITNESSES

I DO not know whether the witnesses for the defence and for the prosecution were separated into groups by the President, and whether it was arranged to call them in certain order. But no doubt it was so. I only know that the witnesses for the prosecution were called first. I repeat I don't intend to describe all the questions step by step. Besides, my account would be to some extent superfluous, because in the speeches for the prosecution and for the defence the whole course of the evidence was brought together and set in a strong and significant light, and I took down parts of those two remarkable speeches in full, and will quote them in due course, together with one extraordinary and quite unexpected episode, which occurred before the final speeches, and undoubtedly influenced the sinister and fatal outcome of the trial.

I will only observe that from the first moments of the trial one peculiar characteristic of the case was conspicuous and observed by all, that is, the overwhelming strength of the prosecution as compared with the arguments the defence had to rely upon. Everyone realised it from the first moment that the facts began to group themselves round a single point, and the whole horrible and bloody crime was gradually revealed. Everyone, perhaps, felt from the first that the case was beyond dispute, that there was no doubt about it, that there could be really no discussion, and that the defence was only a matter of form, and that the prisoner was guilty, obviously and conclusively guilty. I imagine that even the ladies, who were so impatiently longing for the acquittal of the interesting prisoner, were at the same time, without exception, convinced of his guilt. What's more, I believe they would have been mortified if his guilt had not been so firmly established, as that would have lessened the effect of the closing scene of the criminal's acquittal. That he would be acquitted all the ladies, strange to say, were firmly persuaded up to the very last moment. "He is guilty, but he will be acquitted, from motives of humanity, in accordance with the new ideas, the new sentiments that had come into fashion," and so on, and so on. And that was why they had crowded into the court so impatiently. The men were more interested in the contest between the prosecutor and the famous Fetyukovitch. All were wondering and asking themselves what could even a talent like Fetyukovitch's make of such a desperate case; and so they followed his achievements, step by step, with concentrated attention.

But Fetyukovitch remained an enigma to all up to the very end, up to his speech. Persons of experience suspected that he had some design, that he was working towards some object, but it was almost impossible to guess what it was. His confidence and self-reliance were unmistakable, however. Everyone noticed with pleasure, moreover, that he, after so short a stay, not more than three days, perhaps, among us, had so wonderfully succeeded in mastering the case and "had studied it to a nicety". People described with relish, afterwards, how cleverly he had "taken down" all the witnesses for the prosecution, and as far as possible perplexed them and, what's more, had aspersed their reputation and so depreciated the value of their evidence. But it was supposed that he did this rather by way of sport, so to speak, for professional glory, to show nothing had been omitted of the accepted methods, for all were convinced that he could do no real good by such disparagement of the witnesses, and probably was more aware of this than anyone, having some idea of his own in the background, some concealed weapon of defence, which he would suddenly reveal when the time came. But meanwhile, conscious of his strength, he seemed to be diverting himself.

So, for instance, when Grigory, Fyodor Pavlovitch's old servant, who had given the most damning piece of evidence about the open door, was examined, the counsel for the defence positively fastened upon him when his turn came to question him. It must be noted that Grigory entered the hall with a composed and almost stately air, not the least disconcerted by the majesty of the court or the vast audience listening to him. He gave evidence with as much confidence as though he had been talking with his Marfa, only perhaps more respectfully. It was impossible to make him contradict himself. The prosecutor questioned him first in detail about the family life of the Karamazovs. The family picture stood out in lurid colours. It was plain to ear and eye that the witness was guileless and impartial. In spite of his profound reverence for the memory of his deceased master, he yet bore witness that he had been unjust to Mitya and "hadn't brought up his children as he should. He'd have been devoured by lice when he was little if it hadn't been for me," he added, describing Mitya's early childhood. "It wasn't fair either of the father to wrong his son over his mother's property, which was by right his."

In reply to the prosecutor's question what grounds he had for asserting that Fyodor Pavlovitch had wronged his son in their money relations, Grigory, to the surprise of everyone, had no proof at all to bring forward, but he still persisted that the arrangement with the son was "unfair", and that he ought "to have paid him several thousand roubles more". I must note, by the way, that the prosecutor asked this question: whether Fyodor Pavlovitch had really kept back part of Mitya's inheritance with marked persistence of all the witnesses who could be asked it, not excepting Alyosha and Ivan, but he obtained no exact information from anyone; all alleged that it was so, but were unable to bring forward any distinct proof. Grigory's description of the scene at the dinner-table, when Dmitri had burst in and beaten his father, threatening to come back to kill him, made a sinister impression on the court, especially as the old servant's composure in telling it, his parsimony of words and peculiar phraseology were as effective as eloquence. He observed that he was not angry with Mitya for having knocked him down and struck him on the face; he had forgiven him long ago, he said. Of the deceased Smerdyakov he observed, crossing himself, that he was a lad of ability, but stupid and afflicted, and, worse still, an infidel, and that it was Fyodor Pavlovitch and his elder son who had taught him to be so. But he defended Smerdyakov's honesty almost with warmth, and related how Smerdyakov had once found the master's money in the yard, and, instead of concealing it, had taken it to his master, who had rewarded him with a "gold piece" for it, and trusted him implicitly from that time forward. He maintained obstinately that the door into the garden had been open. But he was asked so many questions that I can't recall them all.

At last the counsel for the defence began to cross-examine him, and the first question he asked was about the envelope in which Fyodor Pavlovitch was supposed to have put three thousand roubles for "a certain person". "Have you ever seen it, you, who were for so many years in close attendance on your master?" Grigory answered that he had not seen it and had never heard of the money from anyone "till everybody was talking about it". This question about the envelope Fetyukovitch put to everyone who could conceivably have known of it, as persistently as the prosecutor asked his question about Dmitri's inheritance, and got the same answer from all, that no one had seen the envelope, though many had heard of it. From the beginning everyone noticed Fetyukovitch's persistence on this subject.

"Now, with your permission I'll ask you a question," Fetyukovitch said, suddenly and unexpectedly. "Of what was that balsam, or, rather, decoction, made, which, as we learn from the preliminary inquiry, you used on that evening to rub your lumbago, in the hope of curing it?"

Grigory looked blankly at the questioner, and after a brief silence muttered "there was saffron in it".

"Nothing but saffron? Don't you remember any other ingredient?"

"There was milfoil in it, too."

"And pepper perhaps?" Fetyukovitch queried.

"Yes, there was pepper, too."

"Etcetera. And all dissolved in vodka?"

"In spirit."

There was a faint sound of laughter in the court.

"You see, in spirit. After rubbing your back, I believe you drank what was left in the bottle with a certain pious prayer, only known to your wife?"

"I did."

"Did you drink much? Roughly speaking, a wineglass or two?"

"It might have been a tumblerful."

"A tumblerful, even. Perhaps a tumbler and a half?"

Grigory did not answer. He seemed to see what was meant.

"A glass and a half of neat spirit—is not at all bad, don't you think? You might see the gates of heaven open, not only the door into the garden?"

Grigory remained silent. There was another laugh in the court. The President made a movement.

"Do you know for a fact," Fetyukovitch persisted, "whether you were awake or not when you saw the open door?"

"I was on my legs."

"That's not a proof that you were awake." (There was again laughter in the court.) "Could you have answered at that moment, if anyone had asked you a question—for instance, what year it is?"

"I don't know."

"And what year is it, *anno Domini*, do you know?"

Grigory stood with a perplexed face, looking straight at his tormentor. Strange to say, it appeared he really did not know what year it was.

"But perhaps you can tell me how many fingers you have on your hands?"

"I am a servant," Grigory said suddenly, in a loud and distinct voice. "If my betters think fit to make game of me, it is my duty to suffer it."

Fetyukovitch was a little taken aback, and the President intervened, reminding him that he must ask more relevant questions. Fetyukovitch bowed with dignity and said that he had no more questions to ask of the witness. The public and the jury, of course, were left with a grain of doubt in their minds as to the evidence of a man who might, while undergoing a certain cure, have seen "the gates of heaven", and who did not even know what year he was living in. But before Grigory left the box another episode occurred. The President, turning to the prisoner, asked him whether he had any comment to make on the evidence of the last witness.

"Except about the door, all he has said is true," cried Mitya, in a loud voice. "For combing the lice off me, I thank him; for forgiving my blows, I thank him. The old man has been honest all his life and as faithful to my father as seven hundred poodles."

"Prisoner, be careful in your language," the President admonished him.

"I am not a poodle," Grigory muttered.

"All right, it's I am a poodle myself," cried Mitya. "If it's an insult, I take it to myself and I beg his pardon. I was a beast and cruel to him. I was cruel to Æsop, too."

"What Æsop?" the President asked sternly again.

"Oh, Pierrot . . . my father, Fyodor Pavlovitch."

The President again and again warned Mitya impressively and very sternly to be more careful in his language.

"You are injuring yourself in the opinion of your judges."

The counsel for the defence was equally clever in dealing with the evidence of Rakitin. I may remark that Rakitin was one of the leading witnesses and one to whom the prosecutor attached great significance. It appeared that he knew everything; his knowledge was amazing, he had been everywhere, seen everything, talked to everybody, knew every detail of the biography of Fyodor Pavlovitch and all the Karamazovs. Of the envelope, it is true, he had only heard from Mitya himself. But he described minutely Mitya's exploits in the "Metropolis", all his compromising doings and sayings, and told the story of Cap-

tain Snegiryov's "wisp of tow". But even Rakitin could say
nothing positive about Mitya's inheritance, and confined himself to contemptuous generalities.

"Who could tell which of them was to blame, and which
was in debt to the other, with their crazy Karamazov way of
muddling things so that no one could make head or tail of it."
He attributed the tragic crime to the habits that had become
ingrained by ages of serfdom and the distressed condition of
Russia, due to the lack of appropriate institutions. He was,
in fact, allowed some latitude of speech. This was the first occasion on which Rakitin showed what he could do, and attracted
notice. The prosecutor knew that the witness was preparing a
magazine article on the case, and afterwards in his speech, as
we shall see later, quoted some ideas from the article, showing
that he had seen it already. The picture drawn by the witness
was a gloomy and sinister one, and greatly strengthened the case
for the prosecution. Altogether, Rakitin's discourse fascinated,
the public by its independence and the extraordinary nobility of
its ideas. There were even two or three outbreaks of applause
when he spoke of serfdom and the distressed condition of Russia.

But Rakitin, in his youthful ardour, made a slight blunder,
of which the counsel for the defence at once adroitly took
advantage. Answering certain questions about Grushenka, and
carried away by the loftiness of his own sentiments and his
success, of which he was, of course, conscious, he went so far as
to speak somewhat contemptuously of Agrafena Alexandrovna
as "the kept mistress of Samsonov". He would have given a
good deal to take back his words afterwards, for Fetyukovitch
caught him out over it at once. And it was all because Rakitin
had not reckoned on the lawyer having been able to become so
intimately acquainted with every detail in so short a time.

"Allow me to ask," began the counsel for the defence, with
the most affable and even respectful smile, "you are, of course,
the same Mr. Rakitin whose pamphlet, 'The Life of the Deceased
Elder, Father Zossima', published by the diocesan authorities,
full of profound and religious reflections and preceded by an
excellent and devout dedication to the Bishop, I have just read
with such pleasure?"

"I did not write it for publication . . . it was published afterwards," muttered Rakitin, for some reason fearfully disconcerted and almost ashamed.

"Oh, that's excellent! A thinker like you can, and indeed
ought to, take the widest view of every social question. Your

most instructive pamphlet has been widely circulated through the patronage of the Bishop, and has been of appreciable service. . . . But this is the chief thing I should like to learn from you. You stated just now that you were very intimately acquainted with Madame Svyetlov." (It must be noted that Grushenka's surname was Svyetlov. I heard it for the first time that day, during the case.)

"I cannot answer for all my acquaintances. . . , I am a young man . . . and who can be responsible for everyone he meets?" cried Rakitin, flushing all over.

"I understand, I quite understand," cried Fetyukovitch, as though he, too, were embarrassed and in haste to excuse himself. "You, like any other, might well be interested in an acquaintance with a young and beautiful woman who would readily entertain the *élite* of the youth of the neighbourhood, but . . . I only wanted to know . . . it has come to my knowledge that Madame Svyetlov was particularly anxious a couple of months ago to make the acquaintance of the younger Karamazov, Alexey Fyodorovitch, and promised you twenty-five roubles if you would bring him to her in his monastic dress. And that actually took place on the evening of the day on which the terrible crime, which is the subject of the present investigation, was committed. You brought Alexey Karamazov to Madame Svyetlov, and did you receive the twenty-five roubles from Madame Svyetlov as a reward? That's what I wanted to hear from you.'

"It was a joke. . . . I don't see of what interest that can be to you. . . . I took it for a joke . . . meaning to give it back later . . ."

"Then you did take . . . But you have not given it back yet . . . or have you?"

"That's of no consequence," muttered Rakitin, "I refuse to answer such questions. . . . Of course I shall give it back."

The President intervened, but Fetyukovitch declared he had no more questions to ask of the witness. Mr. Rakitin left the witness-box not absolutely without a stain upon his character. The effect left by the lofty idealism of his speech was somewhat marred, and Fetyukovitch's expression, as he watched him walk away, seemed to suggest to the public "this is a specimen of the lofty-minded persons who accuse him". I remember that this incident, too, did not pass off without an outbreak from Mitya. Enraged by the tone in which Rakitin had referred to Grushenka, he suddenly shouted "Bernard!" When, after Rakitin's cross-

THE BROTHERS KARAMAZOV

examination, the President asked the prisoner if he had anything to say, Mitya cried loudly:

"Since I've been arrested, he has borrowed money from me!
He is a contemptible Bernard and opportunist, and he doesn't
believe in God; he took the Bishop in!"

Mitya, of course, was pulled up again for the intemperance of
his language, but Rakitin was done for. Captain Snegiryov's
evidence was a failure, too, but from quite a different reason.
He appeared in ragged and dirty clothes, muddy boots, and in
spite of the vigilance and expert observation of the police officers,
he turned out to be hopelessly drunk. On being asked about
Mitya's attack upon him, he refused to answer.

"God bless him. Ilusha told me not to. God will make it
up to me yonder."

"Who told you not to tell? Of whom are you talking?"

"Ilusha, my little son. 'Father, father, how he insulted you!'
He said that at the stone. Now he is dying . . ."

The captain suddenly began sobbing, and plumped down on
his knees before the President. He was hurriedly led away
amidst the laughter of the public. The effect prepared by the
prosecutor did not come off at all.

Fetyukovitch went on making the most of every opportunity,
and amazed people more and more by his minute knowledge of
the case. Thus, for example, Trifon Borissovitch made a great
impression, of course very prejudicial to Mitya. He calculated
almost on his fingers that on his first visit to Mokroe, Mitya
must have spent three thousand roubles, "or very little less.
Just think what he squandered on those gypsy girls alone! And
as for our lousy peasants, it wasn't a case of flinging half a
rouble in the street, he made them presents of twenty-five
roubles each, at least; he didn't give them less. And what a
lot of money was simply stolen from him! And if anyone did
steal, he did not leave a receipt. How could one catch the thief
when he was flinging his money away all the time? Our peasants
are robbers, you know; they have no care for their souls. And
the way he went on with the girls, our village girls! They're
completely set up since then, I tell you, they used to be
poor." He recalled, in fact, every item of expense and added
it all up. So the theory that only fifteen hundred had been
spent and the rest had been put aside in a little bag seemed
inconceivable.

"I saw three thousand as clear as a penny in his hands, I
saw it with my own eyes; I should think I ought to know how

to reckon money," cried Trifon Borissovitch, doing his best to satisfy "his betters".

When Fetyukovitch had to cross-examine him, he scarcely tried to refute his evidence, but began asking him about an incident at the first carousal at Mokroe, a month before the arrest, when Timofey and another peasant called Akim had picked up from the floor in the passage a hundred roubles dropped by Mitya when he was drunk, and had given them to Trifon Borissovitch, and received a rouble each from him for doing so. "Well," asked the lawyer, "did you give that hundred roubles back to Mr. Karamazov?" Trifon Borissovitch shuffled in vain. . . . He was obliged, after the peasants had been examined, to admit the finding of the hundred roubles, only adding that he had religiously returned it all to Dmitri Fyodorovitch "in perfect honesty, and it's only because his honour was in liquor at the time, he wouldn't remember it". But, as he had denied the incident of the hundred roubles till the peasants had been called to prove it, his evidence as to returning the money to Mitya was naturally regarded with great suspicion. So one of the most dangerous witnesses brought forward by the prosecution was again discredited.

The same thing happened with the Poles. They took up an attitude of pride and independence; they vociferated loudly that they had both been in the service of the Crown, and that "Pan Mitya" had offered them three thousand "to buy their honour", and that they had seen a large sum of money in his hands. Pan Mussyalovitch introduced a terrible number of Polish words into his sentences, and seeing that this only increased his consequence in the eyes of the President and the prosecutor, grew more and more pompous, and ended by talking in Polish altogether. But Fetyukovitch caught them, too, in his snares. Trifon Borissovitch, recalled, was forced, in spite of his evasions, to admit that Pan Vrublevsky had substituted another pack of cards for the one he had provided, and that Pan Mussyalovitch had cheated during the game. Kalganov confirmed this, and both the Poles left the witness-box with damaged reputations, amidst laughter from the public.

Then exactly the same thing happened with almost all the most dangerous witnesses. Fetyukovitch succeeded in casting a slur on all of them, and dismissing them with a certain derision. The lawyers and experts were lost in admiration, and were only at a loss to understand what good purpose could be served by it, for all, I repeat, felt that the case for the prosecution could

Keto Saito.

not be refuted, but was growing more and more tragically over-whelming. But from the confidence of the "great magician" they saw that he was serene, and they waited, feeling that "such a man" had not come from Petersburg for nothing, and that he was not a man to return unsuccessful.

CHAPTER III

THE MEDICAL EXPERTS AND A POUND OF NUTS

THE evidence of the medical experts, too, was of little use to the prisoner. And it appeared later that Fetyukovitch had not reckoned much upon it. The medical line of defence had only been taken up through the insistence of Katerina Ivanovna, who had sent for a celebrated doctor from Moscow on purpose. The case for the defence could, of course, lose nothing by it and might, with luck, gain something from it. There was, however, an element of comedy about it, through the difference of opinion of the doctors. The medical experts were the famous doctor from Moscow, our doctor, Herzenstube, and the young doctor, Varvinsky. The two latter appeared also as witnesses for the prosecution.

The first to be called in the capacity of expert was Doctor Herzenstube. He was a grey and bald old man of seventy, of middle height and sturdy build. He was much esteemed and respected by everyone in the town. He was a conscientious doctor and an excellent and pious man, a Herrnhuter or Moravian brother, I am not quite sure which. He had been living amongst us for many years and behaved with wonder-ful dignity. He was a kind-hearted and humane man. He treated the sick poor and peasants for nothing, visited them in their slums and huts, and left money for medicine, but he was as obstinate as a mule. If once he had taken an idea into his head, there was no shaking it. Almost everyone in the town was aware, by the way, that the famous doctor had, within the first two or three days of his presence among us, uttered some extremely offensive allusions to Doctor Herzenstube's qualifica-tions. Though the Moscow doctor asked twenty-five roubles for a visit, several people in the town were glad to take advantage of his arrival, and rushed to consult him regardless of expense. All these had, of course, been previously patients of Doctor Herzenstube, and the celebrated doctor had criticised his treatment with extreme harshness. Finally, he had asked the patients as soon as he saw them: "Well, who has been cramming you with nostrums? Herzenstube? He, he!" Doctor Herzenstube, of course, heard all this, and now all the three doctors made their appearance, one after another, to be examined.

Doctor Herzenstube roundly declared that the abnormality of the prisoner's mental faculties was self-evident. Then giving his grounds for this opinion, which I omit here, he added that the abnormality was not only evident in many of the prisoner's actions in the past but was apparent even now at this very moment. When he was asked to explain how it was apparent now at this moment, the old doctor, with simple-hearted direct-ness, pointed out that the prisoner on entering the court had "an extraordinary air, remarkable in the circumstances"; that he had "marched in like a soldier, looking straight before him, though it would have been more natural for him to look to the left where, among the public, the ladies were sitting, seeing that he was a great admirer of the fair sex and must be thinking much of what the ladies are saying of him now," the old man concluded in his peculiar language.

I must add that he spoke Russian readily, but every phrase was formed in German style, which did not, however, trouble him, for it had always been a weakness of his to believe that he spoke Russian perfectly, better indeed than Russians. And he was very fond of using Russian proverbs, always declaring that the Russian proverbs were the best and most expressive sayings in the whole world. I may remark, too, that in conversation, through absent-mindedness he often forgot the most ordinary words, which sometimes went out of his head, though he knew them perfectly. The same thing happened, though, when he spoke German, and at such times he always waved his hand before his face as though trying to catch the lost word, and no one could induce him to go on speaking till he had found the missing word. His remark that the prisoner ought to have looked at the ladies on entering roused a whisper of amusement in the audience. All our ladies were very fond of our old doctor; they knew, too, that having been all his life a bachelor and a religious man of exemplary conduct, he looked upon women as lofty creatures. And so his unexpected observation struck everyone as very queer.

The Moscow doctor, being questioned in his turn, definitely and emphatically repeated that he considered the prisoner's mental condition abnormal in the highest degree. He talked at length and with erudition of "aberration" and "mania", and argued that, from all the facts collected, the prisoner had undoubtedly been in a condition of aberration for several days before his arrest, and, if the crime had been committed by him, it must, even if he were conscious of it, have been almost involuntary, as he had not the power to control the morbid impulse that possessed him.

But apart from temporary aberration, the doctor diagnosed mania, which promised, in his words, to lead to complete insanity in the future. (It must be noted that I report this in my own words, the doctor made use of very learned and professional language.) "All his actions are in contravention of common sense and logic," he continued. "Not to refer to what I have not seen, that is, the crime itself and the whole catastrophe, the day before yesterday, while he was talking to me, he had an unaccountably fixed look in his eye. He laughed unexpectedly when there was nothing to laugh at. He showed continual and inexplicable irritability, using strange words, 'Bernard!' 'Ethics!' and others equally inappropriate." But the doctor detected mania, above all, in the fact that the prisoner could not even speak of the three thousand roubles, of which he considered himself to have been cheated, without extraordinary irritation, though he could speak comparatively lightly of other misfortunes and grievances. According to all accounts, he had even in the past, whenever the subject of the three thousand roubles was touched on, flown into a perfect frenzy, and yet he was reported to be a disinterested and not grasping man.

"As to the opinion of my learned colleague," the Moscow doctor added ironically in conclusion, "that the prisoner would, on entering the court, have naturally looked at the ladies and not straight before him, I will only say that, apart from the playfulness of this story, it is radically unsound. For though I fully agree that the prisoner, on entering the court where his fate will be decided, would not naturally look straight before him in that fixed way, and that that may really be a sign of his abnormal mental condition, at the same time I maintain that he would naturally not look to the left at the ladies, but, on the contrary, to the right to find his legal adviser, on whose help all his hopes rest and on whose defence all his future depends." The doctor expressed his opinion positively and emphatically.

But the unexpected pronouncement of Doctor Varvinsky gave the last touch of comedy to the difference of opinion

375

between the experts. In his opinion the prisoner was now, and had been all along, in a perfectly normal condition, and, although he certainly must have been in a nervous and exceedingly excited state before his arrest, this might have been due to several perfectly obvious causes, jealousy, anger, continual drunkenness, and so on. But this nervous condition would not involve the mental aberration of which mention had just been made. As to the question whether the prisoner should have looked to the left or to the right on entering the court, "in his modest opinion" the prisoner would naturally look straight before him on entering the court, as he had in fact done, as that was where the judges, on whom his fate depended, were sitting. So that it was just by looking straight before him that he showed his perfectly normal state of mind at the present. The young doctor concluded his "modest" testimony with some heat.

"Bravo, doctor!" cried Mitya, from his seat, "just so!"

Mitya, of course, was checked, but the young doctor's opinion had a decisive influence on the judges and on the public, and, as appeared afterwards, everyone agreed with him. But Doctor Herzenstube, when called as a witness, was quite unexpectedly of use to Mitya. As an old resident in the town who had known the Karamazov family for years, he furnished some facts of great value for the prosecution, and suddenly, as though recalling something, he added:

"But the poor young man might have had a very different life, for he had a good heart both in childhood and after childhood, that I know. But the Russian proverb says: 'If a man has one head, it's good, but if another clever man comes to visit him, it would be better still, for then there will be two heads and not only one.' "

"One head is good, but two are better," the prosecutor put in impatiently. He knew the old man's habit of talking slowly and deliberately, regardless of the impression he was making and of the delay he was causing, and highly prizing his flat, dull and always gleefully complacent German wit. The old man was fond of making jokes.

"Oh, yes, that's what I say," he went on stubbornly. "One head is good, but two are much better, but he did not meet another head with wits, and his wits went. Where did they go? I've forgotten the word." He went on, passing his hand before his eyes: "Oh yes, *spazieren.*"

"Wandering?"

"Oh yes, wandering, that's what I say. Well, his wits went

wandering and fell in such a deep hole that he lost himself. And yet he was a grateful and sensitive boy. Oh, I remember him very well, a little chap so high, left neglected by his father in the back yard, when he ran about without boots on his feet, and his little breeches hanging by one button.''

A note of feeling and tenderness suddenly came into the honest old man's voice. Fetyukovitch positively started, as though scenting something and caught at it instantly.

"Oh yes, I was a young man then. . . . I was . . . well, I was forty-five then, and had only just come here. And I was so sorry for the boy then; I asked myself why shouldn't I buy him a pound of . . . a pound of what? I've forgotten what it's called. A pound of what children are very fond of, what is it, what is it?'' The doctor began waving his hands again. "It grows on a tree and is gathered and given to everyone . . .''

"Apples?''

"Oh, no no. You have a dozen of apples, not a pound. . . . No, there are a lot of them, and all little. You put them in the mouth and crack.''

"Nuts?''

"Quite so, nuts, I say so.'' The doctor repeated in the calmest way as though he had been at no loss for a word. "And I bought him a pound of nuts, for no one had ever bought the boy a pound of nuts before. And I lifted my finger and said to him: 'Boy, *Gott der Vater.*' He laughed and said: '*Gott der Vater.*' . . . '*Gott der Sohn.*' He laughed again and lisped '*Gott der Sohn.*' '*Gott der heilige Geist.*' Then he laughed and said as best he could: '*Gott der heilige Geist.*' I went away, and two days after I happened to be passing, and he shouted to me of himself: 'Uncle, *Gott der Vater, Gott der Sohn,*' and he had only forgotten '*Gott der heilige Geist*'. But I reminded him of it and I felt very sorry for him again. But he was taken away, and I did not see him again. Twenty-three years passed I am sitting one morning in my study, a white-haired old man, when there walks into the room a blooming young man, whom I should never have recognised, but he held up his finger and said, laughing, '*Gott der Vater, Gott der Sohn,* and *Gott der heilige Geist.* I have just arrived and have come to thank you for that pound of nuts, for no one else ever bought me a pound of nuts; you are the only one that ever did.' And then I remembered my happy youth and the poor child in the yard, without boots on his feet, and my heart was touched and I said, 'You are a grateful young man, for you have remembered all your life the pound of nuts I bought you in your childhood.' And I embraced him and blessed him. And I shed tears. He laughed, but he shed tears, too . . . for the Russian often laughs when he ought to be weeping. But he did weep; I saw it. And now, alas! . . ."

"And I am weeping now, German, I am weeping now, too, you saintly man," Mitya cried suddenly.

In any case the anecdote made a certain favourable impression on the public. But the chief sensation in Mitya's favour was created by the evidence of Katerina Ivanovna, which I will describe directly. Indeed, when the witnesses *à décharge*, that is, called by the defence, began giving evidence, fortune seemed all at once markedly more favourable to Mitya, and what was particularly striking, this was a surprise even to the counsel for the defence. But before Katerina Ivanovna was called, Alyosha was examined, and he recalled a fact which seemed to furnish positive evidence against one important point made by the prosecution.

CHAPTER IV

FORTUNE SMILES ON MITYA

IT came quite as a surprise even to Alyosha himself. He was not required to take the oath, and I remember that both sides addressed him very gently and sympathetically. It was evident that his reputation for goodness had preceded him. Alyosha gave his evidence modestly and with restraint, but his warm sympathy for his unhappy brother was unmistakable. In answer to one question, he sketched his brother's character as that of a man, violent-tempered perhaps and carried away by his passions, but at the same time honourable, proud and generous, capable of self-sacrifice, if necessary. He admitted, however, that, through his passion for Grushenka and his rivalry with his father, his brother had been of late in an intolerable position. But he repelled with indignation the suggestion that his brother might have committed a murder for the sake of gain, though he recognised that the three thousand roubles had become almost an obsession with Mitya; that he looked upon them as part of the inheritance he had been cheated of by his father, and that, indifferent as he was to money as a rule, he could not even speak of. that three thousand without fury. As for the rivalry of the two "ladies", as the prosecutor expressed it—that is, of Grushenka and Katya—he answered evasively and was even unwilling to answer one or two questions altogether.

"Did your brother tell you, anyway, that he intended to kill your father?" asked the prosecutor. "You can refuse to answer if you think necessary," he added.

"He did not tell me so directly," answered Alyosha.

"How so? Did he indirectly?"

"He spoke to me once of his hatred for our father and his fear that at an extreme moment . . . at a moment of fury, he might perhaps murder him."

"And you believed him?"

"I am afraid to say that I did. But I never doubted that some higher feeling would always save him at the fatal moment, as it has indeed saved him, for it was not he killed my father," Alyosha said firmly, in a loud voice that was heard throughout the court.

The prosecutor started like a war-horse at the sound of a trumpet.

"Let me assure you that I fully believe in the complete sincerity of your conviction and do not explain it by or identify it with your affection for your unhappy brother. Your peculiar view of the whole tragic episode is known to us already from the preliminary investigation. I won't attempt to conceal from you that it is highly individual and contradicts all the other evidence collected by the prosecution. And so I think it essential to press you to tell me what facts have led you to this conviction of your brother's innocence and of the guilt of another person against whom you gave evidence at the preliminary inquiry."

"I only answered the questions asked me at the preliminary inquiry," replied Alyosha, slowly and calmly. "I made no accusation against Smerdyakov of myself."

"Yet you gave evidence against him?"

"I was led to do so by my brother Dmitri's words. I was told what took place at his arrest and how he had pointed to Smerdyakov before I was examined. I believe absolutely that my brother is innocent, and if he didn't commit the murder, then . . ."

"Then Smerdyakov? Why Smerdyakov? And why are you so completely persuaded of your brother's innocence?"

"I cannot help believing my brother. I know he wouldn't lie to me. I saw from his face he wasn't lying."

"Only from his face? Is that all the proof you have?"

"I have no other proof."

"And of Smerdyakov's guilt have you no proof whatever but your brother's word and the expression of his face?"

"No, I have no other proof."

The prosecutor dropped the examination at this point. The impression left by Alyosha's evidence on the public was most disappointing. There had been talk about Smerdyakov before the trial; someone had heard something, someone had pointed out something else; it was said that Alyosha had gathered together some extraordinary proofs of his brother's innocence and Smerdyakov's guilt, and after all there was nothing, no evidence except certain moral convictions so natural in a brother.

But Fetyukovitch began his cross-examination. On his asking Alyosha when it was that the prisoner had told him of his hatred for his father and that he might kill him, and whether he had heard it, for instance, at their last meeting before the catastrophe, Alyosha started as he answered, as though only just recollecting and understanding something.

"I remember one circumstance now which I'd quite forgotten myself. It wasn't clear to me at the time, but now . . ."

And, obviously only now for the first time struck by an idea, he recounted eagerly how, at his last interview with Mitya that evening under the tree, on the road to the monastery, Mitya had struck himself on the breast, "the upper part of the breast", and had repeated several times that he had a means of regaining his honour, that that means was here, here on his breast. "I thought, when he struck himself on the breast, he meant that it was in his heart," Alyosha continued, "that he might find in his heart strength to save himself from some awful disgrace which was awaiting him and which he did not dare confess even to me. I must confess I did think at the time that he was speaking of our father, and that the disgrace he was shuddering at was the thought of going to our father and doing some violence to him. Yet it was just then that he pointed to something on his breast, so that I remember the idea struck me at the time that the heart is not on that part of the breast, but below, and that he struck himself much too high, just below the neck, and kept pointing to that place. My idea seemed silly to me at the time, but he was perhaps pointing then to that little bag in which he had fifteen hundred roubles!"

"Just so," Mitya cried from his place. "That's right, Alyosha, it was the little bag I struck with my fist."

Fetyukovitch flew to him in hot haste entreating him to keep quiet, and at the same instant pounced on Alyosha. Alyosha, carried away himself by his recollection, warmly expressed his theory that this disgrace was probably just that fifteen hundred roubles on him, which he might have returnerd to Katerina Ivanovna as half of what he owed her, but which he had yet determined not to repay her and to use for another purpose—namely, to enable him to elope with Grushenka, if she consented.

"It is so, it must be so," exclaimed Alyosha, in sudden excitement. "My brother cried several times that half of the disgrace, half of it" (he said *half* several times), "he could free himself from at once, but that he was so unhappy in his weakness of will that he wouldn't do it . . . that he knew beforehand he was incapable of doing it!"

"And you clearly, confidently remember that he struck himself just on this part of the breast?" Fetyukovitch asked eagerly.

"Clearly and confidently, for I thought at the time, 'Why does he strike himself up there when the heart it lower down?' and the thought seemed stupid to me at the time . . . I remember it seeming stupid . . . it flashed through my mind. That's what brought it back to me just now. How could I have forgotten it till now? It was that little bag he meant when he said he had the means but wouldn't give back that fifteen hundred. And when he was arrested at Mokroe he cried out—I know, I was told it—that he considered it the most disgraceful act of his life that when he had the means of repaying Katerina Ivanovna half (half, note!) what he owed her, he yet could not bring himself to repay the money and preferred to remain a thief in her eyes rather than part with it. And what torture, what torture that debt has been to him!" Alyosha exclaimed in conclusion.

The prosecutor, of course, intervened. He asked Alyosha to describe once more how it had all happened, and several times insisted on the question, "Had the prisoner seemed to point to anything? Perhaps he had simply struck himself with his fist on the breast?"

"But it was not with his fist," cried Alyosha; "he pointed with his fingers and pointed here, very high up. . . . How could I have so completely forgotten it till this moment!"

The President asked Mitya what he had to say to the last witness's evidence. Mitya confirmed it, saying that he had been pointing to the fifteen hundred roubles which were on his breast, just below the neck, and that that was, of course, the disgrace,

381

"A disgrace I cannot deny, the most shameful act of my whole life," cried Mitya. "I might have repaid it and didn't repay it. I preferred to remain a thief in her eyes rather than give it back. And the most shameful part of it was that I knew beforehand I shouldn't give it back! You are right, Alyosha! Thanks, Alyosha!"

So Alyosha's cross-examination ended. What was important and striking about it was that one fact at least had been found, and even though this were only one tiny bit of evidence, a mere hint at evidence, it did go some little way towards proving that the bag had existed and had contained fifteen hundred roubles and that the prisoner had not been lying at the preliminary inquiry when he alleged at Mokroe that those fifteen hundred roubles were "his own". Alyosha was glad. With a flushed face he moved away to the seat assigned to him. He kept repeating to himself: "How was it I forgot? How could I have forgotten it? And what made it come back to me now?"

Katerina Ivanovna was called to the witness-box. As she entered something extraordinary happened in the court. The ladies clutched their lorgnettes and opera-glasses. There was a stir among the men: some stood up to get a better view. Everybody alleged afterwards that Mitya had turned "white as a sheet" on her entrance. All in black, she advanced modestly, almost timidly. It was impossible to tell from her face that she was agitated; but there was a resolute gleam in her dark and gloomy eyes. I may remark that many people mentioned that she looked particularly handsome at that moment. She spoke softly but clearly, so that she was heard all over the court. She expressed herself with composure, or at least tried to appear composed. The President began his examination discreetly and very respectfully, as though afraid to touch on "certain chords", and showing consideration for her great unhappiness. But in answer to one of the first questions Katerina Ivanovna replied firmly that she had been formerly betrothed to the prisoner "until he left me of his own accord . . ." she added quietly. When they asked her about the three thousand she had entrusted to Mitya to post to her relations, she said firmly: "I didn't give him the money simply to send it off. I felt at the time that he was in great need of money. . . . I gave him the three thousand on the understanding that he should post it within the month if he cared to. There was no need for him to worry himself about that debt afterwards."

I will not repeat all the questions asked her and all her

answers in detail. I will only give the substance of her
evidence.

"I was firmly convinced that he would send off that sum as
soon as he got money from his father," she went on. "I have
never doubted his disinterestedness and his honesty . . . his
scrupulous honesty . . . in money matters. He felt quite
certain that he would receive the money from his father, and
spoke to me several times about it. I knew he had a feud with
his father and have always believed that he had been unfairly
treated by his father. I don't remember any threat uttered by
him against his father. He certainly never uttered any such
threat before me. If he had come to me at that time, I should
have at once relieved his anxiety about that unlucky three
thousand roubles, but he had given up coming to see me . . .
and I myself was put in such a position . . . that I could not
invite him. . . . And I had no right, indeed, to be exacting as
to that money," she added suddenly, and there was a ring of
resolution in her voice. "I was once indebted to him for assistance in money for more than three thousand, and I took it,
although I could not at that time foresee that I should ever be
in a position to repay my debt."

There was a note of defiance in her voice. It was then
Fetyukovitch began his cross-examination.

"Did that take place not here but at the beginning of your
acquaintance?" Fetyukovitch suggested cautiously, feeling his
way, instantly scenting something favourable. I must mention
in parenthesis that, though Fetyukovitch had been brought
from Petersburg partly at the instance of Katerina Ivanovna
herself, he knew nothing about the episode of the five thousand
roubles given her by Mitya, and of her "bowing to the ground
to him". She concealed this from him and said nothing about
it, and that was strange. It may be pretty certainly assumed
that she herself did not know till the very last minute whether
she would speak of that episode in the court, and waited for the
inspiration of the moment.

"No, I can never forget those moments." She began telling
her story. She told everything, the whole episode that Mitya
had told Alyosha, and her bowing to the ground, and her reason.
She told about her father and her going to Mitya, and did not
in one word, in a single hint, suggest that Mitya had himself,
through her sister, proposed they should "send him Katerina
Ivanovna" to fetch the money. She generously concealed that
and was not ashamed to make it appear as though she had of

her own impulse run to the young officer, relying on something . . . to beg him for the money. It was something tremendous! I turned cold and trembled as I listened. The court was hushed, trying to catch each word. It was something unexampled. Even from such a self-willed and contemptuously proud girl as she was, such an extremely frank avowal, such sacrifice, such self-immolation, seemed incredible. And for what, for whom? To save the man who had deceived and insulted her and to help, in however small a degree, in saving him, by creating a strong impression in his favour. And, indeed, the figure of the young officer who, with a respectful bow to the innocent girl, handed her his last five thousand roubles—all he had in the world—was thrown into a very sympathetic and attractive light, but . . . I had a painful misgiving at heart! I felt that calumny might come of it later (and it did, in fact, it did). It was repeated all over the town afterwards with spiteful laughter that the story was perhaps not quite complete—that is, in the statement that the officer had let the young lady depart "with nothing but a respectful bow". It was hinted that something was here omitted.

"And even if nothing had been omitted, if this were the whole story," the most highly respected of our ladies maintained, "even then it's very doubtful whether it was creditable for a young girl to behave in that way, even for the sake of saving her father."

And can Katerina Ivanovna, with her intelligence, her morbid sensitiveness, have failed to understand that people would talk like that? She must have understood it, yet she made up her mind to tell everything. Of course, all these nasty little suspicions as to the truth of her story only arose afterwards and at the first moment all were deeply impressed by it. As for the judges and the lawyers, they listened in reverent, almost shamefaced silence to Katerina Ivanovna. The prosecutor did not venture upon even one question on the subject. Fetyukovitch made a low bow to her. Oh, he was almost triumphant! Much ground had been gained. For a man to give his last five thousand on a generous impulse and then for the same man to murder his father for the sake of robbing him of three thousand —the idea seemed too incongruous. Fetyukovitch felt that now the charge of theft, at least, was as good as disproved. "The case" was thrown into quite a different light. There was a wave of sympathy for Mitya. As for him. . . . I was told that once

or twice, while Katerina Ivanovna was giving her evidence, he
jumped up from his seat, sank back again, and hid his face in
his hands. But when she had finished, he suddenly cried in a
sobbing voice:

"Katya, why have you ruined me?" and his sobs were
audible all over the court. But he instantly restrained himself,
and cried again:

"Now I am condemned!"

Then he sat rigid in his place, with his teeth clenched and his
arms across his chest. Katerina Ivanovna remained in the
court and sat down in her place. She was pale and sat with her
eyes cast down. Those who were sitting near her declared that
for a long time she shivered all over as though in a fever.
Grushenka was called.

I am approaching the sudden catastrophe which was perhaps
the final cause of Mitya's ruin. For I am convinced, so is
everyone—all the lawyers said the same afterwards—that if
the episode had not occurred, the prisoner would at least have
been recommended to mercy. But of that later. A few words
first about Grushenka.

She, too, was dressed entirely in black, with her magnificent
black shawl on her shoulders. She walked to the witness-box
with her smooth, noiseless tread, with the slightly swaying gait
common in women of full figure. She looked steadily at the
President, turning her eyes neither to the right nor to the left.
To my thinking she looked very handsome at that moment, and
not at all pale, as the ladies alleged afterwards. They declared,
too, that she had a concentrated and spiteful expression. I
believe that she was simply irritated and painfully conscious of
the contemptuous and inquisitive eyes of our scandal-loving
public. She was proud and could not stand contempt. She was
one of those people who flare up, angry and eager to retaliate,
at the mere suggestion of contempt. There was an element of
timidity, too, of course, and inward shame at her own timidity,
so it was not strange that her tone kept changing. At one
moment it was angry, contemptuous and rough, and at another
there was a sincere note of self-condemnation. Sometimes she
spoke as though she were taking a desperate plunge; as though
she felt, "I don't care what happens, I'll say it. . . ." *Apropos*
of her acquaintance with Fyodor Pavlovitch, she remarked
curtly: "That's all nonsense, and was it my fault that he
would pester me?" But a minute later she added: "It was
all my fault. I was laughing at them both—at the old man and

385

at him, too—and I brought both of them to this. It was all on account of me it happened."

Samsonov's name came up somehow. "That's nobody's business," she snapped at once, with a sort of insolent defiance. "He was my benefactor; he took me when I hadn't a shoe to my foot, when my family had turned me out." The President reminded her, though very politely, that she must answer the questions directly, without going off into irrelevant details. Grushenka crimsoned and her eyes flashed.

The envelope with the notes in it she had not seen, but had only heard from "that wicked wretch" that Fyodor Pavlovitch had an envelope with notes for three thousand in it. "But that was all foolishness. I was only laughing. I wouldn't have gone to him for anything."

"To whom are you referring 'as that wicked wretch'?" inquired the prosecutor.

"The lackey, Smerdyakov, who murdered his master and hanged himself last night."

She was, of course, at once asked what ground she had for such a definite accusation; but it appeared that she, too, had no grounds for it.

"Dmitri Fyodorovitch told me so himself; you can believe him. The woman who came between us has ruined him; she is the cause of it all, let me tell you," Grushenka added. She seemed to be quivering with hatred, and there was a vindictive note in her voice.

She was again asked to whom she was referring.

"The young lady, Katerina Ivanovna there. She sent for me, offered me chocolate, tried to fascinate me. There's not much true shame about her, I can tell you that . . ."

At this point the President checked her sternly, begging her to moderate her language. But the jealous woman's heart was burning, and she did not care what she did.

"When the prisoner was arrested at Mokroe," the prosecutor asked, "everyone saw and heard you run out of the next room and cry out: 'It's all my fault. We'll go to Siberia together!' So you already believed him to have murdered his father?"

"I don't remember what I felt at the time," answered Grushenka. "Everyone was crying out that he had killed his father, and I felt that it was my fault, that it was on my account he had murdered him. But when he said he wasn't guilty, I believed him at once, and I believe him now and always shall believe him. He is not the man to tell a lie."

Fetyukovitch began his cross-examination. I remember that among other things he asked about Rakitin and the twenty-five roubles "you paid him for bringing Alexey Fyodorovitch Karamazov to see you."

"There was nothing strange about his taking the money," sneered Grushenka, with angry contempt. "He was always coming to me for money: he used to get thirty roubles a month at least out of me, chiefly for luxuries: he had enough to keep him without my help."

"What led you to be so liberal to Mr. Rakitin?" Fetyukovitch asked, in spite of an uneasy movement on the part of the President.

"Why, he is my cousin. His mother was my mother's sister. But he's always besought me not to tell anyone here of it, he is so dreadfully ashamed of me."

This fact was a complete surprise to everyone; no one in the town nor in the monastery, not even Mitya, knew of it. I was told that Rakitin turned purple with shame where he sat. Grushenka had somehow heard before she came into the court that he had given evidence against Mitya, and so she was angry. The whole effect on the public, of Rakitin's speech, of his noble sentiments, of his attacks upon serfdom and the political disorder of Russia, was this time finally ruined. Fetyukovitch was satisfied: it was another godsend. Grushenka's cross-examination did not last long and, of course, there could be nothing particularly new in her evidence. She left a very disagreeable impression on the public; hundreds of contemptuous eyes were fixed upon her, as she finished giving her evidence and sat down again in the court, at a good distance from Katerina Ivanovna. Mitya was silent throughout her evidence. He sat as though turned to stone, with his eyes fixed on the ground.

Ivan was called to give evidence.

CHAPTER V

A SUDDEN CATASTROPHE

I MAY note that he had been called before Alyosha. But the usher of the court announced to the President that, owing to an attack of illness or some sort of fit, the witness could not appear at the moment, but was ready to give his evidence as soon as he recovered. But no one seemed to have heard it and it only came out later.

His entrance was for the first moment almost unnoticed. The principal witnesses, especially the two rival ladies, had already been questioned. Curiosity was satisfied for the time; the public was feeling almost fatigued. Several more witnesses were still to be heard, who probably had little information to give after all that had been given. Time was passing. Ivan walked up with extraordinary slowness, looking at no one, and with his head bowed, as though plunged in gloomy thought. He was irreproachably dressed, but his face made a painful impression, on me at least: there was an earthy look in it, a look like a dying man's. His eyes were lustreless; he raised them and looked slowly round the court. Alyosha jumped up from his seat and moaned "Ah!" I remember that, but it was hardly noticed.

The President began by informing him that he was a witness not on oath, that he might answer or refuse to answer, but that, of course, he must bear witness according to his conscience, and so on and so on. Ivan listened and looked at him blankly, but his face gradually relaxed into a smile, and as soon as the President, looking at him in astonishment, finished, he laughed outright.

"Well, and what else?" he asked in a loud voice.

There was a hush in the court; there was a feeling of something strange. The President showed signs of uneasiness.

"You . . . are perhaps still unwell?" he began, looking everywhere for the usher.

"Don't trouble yourself, your excellency, I am well enough and can tell you something interesting," Ivan answered, with sudden calmness and respectfulness.

"You have some special communication to make?" the President went on, still mistrustfully.

Ivan looked down, waited a few seconds and, raising his head, answered, almost stammering:

"No . . . I haven't. I have nothing particular."

They began asking him questions. He answered, as it were reluctantly, with extreme brevity, with a sort of disgust which grew more and more marked, though he answered rationally. To many questions he answered that he did not know. He knew nothing of his father's money relations with Dmitri. "I wasn't interested in the subject," he added. Threats to murder his father he had heard from the prisoner. Of the money in the envelope he had heard from Smerdyakov.

"The same thing over and over again," he interrupted suddenly, with a look of weariness. "I have nothing particular to tell the court."

"I see you are unwell and understand your feelings," the President began.

He turned to the prosecutor and the counsel for the defence to invite them to examine the witness, if necessary, when Ivan suddenly asked in an exhausted voice:

"Let me go, your excellency, I feel very ill."

And with these words, without waiting for permission, he turned to walk out of the court. But after taking four steps he stood still, as though he had reached a decision, smiled slowly, and went back.

"I am like the peasant girl, your excellency . . . you know. How does it go? 'I'll stand up if I like, and I won't if I don't.' They were trying to put on her sarafan to take her to church to be married, and she said, 'I'll stand up if I like, and I won't if I don't.' . . . It's in some book about the peasantry."

"What do you mean by that?" the President asked severely.

"Why, this," Ivan suddenly pulled out a roll of notes. "Here's the money . . . the notes that lay in that envelope" (he nodded towards the table on which lay the material evidence) "for the sake of which our father was murdered. Where shall I put them? Mr. Superintendent, take them."

The usher of the court took the whole roll and handed it to the President.

"How could this money have come into your possession if it is the same money?" the President asked wonderingly.

"I got them from Smerdyakov, from the murderer, yesterday. . . . I was with him just before he hanged himself. It was he, not my brother, killed our father. He murdered him and I incited him to do it . . . Who doesn't desire his father's death?"

"Are you in your right mind?" broke involuntarily from the President.

"I should think I am in my right mind . . . in the same nasty mind as all of you . . . as all these . . . ugly faces." He turned suddenly to the audience. "My father has been murdered and they pretend they are horrified," he snarled, with furious contempt. "They keep up the sham with one another. Liars! They all desire the death of their fathers. One reptile

389

devours another. . . . If there hadn't been a murder, they'd have been angry and gone home ill-humoured. It's a spectacle they want! *Panem et circenses.* Though I am one to talk! Have you any water? Give me a drink for Christ's sake!" He suddenly clutched his head.

The usher at once approached him. Alyosha jumped up and cried, "He is ill. Don't believe him: he has brain fever." Katerina Ivanovna rose impulsively from her seat and, rigid with horror, gazed at Ivan. Mitya stood up and greedily looked at his brother and listened to him with a wild, strange smile.

"Don't disturb yourselves. I am not mad, I am only a murderer," Ivan began again. "You can't expect eloquence from a murderer," he added suddenly for some reason and laughed a queer laugh.

The prosecutor bent over to the President in obvious dismay. The two other judges communicated in agitated whispers. Fetyukovitch pricked up his ears as he listened: the hall was hushed in expectation. The President seemed suddenly to recollect himself.

"Witness, your words are incomprehensible and impossible here. Calm yourself, if you can, and tell your story . . . if you really have something to tell. How can you confirm your statement . . . if indeed you are not delirious?"

"That's just it. I have no proof. That cur Smerdyakov won't send you proofs from the other world . . . in an envelope. You think of nothing but envelopes—one is enough. I've no witnesses . . . except one, perhaps," he smiled thoughtfully.

"Who is your witness?"

"He has a tail, your excellency, and that would be irregular! *Le diable n'existe point!* Don't pay attention: he is a paltry, pitiful devil," he added suddenly. He ceased laughing and spoke, as it were, confidentially. "He is here somewhere, no doubt—under that table with the material evidence on it, perhaps. Where should he sit if not there? You see, listen to me. I told him I don't want to keep quiet, and he talked about the geological cataclysm . . . idiocy! Come, release the monster . . . he's been singing a hymn. That's because his heart is light! It's like a drunken man in the street bawling how 'Vanka went to Petersburg', and I would give a quadrillion quadrillions for two seconds of joy. You don't know me! Oh, how stupid all this business is! Come, take me instead of him! I didn't come for nothing. . . . Why, why is everything so stupid? . . ."

And he began slowly, and as it were reflectively, looking

round him again. But the court was all excitement by now. Alyosha rushed towards him, but the court usher had already seized Ivan by the arm.

"'What are you about?" he cried, staring into the man's face, and suddenly seizing him by the shoulders, he flung him violently to the floor. But the police were on the spot and he was seized. He screamed furiously. And all the time he was being removed, he yelled and screamed something incoherent.

The whole court was thrown into confusion. I don't remember everything as it happened. I was excited myself and could not follow. I only know that afterwards, when everything was quiet again and everyone understood what had happened, the court usher came in for a reprimand, though he very reasonably explained that the witness had been quite well, that the doctor had seen him an hour ago, when he had a slight attack of giddiness, but that, until he had come into the court, he had talked quite consecutively, so that nothing could have been foreseen—that he had, in fact, insisted on giving evidence. But before everyone had completely regained their composure and recovered from this scene, it was followed by another. Katerina Ivanovna had an attack of hysterics. She sobbed, shrieking loudly, but refused to leave the court, struggled, and besought them not to remove her. Suddenly she cried to the President:

"There is more evidence I must give at once . . . at once! Here is a document, a letter . . . take it, read it quickly, quickly! It's a letter from that monster . . . that man there, there!" she pointed to Mitya. "It was he killed his father, you will see that directly. He wrote to me how he would kill his father! But the other one is ill, he is ill, he is delirious!" she kept crying out, beside herself.

The court usher took the document she held out to the President, and she, dropping into her chair, hiding her face in her hands, began convulsively and noiselessly sobbing, shaking all over, and stifling every sound for fear she should be ejected from the court. The document she had handed up was that letter Mitya had written at the Metropolis tavern, which Ivan had spoken of as a "mathematical proof". Alas! its mathematical conclusiveness was recognised, and had it not been for that letter, Mitya might have escaped his doom or, at least, that doom would have been less terrible. It was, I repeat, difficult to notice every detail. What followed is still confused to my mind. The President must, I suppose, have at once passed on the document to the judges, the jury, and the lawyers on both sides. I only remember how they began examining the witness. On being gently asked by the President whether she had recovered sufficiently, Katerina Ivanovna exclaimed impetuously:

"I am ready, I am ready! I am quite equal to answering you," she added, evidently still afraid that she would somehow be prevented from giving evidence. She was asked to explain in detail what this letter was and under what circumstances she received it.

"I received it the day before the crime was committed, but he wrote it the day before that, at the tavern—that is, two days before he committed the crime. Look, it is written on some sort of bill!" she cried breathlessly. "He hated me at that time, because he had behaved contemptibly and was running after that creature . . . and because he owed me that three thousand. . . . Oh! he was humiliated by that three thousand on account of his own meanness! This is how it happened about that three thousand. I beg you, I beseech you, to hear me. Three weeks before he murdered his father, he came to me one morning. I knew he was in want of money, and what he wanted it for. Yes, yes—to win that creature and carry her off. I knew then that he had been false to me and meant to abandon me, and it was I, I, who gave him that money, who offered it to him on the pretext of his sending it to my sister in Moscow. And as I gave it him, I looked him in the face and said that he could send it when he liked, 'in a month's time would do'. How, how could he have failed to understand that I was practically telling him to his face, 'You want money to be false to me with your creature, so here's the money for you. I give it to you myself. Take it, if you have so little honour as to take it!' I wanted to prove what he was, and what happened? He took it, he took it, and squandered it with that creature in one night. . . . But he knew, he knew that I knew all about it. I assure you he understood, too, that I gave him that money to test him, to see whether he was so lost to all sense of honour as to take it from me. I looked into his eyes and he looked into mine, and he understood it all and he took it—he carried off my money!"

"That's true, Katya," Mitya roared suddenly, "I looked into your eyes and I knew that you were dishonouring me, and yet I took your money. Despise me as a scoundrel, despise me, all of you! I've deserved it!"

"Prisoner," cried the President, "another word and I will order you to be removed."

"That money was a torment to him," Katya went on with

impulsive haste. "He wanted to repay it me. He wanted to, that's true; but he needed money for that creature, too. So he murdered his father, but he didn't repay me, and went off with her to that village where he was arrested. There, again, he squandered the money he had stolen after the murder of his father. And a day before the murder he wrote me this letter. He was drunk when he wrote it. I saw it at once, at the time. He wrote it from spite, and feeling certain, positively certain, that I should never show it to anyone, even if he did kill him, or else he wouldn't have written it. For he knew I shouldn't want to avenge myself and ruin him! But read it, read it attentively—more attentively, please—and you will see that he had described it all in his letter, all beforehand, how he would kill his father and where his money was kept. Look, please, don't overlook that, there's one phrase there, 'I shall kill him as soon as Ivan has gone away'. So he thought it all out beforehand how he would kill him," Katerina Ivanovna pointed out to the court with venomous and malignant triumph. Oh! it was clear she had studied every line of that letter and detected every meaning underlining it. "If he hadn't been drunk, he wouldn't have written to me; but, look, everything is written there beforehand, just as he committed the murder after. A complete programme of it!" she exclaimed frantically.

She was reckless now of all consequences to herself, though, no doubt, she had foreseen them even a month ago, for even then, perhaps, shaking with anger, she had pondered whether to show it at the trial or not. Now she had taken the fatal plunge. I remember that the letter was read aloud by the clerk, directly afterwards, I believe. It made an overwhelming impression. They asked Mitya whether he admitted having written the letter.

"It's mine, mine!" cried Mitya. "I shouldn't have written it if I hadn't been drunk! . . . We've hated each other for many things, Katya, but I swear, I swear I loved you even while I hated you, and you didn't love me!"

He sank back on his seat, wringing his hands in despair. The prosecutor and counsel for the defence began cross-examining her, chiefly to ascertain what had induced her to conceal such a document and to give her evidence in quite a different tone and spirit just before.

"Yes, yes. I was telling lies just now. I was lying against my honour and my conscience, but I wanted to save him, for he has hated and despised me so!" Katya cried madly. "Oh, he has despised me so horribly, he has always despised me, and do you know, he has despised me from the very moment that I bowed down to him for that money. I saw that. . . . I felt it at once at the time, but for a long time I wouldn't believe it. How often I have read it in his eyes 'you came of yourself, though'. Oh, he didn't understand, he had no idea why I ran to him, he can suspect nothing but baseness, he judged me by himself, he thought everyone was like himself!'' Katya hissed furiously, in a perfect frenzy. "And he only wanted to marry me because I'd inherited a fortune, because of that, because of that! I always suspected it was because of that! Oh, he is a brute! He was always convinced that I should be trembling with shame all my life before him, because I went to him then, and that he had a right to despise me for ever for it, and so to be superior to me—that's why he wanted to marry me! That's so, that's all so! I tried to conquer him by my love—a love that knew no bounds. I even tried to forgive his faithlessness; but he understood nothing, nothing! How could be understand indeed? He is a monster! I only received that letter the next evening: it was brought me from the tavern—and only that morning, only that morning I wanted to forgive him everything, everything—even his treachery!''

The President and the prosecutor, of course, tried to calm her. I can't help thinking that they felt ashamed of taking advantage of her hysteria and of listening to such avowals. I remember hearing them say to her: "We understand how hard it is for you; be sure we are able to feel for you,'' and so on, and so on. And yet they dragged the evidence out of the raving, hysterical woman. She described at last with extraordinary clearness, which is so often seen, though only for a moment, in such overwrought states, how Ivan had been nearly driven out of his mind during the last two months trying to save "the monster and murderer'', his brother.

"He tortured himself,'' she exclaimed, "he was always trying to minimise his brother's guilt and confessing to me that he, too, had never loved his father, and perhaps desired his death himself. Oh, he has a tender, over-tender conscience! He tormented himself with his conscience! He told me everything, everything! He came every day and talked to me as his only friend. I have the honour to be his only friend!'' she cried suddenly with a sort of defiance, and her eyes flashed. "He had been twice to see Smerdyakov. One day he came to me and said: 'If it was not my brother, but Smerdyakov committed the murder' (for the legend was circulating everywhere that Smerdyakov had done it), 'perhaps I too am guilty, for Smerdyakov knew I didn't like my father and perhaps believed that I desired my father's death.' Then I brought out that letter and showed it him. He was entirely convinced that his brother had done it, and he was overwhelmed by it. He couldn't endure the thought that his own brother was a parricide! Only a week ago I saw that it was making him ill. During the last few days he has talked incoherently in my presence. I saw his mind was giving way. He walked about, raving; he was seen muttering in the streets. The doctor from Moscow, at my request, examined him the day before yesterday and told me that he was on the eve of brain fever—and all on his account, on account of this monster! And last night he learnt that Smerdyakov was dead! It was such a shock that it drove him out of his mind . . . and all through this monster, all for the sake of saving the monster!"

Oh, of course, such an outpouring, such an avowal is only possible once in a lifetime—at the hour of death, for instance, on the way to the scaffold! But it was in Katya's character, and it was such a moment in her life. It was the same impetuous Katya who had thrown herself on the mercy of a young profligate to save her father; the same Katya who had just before, in her pride and chastity, sacrificed herself and her maidenly modesty before all these people, telling of Mitya's generous conduct, in the hope of softening his fate a little. And now, again, she sacrificed herself; but this time it was for another, and perhaps only now—perhaps only at this moment—she felt and knew how dear that other was to her! She had sacrificed herself in terror for him, conceiving all of a sudden that he had ruined himself by his confession that it was he who had committed the murder, not his brother, she had sacrificed herself to save him, to save his good name, his reputation!

And yet one terrible doubt occurred to one—was she lying in her description of her former relations with Mitya?—that was the question. No, she had not intentionally slandered him when she cried that Mitya despised her for her bowing down to him! She believed it herself. She had been firmly convinced, perhaps ever since that bow, that the simple-hearted Mitya, who even then adored her, was laughing at her and despising her. She had loved him with an hysterical, "lacerated" love only from pride, from wounded pride, and that love was not like love, but more like revenge. Oh! perhaps that lacerated love would have grown into real love, perhaps Katya longed for nothing more than that, but Mitya's faithlessness had wounded her to the bottom of her heart, and her heart could not forgive him. The moment of revenge had come upon her suddenly, and all that had been accumulating so long and so painfully in the offended woman's breast burst out all at once and unexpectedly. She betrayed Mitya, but she betrayed herself, too. And no sooner had she given full expression to her feelings than the tension, of course, was over and she was overwhelmed with shame. Hysterics began again: she fell on the floor, sobbing and screaming. She was carried out. At that moment Grushenka, with a wail, rushed towards Mitya before they had time to prevent her.

"Mitya," she wailed, "your serpent has destroyed you! There, she has shown you what she is!" she shouted to the judges, shaking with anger. At a signal from the President they seized her and tried to remove her from the court. She wouldn't allow it. She fought and struggled to get back to Mitya. Mitya uttered a cry and struggled to get to her. He was overpowered.

Yes, I think the ladies who came to see the spectacle must have been satisfied—the show had been a varied one. Then I remember the Moscow doctor appeared on the scene. I believe the President had previously sent the court usher to arrange for medical aid for Ivan. The doctor announced to the court that the sick man was suffering from a dangerous attack of brain fever and that he must be at once removed. In answer to questions from the prosecutor and the counsel for defence he said that the patient had come to him of his own accord the day before yesterday and that he had warned him that he had such an attack coming on, but he had not consented to be looked after. "He was certainly not in a normal state of mind: he told me himself that he saw visions when he was awake, that he met several persons in the street, who were dead, and that Satan visited him every evening," said the doctor, in conclusion. Having given his evidence, the celebrated doctor withdrew. The letter produced by Katerina Ivanovna was added to the material proofs. After some deliberation, the judges decided to proceed with the trial and to enter both the unexpected pieces of evidence (given by Ivan and Katerina Ivanovna) on the protocol.

But I will not detail the evidence of the other witnesses, who only repeated and confirmed what had been said before, though all with their characteristic peculiarities. I repeat, all was brought together in the prosecutor's speech, which I shall quote immediately. Everyone was excited, everyone was electrified

by the late catastrophe, and all were awaiting the speeches for the prosecution and the defence with intense impatience. Fetyukovitch was obviously shaken by Katerina Ivanovna's evidence. But the prosecutor was triumphant. When all the evidence had been taken, the court was adjourned for almost an hour. I believe it was just eight o'clock when the President returned to his seat and our prosecutor, Ippolit Kirillovitch, began his speech.

CHAPTER VI

THE PROSECUTOR'S SPEECH. SKETCHES OF CHARACTER

IPPOLIT KIRILLOVITCH began his speech, trembling with nervousness, with cold sweat on his forehead, feeling hot and cold all over by turns. He described this himself afterwards. He regarded this speech as his *chef-d'œuvre*, the *chef-d'œuvre* of his whole life, as his swan-song. He died, it is true, nine months later of rapid consumption, so that he had the right, as it turned out, to compare himself to a swan singing his last song. He had put his whole heart and all the brain he had into that speech. And poor Ippolit Kirillovitch unexpectedly revealed that at least some feeling for the public welfare and "the eternal question" lay concealed in him. Where his speech really excelled was in its sincerity. He genuinely believed in the prisoner's guilt; he was accusing him not as an official duty only, and in calling for vengeance he quivered with a genuine passion "for the security of society". Even the ladies in the audience, though they remained hostile to Ippolit Kirillovitch, admitted that he made an extraordinary impression on them. He began in a breaking voice, but it soon gained strength and filled the court to the end of his speech. But as soon as he had finished, he almost fainted.

"Gentlemen of the jury," began the prosecutor, "this case has made a stir throughout Russia. But what is there to wonder at, what is there so peculiarly horrifying in it for us? We are so accustomed to such crimes! That's what is so horrible, that such dark deeds have ceased to horrify us. What ought to horrify us is that we are so accustomed to it, and not this or that isolated crime. What are the causes of our indifference, our lukewarm attitude to such deeds, to such signs of the times, ominous of an unenviable future? Is it our cynicism, is it the

premature exhaustion of intellect and imagination in a society
that is sinking into decay, in spite of its youth? Is it that our
moral principles are shattered to their foundatons, or is it, perhaps, a complete lack of such principles among us? I cannot
answer such questions; nevertheless they are disturbing, and
every citizen not only must but ought to be harassed by them.
Our newborn and still timid press has done good service to the
public already, for without it we should never have heard of the
horrors of unbridled violence and moral degradation which are
continually made known by the press, not merely to those who
attend the new jury courts established in the present reign, but
to everyone. And what do we read almost daily? Of things
beside which the present case grows pale, and seems almost
commonplace. But what is most important is that the majority
of our national crimes of violence bear witness to a widespread
evil, now so general among us that it is difficult to contend
against it.

"One day we see a brilliant young officer of high society, at
the very outset of his career, in a cowardly underhand way,
without a pang of conscience, murdering an official who had
once been his benefactor, and the servant girl, to steal his own
IOU and what ready money he could find on him; 'it will come
in handy for my pleasures in the fashionable world and for my
career in the future'. After murdering them, he puts pillows
under the head of each of his victims; he goes away. Next, a
young hero 'decorated for bravery' kills the mother of his chief
and benefactor, like a highwayman, and to urge his companions
to join him he asserts that 'she loves him like a son, and so will
follow all his directions and take no precautions'. Granted that
he is a monster, yet I dare not say in these days that he is
unique. Another man will not commit the murder, but will feel
and think like him, and is as dishonourable in soul. In silence,
alone with his conscience, he asks himself perhaps: 'What is
honour, and isn't the condemnation of bloodshed a prejudice?'

"Perhaps people will cry out against me that I am morbid,
hysterical, that it is monstrous slander, that I am exaggerating.
Let them say so—and heavens! I should be the first to rejoice
if it were so! Oh, don't believe me, think of me as morbid, but
remember my words; if only a tenth, if only a twentieth part
of what I say is true—even so it's awful! Look how our young
people commit suicide, without asking themselves Hamlet's
question what there is beyond, without a sign of such a question,
as though all that relates to the soul and to what awaits us

beyond the grave had long been erased in their minds and buried under the sands. Look at our vice, at our profligates. Fyodor Pavlovitch, the luckless victim in the present case, was almost an innocent babe compared with many of them. And yet we all knew him, 'he lived among us!' . . .

"Yes, one day perhaps the leading intellects of Russia and of Europe will study the psychology of Russian crime, for the subject is worth it. But this study will come later, at leisure, when all the tragic topsy-turvydom of to-day is further behind us, so that it's possible to examine it with more insight and more impartiality than I can do. Now we are either horrified or pretend to be horrified, though we really gloat over the spectacle, and love strong and eccentric sensations which tickle our cynical, pampered idleness. Or, like little children, we brush the dreadful ghosts away and hide our heads in the pillow so as to return to our sports and merriment as soon as they have vanished. But we must one day begin life in sober earnest, we must look at ourselves as a society; it's time we tried to grasp something of our social position, or at least to make a beginning in that direction.

"A great writer* of the last epoch, comparing Russia to a swift troika galloping to an unknown goal, exclaims: 'Oh, troika, birdlike troika, who invented thee?' and adds, in proud ecstasy, that all the peoples of the world stand aside respectfully to make way for the recklessly galloping troika to pass. That may be, they may stand aside, respectfully or no, but in my poor opinion the great writer ended his book in this way either in an access of childish and naïve optimism, or simply in fear of the censorship of the day. For if the troika were drawn by his heroes, Sobakevitch, Nozdryov, Tchitchikov, it could reach no rational goal, whoever might be driving it. And those were the heroes of an older generation, ours are worse specimens still . . ."

At this point Ippolit Kirillovitch's speech was interrupted by applause. The liberal significance of this simile was appreciated. The applause was, it's true, of brief duration, so that the President did not think it necessary to caution the public, and only looked severely in the direction of the offenders. But Ippolit Kirillovitch was encouraged; he had never been applauded before! He had been all his life unable to get a hearing, and now he suddenly had an opportunity of securing the ear of all Russia.

* Gogol is meant.

399

"What, after all, is this Karamazov family, which has gained such an unenviable notoriety throughout Russia?" he continued. "Perhaps I am exaggerating, but it seems to me that certain fundamental features of the educated class of to-day are reflected in this family picture—only, of course, in miniature, 'like the sun in a drop of water'. Think of that unhappy, vicious, unbridled old man, who has met with such a melancholy end, the head of a family! Beginning life of noble birth, but in a poor dependent position, through an unexpected marriage he came into a small fortune. A petty knave, a toady and buffoon, of fairly good, though undeveloped, intelligence, he was, above all, a moneylender, who grew bolder with growing prosperity. His abject and servile characteristics disappeared, his malicious and sarcastic cynicism was all that remained. On the spiritual side he was undeveloped, while his vitality was excessive. He saw nothing in life but sensual pleasure, and he brought his children up to be the same. He had no feelings for his duties as a father. He ridiculed those duties. He left his little children to the servants, and was glad to be rid of them, forgot about them completely. The old man's maxim was: *Après moi le déluge!* He was an example of everything that is opposed to civic duty, of the most complete and malignant individualism. 'The world may burn for aught I care, so long as I am all right,' and he was all right; he was content, he was eager to go on living in the same way for another twenty or thirty years. He swindled his own son and spent his money, his maternal inheritance, on trying to get his mistress from him. No, I don't intend to leave the prisoner's defence altogether to my talented colleague from Petersburg. I will speak the truth myself, I can well understand what resentment he had heaped up in his son's heart against him.

"But enough, enough of that unhappy old man; he has paid the penalty. Let us remember, however, that he was a father, and one of the typical fathers of to-day. Am I unjust, indeed, in saying that he is typical of many modern fathers? Alas! many of them only differ in not openly professing such cynicism, for they are better educated, more cultured, but their philosophy is essentially the same as his. Perhaps I am a pessimist, but you have agreed to forgive me. Let us agree beforehand, you need not believe me, but let me speak. Let me say what I have to say, and remember something of my words.

"Now for the children of this father, this head of a family. One of them is the prisoner before us, all the rest of my speech

400

will deal with him. Of the other two I will speak only cursorily.

"The elder is one of those modern young men of brilliant education and vigorous intellect, who has lost all faith in everything. He has denied and rejected much already, like his father. We have all heard him, he was a welcome guest in local society. He never concealed his opinions, quite the contrary in fact, which justifies me in speaking rather openly of him now, of course, not as an individual, but as a member of the Karamazov family. Another personage closely connected with the case died here by his own hand last night. I mean an afflicted idiot, formerly the servant, and possibly the illegitimate son of Fyodor Pavlovitch, Smerdyakov. At the preliminary inquiry, he told me with hysterical tears how the young Ivan Karamazov had horrified him by his spiritual audacity. 'Everything in the world is lawful according to him, and nothing must be forbidden in the future—that is what he always taught me.' I believe that idiot was driven out of his mind by this theory, though, of course, the epileptic attacks from which he suffered, and this terrible catastrophe, have helped to unhinge his faculties. But he dropped one very interesting observation. which would have done credit to a more intelligent observer, and that is, indeed, why I've mentioned it: 'If there is one of the sons that is like Fyodor Pavlovitch in character, it is Ivan Fyodorovitch.'

"With that remark I conclude my sketch of his character, feeling it indelicate to continue further. Oh, I don't want to draw any further conclusions and croak like a raven over the young man's future. We've seen to-day in this court that there are still good impulses in his young heart, that family feeling has not been destroyed in him by lack of faith and cynicism, which has come to him rather by inheritance than by the exercise of independent thought.

"Then the third son. Oh, he is a devout and modest youth, who does not share his elder brother's gloomy and destructive theory of life. He has sought to cling to the 'ideas of the people', or to what goes by that name in some circles of our intellectual classes. He clung to the monastery, and was within an ace of becoming a monk. He seems to me to have betrayed unconsciously, and so early, that timid despair which leads so many in our unhappy society, who dread cynicism and its corrupting influences, and mistakenly attribute all the mischief to European enlightenment, to return to their 'native soil', as they say, to the bosom, so to speak, of their mother earth, like frightened children, yearning to fall asleep on the withered bosom of their decrepit mother, and to sleep there for ever, only to escape the horrors that terrify them.

"For my part I wish the excellent and gifted young man every success; I trust that his youthful idealism and impulse towards the ideas of the people may never degenerate, as often happens, on the moral side into gloomy mysticism, and on the political into blind Chauvinism—two elements which are even a greater menace to Russia than the premature decay, due to mis-understanding and gratuitous adoption of European ideas, from which his elder brother is suffering."

Two or three people clapped their hands at the mention of Chauvinism and mysticism. Ippolit Kirillovitch had been, indeed, carried away by his own eloquence. All this had little to do with the case in hand, to say nothing of the fact of its being somewhat vague, but the sickly and consumptive man was overcome by the desire to express himself once in his life. People said afterwards that he was actuated by unworthy motives in his criticism of Ivan, because the latter had on one or two occasions got the better of him in argument, and Ippolit Kirillovitch, remembering it, tried now to take his revenge. But I don't know whether it was true. All this was only introduc-tory, however, and the speech passed to more direct considera-tion of the case.

"But to return to the eldest son," Ippolit Kirillovitch went on. "He is the prisoner before us. We have his life and his actions, too, before us; the fatal day has come and all has been brought to the surface. While his brothers seem to stand for 'Europeanism' and 'the principles of the people', he seems to represent Russia *as she is*. Oh, not all Russia, not all! God preserve us, if it were! Yet, here we have her, our mother Russia, the very scent and sound of her. Oh, he is spontaneous, he is a marvellous mingling of good and evil, he is a lover of culture and Schiller, yet he brawls in taverns and plucks out the beards of his boon companions. Oh, he, too, can be good and noble, but only when all goes well with him. What is more, he can be carried off his feet, positively carried off his feet by noble ideas, but only if they come of themselves, if they fall from heaven for him, if they need not be paid for. He dislikes paying for anything, but is very fond of receiving, and that's so with him in everything. Oh, give him every possible good in life (he couldn't be content with less), and put no obstacle in his way, and he will show that he, too, can be noble. He is not greedy, no, but he must have money, a great deal of money, and you will see how generously, with what scorn of filthy lucre, he will fling it all away in the reckless dissipation of one night. But if he has not money, he will show what he is ready to do to get it when he is in great need of it. But all this later. Let us take events in their chronological order.

"First, we have before us a poor abandoned child, running about the back-yard 'without boots on his feet', as our worthy and esteemed fellow-citizen, of foreign origin, alas! expressed it just now. I repeat it again, I yield to no one the defence of the criminal. I am here to accuse him, but to defend him also. Yes, I, too, am human! I, too, can weigh the influence of home and childhood on the character. But the boy grows up and becomes an officer; for a duel and other reckless conduct he is exiled to one of the remote frontier towns of Russia. There he led a wild life as an officer. And, of course, he needed money, money before all things, and so after prolonged disputes he came to a settlement with his father, and the last six thousand was sent him. A letter is in existence in which he practically gives up his claim to the rest and settles his conflict with his father over the inheritance on the payment of this six thousand.

"Then came his meeting with a young girl of lofty character and brilliant education. Oh, I do not venture to repeat the details; you have only just heard them. Honour, self-sacrifice were shown there, and I will be silent. The figure of the young officer, frivolous and profligate, doing homage to true nobility and a lofty ideal, was shown in a very sympathetic light before us. But the other side of the medal was unexpectedly turned to us immediately after in this very court. Again I will not venture to conjecture why it happened so, but there were causes. The same lady, bathed in tears of long-concealed indignation, alleged that he, he of all men, had despised her for her action, which, though incautious, reckless perhaps, was still dictated by lofty and generous motives. He, he, the girl's betrothed, looked at her with that smile of mockery, which was more insufferable from him than from anyone. And knowing that he had already deceived her (he had deceived her, believing that she was bound to endure everything from him, even treachery), she intentionally offered him three thousand roubles, and clearly, too clearly, let him understand that she was offering him money to deceive her. 'Well, will you take it or not, are you so lost to shame?' was the dumb question in her scrutinising eyes. He looked at her, saw clearly what was in her mind

403

(she's admitted here before you that he understood it all), appropriated that three thousand unconditionally, and squandered it in two days with the new object of his affections.

"What are we to believe then? The first legend of the young officer sacrificing his last farthing in a noble impulse of generosity and doing reverence to virtue, or this other revolting picture? As a rule, between two extremes one has to find the mean, but in the present case this is not true. The probability is that in the first case he was genuinely noble, and in the second as genuinely base. And why? Because he was of the broad Karamazov character—that's just what I am leading up to—capable of combining the most incongruous contradictions, and capable of the greatest heights and of the greatest depths. Remember the brilliant remark made by a young observer who has seen the Karamazov family at close quarters—Mr. Rakitin: 'The sense of their own degradation is as essential to these reckless, unbridled natures as the sense of their lofty generosity.' And that's true, they need continually this unnatural mixture. Two extremes at the same moment, or they are miserable and dissatisfied and their existence is incomplete. They are wide, wide as mother Russia; they include everything and put up with everything.

"By the way, gentlemen of the jury, we've just touched upon that three thousand roubles, and I will venture to anticipate things a little. Can you conceive that a man like that, on receiving that sum and in such a way, at the price of such shame, such disgrace, such utter degradation, could have been capable that very day of setting apart half that sum, that very day, and sewing it up in a little bag, and would have had the firmness of character to carry it about with him for a whole month afterwards, in spite of every temptation and his extreme need of it! Neither in drunken debauchery in taverns, nor when he was flying into the country, trying to get from God knows whom, the money so essential to him to remove the object of his affections from being tempted by his father, did he bring himself to touch that little bag! Why, if only to avoid abandoning his mistress to the rival of whom he was so jealous, he would have been certain to have opened that bag and to have stayed at home to keep watch over her, and to await the moment when she would say to him at last 'I am yours', and to fly with her far from their fatal surroundings.

"But no, he did not touch his talisman, and what is the reason he gives for it? The chief reason, as I have just said, was that when she would say 'I am yours, take me where you will', he might have the wherewithal to take her. But that first reason, in the prisoner's own words, was of little weight beside the second. 'While I have that money on me,' he said, 'I am a scoundrel, not a thief, for I can always go to my insulted betrothed, and, laying down half the sum I have fraudulently appropriated, I can always say to her, "You see, I've squandered half your money, and shown I am a weak and immoral man, and, if you like, a scoundrel" (I use the prisoner's own expressions), "but though I am a scoundrel, I am not a thief, for if I had been a thief, I shouldn't have brought you back this half of the money, but should have taken it as I did the other half!" A marvellous explanation! This frantic but weak man, who could not resist the temptation of accepting the three thousand roubles at the price of such disgrace, this very man suddenly develops the most stoical firmness, and carries about a thousand roubles without daring to touch it. Does that fit in at all with the character we have analysed? No, and I venture to tell you how the real Dmitri Karamazov would have behaved in such circumstances if he really had brought himself to put away the money.

"At the first temptation—for instance, to entertain the woman with whom he had already squandered half the money—he would have unpicked his little bag and have taken out some hundred roubles, for why should he have taken back precisely half the money, that is, fifteen hundred roubles; why not fourteen hundred? He could just as well have said then that he was not a thief, because he brought back fourteen hundred roubles. Then another time he would have unpicked it again and taken out another hundred, and then a third, and then a fourth, and before the end of the month he would have taken the last note but one, feeling that if he took back only a hundred it would answer the purpose, for a thief would have stolen it all. And then he would have looked at this last note, and have said to himself: 'It's really not worth while to give back one hundred; let's spend that, too!' That's how the real Dmitri Karamazov, as we know him, would have behaved. One cannot imagine anything more incongruous with the actual fact than this legend of the little bag. Nothing could be more inconceivable. But we shall return to that later."

After touching upon what had come out in the proceedings concerning the financial relations of father and son, and arguing again and again that it was utterly impossible, from the facts

known, to determine which was in the wrong, Ippolit Kirillovitch passed to the evidence of the medical experts in reference
to Mitya's fixed idea about the three thousand owing him.

CHAPTER VII

AN HISTORICAL SURVEY

'THE medical experts have striven to convince us that the
prisoner is out of his mind and, in fact, a maniac. I maintain that he is in his right mind, and that if he had not been,
he would have behaved more cleverly. As for his being a
maniac, that I would agree with, but only in one point, that is,
his fixed idea about the three thousand. Yet I think one might
find a much simpler cause than his tendency to insanity. For
my part I agree thoroughly with the young doctor who maintained that the prisoner's mental faculties have always been
normal, and that he has only been irritable and exasperated.
The object of the prisoner's continual and violent anger was not
the sum itself; there was a special motive at the bottom of it.
That motive is jealousy!"

Here Ippolit Kirillovitch described at length the prisoner's
fatal passion for Grushenka. He began from the moment when
the prisoner went to the "young person's" lodgings "to beat
her"—"I use his own expression," the prosecutor explained—
"but instead of beating her, he remained there, at her feet.
That was the beginning of the passion. At the same time the
prisoner's father was captivated by the same young person—
a strange and fatal coincidence, for they both lost their hearts
to her simultaneously, though both had known her before. And
she inspired in both of them the most violent, characteristically
Karamazov passion. We have her own confession: 'I was
laughing at both of them.' Yes, the sudden desire to make a
jest of them came over her, and she conquered both of them at
once. The old man, who worshipped money, at once set aside
three thousand roubles as a reward for one visit from her, but
soon after that, he would have been happy to lay his property
and his name at her feet, if only she would become his lawful
wife. We have good evidence of this. As for the prisoner, the
tragedy of his fate is evident; it is before us. But such was the
young person's 'game'. The enchantress gave the unhappy

406

young man no hope until the last moment, when he knelt before her, stretching out hands that were already stained with the blood of his father and rival. It was in that position that he was arrested. 'Send me to Siberia with him, I have brought him to this, I am most to blame,' the woman herself cried, in genuine remorse at the moment of his arrest.

"The talented young man, to whom I have referred already, Mr. Rakitin, characterised this heroine in brief and impressive terms: 'She was disillusioned early in life, deceived and ruined by a betrothed, who seduced and abandoned her. She was left in poverty, cursed by her respectable family, and taken under the protection of a wealthy old man, whom she still, however, considers as her benefactor. There was perhaps much that was good in her young heart, but it was embittered too early. She became prudent and saved money. She grew sarcastic and resentful against society.' After this sketch of her character it may well be understood that she might laugh at both of them simply from mischief, from malice.

"After a month of hopeless love and moral degradation, during which he betrayed his betrothed and appropriated money entrusted to his honour, the prisoner was driven almost to frenzy, almost to madness by continual jealousy—and of whom? His father! And the worst of it was that the crazy old man was alluring and enticing the object of his affection by means of that very three thousand roubles, which the son looked upon as his own property, part of his inheritance from his mother, of which his father was cheating him. Yes, I admit it was hard to bear! It might well drive a man to madness. It was not the money, but the fact that this money was used with such revolting cynicism to ruin his happiness!"

Then the prosecutor went on to describe how the idea of murdering his father had entered the prisoner's head, and illustrated his theory with facts.

"At first he only talked about it in taverns—he was talking about it all that month. Ah, he likes being always surrounded with company, and he likes to tell his companions everything, even his most diabolical and dangerous ideas; he likes to share every thought with others, and expects, for some reason, that those he confides in will meet him with perfect sympathy, enter into all his troubles and anxieties, take his part and not oppose him in anything. If not, he flies into a rage and smashes up everything in the tavern. [Then followed the anecdote about Captain Snegiryov.] Those who heard the prisoner began to think at last that he might mean more than threats, and that such a frenzy might turn threats into actions."

Here the prosecutor described the meeting of the family at the monastery, the conversations with Alyosha, and the horrible scene of violence when the prisoner had rushed into his father's house just after dinner.

"I cannot positively assert," the prosecutor continued, "that the prisoner fully intended to murder his father before that incident. Yet the idea had several times presented itself to him, and he had deliberated on it—for that we have facts, witnesses, and his own words. I confess, gentlemen of the jury," he added, "that till to-day I have been uncertain whether to attribute to the prisoner conscious premeditation. I was firmly convinced that he had pictured the fatal moment beforehand, but had only pictured it, contemplating it as a possibility. He had not definitely considered when and how he might commit the crime.

"But I was only uncertain till to-day, till that fatal document was presented to the court just now. You yourselves heard that young lady's exclamation: 'It is the plan, the programme of the murder!' That is how she defined that miserable, drunken letter of the unhappy prisoner. And, in fact, from that letter we see that the whole fact of the murder was premeditated. It was written two days before, and so we know now for a fact that, forty-eight hours before the perpetration of his terrible design, the prisoner swore that, if he could not get money next day, he would murder his father in order to take the envelope with the notes from under his pillow, as soon as Ivan had left. 'As soon as Ivan had gone away'—you hear that; so he had thought everything out, weighing every circumstance, and he carried it all out just as he had written it. The proof of pre-meditation is conclusive; the crime must have been committed for the sake of the money, that is stated clearly, that is written and signed. The prisoner does not deny his signature.

"I shall be told he was drunk when he wrote it. But that does not diminish the value of the letter, quite the contrary; he wrote when drunk what he had planned when sober. Had he not planned it when sober, he would not have written it when drunk. I shall be asked: 'Then why did he talk about it in taverns?' A man who premeditates such a crime is silent and keeps it to himself. Yes, but he talked about it before he had formed a plan, when he had only the desire, only the impulse to it. Afterwards he talked less about it. On the evening he wrote that letter at the Metropolis tavern, contrary to his custom he was silent, though he had been drinking. He did not play billiards, he sat in a corner, talked to no one. He did indeed turn a shopman out of his seat, but that was done almost unconsciously, because he could never enter a tavern without making a disturbance. It is true that after he had taken the final decision, he must have felt apprehensive that he had talked too much about his design beforehand, and that this might lead to his arrest and prosecution afterwards. But there was nothing for it; he could not take his words back, but his luck had served him before, it would serve him again. He believed in his star, you know! I must confess, too, that he did a great deal to avoid the fatal catastrophe. 'To-morrow I shall try and borrow the money from everyone,' as he writes in his peculiar language, 'and if they won't give it to me, there will be bloodshed.' ''

Here Ippolit Kirillovitch passed to a detailed description of all Mitya's efforts to borrow the money. He described his visit to Samsonov, his journey to Lyagavy. "Harassed, jeered at, hungry, after selling his watch to pay for the journey (though he tells us he had fifteen hundred roubles on him—a likely story!), tortured by jealousy at having left the object of his affections in the town, suspecting that she would go to Fyodor Pavlovitch in his absence, he returned at last to the town, to find, to his joy, that she had not been near his father. He accompanied her himself to her protector. (Strange to say, he doesn't seem to have been jealous of Samsonov, which is psychologically interesting.) Then he hastens to his ambush in the back gardens, and there learns that Smerdyakov is in a fit, that the other servant is ill—the coast is clear and he knows the 'signals'—what a temptation! Still he resists it; he goes off to a lady who has for some time been residing in the town, and who is highly esteemed among us, Madame Hohlakov. That lady, who had long watched his career with compassion, gave him the most judicious advice, to give up his dissipated life, his unseemly love-affair, the waste of his youth and vigour in pothouse debauchery, and to set off to Siberia to the gold-mines: 'that would be an outlet for your turbulent energies, your romantic character, your thirst for adventure'.''

After describing the result of this conversation and the moment when the prisoner learnt that Grushenka had not remained at Samsonov's, the sudden frenzy of the luckless man, worn out with jealousy and nervous exhaustion, at the thought that she had deceived him and was now with his father, Ippolit

Kirillovitch concluded by dwelling upon the fatal influence of chance. "Had the maid told him that her mistress was at Mokroe with her former lover, nothing would have happened. But she lost her head, she could only swear and protest her ignorance, and if the prisoner did not kill her on the spot, it was only because he flew in pursuit of his false mistress.

"But note, frantic as he was, he took with him a brass pestle. Why that? Why not some other weapon? But since he had been contemplating his plan and preparing himself for it for a whole month, he would snatch up anything like a weapon that caught his eye. He had realised for a month past that any object of the kind would serve as a weapon, so he instantly, without hesitation, recognised that it would serve his purpose. So it was by no means unconsciously, by no means involuntarily, that he snatched up that fatal pestle. And then we find him in his father's garden—the coast is clear, there are no witnesses, darkness and jealousy. The suspicion that she was there, with him, with his rival, in his arms, and perhaps laughing at him at that moment—took his breath away. And it was not mere suspicion, the deception was open, obvious. She must be there, in that lighted room, she must be behind the screen; and the unhappy man would have us believe that he stole up to the window, peeped respectfully in, and discreetly withdrew, for fear something terrible and immoral should happen. And he tries to persuade us of that, us, who understand his character, who know his state of mind at the moment, and that he knew the signals by which he could at once enter the house." At this point Ippolit Kirillovitch broke off to discuss exhaustively the suspected connection of Smerdyakov with the murder. He did this very circumstantially, and everyone realised that, although he professed to despise that suspicion, he thought the subject of great importance.

CHAPTER VIII

A TREATISE ON SMERDYAKOV

"TO begin with, what was the source of this suspicion?" Ippolit Kirillovitch began. "The first person who cried out that Smerdyakov had committed the murder was the prisoner himself at the moment of his arrest, yet from that time to this he had not brought forward a single fact to confirm the charge, nor the faintest suggestion of a fact. The charge is confirmed by three persons only—the two brothers of the prisoner and Madame Svyetlov. The elder of these brothers expressed his suspicions only to-day, when he was undoubtedly suffering from brain fever. But we know that for the last two months he has completely shared our conviction of his brother's guilt and .lid not attempt to combat that idea. But of that later. The younger brother has admitted that he has not the slightest fact to support his notion of Smerdyakov's guilt, and has only been led to that conclusion from the prisoner's own words and the expression of his face. Yes, that astounding piece of evidence has been brought forward twice to-day by him. Madame Svyetlov was even more astounding. 'What the prisoner tells you, you must believe; he is not a man to tell a lie.' That is all the evidence against Smerdyakov produced by these three persons, who are all deeply concerned in the prisoner's fate. And yet the theory of Smerdyakov's guilt has been noised about, has been and is still maintained. Is it credible? Is it conceivable?''

Here Ippolit Kirillovitch thought it necessary to describe the personality of Smerdyakov, ''who had cut short his life in a fit of insanity''. He depicted him as a man of weak intellect, with a smattering of education, who had been thrown off his balance by philosophical ideas above his level and certain modern theories of duty, which he learnt in practice from the reckless life of his master, who was also perhaps his father—Fyodor Pavlovitch; and, theoretically, from various strange philosophical conversations with his master's elder son, Ivan Fyodorovitch, who readily indulged in this diversion, probably feeling dull or wishing to amuse himself at the valet's expense. He spoke to me himself of his spiritual condition during the last few days at his father's house,'' Ippolit Kirillovitch explained; ''but others too have borne witness to it—the prisoner himself, his brother, and the servant Grigory—that is, all who knew him well.

''Moreover, Smerdyakov, whose health was shaken by his attacks of epilepsy, had not the courage of a chicken. 'He fell at my feet and kissed them,' the prisoner himself has told us, before he realised how damaging such a statement was to himself. 'He is an epileptic chicken,' he declared about him in his characteristic language. And the prisoner chose him for his confidant (we have his own word for it) and he frightened him into consenting at last to act as a spy for him. In that capacity he deceived his master, revealing to the prisoner the existence of the envelope with the notes in it and the signals by means of which he could get into the house. How could he help telling him, indeed? 'He would have killed me, I could see that he would have killed me,' he said at the inquiry, trembling and shaking even before us, though his tormentor was by that time arrested and could do him no harm. 'He suspected me at every instant. In fear and trembling I hastened to tell him every secret to pacify him, that he might see that I had not deceived him and let me off alive.' Those are his own words. I wrote them down and I remember them. 'When he began shouting at me, I would fall on my knees.'

"He was naturally very honest and enjoyed the complete confidence of his master, ever since he had restored him some money he had lost. So it may be supposed that the poor fellow suffered pangs of remorse at having deceived his master, whom he loved as his benefactor. Persons severely afflicted with epilepsy are, so the most skilful doctors tell us, always prone to continual and morbid self-reproach. They worry over their 'wickedness', they are tormented by pangs of conscience, often entirely without cause; they exaggerate and often invent all sorts of faults and crimes. And here we have a man of that type who had really been driven to wrong-doing by terror and intimidation.

"He had, besides, a strong presentiment that something terrible would be the outcome of the situation that was developing before his eyes. When Ivan Fyodorovitch was leaving for Moscow, just before the catastrophe, Smerdyakov besought him to remain, though he was too timid to tell him plainly what he feared. He confined himself to hints, but his hints were not understood.

"It must be observed that he looked on Ivan Fyodorovitch as a protector, whose presence in the house was a guarantee that no harm would come to pass. Remember the phrase in Dmitri Karamazov's drunken letter, 'I shall kill the old man, if only Ivan goes away'. So Ivan Fyodorovitch's presence seemed to everyone a guarantee of peace and order in the house.

"But he went away, and within an hour of his young master's departure Smerdyakov was taken with an epileptic fit. But that's perfectly intelligible. Here I must mention that Smerdyakov, oppressed by terror and despair of a sort, had felt during those last few days that one of the fits from which he had suffered before at moments of strain, might be coming

412

upon him again. The day and hour of such an attack cannot, of course, be foreseen, but every epileptic can feel beforehand that he is likely to have one. So the doctors tell us. And so, as soon as Ivan Fyodorovitch had driven out of the yard, Smerdyakov, depressed by his lonely and unprotected position, went to the cellar. He went down the stairs wondering if he would have a fit or not, and what if it were to come upon him at once? And that very apprehension, that very wonder, brought on the spasm in his throat that always precedes such attacks, and he fell unconscious into the cellar. And in this perfectly natural occurrence people try to detect a suspicion, a hint that he was shamming an attack *on purpose*. But, if it were on purpose, the question arises at once, what was his motive? What was he reckoning on? What was he aiming at? I say nothing about medicine: science, I am told, may go astray: the doctors were not able to discriminate between the counterfeit and the real. That may be so, but answer me one question: what motive had he for such a counterfeit? Could he, had he been plotting the murder, have desired to attract the attention of the household by having a fit just before?

"You see, gentlemen of the jury, on the night of the murder, there were five persons in Fyodor Pavlovitch's—Fyodor Pavlovitch himself (but he did not kill himself, that's evident); then his servant, Grigory, but he was almost killed himself; the third person was Grigory's wife, Marfa Ignatyevna, but it would be simply shameful to imagine her murdering her master. Two persons are left—the prisoner and Smerdyakov. But, if we are to believe the prisoner's statement that he is not the murderer, then Smerdyakov must have been, for there is no other alternative, no one else can be found. That is what accounts for the artful, astounding accusation against the unhappy idiot who committed suicide yesterday. Had a shadow of suspicion rested on anyone else, had there been any sixth person, I am persuaded that even the prisoner would have been ashamed to accuse Smerdyakov, and would have accused that sixth person, for to charge Smerdyakov with that murder is perfectly absurd.

"Gentlemen, let us lay aside psychology, let us lay aside medicine, let us even lay aside logic, let us turn only to the facts and see what the facts tell us. If Smerdyakov killed him, how did he do it? Alone or with the assistance of the prisoner? Let us consider the first alternative—that he did it alone. If he had killed him it must have been with some object, for some advantage to himself. But not having a shadow of the motive

413

that the prisoner had for the murder—hatred, jealousy, and so on—Smerdyakov could only have murdered him for the sake of gain, in order to appropriate the three thousand roubles he had seen his master put in the envelope. And yet he tells another person—and a person most closely interested, that is, the prisoner—everything about the money and the signals, where the envelope lay, what was written on it, what it was tied up with, and, above all, told him of those signals by which he could enter the house. Did he do this simply to betray himself, or to invite to the same enterprise one who would be anxious to get that envelope for himself? 'Yes,' I shall be told, 'but he betrayed it from fear.' But how do you explain this? A man who could conceive such an audacious, savage act, and carry it out, tells facts which are known to no one else in the world, and which, if he held his tongue, no one would ever have guessed!

"No, however cowardly he might be, if he had plotted such a crime, nothing would have induced him to tell anyone about the envelope and the signals, for that was as good as betraying himself beforehand. He would have invented something, he would have told some lie if he had been forced to give information, but he would have been silent about that. For, on the other hand, if he had said nothing about the money but had committed the murder and stolen the money, no one in the world could have charged him with murder for the sake of robbery, since no one but he had seen the money, no one but he knew of its existence in the house. Even if he had been accused of the murder, it could only have been thought that he had committed it from some other motive. But since no one had observed any such motive in him beforehand, and everyone saw, on the contrary, that his master was fond of him and honoured him with his confidence, he would, of course, have been the last to be suspected. People would have suspected first the man who had a motive, a man who had himself declared he had such motives, who had made no secret of it; they would, in fact, have suspected the son of the murdered man, Dmitri Fyodorovitch. Had Smerdyakov killed and robbed him, and the son been accused of it, that would, of course, have suited Smerdyakov. Yet are we to believe that, though plotting the murder, he told that son, Dmitri, about the money, the envelope, and the signals? Is that logical? Is that clear?

"When the day of the murder planned by Smerdyakov came, we have him falling downstairs in a *feigned* fit—with what object? In the first place that Grigory, who had been intending

414

to take his medicine, might put it off and remain on guard, seeing there was no one to look after the house, and, in the second place, I suppose, that his master, seeing that there was no one to guard him, and in terror of a visit from his son, might redouble his vigilance and precaution. And, most of all, I suppose that he, Smerdyakov, disabled by the fit, might be carried from the kitchen, where he always slept, apart from all the rest, and where he could go in and out as he liked, to Grigory's room at the other end of the lodge, where he was always put, shut off by a screen three paces from their own bed. This was the immemorial custom established by his master and the kind-hearted Marfa Ignatyevna, whenever he had a fit. There, lying behind the screen, he would most likely, to keep up the sham, have begun groaning, and so keeping them awake all night (as Grigory and his wife testified). And all this, we are to believe, that he might more conveniently get up and murder his master!

"But I shall be told that he shammed illness on purpose that he might not be suspected and that he told the prisoner of the money and the signals to tempt him to commit the murder, and when he had murdered him and had gone away with the money, making a noise, most likely, and waking people, Smerdyakov got up, am I to believe, and went in—what for? To murder his master a second time and carry off the money that had already been stolen? Gentlemen, are you laughing? I am ashamed to put forward such suggestions, but, incredible as it seems, that's just what the prisoner alleges. When he had left the house, had knocked Grigory down and raised an alarm, he tells us Smerdyakov got up, went in and murdered his master and stole the money! I won't press the point that Smerdyakov could hardly have reckoned on this beforehand, and have foreseen that the furious and exasperated son would simply come to peep in respectfully, though he knew the signals, and beat a retreat, leaving Smerdyakov his booty. Gentlemen of the jury, I put this question to you in earnest: When was the moment when Smerdyakov could have committed his crime? Name that moment, or you can't accuse him.

"But, perhaps, the fit was a real one, the sick man suddenly recovered, heard a shout, and went out. Well—what then? He looked about him and said: 'Why not go and kill the master?' And how did he know what had happened, since he had been lying unconscious till that moment? But there's a limit to these flights of fancy.

" 'Quite so,' some astute people will tell me, 'but what if they

415

were in agreement? What if they murdered him together and shared the money—what then?' A weighty question, truly! And the facts to confirm it are astounding. One commits the murder and takes all the trouble while his accomplice lies on one side shamming a fit, apparently to arouse suspicion in everyone, alarm in his master and alarm in Grigory. It would be interesting to know what motives could have induced the two accomplices to form such an insane plan.

"But perhaps it was not a case of active complicity on Smerdyakov's part, but only of passive acquiescence; perhaps Smerdyakov was intimidated and agreed not to prevent the murder, and foreseeing that he would be blamed for letting his master be murdered, without screaming for help or resisting, he may have obtained permission from Dmitri Karamazov to get out of the way by shamming a fit—'you may murder him as you like; it's nothing to me'. But as this attack of Smerdyakov's was bound to throw the household into confusion, Dmitri Karamazov could never have agreed to such a plan. I will waive that point, however. Supposing that he did agree, it would still follow that Dmitri Karamazov is the murderer and the instigator, and Smerdyakov is only a passive accomplice, and not even an accomplice but merely acquiesced against his will through terror.

"But what do we see? As soon as he is arrested the prisoner instantly throws all the blame on Smerdyakov, not accusing him of being his accomplice but of being himself the murderer. 'He did it alone,' he says. 'He murdered and robbed him. It was the work of his hands. Strange sort of accomplices who begin to accuse one another at once! And think of the risk for Karamazov. After committing the murder while his accomplice lay in bed, he throws the blame on the invalid, who might well have resented it and in self-preservation might well have confessed the truth. For he might well have seen that the court would at once judge how far he was responsible, and so he might well have reckoned that if he were punished, it would be far less severely than the real murderer. But in that case he would have been certain to make a confession, yet he has not done so. Smerdyakov never hinted at their complicity, though the actual murderer persisted in accusing him and declaring that he had committed the crime alone.

"What's more, Smerdyakov at the inquiry volunteered the statement that it was *he* who had told the prisoner of the envelope of notes and of the signals, and that, but for him, he

would have known nothing about them. If he had really been
a guilty accomplice, would he so readily have made this statement at the inquiry? On the contrary, he would have tried to
conceal it, to distort the facts or minimise them. But he was far
from distorting or minimising them. No one but an innocent
man, who had no fear of being charged with complicity, could
have acted as he did. And in a fit of melancholy arising from
his disease and this catastrophe he hanged himself yesterday.
He left a note written in his peculiar language: 'I destroy myself
of my own will and inclination so as to throw no blame on anyone.' What would it have cost him to add: 'I am the murderer,
not Karamazov'? But that he did not add. Did his conscience
lead him to suicide and not to avowing his guilt?

"And what followed? Notes for three thousand roubles were
brought into the court just now, and we were told that they
were the same that lay in the envelope now on the table before
us, and that the witness had received them from Smerdyakov
the day before. But I need not recall the painful scene, though
I will make one or two comments, selecting such trivial ones as
might not be obvious at first sight to everyone, and so may be
overlooked. In the first place, Smerdyakov must have given
back the money and hanged himself yesterday from remorse.
And only yesterday he confessed his guilt to Ivan Karamazov,
as the latter informs us. If it were not so, indeed, why should
Ivan Fyodorovitch have kept silence till now? And so, if he
has confessed, then why, I ask again, did he not avow the whole
truth in the last letter he left behind, knowing that the innocent
prisoner had to face this terrible ordeal the next day?

"The money alone is no proof. A week ago, quite by chance,
the fact came to the knowledge of myself and two other persons
in this court that Ivan Fyodorovitch had sent two five-per-cent.
coupons of five thousand each—that is, ten thousand in all—to
the chief town of the province to be changed. I only mention
this to point out that anyone may have money, and that it
can't be proved that these notes are the same as were in Fyodor
Pavlovitch's envelope.

"Ivan Karamazov, after receiving yesterday a communication of such importance from the real murderer, did not stir.
Why didn't he report it at once? Why did he put it all off
till morning? I think I have a right to conjecture why. His
health had been giving way for a week past: he had admitted
to a doctor and to his most intimate friends that he was suffering from hallucinations and seeing phantoms of the dead: he

was on the eve of the attack of brain fever by which he has been stricken down to-day. In this condition he suddenly heard of Smerdyakov's death, and at once reflected: 'The man is dead, I can throw the blame on him and save my brother. I have money. I will take a roll of notes and say that Smerdyakov gave them me before his death.' You will say that was dishonourable: it's dishonourable to slander even the dead, and even to save a brother. True, but what if he slandered him unconsciously? What if, finally unhinged by the sudden news of the valet's death, he imagined it really was so? You saw the recent scene: you have seen the witness's condition. He was standing up and was speaking, but where was his mind?

"Then followed the document, the prisoner's letter written two days before the crime and containing a complete programme of the murder. Why, then, are we looking for any other programme? The crime was committed precisely according to this programme, and by no other than the writer of it. Yes, gentlemen of the jury, it went off without a hitch! He did not run respectfully and timidly away from his father's window, though he was firmly convinced that the object of his affections was with him. No, that is absurd and unlikely! He went in and murdered him. Most likely he killed him in anger, burning with resentment, as soon as he looked on his hated rival. But having killed him, probably with one blow of the brass pestle, and having convinced himself, after careful search, that she was not there, he did not, however, forget to put his hand under the pillow and take out the envelope, the torn cover of which lies now on the table before us.

"I mention this fact that you may note one, to my thinking, very characteristic circumstance. Had he been an experienced murderer and had he committed the murder for the sake of gain only, would he have left the torn envelope on the floor as it was found, beside the corpse? Had it been Smerdyakov, for instance, murdering his master to rob him, he would have simply carried away the envelope with him, without troubling himself to open it over his victim's corpse, for he would have known for certain that the notes were in the envelope—they had been put in and sealed up in his presence—and had he taken the envelope with him, no one would ever have known of the robbery. I ask you, gentlemen, would Smerdyakov have behaved in that way? Would he have left the envelope on the floor?

"No, this was the action of a frantic murderer, a murderer who was not a thief and had never stolen before that day, who

418

snatched the notes from under the pillow, not like a thief stealing them, but as though seizing his own property from the thief
who had stolen it. For that was the idea which had become
almost an insane obsession in Dmitri Karamazov in regard to
that money. And pouncing upon the envelope, which he had
never seen before, he tore it open to make sure whether the
money was in it, and ran away with the money in his pocket,
even forgetting to consider that he had left an astounding piece
of evidence against himself in that torn envelope on the floor.
All because it was Karamazov, not Smerdyakov, he didn't
think, he didn't reflect, and how should he? He ran away; he
heard behind him the servant cry out; the old man caught him,
stopped him and was felled to the ground by the brass pestle.

"The prisoner, moved by pity, leapt down to look at him.
Would you believe it, he tells us that he leapt down out of pity,
out of compassion, to see whether he could do anything for him.
Was that a moment to show compassion? No; he jumped down
simply to make certain whether the only witness of his crime
were dead or alive. Any other feeling, any other motive would
be unnatural. Note that he took trouble over Grigory, wiped
his head with his handkerchief and, convincing himself he was
dead, he ran to the house of his mistress, dazed and covered
with blood. How was it he never thought that he was covered
with blood and would be at once detected? But the prisoner
himself assures us that he did not even notice that he was
covered with blood. That may be believed, that is very possible,
that always happens at such moments with criminals. On one
point they will show diabolical cunning, while another will
escape them altogether. But he was thinking at that moment
of one thing only—where was *she?* He wanted to find out at
once where she was, so he ran to her lodging and learnt an unexpected and astounding piece of news—she had gone off to
Mokroe to meet her first lover.

CHAPTER IX

THE GALLOPING TROIKA. THE END OF THE PROSECUTOR'S SPEECH

IPPOLIT KIRILLOVITCH had chosen the historical method
of exposition, beloved by all nervous orators, who find in its
limitations a check on their own eager rhetoric. At this moment

in his speech he went off into a dissertation on Grushenka's "first lover", and brought forward several interesting thoughts on this theme.

"Karamazov, who had been frantically jealous of everyone, collapsed, so to speak, and effaced himself at once before this first lover. What makes it all the more strange is that he seems to have hardly thought of this formidable rival. But he had looked upon him as a remote danger, and Karamazov always lives in the present. Possibly he regarded him as a fiction. But his wounded heart grasped instantly that the woman had been concealing this new rival and deceiving him, because he was anything but a fiction to her, because he was the one hope of her life. Grasping this instantly, he resigned himself.

"Gentlemen of the jury, I cannot help dwelling on this unexpected trait in the prisoner's character. He suddenly evinces an irresistible desire for justice, a respect for woman and a recognition of her right to love. And all this at the very moment when he had stained his hands with his father's blood for her sake! It is true that the blood he had shed was already crying out for vengeance, for, after having ruined his soul and his life in this world, he was forced to ask himself at that same instant what he was and what he could be *now* to her, to that being, dearer to him that his own soul, in comparison with that former lover who had returned penitent, with new love, to the woman he had once betrayed, with honourable offers, with the promise of a reformed and happy life. And he, luckless man, what could he give her now, what could he offer her?

"Karamazov felt all this, knew that all ways were barred to him by his crime and that he was a criminal under sentence, and not a man with life before him! This thought crushed him. And so he instantly flew to one frantic plan, which, to a man of Karamazov's character, must have appeared the one inevitable way out of his terrible position. That way out was suicide. He ran for the pistols he had left in pledge with his friend Perhotin and on the way, as he ran, he pulled out of his pocket the money, for the sake of which he had stained his hands with his father's gore. Oh, now he needed money more than ever. Karamazov would die, Karamazov would shoot himself and it should be remembered! To be sure, he was a poet and had burnt the candle at both ends ɩll his life. 'To her, to her! and there, oh there, I will give a feast to the whole world, such as never was before, that will be remembered and talked of long after! In the midst of shouts of wild merriment, reckless gypsy songs and dances I shall raise the glass and drink to the woman I adore and her new-found happiness! And then, on the spot, at her feet, I shall dash out my brains before her and punish myself! She will remember Mitya Karamazov sometimes, she will see how Mitya loved her, she will feel for Mitya!'

"Here we see in excess a love of effect, a romantic despair and sentimentality, and the wild recklessness of the Karamazovs. Yes, but there is something else, gentlemen of the jury, something that cries out in the soul, throbs incessantly in the mind, and poisons the heart unto death—that *something* is conscience, gentlemen of the jury, its judgment, its terrible torments! The pistol will settle everything, the pistol is the only way out! But *beyond*—I don't know whether Karamazov wondered at that moment 'What lies beyond', and whether Karamazov could, like Hamlet, wonder 'What lies beyond'. No, gentlemen of the jury, they have their Hamlets, but we still have our Karamazovs!"

Here Ippolit Kirillovitch drew a minute picture of Mitya's preparations, the scene at Perhotin's, at the shop, with the drivers. He quoted numerous words and actions, confirmed by witnesses, and the picture made a terrible impression on the audience. The guilt of this harassed and desperate man stood out clear and convincing, when the facts were brought together.

"What need had he of precaution? Two or three times he almost confessed, hinted at it, all but spoke out." (Then followed the evidence given by witnesses.) "He even cried out to the peasant who drove him, 'Do you know, you are driving a murderer!' But it was impossible for him to speak out, he had to get to Mokroe and there to finish his romance. But what was awaiting the luckless man? Almost from the first minute at Mokroe he saw that his invincible rival was perhaps by no means so invincible, that the toast to their new-found happiness was not desired and would not be acceptable. But you know the facts, gentlemen of the jury, from the preliminary inquiry. Karamazov's triumph over his rival was complete and his soul passed into quite a new phase, perhaps the most terrible phase through which his soul has passed or will pass.

"One may say with certainty, gentlemen of the jury," the prosecutor continued, "that outraged nature and the criminal heart bring their own vengeance more completely than any earthly justice. What's more, justice and punishment on earth positively alleviate the punishment of nature and are, indeed, essential to the soul of the criminal at such moments, as its salvation from despair. For I cannot imagine the horror and moral suffering of Karamazov when he learnt that she loved him, that for his sake she had rejected her first lover, that she was summoning him, Mitya, to a new life, that she was promising him happiness—and when? When everything was over for him and nothing was possible!

"By the way, I will note in parenthesis a point of importance for the light it throws on the prisoner's position at the moment. This woman, this love of his, had been till the last moment, till the very instant of his arrest, a being unattainable, passionately desired by him but unattainable. Yet why did he not shoot himself then, why did he relinquish his design and even forget where his pistol was? It was just that passionate desire for love and the hope of satisfying it that restrained him. Throughout their revels he kept close to his adored mistress, who was at the banquet with him and was more charming and fascinating to him than ever—he did not leave her side, abasing himself in his homage before her.

"His passion might well, for a moment, stifle not only the fear of arrest but even the torments of conscience. For a moment, oh, only for a moment. I can picture the state of mind of the criminal hopelessly enslaved by these influences—first, the influence of drink, of noise and excitement, of the thud of the dance and the scream of the song, and of her, flushed with wine, singing and dancing and laughing to him! Secondly, the hope in the background that the fatal end might still be far off, that not till next morning, at least, they would come and take him. So he had a few hours and that's much, very much! In a few hours one can think of many things. I imagine that he felt something like what criminals feel when they are being taken to the scaffold. They have another long, long street to pass down and at walking pace, past thousands of people. Then there will be a turning into another street and only at the end of that street the dread place of execution! I fancy that at the beginning of the journey the condemned man, sitting on his shameful cart, must feel that he has infinite life still before him. The houses recede, the cart moves on—oh, that's nothing, it's still far to the turning into the second street and he still looks boldly to right and to left at those thousands of callously curious people with their eyes fixed on him, and he still fancies that he is just such a man as they. But now the turning comes to the next street. Oh, that's nothing, nothing, there's still a whole street before him, and however many houses have been passed, he will still think there are many left. And so to the very end, to the very scaffold.

"This, I imagine, is how it was with Karamazov then. 'They've not had time yet,' he must have thought. 'I may still find some way out, oh, there's still time to make some plan of defence, and now, now—she is so fascinating!'

"His soul was full of confusion and dread, but he managed, however, to put aside half his money and hide it somewhere—I cannot otherwise explain the disappearance of quite half of the three thousand he had just taken from his father's pillow. He had been in Mokroe more than once before, he had caroused there for two days together already, he knew the old big house with all its passages and outbuildings. I imagine that part of the money was hidden in that house, not long before the arrest, in some crevice, under some floor, in some corner, under the roof. With what object? I shall be asked. Why, the catastrophe may take place at once, of course; he hadn't yet considered how to meet it, he hadn't the time, his head was throbbing and his heart was with *her*, but money—money was indispensable in any case! With money a man is always a man. Perhaps such foresight at such a moment may strike you as unnatural? But he assures us himself that a month before, at a critical and exciting moment, he had halved his money and sewn it up in a little bag. And though that was not true, as we shall prove directly, it shows the idea was a familiar one to Karamazov, he had contemplated it. What's more, when he declared at the inquiry that he had put fifteen hundred roubles in a bag (which never existed) he may have invented that little bag on the inspiration of the moment, because he had two hours before divided his money and hidden half of it at Mokroe till morning, in case of emergency, simply not to have it on himself. Two extremes, gentlemen of the jury, remember that Karamazov can contemplate two extremes and both at once.

"We have looked in the house, but we haven't found the money. It may still be there or it may have disappeared next day and be in the prisoner's hands now. In any case, he was at her side, on his knees before her, she was lying on the bed, he had his hands stretched out to her and he had so entirely forgotten everything that he did not even hear the men coming to arrest him. He hadn't time to prepare any line of defence in his mind. He was caught unawares and confronted with his judges, the arbiters of his destiny.

"Gentlemen of the jury, there are moments in the execution

of our duties when it is terrible for us to face a man, terrible on his account, too! The moments of contemplating that animal fear, when the criminal sees that all is lost, but still struggles, still means to struggle, the moments when every instinct of self-preservation rises up in him at once and he looks at you with questioning and suffering eyes, studies you, your face, your thoughts, uncertain on which side you will strike, and his distracted mind frames thousands of plans in an instant, but he is still afraid to speak, afraid of giving himself away! This purgatory of the spirit, this animal thirst for self-preservation, these humiliating moments of the human soul, are awful, and sometimes arouse horror and compassion for the criminal even in the lawyer. And this was what we all witnessed then.

"At first he was thunderstruck and in his terror dropped some very compromising phrases. 'Blood! I've deserved it!' But he quickly restrained himself. He had not prepared what he was to say, what answer he was to make, he had nothing but a bare denial ready. 'I am not guilty of my father's death.' That was his fence for the moment and behind it he hoped to throw up a barricade of some sort. His first compromising exclamations he hastened to explain by declaring that he was responsible for the death of the servant Grigory only. 'Of that bloodshed I am guilty, but who has killed my father, gentlemen, who has killed him? Who can have killed him, *if not I?*' Do you hear, he asked us that, us, who had come to ask him that question! Do you hear that phrase uttered with such premature haste—'if not I'—the animal cunning, the naïveté, the Karamazov impatience of it? 'I didn't kill him and you mustn't think I did! I wanted to kill him, gentlemen, I wanted to kill him,' he hastens to admit (he was in a hurry, in a terrible hurry), 'but still I am not guilty, it is not I murdered him.' He concedes to us that he wanted to murder him, as though to say: 'You can see for yourselves how truthful I am, so you'll believe all the sooner that I didn't murder him.' Oh, in such cases the criminal is often amazingly shallow and credulous.

"At that point one of the lawyers asked him, as it were incidentally, the most simple question, 'Wasn't it Smerdyakov killed him?' Then, as we expected, he was horribly angry at our having anticipated him and caught him unawares, before he had time to pave the way to choose and snatch the moment when it would be most natural to bring in Smerdyakov's name. He rushed at once to the other extreme, as he always does, and began to assure us that Smerdyakov could not have killed him, was not capable of it. But don't believe him, that was only his cunning; he didn't really give up the idea of Smerdyakov; on the contrary, he meant to bring him forward again; for, indeed, he had no one else to bring forward, but he would do that later, because for the moment that line was spoiled for him. He would bring him forward perhaps next day, or even a few days later, choosing an opportunity to cry out to us, 'You know I was more sceptical about Smerdyakov than you, you remember that yourselves, but now I am convinced. He killed him, he must have done!' And for the present he falls back upon a gloomy and irritable denial. Impatience and anger prompted him, however, to the most inept and incredible explanation of how he looked into his father's window and how he respectfully withdrew. The worst of it was that he was unaware of the position of affairs, of the evidence given by Grigory.

"We proceeded to search him. The search angered, but encouraged him, the whole three thousand had not been found on him, only half of it. And no doubt only at that moment of angry silence, the fiction of the little bag first occurred to him. No doubt he was conscious himself of the improbability of the story and strove painfully to make it sound more likely, to weave it into a romance that would sound plausible. In such cases the first duty, the chief task of the investigating lawyers, is to prevent the criminal being prepared, to pounce upon him unexpectedly so that he may blurt out his cherished ideas in all their simplicity, improbability and inconsistency. The criminal can only be made to speak by the sudden and apparently incidental communication of some new fact, of some circumstance of great importance in the case, of which he had no previous idea and could not have foreseen. We had such a fact in readiness—that was Grigory's evidence about the open door through which the prisoner had run out. He had completely forgotten about that door and had not even suspected that Grigory could have seen it.

"The effect of it was amazing. He leapt up and shouted to us, 'Then Smerdyakov murdered him, it was Smerdyakov!' and so betrayed the basis of the defence he was keeping back, and betrayed it in its most improbable shape, for Smerdyakov could only have committed the murder after he had knocked Grigory down and run away. When we told him that Grigory saw the door was open before he fell down, and had heard Smerdyakov behind the screen as he came out of his bedroom —Karamazov was positively crushed. My esteemed and witty

425

colleague, Nikolay Parfenovitch, told me afterwards that he was almost moved to tears at the sight of him. And to improve matters, the prisoner hastened to tell us about the much-talked-of little bag—so be it, you shall hear this romance!

"Gentlemen of the jury, I have told you already why I consider this romance not only an absurdity but the most improbable invention that could have been brought forward in the circumstances. If one tried for a bet to invent the most unlikely story, one could hardly find anything more incredible. The worst of such stories is that the triumphant romancers can always be put to confusion and crushed by the very details in which real life is so rich and which these unhappy and involuntary story-tellers neglect as insignificant trifles. Oh, they have no thought to spare for such details, their minds are concentrated on their grand invention as a whole and fancy anyone daring to pull them up for a trifle! But that's how they are caught. The prisoner was asked the question, 'Where did you get the stuff for your little bag and who made it for you?' 'I made it myself.' 'And where did you get the linen?' The prisoner was positively offended, he thought it almost insulting to ask him such a trivial question, and would you believe it, his resentment was genuine! But they are all like that. 'I tore it off my shirt.' 'Then we shall find that shirt among your linen to-morrow, with a piece torn off.' And only fancy, gentlemen of the jury, if we really had found that torn shirt (and how could we have failed to find it in his chest of drawers or trunk?) that would have been a fact, a material fact in support of his statement! But he was incapable of that reflection. 'I don't remember, it may not have been off my shirt, I sewed it up in one of my landlady's caps.' 'What sort of a cap?' 'It was an old cotton rag of hers lying about.' 'And do you remember that clearly?' 'No, I don't.' And he was angry, very angry, and yet imagine not remembering it! At the most terrible moments of man's life, for instance when he is being led to execution, he remembers just such trifles. He will forget anything but some green roof that has flashed past him on the road, or a jackdaw on a cross—that he will remember. He concealed the making of that little bag from his household, he must have remembered his humiliating fear that someone might come in and find him needle in hand, how at the slightest sound he slipped behind the screen (there is a screen in his lodgings).

"But, gentlemen of the jury, why do I tell you all this, all these details, trifles?" cried Ippolit Kirillovitch suddenly. "Just because the prisoner still persists in these absurdities to this moment. He has not explained anything since that fatal night two months ago, he has not added one actual illuminating fact to his former fantastic statements; all those are trivialities. 'You must believe it on my honour.' Oh, we are glad to believe it, we are eager to believe it, even if only on his word of honour! Are we jackals thirsting for human blood? Show us a single fact in the prisoner's favour and we shall rejoice; but let it be a substantial, real fact, and not a conclusion drawn from the prisoner's expression by his own brother, or that when he beat himself on the breast he must have meant to point to the little bag, in the darkness, too. We shall rejoice at the new fact, we shall be the first to repudiate our charge, we shall hasten to repudiate it. But now justice cries out and we persist, we cannot repudiate anything."

Ippolit Kirillovitch passed to his final peroration. He looked as though he were in a fever, he spoke of the blood that cried for vengeance, the blood of the father murdered by his son, with the base motive of robbery! He pointed to the tragic and glaring consistency of the facts.

"And whatever you may hear from the talented and celebrated counsel for the defence," Ippolit Kirillovitch could not resist adding, "whatever eloquent and touching appeals may be made to your sensibilities, remember that at this moment you are in a temple of justice. Remember that you are the champions of our justice, the champions of our holy Russia, of her principles, her family, everything that she holds sacred! Yes, you represent Russia here at this moment, and your verdict will be heard not in this hall only but will re-echo throughout the whole of Russia, and all Russia will hear you, as her champions and her judges, and she will be encouraged or disheartened by your verdict. Do not disappoint Russia and her expectations. Our fatal troika dashes on in her headlong flight perhaps to destruction and in all Russia for long past men have stretched out imploring hands and called a halt to its furious reckless course. And if other nations stand aside from that troika that may be, not from respect, as the poet would fain believe, but simply from horror. From horror, perhaps from disgust. And well it is that they stand aside, but, maybe, they will cease one day to do so and will form a firm wall confronting the hurrying apparition and will check the frenzied rush of our lawlessness, for the sake of their own safety, enlightenment and civilisation. Already we have heard voices of alarm from Europe, they already begin to sound. Do not tempt them! Do not heap up their growing hatred by a sentence justifying the murder of a father by his son!"

Though Ippolit Kirillovitch was genuinely moved, he wound up his speech with this rhetorical appeal—and the effect produced by him was extraordinary. When he had finished his speech, he went out hurriedly and, as I have mentioned before, almost fainted in the adjoining room. There was no applause in the court, but serious persons were pleased. The ladies were not so well satisfied, though even they were pleased with his eloquence, especially as they had no apprehensions as to the upshot of the trial and had full trust in Fetyukovitch. "He will speak at last and of course carry all before him."

Everyone looked at Mitya; he sat silent through the whole of the prosecutor's speech, clenching his teeth, with his hands clasped, and his head bowed. Only from time to time he raised his head and listened, especially when Grushenka was spoken of. When the prosecutor mentioned Rakitin's opinion of her, a smile of contempt and anger passed over his face and he murmured rather audibly: "The Bernards!" When Ippolit Kirillovitch described how he had questioned and tortured him at Mokroe, Mitya raised his head and listened with intense curiosity. At one point he seemed about to jump up and cry out, but controlled himself and only shrugged his shoulders disdainfully. People talked afterwards of the end of the speech, of the prosecutor's feat in examining the prisoner at Mokroe and jeered at Ippolit Kirillovitch. "The man could not resist boasting of his cleverness," they said.

The court was adjourned, but only for a short interval, a quarter of an hour or twenty minutes at most. There was a hum of conversation and exclamations in the audience. I remember some of them.

"A weighty speech," a gentleman in one group observed gravely.

"He brought in too much psychology," said another voice.

"But it was all true, the absolute truth!"

"Yes, he is first-rate at it."

"He summed it all up."

"Yes, he summed us up, too," chimed in another voice. "Do you remember, at the beginning of his speech, making out we were all like Fyodor Pavlovitch?"

"And at the end, too. But that was all rot."

"And obscure too."

428

"He was a little too much carried away."

"It's unjust, it's unjust."

"No, it was smartly done, anyway. He's had long to wait, but he's had his say, ha-ha!"

"What will the counsel for the defence say?"

In another group I heard:

"He had no business to make a thrust at the Petersburg man like that; 'appealing to your sensibilities'—do you remember?"

"Yes, that was awkward of him."

"He was in too great a hurry."

"He is a nervous man."

"We laugh, but what must the prisoner be feeling?"

"Yes, what must it be for Mitya?"

In a third group:

"What lady is that, the fat one, with the lorgnette, sitting at the end?"

"She is a general's wife, divorced, I know her."

"'That's why she has the lorgnette."

"She is not good for much."

"Oh no, she is a piquante little woman."

"Two places beyond her there is a little fair woman, she is prettier."

"They caught him smartly at Mokroe, didn't they, eh?"

"Oh, it was smart enough. We've heard it before, how often he has told the story at people's houses!"

"And he couldn't resist doing it now. That's vanity."

"He is a man with a grievance, he-he!"

"Yes, and quick to take offence. And there was too much rhetoric, such long sentences."

"Yes, he tries to alarm us, he kept trying to alarm us. Do you remember about the troika? Something about 'They have Hamlets, but we have, so far, only Karamazovs!' That was cleverly said!"

"That was to propitiate the Liberals. He is afraid of them."

"Yes, and he is afraid of the lawyer, too."

"Yes, what will Fetyukovitch say?"

"Whatever he says, he won't get round our peasants."

"Don't you think so?"

A fourth group:

"What he said about the troika was good, that piece about the other nations."

"And that was true what he said about other nations not standing it."

"What do you mean?"

"Why, in the English Parliament a Member got up last week and speaking about the Nihilists asked the Ministry whether it was not high time to intervene, to educate this barbarous people. Ippolit was thinking of him, I know he was. He was talking about that last week."

"Not an easy job."

"Not an easy job? Why not?"

"Why, we'd shut up Kronstadt and not let them have any corn. Where would they get it?"

"In America. They get it from America now."

"Nonsense!"

But the bell rang, all rushed to their places. Fetyukovitch mounted the tribune.

CHAPTER X

THE SPEECH FOR THE DEFENCE. AN ARGUMENT THAT CUTS BOTH WAYS

ALL was hushed as the first words of the famous orator rang out. The eyes of the audience were fastened upon him. He began very simply and directly, with an air of conviction, but not the slightest trace of conceit. He made no attempt at eloquence, at pathos, or emotional phrases. He was like a man speaking in a circle of intimate and sympathetic friends. His voice was a fine one, sonorous and sympathetic, and there was something genuine and simple in the very sound of it. But everyone realised at once that the speaker might suddenly rise to genuine pathos and "pierce the heart with untold power". His language was perhaps more irregular than Ippolit Kirillovitch's, but he spoke without long phrases, and, indeed, with more precision. One thing did not please the ladies: he kept bending forward, especially at the beginning of his speech, not exactly bowing but as though he were about to dart at his listeners, bending his long spine in half, as though there were a spring in the middle that enabled him to bend almost at right angles.

At the beginning of his speech he spoke rather disconnectedly, without system, one may say, dealing with facts separately, though, at the end, these facts formed a whole. His speech might be divided into two parts, the first consisting of criticism in refutation of the charge, sometimes malicious and sarcastic. But in the second half he suddenly changed his tone, and even his manner, and at once rose to pathos. The audience seemed on the look-out for it, and quivered with enthusiasm.

He went straight to the point, and began by saying that although he practised in Petersburg, he had more than once visited provincial towns to defend prisoners of whose innocence he had a conviction or at least a preconceived idea. "That is what has happened to me in the present case," he explained. "From the very first accounts in the newspapers I was struck by something which strongly prepossessed me in the prisoner's favour. What interested me most was a fact which often occurs in legal practice, but rarely, I think, in such an extreme and peculiar form as in the present case. I ought to formulate that peculiarity only at the end of my speech, but I will do so at the very beginning, for it is my weakness to go to work directly, not keeping my effects in reserve and economising my material. That may be imprudent on my part, but at least it's sincere. What I have in my mind is this: there is an overwhelming chain of evidence against the prisoner and at the same time not one fact that will stand criticism, if it is examined separately. As I followed the case more closely in the papers my idea was more and more confirmed, and I suddenly received from the prisoner's relatives a request to undertake his defence. I at once hurried here, and here I became completely convinced. It was to break down this terrible chain of facts, and to show that each piece of evidence taken separately was unproved and fantastic, that I undertook the case."

So Fetyukovitch began.

"Gentlemen of the jury," he suddenly protested, "I am new to this district. I have no preconceived ideas. The prisoner, a man of turbulent and unbridled temper, has not insulted me. But he has insulted perhaps hundreds of persons in this town, and so prejudiced many people against him beforehand. Of course I recognise that the moral sentiment of local society is justly excited against him. The prisoner is of turbulent and violent temper. Yet he was received in society here; he was even welcome in the family of my talented friend, the prosecutor."

(N.B. At these words there were two or three laughs in the audience, quickly suppressed, but noticed by all. All of us knew that the prosecutor received Mitya against his will, solely because he had somehow interested his wife—a lady of the highest virtue and moral worth, but fanciful, capricious, and fond of opposing her husband, especially in trifles. Mitya's visits, however, had not been frequent.)

"Nevertheless I venture to suggest," Fetyukovitch continued, "that in spite of his independent mind and just character, my opponent may have formed a mistaken prejudice against my unfortunate client. Oh, that is so natural; the unfortunate man has only too well deserved such prejudice. Outraged morality, and still more outraged taste, is often relentless. We have, in the talented prosecutor's speech, heard a stern analysis of the prisoner's character and conduct, and his severe critical attitude to the case was evident. And, what's more, he went into psychological subtleties into which he could not have entered if he had the least conscious and malicious prejudice against the prisoner. But there are things which are even worse, even more fatal in such cases, than the most malicious and consciously unfair attitude. It is worse if we are carried away by the artistic instinct, by the desire to create, so to speak, a romance especially if God has endowed us with psychological insight. Before I started on my way here, I was warned in Petersburg, and was myself aware, that I should find a talented opponent whose psychological insight and subtlety had gained him peculiar renown in legal circles of recent years. But profound as psychology is, it's a knife that cuts both ways." (Laughter among the public.) "You will, of course, forgive me my comparison; I can't boast of eloquence. But I will take as an example any point in the prosecutor's speech.

"The prisoner, running away in the garden in the dark, climbed over the fence, was seized by the servant, and knocked him down with a brass pestle. Then he jumped back into the garden and spent five minutes over the man, trying to discover whether he had killed him or not. And the prosecutor refuses to believe the prisoner's statement that he ran to old Grigory out of pity. 'No,' he says, 'such sensibility is impossible at such a moment, that's unnatural; he ran to find out whether the only witness of his crime was dead or alive, and so showed that he had committed murder, since he would not. have run back for any other reason.'

"Here you have psychology; but let us take the same method and apply it to the case the other way round, and our result will be no less probable. The murderer, we are told, leapt down to find out, as a precaution, whether the witness was alive or not, yet he had left in his murdered father's study, as the prosecutor himself argues, an amazing piece of evidence in the shape of a torn envelope, with an inscription that there had been three thousand roubles in it. 'If he had carried that envelope away with him, no one in the world would have known of that envelope and of the notes in it, and that the money had been stolen by the prisoner.' Those are the prosecutor's own words. So on one side you see a complete absence of precaution, a man who has lost his head and run away in a fright, leaving that clue on the floor, and two minutes later, when he has killed another man, we are entitled to assume the most heartless and calculating foresight in him. But even admitting this was so, it is psychological subtlety, I suppose, that discerns that under certain circumstances I become as bloodthirsty and keen-sighted as a Caucasian eagle, while at the next I am as timid and blind as a mole. But if I am so bloodthirsty and cruelly calculating that when I kill a man I only run back to find out whether he is alive to witness against me, why should I spend five minutes looking after my victim at the risk of encountering other witnesses? Why soak my handkerchief, wiping the blood off his head so that it may be evidence against me later? If he were so cold-hearted and calculating, why not hit the servant on the head again and again with the same pestle so as to kill him outright and relieve himself of all anxiety about the witness?

"Again, though he ran to see whether the witness was alive, he left another witness on the path, that brass pestle which he had taken from the two women, and which they could always recognise afterwards as theirs, and prove that he had taken it from them. And it is not as though he had forgotten it on the path, dropped it through carelessness or haste—no, he had flung away his weapon, for it was found fifteen paces from where Grigory lay. Why did he do so? Just because he was grieved at having killed a man, an old servant; and he flung away the pestle with a curse, as a murderous weapon. That's how it must have been, what other reason could he have had for throwing it so far? And if he were capable of feeling grief and pity at having killed a man, it shows that he was innocent of his father's murder. Had he murdered him, he would never have run to another victim out of pity; then he would have felt differently; his thoughts would have been centred on self-preservation. He would have had none to spare for pity, that is beyond doubt. On the contrary, he would have broken his skull instead of

THE BROTHERS KARAMAZOV

spending five minutes looking after him. There was room for
pity and good-feeling just because his conscience had been clear
till then. Here we have a different psychology. I have purposely resorted to this method, gentlemen of the jury, to show
that you can prove anything by it. It all depends on who makes
use of it. Psychology lures even most serious people into
romancing, and quite unconsciously. I am speaking of the
abuse of psychology, gentlemen."

Sounds of approval and laughter, at the expense of the
prosecutor, were again audible in the court. I will not repeat
the speech in detail; I will only quote some passages from it,
some leading points.

CHAPTER XI

THERE WAS NO MONEY. THERE WAS NO ROBBERY

THERE was one point that struck everyone in Fetyukovitch's speech. He flatly denied the existence of the fatal
three thousand roubles, and consequently the possibility of their
having been stolen.

"Gentlemen of the jury," he began. "Every new and unprejudiced observer must be struck by a characteristic peculiarity in the present case, namely, the charge of robbery, and
the complete impossibility of proving that there was anything to
be stolen. We are told that money was stolen—three thousand
roubles—but whether those roubles ever existed, nobody knows.
Consider, how have we heard of that sum, and who has seen the
notes? The only person who saw them, and stated that they
had been put in the envelope, was the servant, Smerdyakov.
He had spoken of it to the prisoner and his brother, Ivan
Fyodorovitch, before the catastrophe. Madame Svyetlov, too,
had been told of it. But not one of these three persons had
actually seen the notes, no one but Smerdyakov had seen them.

"Here the question arises, if it's true that they did exist, and
that Smerdyakov had seen them, when did he see them for the
last time? What if his master had taken the notes from under
his bed and put them back in his cash-box without telling him?
Note, that according to Smerdyakov's story the notes were kept
under the mattress; the prisoner must have pulled them out,
and yet the bed was absolutely unrumpled; that is carefully
recorded in the protocol. How could the prisoner have found

434

the notes without disturbing the bed? How could he have helped soiling with his blood-stained hands the fine and spotless linen with which the bed had been purposely made?

"But I shall be asked: what about the envelope on the floor? Yes, it's worth saying a word or two about that envelope. I was somewhat surprised just now to hear the highly talented prosecutor declare of himself—of himself, observe—that but for that envelope, but for its being left on the floor, no one in the world would have known of the existence of that envelope and the notes in it, and therefore of the prisoner's having stolen it. And so that torn scrap of paper is, by the prosecutor's own admission, the sole proof on which the charge of robbery rests, 'otherwise no one would have known of the robbery, nor perhaps even of the money'. But is the mere fact that that scrap of paper was lying on the floor a proof that there was money in it, and that that money had been stolen? Yet, it will be objected, Smerdyakov had seen the money in the envelope. But when, when had he seen it for the last time? I ask you that. I talked to Smerdyakov, and he told me that he had seen the notes two days before the catastrophe. Then why not imagine that old Fyodor Pavlovitch, locked up alone in impatient and hysterical expectation of the object of his adoration, may have whiled away the time by breaking open the envelope and taking out the notes? 'What's the use of the envelope?' he may have asked himself, 'she won't believe the notes are there, but when I show her the thirty rainbow-coloured notes in one roll, it will make more impression, you may be sure, it will make her mouth water.' And so he tears open the envelope, takes out the money, and flings the envelope on the floor, conscious of being the owner and untroubled by any fears of leaving evidence.

"Listen, gentlemen, could anything be more likely than this theory and such an action? Why is it out of the question? But if anything of the sort could have taken place, the charge of robbery falls to the ground; if there was no money, there was no theft of it. If the envelope on the floor may be taken as evidence that there had been money in it, why may I not maintain the opposite, that the envelope was on the floor because the money had been taken from it by the owner?

"But I shall be asked: what became of the money if Fyodor Pavlovitch took it out of the envelope, since it was not found when the police searched the house? In the first place, part of the money was found in the cash-box, and secondly, he might have taken it out that morning or the evening before to make

435

some other use of it, to give or send it away; he may have changed his idea, his plan of action completely, without thinking it necessary to announce the fact to Smerdyakov beforehand. And if there is the barest possibility of such an explanation, how can the prisoner be so positively accused of having committed murder for the safe of robbery, and of having actually carried out that robbery? This is encroaching on the domain of romance. If it is maintained that something has been stolen, the thing must be produced, or at least its existence must be proved beyond doubt. Yet no one had ever seen these notes.

"Not long ago in Petersburg a young man of eighteen, hardly more than a boy, who carried on a small business as a coster-monger, went in broad daylight into a money-changer's shop with an axe, and with extraordinary, typical audacity killed the master of the shop and carried off fifteen hundred roubles. Five hours later he was arrested, and, except fifteen roubles he had already managed to spend, the whole sum was found on him. Moreover, the shopman, on his return to the shop after the murder, informed the police not only of the exact sum stolen but even of the notes and gold coins of which that sum was made up, and those very notes and coins were found on the criminal. This was followed by a full and genuine confession on the part of the murderer. That's what I call evidence, gentlemen of the jury! In that case, I know, I see, I touch the money, and cannot deny its existence. Is it the same in the present case? And yet it is a question of life and death.

"Yes, I shall be told, but he was carousing that night squandering money; he was shown to have had fifteen hundred roubles—where did he get the money? But the very fact that only fifteen hundred could be found, and the other half of the sum could nowhere be discovered, shows that that money was not the same, and had never been in any envelope. By strict calculation of time it was proved at the preliminary inquiry that the prisoner ran straight from these women servants to Per-hotin's without going home, and that he had been nowhere. So he had been all the time in company and therefore could not have divided the three thousand in half and hidden half in the town. It's just this consideration that has led the prosecutor to assume that the money is hidden in some crevice at Mokroe. Why not in the dungeons of the castle of Udolpho, gentlemen? Isn't this supposition really too fantastic and too romantic? And observe, if that supposition breaks down, the whole charge of robbery is scattered to the winds, for in that case what could

have become of the other fifteen hundred roubles? By what miracle could they have disappeared, since it's proved that the prisoner went nowhere else? And we are ready to ruin a man's life with such tales!

"I shall be told that he could not explain where he got the fifteen hundred that he had, and everyone knew that he was without money before that night. Who knew it, pray? The prisoner has made a clear and unflinching statement of the source of that money, and if you will have it so, gentlemen of the jury, nothing can be more probable than that statement, and more consistent with the temper and spirit of the prisoner. The prosecutor is charmed with his own romance. A man of weak will, who had brought himself to take the three thousand so insultingly offered by his betrothed, could not, we are told, have set aside half and sewn it up, but would, even if he had done so, have unpicked it every two days and taken out a hundred, and so would have spent it all in a month. All this, you will remember, was put forward in a tone that brooked no contradiction. But what if the thing happened quite differently? What if you've been weaving a romance, and about quite a different kind of man? That's just it, you have invented quite a different man!

"I shall be told, perhaps, there are witnesses that he spent on one day all that three thousand given him by his betrothed a month before the catastrophe, so he could not have divided the sum in half. But who are the witnesses? The value of their evidence has been shown in court already. Besides, in another man's hand a crust always seems larger, and no one of these witnesses counted that money; they all judged simply at sight. And the witness Maximov has testified that the prisoner had twenty thousand in his hand. You see, gentlemen of the jury, psychology is a two-edged weapon. Let me turn the other edge now and see what comes of it.

"A month before the catastrophe the prisoner was entrusted by Katerina Ivanovna with three thousand roubles to send off by post. But the question is: is it true that they were entrusted to him in such an insulting and degrading way as was proclaimed just now? The first statement made by the young lady on the subject was different, perfectly different. In the second statement we heard only cries of resentment and revenge, cries of long-concealed hatred. And the very fact that the witness gave her first evidence incorrectly gives us a right to conclude that her second piece of evidence may have been incorrect also.

The prosecutor will not, dare not (his own words) touch on that story. So be it. I will not touch on it either, but will only venture to observe that if a lofty and high-principled person, such as that highly respected young lady unquestionably is, if such a person, I say, allows herself suddenly in court to contradict her first statement, with the obvious motive of ruining the prisoner, it is clear that this evidence has been given not impartially, not coolly. Have not we the right to assume that a revengeful woman might have exaggerated much? Yes, she may well have exaggerated, in particular, the insult and humiliation of her offering him the money. No, it was offered in such a way that it was possible to take it, especially for a man so easy-going as the prisoner; above all, as he expected to receive shortly from his father the three thousand roubles that he reckoned was owing to him. It was unreflecting of him, but it was just his irresponsible want of reflection that made him so confident that his father would give him the money, that he would get it, and so could always despatch the money entrusted to him and repay the debt.

"But the prosecutor refuses to allow that he could the same day have set aside half the money and sewn it up in a little bag. That's not his character, he tells us, he couldn't have had such feelings. But yet he talked himself of the broad Karamazov nature; he cried out about the two extremes which a Karamazov can contemplate at once. Karamazov is just such a two-sided nature, fluctuating between two extremes, that even when moved by the most violent craving for riotous gaiety, he can pull himself up, if something strikes him on the other side. And on the other side is love—that new love which had flamed up in his heart, and for that love he needed money; oh, far more than for carousing with his mistress. If she were to say to him: 'I am yours, I won't have Fyodor Pavlovitch,' then he must have money to take her away. That was more important than carousing. Could a Karamazov fail to understand it? That anxiety was just what he was suffering from—what is there improbable in his laying aside that money and concealing it in case of emergency?

"But time passed, and Fyodor Pavlovitch did not give the prisoner the expected three thousand; on the contrary, the latter heard that he meant to use this sum to seduce the woman he, the prisoner, loved. 'If Fyodor Pavlovitch doesn't give the money,' he thought, 'I shall be put in the position of a thief before Katerina Ivanovna.' And then the idea presented itself to him that he would go to Katerina Ivanovna, lay before her the fifteen hundred roubles he still carried round his neck, and say: 'I am a scoundrel, but not a thief.' So here we have already a twofold reason why he should guard that sum of money as the apple of his eye, why he shouldn't unpick the little bag, and spend it a hundred at a time. Why should you deny the prisoner a sense of honour? Yes, he has a sense of honour, granted that it's misplaced, granted it's often mistaken, yet it exists and amounts to a passion, and he has proved that.

"But now the affair becomes even more complex; his jealous torments reach a climax, and those same two questions torture his fevered brain more and more: 'If I repay Katerina Ivanovna, where can I find the means to go off with Grushenka?' If he behaved wildly, drank, and made disturbances in the taverns in the course of that month, it was perhaps because he was wretched and strained beyond his powers of endurance. These two questions became so acute that they drove him at last to despair. He sent his younger brother to beg for the last time for the three thousand roubles, but without waiting for a reply, burst in himself and ended by beating the old man in the presence of witnesses. After that he had no prospect of getting it from anyone; his father would not give it him after that beating.

"The same evening he struck himself on the breast, just on the upper part of the breast where the little bag was, and swore to his brother that he had the means of not being a scoundrel, but that still he would remain a scoundrel, for he foresaw that he would not use that means, that he wouldn't have the character, that he wouldn't have the will-power to do it. Why, why does the prosecutor refuse to believe the evidence of Alexey Karamazov, given so genuinely and sincerely, so spontaneously and convincingly? And why, on the contrary, does he force me to believe in money hidden in a crevice, in the dungeons of the castle of Udolpho?

"The same evening, after his talk with his brother, the prisoner wrote that fatal letter, and that letter is the chief, the most stupendous proof of the prisoner having committed robbery! 'I shall beg from everyone, and if I don't get it I shall murder my father and shall take the envelope with the pink ribbon on it from under his mattress as soon as Ivan has gone.' A full programme of the murder, we are told, so it must have been he. 'It has all been done as he wrote,' cries the prosecutor.

"But in the first place, it's the letter of a drunken man and

439

written in great irritation; secondly, he writes of the envelope
from what he has heard from Smerdyakov again, for he has not
seen the envelope himself; and thirdly, he wrote it indeed, but
how can you prove that he did it? Did the prisoner take the
envelope from under the pillow, did he find the money, did that
money exist indeed? And was it to get money that the prisoner
ran off, if you remember? He ran off post-haste not to steal,
but to find out where she was, the woman who had crushed
him. He was not running to carry out a programme, to carry
out what he had written, that is, not for an act of premeditated
robbery, but he ran suddenly, spontaneously, in a jealous fury.
Yes! I shall be told, but when he got there and murdered him
he seized the money, too. But did he murder him after all?
The charge of robbery I repudiate with indignation. A man
cannot be accused of robbery if it's impossible to state accurately what he has stolen; that's an axiom. But did he murder
him without robbery, did he murder him at all? Is that proved?
Isn't that, too, a romance?''

CHAPTER XII

AND THERE WAS NO MURDER EITHER

"ALLOW me, gentlemen of the jury, to remind you that a
man's life is at stake and that you must be careful. We
have heard the prosecutor himself admit that until to-day he
hesitated to accuse the prisoner of a full and conscious premeditation of the crime; he hesitated till he saw that fatal drunken
letter which was produced in court to-day. 'All was done as
written.' But, I repeat again, he was running to her, to seek
her, solely to find out where she was. That's a fact that can't
be disputed. Had she been at home, he would not have run
away, but would have remained at her side, and so would not
have done what he promised in the letter. He ran unexpectedly
and accidentally, and by that time very likely he did not even
remember his drunken letter. 'He snatched up the pestle,' they
say, and you will remember how a whole edifice of psychology
was built on that pestle—why he was bound to look at that
pestle as a weapon, to snatch it up, and so on, and so on. A
very commonplace idea occurs to me at this point: What if that
pestle had not been in sight, had not been lying on the shelf
from which it was snatched by the prisoner, but had been put

away in a cupboard? It would not have caught the prisoner's eye, and he would have run away without a weapon, with empty hands and then he would certainly not have killed anyone. How then can I look upon the pestle as a proof of premeditation?

"Yes, but he talked in the taverns of murdering his father, and two days before, on the evening when he wrote his drunken letter, he was quiet and only quarrelled with a shopman in the tavern, because a Karamazov could not help quarrelling, forsooth! But my answer to that is, that if he were planning such a murder in accordance with his letter, he certainly would not have quarrelled even with a shopman, and probably would not have gone into the tavern at all, because a person plotting such a crime seeks quiet and retirement, seeks to efface himself, to avoid being seen and heard, and that not from calculation but from instinct. Gentlemen of the jury, the psychological method is a two-edged weapon, and we, too, can use it. As for all this shouting in taverns throughout the month, don't we often hear children, or drunkards coming out of taverns shout: 'I'll kill you'? but they don't murder anyone. And that fatal letter—isn't that simply drunken irritability, too? Isn't that simply the shout of the brawler outside the tavern: 'I'll kill you! I'll kill the lot of you!'? Why not, why could it not be that? What reason have we to call that letter 'fatal' rather than absurd? Because his father has been found murdered, because a witness saw the prisoner running out of the garden with a weapon in his hand, and was knocked down by him: therefore, we are told, everything was done as he had planned in writing, and the letter was not 'absurd' but 'fatal'.

"Now, thank God! we've come to the real point: 'since he was in the garden, he must have murdered him.' In those few words: 'since he *was*, then he *must*' lies the whole case for the prosecution. He was there, so he must have. And what if there is no *must* about it, even if he were there? Oh, I admit that the chain of evidence—the coincidences—are really suggestive. But examine all these facts separately, regardless of their connection. Why, for instance, does the prosecution refuse to admit the truth of the prisoner's statement that he ran away from his father's window? Remember the sarcasms in which the prosecutor indulged at the expense of the respectful and 'pious' sentiments which suddenly came over the murderer. But what if there were something of the sort, a feeling of religious awe, if not of filial respect? 'My mother must have been praying for me at that moment,' were the prisoner's words at the preliminary inquiry, and so he ran away as soon as he convinced himself that Madame Svyetlov was not in his father's house. 'But he could not convince himself by looking through the window,' the prosecutor objects. But why couldn't he? Why? The window opened at the signals given by the prisoner. Some word might have been uttered by Fyodor Pavlovitch, some exclamation which showed the prisoner that she was not there. Why should we assume everything as we imagine it, as we make up our minds to imagine it? A thousand things may happen in reality which elude the subtlest imagination.

"'Yes, but Grigory saw the door open and so the prisoner certainly was in the house, therefore he killed him.' Now about that door, gentlemen of the jury. . . . Observe that we have only the statement of one witness as to that door, and he was at the time in such a condition that . . . But supposing the door was open; supposing the prisoner had lied in denying it, from an instinct of self-defence, natural in his position; supposing he did go into the house—well, what then? How does it follow that because he was there he committed the murder? He might have dashed in, run through the rooms; might have pushed his father away; might have struck him; but as soon as he had made sure Madame Svyetlov was not there, he may have run away rejoicing that she was not there and that he had not killed his father. And it was perhaps just because he had escaped from the temptation to kill his father, because he had a clear conscience and was rejoicing at not having killed him, that he was capable of a pure feeling, the feeling of pity and compassion, and leapt off the fence a minute later to the assistance of Grigory after he had, in his excitement, knocked him down.

"With terrible eloquence the prosecutor has described to us the dreadful state of the prisoner's mind at Mokroe when love again lay before him calling him to new life, while love was impossible for him because he had his father's blood-stained corpse behind him and beyond that corpse—retribution. And yet the prosecutor allowed him love, which he explained, according to his method, talking about his drunken condition, about a criminal being taken to execution, about it being still far off, and so on and so on. But again I ask, Mr. Prosecutor, have you not invented a new personality? Is the prisoner so coarse and heartless as to be able to think at that moment of love and of dodges to escape punishment, if his hands were really stained with his father's blood? No, no, no! As soon as it was made plain to him that she loved him and called him to her side, promising him new happiness, oh! then, I protest he must have felt the impulse to suicide doubled, trebled, and must have killed himself, if he had his father's murder on his conscience. Oh, no! he would not have forgotten where his pistols lay! I know the prisoner: the savage, stony heartlessness ascribed to him by the prosecutor is inconsistent with his character. He would have killed himself, that's certain. He did not kill himself just because 'his mother's prayers had saved him', and he was innocent of his father's blood. He was troubled, he was grieving that night at Mokroe only about old Grigory and praying to God that the old man would recover, that his blow had not been fatal, and that he would not have to suffer for it. Why not accept such an interpretation of the facts? What trustworthy proof have we that the prisoner is lying?

"But we shall be told at once again: 'There is his father's corpse! If he ran away without murdering him, who did murder him?' Here, I repeat, you have the whole logic of the prosecution. Who murdered him, if not he? There's no one to put in his place.

"Gentlemen of the jury, is that really so? Is it positively, actually true that there is no one else at all? We've heard the prosecutor count on his fingers all the persons who were in that house that night. They were five in number; three of them, I agree, could not have been responsible—the murdered man himself, old Grigory, and his wife. There are left then the prisoner and Smerdyakov, and the prosecutor dramatically exclaims that the prisoner pointed to Smerdyakov because he had no one else to fix on, that had there been a sixth person, even a phantom of a sixth person, he would have abandoned the charge against Smerdyakov at once in shame and have accused that other. But, gentlemen of the jury, why may I not draw the very opposite conclusion? There are two persons—the prisoner and Smerdyakov. Why can I not say that you accuse my client simply because you have no one else to accuse? And you have no one else only because you have determined to exclude Smerdyakov from all suspicion.

"It's true, indeed, Smerdyakov is accused only by the prisoner, his two brothers, and Madame Svyetlov. But there are others who accuse him: there are vague rumours of a question, of a suspicion, an obscure report, a feeling of expectation. Finally, we have the evidence of a combination of facts very suggestive, though, I admit, inconclusive. In the first place we have precisely on the day of the catastrophe that fit, for the genuineness of which the prosecutor, for some reason, has felt obliged to make a careful defence. Then Smerdyakov's sudden suicide on the eve of the trial. Then the equally startling evidence given in court to-day by the elder of the prisoner's brothers, who had believed in his guilt, but has to-day produced a bundle of notes and proclaimed Smerdyakov as the murderer. Oh, I fully share the court's and the prosecutor's conviction that Ivan Karamazov is suffering from brain fever, that his statement may really be a desperate effort, planned in delirium, to save his brother by throwing the guilt on the dead man. But again Smerdyakov's name is pronounced, again there is a suggestion of mystery. There is something unexplained, incomplete. And perhaps it may one day be explained. But we won't go into that now. Of that later.

"The court has resolved to go on with the trial, but, meantime, I might make a few remarks about the character-sketch of Smerdyakov drawn with subtlety and talent by the prosecutor. But while I admire his talent I cannot agree with him. I have visited Smerdyakov, I have seen him and talked to him, and he made a very different impression on me. He was weak in health, it is true; but in character, in spirit, he was by no means the weak man the prosecutor has made him out to be. I found in him no trace of the timidity on which the prosecutor so insisted. There was no simplicity about him, either. I found in him, on the contrary, an extreme mistrustfulness concealed under a mask of naïveté, and an intelligence of considerable range. The prosecutor was too simple in taking him for weak-minded. He made a very definite impression on me: I left him with the conviction that he was a distinctly spiteful creature, excessively ambitious, vindictive, and intensely envious. I made some inquiries: he resented his parentage, was ashamed of it, and would clench his teeth when he remembered that he was the son of 'stinking Lizaveta'. He was disrespectful to the servant Grigory and his wife, who had cared for him in his childhood. He cursed and jeered at Russia. He dreamed of going to France and becoming a Frenchman. He used often to say that he hadn't the means to do so. I fancy he loved no one but himself and had a strangely high opinion of himself. His conception of culture was limited to good clothes, clean shirt-fronts and polished boots. Believing himself to be the illegitimate son of Fyodor Pavlovitch (there is evidence of this) he might well have resented his position, compared with that of his master's legitimate sons. They had everything, he nothing. They had all the rights, they had the inheritance, while he was only the cook. He told me himself that he had helped Fyodor Pavlovitch to put the notes in the envelope. The destination of that sum—a sum which would have made his career—must have been hateful to him. Moreover, he saw three thousand roubles in new rainbow-coloured notes (I asked him about that on purpose). Oh, beware of showing an ambitious and envious man a large sum of money at once! And it was the first time he had seen so much money in the hands of one man. The sight of the rainbow-coloured notes may have made a morbid impression on his imagination, but with no immediate results.

"The talented prosecutor, with extraordinary subtlety, sketched for us all the arguments for and against the hypothesis of Smerdyakov's guilt, and asked us in particular what motive he had in feigning a fit. But he may not have been feigning at all, the fit may have happened quite naturally, but it may have passed off quite naturally, and the sick man may have recovered, not completely perhaps, but still regaining consciousness, as happens with epileptics.

"The prosecutor asks at what moment could Smerdyakov have committed the murder. But it is very easy to point out that moment. He might have waked up from deep sleep (for he was only asleep—an epileptic fit is always followed by a deep sleep) at that moment when the old Grigory shouted at the top of his voice 'Parricide!' That shout in the dark and stillness may have waked Smerdyakov whose sleep may have been less sound at the moment: he might naturally have waked up an hour before.

"Getting out of bed, he goes almost unconsciously and with no definite motive towards the sound to see what's the matter. His head is still clouded with his attack, his faculties are half asleep; but, once in the garden, he walked to the lighted windows and he hears terrible news from his master, who would be, of course, glad to see him. His mind sets to work at once. He hears all the details from his frightened master, and gradually in his disordered brain there shapes itself an idea—terrible, but seductive and irresistibly logical. To kill the old man, take the three thousand and throw all the blame on to his young master. A terrible lust of money, of booty, might seize upon him as he realised his security from detection. Oh! these sudden and irresistible impulses come so often when there is a favourable opportunity, and especially with murderers who have had

445

no idea of committing a murder beforehand. And Smerdyakov
may have gone in and carried out his plan. With what weapon?
Why, with any stone picked up in the garden. But what for,
with what object? Why, the three thousand which means a
career for him. Oh, I am not contradicting myself—the money
may have existed. And perhaps Smerdyakov alone knew where
to find it, where his master kept it. And the covering of the
money—the torn envelope on the floor?

"Just now, when the prosecutor was explaining his subtle
theory that only an inexperienced thief like Karamazov would
have left the envelope on the floor, and not one like Smerdyakov, who would have avoided leaving a piece of evidence
against himself, I thought as I listened that I was hearing something very familiar, and, would you believe it, I have heard
that very argument, that very conjecture, of how Karamazov
would have behaved, precisely two days before, from Smerdyakov himself. What's more, it struck me at the time. I
fancied that there was an artificial simplicity about him; that he
was in a hurry to suggest this idea to me that I might fancy it
was my own. He insinuated, as it were. Did he not insinuate
the same idea at the inquiry and suggest it to the talented
prosecutor?

"I shall be asked: 'What about the old woman, Grigory's
wife? She heard the sick man moaning close by, all night.'
Yes, she heard it, but that evidence is extremely unreliable. I
knew a lady who complained bitterly that she had been kept
awake all night by a dog in the yard. Yet the poor beast, it
appeared, had only yelped once or twice in the night. And
that's natural. If anyone is asleep and hears a groan he wakes
up, annoyed at being waked, but instantly falls asleep again.
Two hours later, again a groan, he wakes up and falls asleep
again; and the same thing again two hours later—three times
altogether in the night. Next morning the sleeper wakes up
and complains that someone has been groaning all night and
keeping him awake. And it is bound to seem so to him: the
intervals of two hours of sleep he does not remember, he only
remembers the moments of waking, so he feels he has been
waked up all night.

"But why, why, asks the prosecutor, did not Smerdyakov
confess in his last letter? Why did his conscience prompt him
to one step and not to both? But, excuse me, conscience
implies penitence, and the suicide may not have felt penitence,
but only despair. Despair and penitence are two very different

things. Despair may be vindictive and irreconcilable, and the suicide, laying his hands on himself, may well have felt redoubled hatred for those whom he had envied all his life.

"Gentlemen of the jury, beware of a miscarriage of justice! What is there unlikely in all I have put before you just now? Find the error in my reasoning; find the impossibility, the absurdity. And if there is but a shade of possibility, but a shade of probability in my propositions, do not condemn him. And is there only a shade? I swear by all that is sacred, I fully believe in the explanation of the murder I have just put forward. What troubles me and makes me indignant is that of all the mass of facts heaped up by the prosecution against the prisoner, there is not a single one certain and irrefutable. And yet the unhappy man is to be ruined by the accumulation of these facts. Yes, the accumulated effect is awful: the blood, the blood dripping from his fingers, the blood-stained shirt, the dark night resounding with the shout 'Parricide!' and the old man falling with a broken head. And then the mass of phrases, statements, gestures, shouts! Oh! this has so much influence, it can so bias the mind; but, gentlemen of the jury, can it bias your minds? Remember, you have been given absolute power to bind and to loose, but the greater the power, the more terrible its responsibility.

"I do not draw back one iota from what I have said just now, but suppose for one moment I agreed with the prosecution that my luckless client had stained his hands with his father's blood. This is only an hypothesis, I repeat; I never for one instant doubt of his innocence. But, so be it, I assume that my client is guilty of parricide. Even so, hear what I have to say. I have it in my heart to say something more to you, for I feel that there must be a great conflict in your hearts and minds. . . . Forgive my referring to your hearts and minds, gentlemen of the jury, but I want to be truthful and sincere to the end. Let us all be sincere!"

At this point the speech was interrupted by rather loud applause. The last words, indeed, were pronounced with a note of such sincerity that everyone felt that he really might have something to say, and that what he was about to say would be of the greatest consequence. But the President, hearing the applause, in a loud voice threatened to clear the court if such an incident were repeated. Every sound was hushed and Fetyuko-vitch began in a voice full of feeling quite unlike the tone he had used hitherto.

447

CHAPTER XIII

A CORRUPTER OF THOUGHT

"IT'S not only the accumulation of facts that threatens my client with ruin, gentlemen of the jury," he began, "what is really damning for my client is one fact—the dead body of his father. Had it been an ordinary case of murder you would have rejected the charge in view of the triviality, the incompleteness, and the fantastic character of the evidence, if you examine each part of it separately; or, at least, you would have hesitated to ruin a man's life simply from the prejudice against him which he has, alas! only too well deserved. But it's not an ordinary case of murder, it's a case of parricide. That impresses men's minds, and to such a degree that the very triviality and incompleteness of the evidence become less trivial and less incomplete even to an unprejudiced mind. How can such a prisoner be acquitted? What if he committed the murder and gets off unpunished? That is what everyone, almost involuntarily, instinctively, feels at heart.

"Yes, it's a fearful thing to shed a father's blood—the father who has begotten me, loved me, not spared his life for me, grieved over my illness from childhood up, troubled all his life for my happiness, and has lived in my joys, in my successes. To murder such a father—that's inconceivable. Gentlemen of the jury, what is a father—a real father? What is the meaning of that great word? What is the great idea in that name? We have just indicated in part what a true father is and what he ought to be. In the case in which we are now so deeply occupied and over which our hearts are aching—in the present case, the father, Fyodor Pavlovitch Karamazov, did not correspond to that conception of a father to which we have just referred. That's the misfortune. And indeed some fathers are a misfortune. Let us examine this misfortune rather more closely: we must shrink from nothing, gentlemen of the jury, considering the importance of the decision you have to make. It's our particular duty not to shrink from any idea, like children or frightened women, as the talented prosecutor happily expresses it.

"But in the course of his heated speech my esteemed opponent (and he was my opponent before I opened my lips) exclaimed

several times: 'Oh, I will not yield the defence of the prisoner
to the lawyer who has come down from Petersburg. I accuse,
but I defend also!' He exclaimed that several times, but
forgot to mention that if this terrible prisoner was for twenty-
three years so grateful for a mere pound of nuts given him by
the only man who had been kind to him, as a child in his father's
house, might not such a man well have remembered for twenty-
three years how he ran in his father's backyard, 'without boots
on his feet and with his little trousers hanging by one button'—
to use the expression of the kind-hearted doctor, Herzenstube?

"Oh, gentlemen of the jury, why need we look more closely at
this misfortune, why repeat what we all know already? What
did my client meet with when he arrived here, at his father's
house, and why depict my client as a heartless egoist and
monster? He is uncontrolled, he is wild and unruly—we are
trying him now for that—but who is responsible for his life?
Who is responsible for his having received such an unseemly
bringing up, in spite of his excellent disposition and his grateful
and sensitive heart? Did anyone train him to be reasonable?
Was he enlightened by study? Did anyone love him ever so
little in his childhood? My client was left to the care of Providence like a beast of the field. He thirsted perhaps to see his
father after long years of separation. A thousand times perhaps
he may, recalling his childhood, have driven away the loathsome
phantoms that haunted his childish dreams and with all his heart
he may have longed to embrace and to forgive his father! And
what awaited him? He was met by cynical taunts, suspicions
and wrangling about money. He heard nothing but revolting
talk and vicious precepts uttered daily over the brandy, and at
last he saw his father seducing his mistress from him with his
own money. Oh, gentlemen of the jury, that was cruel and
revolting! And that old man was always complaining of the
disrespect and cruelty of his son. He slandered him in society,
injured him, calumniated him, bought up his unpaid debts to
get him thrown into prison.

"Gentlemen of the jury, people like my client, who are fierce,
unruly, and uncontrolled on the surface, are sometimes, most
frequently indeed, exceedingly tender-hearted, only they don't
express it. Don't laugh, don't laugh at my idea! The talented
prosecutor laughed mercilessly just now at my client for loving
Schiller—loving the sublime and beautiful! I should not have
laughed at that in his place. Yes, such natures—oh, let me
speak in defence of such natures, so often and so cruelly mis-

understood—these natures often thirst for tenderness, goodness, and justice, as it were, in contrast to themselves, their unruliness, their ferocity—they thirst for it unconsciously. Passionate and fierce on the surface, they are painfully capable of loving woman, for instance, and with a spiritual and elevated love. Again do not laugh at me, this is very often the case in such natures. But they cannot hide their passions—sometimes very coarse—and that is conspicuous and is noticed, but the inner man is unseen. Their passions are quickly exhausted, but by the side of a noble and lofty creature that seemingly coarse and rough man seeks a new life, seeks to correct himself, to be better, to become noble and honourable, 'sublime and beautiful', however much the expression has been ridiculed.

"I said just now that I would not venture to touch upon my client's engagement. But I may say half a word. What we heard just now was not evidence, but only the scream of a frenzied and revengeful woman, and it was not for her—oh, not for her!—to reproach him with treachery, for she has betrayed him! If she had had but a little time for reflection she would not have given such evidence. Oh, do not believe her! No, my client is not a monster, as she called him!

"The Lover of Mankind on the eve of His Crucifixion said: 'I am the Good Shepherd. The good shepherd lays down his life for his sheep, so that not one of them might be lost.' Let not a man's soul be lost through us!

"I asked just now what does 'father' mean, and exclaimed that it was a great word, a precious name. But one must use words honestly, gentlemen, and I venture to call things by their right names: such a father as old Karamazov cannot be called a father and does not deserve to be. Filial love for an unworthy father is an absurdity, an impossibility. Love cannot be created from nothing: only God can create something from nothing.

" 'Fathers, provoke not your children to wrath,' the apostle writes, from a heart glowing with love. It's not for the sake of my client that I quote these sacred words, I mention them for all fathers. Who has authorised me to preach to fathers? No one. But as a man and a citizen I make my appeal—*vivos voco!* We are not long on earth, we do many evil deeds and say many evil words. So let us all catch a favourable moment when we are all together to saw a good word to each other. That's what I am doing: while I am in this place I take advantage of my opportunity. Not for nothing is this tribune given us by the highest authority—all Russia hears us! I am not speaking only for the fathers here present, I cry aloud to all fathers: 'Fathers, provoke not your children to wrath.' Yes, let us first fulfil Christ's injunction ourselves and only then venture to expect it of our children. Otherwise we are not fathers but enemies of our children, and they are not our children but our enemies, and we have made them our enemies ourselves. 'What measure ye mete it shall be measured unto you again'—it's not I who say that, it's the Gospel precept, measure to others according as they measure to you. How can we blame children if they measure us according to our measure?

"Not long ago a servant girl in Finland was suspected of having secretly given birth to a child. She was watched, and a box of which no one knew anything was found in the corner of the loft, behind some bricks. It was opened and inside was found the body of a new-born child which she had killed. In the same box were found the skeletons of two other babies which, according to her own confession, she had killed at the moment of their birth.

"Gentlemen of the jury, was she a mother to her children? She gave birth to them, indeed; but was she a mother to them? Would anyone venture to give her the sacred name of mother? Let us be bold, gentlemen, let us be audacious even: it's our duty to be so at this moment and not to be afraid of certain words and ideas like the Moscow women in Ostrovsky's play, who are scared at the sound of certain words. No, let us prove that the progress of the last few years has touched even us, and let us say plainly, the father is not merely he who begets the child, but he who begets it and does his duty by it.

"Oh, of course, there is the other meaning, there is the other interpretation of the word 'father', which insists that any father, even though he be a monster, even though he be the enemy of his children, still remains my father simply because he begot me. But this is, so to say, the mystical meaning which I cannot comprehend with my intellect, but can only accept by faith, or, better to say, *on faith*, like many other things which I do not understand, but which religion bids me believe. But in that case let it be kept outside the sphere of actual life. In the sphere of actual life, which has, indeed, its own rights, but also lays upon us great duties and obligations, in that sphere, if we want to be humane—Christian, in fact—we must, or ought to, act only upon convictions justified by reason and experience, which have been passed through the crucible of analysis; in a word, we must act rationally, and not as though in dream and delirium, that we may not do harm, that we may not ill-treat and ruin a man. Then it will be real Christian work, not only mystic, but rational and philanthropic." . . .

There was violent applause at this passage from many parts of the court, but Fetyukovitch waved his hands as though imploring them to let him finish without interruption. The court relapsed into silence at once. The orator went on.

"Do you suppose, gentlemen, that our children as they grow up and begin to reason can avoid such questions? No, they cannot, and we will not impose on them an impossible restriction. The sight of an unworthy father involuntarily suggests tormenting questions to a young creature, especially when he compares him with the excellent fathers of his companions. The conventional answer to this question is: 'He begot you, and you are his flesh and blood, and therefore you are bound to love him.' The youth involuntarily reflects: 'But did he love me when he begot me?' he asks, wondering more and more. 'Was it for my sake he begot me? He did not know me, not even my sex, at that moment, at the moment of passion, perhaps, inflamed by wine, and he has only transmitted to me a propensity to drunkenness—that's all he's done for me. . . . Why am I bound to love him, simply for begetting me when he has cared nothing for me all my life after?'

"Oh, perhaps those questions strike you as coarse and cruel, but do not expect an impossible restraint from a young mind. 'Drive nature out of the door and it will fly in at the window,' and, above all, let us not be afraid of words, but decide the question according to the dictates of reason and humanity and not of mystic ideas. How shall it be decided? Why, like this. Let the son stand before his father and ask him: 'Father, tell me, why must I love you? Father, show me that I must love you,' and if that father is able to answer him and show him good reason, we have a real, normal, parental relation, not resting on mystical prejudice but on a rational, responsible and strictly humanitarian basis. But if he does not, there's an end to the family tie. He is not a father to him, and the son has a right to look upon him as a stranger, and even an enemy. Our tribune, gentlemen of the jury, ought to be a school of true and sound ideas."

(Here the orator was interrupted by irrepressible and almost frantic applause. Of course, it was not the whole audience, but a good half of it applauded. The fathers and mothers present

452

applauded. Shrieks and exclamations were heard from the gallery, where the ladies were sitting. Handkerchiefs were waved. The President began ringing his bell with all his might. He was obviously irritated by the behaviour of the audience, but did not venture to clear the court as he had threatened. Even persons of high position, old men with stars on their breasts, sitting on specially reserved seats behind the judges applauded the orator and waved their handkerchiefs. So that when the noise died down, the President confined himself to repeating his stern threat to clear the court, and Fetyukovitch, excited and triumphant, continued his speech.)

"Gentlemen of the jury, you remember that awful night of which so much has been said to-day, when the son got over the fence and stood face to face with the enemy and persecutor who had begotten him. I insist most emphatically it was not for money he ran to his father's house: the charge of robbery is an absurdity, as I proved before. And it was not to murder him he broke into the house, oh no! If he had had that design he would, at least, have taken the precaution of arming himself beforehand. The brass pestle he caught up instinctively without knowing why he did it. Granted that he deceived his father by tapping at the window, granted that he made his way in— I've said already that I do not for a moment believe that legend, but let it be so, let us suppose it for a moment. Gentlemen, I swear to you by all that's holy, if it had not been his father, but an ordinary enemy, he would, after running through the rooms and satisfying himself that the woman was not there, have made off, post-haste, without doing any harm to his rival. He would have struck him, pushed him away perhaps, nothing more, for he had no thought and no time to spare for that. What he wanted to know was where she was. But his father, his father! The mere sight of the father who had hated him from his child-hood, had been his enemy, his persecutor, and now his unnatural rival, was enough! A feeling of hatred came over him involun-tarily, irresistibly, clouding his reason. It all surged up in one moment! It was an impulse of madness and insanity, but also an impulse of nature, irresistibly and unconsciously (like every-thing in nature) avenging the violation of its eternal laws.

"But the prisoner even then did not murder him—I maintain that, I cry that aloud!—no, he only brandished the pestle in a burst of indignant disgust, not meaning to kill him, not knowing that he would kill him. Had he not had this fatal pestle in his hand, he would have only knocked his father down perhaps, but would not have killed him. As he ran away, he did not know whether he had killed the old man. Such a murder is not a murder. Such a murder is not a parricide. No, the murder of such a father cannot be called parricide. Such a murder can only be reckoned parricide by prejudice.

"But I appeal to you again and again from the depths of my soul; did this murder actually take place? Gentlemen of the jury, if we convict and punish him, he will say to himself: 'These people have done nothing for my bringing up, for my education, nothing to improve my lot, nothing to make me better, nothing to make me a man. These people have not given me to eat and to drink, have not visited me in prison and nakedness, and here they have sent me to penal servitude. I am quits. I owe them nothing now, and owe no one anything for ever. They are wicked and I will be wicked. They are cruel and I will be cruel.' That is what he will say, gentlemen of the jury. And I swear, by finding him guilty you will only make it easier for him: you will ease his conscience, he will curse the blood he has shed and will not regret it. At the same time you will destroy in him the possibility of becoming a new man, for he will remain in his wickedness and blindness all his life.

"But do you want to punish him fearfully, terribly, with the most awful punishment that could be imagined, and at the same time to save him and regenerate his soul? If so, overwhelm him with your mercy! You will see, you will hear how he will tremble and be horror-stricken. 'How can I endure this mercy? How can I endure so much love? Am I worthy of it?' That's what he will exclaim.

"Oh, I know, I know that heart, that wild but grateful heart, gentlemen of the jury! It will bow before your mercy; it thirsts for a great and loving action, it will melt and mount upwards. There are souls which, in their limitation, blame the whole world. But subdue such a soul with mercy, show it love, and it will curse its past, for there are many good impulses in it. Such a heart will expand and see that God is merciful and that men are good and just. He will be horror-stricken; he will be crushed by remorse and the vast obligation laid upon him henceforth. And he will not say then: 'I am quits,' but will say, 'I am guilty in the sight of all men and am more unworthy than all'. With tears of penitence and poignant, tender anguish, he will exclaim: 'Others are better than I, they wanted to save me, not to ruin me!' Oh, this act of mercy is so easy for you, for in the absence of anything like real evidence it will be too awful

454

for you to pronounce: 'Yes, he is guilty.'

"Better acquit ten guilty men than punish one innocent man! Do you hear, do you hear that majestic voice from the past century of our glorious history? It is not for an insignificant person like me to remind you that the Russian court does not exist for the punishment only, but also for the salvation of the criminal! Let other nations think of retribution and the letter of the law, we will cling to the spirit and the meaning—the salvation and the reformation of the lost. If this is true, if Russia and her justice are such, she may go forward with good cheer! Do not try to scare us with your frenzied troikas from which all the nations stand aside in disgust. Not a runaway troika but the stately chariot of Russia will move calmly and majestically to its goal. In your hands is the fate of my client, in your hands is the fate of Russian justice. You will defend it, you will save it, you will prove that there are men to watch over it, that it is in good hands!"

CHAPTER XIV

THE PEASANTS STAND FIRM

THIS was how Fetyukovitch concluded his speech, and the enthusiasm of the audience burst like an irresistible storm. It was out of the question to stop it: the women wept, many of the men wept too, even two important personages shed tears. The President submitted, and even postponed ringing his bell. The suppression of such enthusiasm would be the suppression of something sacred, as the ladies cried afterwards. The orator himself was genuinely touched.

And it was at this moment that Ippolit Kirillovitch got up to make certain objections. People looked at him with hatred. "What? What's the meaning of it? He positively dares to make objections," the ladies babbled. But if the whole world of ladies, including his wife, had protested he could not have been stopped at that moment. He was pale, he was shaking with emotion, his first phrases were even unintelligible, he gasped for breath, could hardly speak clearly, lost the thread. But he soon recovered himself. Of this new speech of his I will quote only a few sentences.

"... I am reproached with having woven a romance. But

what is this defence if not one romance on the top of another? All that was lacking was poetry. Fyodor Pavlovitch, while waiting for his mistress, tears open the envelope and throws it on the floor. We are even told what he said while engaged in this strange act. Is not this a flight of fancy? And what proof have we that he had taken out the money? Who heard what he said? The weak-minded idiot, Smerdyakov, transformed into a Byronic hero, avenging society for his illegitimate birth—isn't this a romance in the Byronic style? And the son who breaks into his father's house and murders him without murdering him is not even a romance—this is a sphinx setting us a riddle which he cannot solve himself. If he murdered him, he murdered him, and what's the meaning of his murdering him without having murdered him—who can make head or tail of this?

"Then we are admonished that our tribune is a tribune of true and sound ideas and from this tribute of 'sound ideas' is heard a solemn declaration that to call the murder of a father 'parricide' is nothing but a prejudice! But if parricide is a prejudice, and if every child is to ask his father why he is to love him, what will become of us? What will become of the foundations of society? What will become of the family? Parricide, it appears, is only a bogey of Moscow merchants' wives. The most precious, the most sacred guarantees for the destiny and future of Russian justice are presented to us in a perverted and frivolous form, simply to attain an object—to obtain the justification of something which cannot be justified. 'Oh, crush him by mercy,' cries the counsel for the defence; but that's all the criminal wants, and to-morrow it will be seen how much he is crushed. And is not the counsel for the defence too modest in asking only for the acquittal of the prisoner? Why not found a charity in the honour of the parricide to commemorate his exploit among future generations? Religion and the Gospel are corrected—that's all mysticism, we are told, and ours is the only true Christianity which has been subjected to the analysis of reason and common sense. And so they set up before us a false semblance of Christ! 'What measure ye mete so it shall be meted unto you again,' cries the counsel for the defence, and instantly deduces that Christ teaches us to measure as it is measured to us—and this from the tribune of truth and sound sense? We peep into the Gospel only on the eve of making speeches, in order to dazzle the audience by our acquaintance with what is, anyway, a rather original composition, which may be of use to produce a certain effect—all to serve the purpose! But what Christ commands us is something very different: He bids us beware of doing this, because the wicked world does this, but we ought to forgive and to turn the other cheek, and not to measure to our persecutors as they measure for us. This is what our God has taught us and not that to forbid children to murder their fathers is a prejudice. And we will not from the tribune of truth and good sense correct the Gospel of our Lord, Whom the counsel for the defence deigns to call only 'the crucified lover of humanity', in opposition to all orthodox Russia, which calls to Him: 'For Thou art our God!' "

At this the President intervened and checked the over-zealous speaker, begging him not to exaggerate, not to overstep the bounds, and so on, as presidents always do in such cases. The audience, too, was uneasy. The public was restless: there were even exclamations of indignation. Fetyukovitch did not so much as reply; he only mounted the tribune to lay his hand on his heart and, with an offended voice, utter a few words full of dignity. He only touched again, lightly and ironically, on "romancing" and "psychology", and in an appropriate place quoted: "Jupiter, you are angry, therefore you are wrong," which provoked a burst of approving laughter in the audience, for Ippolit Kirillovitch was by no means like Jupiter. Then, à propos of the accusation that he was teaching the young generation to murder their fathers, Fetyukovitch observed, with great dignity, that he would not even answer. As for the prosecutor's charge of uttering unorthodox opinions, Fetyukovitch hinted that it was a personal insinuation and that he had expected in this court to be secure from accusations "damaging to my reputation as a citizen and a loyal subject". But at these words the President pulled him up, too, and Fetyukovitch concluded his speech with a bow, amid a hum of approbation in the court. And Ippolit Kirillovitch was, in the opinion of our ladies, "crushed for good".

Then the prisoner was allowed to speak. Mitya stood up, but said very little. He was fearfully exhausted, physically and mentally. The look of strength and independence with which he had entered in the morning had almost disappeared. He seemed as though he had passed through an experience that day which had taught him for the rest of his life something very important he had not understood till then. His voice was weak, he did not shout as before. In his words there was a new

THE BROTHERS KARAMAZOV

note of humility, defeat and submission.

"What am I to say, gentlemen of the jury? The hour of judgment has come for me, I feel the hand of God upon me! The end has come to an erring man! But, before God, I repeat to you, I am innocent of my father's blood! For the last time I repeat, it wasn't I killed him! I was erring, but I loved what is good. Every instant I strove to reform, but I lived like a wild beast. I thank the prosecutor, he told me many things about myself that I did not know; but it's not true that I killed my father, the prosecutor is mistaken. I thank my counsel, too. I cried listening to him; but it's not true that I killed my father, and he needn't have supposed it. And don't believe the doctors. I am perfectly sane, only my heart is heavy. If you spare me, if you let me go, I will pray for you. I will be a better man. I give you my word before God I will! And if you will condemn me, I'll break my sword over my head myself and kiss the pieces. But spare me, do not rob me of my God! I know myself, I shall rebel! My heart is heavy, gentlemen . . . spare me!"

He almost fell back in his place: his voice broke: he could hardly articulate the last phrase. Then the judges proceeded to put the questions and began to ask both sides to formulate their conclusions. But I will not describe the details. At last the jury rose to retire for consultation. The President was very tired, and so his last charge to the jury was rather feeble. "Be impartial, don't be influenced by the eloquence of the defence, but yet weigh the arguments. Remember that there is a great responsibility laid upon you," and so on and so on.

The jury withdrew and the court adjourned. People could get up, move about, exchange their accumulated impressions, refresh themselves at the buffet. It was very late, almost one o'clock in the night, but nobody went away: the strain was so great that no one could think of repose. All waited with sinking hearts; though that is, perhaps, too much to say, for the ladies were only in a state of hysterical impatience and their hearts were untroubled. An acquittal, they thought, was inevitable. They all prepared themselves for a dramatic moment of general enthusiasm. I must own there were many among the men, too, who were convinced that an acquittal was inevitable. Some were pleased, others frowned, while some were simply dejected, not wanting him to be acquitted. Fetyukovitch himself was confident of his success. He was surrounded by people congratulating him and fawning upon him.

"There are," he said to one group, as I was told afterwards, "there are invisible threads binding the counsel for the defence with the jury. One feels during one's speech if they are being formed. I was aware of them. They exist. Our cause is won. Set your mind at rest."

"What will our peasants say now?" said one stout, cross-looking, pock-marked gentleman, a landowner of the neighbourhood, approaching a group of gentlemen engaged in conversation.

"But they are not all peasants. There are four government clerks among them."

"Yes, there are clerks," said a member of the district council, joining the group.

"And do you know that Nazaryev, the merchant with the medal, a juryman?"

"What of him?"

"He is a man with brains."

"But he never speaks."

"He is no great talker, but so much the better. There's no need for the Petersburg man to teach him: he could teach all Petersburg himself. He's the father of twelve children. Think of that!"

"Upon my word, you don't suppose they won't acquit him?" one of our young officials exclaimed in another group.

"They'll acquit him for certain," said a resolute voice.

"It would be shameful, disgraceful, not to acquit him!" cried the official. "Suppose he did murder him—there are fathers *and* fathers! And, besides, he was in such a frenzy. . . . He really may have done nothing but swing the pestle in the air, and so knocked the old man down. But it was a pity they dragged the valet in. That was simply an absurd theory! If I'd been in Fetyukovitch's place, I should simply have said straight out: 'He murdered him; but he is not guilty, hang it all!'"

"That's what he did, only without saying, 'Hang it all!'"

"No, Mihail Semyonovitch, he almost said that, too," put in a third voice.

"Why, gentlemen, in Lent an actress was acquitted in our town who had cut the throat of her lover's lawful wife."

"Oh, but she did not finish cutting it."

"That makes no difference. She began cutting it."

"What did you think of what he said about children? Splendid, wasn't it?"

"Splendid!"

"And about mysticism, too!"

"Oh, drop mysticism, do!" cried someone else; "think of Ippolit and his fate from this day forth. His wife will scratch his eyes out to-morrow for Mitya's sake."

"Is she here?"

"What an idea! If she'd been here she'd have scratched them out in court. She is at home with toothache. He, he, he!"

"He, he, he!"

In a third group:

"I daresay they will acquit Mitenka, after all."

"I should not be surprised if he turns the 'Metropolis' upside down to-morrow. He will be drinking for ten days!"

"Oh, the devil!"

"The devil's bound to have a hand in it. Where should he be if not here?"

"Well, gentlemen, I admit it was eloquent. But still it's not the thing to break your father's head with a pestle! Or what are we coming to?"

"The chariot! Do you remember the chariot?"

"Yes; he turned a cart into a chariot!"

"And to-morrow he will turn a chariot into a cart, just to suit his purpose."

"What cunning chaps there are nowadays. Is there any justice to be had in Russia?"

But the bell rang. The jury deliberated for exactly an hour, neither more nor less. A profound silence reigned in the court as soon as the public had taken their seats. I remember how the jurymen walked into the court. At last! I won't repeat the questions in order, and, indeed, I have forgotten them. I remember only the answer to the President's first and chief question: "Did the prisoner commit the murder for the sake of robbery and with premeditation?" (I remember the exact words.) There was a complete hush. The foreman of the jury, the youngest of the clerks, pronounced, in a clear, loud voice, amidst the deathlike stillness of the court:

"Yes, guilty!"

And the same answer was repeated to every question: "Yes, guilty!" and without the slightest extenuating comment. This no one had expected; almost everyone had reckoned upon a recommendation to mercy, at least. The deathlike silence in the court was not broken—all seemed petrified: those who desired his conviction as well as those who had been eager for his acquittal. But that was only for the first instant, and it was followed by a fearful hubbub. Many of the men in the audience were pleased. Some were rubbing their hands with no attempt to conceal their joy. Those who disagreed with the verdict seemed crushed, shrugged their shoulders, whispered, but still seemed unable to realise this. But how shall I describe the state the ladies were in? I thought they would create a riot. At first they could scarcely believe their ears. Then suddenly the whole court rang with exclamations: "What's the meaning of it? What next?" They leapt up from their places. They seemed to fancy that it might be at once reconsidered and reversed. At that instant Mitya suddenly stood up and cried in a heart-rending voice, stretching his hands out before him:

"I swear by God and the dreadful Day of Judgment I am not guilty of my father's blood! Katya, I forgive you! Brothers, friends, have pity on the other woman!"

He could not go on, and broke into a terrible sobbing wail that was heard all over the court in a strange, unnatural voice unlike his own. From the farthest corner at the back of the gallery came a piercing shriek—it was Grushenka. She had succeeded in begging admittance to the court again before the beginning of the lawyers' speeches. Mitya was taken away. The passing of the sentence was deferred till next day. The whole court was in a hubbub, but I did not wait to hear. I only remember a few exclamations I heard on the steps as I went out.

"He'll have a twenty years' trip to the mines!"

"Not less."

"Well, our peasants have stood firm."

"And have done for our Mitya."

EPILOGUE

CHAPTER I

PLANS FOR MITYA'S ESCAPE

VERY early, at nine o'clock in the morning, five days after the trial, Alyosha went to Katerina Ivanovna's to talk over a matter of great importance to both of them, and to give her a message. She sat and talked to him in the very room in which she had once received Grushenka. In the next room Ivan Fyodorovitch lay unconscious in a high fever. Katerina Ivanovna had immediately after the scene at the trial ordered the sick and unconscious man to be carried to her house, disregarding the inevitable gossip and general disapproval of the public. One of the two relations who lived with her had departed to Moscow immediately after the scene at the court, the other remained. But if both had gone away, Katerina Ivanovna would have adhered to her resolution, and would have gone on nursing the sick man and sitting by him day and night. Varvinsky and Herzenstube were attending him. The famous doctor had gone back to Moscow, refusing to give an opinion as to the probable end of the illness. Though the doctors encouraged Katerina Ivanovna and Alyosha, it was evident that they could not yet give them positive hopes of recovery.

Alyosha came to see his sick brother twice a day. But this time he had specially urgent business, and he foresaw how difficult it would be to approach the subject, yet he was in great haste. He had another engagement that could not be put off for that same morning, and there was need of haste.

They had been talking for a quarter of an hour. Katerina Ivanovna was pale and terribly fatigued, yet at the same time in a state of hysterical excitement. She had a presentiment of the reason why Alyosha had come to her.

"Don't worry about his decision," she said, with confident emphasis to Alyosha. "One way or another he is bound to come to it. He must escape. That unhappy man, that hero of honour and principle—not he, not Dmitri Fyodorovitch, but the man lying the other side of that door, who has sacrificed himself for

462

his brother," Katya added, with flashing eyes, "told me the whole plan of escape long ago. You know he has already entered into negotiations. . . . I've told you something already. . . . You see, it will probably come off at the third *étape* from here, when the party of prisoners is being taken to Siberia. Oh, it's a long way off yet. Ivan Fyodorovitch has already visited the superintendent of the third *étape*. But we don't know yet who will be in charge of the party, and it's impossible to find that out so long beforehand. To-morrow perhaps I will show you in detail the whole plan which Ivan Fyodorovitch left me on the eve of the trial in case of need. . . . That was when—do you remember?—you found us quarrelling. He had just gone downstairs, but seeing you I made him come back; do you remember? Do you know what we were quarrelling about then?"

"No, I don't," said Alyosha.

"Of course he did not tell you. It was about that plan of escape. He had told me the main idea three days before, and we began quarrelling about it at once and quarrelled for three days. We quarrelled because when he told me that if Dmitri Fyodorovitch were convicted he would escape abroad with that creature, I felt furious at once—I can't tell you why, I don't know myself why. . . . Oh, of course, I was furious then about that creature, and that she, too, should go abroad with Dmitri!" Katerina Ivanovna exclaimed suddenly, her lips quivering with anger. "As soon as Ivan Fyodorovitch saw that I was furious about that woman, he instantly imagined I was jealous of Dmitri, and that I still loved Dmitri. That is how our first quarrel began. I would not give an explanation, I could not ask forgiveness. I could not bear to think that such a man could suspect me of still loving that . . . and when I myself had told him long before that I did not love Dmitri, that I loved no one but him! It was only resentment against that creature that made me angry with him. Three days later, on the evening you came, he brought me a sealed envelope, which I was to open at once if anything happened to him. Oh, he foresaw his illness! He told me that the envelope contained the details of the escape, and that if he died or was taken dangerously ill, I was to save Mitya alone. Then he left me money, nearly ten thousand—those notes to which the prosecutor referred in his speech, having learnt from someone that he had sent them to be changed. I was tremendously impressed to find that Ivan Fyodorovitch had not given up his idea of saving his brother, and was confiding this plan of escape to me, though he was still jealous of me and still convinced that I loved Mitya. Oh, that was a sacrifice! No, you cannot understand the greatness of such self-sacrifice, Alexey Fyodorovitch. *I* wanted to fall at his feet in reverence, but I thought at once that he would take it only for my joy at the thought of Mitya's being saved (and he certainly would have imagined that!), and I was so exasperated at the mere possibility of such an unjust thought on his part that I lost my temper again, and instead of kissing his feet, flew into a fury again! Oh, I am unhappy! It's my character, my awful, unhappy character! Oh, you will see, I shall end by driving him, too, to abandon me for another with whom he can get on better, like Dmitri. But . . . no, I could not bear it, I should kill myself. And when you came in then, and when I called to you and told him to come back, I was so enraged by the look of contempt and hatred he turned on me that—do you remember?—I cried out to you that it was he, he alone who had persuaded me that his brother Dmitri was a murderer! I said that malicious thing on purpose to wound him again. He had never, never persuaded me that his brother was a murderer. On the contrary, it was I who persuaded him! Oh, my vile temper was the cause of everything! I paved the way to that hideous scene at the trial. He wanted to show me that he was an honourable man, and that, even if I loved his brother, he would not ruin him for revenge or jealousy. So he came to the court . . . I am the cause of it all, I alone am to blame!"

Katya never had made such confessions to Alyosha before, and he felt that she was now at that stage of unbearable suffering when even the proudest heart painfully crushes its pride and falls vanquished by grief. Oh, Alyosha knew another terrible reason of her present misery, though she had carefully concealed it from him during those days since the trial; but it would have been for some reason too painful to him if she had been brought so low as to speak to him now about that. She was suffering for her "treachery" at the trial, and Alyosha felt that her conscience was impelling her to confess it to him, to him, Alyosha, with tears and cries and hysterical writhings on the floor. But he dreaded that moment and longed to spare her. It made the commission on which he had come even more difficult. He spoke of Mitya again.

"It's all right, it's all right, don't be anxious about him!" she began again, sharply and stubbornly. "All that is only momentary, I know him, I know his heart only too well. You may be sure he will consent to escape. It's not as though it

464

would be immediately; he will have time to make up his mind to it. Ivan Fyodorovitch will be well by that time and will manage it all himself, so that I shall have nothing to do with it. Don't be anxious; he will consent to run away. He has agreed already: do you suppose he would give up that creature? And they won't let her go to him, so he is bound to escape. It's you he's most afraid of, he is afraid you won't approve of his escape òn moral grounds. But you must generously *allow* it, if your sanction is so necessary," Katya added viciously. She paused and smiled.

"He talks about some hymn," she went on again, "some cross he has to bear, some duty; I remember Ivan Fyodorovitch told me a great deal about it, and if you knew how he talked!" Katya cried suddenly, with feeling she could not repress, "if you knew how he loved that wretched man at the moment he told me, and how he hated him, perhaps, at the same moment. And I heard his story and his tears with sneering disdain. Brute! Yes, I am a brute. I am responsible for his fever. But that man in prison is incapable of suffering," Katya concluded irritably. "Can such a man suffer? Men like him never suffer!"

There was a note of hatred and contemptuous repulsion in her words. And yet it was she who had betrayed him. "Perhaps because she feels how she's wronged him she hates him at moments," Alyosha thought to himself. He hoped that it was only "at moments". In Katya's last words he detected a challenging note, but he did not take it up.

"I sent for you this morning to make you promise to persuade him yourself. Or do you, too, consider that to escape would be dishonourable, cowardly, or something . . . unchristian, perhaps?" Katya added, even more defiantly.

"Oh no. I'll tell him everything," muttered Alyosha. "He asks you to come and see him to-day," he blurted out suddenly, looking her steadily in the face. She started, and drew back a little from him on the sofa.

"Me? Can that be?" she faltered, turning pale.

"It can and ought to be!" Alyosha began emphatically, growing more animated. "He needs you particularly just now. I would not have opened the subject and worried you if it were not necessary. He is ill, he is beside himself, he keeps asking for you. It is not to be reconciled with you that he wants you, but only that you would go and show yourself at his door. So much has happened to him since that day. He realises that he has injured you beyond all reckoning. He does not ask your forgiveness; 'it's impossible to forgive me,' he says himself, but only that you would show yourself in his doorway.''

"It's so sudden . . ." faltered Katya. "I had a presentiment all these days that you would come with that message. I knew he would ask me to come. It's impossible!"

"Let it be impossible, but do it. Only think, he realises for the first time how he has wounded you, the first time in his life; he had never grasped it before so fully. He said: 'If she refuses to come I shall be unhappy all my life.' Do you hear? though he is condemned to penal servitude for twenty years, he is still planning to be happy—is not that piteous? Think—you must visit him; though he is ruined, he is innocent," broke like a challenge from Alyosha. "His hands are clean, there is no blood on them! For the sake of his infinite sufferings in the future visit him now. Go, greet him on his way into the darkness—stand at his door, that is all. . . . You ought to do it, you ought to!" Alyosha concluded, laying immense stress on the word "ought".

"I ought to . . . but I cannot . . ." Katya moaned. "He will look at me. . . . I can't."

"Your eyes ought to meet. How will you live all your life if you don't make up your mind to do it now?"

"Better suffer all my life."

"You ought to go, you ought to go," Alyosha repeated, with merciless emphasis.

"But why to-day, why at once? . . . I can't leave our patient . . ."

"You can for a moment. It will only be a moment. If you don't come, he will be in delirium by to-night. I would not tell you a lie; have pity on him!"

"Have pity on *me!*" Katya said, with bitter reproach, and she burst into tears.

"Then you will come," said Alyosha firmly, seeing her tears. "I'll go and tell him you will come directly."

"No, don't tell him so on any account," cried Katya in alarm. "I will come, but don't tell him beforehand, for perhaps I may go, but not go in . . . I don't know yet . . ."

Her voice failed her. She gasped for breath. Alyosha got up to go.

"And what if I meet anyone?" she said suddenly, in a low voice, turning white again.

"That's just why you must go now, to avoid meeting any-

one. There will be no one there, I can tell you that for certain.
We will expect you," he concluded emphatically, and went out
of the room.

CHAPTER II

FOR A MOMENT THE LIE BECOMES TRUTH

HE hurried to the hospital where Mitya was lying now. The
day after his fate was determined, Mitya had fallen ill with
nervous fever, and was sent to the prison division of the town
hospital. But at the request of several persons (Alyosha,
Madame Hohlakov, Lise, etc.), Doctor Varvinsky had put
Mitya not with other prisoners but in a separate little room,
the one where Smerdyakov had been. It is true that there was
a sentinel at the other end of the corridor, and there was a
grating over the window, so that Varvinsky could be at ease
about the indulgence he had shown, which was not quite legal,
indeed; but he was a kind-hearted and compassionate young
man. He knew how hard it would be for a man like Mitya to
pass at once so suddenly into the society of robbers and murderers, and that he must get used to it by degrees. The visits of
relations and friends were informally sanctioned by the doctor
and overseer, and even by the police captain. But only Alyosha
and Grushenka had visited Mitya. Rakitin had tried to force
his way in twice, but Mitya persistently begged Varvinsky not
to admit him.

Alyosha found him sitting on his bed in a hospital dressing-
gown, rather feverish, with a towel, soaked in vinegar and
water, on his head. He looked at Alyosha as he came in with
an undefined expression, but there was a shade of something like
dread discernible in it. He had become terribly preoccupied
since the trial; sometimes he would be silent for half an hour
together, and seemed to be pondering something heavily and
painfully, oblivious of everything about him. If he roused himself from his brooding and began to talk, he always spoke with
a kind of abruptness and never of what he really wanted to say.
He looked sometimes with a face of suffering at his brother. He
seemed to be more at ease with Grushenka than with Alyosha.
It is true, he scarcely spoke to her at all, but as soon as she
came in, his whole face lighted up with joy.

Alyosha sat down beside him on the bed in silence. This time
Mitya was waiting for Alyosha in suspense, but he did not dare

ask him a question. He felt it almost unthinkable that Katya would consent to come, and at the same time he felt that if she did not come, something inconceivable would happen. Alyosha understood his feelings.

"Trifon Borissovitch," Mitya began nervously, "has pulled his whole inn to pieces, I am told. He's taken up the flooring, pulled apart the planks, split up all the gallery, I am told. He is seeking treasure all the time—the fifteen hundred roubles which the prosecutor said I'd hidden there. He began playing these tricks, they say, as soon as he got home. Serve him right, the swindler! The guard here told me yesterday; he comes from there."

"Listen," began Alyosha. "She will come, but I don't know when. Perhaps to-day, perhaps in a few days, that I can't tell. But she will come, she will, that's certain."

Mitya started, would have said something, but was silent. The news had a tremendous effect on him. It was evident that he would have liked terribly to know what had been said, but he was again afraid to ask. Something cruel and contemptuous from Katya would have cut him like a knife at that moment.

"This was what she said among other things: that I must be sure to set your conscience at rest about escaping. If Ivan is not well by then she will see to it all herself."

"You've spoken of that already," Mitya observed musingly.

"And you have repeated it to Grusha," observed Alyosha.

"Yes," Mitya admitted. "She won't come this morning." He looked timidly at his brother. "She won't come till the evening. When I told her yesterday that Katya was taking measures, she was silent, but she set her mouth. She only whispered, 'Let her!' She understood that it was important. I did not dare to try her further. She understands now, I think, that Katya no longer cares for me, but loves Ivan."

"Does she?" broke from Alyosha.

"Perhaps she does not. Only she is not coming this morning," Mitya hastened to explain again; "I asked her to do something for me. You know, Ivan is superior to all of us. He ought to live, not us. He will recover."

"Would you believe it, though Katya is alarmed about him, she scarcely doubts of his recovery?" said Alyosha.

"That means that she is convinced he will die. It's because she is frightened she's so sure he will get well."

"Ivan has a strong constitution, and I, too, believe there's every hope that he will get well," Alyosha observed anxiously

"Yes, he will get well. But she is convinced that he will die. She has a great deal of sorrow to bear . . ." A silence followed. A grave anxiety was fretting Mitya.

"Alyosha, I love Grusha terribly," he said suddenly in a shaking voice, full of tears.

"They won't let her go out there to you," Alyosha put in at once.

"And there is something else I wanted to tell you," Mitya went on, with a sudden ring in his voice. "If they beat me on the way or out there, I won't submit to it. I shall kill someone, and shall be shot for it. And this will be going on for twenty years! They speak to me rudely as it is. I've been lying here all night, passing judgment on myself. I am not ready! I am not able to resign myself. I wanted to sing a 'hymn'; but if a guard speaks rudely to me, I have not the strength to bear it. For Grusha I would bear anything . . . anything except blows. . . . But she won't be allowed to come there."

Alyosha smiled gently.

"Listen, brother, once for all," he said. "This is what I think about it. And you know that I would not tell you a lie. Listen: you are not ready, and such a cross is not for you. What's more, you don't need such a martyr's cross when you are not ready for it. If you had murdered our father, it would grieve me that you should reject your punishment. But you are innocent, and such a cross is too much for you. You wanted to make yourself another man by suffering. I say, only remember that other man always, all your life and wherever you go; and that will be enough for you. Your refusal of that great cross will only serve to make you feel all your life an even greater duty, and that constant feeling will do more to make you a new man, perhaps, than if you went there. For there you would not endure it and would repine, and perhaps at last would say: 'I am quits.' The lawyer was right about that. Such heavy burdens are not for all men. For some they are impossible. These are my thoughts about it, if you want them so much. If other men would have to answer for your escape, officers or soldiers, then I would not have 'allowed' you," smiled Alyosha. "But they declare—the superintendent of that *étape* told Ivan himself—that if it's well managed there will be no great inquiry, and that they can get off easily. Of course, bribing is dishonest even in such a case, but I can't undertake to judge about it, because if Ivan and Katya commissioned me to act for you, I know I should go and give bribes. I must tell you the truth. And so I can't judge of your own action. But let me assure you that I shall never condemn you. And it would be a strange thing if I could judge you in this. Now I think I've gone into everything."

"But I do condemn myself!" cried Mitya. "I shall escape, that was settled apart from you; could Mitya Karamazov do anything but run away? But I shall condemn myself, and I will pray for my sin for ever. That's how the Jesuits talk, isn't it? Just as we are doing?"

"Yes." Alyosha smiled gently.

"I love you for always telling the whole truth and never hiding anything," cried Mitya, with a joyful laugh. "So I've caught my Alyosha being Jesuitical. I must kiss you for that. Now listen to the rest; I'll open the other side of my heart to you. This is what I planned and decided. If I run away, even with money and a passport, and even to America, I should be cheered up by the thought that I am not running away for pleasure, not for happiness, but to another exile as bad, perhaps, as Siberia. It is as bad, Alyosha, it is! I hate that America, damn it, already. Even though Grusha will be with me. Just look at her; is she an American? She is Russian, Russian to the marrow of her bones; she will be homesick for the mother country, and I shall see every hour that she is suffering for my sake, that she has taken up that cross for me. And what harm has she done? And how shall I, too, put up with the rabble out there, though they may be better than I, every one of them? I hate that America already! And though they may be wonderful at machinery, every one of them, damn them, they are not of my soul. I love Russia, Alyosha, I love the Russian God, though I am a scoundrel myself. I shall choke there!" he exclaimed, his eyes suddenly flashing. His voice was trembling with tears. "So this is what I've decided, Alyosha, listen," he began again, mastering his emotion. "As soon as I arrive there with Grusha, we will set to work at once on the land, in solitude, somewhere very remote, with wild bears. There must be some remote parts even there. I am told there are still Redskins there, somewhere, on the edge of the horizon. So to the country of the 'Last of the Mohicans', and there we'll tackle the grammar at once, Grusha and I. Work and grammar—that's how we'll spend three years. And by that time we shall speak English like any Englishman. And as soon as we've learnt it—good-bye to America! We'll run here to Russia as American citizens. Don't be uneasy—we would not come to this little town. We'd hide somewhere, a long way off, in the north or in the south. I shall be changed by that time, and she will, too, in America. The doctors shall make me some sort of wart on my face—what's the use of their being so mechanical!—or else I'll put out one eye, let my beard grow a yard, and I shall turn grey, fretting for Russia. I dare say they won't recognise us. And if they do, let them send us to Siberia— I don't care. It will show it's our fate. We'll work on the land here, too, somewhere in the wilds, and I'll make up as an American all my life. But we shall die on our own soil. That's my plan, and it shan't be altered. Do you approve?"

"Yes," said Alyosha, not wanting to contradict him. Mitya paused for a minute and said suddenly:

"And how they worked it up at the trial! Didn't they work it up!"

"If they had not, you would have been convicted just the same," said Alyosha, with a sigh.

"Yes, people are sick of me here! God bless them, but it's hard," Mitya moaned miserably. Again there was silence for a minute.

"Alyosha, put me out of my misery at once!" he exclaimed suddenly. "Tell me, is she coming now, or not? Tell me. What did she say? How did she say it?"

"She said she would come, but I don't know whether she will come to-day. It's hard for her, you know." Alyosha looked timidly at his brother.

"I should think it is hard for her! Alyosha, it will drive me out of my mind. Grusha keeps looking at me. She understands. My God, calm my heart: what is it I want? I want Katya! Do I understand what I want? It's the headstrong, evil Karamazov spirit! No, I am not fit for suffering. I am a scoundrel, that's all one can say."

"Here she is!" cried Alyosha.

At that instant Katya appeared in the doorway. For a moment she stood still, gazing at Mitya with a dazed expression. He leapt impulsively to his feet, and a scared look came into his face. He turned pale, but a timid, pleading smile appeared on his lips at once, and with an irresistible impulse he held out both hands to Katya. Seeing it, she flew impetuously to him. She seized him by the hands, and almost by force made him sit down on the bed. She sat down beside him, and still keeping his hands pressed them violently. Several times they both strove to speak, but stopped short and again gazed speech-less with a strange smile, their eyes fastened on one another. So passed two minute

"Have you forgiven me?" Mitya faltered at last, and at the same moment turning to Alyosha, his face working with joy, he cried: "Do you hear what I am asking, do you hear?"

"That's what I loved you for, that you are generous at heart!" broke from Katya. "My forgiveness is no good to you, nor yours to me; whether you forgive me or not, you will always be a sore place in my heart, and 1 in yours—sc it must be . . ." She stopped to take breath. "What have I come for?" she began again, with nervous haste: "to embrace your feet, to press your hands like this, till it hurts—you remember how in Moscow I used to squeeze them—to tell you again that you are my god, my joy, to tell you that I love you madly," she moaned in anguish, and suddenly pressed his hand greedily to her lips. Tears streamed from her eyes. Alyosha stood speech-less and confounded; he had never expected what he was seeing.

"Love is over, Mitya!" Katya began again, "but the past is painfully dear to me. Know that will always be so. But now let what might have been come true for one minute," she faltered, with a drawn smile, looking into his face joyfully again. "You love another woman, and I love another man, and yet I shall love you for ever, and you will love me; do you know that? Do you hear? Love me, love me all your life!" she cried, with a quiver almost of menace, in her voice.

"I shall love you, and . . . do you know, Katya," Mitya began, drawing a deep breath at each word, "do you know, five days ago, that same evening, I loved you. . . . When you fell down and were carried out . . . All my life! So it will be, so it will always be . . ."

So they murmured to one another frantic words, almost meaningless, perhaps not even true, but at that moment it was all true, and they both believed what they said implicitly.

"Katya," cried Mitya suddenly, "do you believe I murdered him? I know you don't believe it now, but then . . . when you gave evidence. . . . Surely, surely you did not believe it!"

"I did not believe it even then. I've never believed it. I hated you, and for a moment I persuaded myself. While I was giving evidence I persuaded myself and believed it, but when I'd finished speaking I left off believing it at once. Don't doubt that! I have forgotten that I came here to punish myself," she said, with a new expression in her voice, quite unlike the loving tones of a moment before.

"Woman, yours is a heavy burden," broke, as it were, involuntarily from Mitya.

"Let me go," she whispered. "I'll come again. It's more than I can bear now."

She was getting up from her place, but suddenly uttered a loud scream and staggered back. Grushenka walked suddenly and noiselessly into the room. No one had expected her. Katya moved swiftly to the door, but when she reached Grushenka she stopped suddenly, turned as white as chalk and moaned softly, almost in a whisper:

"Forgive me!"

Grushenka stared at her and, pausing for an instant, in a vindictive, venomous voice, answered:

"We are full of hatred, my girl, you and I! We are both full of hatred! As though we could forgive one another! Save him, and I'll worship you all my life."

"You won't forgive her!" cried Mitya, with frantic reproach.

"Don't be anxious, I'll save him for you!" Katya whispered rapidly, and she ran out of the room.

"And you could refuse to forgive her when she begged your forgiveness herself?" Mitya exclaimed bitterly again.

"Mitya, don't dare to blame her; you have no right to!" Alyosha cried hotly.

"Her proud lips spoke, not her heart," Grushenka brought out in a tone of disgust. "If she saves you I'll forgive her everything . . ."

She stopped speaking, as though suppressing something. She could not yet recover herself. She had come in, as appeared afterwards, accidentally, with no suspicion of what she would meet.

"Alyosha, run after her!" Mitya cried to his brother; "tell her . . . I don't know . . . don't let her go away like this!"

"I'll come to you again at nightfall," said Alyosha, and he ran after Katya. He overtook her outside the hospital grounds. She was walking fast, but as soon as Alyosha caught her up she said quickly:

"No, before that woman I can't punish myself! I asked her forgiveness because I wanted to punish myself to the bitter end. She would not forgive me. . . . I like her for that!" she added, in an unnatural voice, and her eyes flashed with fierce resentment.

y brother did not expect this in the least," muttered
ıa. "He was sure she would not come . . ."
) doubt. Let us leave that," she snapped. "Listen: I
ʒo with you to the funeral now. I've sent them flowers.
ʒ they still have money. If necessary, tell them I'll never
on them. . . . Now leave me, leave me, please. You are
; it is—the bells are ringing for the service. . . . Leave
ease !"

CHAPTER III

ILUSHA'S FUNERAL. THE SPEECH AT THE STONE

H E really was late. They had waited for him and had already
decided to bear the pretty flower-decked little coffin to the
church without him. It was the coffin of poor little Ilusha. He
had died two days after Mitya was sentenced. At the gate of
the house Alyosha was met by the shouts of the boys, Ilusha's
schoolfellows. They had all been impatiently expecting him and
were glad that he had come at last. There were about twelve
of them, they all had their school-bags or satchels on their
shoulders. "Father will cry, be with father," Ilusha had told
them as he lay dying, and the boys remembered it. Kolya
Krassotkin was the foremost of them.

"How glad I am you've come, Karamazov !" he cried, holding out his hand to Alyosha. "It's awful here. It's really
horrible to see it. Snegiryov is not drunk, we know for a fact
he's had nothing to drink to-day, but he seems as if he were
drunk . . . I am always manly, but this is awful. Karamazov,
if I am not keeping you, one question before you go in?"

"What is it, Kolya?" said Alyosha.

"Is your brother innocent or guilty? Was it he killed your
father or was it the valet? As you say, so it will be. I haven't
slept for the last four nights for thinking of it."

"The valet killed him, my brother is innocent," answered
Alyosha.

"That's what I said," cried Smurov.

"So he will perish an innocent victim!" exclaimed Kolya;
"though he is ruined he is happy! I could envy him!"

"What do you mean? How can you? Why?" cried
Alyosha, surprised.

"Oh, if I, too, could sacrifice myself some day for truth !"
said Kolya, with enthusiasm.

474

"But not in such a cause, not with such disgrace and such horror!" said Alyosha.

"Of course . . . I should like to die for all humanity, and as for disgrace, I don't care about that—our names may perish. I respect your brother!"

"And so do I!" the boy, who had once declared that he knew who had founded Troy, cried suddenly and unexpectedly, and he blushed up to his ears like a peony as he had done on that occasion.

Alyosha went into the room. Ilusha lay with his hands folded and his eyes closed in a blue coffin with a white frill round it. His thin face was hardly changed at all, and strange to say there was no smell of decay from the corpse. The expression of his face was serious and, as it were, thoughtful. His hands, crossed over his breast, looked particularly beautiful, as though chiselled in marble. There were flowers in his hands and the coffin, inside and out, was decked with flowers, which had been sent early in the morning by Lise Hohlakov. But there were flowers too from Katerina Ivanovna, and when Alyosha opened the door, the captain had a bunch in his trembling hands and was strewing them again over his dear boy. He scarcely glanced at Alyosha when he came in, and he would not look at anyone, even at his crazy weeping wife, "mamma", who kept trying to stand on her crippled legs to get a nearer look at her dead boy. Nina had been pushed in her chair by the boys close up to the coffin. She sat with her head pressed to it and she too was no doubt quietly weeping. Snegiryov's face looked eager, yet bewildered and exasperated. There was something crazy about his gestures and the words that broke from him. "Old man, dear old man!" he exclaimed every minute, gazing at Ilusha. It was his habit to call Ilusha "old man", as a term of affection when he was alive.

"Father, give me a flower, too; take that white one out of his hand and give it me," the crazy mother begged, whimpering. Either because the little white rose in Ilusha's hand had caught her fancy or that she wanted one from his hand to keep in memory of him, she moved restlessly, stretching out her hands for the flower.

"I won't give it to anyone, I won't give you anything," Snegiryov cried callously. "They are his flowers, not yours! Everything is his, nothing is yours!"

"Father, give mother a flower!" cried Nina, lifting her face wet with tears.

"I won't give away anything and to her less than anyone!

She didn't love Ilusha. She took away his little cannon and he gave it to her," the captain broke into loud sobs at the thought of how Ilusha had given up his cannon to his mother. The poor, crazy creature was bathed in noiseless tears, hiding her face in her hands.

The boys, seeing that the father would not leave the coffin and that it was time to carry it out, stood round it in a close circle and began to lift it up.

"I don't want him to be buried in the churchyard," Snegiryov wailed suddenly; "I'll bury him by the stone, by our stone! Ilusha told me to. I won't let him be carried out!"

He had been saying for the last three days that he would bury him by the stone, but Alyosha, Krassotkin, the landlady, her sister and all the boys interfered.

"What an idea, bury him by an unholy stone, as though he had hanged himself," the old landlady said sternly. "There in the churchyard the ground has been crossed. He'll be prayed for there. One can hear the singing in church and the deacon reads so plainly and verbally that it will reach him every time just as though it were read over his grave."

At last the captain made a gesture of despair as though to say, "Take him where you will". The boys raised the coffin, but as they passed the mother, they stopped for a moment and lowered it that she might say good-bye to Ilusha. But on seeing that precious little face, which for the last three days she had only looked at from a distance, she trembled all over and her grey head began twitching spasmodically over the coffin.

"Mother, make the sign of the cross over him, give him your blessing, kiss him," Nina cried to her. But her head still twitched like an automaton and with a face contorted with bitter grief she began, without a word, beating her breast with her fist. They carried the coffin past her. Nina pressed her lips to her brother's for the last time as they bore the coffin by her. As Alyosha went out of the house he begged the landlady to look after those who were left behind, but she interrupted him before he had finished.

"To be sure, I'll stay with them, we are Christians, too." The old woman wept as she said it.

They had not far to carry the coffin to the church, not more than three hundred paces. It was a still clear day, with a slight frost. The church bells were still ringing. Snegiryov ran fussing and distracted after the coffin, in his short old summer overcoat, with his head bare and his soft, old, wide-brimmed hat in his hand. He seemed in a state of bewildered anxiety. At one moment he stretched out his hand to support the head of the coffin and only hindered the bearers, at another he ran alongside and tried to find a place for himself there. A flower fell on the snow and he rushed to pick it up as though everything in the world depended on the loss of that flower.

"And the crust of bread, we've forgotten the crust!" he cried suddenly in dismay. But the boys reminded him at once that he had taken the crust of bread already and that it was in his pocket. He instantly pulled it out and was reassured.

"Ilusha told me to, Ilusha," he explained at once to Alyosha. "I was sitting by him one night and he suddenly told me: 'Father, when my grave is filled up crumble a piece of bread on it so that the sparrows may fly down, I shall hear and it will cheer me up not to be lying alone.' "

"That's a good thing," said Alyosha, "we must often take some."

"Every day, every day!" said the captain quickly, seeming cheered at the thought.

They reached the church at last and set the coffin in the middle of it. The boys surrounded it and remained reverently standing so, all through the service. It was an old and rather poor church. Many of the ikons were without settings, but such churches are the best for praying in. During the mass Snegiryov became somewhat calmer, though at times he had outbursts of the same unconscious and, as it were, incoherent anxiety. At one moment he went up to the coffin to set straight the cover or the wreath, when a candle fell out of the candlestick he rushed to replace it and was a fearful time fumbling over it, then he subsided and stood quietly by the coffin with a look of blank uneasiness and perplexity. After the Epistle he suddenly whispered to Alyosha, who was standing beside him, that the Epistle had not been read properly, but did not explain what he meant. During the prayer, "Like the Cherubim", he joined in the singing but did not go on to the end. Falling on his knees, he pressed his forehead to the stone floor and lay so for a long while.

At last came the funeral service itself and candles were distributed. The distracted father began fussing about again, but the touching and impressive funeral prayers moved and roused his soul. He seemed suddenly to shrink together and broke into rapid, short sobs, which he tried at first to smother, but at last he sobbed aloud. When they began taking leave of the dead and closing the coffin, he flung his arms about, as though he would not allow them to cover Ilusha, and began greedily and persistently kissing his dead boy on the lips. At last they succeeded in persuading him to come away from the step, but suddenly he impulsively stretched out his hand and snatched a few flowers from the coffin. He looked at them and a new idea seemed to dawn upon him, so that he apparently forgot his grief for a minute. Gradually he seemed to sink into brooding and did not resist when the coffin was lifted up and carried to the grave. It was an expensive one in the churchyard close to the church, Katerina Ivanovna had paid for it. After the customary rites the grave-diggers lowered the coffin. Snegiryov with his flowers in his hands bent down so low over the open grave that the boys caught hold of his coat in alarm and pulled him back. He did not seem to understand fully what was happening. When they began filling up the grave, he suddenly pointed anxiously at the falling earth and began trying to say something, but no one could make out what he meant, and he stopped suddenly. Then he was reminded that he must crumble the bread and he was awfully excited, snatched up the bread and began pulling it to pieces and flinging the morsels on the grave.

"Come, fly down, birds, fly down, sparrows!" he muttered anxiously.

One of the boys observed that it was awkward for him to crumble the bread with the flowers in his hands and suggested he should give them to someone to hold for a time. But he would not do this and seemed indeed suddenly alarmed for his flowers, as though they wanted to take them from him altogether. And after looking at the grave and, as it were, satisfying himself that everything had been done and the bread had been crumbled, he suddenly, to the surprise of everyone, turned, quite composedly even, and made his way homewards. But his steps became more and more hurried, he almost ran. The boys and Alyosha kept up with him.

"The flowers are for mamma, the flowers are for mamma! I was unkind to mamma," he began exclaiming suddenly.

Someone called to him to put on his hat, as it was cold. But he flung the hat in the snow as though he were angry and kept repeating, "I won't have the hat, I won't have the hat". Smurov picked it up and carried it after him. All the boys were crying, and Kolya and the boy who discovered about Troy most of all. Though Smurov, with the captain's hat in his hand, was crying bitterly too, he managed, as he ran, to snatch up a piece of red brick that lay on the snow of the path, to fling it at the flock of sparrows that was flying by. He missed them, of course, and went on crying as he ran. Half-way, Snegiryov suddenly stopped, stood still for half a minute, as though struck by something, and suddenly turning back to the church, ran towards the deserted grave. But the boys instantly overtook him and caught hold of him on all sides. Then he fell helpless on the snow as though he had been knocked down, and struggling, sobbing, and wailing, he began crying out, "Ilusha, old man, dear old man!" Alyosha and Kolya tried to make him get up, soothing and persuading him.

"Captain, give over, a brave man must show fortitude," muttered Kolya.

"You'll spoil the flowers," said Alyosha, "and mamma is expecting them, she is sitting crying because you would not give her any before. Ilusha's little bed is still there . . ."

"Yes, yes, mamma!" Snegiryov suddenly recollected, "they'll take away the bed, they'll take it away," he added as though alarmed that they really would. He jumped up and ran homewards again. But it was not far off and they all arrived together. Snegiryov opened the door hurriedly and called to his wife, with whom he had so cruelly quarrelled just before:

"Mamma, poor crippled darling, Ilusha has sent you these flowers," he cried, holding out to her a little bunch of flowers that had been frozen and broken while he was struggling in the snow. But at that instant he saw in the corner, by the little bed, Ilusha's little boots, which the landlady had put tidily side by side. Seeing the old, patched, rusty-looking, stiff boots he flung up his hands and rushed to them, fell on his knees, snatched up one boot and, pressing his lips to it, began kissing it greedily, crying, "Ilusha, old man, dear old man, where are your little feet?"

"Where have you taken him away? Where have you taken him?" the lunatic cried in a heart-rending voice. Nina, too, broke into sobs. Kolya ran out of the room, the boys followed him. At last Alyosha too went out.

"Let them weep," he said to Kolya, "it's no use trying to comfort them just now. Let us wait a minute and then go back."

"No, it's no use, it's awful," Kolya assented. "Do you know, Karamazov," he dropped his voice so that no one could hear them, "I feel dreadfully sad, and if it were only possible to bring him back, I'd give anything in the world to do it."

"Ah, so would I," said Alyosha.

"What do you think, Karamazov, had we better come back here to-night? He'll be drunk, you know."

"Perhaps he will. Let us come together, you and I, that will be enough, to spend an hour with them, with the mother and Nina. If we all come together we shall remind them of everything again," Alyosha suggested.

"The landlady is laying the table for them now—there'll be a funeral dinner or something, the priest is coming; shall we go back to it, Karamazov?"

"Of course," said Alyosha.

"It's all so strange, Karamazov, such sorrow and then pancakes after it, it all seems so unnatural in our religion."

"They are going to have salmon, too," the boy who had discovered about Troy observed in a loud voice.

"I beg you most earnestly, Kartashov, not to interrupt again with your idiotic remarks, especially when one is not talking to you and doesn't care to know whether you exist or not!" Kolya snapped out irritably. The boy flushed crimson but did not dare to reply.

Meantime they were strolling slowly along the path and suddenly Smurov exclaimed:

"There's Ilusha's stone, under which they wanted to bury him."

They all stood still by the big stone. Alyosha looked and the whole picture of what Snegiryov had described to him that day, how Ilusha, weeping and hugging his father, had cried, "Father, father, how he insulted you!" rose at once before his imagination. A sudden impulse seemed to come into his soul. With a serious and earnest expression he looked from one to another of the bright, pleasant faces of Ilusha's schoolfellows, and suddenly said to them:

"Boys, I should like to say one word to you, here at this place."

The boys stood round him and at once bent attentive and expectant eyes upon him.

"Boys, we shall soon part. I shall be for some time with my two brothers, of whom one is going to Siberia and the other is lying at death's door. But soon I shall leave this town, perhaps for a long time, so we shall part. Let us make a compact, here, at Ilusha's stone that we will never forget Ilusha and one another. And whatever happens to us later in life, if we don't meet for twenty years afterwards, let us always remember how we buried the poor boy at whom we once threw stones, do you

remember, by the bridge? and afterwards we all grew so fond of him. He was a fine boy, a kind-hearted, brave boy, he felt for his father's honour and resented the cruel insult to him and stood up for him. And so, in the first place, we will remember him, boys, all our lives. And even if we are occupied with most important things, if we attain to honour or fall into great misfortune—still let us remember how good it was once here, when we were all together, united by a good and kind feeling which made us, for the time we were loving that poor boy, better perhaps than we are. My little doves—let me call you so, for you are very like them, those pretty blue birds, at this minute as I look at your good dear faces. My dear children, perhaps you won't understand what I am saying to you, because I often speak very unintelligibly, but you'll remember it all the same and will agree with my words some time. You must know that there is nothing higher and stronger and more wholesome and good for life in the future than some good memory, especially a memory of childhood, of home. People talk to you a great deal about your education, but some good, sacred memory, preserved from childhood, is perhaps the best education. If a man carries many such memories with him into life, he is safe to the end of his days, and if one has only one good memory left in one's heart, even that may some time be the means of saving us. Perhaps we may even grow wicked later on, may be unable to refrain from a bad action, may laugh at men's tears and at those people who say, as Kolya did just now, 'I want to suffer for all men', and may even jeer spitefully at such people. But however bad we may become—which God forbid!—yet, when we recall how we buried Ilusha, how we loved him in his last days, and how we have been talking like friends all together, at this stone, the cruellest and most mocking of us—if we do become so—will not dare to laugh inwardly at having been kind and good at this moment! What's more, perhaps, that one memory may keep him from great evil and he will reflect and say, 'Yes, I was good and brave and honest then!' Let him laugh to himself, that's no matter, a man often laughs at what's good and kind. That's only from thoughtlessness. But I assure you, boys, that as he laughs he will say at once in his heart, 'No, I do wrong to laugh, for that's not a thing to laugh at'.''

"That will be so, I understand you, Karamazov!" cried Kolya, with flashing eyes.

The boys were excited and they, too, wanted to say something, but they restrained themselves, looking with intentness and emotion at the speaker.

"I say this in case we become bad," Alyosha went on, "but there's no reason why we should become bad, is there, boys? Let us be, first and above all, kind, then honest and then let us never forget each other! I say that again. I give you my word for my part that I'll never forget one of you. Every face looking at me now I shall remember even for thirty years. Just now Kolya said to Kartashov that we did not care to know whether he exists or not. But I cannot forget that Kartashov exists and that he is not blushing now as he did when he discovered the founders of Troy, but is looking at me with his jolly, kind dear little eyes. Boys, my dear boys, let us all be generous and brave like Ilusha, clever, brave and generous like Kolya (though he will be ever so much cleverer when he is grown up), and let us all be as modest, as clever and sweet at Kartashov. But why am I talking about those two? You are all dear to me, boys, from this day forth I have a place in my heart for you all, and I beg you to keep a place in your hearts for me! Well, and who has united us in this kind, good feeling which we shall remember and intend to remember all our lives? Who, if not Ilusha, the good boy, the dear boy, precious to us for ever! Let us never forget him. May his memory live for ever in our hearts from this time forth!"

"Yes, yes, for ever, for ever!" the boys cried in their ringing voices, with softened faces.

"Let us remember his face and his clothes and his poor little boots, his coffin and his unhappy, sinful father, and how boldly he stood up for him alone against the whole school."

"We will remember, we will remember," cried the boys. "He was brave, he was good!"

"Ah, how I loved him!" exclaimed Kolya.

"Ah, children, ah, dear friends, don't be afraid of life! How good life is when one does something good and just!"

"Yes, yes," the boys repeated enthusiastically.

"Karamazov, we love you!" a voice, probably Kartashov's, cried impulsively.

"We love you, we love you!" they all caught it up. There were tears in the eyes of many of them.

"Hurrah for Karamazov!" Kolya shouted ecstatically.

"And may the dead boy's memory live for ever!" Alyosha added again, with feeling.

"For ever!" the boys chimed in again.

"Karamazov, ' cried Kolya, "can it be true what's taught us in religion, that we shall all rise again from the dead and shall live and see each other again, all, Ilusha too?"

"Certainly we shall all rise again, certainly we shall see each other and shall tell each other with joy and gladness all that has happened!" Alyosha answered, half laughing, half enthusiastic.

"Ah, how splendid it will be!" broke from Kolya.

"Well, now we will finish talking and go to his funeral dinner. Don't be put out at our eating pancakes—it's a very old custom and there's something nice in that!" laughed Alyosha. "Well, let us go! And now we go hand in hand."

"And always so, all our lives hand in hand! Hurrah for Karamazov!" Kolya cried once more rapturously and once more the boys took up his exclamation:

"Hurrah for Karamazov!"

This book, designed by
William B. Taylor
is a production of
Edito-Service S.A., Geneva

Printed in Switzerland